READER'S DIGEST
CONDENSED BOOKS

www.readersdigest.co.uk

The Reader's Digest Association Limited
11 Westferry Circus
Canary Wharf London E14 4HE

For information as to ownership of
copyright in the material of this book,
and acknowledgments, see last page.

READER'S DIGEST CONDENSED BOOKS

Selected and edited
by Reader's Digest

CONDENSED BOOKS DIVISION
THE READER'S DIGEST ASSOCIATION LIMITED, LONDON

CONTENTS

One day in 1958, a man wakes up unable to remember anything about his life or his identity. As he desperately pieces together clues to his past, he realises his fate is bound up with that of the Jupiter-C rocket soon to be launched from Cape Canaveral. A gripping thriller from one of Britain's greatest storytellers about the men and women at the heart of America's bid for supremacy in space.

PUBLISHED BY MACMILLAN

Actress Elfrida Phipps has planned her retirement in a pretty Hampshire village with the same zest that she brings to everything in life. But her carefree existence is interrupted one autumn day when she hears shocking news about a dear friend. A poignant best seller set against the vivid scenery of a Scottish winter and filled with the magic and joy of the Christmas season.

PUBLISHED BY HODDER & STOUGHTON

HIGH RISK   page 277

Matt Dickinson

Daybreak TV, run by tycoon Sebastian Turner,
is one of London's most successful television
stations. When Sebastian makes a bid to climb
Everest, the station follows him every step of
the way. Among the millions of viewers avidly
awaiting news of his progress is his TV-
presenter wife, Josie. For her it is the start of
a real-life drama that will test her courage to
the very limit. A superb story of high-altitude
adventure and knife-edged suspense.

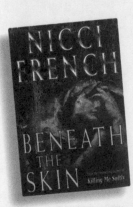

PUBLISHED BY HUTCHINSON

BENEATH THE SKIN   page 395

Nicci French

Zoë, a young teacher, has recently moved
to London; Jennifer, mother of three, is
busy redesigning her home; Nadia, a
children's entertainer, is trying to sort out
her life. Three women with little in
common—except the man who wants to
kill them and who sends terrifying letters
forewarning of his plans. A taut thriller set
in the claustrophobic, sweltering heat of a
London summer.

PUBLISHED BY MICHAEL JOSEPH

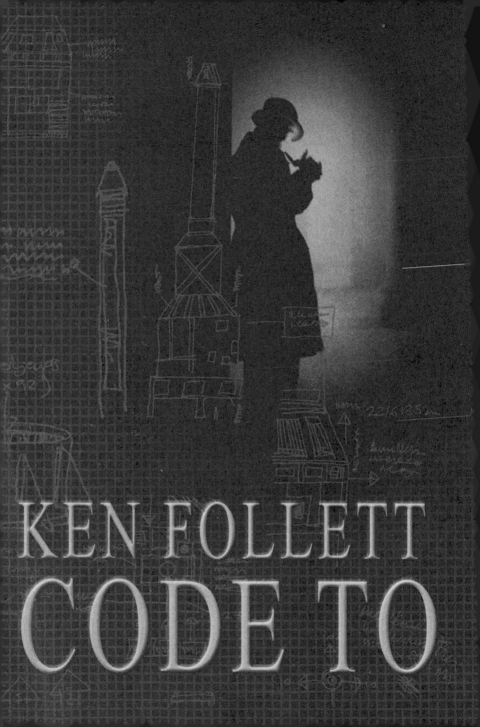

ZERO

A man wakes up on the floor of a public toilet in Washington, scared and hung over, unable to work out his identity or what has happened to him. All the evidence suggests he is a drunken tramp—yet he knows that can't be true.

Who is he and how did he lose his memory? As he unearths answers, his fear grows. He realises he must, in the depths of his mind, hold information so secret that it has made him a target . . .

Historical note: *The launch of the first American space satellite, Explorer I, was originally scheduled for Wednesday January 29, 1958. Late that evening, it was postponed to the following day. The reason given was the weather. Observers at Cape Canaveral were puzzled: it was a perfect, sunny Florida day. Next night, there was another postponement, and the same reason was given.*

The launch was finally attempted on Friday, January 31.

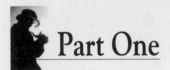 # Part One

5.00am: He woke up scared.

Worse than that: he was terrified. His heart was pounding, his breath came in gasps and his body was taut. It was like a nightmare, except that waking brought no sense of relief. He felt that something dreadful had happened, but he did not know what it was.

He opened his eyes. A faint light illuminated his surroundings, and he made out vague shapes. Somewhere near by, water ran. He tried to make himself calm and attempted to think straight. He was lying on a hard floor. He was cold, and he had some kind of hangover, with a headache and a dry mouth and a feeling of nausea.

He sat upright, shaking with fear. There was an unpleasant smell of disinfectant. He recognised the outline of a row of washbasins. He was in a public toilet.

He felt disgusted. He had been sleeping on the floor of a men's room. What the hell had happened to him? He concentrated. He was

9

fully dressed, wearing some kind of topcoat and heavy boots, though he had a feeling that these were not his clothes. His panic was subsiding, but in its place came a deeper fear.

He needed light. He got to his feet and peered into the gloom. Holding his arms out in front of him in case of invisible obstacles, he made his way to a wall. Then he walked crabwise, his hands exploring. He found a cold glassy surface he guessed was a mirror, then a towel roller. At last his fingertips touched a switch, and he turned it on.

Bright light flooded white-tiled walls. In a corner was what looked like a bundle of old clothes. He asked himself how he got here. What had happened last night? He could not remember. *He could not remember anything at all.*

What was his name? He did not know.

He turned towards the mirror. He saw a filthy hobo, dressed in rags, with matted hair, a dirty face and a crazy stare. Then he was hit by a terrible revelation. The hobo was himself. In a voice that shook with terror, he shouted, 'Who am I?'

The bundle of old clothes moved and a voice mumbled, 'You're a bum, Luke. Pipe down.'

His name was Luke. He was grateful for the knowledge. A name was not much, but it gave him a focus. He stared at his companion. The man wore a ripped tweed coat with string for a belt. He rubbed his eyes and muttered, 'My head hurts.'

Luke said, 'Who are you?'

'I'm Pete, you retard, can't you see?'

Luke swallowed. 'I've lost my memory!'

'I ain't surprised. You drank most of a bottle of bourbon yesterday. It's a miracle you didn't lose your entire mind.'

Bourbon would explain the hangover, Luke thought. 'But why would I drink a whole bottle?'

Pete laughed. 'That's about the dumbest question I ever heard. To get drunk, of course!'

Luke was appalled. He was a drunken bum who slept in public toilets. He bent over a washbasin, ran the cold water, and drank from the tap. It made him feel better. He wiped his mouth, then forced himself to look in the mirror again. The reflection showed a man in his late thirties, with dark hair and blue eyes. He had no beard or moustache, just a heavy growth of dark stubble.

He turned back to his companion. 'Luke what?' he said. 'What's my last name?'

'How the hell am I supposed to know?' Pete got to his feet. 'I need some breakfast.'

Luke realised he was hungry. He searched his pockets for money. All were empty. 'I think I'm broke,' he said.

'No kidding,' Pete said sarcastically. 'Come on.' He stumbled through a doorway. Luke followed.

When he emerged into the light, he suffered another shock. He was in a huge temple, empty and eerily silent. Mahogany benches stood in rows on the marble floor, like church pews waiting for a ghostly congregation. The insane thought crossed Luke's mind that he had been the sacrificial victim in a weird rite that had left him with no memory. 'What is this place?' he asked.

'Union Station, Washington, DC,' said Pete.

Luke felt foolish. He was in a grandiose train station, early in the morning before it filled up with passengers. He had scared himself, like a child imagining monsters in a dark bedroom.

Pete headed for an arch marked EXIT, and Luke hurried after him.

An aggressive voice called, 'Hey! Hey, you!'

Pete said, 'Oh-oh.' He quickened his step.

A stout man in a railroad uniform bore down on them, full of righteous indignation. 'You bums been sleeping here, ain't you?' he said. 'You know that ain't allowed.'

Luke suppressed a retort and walked faster.

'This ain't a flophouse,' the man went on. 'Now scat.' He shoved Luke's shoulder.

Luke turned suddenly. 'Don't touch me!' he said.

The man took a big step backward, looking scared.

Pete took Luke's arm. 'Let's go.'

They passed through the arch. It was dark outside. The air was bitterly cold, and Luke drew his ragged clothes closer about him. It was winter, maybe January or February. He wondered what year it was. Pete turned left, apparently sure where he was going. Luke followed.

'Where are we headed?' he asked.

'I know a gospel shop on H Street where we can get free breakfast, so long as you don't mind singing a hymn or two.'

'I'm starving—I'll sing a whole oratorio.'

Luke's mind seethed with anxious questions. How long had he been a drunk? Did he have any family? Where had he met Pete? But Pete was taciturn, and Luke controlled his impatience, hoping Pete might be more forthcoming when he had some food inside him.

11

They came to a small church between a cinema and a liquor store. They entered by a side door and went down to the basement. At one end of a long low room Luke saw a piano and a small pulpit; at the other, a kitchen range. In between were trestle tables with benches. At the kitchen end, a woman stirred a big pot. Beside her, a grey-bearded man wearing a clerical collar looked up from a coffee urn and smiled. 'Come in, come in,' he said cheerfully.

'Morning, Pastor Lonegan,' Pete said.

'You're a little early for breakfast, but there's fresh coffee.' The pastor poured it into thick mugs. 'Milk and sugar?'

Luke did not know whether he liked milk and sugar in his coffee. 'Yes, thank you,' he said, guessing. He sipped the coffee. It tasted sickeningly creamy and sweet. He guessed he normally took it black. But it assuaged his hunger, and he drank it all quickly.

Luke and Pete sat at a table and Luke studied his companion. Until now, he had noticed only the dirty face and ragged clothes. Now he saw that Pete had none of the marks of a long-term drunk: no broken veins, no flaking skin, no cuts or bruises. Perhaps he was too young—only about twenty-five, Luke guessed. He had a dark red birthmark that ran from his right ear to his jaw line.

'What are you staring at?' Pete said.

Luke shrugged and did not reply. On the table was a newspaper folded open at the crossword, and a pencil. Luke picked up the pencil, and started to fill in the answers.

More bums drifted in. Luke got all the crossword clues but one, 'Small place in Denmark,' six letters. Pastor Lonegan looked over his shoulder and said quietly to his wife, 'Oh, what a noble mind is here o'erthrown!' Luke immediately got the clue. HAMLET, he wrote in. Then he thought, How did I know that?

He unfolded the paper and looked at the front page. It was dated Wednesday, January 29, 1958. His eye was caught by the headline: US MOON STAYS EARTHBOUND.

Cape Canaveral, Tuesday: The US Navy abandoned a second attempt to launch its space rocket, Vanguard, after technical problems. American hopes of launching a satellite to rival the Soviet Sputnik now rest with the Army's Jupiter missile.

The piano sounded a strident chord. Mrs Lonegan was playing a familiar hymn, 'What a Friend we have in Jesus'. Luke joined in the singing, pleased he could remember the song. Bourbon had a strange effect, he thought. He could do the crossword and sing a hymn from memory, but he did not know his mother's name.

After the hymn, they said grace. Then the men lined up and Mrs Lonegan served them hot oatmeal. Luke ate three bowls. Afterwards, feeling better, he approached the pastor. 'Sir, have you seen me here before? I've lost my memory.'

Lonegan looked at him. 'I don't believe I have. How old are you?'

'I don't know,' Luke said, feeling foolish.

'Late thirties, I'd say. You haven't been living rough very long. It takes its toll on a man. But you're alert enough to do a crossword puzzle. Quit drinking now, and you could lead a normal life again.'

Luke wondered how many times the pastor had said that. 'I'm going to try,' he promised.

'If you need help, just ask.' A young man who appeared to be mentally handicapped was patting Lonegan's arm, and he turned to him with a patient smile.

Luke spoke to Pete. 'How long have you known me?'

'I don't know. You been around a while. Relax, will you? Your memory will come back sooner or later.'

'I have to find out where I'm from.'

Pete hesitated. 'What we need is a beer. Help us think straight.' He turned for the door.

Luke grabbed his arm. 'I don't want a beer,' he said decisively. Pete did not want him to dig into his past, it seemed. 'In fact, I think I'd like to be alone for a while.'

'What are you, Greta Garbo?'

'I'm serious.'

'You need me to look out for you. You can't make it on your own. Hell, you can't even remember how old you are.'

Pete had a desperate look in his eyes, but Luke was unmoved. 'I appreciate your concern, but you're not helping me find out who I am.'

Pete shrugged. 'You got a right. See you around, maybe.'

'Maybe.'

Pete went out. Luke thanked Pastor Lonegan, then went up the stairs and out into the street. Pete was on the next block, speaking to a man in a green gaberdine raincoat—begging the price of a beer, Luke guessed. He turned and walked in the opposite direction.

It was still dark. Luke's feet were cold. He realised he wasn't wearing socks. As he hurried on, a light flurry of snow fell. After a few minutes, he eased his pace. He had no reason to rush.

6.00AM: ELSPETH WOKE up worrying about Luke. She lay in bed for a few moments, her heart heavy with concern for the man she loved. Then she switched on the bedside lamp and sat upright.

Her motel room was decorated with a space-programme theme. The floor lamp was shaped like a rocket, and the pictures on the wall showed planets, crescent moons and orbital paths in a wildly unrealistic night sky. The Starlite was one of a cluster of new motels that had sprouted in the area of Cocoa Beach, Florida, eight miles south of Cape Canaveral. The decorator had obviously thought the space theme appropriate, but it made Elspeth feel as if she were borrowing the bedroom of a ten-year-old boy.

She picked up the bedside phone and dialled Anthony Carroll's office in Washington, DC. At the other end, the phone rang unanswered. She tried his home number with the same result. Had something gone wrong? She felt sick with fear. She would call his office again in half an hour.

As she showered, she thought about Luke and Anthony when she had first known them. They were at Harvard and she was at Radcliffe, before the war. Best friends, Luke and Anthony had made an odd couple. Both were tall and athletic, but there the resemblance ended. The Radcliffe girls had called them Beauty and the Beast. Luke was Beauty, with his wavy black hair and elegant clothes. Anthony was not handsome, but girls were attracted to his energy and intense enthusiasm.

Elspeth showered quickly. In her bathrobe, she sat at the dressing table to do her make-up. She had been sitting at a dressing table wearing a bathrobe the first time she ever spoke to Luke. It was during a panty raid by a group of Harvard boys. By chance, Luke had come to her room. He was a maths major, like her. Once alone with her, Luke had seemed embarrassed. She had smiled, pointed to the closet, and said, 'Top drawer.' He had taken a pair of pretty white panties with a lace edging. The next day he asked her for a date.

She tried to concentrate on her make-up. The job was more difficult than usual this morning, because she had slept badly. She had a maths degree from Radcliffe, but still she was expected to look like a mannequin at work. She brushed her hair. It was reddish-brown, and cut in the fashionable style: chin-length and turned under at the back. She dressed quickly in a green-and-tan striped shirtwaist.

She picked up the phone and dialled Anthony's office again. There was no reply.

1941: ELSPETH TWOMEY had fallen in love with Luke the first time he kissed her.

That had been six months ago, and the feeling had grown stronger since. Now she was seeing Luke almost every day. They were both in their senior year. Every day they either met for lunch or studied together. Weekends they spent almost all their time together.

It was not uncommon for Radcliffe girls to get engaged in their final year, to a Harvard boy or a young professor. But Luke had never spoken about marriage.

She looked at him now, sitting in a booth at the back of Flanagan's Bar, arguing with Bern Rothsten, a graduate student. Bern was a communist, like many Harvard students and professors. 'Your father's a banker,' he said to Luke with disdain. 'You'll be a banker, too. Of course you think capitalism is great.'

Elspeth saw a flush rise at Luke's throat. His father had recently been featured in a *Time* magazine article as one of ten men who had become millionaires since the Depression.

Luke said, 'Banking is an honourable job. Bankers help people.'

'Like they did in 1929.'

'They make mistakes. Soldiers make mistakes—they shoot the wrong people—but I don't accuse you of being a murderer.'

It was Bern's turn to look wounded. He had fought in the Spanish Civil War—he was older than the rest of them—and Elspeth now guessed he was remembering some tragic error.

Luke added, 'Anyway, I don't aim to be a banker.'

Bern's dowdy girlfriend, Peg, leaned forward, interested. Like Bern she was intense in her convictions, but she did not have his sarcastic tongue. 'What, then?'

'A scientist. I want to explore beyond our planet.'

Bern laughed scornfully. 'Space rockets! A schoolboy fantasy.'

Elspeth leaped to Luke's defence. 'Knock it off, Bern. You don't know what you're talking about.'

'I think it's going to happen,' Luke said. 'And I believe science will do more than communism for ordinary people in our lifetime.'

Elspeth winced. She felt Luke was naive about politics. 'The benefits of science are restricted to the privileged elite,' she said.

'That's not true,' Luke said.

A tall figure cast a shadow over the table. 'Are you kids old enough to drink alcoholic liquor?' It was Anthony Carroll. With him was someone so striking that Elspeth uttered an involuntary murmur of surprise. She was a small girl, fashionably dressed in a short red jacket, with curls of dark hair escaping from under a little red hat. 'Meet Billie Josephson,' said Anthony.

Luke stood up to shake hands and knocked over a glass. It was unusual for him to be clumsy, and Elspeth realised with annoyance that he was taken with Miss Josephson. 'I'm surprised,' he said, giving her his most charming smile. 'When Anthony said his date was called Billie, I imagined someone six feet tall and built like a wrestler.'

Billie laughed and slid into the booth beside Luke. 'My name is Bilhah,' she said. 'It's biblical, she was the handmaiden of Jacob and the mother of Dan. But I was brought up in Dallas, where they called me Billie-Jo.'

Anthony sat next to Elspeth and said quietly, 'Isn't she pretty?'

Billie was not exactly pretty, Elspeth thought. She had a sharp nose and large, intense, dark-brown eyes. It was the whole package that was so stunning: the angle of the hat, the Texas accent, and most of all her animation. While she talked to Luke, telling him some tall story, she smiled, frowned, and pantomimed all kinds of emotion.

'She's cute,' Elspeth said to Anthony. 'How did you meet her?'

'I noticed her in the Fogg Museum. She was wearing a green coat with brass buttons and a beret. I thought she looked like a toy soldier fresh out of the box.'

Billie was not a toy, Elspeth thought. She was more dangerous than that. Billie laughed at something Luke had said and swiped his arm in mock admonishment. Irritated, Elspeth interrupted them and said to Billie, 'Are you planning to beat the curfew tonight?'

Radcliffe girls were supposed to be in their dormitories by ten o'clock. To stay out later they had to put their name in a book with details of where they planned to go and what time they would be back. Billie said, 'I'm supposed to be spending the night with a visiting aunt who has taken a suite at the Ritz. What's your story?'

'No story, just a ground-floor window that will be left open.'

Billie said, 'In fact, I'm staying with friends of Anthony's.'

'Some people my mother knows, who have a large apartment,' Anthony said to Elspeth. 'Don't give me that old-fashioned look, they're terribly respectable.'

'I should hope so.' Elspeth said primly, and she had the satisfaction of seeing Billie blush. Turning to Luke, she said, 'Honey, what time's the movie?'

He looked at his wristwatch. 'We've got to go,' he said.

Luke had borrowed a Ford roadster for the weekend. They drove into Boston to see Alfred Hitchcock's latest film, *Suspicion*.

Around midnight they returned to Cambridge and pulled off Memorial Drive to park facing the Charles River, next to the boathouse. The car had no heater, and Elspeth turned up the fur collar of her coat and leaned against Luke for warmth.

They talked about the movie. Elspeth thought that in real life the Joan Fontaine character, a repressed girl brought up by stuffy parents, would never be attracted to the kind of ne'er-do-well Cary Grant had played. Luke said, 'But that's why she fell for him—because he was dangerous.'

Elspeth looked at the reflection of the moon on the water. Billie Josephson was dangerous, she thought.

Luke changed the subject. 'This afternoon, Professor Davies told me I could do my master's degree right here at Harvard.'

'What made him say that?'

'I mentioned that I was hoping to go to Columbia. He said, "What for? Stay here!" I explained that my family's in New York.'

Luke was the eldest of four children. His mother was French. Elspeth knew that Luke was fond of his two teenage brothers and doted on his eleven-year-old sister.

'Professor Davies is a bachelor,' she said. 'He lives for his work.'

'Have you thought about doing a master's?' he asked. 'You're a better mathematician than most of the Harvard men.'

'I've always wanted to work at the State Department.'

'That would mean living in Washington.'

Elspeth was sure Luke was just thinking aloud, but he seemed dismayed that they might move to different cities.

'Have you ever been in love?' he said suddenly.

'When I was seventeen, there was a steelworks dispute in Chicago.' she said. 'I was very political in those days. I went to help as a volunteer. I worked for a young organiser called Jack Largo, and I fell in love with him.'

'And he with you?'

'Goodness, no. He was twenty-five; he thought of me as a kid.' She hesitated. 'He kissed me once, though. We were packing leaflets, and I said something that made him laugh. "You're a gem, Ellie," he said. Then he kissed me. I nearly died of joy. But he just went on packing leaflets as though nothing had changed.'

'Are you still in touch with him?'

She shook her head. 'He was killed.' She fought back sudden tears. 'Two off-duty policemen, hired by the steelworks, got him in an alley and beat him to death with iron bars.'

'No!' Luke stared at her.

'Everyone in town knew who had done it, but nobody was arrested.'

He took her hand. 'I've read about that kind of stuff in the papers but it never seemed real.'

'It's real. The mills must keep rolling. Anyone who gets in the way has to be rubbed out.'

'You make it sound as if industry were no better than organised crime.'

'I don't see a big difference. But I don't get involved any more. That was enough.' Luke had started talking about love, but she had stupidly moved the conversation on to politics. She switched back. 'What about you?' she said. 'Have you ever been in love?'

'I don't think I know what love is.' It was a typical boy's answer. But then he kissed her and she relaxed. After a while he drew away from her and sighed. 'I wonder how married people ever get bored. They never have to stop.'

'Their children stop them, I guess,' she said with a laugh.

'Do you want to have children, some day?'

She felt her breath come faster. 'Of course I do.'

He turned to her with a serious expression. 'I'd like four. How would you feel about that? Having four children?'

She smiled happily. 'If they were yours, I'd love it,' she said.

He kissed her again.

Soon it became too cold to stay where they were, and reluctantly they drove back towards the Radcliffe dorms. As they were passing through Harvard Square, a figure waved to them from the side of the road. 'Is that Anthony?' Luke said incredulously.

It was, Elspeth saw. Billie was with him.

Luke pulled over, and Anthony came to the window. 'I'm glad I spotted you,' he said. 'I need a favour. My friends have gone away— they must have got the dates mixed up. Billie has nowhere to go.'

Billie had lied about where she was spending the night, Elspeth recalled. Now she could not return to her dorm without revealing her deception.

'I took her to the House.' He meant Cambridge House, where he and Luke lived. 'I thought she could sleep in our room, and Luke and I could spend the night in the library.'

Elspeth said, 'You're crazy.'

Luke put in, 'It's been done before. So what went wrong?'

'We were seen.'

'Oh, no,' Elspeth said. For a girl to be found in a man's room was a serious offence. Both of them could be expelled.

Luke said, 'Who saw you?'

'Geoff Pidgeon and a whole bunch of men. It was half dark and they were all drunk. I'll talk to them in the morning.'

Luke nodded. 'What are you going to do now?'

'Billie has a cousin who lives in Newport, Rhode Island. Would you drive her there?'

'What?' said Elspeth. 'But it's fifty miles away!'

'What do you say, Luke?' Anthony asked.

'Of course,' Luke said.

Elspeth had known he would comply. It was a matter of honour for him to help a friend. But she was angry all the same.

'Hey, thanks,' Anthony said lightly.

'No problem,' Luke said. 'Well, there is a problem. This car is a two-seater.'

Elspeth opened the door and got out. 'Be my guest,' she said sulkily. She hated the thought of Luke spending two hours in this little car with sexy Billie Josephson.

Luke sensed her displeasure and said, 'Elspeth, get back in, I'll drive you home first.'

'No need,' she said. 'Anthony can walk me to the dorm.'

'I don't know how to thank you,' Billie said to Elspeth. She got into the car and closed the door.

Luke waved and drove off.

Anthony and Elspeth stood and watched the car recede into the darkness.

6.30AM: DAYLIGHT CREPT stealthily over the cold city. Men and women came out of houses, narrowing their eyes against the biting wind, and hurried towards the warmth and bright lights of offices.

Luke had no destination: one street was as good as another when none of them meant anything. He began to study the people he passed. He kept hoping that one of them would stop, and say, 'Luke, what happened to you? Come home with me, let me help you!' He began to feel he was not going to be lucky. Walking around fantasising about a lucky break was no kind of strategy. He needed a plan.

He wondered if he might be a Missing Person. There was a list, he felt sure, of such people. Who kept the list? It had to be the police. Or, if not, they would know.

He seemed to remember passing a precinct house a few minutes earlier. He turned abruptly to go back. As he did so, he bumped into a young man in an olive-coloured gabardine raincoat. He had a feeling he might have seen the man before. Their eyes met, but the man looked away, and walked on. Swallowing his disappointment, Luke tried to retrace his steps. It was difficult, because he had turned corners and crossed streets more or less at random. However, he had to come across a police station sooner or later.

Soon he had completely lost his way. He was on a street of cheap shops. He stopped suddenly and looked back. Thirty yards behind him, he saw the man in a green gabardine raincoat, watching the TV in a store window. Luke frowned, thinking, 'Is he shadowing me?'

It was easy enough to check. Luke walked to the end of the block, crossed the street, and walked back along the other side. When he reached the far end he stood at the kerb and looked both ways. The olive raincoat was thirty yards behind him. Luke crossed again. To allay suspicion, he studied doors as if looking for a street number. The raincoat followed.

Luke was mystified, but his heart leaped with hope. A man who was following him must know something about him—maybe even his identity.

For a real test to see if he was being followed, he needed to travel in a vehicle, forcing his shadow to do the same. Now he needed the bus fare. He began to look at his surroundings with different eyes. He saw newsstands to be robbed, handbags that could be snatched, pockets ready to be picked. He stepped inside a coffee shop.

His eyes raked the tables, looking for change left as tips. He approached the counter. A radio was playing the news. 'Rocket experts claim America has one last chance of catching up with the Russians in the race to control outer space.'

The counterman was making espresso coffee, and a delicious fragrance make Luke's nostrils flare.

What would a bum say? 'Any stale doughnuts?' he asked.

'Get out of here,' the man said roughly.

Luke saw what he needed. Beside the till, within easy reach, was a can with a slit in the top and the label saying: REMEMBER THOSE WHO CANNOT SEE. Now Luke just had to distract the counterman.

'Gimme a dime?' he said.

The man said, 'OK, that's it, you get the bum's rush.' But he had to duck under the counter to get out, and for a second he could not see Luke. In that moment, Luke took the collection box and slipped it inside his coat.

The counterman grabbed Luke by the collar and propelled him rapidly across the café. At the door the man gave him a painful kick.

In an alleyway, Luke busted the can open. The money inside, mostly pennies, amounted to two or three dollars, he guessed. He put it in his coat pocket and returned to the street. He thanked heaven for charity and made a silent promise to give three bucks to the blind if he ever got straight. All right, he thought, thirty bucks.

The man in the olive raincoat was standing by a newsstand.

A bus pulled up a few yards away. Luke had no idea where it went, but he boarded. The driver gave him a hard look. 'The fare is seventeen cents, unless you got a token,' he said. Luke paid with some of the change he had stolen. As he walked towards the back of the bus, he looked anxiously out of the window. The man in the raincoat was walking away. Luke frowned. The man should have been trying to hail a taxicab. Maybe he was not a shadow, after all.

The bus pulled away, and Luke took a seat.

At the third stop, Luke got off the bus. He looked up and down the street. There was no sign of the man in the olive raincoat. As he hesitated, he noticed that one of the passengers who had got off the bus with him had paused in a shop doorway and was fumbling in his pockets. As Luke watched, he lit a cigarette and took a long, satisfying drag. He was a tall man, wearing a grey Homburg hat.

Luke realised he had seen him before.

7.00AM: ANTHONY CARROLL drove along Constitution Avenue in a five-year-old Cadillac Eldorado. He pulled into the parking lot of Q Building in Alphabet Row, a strip of barracks-like structures hastily erected, during the war, on parkland near the Lincoln Memorial. He had spent much of the war here, working for the Office of Strategic Services, precursor of the CIA. A multimillion-dollar CIA headquarters was under construction across the Potomac River in Langley, Virginia. When it was completed, Alphabet Row would be demolished.

Anthony was a hugely powerful figure within the Agency. He was Head of Technical Services, a euphemistic name for the division responsible for burglary, phone tapping, and other illegal activities. Its nickname was Dirty Tricks. Anthony's position was founded on his record as a war hero, and a series of Cold War coups. However, he had enemies: pen-pushers who disliked the whole notion of the government doing secret operations. They were ready to destroy him as soon as he made a slip. And today his neck was stuck out further than ever before.

As he strode into the building, he focused on the problem of the day: Dr Claude Lucas, known as Luke, the most dangerous man in America, the one who threatened everything Anthony had lived for.

He had been at the office most of the night, and had gone home only to shave and change his shirt. The guard in the lobby said, 'Mr Maxell's in your office, sir.'

Anthony frowned. Pete Maxell was supposed to be with Luke. Had something gone wrong? He ran up the stairs.

Pete was sitting in the chair opposite Anthony's desk, still dressed in ragged clothes, a smear of dirt partly covering his birthmark. As Anthony walked in he jumped up, looking scared.

'What happened?' Anthony said.

'Luke decided he wanted to be alone. But Simons has him under surveillance, and Betts is there for back-up.'

'What about his memory.'

'Completely gone.'

Anthony took off his coat and sat behind his desk. He looked at the man opposite. Pete was a good agent, but inexperienced. However, he was fanatically loyal to Anthony.

Anthony said, 'Tell me exactly what happened.'

Pete sat down again. 'He woke up crazy, yelling 'Who am I?' and stuff like that. I made a mistake: I called him Luke.'

Anthony had told Pete to observe Luke but not to give him any information. 'No matter—it's not his real name.'

'Then he asked who I was, and I said, "I'm Pete." It just came out, I was so concerned to stop him yelling. He asked questions. 'How long have I been like this? Do I have any family? I kept trying to steer him away from enquiring into his past. But I think he figured out what I was doing.'

'Where is he *now*?' Anthony asked.

'I don't know. Steve will call in as soon as he gets a chance.'

'When he does, get back there and join up with him. Whatever happens, Luke mustn't get away from us.'

The white phone on Anthony's desk rang, his direct line. He stared at it. Not many people had the number. He picked it up.

'It's me,' said Elspeth's voice. 'What's happened?'

'Relax,' he said. 'Everything is under control.'

7.30AM: THE SHADOW followed Luke for a quarter of a mile. It was now full light and, although the street was busy, Luke easily kept track of the grey Homburg hat, but after he crossed Pennsylvania Avenue it disappeared from view. Once again, he wondered if he might be imagining things. But a minute later he spotted the green raincoat coming out of a bakery.

'You again,' he said under his breath. There was no further room for doubt: two people were following him in a smoothly executed relay operation. They had to be professionals. He tried to figure out what that meant. They could be spies, KGB or CIA, although it seemed unlikely that a deadbeat could be involved in espionage.

He decided he would split the team then confront one of the men. He stepped into a shop and bought a pack of Pall Malls. When he went outside, Raincoat had disappeared and Homburg had taken over again. He walked to the end of the block and turned the corner.

A Coca-Cola truck was parked at the kerb, and the driver was unloading crates. Luke walked to the far side of the truck, dropped to the ground and rolled under it. Looking along the sidewalk at ground level, he picked out the blue suit pants and tan oxfords of his shadow.

The man quickened his pace, presumably concerned that Luke had disappeared. He walked around the truck, then returned to the sidewalk and broke into a run.

Luke was pleased. He did not know how he had learned this game, but he seemed to be good at it. He crawled to the front of the truck and scrambled to his feet. Homburg was still hurrying away.

Luke crossed the sidewalk and turned the corner. He stood in the doorway of an electrical store, opened the pack of cigarettes, and took one out.

Raincoat appeared. He spotted Luke, gave a nervous start, and continued walking, edging to the outside of the sidewalk.

Luke stepped into his path and said, 'Got a light, buddy?'

Raincoat hesitated, then stopped. 'Sure,' he said, trying to act casual. He reached into the pocket of his raincoat, took out a book of matches and struck one.

Luke said, 'You know who I am, don't you?'

The man stared at Luke, dumbstruck, until the match burned down. Then he dropped it and said, 'I don't know what you're talking about, pal.'

'You're following me,' Luke said. 'You must know who I am.'

'I'm not following anyone.'

The man tried to walk past Luke. Luke moved sideways, blocking his path. 'Excuse me, please,' Raincoat said.

Frustrated, Luke grabbed him by the lapels of the raincoat and slammed him against the shop window, rattling the glass.

'Get your damn hands off me,' the man said. 'I'm not following you.'

'Who am I?' Luke screamed at him. 'Tell me, who am I?'

'How should I know?'

Luke took the man by the throat. 'You're going to tell me.'

Behind Luke, the frightened voice of a passer-by said, 'Hey, what's going on here?'

Luke let his hands fall to his side. Raincoat backed away. 'You crazy bastard,' he said. 'You're out of your mind.'

'You're lying,' Luke yelled. He reached out to grab the man again.

Raincoat turned and ran away. Luke could have chased him, but he hesitated. What was the point?

After a moment, Luke walked away, heading in the direction opposite to that taken by his two shadows. 'Great job,' he said to himself. 'You achieved precisely nothing.'

And he was alone again.

8.00AM: DR BILLIE JOSEPHSON was running late. She had got her mother up and sat her in the kitchen with coffee. She woke her seven-year-old, Larry, then returned to the kitchen.

Her mother, a small, plump woman of seventy known as Becky-Ma, had the radio on loud. Perry Como was singing 'Catch a Falling Star'. Billie put bread in the toaster for her mother and poured corn-flakes into a bowl for Larry. Then she made a peanut butter and jelly sandwich for Larry's lunch. She put the lunch box in his school bag and added his baseball glove, a present from his father.

On the radio, a reporter was interviewing sightseers on the beach near Cape Canaveral who were hoping to see a rocket launch.

Larry came into the kitchen. She got him started on his cornflakes, and began to scramble eggs.

The radio reporter was interviewing an army spokesman. 'What if the rocket goes off course and crash-lands right here on the beach?'

'There's no danger of that,' came the reply. 'Every rocket has a self-destruct mechanism. If it veers off course it will be blown up in midair.'

'But how can you blow it up after it's already taken off?'

'The explosive device is triggered by a radio signal sent by the range safety officer.'

Larry said, 'Can I take the yoghurt pot to school?'

'No, you can't. It's half full,' she told him.

'But I have to take some containers! Miss Page will be mad if I don't.' He was near to tears with the suddenness of a seven-year-old.

'What do you need containers for?'

'To make a space rocket! She told us last week.'

Billie sighed. 'Larry, if you had told *me* last week, I would have saved a whole bunch for you. What kind of containers do you want?'

'Rocket shape.'

Billie went around the house and got a cardboard detergent container, a liquid soap bottle, and an ice-cream tub. Most of the packages showed families using the products—a pretty housewife, two kids, and a pipe-smoking father in the background. She had never lived in a family like that. Her father, a poor tailor in Dallas, had died when she was a baby, and her mother had brought up five children in poverty. Billie herself had been divorced since Larry was two.

She put all the containers in a bag for Larry to carry to school.

'Oh, boy, I bet I have more than anyone,' he said. 'Thanks, Mom.'

A car horn tooted outside, and Billie quickly checked her appearance in the glass of a cupboard door. Her curly black hair had been hastily combed, she had no make-up on and she was wearing an oversize pink sweater . . . but the effect was kind of sexy.

The back door opened and Roy Brodsky came in. Roy was Larry's best friend. He was followed by his father, Harold, a good-looking man with soft brown eyes. Harold Brodsky was a widower, who taught chemistry at the George Washington University. Billie and Harold were dating. He looked at her adoringly and said, 'My God, you look gorgeous.' She grinned and kissed his cheek.

Like Larry, Roy had a bag full of cartons. Billie said to Harold, 'Did you have to empty half the containers in your kitchen?'

'Yes. I have little bowls of soap flakes, and six toilet rolls without the cardboard cylinder.'

'Darn, I never thought of toilet rolls!'

He laughed. 'I wonder, would you like to have dinner at my place tonight?'

She was surprised. 'You're going to cook?'

'Not exactly. I thought I'd ask Mrs Riley to make a casserole. Roy's going to a cousin's birthday party tonight, and he'll sleep over. We'll have a chance to talk without interruption.'

'That'll be great,' Billie said.

'I'll pick you up around eight. Come on, boys,' He shepherded the children out through the back door.

Billie cleared the table. Rushing now, she stripped the beds and bundled the sheets into a laundry bag. She showed Becky-Ma the bag and said, 'Hand this to the laundry man when he calls, OK, Ma?'

Her mother said, 'I don't have any of my heart pills left.'

'Jesus Christ!' She rarely swore in front of her mother, but she was at the end of her rope. 'Ma, I have a busy day at work today and I don't have time to go to the pharmacist!'

'I can't help it, I ran out.' She started to cry.

Billie relented immediately. 'I'm sorry, Ma,' she said. Five years ago, when the three of them had set up house together, Ma had helped take care of Larry. But nowadays she was barely able to look after him when he came home from school.

The phone rang. She picked it up. It was Bern Rothsten, her ex-husband. Billie got on well with him, despite the divorce. 'Hey, Bern—you're up early.'

'Yeah. Have you heard from Luke?'

'Luke Lucas? Lately? No—is something wrong?'

'I don't know, maybe.'

Bern and Luke shared the intimacy of rivals. When they were young they had argued endlessly yet they had remained close at college and all through the war. 'What's happened?' Billie said.

'He called me on Monday. I was kind of surprised. I don't hear from him often.'

'Nor do I.' Billie struggled to remember. 'Last time I saw him was a couple of years ago, I think. Why did he call you?'

'He was coming to Washington and wanted to see me. Something had happened.'

'Did he tell you what?'

'Not really. He just said, "It's like the stuff we did in the war."'

Billie frowned anxiously. Luke and Bern had been in OSS during the war, working behind enemy lines, helping the French Resistance. 'What do you think he meant?'

'I don't know. He said he would call me when he reached

Washington. He checked into the Carlton on Monday night. Now it's Wednesday, and he hasn't called. Call me if you hear from him, OK?'

'Sure, of course.'

'Be seeing you.'

'Bye.' Billie hung up. Then she sat at the kitchen table, her chores forgotten, thinking about Luke.

1941: ROUTE 138 MEANDERED south through Massachusetts towards Rhode Island. The old Ford had no heater. Billie was wrapped up in coat, scarf and gloves, but her feet were numb. However, it was no great hardship to spend a couple of hours in a car alone with Luke Lucas, even if he was someone else's boyfriend.

They talked about the war in Europe. That morning in Radcliffe Yard, rival student groups had handed out leaflets, the Interventionists passionately advocating that America should enter the war, the America Firsters opposing it.

'I have cousins in Paris,' Luke said. 'I'd like us to go over there and rescue them. But that's a personal reason.'

'I have a personal reason too: I'm Jewish,' Billie said. 'But rather than send Americans to die in Europe, I'd open our doors to refugees. Save lives instead of killing people.'

'That's what Anthony believes.'

Billie was still fuming about the night's fiasco. 'Anthony should have made sure we could stay at his friends' apartment,' she said.

She was hoping for sympathy from Luke, but he disappointed her. 'I guess you both were a little too casual about the whole thing.'

Billie was stung. 'I think Anthony had a duty to protect my reputation.'

'Yes, but so did you.'

She was surprised he was so critical. 'I'll never do that again, with any man,' she said vehemently.

'Could I ask you a personal question?' Luke met her eyes for a moment. 'Are you in love with Anthony?'

'I'm fond of him, I enjoy his company, but I don't love him.' She thought about Luke's girlfriend, the most striking beauty on campus. 'What about you? Are you in love with Elspeth?'

'To be honest, this is as close to love as I've ever come, but I don't know if it's the real thing.'

'Didn't you put Elspeth in a vulnerable situation tonight, too, keeping her out in your car until the early hours?'

To her surprise, he laughed appreciatively. 'You're right, and I'm a pompous idiot,' he said. 'We all took risks.'

'That's the truth.' She shuddered. 'I don't know what I'd do if I got thrown out.'

'Study somewhere else, I guess.'

She shook her head. 'I'm on a scholarship. My father's dead, my mother's a penniless widow. I couldn't study anywhere without a scholarship. Why do you look surprised?'

'I have to say you don't dress like a scholarship girl.'

'It's the Leavenworth Award,' she explained.

'Wow.' The Leavenworth was a famously generous grant and thousands of outstanding students applied for it. 'You must be a genius.'

'I don't know about that,' she said. 'I'm not smart enough to make sure I have a place to stay the night.'

'On the other hand, being thrown out of college is not the worst thing in the world.'

'It would be the end of the world for me. I want to help sick people get well.'

'You're going to be a doctor?'

'Psychologist. I want to understand how the mind works. It's so mysterious and complicated. Things like logic, the way we think. Imagining something that isn't there in front of us—animals can't do that.'

He nodded. 'And why is it just about everyone can recognise a musical octave?' he said.

'You find it interesting, too.' She was pleased.

'What did your father die of?' he asked.

Billie swallowed hard. Sudden grief overwhelmed her. She struggled against tears.

'I'm really sorry,' Luke said. 'I didn't mean to upset you.'

'Not your fault,' she said. 'He lost his mind. One Sunday morning he went bathing in the Trinity River. He hated water, and he couldn't swim. I think he wanted to die. The coroner thought so too, but the jury took pity on us and called it an accident, so that we'd get the life insurance. It was a hundred dollars. We lived on that for about a year.' She took a deep breath. 'Let's talk about something else. Tell me about why you want to explore outer space.'

'I think it's the most exciting adventure mankind has ever had.'

'And I want to map the mind.' She smiled. 'We have something in common—big ideas.'

He laughed, then braked. 'Hey, we're coming to a fork in the road.'

She switched on the flashlight and looked at the map on her knee. 'You'll have to pull up, I can't find it.'

He stopped the car and leaned across to look at the map. 'Maybe we're here,' he said, pointing.

Instead of looking at the map, she found herself staring at his face. His hair fell forward over his left eye. Without thinking, Billie lifted her hand and stroked his cheek with the outside edge of her little finger. She saw bewilderment and desire in his eyes. 'Which way do we go?' she murmured.

He moved away suddenly and put the car in gear. 'We take . . .' He cleared his throat. 'We take the left fork. Why did you do that?'

'I don't know,' she said. 'I didn't intend to, it just happened.'

He took a bend too fast. 'I don't want to feel like this about you,' he said.

She was suddenly breathless. 'Like what?'

'Never mind.'

'We're here,' Billie said. They stopped outside a neat one-storey frame house with gingerbread eaves. 'Come in. Denny will make some coffee to keep you awake on the return trip.'

'No, thanks,' he said. 'I'll just wait here until you're safely inside.'

'You've been very kind to me.' She held out her hand to shake.

'Are we friends?' he said, taking her hand.

She lifted his hand to her face, kissed it, and pressed it against her cheek, closing her eyes. After a moment he moved his hand behind her head, pulled her to him, and they kissed. She held the lapel of his rough tweed coat and pulled him closer. Then she heard Denny's voice. 'Who's out there?'

She pulled away from Luke and looked out. There were lights on in the house, and Denny stood in the doorway, wearing a purple silk dressing gown.

She turned back to Luke. 'I could fall in love with you in about twenty minutes, but I don't think we can be friends.' She took a deep breath, and got out of the car.

'Billie?' said Denny. 'What are you doing here?'

She crossed the yard, stepped on to the porch and fell into his arms. 'Oh, Denny, I love that man, and he belongs to someone else!'

She heard the car move, and turned to wave. As it swung by, she saw Luke's face, and the glint of something shiny on his cheeks.

Then he disappeared into the darkness.

8.30AM: SIX AGENTS were gathered in Anthony Carroll's office, a large, bare room with cheap wartime furniture. Anthony liked the spartan look.

Secret agents in America had never been as powerful as they were in January 1958. The Director of the CIA, Allen Dulles, was the brother of John Foster Dulles, Eisenhower's Secretary of State. The CIA's Plans Directorate—also known as CS, for Clandestine Services—had carried out coups against left-leaning governments in Iran and Guatemala, and the White House had been delighted at how cheap and bloodless these were by comparison with the war in Korea.

Within the Plans Directorate was Technical Services, the division that Anthony headed. The fact that the CIA was prohibited, by law, from operating within the United States was no more than a minor inconvenience to Technical Services. Theoretically it was a training division, but 'training' served as an all-purpose cover for covert actions inside the USA. Just about anything Anthony wanted to do, from bugging the phones of union bosses to testing truth drugs on prison inmates, could be labelled a training exercise. The surveillance of Luke was no exception.

Pete Maxell passed around a mugshot of Luke while Anthony briefed the agents: 'Our target today is a middle-ranking State Department employee with a high security clearance. He's having some kind of nervous breakdown. He flew in from Paris on Monday, spent Monday night in the Carlton Hotel, and went on a drinking binge on Tuesday. He stayed out all last night and went to a shelter for homeless people this morning. The security risk is obvious.'

Anthony's office door opened, and Carl Hobart came in. A plump, bald man with spectacles, he was Anthony's immediate boss. Anthony groaned inwardly and continued with his briefing. 'But before we tip our hand, we want to see what the subject does, where he goes—who he contacts. A case like this, he may just be having trouble with his wife. But it could be that he's giving information to the other side, and now the strain has gotten to be too much for him. If he's involved in some kind of treason, we need all the information we can get before we pick him up.'

Hobart interrupted. 'What's this?'

Anthony turned to him slowly. 'A little exercise. We're conducting surveillance on a suspect diplomat.'

'Give it to the FBI,' Hobart said. 'It's the their job, not ours.'

'A case like this can unlock a horde of information if we handle it right, but the Feds are only interested in getting publicity for putting Reds in the electric chair. Anyway, when was the last time the FBI gave us anything?'

'The last time was never,' Hobart said. 'But I've got another assignment for you. The White House has called for a report on ways to deal with a rebel group in Cuba. There's a top level meeting later this morning. I need you and all your experienced people to brief me.'

'You're asking me for a briefing on Fidel Castro?'

'Of course not. I know all about Castro. What I need from you are practical ideas for dealing with insurgency.'

Anthony despised this kind of mealy-mouthed talk. 'Why don't you say what you mean? You want to know how to take them out.'

'Maybe.'

Anthony laughed scornfully. 'Well, what else would we do—start a Sunday School for them?'

'That's for the White House to decide. Our job is to present options. You can give me some suggestions.'

Anthony was worried. He had no time for distractions today, and he needed all his best people to keep an eye on Luke. 'I'll see what I can do,' he said.

'My conference room, with all your most experienced agents, at ten o'clock—and no excuses.' He turned away.

Anthony made a decision. 'Watch my lips,' he said.

Reluctantly, Hobart stared at Anthony's face.

Enunciating carefully, Anthony said, 'No.'

Hobart's bald head reddened. 'You'll hear more about this,' he said. 'A lot more.' He went out and slammed the door.

'Back to work,' Anthony said. 'Now Simons and Betts are with the subject at this moment, but they're due to be relieved in a few minutes by Rifenberg and Horwitz. We'll run four shifts of six hours each, with a back-up team always on call. That's all for now.'

The agents trooped out. Anthony stayed at his desk, trying to be patient. Office politics infuriated him. After five minutes the phone rang and he picked it up. 'Carroll here.'

'You've been upsetting Carl Hobart again.' It was George Cooperman, Deputy Chief of Operations and a wartime comrade of Anthony's. He was Hobart's immediate superior. 'Get yourself over here.'

'Coming.' Anthony hung up. He opened his desk drawer and took out an envelope. Then he put on his coat and walked to

Cooperman's office, which was in P Building, next door.

Cooperman was a tall, gaunt man of fifty. He was reading the Moscow newspaper *Pravda*. He threw it down and growled, 'What's your excuse this time?'

Anthony tossed the envelope on to the desk. Cooperman looked inside. 'Blueprints,' he said. 'Of a rocket. So what?'

'I took them from the surveillance subject. He's a spy.'

'And you chose not to tell Hobart that.'

'I want to follow this guy around until he reveals his whole network. Hobart would hand the case over to the FBI, who would throw him in jail, and his network would fade to black.'

'You're right. Still, I need you at this meeting. I'm chairing it. But you can let your team carry on the surveillance. If anything happens they can get you out of the conference room.'

'Thanks, George.'

Anthony got up to leave. Cooperman said, 'And make damn sure you run this surveillance right. If you screw up on top of insulting your boss, I may not be able to protect you.'

Back in his office, Anthony found Pete with the team that had been shadowing Luke: Simons, in a navy topcoat, and Betts wearing a green raincoat. Also there were the team that should have relieved them. 'What the hell is this?' Anthony said. 'Who's with Luke?'

Simons was carrying a grey Homburg hat, which shook as his hand trembled. 'Nobody,' he said.

'What happened?' Anthony roared. 'What happened?'

Pete answered. 'We, uh . . .' He swallowed. 'We've lost him.'

Part Two

10.00am: The Georgetown Mind Hospital was a redbrick Victorian mansion with a modern extension at the back. Billie Josephson parked her red Thunderbird and hurried into the building.

She hated to arrive this late. It seemed disrespectful of her work and her colleagues. She was late because of her mother. Billie had gone to get the heart pills and returned home to find Becky-Ma lying on her bed, fully dressed, gasping for breath. The doctor had come, but he had nothing new to say. Becky-Ma had a weak heart. If she felt breathless, she should lie down. She must remember to take her pills. Stress was bad for her. Billie resolved anew to walk on eggshells around her mother.

She stopped by the admissions office and glanced at the overnight register. A new patient had been brought in late yesterday, after she had left: Joseph Bellow, a schizophrenic. Surprisingly, the patient had been discharged during the night. That was odd.

She passed through the day room on the way to her office. The subjects of Billie's research sat around, some watching TV or playing games, a few gazing vacantly into space. She waved to Tom, a young man with aphasia. 'How are you, Tommy?' she called. He grinned and waved back. He could read body language well, and often responded as if he knew what people were saying, so it had taken Billie months to figure out that he did not understand a single word.

Through the glass wall of an interview room she saw Ronald, a brilliant architect who had suffered head injuries in a car crash. He could look at a group of objects on a tray and say whether there were three or four of them, but if there were twelve and he had to count them, he had trouble. This suggested to Billic that the ability to see at a glance how many items are in a small group is a separate skill from the ability to count.

In this way, she was slowly charting the depths of the mind, locating memory here, language there, mathematics somewhere else. If the disability was related to brain damage, she could speculate that the normal ability was located in the damaged part of the brain. Eventually, her conceptual picture of the mind's functions would be mapped onto a physical diagram of the human brain. At her present rate of progress, it would take about two hundred years. With a team of psychologists she could progress much faster. She might see the map completed in her lifetime. That was her ambition.

She went up the stairs, thinking about the mystery patient, Joseph Bellow. Why had he been discharged in the middle of the night?

She reached her office and looked out of the window onto a building site. A new wing was being added to the hospital—and a new post was to be created to go with it: Director of Research. Billie had applied for the job, but so had one of her colleagues, Dr Leonard Ross. Len was older, but Billie had wider experience and had published more. She wanted the job badly.

On the building site she noticed, among the workmen, a small group of men in business clothes. Looking more closely, she saw that Len Ross was with them.

She spoke to her secretary. 'Who are those guys being shown around by Len Ross?'

'They're from the Sowerby Foundation.'

The Foundation was financing the new post. They would have a big say in who got the job. 'Did we know they were coming?'

'Len said he had sent you a note. He came by this morning, but you weren't here.'

There had never been a note, Billie felt sure. Len had deliberately failed to warn her. And she had been late. 'Damn,' Billie said. She rushed out to join the party on the building site.

She did not think about Joseph Bellow again for several hours.

11.00AM: AS LUKE NEGOTIATED the grid of streets leading to Union Station, he found himself checking, every minute or two, to see whether he was being followed. He had lost his shadows more than an hour ago, but they might now be searching for him. The thought made him fearful and bewildered. Who were they and what were they doing? He had to find out.

But first he had to clean himself up. His plan was to steal a suitcase from a train passenger. It would not be easy. His dirty, ragged clothing would stand out in a crowd of respectable travellers. If he were arrested, the police would never believe he was anything but a deadbeat. He would end up in jail. It was not prison itself that scared him, so much as the prospect of weeks or months of ignorance and confusion, not knowing who he was and helpless to find out.

Thinking ahead, he figured that after the theft he would have to disappear fast. He needed a car. The knowledge of how to steal one came to his mind immediately.

Close to the station, the street was lined with parked cars. He slowed his pace as a car pulled into a slot ahead of him. It was a blue and white Buick, new but not ostentatious. It would do fine. The starter would be operated with a key, not a handle, but it would be easy to pull out a couple of wires behind the dash and bypass the ignition. He wondered how he knew that.

A man in a dark topcoat got out of the Buick, took a briefcase from the trunk, locked the car, and headed for the station.

Luke waited until there was no one around, then he walked to the driver's door. Pressing his hands flat against the glass of the window, he pushed down. Nothing happened. He stood on tiptoe, to add the weight of his body to the pressure on the window mechanism. At last the pane of glass slid slowly down. When the window was fully open, he reached in and unlocked the door. He opened it, wound up the window, and closed the door. Now he was ready for a fast getaway.

He considered starting the car and leaving the engine running, but that might draw the attention of a passing patrolman.

He returned to Union Station. The best time to steal a suitcase would be immediately after the arrival of a large, crowded train. when the concourse was thronged with hurrying people. He studied the information board. An express from New York was due in a few minutes. He hurried to the gate and waited.

As the passengers emerged, he watched them intently. He was looking for a man his own size and build.

At least a hundred passengers came out before Luke saw his mark. He was Luke's height, build and age. His grey topcoat was unbuttoned to show a tweed sports jacket and flannel pants—which meant he probably had a business suit in the tan leather suitcase he carried.

Luke shoved his way through the crowd until he was directly behind the man. Then he tripped him.

The man cried out and fell forward. He let go of both briefcase and suitcase, and crashed into a woman in a fur coat. She, too, stumbled, giving a little scream, and fell to the ground. While other passengers gathered around, trying to help, Luke calmly picked up the tan suitcase and walked away.

At the exit, he glanced back. A tall man was scanning the concourse, as if looking for something. His head swivelled suddenly towards Luke. Luke stepped quickly through the door.

Outside, he walked to the Buick. He looked back towards the station. The tall man was running across the traffic circle in front of the station, heading Luke's way.

Luke opened the driver's door and slung the bag onto the back seat. Then he got in and slammed the door. He reached under the dash and found the wires on either side of the ignition lock. He pulled them out and touched them together. Nothing happened. There was another wire to the right of the ignition. He pulled it out and touched it to the wire on the left.

The engine started. He put the transmission into drive, released the parking brake, and pulled out. Then he drove off.

A smile crossed his face. Unless he was very unlucky, he had a complete set of fresh clothes in the bag. He felt he had begun to take charge of his life. Now he needed somewhere to shower and change.

12 NOON: THE COUNTDOWN stood at X minus 630 minutes, and Cape Canaveral was buzzing. The Explorer team had built and launched many missiles, but this would be the first of them to break free of the Earth's pull and fly beyond the atmosphere. For most of the team, tonight's launch would be the fulfilment of a lifetime's hopes. Elspeth felt the same way.

They were based in Hangar D and Hangar R, which were side by side. Elspeth was in Hangar R. She had a desk in the office of her boss, Willy Fredrickson, the launch conductor. Her job was to prepare and distribute the launch timetable.

Trouble was, the timetable changed constantly. Nobody in America had sent a rocket into space before. New problems arose all the time, and the engineers were forever improvising ways to jury-rig a component. Here, duct tape was called missile tape. So Elspeth produced regular updates of the timetable and distributed them. The job required her to go everywhere and know almost everything. Her title was secretary, and she was paid a secretary's wages, but no one could have done the job without a science degree.

She set out to distribute her noon update. She was rushed off her feet today, but that suited her: it stopped her worrying constantly about Luke and phoning Anthony every four minutes. She went first to the press department. The missile men had learned, from bitter experience, that a routine postponement could be made to look like a failure when the newspapers reported it. So they had a deal with all the major news organisations. They gave advance notification of launches only on condition that nothing would be published until there was 'fire in the tail', which meant the rocket engine had been ignited.

It was an all-male office, and several men stared at Elspeth as she walked across the pressroom. She knew she was attractive, but there was something formidable about her that made men who were inclined to whistle, or call her 'Honeybunch', think again.

In the Missile Firing Laboratory she found five shirtsleeved scientists at a bench, staring worriedly at a flat piece of metal that looked as if it had been in a fire. The group leader, Dr Keller, said, 'Good afternoon, Elspeth.' He spoke in heavily accented English. Like most of the scientists, he was a German who had been captured at the end of the war and brought to America to work on the missile programme.

She handed him a copy of her update and he took it. Elspeth nodded at the object on the table and said, 'What's that?'

'A jet vane. The burning fuel erodes the metal,' he explained. 'This always happens, to some extent. But with normal alcohol fuel the vanes last long enough to do their job. Today we are using a new fuel, which has a longer burning time, but it may erode the vanes so much that they become ineffective for steering. We have not had time to run sufficiently many tests on it.'

'Is this is going to delay the launch?' she asked. She felt she could not stand a postponement. The suspense was already killing her.

'That's what we're trying to decide. I think our answer is going to be: Let's take the chance.' The others nodded gloomily.

'I'll keep my fingers crossed,' Elspeth said.

She went outside into the scorching Florida sun, crossed a dusty apron and entered Hangar D. In the telemetry room she saw Hans Mueller, known as Hank. He pointed a finger at her and said, 'One hundred thirty-five.'

It was a game they played. She had to say what was unusual about the number. 'Too easy,' she said. 'Take the first digit, add the square of the second, plus the cube of the third, and you get the number you first thought of.'

'Correct! You win the big prize.' He fished a dime out of his pocket.

She took it. 'I'll give you a chance to win it back,' she said. 'One hundred thirty-six.'

'Ah.' He frowned. 'Wait. Sum the cubes of its digits and you get two hundred forty-four. Repeat the process, and you get the number you first thought of.'

She gave him back his dime, and a copy of her update.

She found Willy Fredrickson in the communications room with two army technicians. The teletype machine was not working and Willy was frustrated. But he gave her a grateful look as he took the update, and said, 'Elspeth, you are twenty-two carat gold.'

A moment later, two men approached Willy: a young army officer carrying a chart, and Stimmens, one of the scientists. The officer said, 'We got a problem.' He handed Willy the chart. 'The jet stream has moved south, and it's blowing at one forty-six knots.'

Elspeth's heart sank. The jet stream was a wind in the stratosphere between 30,000 and 40,000 feet. It did not normally extend over Cape Canaveral, but it could move. And if it was too fierce, it might throw the missile off course.

Willy turned to Stimmens. 'We've allowed for this, haven't we?'

'Not really,' Stimmens said. 'We figure the missile can withstand winds up to one twenty knots, no higher.'

Willy turned back to the officer. 'What's the forecast for tonight?'
'Up to one seventy-seven knots.'

Willy ran a hand over his head. Elspeth knew what he was thinking. The launch might have to be postponed. 'Send up a weather
balloon,' he ordered. 'We'll review the forecast again at five o'clock.'

Elspeth made a note to add the meeting to her timetable, then she
left, feeling despondent. They could solve engineering problems, but
there was nothing they could do about the weather.

Outside, she got into a Jeep and drove to Launch Complex 26. She
pulled up outside the blockhouse and looked across to Launch Pad
26B. The gantry was a derrick from an oil rig, adapted for this purpose and coated with orange rust-resistant paint to protect it from
corrosion by the humid, salty Florida air. The long white pencil of
the Jupiter-C rocket seemed caught in the tangle of orange girders
like a dragonfly in a spider's web. The men called it 'she', despite its
phallic shape, and Elspeth, too, thought of the rocket as female. A
bridal veil of canvas had concealed the upper stages from prying eyes
since it arrived here, but that had now been removed, and the missile
stood fully revealed, sunshine gleaming off its spotless paintwork.

The scientists knew that the eyes of the world were on them. Four
months ago, the Soviet Union had stunned the world by sending up
the world's first space satellite, the Sputnik. A month later they had
sent up a second satellite, Sputnik 2, with a dog on board.
Americans were devastated. A dog today, a man tomorrow.

President Eisenhower promised an American satellite before the
end of the year. Early in December the US Navy launched the
Vanguard rocket. It rose a few feet, burst into flames, toppled sideways and smashed to pieces. IT'S A FLOPNIK! said one headline.

The Jupiter-C was America's last hope. There was no third rocket.
If this failed today, the United States was out of the space race. The
American space programme would be in total disarray, and the
USSR would control outer space for the foreseeable future.

All that, Elspeth thought, resting on this one rocket.

Vehicles were banned from the launch-pad area, except for essential ones such as fuel trucks, so she left her car and walked across the
open space. At the back of the derrick was a long steel cabin containing offices and machinery. Elspeth entered by a metal door.

The gantry supervisor, Harry Lane, sat on a folding chair studying
a blueprint. 'Hi, Harry,' she said brightly.

He grunted. He did not like to see women around the launch pad, an... ...d him from letting her know it.

...l table and left. Driving back to
the... ...rfect excuse for calling Anthony.
Sh... ...am, then ask about Luke.

...y's direct line and got him right
av... ...ostponed until tomorrow. There
ar... ...'

...p there.'

...am. The postponement isn't def-
in... ...ng at five. How's Luke?'

...'e've lost him.'

...hat?'

...re in trouble.'

...t back to Cambridge House, and
...fell into bed in his underwear. The
...shaking him, saying, 'Get up!'
...time?' he mumbled.
...waiting for you downstairs.'
...ogged his memory. He did not love
...e with Billie. It would make a train
...lspeth's, Billie's and Anthony's.
...ir of flannels, a sweater and tennis

...bby, the only part of the building
...i spacious hall with a fireplace and
...e-catching as ever, in a wool dress
...ig hat. She laughed when she saw
...ho can't wake up!'
...ed into a chair. 'It took hours to get

...u're supposed to take me to lunch,'

...tiful but he did not love her. He felt

...even shaved.'
...r face, and he realised that she knew
...ong. But her reply was carefree. 'Of
course,' she said.

'I'm sorry you got dressed up for nothing,' he said miserably.

'It wasn't for nothing—I saw you. And your fellow housemen seemed to like my outfit.' She stood up. 'Anyway, Professor and Mrs Durkham are having a party. I'll go there.'

Luke stood and helped her into her coat. 'We could meet later. He had to tell her today—it would be deceitful to let any more time pass without revealing the truth.'

'That'll be fine,' she said gaily. 'Pick me up at six.'

Luke returned woefully to his room. 'Has anyone said anything about last night?' he asked Anthony.

'Not a thing.'

'Billie's quite a gal,' Luke said.

'Isn't she great?' Anthony said. Luke observed with dismay the look of pride on his room-mate's face. To steal someone else's girl-friend was despicable in any circumstances, but the fact that Anthony was obviously crazy about Billie made everything even worse.

Luke groaned, and Anthony said, 'What's the matter?'

'I'm not in love with Elspeth any more. I think I have to end it. I feel like a heel.'

Anthony looked shocked. 'That's too bad. You two are quite an item. Have you proposed?'

'No, but we've talked about how many children we'll have.'

'You're still not engaged.'

'I guess you're right, but all the same I feel like a heel.'

There was a tap at the door, and a man Luke had never seen before came in. He was carrying two envelopes.

'The Dean of Students has asked me to hand you these notes in person.' He gave them an envelope each and left.

Anthony ripped open his envelope. 'Damn it.'

Luke opened his and read the short note inside asking him to come to the Dean's study at three o'clock that afternoon. Such letters always meant disciplinary trouble. Someone had reported to Dean Ryder that there had been a girl in the House last night. Anthony would probably be expelled.

There was another knock at the door, and in came Geoff Pidgeon, the amiable, chubby occupant of the room opposite. 'Didn't I just see the Dean's clerk?'

Luke waved his letter. 'Too damn right.'

'You know,' Geoff said to Anthony, 'I haven't said a word to anyone about seeing you with that girl.

'But who did? The only sneak in the House is Jenkins and he's away for the weekend.'

'No, he's not,' Pidgeon said. 'He changed his plans.'

'Then it's him,' Anthony said. 'I'm going to strangle that son of a bitch with my own hands.'

'I wonder if Elspeth and Billie have had letters,' Luke said.

Pidgeon said, 'If Jenkins knows their names, we can be sure he reported them.'

'Elspeth is safe,' Luke said. 'She wasn't here. But Billie could be expelled. Then she'll lose her scholarship. She explained it to me last night. She won't be able to study anywhere else.'

'I can't worry about Billie now,' Anthony said. 'I have to figure out what I'm going to do.'

Luke was shocked. Anthony had got Billie into trouble, and by Luke's code he should be more worried about her than about himself. But Luke saw an pretext to talk to Billie, and he could not resist it. Suppressing a guilty feeling, he said, 'Why don't I go to the girls' dorm and see whether Billie's back from Newport yet?'

'Would you?' Anthony said. 'Thanks.'

Luke shaved and changed his clothes. It was two o'clock when he reached the Radcliffe dormitory. A uniformed maid let him into the lobby. He asked for Billie. The maid sat at a desk, picked up a speaking-tube of the kind used on ships, blew into the mouthpiece, and said, 'Visitor for Miss Josephson.'

Billie came down wearing a dove-grey cashmere sweater and a plaid skirt. She looked lovely but distraught. She and Elspeth had been summoned to the office of Peter Ryder.

She showed him into the smoking room, where girls were allowed to receive male visitors. 'What am I going to do?' she said. Her face was drawn with distress, but Luke found her even more ravishing than yesterday.

'Anthony could say it was someone else in the room.'

Billie shook her head. 'They wouldn't believe it.' With a bitter smile, she said, 'I'll have to go back to Dallas and be a secretary to an oil man in cowboy boots.'

Two girls burst into the lounge, their faces flushed. 'Have you heard the news?' said one.

Luke shook his head, and Billie said desultorily, 'What's happened?'

'We're at war! The Japanese have bombed Hawaii!'

Luke could hardly take it in. 'Hawaii? What the heck for?'

'Is this true?' asked Billie.

'Everyone's talking about it on the street. People are stopping their cars.'

Two more girls rushed in, talking excitedly. Someone brought a radio downstairs and plugged it in. When it had warmed up they heard an announcer's voice. 'The battleship *Arizona* is reported destroyed and the *Oklahoma* sunk in Pearl Harbor. First reports say that more than one hundred US aircraft were crippled on the ground. American casualties are estimated to be at least two thousand dead and a thousand more injured. No warning was given for the Japanese attack.'

Billie said, 'It means war, doesn't it.'

'You bet it does,' Luke said angrily.

She squeezed his hand. 'I don't want you to be in a war,' she said. There were tears in her eyes. 'I don't want you hurt.'

'I'm so happy you feel that way.' He smiled ruefully. 'The world is falling apart, and I'm happy.' He looked at his watch. 'I suppose we all have to see the Dean, even though we're at war.' Then he was struck by a thought. 'Maybe there is a way for you and Anthony to stay at Harvard.'

ELSPETH WAS NERVOUS when the four of them met outside the Dean's study, but she told herself that she did not need to be afraid. She had broken the curfew last night, but she had not been caught. Anthony and Billie were the ones who were in trouble.

The Dean, summoned them inside. He was a fussy, old-fashioned man in a neat suit of black coat and waistcoat with grey pants. His bow tie was a perfect butterfly, and his oiled hair looked like black paint on a boiled egg. With him was a grey-haired spinster called Iris Rayford who was responsible for the moral welfare of Radcliffe girls.

They sat in a circle of chairs, as if for a tutorial. The Dean lit a cigarette. 'Now, you boys had better tell the truth,' Dean Ryder said. 'What happened in your room last night?'

Anthony ignored Ryder's question and acted as if he were in charge of the proceedings.

'Where's Jenkins?' he said curtly. 'He's the sneak, isn't he? A man has a right to be confronted by his accuser.'

'This isn't a court, Mr Carroll,' the Dean said. 'Miss Rayford and I have been asked to establish the facts. Disciplinary proceedings, if necessary, will follow in due course.'

'Enough of this,' Luke said with an impatient gesture. 'I brought a woman into the House last night, sir.'

The Dean frowned. 'My information is that it was Mr Carroll who invited the woman in.'

'I'm afraid you've been misinformed.'

Anthony said, 'Luke, I don't know what you're doing, but—'

'Let me tell the story,' Luke said. 'I met the girl at the Dew Drop Inn, a waitress there. Her name is Angela Carlotti.'

The Dean said, 'I was told that the person seen in Cambridge House was Miss Bilhah Josephson here.'

'No, sir,' Luke said. 'Miss Josephson is a friend of ours, but she spent last night at the home of a relative in Newport.'

Miss Rayford spoke to Billie. 'Will the relative confirm that?'

Billie shot a bewildered look at Luke, then said, 'Yes.'

Ryder said to Luke, 'Can you produce this . . . waitress?'

'Yes, sir, I can. But I don't intend to bring her into this.'

'In that case, you make it difficult for me to accept your story.'

'I don't think Miss Carlotti's evidence will be necessary.'

'I beg to differ, Mr Lucas.'

Then Luke dropped his bombshell. 'I'm leaving the college tonight, sir. I'm going to join the army tomorrow.'

Elspeth cried, 'No!'

For the first time the Dean did not have an answer. He stared at Luke with his mouth open. Elspeth realised Luke had been clever. The collage could hardly pursue a disciplinary action against a boy who was risking his life for his country. And if there were no investigation, then Billie was safe. A mist of grief obscured her vision. Luke had sacrificed everything—to save Billie.

Ryder was muttering about making his report and leaving others to decide. Miss Rayford wrote down the address of Billie's cousin. But it was all camouflage. They had been outwitted, and they knew it. At last the students were dismissed.

As soon as the door closed, Billie burst into tears. 'Don't go to war, Luke,' she said.

'You saved my life,' Anthony said. 'I'll never forget this.'

Luke turned to Elspeth. When he met her eye he flinched and she realised that her rage must be plainly visible. But she did not care. She stared at him for a moment then she raised her hand and slapped his face, once, very hard.

'You bastard,' she said. Then she turned and walked away.

1.00PM: LUKE WAS LOOKING for a quiet residential street. Driving away from Union Station he headed west. He crossed a river and found himself in a charming suburb of narrow streets lined with trees. He passed a building with a sign that read GEORGETOWN MIND HOSPITAL, and parked the stolen Buick on a dead-end street, facing the way he had come, in case he had to make a fast getaway.

He needed some simple tools: a chisel or screwdriver and a hammer. There was probably a tool kit in the trunk—but the trunk was locked. It took him about thirty seconds to pick the lock. As he had hoped, there were a few tools in a box next to the jack. He chose the largest screwdriver. There was no hammer, but there was a heavy wrench that would serve. He put them in the pocket of his raincoat.

He took the stolen suitcase from the car and walked around the corner. He knew he was conspicuous, a ragged bum walking in a nice neighbourhood. If the local busybody called the cops, he could be in trouble. On the other hand, if all went well he might be washed and shaved and dressed like a respectable citizen in half an hour's time.

He drew level with the first house in the street, crossed a small front yard and knocked at the door.

ROSEMARY SIMS saw a nice blue and white car drive slowly past her house, and she wondered whose it was. She had good eyesight still, and she could watch most of the street from her comfy chair by the first-floor window. So she saw the stranger when he came walking around the corner. 'Strange' was the word. He wore no hat, his raincoat was torn and his shoes were tied up with string.

He went to Mrs Britsky's door and knocked. Mrs Britsky—a widow, living alone—looked out of the window and waved him away.

He went to the next house. Young Jeannie Evans came to the door with baby Rita in her arms. She fished in the pocket of her apron and gave him something, probably a few coins. So he was a beggar.

Old Mr Clark came to the door in his bathrobe. The stranger got nothing out of him.

The owner of the next house, Mr Bonetti, was at work, and his pregnant wife had left five minutes ago, heading for the store. The stranger studied the door and glanced up and down the street.

Mrs Sims turned away from the window and lifted the handset of the phone. Slowly she dialled the number of the local police station.

Luke had to act fast. He inserted the screwdriver between the door and the jamb at the level of the lock. Then he struck the handle with the wrench, trying to force the blade into the socket of the lock. The first blow failed. He wiggled the screwdriver and used the wrench again, hammering as hard as he could. The screwdriver sank in an inch. He pulled sideways on the handle. To his profound relief, the door opened inwards.

He stepped quickly inside and closed the door behind him.

WHEN ROSEMARY SIMS finished dialling the number, she looked out of the window again, but the stranger had vanished. That was quick.

The police answered. Feeling confused, she hung up the phone without speaking.

IT WAS THE HOME of a young couple. They had a new couch and a big TV set in the living room, but they were still using orange crates for storage in the kitchen. An unopened letter on the hall radiator was addressed to Mr G. Bonetti.

Luke went upstairs. Of three bedrooms, only one was furnished. He threw the suitcase on the bed. Inside it he found a carefully folded blue stripe suit, a white shirt and a conservative striped tie. There were dark socks, clean underwear, and a pair of black wing-tips that looked only about half a size too big.

He stripped off his filthy clothes and kicked them into a corner. It gave him an odd feeling, to be naked in the home of strangers. He thought of skipping the shower, but he smelt bad, even to himself.

He crossed the tiny landing to the bathroom. It felt great to stand under the hot water and soap himself all over. When he got out, he dried himself with a pink bath towel and put on undershorts, pants, socks and shoes from the stolen case.

Luke found a safety razor and a shaving brush. He lathered his face and shaved quickly. Mr Bonetti didn't have any cologne, but maybe there was some in the suitcase. After stinking like a pig all morning, he liked the idea of smelling sweet. He found a neat leather toiletry case and unzipped it. No cologne was inside—but there was a hundred dollars in twenties, neatly folded: emergency money. He pocketed the cash, resolving to pay the man back one day.

He put on the shirt, tie and jacket. They fitted well and were of good quality. There was a mirror on the bedroom door. He had not looked at his reflection since early this morning in the men's room at Union Station, when he had been so shocked to see a filthy hobo staring back at him. He stepped up to the mirror, bracing himself.

He saw a tall, fit-looking man in his middle thirties, with black hair and blue eyes. A weary sense of relief swept over him. Take a guy like that, he thought. What would you say he does for a living? His hands were soft and did not look like those of a manual worker. He had a smooth face, one that had not spent much time out in bad weather. His hair was well cut. The guy in the mirror looked comfortable in the clothes of a corporate executive.

There was no hat or coat in the bag. Luke knew he would be conspicuous without either, on a cold January day. He opened the closet. Mr Bonetti had a sports jacket and a black suit he probably wore to church. There was no topcoat, but there was a lightweight raincoat. Luke took it off the hanger and put it on. It was a size small, but wearable. There was no hat, just a tweed cap that was too small. Luke would have to buy a hat, but the cap would serve for an hour or so—

He heard a noise downstairs. He froze, listening.

A young woman's voice said, 'What happened to my front door?'

Another voice, similar, replied, 'Looks like someone tried to break in! Maybe you should call the cops.'

Luke cursed under his breath.

'I don't know . . . looks like the thieves didn't get in.'

'How do you know? Better check if anything's been stolen.'

Luke realised he had to get out of there fast. He opened the bedroom window. There was no convenient tree or drainpipe down which he could climb.

'I'm going to look upstairs. We'll look pretty silly if we call the cops and there's no one here.'

Luke heard footsteps on the stairs. He crossed the landing to the bathroom and stood behind the door.

The footsteps mounted the staircase, crossed the landing and entered the bedroom. A voice said, 'Whose bag is that?'

Luke slipped out of the bathroom and tiptoed down the stairs.

'What kind of burglar brings luggage?'

'I'm calling the cops right now. This is spooky.'

Luke opened the front door and stepped outside.

He smiled. He had done it.

MRS SIMS FROWNED, mystified. The man leaving the Bonetti house had on Mr Bonetti's black raincoat and his tweed cap, but he was larger than Mr Bonetti.

She watched him walk down the street and turn the corner. A

minute later the blue-and-white car she had noticed earlier came around the corner, going too fast. She realised then that the man who had left the house was the beggar she had been watching. He must have broken in and stolen Mr Bonetti's clothes!

As the car passed her window, she read the licence plate and memorised the number.

2.00PM: IN A MENSWEAR store, Luke bought a grey felt hat and a navy wool topcoat. At last, he felt he could look the world in the eye.

Now he was ready to attack his problems. First he had to learn something about memory, what caused amnesia and how long it might last. Where did one go for information? A library. He got a street map of Washington at a newsstand. Prominently displayed was the Central Public Library, at the intersection of New York and Massachusetts Avenues. Luke drove there.

The effect of his new appearance was immediately apparent. The grey-haired librarian behind the counter stood up and said, 'Can I help you, sir?'

'I want to look at books on memory,' Luke said.

'That'll be the psychology section.' She led him up a grand staircase to the next floor and pointed to a corner.

Luke looked along the shelf. There were plenty of books on psychoanalysis, child development, and perception, none of which were any use. He picked out a fat tome called *The Human Brain* and browsed through it, but it seemed highly technical. There were some equations, and a certain amount of statistical material, which he found easy enough to understand.

Then his eye was caught by *An Introduction to the Psychology of Memory* by Bilhah Josephson. He pulled it out and found a chapter on disorders of the memory. He read: 'The common condition in which the patient "loses his memory" is known as "global amnesia". Luke was elated. He was not the only person to whom this had happened.

> Such a patient does not know his identity and will not recognise his own parents or children. However, he remembers a great deal else. He may be able to drive a car, speak foreign languages, and name the Prime Minister of Canada. The condition would be more appropriately called 'autobiographical amnesia'.

This was exactly what had happened to him. He could still check whether he was being tailed and start a stolen car without the key.

Dr Josephson outlined her theory that the brain contained several different memory banks, like separate filing cabinets, for different kinds of information.

The autobiographical memory records events we have experienced personally. The long-term semantic memory holds general knowledge such as the capital of Romania and how to solve quadratic equations. The short-term memory is where we keep a phone number for the few seconds in between looking it up in the phone book and dialling it.

She gave examples of patients who had lost one filing cabinet but retained others, as Luke had. He felt profound relief, and gratitude to the author of the book.

Then he was struck by an inspiration. He was in his thirties, so he must have followed some occupation for a decade. His professional knowledge should still be in his head, lodged in his long-term semantic memory. He ought to be able to use it to figure out his line of work. Thinking back over the last few minutes, he had noticed that he had easily understood the equations and statistics in *The Human Brain*. Maybe he was in a profession that involved numbers: perhaps an accountant or a maths teacher.

He found the maths section and looked along the shelves. A book called *Number Theory* caught his attention. He browsed through it. It was clearly presented, but some years out of date . . . Suddenly he looked up. He had discovered something. He understood number theory. And the book was not written for the curious layman. It was an academic work. He had to be some kind of scientist.

With mounting optimism, he located the chemistry shelf and picked out *Polymer Engineering*. He found it comprehensible but not easy. Next he moved to physics and tried *A Symposium on the Behaviour of Cold and Very Cold Gases*. It was fascinating, like reading a good novel.

His job involved maths and physics. What branch of physics? Cold gases were interesting, but he did not feel that he knew as much as the author of the book. He scanned the shelves and picked out *Principles of Rocket Design*. It was an elementary text, but nevertheless there was an error on the first page he looked at. Reading on, he found two more. 'Yes,' he said aloud, startling a nearby schoolboy who was studying a biology text. If he could recognise mistakes in a textbook, he had to be an expert. He was a rocket scientist.

He hurried to the information desk and asked, 'Is there any kind of list of scientists?'

'Sure,' the librarian said. '*The Dictionary of American Scientists.*'

He found the book easily. He sat and went through the index, searching for anyone named Luke. He found a biologist called Luke Parfitt, an archaeologist called Lucas Dimittry, and a pharmacologist called Luc Fontainebleu, but no physicist. Of course, he thought despondently, he was not even sure that Luke was his name. It was only what he had been called by Pete. For all he knew, his real name might be Percival.

He thought of another approach. Somewhere, there were people who knew him, friends and colleagues who would recognise him. Where did one find scientists? At a university.

He looked up Washington in the encyclopedia. The entry included a list of universities in the city. He picked Georgetown University because he had been in the Georgetown area earlier and knew how to get back there. On his street map, he saw that the university had a large campus. It would probably have a big physics department with dozens of professors. Surely one of them would know him?

Full of hope, he left the library and got back into his car.

2.30PM: WHEN THE CUBA MEETING took a coffee break, Anthony ran back to Q Building for an update from his team.

Pete met him on the stairs. 'Here's a weird report from the police in Georgetown,' he said. 'A housewife came back from the store to find that her home had been broken into and her shower used. The intruder had disappeared, leaving behind a pile of filthy old clothes.'

'At last—a break,' Anthony said. 'Give me the address.'

'You think this is our guy?'

'I'm sure of it! He's fed up with looking like a bum, so he's broken into an empty house, showered, shaved and put on some decent clothes. Come on, let's go. Grab some photos of Luke.'

Anthony left the building with Pete following, and they jumped into his old Cadillac. 'This may need delicate handling,' he said. 'We don't have a hundred men to chase up leads so my plan is to get the Washington Police Department working for us.'

He drove quickly to the address in the police report. It was a small home on a quiet street. A police cruiser was parked outside.

Before going into the house, Anthony studied the opposite side of the street, scrutinising the houses. After a moment he spotted what he was looking for: a face in an upstairs window, watching him. It was an elderly woman, who returned his stare with unabashed curiosity. She was just what he needed, a neighbourhood busybody.

They went to the house that had been broken into. He could see scratches and a little splintering on the door jamb where the lock had been forced. A neat job, he thought. That fitted Luke.

The door was opened by an attractive young woman who was expecting a baby. She took Anthony and Pete into her living room where two men were sitting on the couch, drinking coffee and smoking. One was a uniformed patrolman, the other a detective. An open suitcase was on the coffee table in front of them.

Anthony showed his identification to the cops, but he did not want Mrs Bonetti to know that the CIA was interested in the case, so he said, 'We're colleagues of these police officers.'

The detective was Lewis Hite. 'You know something about this?'

'We may have some information that will help, but first, I need to know what you've got.'

'We got a suitcase belongs to a guy named Rowley Anstruther, from New York. He breaks into Mrs Bonetti's house, takes a shower, and goes away, leaving his suitcase behind. Go figure!'

Anthony looked through the contents of the leather case. There were clean shirts and underwear, but no shoes, pants or jackets. 'Looks like Mr Anstruther arrived in Washington from New York today,' he said.

Mrs Bonetti said, 'How do you know that?'

'The bag contains clean underwear but no laundry,' Hite explained. 'So he probably hasn't yet spent a night away.'

Anthony said, 'I believe some old clothes were also left behind.'

The patrolman said, 'I got 'em.' He lifted a cardboard box from beside the couch.

Anthony recognised the rags Luke had been wearing. 'I don't believe Mr Anstruther came to this house,' he said. 'I think the bag was stolen from him this morning, probably at Union Station. We have a picture of the man we believe stole the suitcase and broke into this house.' Anthony nodded to Pete, who handed Hite a photograph. 'He's six foot one, hundred eighty pounds, athletic build, and may pretend to have lost his memory.'

'So what's the story?' Hite was intrigued. 'This guy wanted Anstruther's clothes and came here to change?'

'Something like that.'

'You think he's still in town.'

'Yes.' Anthony was not as sure as he pretended.

'I presume he's in a car.

'Let's find out.' Anthony turned to Mrs Bonetti. 'What's the name of the white-haired lady who lives across the street, a couple of doors down?'

'Rosemary Sims. We call her Nosy Rosie.'

'Excellent.' He turned to the detective. 'Let's have a word with her.'

They crossed the street and knocked on Mrs Sims's door. She opened it instantly—she had been waiting in the hall. 'I saw him!' she said. 'He went in there looking like a bum, and came out dressed to the nines.'

Hite said, 'Did he have a car, Mrs Sims?'

'Yes, a nice blue and white model.'

'Did you happen to notice the licence plate?' Hite asked.

'Yes,' she said triumphantly. 'I wrote it down.'

3.00PM: LUKE DROVE slowly through the iron gates of Georgetown University. He parked in front of the main entrance, a triple-arched portico marked HEALY HALL. Inside, a receptionist told him the way to the physics department. Following her directions, he found a large laboratory with a group of men who were working with the components of a microwave spectrograph. Judging by their ages, Luke thought they were professors and graduate students. He approached them with an expectant look.

One of the older men asked, 'Can I help you?'

'I hope so,' Luke said. 'Is there a department of geophysics here?'

'Goodness, no,' he said. 'At this university, even physics is considered a minor subject.' The others laughed.

'What about astronomy?'

'Why, yes, of course. Our observatory is famous.'

His spirits lifted. 'Where is it?'

The man gave him directions.

On the flat roof of a small two-storey house was a large revolving observatory, its dome having a sliding roof section. Luke approached it with mounting anticipation.

Inside, the rooms were arranged around a massive central pillar that supported the enormous weight of the dome. Luke opened a door and found an attractive woman about his own age sitting behind a typewriter. 'Good morning,' he said. 'Is the professor in?'

'You mean Father Heyden?'

'Uh, yes.'

'And you are?'

'Um . . . he won't know me,' Luke said. 'That is he will know me, I hope, but not by name.'

The secretary raised her eyebrows, 'Still, you do have a name.'

'Luke. Professor Luke.'

'To which university are you attached, Professor Luke?'

'Look, I didn't come here to be cross-examined. Just tell Father Heyden that Professor Luke, the rocketry physicist, has dropped by and would like a word with him.'

'I'm afraid that won't be possible,' she said firmly.

Luke left the room, slamming the door. He was angry with himself more than with the secretary, who was only protecting her boss. He decided to look around. The building seemed to be deserted. He climbed a wooden stair on the second floor and entered the observatory. It, too, was empty. He stood admiring the large revolving telescope, wondering what he was going to do next.

The secretary came up the stairs. He prepared himself for a row, but instead she spoke sympathetically. 'You're in some kind of trouble, aren't you,' she said.

Her kindness brought a lump to his throat. 'It's very embarrassing,' he said. 'I've lost my memory. I know I'm in the rocketry field, and I was hoping to run into someone who might recognise me.'

'All the faculty are at a lecture on rocket fuels at the Smithsonian Institute.'

Luke felt a surge of hope. 'Where's the Smithsonian Institute?'

'It's downtown, right in the Mall, around 10th Street.'

'What time is the lecture?'

'It started at three.'

Luke checked his watch. It was three thirty. 'Thank you,' he said, and he ran down the stairs and out of the building.

3.30PM: BILLIE WAS FURIOUS with Len Ross for trying to ingratiate himself with the people from the Sowerby Foundation. She was still annoyed that afternoon when the hospital's chief executive asked her to come to his office.

Charles Silverton waved Billie to a chair and said, 'Did you speak to the people from the Sowerby Foundation this morning?'

'Yes. Len was showing them around, and I joined the party.

'Do you think you could have said anything to offend them?'

'I don't think so. We just talked about the new wing.'

'You know, I really wanted you to get the job of Director of Research. Len Ross is a competent scientist, but you're exceptional.'

'The Foundation is backing Len for the job?'

He hesitated. 'I'm afraid they're insisting on it, as a condition of their grant.'

'The hell they are.' Billie was stunned.

'Do you know anyone connected with the Foundation?'

'One of my oldest friends, Anthony Carroll, is a trustee. He's my son's godfather.'

'Why is he on the board? What does he do for a living?'

'He works for the State Department, but his mother is very wealthy, and he's involved with several charities.'

'Does he have a grudge against you?'

Billie had been angry with Anthony after the catastrophe that led to Luke's leaving Harvard, and they never dated again. But she forgave him because of how he behaved towards Elspeth, who had gone into a decline. She had let her academic work slip, and was in danger of failing to graduate. It was Anthony who rescued her. They became close, though the relationship was a friendship rather than a romance. They studied together, and she caught up enough to pass. Anthony won back Billie's respect, and they had been friends ever since.

She told Charles, 'I got kind of mad at him, back in 1941, but we made it up long ago.'

'Maybe someone on the board admires Len's work.'

Billie considered. 'Len's approach is different from mine. He's a Freudian; he looks for psychoanalytical explanations.'

'So there might be a keen Freudian on the board who is against you. Why don't you ask your friend?'

'That's exactly what I'm going to do,' she said.

3.45PM: LUKE CHECKED his watch as he drove along K Street. He would be at the Smithsonian in about ten minutes. He should arrive as the talk was ending. Then he would find out who he was.

He turned right on 9th Street. A few moments later, he heard a police siren blip once. He looked in his rear-view mirror. A police cruiser was on his tail, lights flashing. There were two cops on the front seat. One pointed towards the kerb and mouthed, 'Pull over.'

Luke had almost made it. Could he have committed some minor

traffic violation? If they asked for his driving licence he had no kind of identification and he was driving a stolen car.

Ahead of him on the one-way street was a truck. Without further thought, he pulled around the truck. The cops switched on their siren and followed.

Luke pulled in front of the truck, going fast. Acting on instinct now, he yanked the parking brake and spun the wheel hard to the right. The Buick went into a long skid. The truck swerved left to avoid it. Luke's car came to rest facing the wrong way. He stepped on the gas, heading against the traffic on the one-way street.

Cars veered wildly left and right to avoid a head-on collision. Luke swung right to miss a city bus, then clipped a station wagon. He made it to the next crossing and swung right on to a broad avenue. He raced two blocks, running red lights, then looked in his mirror. There was no sign of the police car.

He turned again, heading south now. It was four o'clock, and he was farther away from the Smithsonian than he had been five minutes ago. He stepped on the gas. His luck changed. All the lights were green. He hit seventy crossing Constitution Avenue, and he was in the park.

He saw the big dark-red building like a castle in a fairy tale. He stopped the car and checked his watch. It was five past four. The audience would be leaving. He cursed and jumped out.

He ran across the grass. The secretary had told him the lecture was in the Aircraft Building around the back. He followed a little path to the side of the building, and found an elaborate iron gateway leading to the museum's back entrance. To his right was what looked like an old aircraft hangar. He went inside.

He looked around. All kinds of aircraft were suspended from the ceiling: old biplanes, a wartime jet, even a hot-air balloon. He spoke to a guard. 'I'm here for the lecture on rocket fuels.'

'You're too late,' the man said. 'The lecture's over.'

'Where was it held? I might still catch the speaker.'

'Far end of the hall,' the man said.

Most of the audience had left the lecture theatre, and attendants were already stacking the metal chairs. But a small knot of eight or nine men remained in a corner, deep in discussion, surrounding a white-haired man who might have been the lecturer.

Luke walked up to the group. The white-haired man glanced at him then looked back to the others. He carried on without a pause.

'Nitromethane is almost impossible to handle. You can't ignore safety factors.'

'You can build safety into your procedures,' said a young man in a tweed suit.

The argument was a familiar one to Luke. A variety of rocket fuels had been tested, many more powerful than the standard combination of alcohol and liquid oxygen, but they had drawbacks.

A man with a southern accent said, 'What about unsymmetrical dimethylhydrazine? I hear they're testing that at the Jet Propulsion Laboratory in Pasadena.'

Luke suddenly said, 'It works, but it's deadly poison.'

They all turned to him. The white-haired man frowned, looking slightly annoyed, resenting the interruption from a stranger.

Then the young man in the tweed suit looked shocked and said, 'My God, what are you doing in Washington, Luke?'

Luke felt so happy he could have wept.

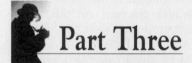 **Part Three**

4:15pm: Luke found he could not speak. The emotion of relief was so strong it seemed to constrict his throat. All day he had forced himself to be calm and rational, but now he was close to breaking point.

The other scientists resumed their conversation, oblivious to his distress, except for the young man, who said, 'Hey, are you OK?'

Luke nodded. After a moment, he managed to say, 'Could we talk?'

'Sure.' He led Luke into a small room with a couple of chairs, a desk and a phone. They sat down. 'What's going on?' said the man.

'I've lost my memory. I still remember my science—that's how I found my way to you guys—but I don't know anything about myself.'

Looking shocked, the young man said, 'Do you know who I am?'

Luke shook his head. 'I'm not even sure of my own name.'

'You're Dr Claude Lucas, but everyone calls you Luke. I'm Will McDermot.'

Luke closed his eyes, overwhelmed by relief and gratitude. 'Thank you, Will. Do you know where I live?'

'Huntsville, Alabama. You work for the Army Ballistic Missile Agency, based at Redstone Arsenal in Huntsville. You're a civilian, though. Your boss is Wernher von Braun.'

'I can't tell you how good it is to know this stuff!'

'I was surprised to see you because your team is about to launch a rocket that will put an American satellite in space for the first time. They're all down in Cape Canaveral.'

'Did I work on that?'

'Yeah. The Explorer. It's the most important launch in the history of the American space programme.'

'I ought to be there for the launch,' Luke said.

'Exactly . . . so do you have any idea why you're not?'

Luke shook his head. 'I woke up this morning in the men's room at Union Station. No idea how I got there.'

Will grinned. 'Sounds like you went to a great party last night!'

'Is that the kind of thing I do? Get so drunk I pass out?'

'I don't know you well enough to answer that. I'd be surprised, though. You know us scientists. Our idea of a party is to sit around drinking coffee and talking about our work.'

That sounded right to Luke. 'I'm going to call Cape Canaveral.'

'Great idea.' Will picked up the phone on the desk and handed the phone to Luke.

Luke got the number from information and dialled. 'This is Dr Lucas.' He felt inordinately pleased to be able to give his name. 'I'd like to speak to someone on the Explorer launch team.'

A moment later a voice said, 'Army security. Colonel Hide speaking.'

'This is Dr Lucas—'

'Luke! At last! Where the hell are you? We've been going crazy! We got Army Security looking for you, the FBI, even the CIA!'

'I'm in Washington. Listen, a strange thing has happened. I lost my memory. I've been wandering around town trying to figure out who I am. Finally I found some physicists who know me.'

'But that's extraordinary. How did it happen?'

'I was hoping you could tell me that, Colonel.'

'OK, well, I'll tell you what I know. Monday morning you took off, saying you had to go to Washington. You flew from Patrick Air Force base, near Cape Canaveral. Marigold made the reservations—'

'Who's Marigold?'

'Your secretary in Huntsville. She booked your usual suite at the Carlton Hotel in Washington.'

'Did I tell anyone the purpose of the trip?'

'Marigold made an appointment for you to see General Sherwood at the Pentagon yesterday—but you didn't keep the appointment.'

'Did I give a reason for wanting to see the general?'

'Apparently not. His area of responsibility is army security—but he's also a friend of your family's.'

'Is the launch going ahead tonight?'

'No, we've got weather problems. It's been postponed until tomorrow night at ten thirty.'

'Do I have friends here in Washington?'

'Sure. One of them's been calling me every hour. Bern Rothsten.' Hide read out a phone number.

Luke scribbled it on a scratch pad. 'I'll call him right away.'

'First you should talk to your wife.'

Luke froze. Wife, he thought. I have a wife. 'What's her name?'

'Elspeth,' Hide said. 'I'll transfer you to her. Hold the line.'

Luke had a nervous sensation in his stomach.

'Elspeth speaking. Luke, is that you?' She had a warm, low voice.

He said, 'Yes, this is Luke. I've lost my memory.'

'I've been so worried. Are you OK?'

He felt grateful for someone who cared how he was. 'I guess I am now,' he said. 'I spent the day trying to find out who I am.'

'Everyone's been looking for you. Where are you now?'

'At the Smithsonian, in the Aircraft Building.'

'Is someone taking care of you?'

'A fellow scientist has been helping me. And I have a number for Bern Rothsten.'

Elspeth said, 'You don't remember why you took off for Washington in such a hurry.'

'No. Obviously I didn't tell you.'

'You said it was better for me not to know. But I was frantic. I called an old friend of ours in Washington, Anthony Carroll. He's in the CIA. He called you at the Carlton Monday night, and arranged to meet him for breakfast on Tuesday morning—but you didn't show up. I'm going to call him now and tell him everything's all right.'

'Obviously something happened to me between Monday evening and Tuesday morning.'

'You ought to see a doctor, get yourself checked out.'

'I feel fine. But there's a lot I want to know. Do we have children?'

'No. We've been trying for a baby ever since we got married, which is four years ago, but we haven't succeeded.'

'Do we know why?'

'No, but we've been talking about adopting.'

'Are my parents alive?'

'Your Mom is. She lives in New York. Your Pa died five years ago.'

Luke felt a sudden wave of grief that seemed to come from nowhere. He had lost his memories of his father, and would never see him again. It seemed unbearably sad.

Elspeth went on, 'You have two brothers and a sister, all younger. Your baby sister Emily is your favourite. She lives in Baltimore.'

'Do you have phone numbers for them?'

'Of course. Hold on while I look them up.'

'I'd like to talk to them, I don't know why.' He heard a muffled sob at the other end of the line. 'Are you crying?'

Elspeth sniffed. 'I'm OK. Suddenly I felt so sorry for you,' she said tearfully. 'It must have been awful.'

'There were some bad moments.'

'Let me give you those numbers.' She read them out.

'I could go on asking you questions all day. Would you fly up here tonight?'

There was a moment of silence. 'My God, why?'

'To figure out this mystery with me. I could use some help—and companionship.'

'Luke, I can't leave Cape Canaveral now. We're about to launch the first American satellite, for heaven's sake! I can't let the team down at a moment like this.'

'I guess not.' He understood, but all the same he was hurt by her refusal. 'Who's Bern Rothsten?'

'He was at Harvard with you and Anthony Carroll.'

'He's been trying to reach me. Maybe he knows what this is about.'

'Call me later, won't you? I'll be at the Starlite Motel tonight.'

'OK.'

'Take care of yourself, Luke, please,' she said earnestly.

'I will, I promise.' He hung up.

He felt emotionally drained. Part of him wanted to go to his hotel and lie down. But he picked up the phone again and called Bern Rothsten. 'This is Luke Lucas,' he said.

'Luke, thank God! What the hell happened to you?'

'I don't really know anything except that I've lost my memory.'

'You lost your memory? Do you know how this happened.'

'No. I was hoping you might have a clue. Why have you been trying to reach me?'

'I was worried. You called me on Monday from Huntsville.'

'Huntsville? I thought I flew from Florida.'

'You did, but you stopped off in Huntsville because you had an errand to run. You said you were on your way here and would call me from the Carlton. But you never did.'

'Something happened to me on Monday night.'

'Yeah. Listen, Billie Josephson is an expert on memory.'

The name rang a bell. 'I think I came across her book in the library.'

'She's also my ex-wife, and an old friend of yours.' Bern gave Luke the number.

'I'm going to call her right away. Bern . . .'

'Yeah.'

'I lose my memory, and it turns out that an old friend of mine is a world expert on memory. Isn't that a hell of a coincidence?'

4.45 PM: BILLIE HAD an hour-long interview with a patient, but she was distracted during it, thinking about the Sowerby Foundation and Anthony Carroll. When it was over, she called Anthony. 'What the hell is going on?' she said abruptly. 'I was passed over for the post of Director of Research here at the hospital. Len Ross got the job. Did you know that?'

'Yeah, I guess I did.'

'I thought I might lose to a highly qualified outsider—Sol Weinberg, from Princeton, or someone of that order. But everyone knows I'm better than Len.'

'Do they?'

'Anthony, come on! You know it yourself. So why didn't I get the job? The foundation is insisting on Len.'

'I guess they have the right.'

'You're part of the foundation. It's very unusual for a trust to interfere in this kind of decision. They normally leave it to the experts. You must know why they took this step.'

'Well, I don't. There hasn't been a meeting about it.'

'Charles was very definite.'

'Most likely, the Director and one or two board members had a chat over a drink at the Cosmos Club. One of them has called Charles and given him the word.'

'Charles was shocked. He can't understand why they would do such a thing.'

'Maybe the Director doesn't approve of women earning high salaries when there are men like Ross trying to support a family.'

'For God's sake! I have a child and an elderly mother to take care of.'

'I didn't say it was logical. Listen, Billie, I have to go.'

She hung up and stared at the phone, trying to sort out her feelings. The conversation rang false to her. It was perfectly plausible that Anthony might not know about machinations among the other board members of the foundation. So why did she disbelieve him? Thinking back, she realised he had been evasive—which was not like him.

Anthony was lying.

WHEN ANTHONY hung up the phone, it rang again immediately. He picked it up and heard Elspeth say, 'I've been on hold for a quarter of an hour.'

'I was talking to Billie, she—'

'Never mind. I just spoke with Luke. He was at the Smithsonian, in the Aircraft Building, with a bunch of physicists.'

'I'm on my way.' Anthony dropped the phone and ran out of the door. Pete saw him and ran after him. They went down to the parking lot and jumped into Anthony's car.

The fact that Luke had spoken with Elspeth dismayed Anthony. Everything was coming unglued. But if he got to Luke, maybe he could hold things together.

It took them four minutes to drive to Independence Avenue and 10th Street. Inside the Aircraft Building, Anthony said, 'I'll go right, you go left.' He walked through the exhibits, scrutinising the faces of the men as they stared up at the aircraft suspended from the ceiling. At the far end of the building he met up with Pete, who made an empty-hands gesture.

The men's room and offices were checked and yielded nothing.

Anthony said, 'This is a catastrophe.'

Outside on Independence Avenue, Anthony saw two cops checking out a car parked on the other side of the road. Anthony went closer and saw that the car was a blue and white Buick with the same licence plate Nosy Rosie had given him.

'Did you just spot this car illegally parked?' he said to them.

'No, we saw a man driving it on 9th Street,' one cop said. 'But he got away from us. Few minutes later, we see the car parked here, but he's gone.'

Anthony took a business card out of his wallet. 'If you get a report of a car stolen near by, would you please call me at this number?'

The cop read the card and said, 'I'll do that, Mr Carroll.'

As Anthony and Pete returned to the yellow Cadillac, Pete said, 'What do you think he'll do now?'

'I don't know.'

Anthony was silent, thinking, while he drove to Q Building. Reaching his office, he said, 'I want you to go with two men to the Carlton Hotel. Take a room, then stake out the lobby. I'll join you there later.'

Anthony shut the door of the office. This really was a catastrophe. Now that Luke knew his identity, there was no telling what else he might find out. If he could find him, he could still patch things up. But he would have to take drastic measures. It would no longer be enough to put Luke under surveillance. He had to solve the problem once and for all.

With a heavy heart, he went to the photograph of President Eisenhower that hung on the wall. He pulled on one side of the frame, and the picture swung out to reveal a safe. He dialled the combination, opened the door, and took out his gun.

It was a Walther P38 automatic. This was the handgun used by the German army in the Second World War. Anthony had been issued with it before he went to North Africa. He also had a silencer that had been specially designed to fit it. He took the silencer from the safe, fitted it over the barrel of the pistol, and screwed it tight. He put on a long camel-hair winter coat, single-breasted, with deep inside pockets. He placed the gun in the right-hand pocket.

He buttoned his coat and went out.

6.00PM: LUKE TOOK A TAXICAB to the Georgetown Mind Hospital and gave his name at the reception desk, saying he had an appointment with Dr Josephson.

She had been charming on the phone: concerned about him, intrigued to know that he had lost his memory, eager to see him as soon as she could. Now she came running down the stairs, a short woman in a white lab coat, with big brown eyes and a flushed expression of excitement. Luke could not help smiling at the sight of her.

'It's so great to see you,' she said, throwing her arms around him.

He felt an impulse to respond to her exuberance but, afraid that he might do something to cause offence, he froze, his hands in the air like the victim of a holdup.

'You don't remember what I'm like,' she said, laughing. 'Relax, I'm almost harmless.'

He let his arms fall around her shoulders. Her small body was soft and round under the lab coat.

'Come on, I'll show you my office.' She led him up the stairs.

Billie had a small room with a plain desk and a steel filing cabinet, but she had made it pretty with flowers and a splashy abstract painting in bright colours. She gave Luke coffee and opened a package of cookies, then asked him about his amnesia.

She made notes as he answered her questions. Luke had had no food for twelve hours, and he ate all the cookies. She smiled and said, 'Want some more?' He shook his head.

'Well, I have a pretty clear picture,' she said. 'You have global amnesia, but otherwise you seem mentally healthy. I can't assess your physical state, but you look all right, just shook up.'

'Is there a cure for this type of amnesia?'

'No, there's not. The process is generally irreversible.'

That was a blow. Luke had hoped that everything might come back to him in a flash.

'Don't be downhearted,' Billie said. 'Sufferers are able to relearn what has been forgotten, so they can usually pick up the threads of their lives and live normally.'

Even while he was hearing horrible news, he found himself watching her with fascination, concentrating on her eyes, which seemed to glow with sympathy. He said, 'What might have caused the amnesia?'

'Brain damage is the first possibility to consider. However, there's no sign of injury.'

'So what else?'

'It can be brought on by prolonged stress, a sudden shock, or drugs. It's also a side effect of some treatments for schizophrenia involving a combination of electric shock and drugs.'

'Any way to tell which affected me?'

'Not conclusively. You need to find out what happened to you between Monday night and this morning. What's your next step?'

Luke stood up. 'I'm going to see Bern Rothsten. He may have some ideas.'

'I'll see you out.'

As they walked down the stairs, Luke asked, 'How long have you been divorced from Bern?'

'Five years. Long enough to become friends again.'

'This is a strange question, but—did you and I ever date?'

'Oh, boy,' said Billie. 'Did we ever.'

1943: ON THE DAY Italy surrendered, Billie bumped into Luke in the lobby of Q Building. At first she did not know him. She saw a thin man of about thirty and her eyes passed over him. Then he spoke. 'Billie? Don't you remember me?'

She knew the voice, of course, and it made her heart beat faster. But he was emaciated. His shirt collar was too large, and his jacket looked as if it were draped over a wire hanger. His eyes were the eyes of an old man. 'Luke,' she said. 'You look terrible,'

'Gee, thanks,' he said, with a tired smile. 'I've lost weight, I know. There's not a lot of food where I've been. What are you doing here?'

'A training course—maps, radio, firearms, unarmed combat.'

He grinned. 'You're not dressed for jujitsu.'

Billie still loved to dress stylishly, despite the war. She could not afford to buy the latest fashions on her army wages, but her father had taught all his children to sew. 'I'll take that as a compliment,' she said. 'Where have you been?'

'Do you have a minute to talk?'

'Of course.'

'Let's go outside.'

It was a warm September afternoon. They walked alongside the reflecting pool. 'How come you're in OSS?' Luke asked.

'Anthony Carroll fixed it,' she said. 'He's Bill Donovan's personal assistant now.' General 'Wild Bill' Donovan was head of OSS. 'He's brought in all his old friends from Harvard. Elspeth is in London, Peg is in Cairo, and I gather you and Bern have been behind enemy lines somewhere.'

'France,' Luke said.

'What was that like?'

'The first man I killed was a Frenchman,' he said abruptly. It was painfully obvious that he needed to talk about it.

'Tell me what happened,' she said.

'He was a cop, a gendarme. Claude, same name as me. He blundered into a farmhouse where my group was meeting. We had maps on the table, rifles stacked in the corner, and Bern was showing the Frenchies how to wire a time bomb.' Luke gave an odd kind of laugh, with no humour in it. 'Damn fool tried to arrest us.'

'What did you do?' Billie whispered.

'Took him outside and shot him in the back of the head.'

'Oh, my God.'

She took his hand and they walked around the long, narrow pool hand in hand. He told her another story, about a woman Resistance fighter who had been captured and tortured, and Billie cried. The afternoon cooled, and still the grim details spilled out of him: cars blown up, German officers assassinated, Jewish families led away to unknown destinations.

Finally he stumbled. 'I'm so tired,' he said. 'I've been sleeping badly.'

She hailed a taxi and took him to his hotel.

He was staying at the Carlton. She recalled that his family was wealthy. He had a corner suite. There was a grand piano in the living room and—something she had never seen before—a telephone extension in the bathroom.

She called room service and ordered chicken soup and scrambled eggs, hot rolls and cold milk. He sat on the couch and began to tell another story. Before he could finish it, the food came.

Billie signed the bill and tipped the waiter. When she turned around, Luke was asleep.

She woke him just long enough to get him into the bedroom and onto the bed. 'Don't leave,' he mumbled, then his eyes closed again.

She took off his boots and loosened his tie, then sat on the edge of the bed watching him for a while, remembering that long drive to Newport almost two years ago.

She slipped off her jacket and skirt. Then, in her underwear and stockings, she lay down on the bed. She got her arms around his shoulders, put his head on her bosom, and held him. 'Everything's all right, now,' she said. 'When you wake up, I'll still be here.'

AT DAWN, when he had been asleep for twelve hours, he got up to go to the bathroom. He got back into bed a couple of minutes later, wearing only his underwear. He put his arms around her and hugged her. 'Something I forgot to tell you, something important,' he said.

'What?'

'In France, I thought about you all the time. Every day.'

'Did you?' she whispered. 'Did you really?' But he did not answer. He had gone back to sleep. She lay in his embrace, thinking about him in France, risking his life and remembering her; and she was so happy she felt her heart would burst.

At eight o'clock in the morning, she called in and said she was sick. It was the first day she had taken off for illness in more than a year in the military. She had a bath, got dressed and ordered coffee and cornflakes from room service.

She was reading the *Washington Post* when Luke came stumbling out of the bedroom in his underwear, his jaw blue with stubble. She smiled at him, happy that he was awake.

'How long did I sleep?

She checked her wristwatch. 'About eighteen hours.'

'I haven't slept like that for a year.' He rubbed his eyes. 'You stayed all night?'

'You asked me to.'

He went to the phone and ordered breakfast from room service.

Billie had never spent the night with a man, so she did not know what to expect in the morning, but this disappointed her. It was so unromantic. She was reminded of her brothers waking up—they, too, emerged stubbly, grouchy and ravenous.

He sat beside her on the couch. 'I talked a lot yesterday.'

'That's the truth. About five hours straight.'

He took her hands. 'I'm so glad we met again.'

Her heart jumped. 'Me, too.'

'I'd like to kiss you.'

She felt a sudden leaping sensation inside, but she held back. The war had brought about a new moral laxity in Washington, but she was not part of it. She clasped her hands in her lap and said, 'I sure don't aim to kiss you until you're dressed.'

He gave her a sceptical look. 'Are you afraid of compromising yourself? We already spent the night together.'

'I stayed here because you begged me to.'

'I appreciate it.'

'Then don't imply I've already compromised myself so that anything else I might do makes no difference.'

He gave a big sigh. 'Well, I didn't intend to imply that. You're making a hell of a fuss about a casual remark.'

'Too darn casual.'

There was a knock at the door.

She did not want a waiter to see her with an undressed man. 'Get in the bedroom.'

He went into the bedroom. Billie opened the suite door and a waitress brought in the room service cart. 'There you go, Miss,' she said.

Billie flushed. There was an insult in that 'Miss'. She signed the bill but did not tip. 'There you go,' she said, and the waitress left.

Billie heard the shower running. She felt exhausted. She had spent hours in the grip of a profound romantic passion, then in a few minutes it had turned sour. How could such things happen? Whatever the reason, he had made her feel cheap.

Well, she thought, if I don't like it, why am I still here?

She put on her hat and left the suite, closing the door quietly behind her.

SHE SAW HIM almost every day for the next four weeks.

At first he was in Q Building for daily debriefing sessions. He would seek her out at lunch time, and they would eat together in the cafeteria or take sandwiches to the park. At the end of the week he asked her for a date, and they saw the movie of *Jane Eyre*. On Sunday they went canoeing on the Potomac. There was a spirit of recklessness in Washington. The city was full of young men on their way to the front or back home on leave. They wanted to gamble, drink, dance and make love because they might never have another chance. The Allies were winning the war, but the bubble of exuberance was burst daily by news of relatives, neighbours and college friends killed and wounded on the front line.

Luke put on a little weight and the haunted look went from his eyes. A little of his boyishness came back.

They talked endlessly and had a major fight about twice a week. Each followed the pattern of their first row, in his hotel suite. He would say something high-handed, or make a decision about their evening's plans without consulting her. She would protest hotly, and he would accuse her of overreacting. She would get angry and, in the heat of the argument, would make some wild assertion she knew to be false. Then he would say there was no point in talking to her, because she was willing to say anything to win an argument. But unlike the first fight when she left, he would walk out. Within minutes, she would be distraught. She would seek him out and beg him to forget it and be friends. At first he would be stony-faced; then she would say something that made him laugh, and he would melt.

But in all that time she did not go to his hotel, and when she kissed him it was a chaste brush of the lips, always in a public place.

On Friday afternoon Luke was waiting for Billie in the lobby of Q Building when she left for the day. She could see by his face that something bad had happened. 'What's wrong?' she said immediately.

'I'm going back to France. I leave on Monday morning. Bern, too.'

Tears came to her eyes. She swallowed hard. 'Two days.'

'I've got to pack.'

'I'll help you.'

They went to his hotel. As soon as they were inside the door she pulled him to her, and tilted her face to be kissed. This time there was nothing chaste about it. Then she slipped off her coat and said, 'Touch my breasts. Please.' And his hands closed over her small breasts. She shut her eyes and concentrated on the sensation.

They broke apart, and she stared at him hungrily, memorising his face. She wanted never to forget the particular blue of his eyes, the lock of dark hair that fell over his forehead, the curve of his jaw. 'I want a photo of you,' she said.

'I might have a family photo. Let me look.' He went into the bedroom. She followed him.

His battered brown leather bag lay on a stand. He took out a silver picture frame that opened up like a book. Inside were two photographs, one on each side. He slipped a picture out and handed it to her. It showed a younger Luke in a polo shirt. With him were an older couple, plus twin boys of around fifteen, and a little girl.

'I can't take this. It's your picture of your family,' she said.

'I want you to have it. That's me, I'm part of my family.'

'Did you take it to France with you?'

'Yes.'

'There are two photos in that frame. Show me the other one.'

He seemed reluctant, but opened it. The second picture had been cut out of the Radcliffe yearbook. It was a photo of Billie.

She burst into tears. He had cut her picture out of the yearbook and carried it, alongside the photo of his family, all that time his life was in such danger.

'Why are you crying?' he said.

'Because you love me,' she replied.

'It's true,' he said. 'I've loved you since Pearl Harbor weekend.'

Her passion turned to rage. 'How can you say that? You left me.'

'If we'd become lovers then, it would have destroyed Anthony.'

'How could you put Anthony's happiness before mine. We could have had each other for two years!' The tears streamed down her cheeks. 'Now we've only got two days—two lousy days!'

'Then stop crying and kiss me again,' he said.

They made love all weekend, frantic with desire and sorrow, knowing they might never meet again.

After Luke left on Monday morning, Billie cried for two days.

Eight weeks later she discovered she was pregnant.

6.30PM: 'YES, WE DATED,' Billie said as they went down the stairs.

They came to the door of the building. 'Were we in love?' Luke asked. He looked hard at her, studying her expression.

'Oh, sure,' she said, and although her tone was light, there was a catch in her voice. 'I thought you were the only man in the world.'

How could he have let a woman like this slip away from him? It seemed a tragedy worse than losing his memory. 'But you learned better and married Bern.'

'Yes.'

'What went wrong with him?'

'Conflicting values. For Bern, politics came above all else.'

'Do you have anyone now?'

'Sure. His name's Harold Brodsky.'

Luke felt foolish. Of course she had someone. 'I guess he shares your values.'

'Yes. The most important thing in his life is his child—he's a widower—and after that comes his academic work.'

'Which is?'

'Iodine chemistry. I feel the same about my work.' She smiled. 'I may not be starry-eyed about men, but I guess I'm still idealistic about unravelling the mysteries of the human mind.'

This brought Luke back to his immediate crisis. 'I wish you could unravel the mystery of my mind.'

'It's strange,' she said. 'Maybe you suffered a cranial injury that left no visible trace. You're not an alcoholic or a drug abuser, I can tell by looking at you.'

'Which leaves . . . ?'

She shook her head. 'You certainly aren't schizophrenic. You couldn't have been given the combination of drugs and electroconvulsive therapy that which could have caused—' She stopped suddenly, looking alluringly startled, mouth open, eyes wide.

'What?' Luke said.

'I just remembered Joseph Bellow. He was admitted late yesterday, after I'd gone home. Then he was discharged in the night—which was real strange.'

'What was wrong with him?'

'He was a schizophrenic.' She paled. 'Let's check his file.'

She turned and ran back up the stairs to a room marked RECORDS OFFICE. Luke followed. There was no one inside. Billie turned on the light, then opened a drawer and pulled out a folder. She read aloud:

'White male, six feet one inch tall, one hundred and eighty pounds, thirty-seven years old.'

'You think it was me,' Luke said.

She nodded. 'The patient was given a treatment that could cause global amnesia.'

'My God.' If she was right, this had been done to him deliberately. That made sense and explained why he had been followed around—presumably to make sure the treatment had worked. 'Who did this?'

'My colleague, Dr Leonard Ross, admitted the patient. A patient should normally be kept under observation for days before any treatment is given. And I can't imagine the medical justification for discharging the patient immediately afterwards. This is very irregular.'

'Sounds like Ross is in trouble.'

Billie sighed. 'If I complain, people will say I'm bitter because he got the job I wanted, Director of Research here.'

'When did that happen?'

'Today.'

Luke was startled. 'A hospital superior must have promised him the promotion in return for doing this irregular treatment.'

'No.' Billie shook her head. 'The trust that's funding the post, the Sowerby Foundation, insisted on Ross for the job.'

'But who at the foundation would want me to lose my memory?'

'I can guess who,' Billie said. 'Anthony Carroll. He's on the board.'

Luke recalled that Anthony was the CIA man mentioned by Elspeth. 'That still leaves the question why.'

'Well at least we have someone to ask,' Billie said, and she picked up the phone and dialled.

'Let me speak to Anthony Carroll,' Billie said. 'This is Dr Josephson. OK, have him call me at home one hour from now.'

'I thought this Anthony was a friend,' Luke said.

'Yeah.' Billie nodded, a worried frown on her face. 'So did I.'

7.30PM: BERN LIVED in a neighbourhood of large homes and foreign embassies. His apartment had an Iberian theme, with ornate Spanish colonial furniture in dark wood. Luke recalled Billie saying that Bern had fought in the Spanish Civil War. It was easy to imagine him as a fighter. His dark hair was receding now, but there was a hard set to his face and a knowing look in his grey eyes.

Bern shook Luke's hand warmly and gave him strong coffee in a small cup. 'What the hell is going on, old buddy?' Bern asked.

Luke sat down and related what he and Billie had discovered at the hospital. Then he said, 'Here's what I think happened to me. I don't know if you're going to buy it, but I'm hoping you can shed some light on the mystery.'

'I'll do what I can.'

'I came to Washington on Monday, to see an army general for some mysterious purpose that I wouldn't tell anyone about. My wife was worried about me and called Anthony, who made a breakfast date with me for Tuesday morning.'

'It makes sense. Anthony's your oldest friend. You were roommates already when I met you.'

'The next bit is more speculative. At breakfast Anthony put something in my coffee to make me fall asleep, then drove me to Georgetown Mind Hospital. He waited until Billie left for the day, checked me in under a false name, then got hold of Dr Len Ross. Using his position as a board member of the Sowerby Foundation, he persuaded Ross to give me a treatment that would destroy my memory.'

Luke waited for Bern to say the whole thing was ludicrous, but he did not. To Luke's surprise he simply said, 'But for God's sake, why?'

Luke began to feel better. If Bern believed him he might help. He said, 'For the moment, let's concentrate on how, rather than why. He checked me out of the hospital, dressed me in rags and dumped me in Union Station with a sidekick to keep an eye on me and make sure the amnesia treatment had worked.'

'But he must have known you'd find out the truth sooner or later.'

'He had to calculate that after a few days or weeks I would figure out who I was. But by then the trail would have gone cold. Billie probably would have forgotten about the mystery patient—and Ross would have destroyed his records.'

Bern nodded thoughtfully. 'A risky plan, but one with a good chance of success.'

'I'm surprised you're not more sceptical.'

Bern shrugged. 'We've all been in secret work. These things happen.'

Luke felt sure Bern was keeping something back. 'Bern, if there's something else you know, for God's sake, tell me.'

'There is something—but I don't want to get anyone into trouble.'

Luke's heart leaped in hope. 'Tell me, please. I'm desperate.'

Bern took a deep breath. 'Towards the end of the war, Billie and Anthony worked on a special project for OSS, the Truth Drug Committee. They were looking for drugs that would affect prisoners under interrogation. After the war, Billie went back to college and did her doctoral thesis on the effects of various legal drugs such as nicotine on people's mental states. When she finally became a professor, she continued to work on the same area, concentrating on how drugs and other factors affect memory.'

'But not for the CIA.'

'That's what I thought. But I was wrong. In 1950, the Agency started a project about mind control codenamed Bluebird. They financed a whole series of legitimate research projects in universities, channelling the money through trusts to conceal their true source. And they financed Billie's work.'

'How did she feel about that?'

'We fought about it. I said it was wrong; the CIA was planning to brainwash people. She said that all scientific knowledge could be used for good or evil; she was doing invaluable research and she didn't care who paid the bill.'

'Is that why you divorced?'

'Sort of. In 1952 I wrote a screenplay about a secret government agency that brainwashed unsuspecting citizens, but I didn't tell Billie. The movie came out in 1953 and was a huge hit. My career was made—I was deluged with offers from the studios.'

'And Billie?'

'I took her to the premiere. She went ape. She said I'd used confidential information I got from her. She was sure the CIA would withdraw her funding. It was the end of our marriage.'

'That's what Billie meant when she said you had a conflict of values.'

'She's right. She should have married you.'

Luke's heart missed a beat. He was curious to know why Bern said that, but he postponed the question. 'I assume the CIA didn't cut off her funding.'

'No.' Bern looked bitterly angry. 'They destroyed my career instead. I was subjected to a loyalty investigation. Of course, I had been a communist, right up until the end of the war, so I made an easy target. I was blacklisted in Hollywood.'

'What did you do?'

'I had a couple of bad years, then I thought of a series of children's books.' He pointed to a bookcase. The bright jackets made a splash of colour. 'I wrote the first story under a pseudonym. The book was a big best seller, and I've written two a year ever since.'

'Now I understand why you didn't react with total incredulity to my story,' Luke said.

'Yes,' Bern said. 'I believe Anthony did this. But I don't have the least idea why.'

8.00PM: BILLIE SAT at her dressing table, freshening her make-up. She could hear television gunfire downstairs: Larry and Becky-Ma were watching *Wagon Train*.

She did not feel like a date with Harold Brodsky tonight. She was angry about not getting the job she wanted, bewildered by what Anthony had done, and confused and threatened to find that the old chemistry between herself and Luke was as powerful as ever.

The phone rang. She jumped up and crossed the room to the extension by the bed, but Larry had already picked up in the hallway. She heard Anthony say, 'This is the CIA. Washington is about to be invaded by an army of bouncing cabbages.'

Larry giggled. 'Uncle Anthony, it's you!'

'If you are approached by a cabbage do not, repeat, do not attempt to reason with it.'

'You're making this up!' Larry laughed.

Billie said, 'Anthony, I'm on the extension.'

Anthony said, 'Get your jammies on, Larry, OK?'

'OK,' said Larry. He hung up.

'Anthony, what the hell are you up to?' Billie asked. 'I could tell you were lying last time we spoke, but I didn't know what the truth was then. Now I do. I know what you did to Luke at my hospital last night. I want an explanation.'

'I can't really talk about this on the phone. If we could meet sometime in the next few days—'

'I want your story right now.'

'I'll explain everything if you'll meet me tomorrow.'

She almost agreed, then she remembered what he had done. 'You went behind my back, right in my own hospital. Tell me the truth right now or I'll go to the FBI the minute I hang up.'

It was dangerous to threaten men—it often made them obstinate. But she knew how the CIA hated and feared interference from the FBI, especially when the Agency was working on the borderline of legality, which was most of the time.

He sighed. 'You may find this hard to believe.'

'Try me.'

'Well, here goes. Luke is a spy, Billie.'

'Don't be absurd.'

'He's an agent for Moscow. He's been passing rocket secrets to the Soviets for years. How do you think they managed to put their Sputnik into orbit while our satellite was still on the laboratory bench? They had the benefit of all our research as well as their own.'

'Anthony, we've both known Luke for twenty years. He'd never betray his country.'

'People do. Remember, when he was with the French Resistance he was working with the communists. They were on our side then, but obviously he continued after the war.'

Billie sat down, feeling stunned. 'Do you have evidence?'

'I have *proof*—top secret blueprints he gave a known KGB officer.'

'But even if all this is true, why did you wipe out his memory?'

'To save his life. The CIA was going to kill him.'

'Why not just put him on trial as a spy?'

'And have the whole world know that our security is so lousy the Soviets have been getting all our rocket secrets for years?'

'So what happened?'

'I persuaded them to try this. Nobody knows except the Director of the CIA and the President. And it would have worked, if only he'd believed that he lost his memory after a night of drinking and lived the life of a bum for a while. I could have kept the lid on. Even he would never have known what secrets he gave away. Is he with you now?'

'No.' Billie felt the hairs prickle on the back of her neck.'

'I need to talk to him before he does himself any more damage.'

Acting on instinct, Billie lied. 'I don't know where he is.'

'You wouldn't hide anything from me, would you?'

'You've already said your organisation wanted to kill Luke. It would be dumb of me to tell you where he is, if I knew. But I don't.'

'Billie, listen to me. I'm his only hope. Tell him to call me, if you want to save his life.'

'I'll think about it,' Billie said, but Anthony had already hung up.

8.30PM: LUKE PUT DOWN the phone with a shaky hand. Bern said, 'What did Billie say? You look like a ghost,'

'Anthony says I'm a Soviet agent,' Luke told him. 'The CIA was going to kill me, but Anthony persuaded them that it would be just as effective to wipe my memory. Could it be true?'

'Hell, no.'

'You can't be sure of that.'

'Yes, I can. Because I *was* a Soviet agent and you ended my career.'

'How?'

Bern stood up. 'I'm going to make you a sandwich.'

Luke realised he was painfully hungry. 'That sounds great.'

They went into the kitchen. Bern opened the refrigerator and took out a loaf of rye bread, butter, corned beef and an onion.

'It was in the war,' Bern said, as he buttered four slices of bread. 'The French Resistance was divided into Gaullists and communists, and they were manoeuvring for position. Roosevelt and Churchill wanted to make sure the communists couldn't win an election. So the Gaullists were getting all the guns and ammunition.'

'How did I feel about that?'

Bern layered corned beef and onion rings on the bread. 'You just wanted to beat the Nazis and go home, but I had another agenda. I wanted to even things up.'

'How?'

'I tipped off the communists about a parachute drop we were expecting, so they could ambush us and steal our ordnance.' He shook his head ruefully. 'They screwed up royally. They attacked us as soon as the stuff hit the ground. So you knew we had been betrayed. And I was the obvious suspect.'

'What did I do?'

'You offered me a deal. I had to stop working for Moscow, right then, and you would keep quiet about what I had done, for ever. We both kept our promises, but our friendship was never the same.'

'If I'd been a communist, I would have covered up for you.'

'Absolutely.'

'So Anthony is mistaken.'

'Or lying.' Bern put the sandwiches on plates. 'Soda?'

'Sure.'

Bern took two bottles of Coke from the refrigerator and opened them. He handed Luke a plate and a bottle, picked up his own, and led the way back into the living room.

Luke finished the sandwich in a few bites.

Bern said, 'If Anthony is lying, what was his real reason for making you lose your memory?'

'It has to be connected with my sudden departure from Cape Canaveral. I must have learned something so important that I had to rush to the Pentagon to talk to them about it. I guess I told Anthony what I had found out and he thought it was so important that he had to wipe my memory of it.'

'I wonder what the hell it was.'

'I guess my first step to finding out is to go to my hotel room and look through my stuff. Maybe I'll find a clue.'

'If Anthony wiped your memory, he must have gone through your possessions too.'

'But there may be something he didn't recognise as relevant.'

'And then?'

'The only other place to look would be Cape Canaveral. I'll fly back tonight or tomorrow morning.'

'Spend the night here,' Bern said. 'My instincts tell me you're in danger. I don't like the idea of you spending the night alone. Go to the Carlton, pick up your stuff, and come back here. I'll take you to the airport in the morning.'

Luke said, 'You've been a heck of a good friend to me over this.'

Bern shrugged. 'We go back a long way.'

'But you just told me that, after that incident in France, our friendship was never the same.'

'That's true.' Bern gave Luke a candid look. 'Your attitude was that a man who betrayed you once would betray you twice.'

'I can believe that,' Luke said thoughtfully. 'I was wrong, though, wasn't I?'

'Yes,' Bern said. 'You were.'

9.30PM: ANTHONY'S YELLOW CADILLAC was parked outside the Carlton Hotel. Pete hurried out of the building and came to the car. 'Ackie called in. Luke is at Bernard Rothsten's place.'

'At last,' Anthony said. He had posted agents outside Bern's building and Billie's house.

Pete added, 'When he leaves, Ackie will follow him on the motorcycle. Do you think he'll come here?'

'He may. I'll wait.' There were two more agents in the hotel lobby who would alert Anthony if Luke should go in by another entrance.

A little later a taxicab pulled into the hotel's driveway, and Luke got out. He was wearing a navy topcoat and a grey hat. Across the street, Ackie Horwitz pulled up on his motorcycle. Anthony got out of his car and strolled towards the hotel entrance.

Luke paid the taxi driver. He glanced at Anthony but did not recognise him.

LUKE KNEW he had been followed from Bern's apartment by a man on a motorcycle. Now he was strung taut, all his senses on alert.

The lobby of the Carlton looked like a grand drawing room, full of reproduction French furniture. It was a luxurious place, designed to soothe the nerves of jangled travellers. It did nothing for Luke.

Scanning the room, he quickly identified two men who had the air of agents: one sitting on a sofa, the other near the elevator. They were dressed in business suits. They definitely were not out for an evening in expensive restaurants and bars. He thought of walking right out again—but where would that leave him? He approached the reception desk, gave his name, and asked for the key to his room. As he turned away, a stranger spoke to him. 'Hey, Luke!'

It was the man who had walked into the hotel behind him.

Luke said, 'I'm afraid I don't know who you are.'

'Anthony Carroll. I'm so glad I've caught up with you at last!' He held out his hand to shake.

Luke tensed. He still didn't know whether Anthony was enemy or friend. He shook hands and said, 'I have a lot of questions to ask you.'

'And I'm ready to answer them.'

Luke paused, wondering where to begin. Anthony did not look like a man who would betray an old friend. He had an open face. In the end, Luke said, 'How could you do this to me? I'm not a spy.'

'It's not that simple. I had to do it—I was trying to save your life.'

'Neither Bern nor Billie believes your story about my working for Moscow.'

'They don't know everything.'

'What do you know that they don't?'

'I'll tell you. But we can't talk here. Shall we go to my office? It's five minutes away.'

'Let's go to my suite,' Luke said.

Anthony hesitated, then said, 'Sure.'

They crossed the lobby. Luke checked the number on his room key: 530. 'Fifth floor,' he said to the elevator operator.

They did not speak as they went up. Luke looked at Anthony's clothes: the old camel-hair coat, the rumpled suit, the nondescript tie. Suddenly, Luke saw that the soft material of the coat sagged slightly on the right side. There was a heavy object in the pocket.

He felt cold with fear. He had not thought that Anthony would have a gun. Trying to keep his face immobile, Luke thought furiously. Could Anthony shoot him right here in the hotel?

As the elevator stopped at the fifth floor, Anthony unbuttoned his coat. For a fast draw, Luke thought. They stepped out. Luke did not know which way to go, but Anthony confidently turned right. He must have been to Luke's room already.

Luke tried to make himself calm. Anthony had the gun, but Luke had guessed Anthony's intentions. It was about even.

They reached the door and Luke took out his key. If he went inside, he was dead.

He unlocked the door and pushed it open. 'Come in,' he said. He stood aside to let his guest enter first.

Anthony hesitated, then walked past Luke through the doorway.

Luke hooked his foot around Anthony's right ankle, put both hands flat on Anthony's shoulder blades, and pushed hard. Anthony went flying. He crashed into a small table, knocking over a vase. In desperation he grabbed at a brass floor lamp, but it fell with him.

Luke pulled the door shut and ran for his life. He hurtled along the corridor, burst through the fire exit to the staircase and ran down. On the next floor, he crashed into a maid carrying a stack of towels. 'I'm sorry,' he called as towels flew everywhere.

ANTHONY KNEW, before he did it, that it was a mistake to enter the room first, but Luke left him no choice. After a stunned moment, he picked himself up and opened the door. Looking out, he saw Luke haring along the corridor. As Anthony gave chase, Luke disappeared into the stairwell.

Anthony followed, running as fast as he could. On the next floor down, he was momentarily delayed by a maid who was kneeling on the floor, picking up scattered towels. He slowed his pace to man-oeuvre around her. As he did so, he heard the elevator arrive.

A couple in evening clothes emerged. Anthony barged past them into the elevator and said, 'Ground floor, and quick about it.'

The man slammed the doors and threw the lever. The elevator descended slowly.

LUKE EMERGED into the lobby next to the elevator doors. His heart sank. The two agents he had spotted earlier were standing in front of the main entrance, blocking his way out. A moment later, the elevator door opened and Anthony stepped out. Luke turned and ran back into the depths of the hotel. Behind him he heard the pounding footsteps of Anthony giving chase. There had to be a back entrance—supplies could not possibly be delivered through the main lobby.

He pushed through a curtain and found himself in a little court-yard decorated like a Mediterranean outdoor café. Barging between the tables, he made it to an exit door, emerging into a kind of butler's pantry. Half a dozen uniformed waiters were heating food in chafing dishes and arranging plates on trays. In the middle of the room was a staircase leading down. Luke pushed through the waiters and took the stairs, ignoring a voice that called, 'Excuse me, sir. You can't go down there!' As Anthony charged after him, the same voice said indignantly, 'What is this, Union Station?'

In the basement was the kitchen, a sweaty purgatory where dozens of chefs cooked for hundreds of people. They were too busy to pay attention to Luke as he dodged between the refrigerators and the ranges. At the back of the kitchen, he found a staircase going up. He guessed it led to the delivery entrance. He raced up the stairs. At the top, he burst through a door into the cold night air.

He was in a dark yard. Fifty yards to his right was a high wire fence with a closed gate. He ran towards it. He heard the door behind him bang open, and guessed that Anthony had come out.

Luke reached the gate. It was closed and secured with a big steel padlock. Heart pounding, he scrambled up the fence. As he reached the top, he heard the discreet cough of a silenced pistol. But he felt nothing. It was a hard shot, a moving target fifty yards away in the dark. He flung himself over the top. The pistol coughed again. He staggered and fell to the ground. He heard a third muffled shot. He sprang to his feet and ran, heading east. At the corner, he looked back. Anthony was nowhere in sight.

He had escaped.

10.30PM: MRS RILEY'S TUNA BAKE was as tasty as promised. For dessert, Harold served cherry pie and ice cream. Billie felt guilty. He was trying so hard to please her, but her mind was on Luke and Anthony, their shared past and their puzzling new entanglement.

After dinner Harold suggested they move to the living room. He produced a bottle of expensive French brandy and poured generous measures into two snifters. Was he trying to stiffen his own courage, Billie wondered, or lower her resistance?

Harold Brodsky was normally an entertaining talker, witty and clever, and she generally laughed a lot when she was with him, but tonight he seemed preoccupied.

He poured himself another brandy. 'I've been thinking about our future,' he said.

Billie's heart sank. He was going to propose. Yesterday she would have accepted him, but today she could hardly think about it.

He took her hand. 'I love you,' he said. 'We get on well, we have the same interests, and we both have a child. But that's not why I want to marry you. I just adore you, for no reason other than you're you. I want us to be together for ever.' He looked at her, then said, 'How do you feel?'

Billie sighed. 'I'm fond of you. Yesterday, I would have said yes, let's get married. But today I met someone from my past, and I remembered what it was like to be in love at the age of twenty-one. I don't feel that way about you, Harold.'

He was not totally discouraged. 'Who does, at our age?'

'Maybe you're right,' she said.

The doorbell rang and Billie's heart leaped.

'Who the heck is that?' Harold said angrily. He got up and went out to the hall.

Billie heard Luke's voice at the door. 'I need to talk to Billie.'

She wondered why she was so inordinately pleased.

Harold said, 'I'm not sure she wants to be disturbed right now.'

'It's important.'

'How did you know she was here?'

'Her mother told me. I'm sorry, I don't have time to dick around.' Billie heard a cry of protest from Harold, and she guessed Luke had forced his way into the house. She went into the hallway. Luke looked very shaken. 'What's happened now?' she said.

'Anthony shot at me.'

Billie was shocked. 'Anthony? My God, what got into him?'

Harold looked scared. 'What's this about a shooting?'

Luke ignored him and said to Billie, 'I'm going to the Pentagon, but I may not be believed. Will you come and back me up?'

'Sure,' she said. She took her coat off the hall stand.

Harold said, 'Billie! We were having a very important conversation.'

Luke said, 'I really need you.'

Billie hesitated. It was hard on Harold. He had obviously been planning this moment for some time. But Luke's life was in danger. 'I'm sorry,' she said to Harold. 'I have to go.' She lifted her face to be kissed, but he turned away.

'Get out of my house, both of you,' Harold said furiously.

11.00PM: ANTHONY FOUND some stationery in the desk drawer of the hotel room Pete had rented. He took out an envelope. From his pocket he took three slugs and three cartridge cases, the rounds he had fired at Luke. He put them into the envelope and sealed it, then stuffed it into his pocket. He would dispose of it later. He was doing damage control. He had very little time, but he had to be meticulous. He needed to wipe out all trace of this incident.

The assistant manager on duty came into the room. He was a small, bald man. 'Sit down, please, Mr Suchard.' Anthony showed the man his CIA identification.

'What can I do for you, Mr Carroll?' Suchard asked.

'First, I want to apologise for the little fracas we had earlier.'

Suchard nodded primly. 'Fortunately, few guests noticed anything.'

'I'm glad we didn't disrupt your fine hotel too much, even over a matter of national security. Of course, I can't give you the details, but I hope I can rely on your discretion.'

'Indeed, you can.'

Anthony took out a roll of bills. 'The State Department has a small fund for compensation in these instances.' He slowly counted five twenties and handed them over.

'Thank you, sir,' said Suchard. 'I'm sure we can handle things.'

'If anyone questions you, it might be best to say you saw nothing.'

'Of course.' Suchard stood up. 'If there's anything else . . .'

'I'll be in touch.' Anthony nodded dismissively, and Suchard left.

Pete came in. 'The head of security at Cape Canaveral is Colonel Bill Hide.' He handed Anthony a slip of paper with the number.

Anthony dialled it and got through. 'This Anthony Carroll, CIA.'

Hide spoke with a slow, unmilitary drawl. 'Well, what can I do for you, Mr Carroll?'

'I'm calling about Dr Lucas.'

'Oh, yes?'

He sounded faintly hostile, and Anthony decided to butter him up. 'I would appreciate your advice, if you could spare a moment, Colonel.'

Hide warmed up. 'Of course, anything I can do.'

'I think you know that Dr Lucas has been behaving strangely. What would you say is his mental state?'

'He seemed normal last time I saw him, but I talked to him a few hours ago and he told me he'd lost his memory.

'There's more to it than that. He stole a car and broke into a house, got into a fight with a cop, stuff like that.'

'My God, he's in worse shape than I thought.'

Hide was buying the story, Anthony thought with relief. He pressed on. 'We think he's not rational, but you know him better than we do. What would you say is going on?'

'Hell, I think he's suffering some kind of breakdown.' This was exactly what Anthony wanted Hide to believe. Hide continued, 'Normally, Luke is as sane as you or me. Obviously something has destabilised him.'

'He seems to think there's some kind of conspiracy against him— but you're saying we shouldn't necessarily credit that.'

'Not for a minute.'

'So we should soft-pedal this stuff. I mean, we shouldn't alert the Pentagon.'

'God, no,' Hide said worriedly. 'In fact, I'd better call them and warn them that Luke seems to have lost his marbles.'

'As you wish. Thank you, Colonel. You've set my mind at rest.'

'You're welcome.'

Anthony hung up and reviewed the situation. There was no evidence left at the hotel. He had prejudiced the Pentagon against any report Luke might make. That just left Billie's hospital.

He stood up. 'I'll be back in an hour,' he said to Pete. 'Take Malone and Curtis and bribe a room service waiter to let you into Luke's suite. I have a feeling he'll come back.'

12 MIDNIGHT: BILLIE drove the red Thunderbird into the parking lot of the Georgetown Mind Hospital and killed the engine. Colonel Lopez from the Pentagon pulled alongside her in a Ford Fairlane.

'He doesn't believe a word I say,' Luke said angrily.

'You can't blame him,' Billie reasoned. 'The assistant manager of the Carlton says no one was chased through the kitchens, and there are no cartridge cases at the loading dock.'

'Anthony cleaned up the evidence.'

'I know that, but Colonel Lopez doesn't.'

They got out of their cars and walked into the building. Billie led the two men up the stairs and along the corridor to the records office.

'I'm going to show you the file of a man named Joseph Bellow, whose physical characteristics match Luke's,' she told the colonel. 'You'll see that he was admitted on Tuesday, treated, then discharged at four o'clock on Wednesday morning. It's very unusual for a schizophrenic patient to be given treatment without observation first and it's unheard of for a patient to be released from a mental hospital at four o'clock in the morning.'

Billie opened the drawer, pulled out the Bellow file and opened it. It was empty. 'Oh, my God,' she said.

Luke stared at the folder in disbelief. 'I saw the papers myself less than six hours ago,'

Lopez stood up with a weary air. 'Well, I guess that's it.'

Luke had the nightmare feeling that he was living in a surreal world in which people could do what they liked to him, and he could never prove it had happened.

'Wait,' Billie said. 'The register will show his admission. It's kept at the reception desk.'

They went down to the lobby. Billie said. 'Let me see the register, please, Charlie.'

'Right away, Dr Josephson.' The young black man behind the counter searched around for a moment. 'Where did that thing go?' he said. 'I know it was here a couple of hours ago.'

Billie's face was like thunder. 'Tell me something. Has Dr Ross been here tonight?'

'Yes, ma'am. He left a few minutes ago.'

'Next time you see him, ask him where the register went.'

Luke turned to Lopez. 'Before we saw you tonight, Colonel, had someone else talked to you about me?'

Lopez hesitated. 'Yes,' he admitted. 'I guess you're entitled to know. We got a call from a Colonel Hide down in Cape Canaveral. He said the CIA had reported that you were behaving irrationally.'

Luke nodded grimly. 'Anthony again.'

Billie said to Lopez, 'I don't blame you for not believing us, when we have no evidence.'

'I didn't say I don't believe you,' Lopez said.

Luke was startled, and looked at the colonel with new hope.

Lopez went on, 'I could believe you imagined that a CIA man chased you around the Carlton. I might even accept that you and the doctor conspired to pretend there used to be a file and it disappeared. But I don't believe that Charlie here is in on the conspiracy. There must be a daily register, and it's gone. I don't think you took it, but who did? Someone has something to hide.'

'So you believe me?' Luke said.

'Something is going on. And it must have to do with that rocket launch. I'm going to order a full security alert at Cape Canaveral.'

'But what about Anthony?'

'I have a friend at the CIA. I'm going to tell him your story, and say I don't know whether it's true or not, but I'm concerned.'

'That's not going to get us far!' Luke protested. 'We need to know what's going on, why they wiped my memory!'

'I agree,' Lopez said. 'But I can't do any more. The rest is up to you.'

'So I'm on my own.' Luke said.

'No, you're not,' said Billie. 'You're not on your own.'

 # Part Four

1.00am: Billie parked her car around the corner from the entrance of the Carlton. 'I'll go first,' she said. 'If there's anyone suspicious in the lobby, I'll come right out again. When you see me take my coat off, you'll know it's all clear.'

Luke was not comfortable with this plan. 'What if Anthony's there?'

'He won't shoot me.' She got out of the car and he watched her go into the hotel. He could see through the glass doors into the lobby. A porter approached her and Luke guessed she was saying, 'I'm Mrs Lucas, my husband will be along in a moment.' Then she took off her coat.

Luke entered the hotel. For the porter's benefit he said, 'I want to make a call before we go upstairs, honey.' Next to the reception desk was a phone booth with a seat. Luke went inside. Billie followed him and closed the door. He put a dime in the slot and called the hotel. He angled the handset so that Billie could hear.

'Sheraton-Carlton, good morning.'

'Room five-thirty, please.'

'Sir, it's past one o'clock—is this an emergency?'

'Dr Lucas asked me to call no matter how late.'

'Very good.'

There was a pause, then a ringing tone. After four rings, the phone was picked up. So Anthony, or one of his men, was lying in wait.

A voice said, 'Hello?' It was not Anthony.

Luke said tipsily, 'Hey, Ronnie, this is Tim. We're waitin' for ya.'

The man grunted with irritation. 'Drunk,' he muttered, as if speaking to someone else. 'You got the wrong room, buddy.' He hung up.

'Someone there,' Billie said.

'Maybe more than one.'

'I know how to get them out. I did it in Lisbon, during the war.'

They left the phone booth. Luke noticed Billie discreetly pick up a book of matches from an ashtray by the elevator. On the fifth floor they found room 530 and went past it. Billie opened a door to reveal a linen closet. 'Perfect,' she said. 'Is there a fire alarm near by?'

Luke looked around and saw an alarm of the type that could be set off by breaking a pane of glass with the little hammer hanging next to it. 'Right there,' he said.

'Good.' In the closet, sheets and blankets stood in neat stacks on slatted wooden shelves. Billie unfolded a blanket and dropped it on the floor. She did the same with several more until she had a pile. She took a breakfast order from a doorknob and lit it with a match. As it flared up, she put the flame to the blankets. 'This is why you should never smoke in bed,' she said.

As the flames blazed up, Billie piled on additional bed linen. Soon smoke began to fill the corridor. 'Time to sound the alarm,' she said. 'We don't want anyone to get hurt.'

Luke broke the fire alarm glass and pressed the large red button inside. A moment later, a loud ringing shattered the silence.

He and Billie retreated along the corridor until they could only just see the door of Luke's suite through the smoke. The corridor filled with people coughing and fumbling through the smoke towards the stairwell.

The door to room 530 opened slowly. Luke saw a tall man step into the corridor: Pete. He drew back to avoid being recognised. The figure hesitated, then joined the rush for the stairs. Two more men came out and followed him.

'All clear,' Luke said, and he and Billie entered the suite.

'Oh, my God,' said Billie. 'It's the same room. I can't believe it.'

He stood still, watching. 'What happened here?' he asked.

She shook her head wonderingly. 'It's hard to imagine that you don't remember.' She walked around. 'There was a grand piano in that corner,' she said. She looked into the bathroom. 'And a phone in here. I had never seen a phone in a bathroom.'

Luke waited.

'You stayed here in the war,' she said at last. 'We made love here.'

He looked into the bedroom. 'On that bed, I guess.'

'Not just on the bed.' She giggled. 'How young we were.'

The thought of making love to this woman was unbearably exciting. 'My God, I wish I could remember,' he said, and his voice sounded thick with desire.

To his surprise, she blushed.

He turned aside and picked up the phone. He dialled the operator. He wanted to make sure the fire did not spread. 'This is Mr Davies. I sounded the alarm,' he said rapidly. 'The fire is in a linen closet near room five-forty.' He hung up.

Billie was looking around, her emotional moment over. 'Your clothes are here,' she said.

Lying on the bed were a grey tweed sports jacket and a pair of charcoal pants. On the floor was a pair of wing-tip shoes. Luke opened the drawer of the bedside table and found a wallet, a cheque-book and a slim appointments diary with a list of phone numbers in the back. He looked quickly through its pages and found the current week, but there were no obvious clues.

A well-worn black leather suitcase rested open on a stand. Luke rummaged through it, finding clean shirts and underwear, a note-book half full of mathematical calculations, and a paperback book.

Billie looked in the bathroom. 'Shaving gear, toiletry bag, tooth-brush, that's all.'

Luke opened all the cupboards and drawers in the bedroom, and Billie did the same in the living room. He found a black wool topcoat and a black Homburg hat in a closet, but nothing else.

'Your phone messages are here on the desk,' Billie said. 'From Bern, from a Colonel Hide, and from someone called Marigold.'

'She's my secretary in Huntsville. Colonel Hide said she had made my flight reservations.'

'I wonder if you told her the purpose of the trip.'

'It's possible.' He looked at the phone numbers in the back of the diary. 'Bingo,' he said. 'Marigold—Home.' He sat at the desk and dialled the number.

The phone was answered by a sleepy woman with a slow Alabama accent.

He said, 'I'm sorry to call so late. Is this Marigold?'

'Dr Lucas! Thank God you've called. What in heaven happened to you? No one knew where you were at—and now I hear tell you lost your memory. Is that so?'

'Yes, but I'm hoping you might help me figure things out.'

'If I can . . .'

'Did I tell you why I suddenly decided to go to Washington on Monday?'

'You sure didn't. You just said you needed to fly to Washington via Huntsville, that you wanted to stop over here for a couple of hours.'

'I wonder why.'

'Then you said something kind of strange. You asked me not to tell anyone that you were coming here.'

'Ah. So it was a secret visit?'

'Yes. And I've kept it secret.'

The fire alarm stopped ringing and Luke realised he had run out of time. 'I have to go now,' he told Marigold. 'Thanks for your help.' He hung up.

'I've packed your stuff,' Billie said.

'Thanks,' he said. He took his own black coat and hat from the closet and put them on. 'Now let's get out of here before the spooks come back.'

THEY DROVE to an all-night diner and ordered coffee. 'I wonder when the first flight to Huntsville leaves in the morning,' Luke said.

'We need the Official Airline Guide,' Billie said. 'I bet Bern has one. It's the kind of thing writers like. They're always looking stuff up.'

'He's probably asleep.'

Billie stood up. 'Then I'll wake him.'

She went to the payphone beside the rest rooms. Luke sipped his coffee, watching her. She looked bewitching, and he ached with desire for her.

She returned and said, 'He's going to join us and bring the book.'

Luke checked his watch. It was 2.00am 'I'll probably go straight to the airport from here. I hope there's an early flight.'

Billie frowned. 'Is there a deadline?'

'There might be. I keep asking myself: what could have made me drop everything and rush to Washington? It has to be something to do with the rocket—a threat to the launch.'

'Sabotage?'

'Yes. And if I'm right, I have to prove it before ten thirty tonight.'

'Do you want me to fly to Huntsville with you?'

'You have to take care of Larry.'

'I can leave him with Bern.'

Luke shook his head. 'I don't think so . . . thanks.'

'You always were an independent son of a gun.'

'It's not that,' he said. He wanted her to understand. 'I'd love you to come with me. That's the trouble—I'd like it too much. Did I always like you so much, or is this new?'

'This is not new. We fight like hell. But we adore one another.'

'You said we were lovers, once. Was it good?'

She looked at him with tears in her eyes. 'The best.'

'Then how come I'm not married to you?'

She began to cry. 'Because . . .' She wiped her face and blurted out, 'You got so mad at me, you didn't speak to me for five years.'

1945: ANTHONY'S PARENTS had a farm near Charlottesville, Virginia. It was a big white timber-framed house with rambling wings that contained a dozen bedrooms.

Luke arrived there on the Friday after Japan surrendered. Anthony's mother showed him to a bedroom where he changed out of his uniform—he now held the rank of major—and put on a black cashmere sports jacket. As he was tying his tie, Anthony looked in. 'Cocktails in the drawing room whenever you're ready,' he said.

'I'll be right there,' Luke said. 'Which room is Billie in?'

'The girls are in the other wing, I'm afraid,' Anthony said. 'The Admiral is old-fashioned about that sort of thing.' His father had spent his life in the navy.

'No problem,' Luke said with a shrug. He had spent the last three years moving around occupied Europe at night: he would be able to find Billie's room in the dark.

When he went downstairs he found all his old friends waiting. As well as Anthony and Billie, there were Elspeth, Bern and Bern's girlfriend Peg. Luke had spent much of the war with Bern and Anthony, and every leave with Billie, but he had not seen Elspeth or Peg since 1941. The Admiral handed him a martini and he took a satisfying gulp. This was a time to celebrate if ever there was one.

Luke studied them over dinner, comparing them with the golden youths who been so worried, four years ago, about being expelled from Harvard. Elspeth was painfully thin after three years on rations in wartime London. Peg, who had been a dowdy girl with a big heart, was now smartly dressed, but her skilfully made-up face looked hardened and cynical. Bern at twenty-seven looked ten years older. This had been his second war and he had been wounded three times. Anthony had seen some action, but had spent most of the war in Washington. Billie had spent two years undercover in Lisbon, and had killed a man there, but she was still a bundle of radiant energy, gay at one moment and fierce at the next.

'We should drink a toast,' Luke said, lifting his wineglass. 'To those who survived—and those who did not.'

They all drank, then Bern said, 'I have another. To the men who broke the back of the Nazi war machine—the Red Army.'

They all drank again, but the Admiral looked displeased.

Coffee was served in the drawing room. Luke handed the cups around. As he offered cream and sugar to Billie, she said in a low voice, 'East wing, last door on the left.'

At ten thirty the Admiral insisted the men move to the billiard room. He poured himself a tumbler of bourbon and took Luke to the locked display rack at the far end of the room to show him his guns.

'I know and respect your family, Luke,' the Admiral said as they examined an Enfield rifle. 'Your father is a very great man.'

'Thank you,' Luke said. His father had spent the war helping to run the Office of Price Administration.

'You'll have to think of your family when you choose a wife, my boy. Whoever becomes Mrs Lucas will have a place waiting for her in the upper reaches of American society. You must pick a girl who can carry that off.'

'I'll bear that in mind, Admiral,' Luke said, putting the rifle back.

The Admiral put a hand on his arm, 'Whatever you do, don't get stuck with that little Jewess—she's not worthy of you.'

Luke gritted his teeth. 'If you'll excuse me, this is something I'd rather discuss with my own father.'

'But your father doesn't know about her, does he?'

Luke flushed. The Admiral had scored a point. Luke and Billie had not met one another's parents. He said, 'Forgive me if I warn you that these remarks are personally offensive to me.'

The room went quiet, but Luke's veiled threat passed over the head of the drunken Admiral. 'I understand that, son, but I may know more about the lady in question than you do.'

'The hell you do,' Luke said.

The Admiral put his arm round Luke's shoulders. 'Look, son, I'm a man, I understand. There's no harm in pronging a little tart, we've all—'

He never finished the sentence. Luke shoved him away. The Admiral staggered back, arms flailing, and his glass of bourbon went flying through the air. He sat down hard on the rug.

Anthony, white-faced, grabbed Luke's arm. 'Luke, for God's sake, what do you think you're doing?'

Bern stepped between them and the fallen Admiral. 'Calm down, both of you,' he said.

'The hell with *calm*,' Luke said. 'What kind of man invites you to his house then insults your girlfriend?'

'She is a tart,' the Admiral said. 'I should know, damn it. I paid for her abortion,'

Luke was stunned. 'Abortion?'

'Yes.' The Admiral struggled to his feet. 'Anthony got her pregnant, and I paid a thousand dollars for her to get rid of the little bastard.' His mouth twisted in a spiteful grin of triumph.

Luke looked at Anthony, but Anthony shook his head. 'I told my father it was my baby, so that he'd give me the money, but it was your child, Luke.'

Luke blushed to the roots of his hair. The drunken old Admiral had made a complete fool of him. He was the ignorant one. He thought he knew Billie, yet she had kept this a secret from him. He had fathered a child, and his girlfriend had had an abortion, and they knew about it but he did not. He was utterly humiliated.

He stormed out of the room, ran up the stairs and along the east wing. He found Billie's room and went in without knocking.

She was lying naked on the bed, reading. For a moment, the sight of her took his breath away. She looked up at him with a happy smile, then her face darkened at his expression.

'The Admiral says he paid for you to have an abortion. Is it true? Answer me!'

She nodded, began to cry and buried her face in her hands.

'So you did deceive me?'

'I'm sorry,' she sobbed. 'I wanted to have your baby with all my heart, but you were in France, and I didn't know if you were ever coming back. I had to decide all on my own.' She raised her voice. 'It was the worst time of my life.'

'You should have told me.'

Her mood changed. She sighed. 'Yes, I know. But Anthony thought I shouldn't tell anyone, and it's not difficult to persuade a girl to keep something like that a secret.'

Luke was maddened by the calm way she talked about her treachery. 'I can't live with this,' he said.

'What do you mean?'

'After you've deceived me over something so important how can I ever trust you again?'

She looked anguished. 'You're going to tell me it's over, aren't you?'

'Yes.'

She began to cry afresh. 'You idiot! You don't know anything, do you, despite the war.'

'The war taught me that nothing counts as much as loyalty.'

'You still haven't learned that when humans are under pressure, we're all willing to lie.'

'Even to people we love?'

'We lie *more* to our loved ones, because we care what they think.'

He despised such easy excuses. 'That's not my philosophy of life.'

'Lucky you,' she said bitterly. 'You come from a happy home, you've never known bereavement or rejection. You had a hard war, but you weren't crippled or tortured. Nothing bad has ever happened to you. Sure, you don't tell lies.'

'If that's how you think of me, you must be glad our relationship is over.'

'No, I'm not glad.' Tears ran down her face. 'I love you. I'm sorry I deceived you, but I'm not going to prostrate myself with guilt because I did a bad thing in a moment of crisis.'

Somewhere in the back of his mind, a small voice told him he was throwing away the most precious thing he had ever had. But he was too angry, too humiliated, and too painfully wounded to listen. He went to the door.

'Don't leave,' she pleaded.

'Go to hell,' he said, and he went out.

2.30AM: 'I CAN'T BELIEVE I gave you up,' Luke said. 'Didn't I understand what you'd been through?'

'It wasn't all your fault,' Billie said wearily. 'I thought it was, at the time, but now I can see my own role in the whole mess.'

'And so you married Bern.'

She laughed. 'I didn't marry Bern because you left me. I married him because he's one of the best men in the world. It took me years to get over you but, when I did, I fell in love with Bern.'

'And you and I became friends again?'

'Slowly. I wrote to you when Larry was born, and you came to see me. Then Anthony had a thirtieth birthday party and you showed up. You were back at Harvard, getting your doctorate, and the rest of us were in Washington—Anthony and Elspeth working for the CIA, me doing research at George Washington University, and Bern writing scripts for National Public Radio.'

'When did I marry Elspeth?'

'Nineteen fifty-four—the year I divorced Bern.'

'Do you know why I married her?'

She hesitated. 'I'm the wrong person to answer that question.'

A white Lincoln Continental pulled up outside and Bern jumped out and came into the diner.

'I'm sorry we woke you,' said Luke.

'Forget it,' Bern said. 'Here.' He tossed a thick booklet onto the table. The cover said: OFFICIAL AIRLINE GUIDE. Luke picked it up.

Billie said, 'Look for Capital Airlines—they fly to the south.'

Luke found it. 'There's a plane that leaves at six fifty-five, but it stops at every small town in Dixie, and gets to Huntsville at two twenty-three this afternoon, local time.'

Bern read over his shoulder. 'The next plane doesn't leave until nine o'clock, but it has fewer stops, so it gets you to Huntsville a few minutes before noon.'

'I'd get the later plane, but I don't relish hanging around Washington any longer than I have to,' Luke said. 'Maybe I could leave here by car, and pick up a plane somewhere down the line. The early flight's first stop is a place called Newport News. Where's that?'

'Near Norfolk, Virginia,' Billie said.

'It lands there at two minutes past eight. Can I get there in time?'

'It's two hundred miles,' Billie said. 'You can make it with an hour to spare.'

Bern said, 'Take my car.

'You'd lend me your car?'

'We've saved each other's lives. A car is nothing. But you have another problem.'

'What's that?'

'I was followed here.'

3.00AM: ANTHONY SAT at the wheel of his Cadillac a block from the diner. It appeared to be a cop hangout: two patrol cars were parked outside, along with Billie's red Thunderbird and Bern's Continental.

Ackie Horwitz had been stationed outside Bern Rothsten's apartment. When Bern left in the middle of the night, Ackie had followed. As soon as Bern arrived at the diner, Ackie had alerted Anthony.

Now Ackie came out of the diner. 'Lucas is in there,' he said to Anthony. 'He has a black coat and a black hat now. Rothsten is with him, and the girl.'

'I'll wait here until Luke comes out, then I'll follow him.'

'Gotcha.' Ackie went to his motorcycle and left.

The door of the diner opened. Billie came out first. The bright lights were behind her, so Anthony could not see her face, but he recognised her small figure. Next came a man in a black coat and black hat: Luke. They went to the red Thunderbird. A man in a trench coat got into the Lincoln. The T-bird moved away, followed by the Lincoln. Anthony waited a few seconds, then pulled out.

Billie headed west, and the Lincoln followed. They came to 14th Street and stopped for a red light. When the light turned green, Billie's Thunderbird suddenly shot forward, while the Lincoln remained stationary. Cursing, Anthony swung round the Lincoln and raced after the others.

Billie zigzagged through the neighbourhood at the back of the White House, shooting red lights, and driving the wrong way on one-way streets. Anthony did the same, but the Cadillac could not match the T-bird for manoeuvrability.

Then luck intervened. Screeching around a corner, Billie ran into a flood. Water was gushing out of a drain and the entire width of the road was two or three inches under. She lost control of her car. The Thunderbird swung round in a wide arc and came to a halt slewed across the street. Anthony pulled across its front, blocking it in. Billie could not get away.

Anthony ran to the passenger side. 'Get out of the car,' he yelled, drawing his gun. The door opened, and the figure in the black coat and hat got out.

Anthony saw immediately that it was not Luke, but Bern. Rage boiled up inside him. 'You idiot!' he screamed at Bern. 'You don't know what you've done!'

'Then tell me, Anthony,' Bern said. 'What have I done?'

Anthony turned away and stuffed the gun back into his coat.

BILLIE LIVED IN ARLINGTON, a leafy suburb on the Virginia side of the Potomac river. Anthony drove along her street. As he passed her house he saw on the other side of the road a Chevrolet belonging to the CIA. He turned a corner and parked.

Billie would be home soon. She knew where Luke had gone but

she would not tell Anthony unless he put her under extraordinary pressure. So that was what he would do.

He walked over to the Chevy. 'I'm going in,' he said to Pete. 'Honk if anyone arrives.'

Anthony walked softly up the driveway and went to the back door. He had lived a life of deception and betrayal, but this, he thought with a surge of self-loathing, was the lowest he had ever sunk.

He knew his way around the house. He checked the living room first, then Billie's bedroom. Both were empty. Next he looked in on Becky-Ma. She was fast asleep. Last he went into Larry's room.

He sat on the edge of the bed and switched on the light. 'Hey, Larry, wake up,' he said. 'Come on.'

The boy's eyes opened. After a disoriented moment, he grinned. 'Uncle Anthony,' he said and he smiled.

4.30AM: BILLIE DROPPED Bern off, then drove home.

She entered her house, hung up her coat and went straight upstairs. She kicked off her shoes and went to check on Larry. When she saw his empty bed, she screamed.

She looked into the bathroom, then Becky-Ma's room. 'Larry,' she yelled. 'Where are you?' She ran downstairs and went into every room. She looked in the garage and the yard. Going back inside, she went into every room again, opening closets and checking under beds, looking into every space large enough to hold a seven-year-old. He had gone.

Becky-Ma came out of her bedroom. 'What's happening?' she said shakily.

'Where's Larry?' Billie shouted.

'In his bed, I thought.'

Fighting down panic, Billie went into Larry's bedroom and studied it. The room was tidy, with no signs of struggle. The teddy-bear pyjamas he had worn last night were neatly folded. His school clothes were gone. It looked as if he had gone with someone he trusted. Anthony.

At first she felt relief. Anthony would not harm Larry. But then she thought again. Wouldn't he? She had to get Larry back fast.

She ran downstairs to call Anthony. Before she got to the phone, it rang. She snatched it up. 'Yes?'

'This is Anthony.'

'How could you be so cruel?' she screamed

'I have to know where Luke is,' he said coolly. 'It's important.'

'He's gone—' She stopped herself. 'Where's Larry?'

'He's with me. He's fine, don't worry. Just tell me what I need to know, and everything will be all right.'

'When I see my son, I'll tell you where Luke is.'

'Don't you trust me?'

'Is that a joke?'

He sighed. 'OK. Meet me at the Jefferson Memorial at seven o'clock.'

She checked her watch. It was after six. 'I'll be there.'

She hung up.

'What is it?' Becky-Ma said. 'What's going on?'

Billie tried to give an impression of calm. 'Larry's with Anthony. I'm going to pick him up now.'

She went upstairs. In her bedroom, she stood on a chair and took a small suitcase from on top of the wardrobe. She placed the case on the bed and opened it. Inside was a Colt 45. They had all been issued with Colts in the war. She had kept hers as a souvenir, but some instinct made her clean and oil it regularly. There was a box of bullets in the case. She loaded the gun.

Then she ran out of the house and jumped into her car.

6.30AM: IT WAS STILL DARK when Luke arrived at Newport News and pulled into the parking lot next to the closed airport terminal. He turned off the engine of Bern's Lincoln and listened to the silence.

Luke had been up for more than twenty-four hours, and he felt desperately weary, but his mind was racing. He was in love with Billie. Now that he was 200 miles away from her, he could admit that to himself. But what about Elspeth? Why had he married her? He had asked Billie that, and she had refused to answer. I'll ask Elspeth, he thought. He checked his watch. He had more than an hour until takeoff. He got out of the car and went to the phone booth.

Elspeth picked up fast, as if she was already awake. Suddenly he felt awkward. 'Uh, good morning, Elspeth.'

'I'm so glad you called,' she said. 'I've been out of my mind with worry. Are you OK?'

'Yes, I'm fine, now. Basically, Anthony caused me to lose my memory, by giving me a combination of electric shock and drugs.'

'Good God. Why would he do a thing like that?'

'He says I'm a Soviet spy.'

'That's absurd.'

'It's what he told Billie.'

'So you've been with Billie?'

Luke heard the note of hostility in Elspeth's voice. 'She's been kind,' he said defensively.

Elspeth changed the subject. 'What are you going to do next?'

'I need to find out what Anthony wanted me to forget.'

'How will you do that?'

'I'd rather not say over the phone.'

'Well, I'm sorry you can't tell me anything.'

'Matter of fact, I called to ask you some things.'

'OK. Fire away.'

'Why can't we have children?'

'We don't know. We've been trying since we got married. Last year, you went to a fertility specialist, but he couldn't find anything wrong. A few weeks ago, I saw a woman doctor in Atlanta. She ran some tests. We're waiting for the results.'

'Would you tell me how we came to get married?'

'Well, I didn't see you for years, then we met again in 1954, in Washington,' she began. 'I was still with the CIA. You were working in Pasadena, but you flew in for Peg's wedding. We were seated together at the breakfast. We talked and talked—it was as if thirteen years had never happened. I had to leave early—I was conductor of the 16th Street Youth Orchestra, and we had a rehearsal. You came with me and afterwards we went back to my place.'

1954: ELSPETH'S APARTMENT was small and uncluttered, with a few pieces of angular modern furniture. Luke made martinis and Elspeth started to cook spaghetti in the tiny kitchen. Luke told her about his job.

'I'm so happy for you,' she said with generous enthusiasm. 'Even back at Harvard, you always wanted to explore outer space.'

He smiled. 'In those days, most people thought it was a foolish dream of science-fiction writers.'

'I guess we still can't be sure it will happen.'

'I think we can,' he said seriously. 'The big problems were solved by German scientists in the war. They built rockets that could be fired in Holland and land on London.'

'I was there, I remember, we called them buzz bombs. So, our missiles are based on the German buzz bombs?'

'More on their V2 rocket, to be exact.'

Luke was not supposed to talk about his work, but this was Elspeth, and anyway she probably had a higher security rating than he did. 'We're building a rocket that can take off in Arizona and explode in Moscow, and if we can do that we can fly to the moon.'

'So it's just the same thing on a larger scale?'

'Yes. We need larger engines, more efficient fuel, that kind of thing. None of these problems is insurmountable. Plus, those German scientists are working for us now.'

'I think I heard that.' She changed the subject. 'And what about life in general?' she asked. 'Are you dating someone?'

'Not right now.' He had dated several girls since his breakup with Billie nine years ago, but none had meant much.

'How about you, Elspeth?' Luke asked. 'Peg's married, Billie's already getting divorced—you've got some catching up to do.'

'Oh, you know about us government girls.' So many young women worked for the government in Washington that they outnumbered single men by five to one. Consequently they were stereotyped as desperate for dates. Luke did not believe Elspeth was like that, but if she wanted to evade his question, she was entitled.

She asked him to watch the stove while she freshened up. He took off his jacket and tie, then stirred the spaghetti sauce.

He heard her call out, 'Luke—could you come here?'

He stepped into the bathroom. Elspeth's dress hung on the back of the door, and she stood in a strapless peach-coloured brassiere and matching half-slip. Her hand was to her face. 'I got soap in my eye, damn it,' she said. 'Would you try to wash it out?'

'Bend down, get your face close to the bowl,' Luke said, encouraging her with his left hand between her shoulder blades. The pale skin of her back was soft and warm to his touch. He cupped water in his right hand and raised it to her eye.

'That helps,' she said.

He rinsed her eye until she said the stinging had stopped. Then he stood her upright and parted her face dry with a clean towel. Her lips parted in a smile. It was the easiest thing in the world to kiss her. She kissed him back, hesitantly at first, then she put her hands behind his neck and pulled his face to hers and kissed him hard.

After a while he picked her up, stepped into the bedroom, and laid her on the bed. When they made love it was slow and intense. 'I've wanted this for so long,' she whispered into his ear; and then she cried out with pleasure, several times, and lay back, exhausted.

Soon Elspeth fell into a deep sleep, but Luke lay awake, thinking about his life. He had always wanted a family, yet here he was, thirty-four and single. Since the war, his career had been his priority, but that was not the real reason he was unmarried. The truth was that only two women had ever touched his heart—Billie and Elspeth. Billie had deceived him, but Elspeth was here beside him.

At daybreak he got up and made coffee. He brought it into the bedroom on a tray, and found Elspeth sitting up in bed, looking sleepily delectable.

'I have something to ask you,' he said taking her hand. 'Will you marry me?'

7.00AM: ANTHONY DROVE up to the Jefferson Memorial with Larry sitting in the front seat between him and Pete. It was still dark, and the area was deserted.

The monument stood on a high platform approached by steps at the rear. 'The statue is nineteen feet high and weighs ten thousand pounds,' he told Larry. 'You can't see it from here, but it's inside those pillars.'

'We should have come in the daytime,' the boy whined.

Anthony had taken Larry out before and they always had a good time. But today Larry knew something was wrong. It was too early and he wanted his mother.

Anthony opened the door. 'Stay here a second, Larry, while I talk to Pete.' The two men got out. Anthony said to Pete, 'I'll wait here. You take the kid and show him the monument. Stay this side, so that she'll see him when she arrives.' He opened the car door again. 'Come on, Larry. Uncle Pete's going to show you the statue.'

Larry got out. With careful politeness, he said, 'After we've seen it, I think I'd like to go home.'

Anthony's breath caught in his throat. Larry's bravery was almost too much. After a moment, Anthony replied in a calm voice, 'We'll check with Mommy. Now go ahead.'

The child took Pete's hand and they walked around the monument towards the steps at the back. A minute later they appeared in front of the pillars, lit by the car's headlights.

Anthony checked his watch. Billie should be here by now. He suffered a pang of doubt. Surely she would come? She was too frightened to call the cops, he felt certain.

He was right. A few moments later, the Thunderbird arrived. It parked twenty yards from Anthony's Cadillac and a small, slight figure jumped out, leaving the engine running.

'Hello, Billie,' said Anthony.

She looked from him to the monument and saw Pete and Larry up on the raised platform.

Anthony walked towards her. 'Don't try anything dramatic—it would upset Larry.'

'Don't talk to me about upsetting him, you son of a bitch.' Her voice cracked with strain. She was near to tears.

'I had to do this.'

'Nobody *has* to do something like this.'

It was a waste of time arguing with her. 'Where's Luke?' he said abruptly.

After a pause she said, 'Luke caught a plane to Huntsville.'

Anthony breathed a deep sigh. He had what he needed. 'Why Huntsville?' he asked. 'Why not Florida?'

'I don't know why.'

Anthony tried to read her face, but it was too dark. 'You're holding something back.'

'I don't care what you think. I'm going to take my son and leave.'

'No, you're not. We're keeping him for a while.'

Billie's voice was a cry of anguish. 'Why? I've told you where Luke went!'

'There may be other ways you can help us.'

'No. It's not fair!'

'You'll live.' He turned away. That was his mistake.

Billie had been half expecting this. As he stepped towards his car, she rushed him. With her right shoulder, she hit him in the small of the back. She weighed only 120 pounds, but she had surprise and rage on her side. He stumbled and fell forward, coming down on his hands and knees.

Billie took the Colt 45 from her coat pocket. As Anthony tried to get up, she dropped to one knee and shoved the barrel of the gun into his mouth. She felt a tooth break.

'I'm going to take the gun out of your mouth,' she said. 'You're going to call to your colleague and tell him what I say.' She took the gun out of Anthony's mouth and pointed it at his left eye. 'Now,' she said. 'Call him.'

Anthony hesitated. She touched the barrel of the pistol to his eyelid.

'Pete!' he shouted.

Pete looked round. 'Where are you?' he said. Anthony and Billie were outside the range of the headlights.

Billie pressed the gun into Anthony's eye. 'Tell him to stay there.'

Anthony shouted, 'Stay where you are!'

'What's happening?' Pete called. 'I can't see you.'

Billie shouted, 'Larry, this is Mom. Get in the T-bird,'

Pete grabbed Larry's arm.

'Uncle Anthony's going to tell the man to let you go.' She pressed the gun barrel harder into Anthony's eye.

'Let the kid go!' Anthony shouted. 'She's got a gun on me!'

'OK!' Pete released Larry's arm.

Larry ran towards Billie. 'Not this way,' she said, struggling to keep her voice calm. 'Get in the car, quickly.'

Larry ran to the Thunderbird and jumped in.

With a lashing movement, Billie hit Anthony on both sides of his face with the gun, as hard as she could. He lay still, groaning. She said, 'Remember that if you're ever tempted to kidnap a child again.'

She backed towards her car, keeping the gun on him. She glanced up at the monument. Pete had not moved.

She got into her car and stuffed the Colt inside her jacket. 'Are you OK?' she asked Larry.

He started to cry. She shoved the gearshift into first and tore away.

8.00AM: BERN POURED warm milk over Larry's cornflakes while Billie beat up an egg for French toast. They were giving their child comfort food, but Billie felt the adults needed comfort too.

'I'm going to kill that son of a bitch Anthony,' Bern muttered, speaking quietly so that Larry would not hear.

Billie's rage had evaporated. Now she was worried and frightened. 'I'm afraid Anthony may try to kill Luke. I didn't think it was possible, a few hours ago—but now I know better.'

Bern dipped a slice of white bread into the egg mixture. 'Luke won't kill easy.'

'But he thinks he's escaped—he doesn't know I've told Anthony where he is. I have to find a way to warn him.'

'Leave a message at the Huntsville airport?'

'It's not reliable enough. I think I have to go there myself.'

Billie picked up the airline guide. Flight 271 left Washington at exactly nine, landing at Huntsville four minutes before noon. Luke's flight did not land until two twenty-three. 'I can do it,' she said, but she hesitated, looking at Larry.

'He'll be OK. I'll take care of him.'

Bern was a trained agent and could protect his kid from just about anything. Billie made a decision. She would go to Huntsville. 'Mommy has to go now,' she said to Larry. 'You have a fun day with Daddy and maybe he'll take you swimming.'

'OK.'

She did not want to make a drama of saying goodbye, for that would scare the child. 'I'll see you later,' she said casually.

As she went out, she heard Bern say, 'I bet you couldn't eat a slice of French toast.'

'I could too,' Larry replied.

 # Part Five

10.45am: Luke's plane refuelled at Winston-Salem, and the passengers got off for a few minutes. Luke called Redstone Arsenal from the terminal and got Marigold, on the phone.

'Dr Lucas!' she said. 'Are you OK?'

'I'm fine, but I only have a minute or two. Is the launch still scheduled for tonight?'

'Yes, ten thirty.'

'I'm on my way to Huntsville—my plane lands at two twenty-three. I'm trying to figure out why I went there on Monday. Do you have any idea what I did there?'

'Well, now, let me see. I met you at the airport in an army car and brought you here to the base. You went into the Computation Lab, then drove yourself down to the south end.'

'What's there, at the south end?'

'The Engineering Building—you sometimes work there.'

'And then?'

'You asked me to drive you home. I waited in the car while you stepped inside for a minute or two. Then I took you to the airport.'

Desperately, Luke cast about for another line of questioning. 'When you met me, was I carrying anything?'

'Just your little suitcase. Oh, and a file.'

'A file?' he said. He swallowed. 'Was it any special kind of file?'

'A standard army file folder, thin cardboard, buff-coloured.'

'And did I still have this file when you took me to the airport?'

A stewardess interrupted. 'Time to board the aircraft, Dr Lucas.'

'I'm coming, I'm coming.' He repeated his question to Marigold.

'I'm trying to remember. You know, I don't believe you had it at the airport.'

'Are you sure?'

'Yes. You must have left that file either at the base or at home.'

Luke's mind was racing. The file was the reason for his trip to Huntsville, he felt sure. It contained the secret he had found out, the one that Anthony was so desperate for him to forget. He had stashed it somewhere for safekeeping. Now, if he could find it, he could discover the secret.

'I think that file could be very important. Could you look around and see if it's there?'

'My lord, Dr Lucas, this is the army! Don't you know there must be a million of them buff-coloured file folders here?'

'Just check around. As soon as I land at Huntsville, I'll go to the house and search there. Then, if I don't find it, I'll come to the base.'

Luke hung up and ran for the plane. Its propellers were already turning.

11.00AM: THE MATS FLIGHT to Huntsville was full of generals. MATS was the Military Air Transport Service. Anthony wore sunglasses to conceal the two black eyes Billie had given him. His lip had stopped bleeding, and the broken tooth showed only when he talked.

Should he simply take the first opportunity to kill Luke? It was temptingly simple. But he worried that he did not know exactly what Luke was up to. He had to make a decision. However, by the time he boarded the plane he had been awake for forty-eight hours straight, and he fell asleep. Next thing he knew, Pete was shaking him awake, as a corporal opened the aircraft door. Huntsville had a civilian airport, but MATS flights came down on the airstrip within Redstone Arsenal.

'I'm going to make some enquiries at the base,' he said to Pete. 'I want you to go to the airport and keep watch. If Luke arrives, try to reach me there.'

At the edge of the airstrip, a young man in the uniform of a lieutenant waited with a card that read: MR CARROLL, STATE DEPARTMENT. Anthony shook his hand. 'Colonel Hickam's compliments, sir,' the lieutenant said and pointed to an olive-drab Ford.

'That'll be fine,' Anthony said. He had called the base before catching his plane, brazenly pretending he was under orders from CIA Director Alan Dulles.

'Colonel Hickam would be glad if you would drop by headquarters at your convenience.' The lieutenant handed Anthony a map. 'The headquarters building is marked on the map. And we have a message, asking you to call Mr Carl Hobart in Washington.'

'Thank you, lieutenant. Where's Dr Claude Lucas's office?'

'That'll be the Computation Laboratory.' He took out a pencil and made a mark on the map.

'Does Dr Lucas have a secretary?'

'Yes—Mrs Marigold Clarke.'

'Lieutenant, this is my colleague Pete Maxell. If he needs to reach me here at the base, what's the best way?'

The lieutenant looked at Pete. 'Sir, you could always leave a message at Colonel Hickam's office, and I would try to get it to Mr Carroll.'

'Good enough,' Anthony said, and got into the Ford. He checked the map, and started out. It was a typical army base. Arrow-straight roads ran through rough woodland broken by neat rectangles of lawn. The buildings were all flat-roofed structures of tan brick. He easily found the Computation Lab.

He went into the building. In an outer office were three small desks. Two were vacant. The third was occupied by a Negro woman of about fifty. 'Good afternoon,' he said.

She looked up. 'Hello! How can I help you?'

'I'm from Colonel Hickam's office,' he said. 'I'm looking for Marigold Clark.'

'That's me.'

'I guess you know that Dr Lucas is on his way here.'

'He called me this morning. His plane lands at two twenty-three.'

That was useful. 'So he'll be here around three.'

'Not necessarily. He said he's going home first.'

That was perfect. Anthony could hardly believe his luck. He could go there and wait, then shoot Luke as soon as he walked in the door. With Elspeth in Florida, the corpse might not be found for days.

'Thank you,' he said to Marigold. He left the room before she could ask his name.

He returned to the car and drove to the headquarters building. He found Colonel Hickam's office. The colonel was out, but a sergeant showed him to an empty room with a phone.

He called Q Building, but did not speak to his boss, Carl Hobart. Instead he asked for Carl's superior, George Cooperman.

'Did you shoot at someone last night?' asked Cooperman.

With an effort, Anthony put on the swashbuckling persona that appealed to Cooperman. 'Aw, hell, who told you that?'

'Some colonel from the Pentagon called Tom Ealy in the Director's office, and Ealy told Carl Hobart.

'There's no proof, I picked up all the slugs.'

'This colonel found a hole in the wall about nine millimetres wide and he guessed what caused it. Did you hit anybody?'

'Unfortunately not.'

'You're supposed to come back immediately.'

'Then it's a good thing I didn't talk to you.'

'Listen, Anthony, I always cut you as much slack as I can, because you get results. But I can't do any more for you on this one. You're on your own from here, buddy.'

'That's how I like it.'

'Good luck.'

Anthony sat staring at the phone. He could disobey orders for only so long. He needed to wrap this up fast.

He called Elspeth. 'Have you talked to Luke?' he asked her.

'He called me at six thirty this morning.' She sounded shaky. 'He wouldn't say where he was going or what he intended to do. But he knows you were responsible for his amnesia.'

'He's on his way to Huntsville. I'm at Redstone Arsenal now. I'm going to your house to wait for him there. Will I be able to get in?'

She answered with another question. 'Are you still trying to protect him?'

'Of course.'

There was a moment's pause, then she said, 'There's a key under the bougainvillea pot in the back yard. Take care of Luke, won't you?'

'I'll do my best.' He hung up.

As he stood up to go, the phone rang.

Only Pete knew he was in Colonel Hickam's office. He picked up.

It was Pete. 'Dr Josephson's here,' he said. 'She just got off a plane. She's sitting in the terminal, like she's waiting.'

'Damn her. She's come to warn him that we're here. You have to get her out of there.'

'How?'

'I don't care—just get rid of her,'

12 NOON: HUNTSVILLE AIRPORT was small but busy. As soon as she arrived, Billie checked on Luke's flight and learned it was running almost an hour late. She had three hours to kill.

A girl in a Capital Airlines uniform approached her. 'Are you Dr Josephson?'

'Yes.'

'I have a phone message for you.' She handed over an envelope.

Billie tore open the envelope and read: *Please call Dr Lucas on Huntsville JE 6-4231.*

She was bewildered. Could Luke be here already? There was only one way to find out. She found a payphone and dialled the number. A man's voice answered: 'Components test lab.'

'Dr Claude Lucas, please.'

'Just one moment.' After a pause the man came back. 'Dr Lucas stepped out for a minute. Who is this, please?'

'Dr Bilhah Josephson, I have a message to call him.'

'Oh, Dr Josephson, I'm so glad we found you! Dr Lucas is very concerned to contact you.'

'What's he doing here? I thought he was still in the air.'

'Army security pulled him off the plane at Norfolk, Virginia, and laid on a special flight. He's been here more than an hour. Can you get yourself down to us?'

'Where are you?'

'The lab is about an hour out of town on the Chattanooga road.'

Billie took a notebook out of her bag. 'Give me directions.'

3.00PM: BILLIE WAS LOST. Leaving the airport in a rented Ford a few minutes before one o'clock, she had driven into the centre of Huntsville then taken Highway 59 towards Chattanooga. She had wondered why the components testing laboratory was an hour away from the base, and imagined it might be for safety reasons.

The landscape gradually became wilder and the roads narrower. The disparity between what she expected and the landmarks she saw around her grew until she threw up her hands in despair. She was furious with herself and with the fool who had given her directions.

After a couple of miles, she came upon a dilapidated feed store with a payphone outside. She pulled over. She still had Luke's message with the phone number. She put a dime in the slot and dialled. The phone was answered immediately.

'May I speak to Dr Claude Lucas?' she said.

'You got the wrong number, honey.'

'Isn't this Huntsville JE 6-4231?'

'Yep. You've reached a payphone in Huntsville airport.'

'A *pay*phone?'

'Yes, ma'am.'

Billie realised she had been hoodwinked. Luke had not been taken off his plane in Norfolk and put on an army flight. That whole story was a lie designed to get her out of the way. With despair in her heart, she wondered if he were still alive. If he was, maybe she could still warn him. She racked her brains. Luke had a secretary at the base, she remembered; a name like a flower . . . Marigold.

She called Redstone Arsenal and asked to speak to Dr Lucas's secretary. A woman with a slow Alabama voice came on the line.

'Is that Marigold?'

'Yes.'

'I'm Dr Josephson, a friend of Dr Lucas. We've spoken before, I think. My name is Billie.'

'Oh, sure, I remember. How are you?'

'Worried. I need to get a message to Luke urgently. Is he with you?'

'No, ma'am. He went to his house.'

'If you see Luke, or if he calls you, would you give him a message from me? Tell him Anthony is in town. He'll understand.'

'I'll do that, Doctor.'

'Thank you.' Billie hung up.

Was there anyone else Luke might talk to? She thought of Elspeth. She called the operator and asked for Cape Canaveral.

3.45PM: EVERYONE WAS bad-tempered at Cape Canaveral. The Pentagon had ordered a security alert. Arriving for work in the morning, staff had been made to wait in line at the gate. Cars had been searched, briefcases opened and lunch pails unpacked. Elspeth was glad of the upset. It meant that nobody noticed she was too distraught to do her job. She did not know where Luke was and she no longer felt sure she could trust Anthony.

When the phone at her desk rang a few minutes before four o'clock, her heart seemed to stop. She snatched up the handset. 'Yes?'

'This is Billie'

'Billie?' Elspeth was taken by surprise. 'Where are you?'

'I'm in Huntsville, trying to contact Luke.'

'What's he doing there?'

'Looking for a file he left here on Monday.'

'He went to Huntsville on Monday? I didn't know that.'

'Nobody knew, except Marigold. Elspeth, do you understand what's going on?'

She laughed humourlessly. 'I thought I did, but not any more.'

'I believe Luke's life is in danger. Anthony shot at him in Washington last night.'

Elspeth went cold. 'Oh, my God.'

'It's too complicated to explain right now. If Luke calls you, will you tell him that Anthony is in Huntsville?'

Elspeth was trying to recover from the shock. 'Of course I will. Billie . . . one more thing. Look after Luke, won't you?'

'What do you mean?' Billie asked. 'You sound like you're going to die.'

Elspeth did not answer. After a moment she broke the connection. A sob came to her throat. She fought fiercely to control herself. Then she dialled her home in Huntsville.

4.00PM: ANTHONY LOOKED out of the front window of Luke's house and saw a Huntsville taxicab pull up at the kerb. He thumbed the safety catch on his gun. His mouth went dry,

The phone rang. He was paralysed by indecision. He looked out of the window and saw Luke getting out of the cab. The call could be trivial or it could be vital information.

He snatched the phone up. 'Yes?'

'This is Elspeth.' Her voice was low. 'He's looking for a file he stashed in Huntsville on Monday.'

Anthony understood in a flash. Luke had copied the blueprints he had brought to Washington. He had made a clandestine stop in Huntsville to hide the copies.

'Who else knows about this?'

'His secretary, Marigold. And Billie—she told me. Maybe others.'

Luke was paying the driver. Anthony was running out of time. 'I have to have that file,' he said to Elspeth.

'That's what I thought.'

'It's not here,' he said. 'I just searched the house.'

'Then it must be at the base.'

'I'll have to follow him while he looks for it.'

Luke was approaching the front door.

'I'm out of time,' Anthony said, and he slammed down the phone.

He heard the key scrape in the lock as he ran through the hall and into the kitchen. He went out of the back door and closed it softly. He slipped the key under the flowerpot.

He reached the street and walked away.

4:30PM: ON TOP OF THE TV in the living room was a bamboo picture frame containing a photograph of a beautiful redhead in an ivory silk wedding dress. Beside her, wearing a grey cutaway, was Luke. He studied Elspeth in the picture. She could have been a movie star.

Luke began to search. A buff-coloured file folder should be easy enough to find. He sat at the desk in the study and looked through the drawers. He found nothing.

Upstairs he opened the closet and saw, with pleasure, the rack of navy blue and grey suits and tweed sports jackets. He had been wearing this stolen suit for more than twenty-four hours, and he was tempted to take five minutes to shower and change into some of his own clothes. But he resisted. There was no time to spare.

He searched the house thoroughly. Everywhere he looked, he learned something about himself and his wife. They liked Glen Miller and Frank Sinatra, they read Hemingway and Scott Fitzgerald, they drank Dewar's scotch and ate All-Bran.

At last he gave up. In a kitchen drawer he found keys to the black Chrysler in the garage. He would drive to the base and search there.

Before leaving, he picked up the mail in the hall and shuffled the envelopes. Desperate for a clue, he ripped them open. One was from a doctor in Atlanta.

Dear Mrs Lucas,

Following your routine checkup, the results of your blood tests have come back from the lab, and everything is normal. However, you are under weight, you suffer insomnia, and when I saw you, you had obviously been crying. These are symptoms of depression. Depression may be caused by changes in body chemistry, by unresolved mental problems such as marital difficulties, or by childhood trauma such as the early death of a parent. In your case, I have no doubt that the condition is related to the tubal ligation you underwent in 1954.

Luke stopped reading. Tubal ligation was a method of sterilisation. When he had asked Elspeth why they could not have children, she had said, 'We don't know. We've been trying since we got married.'

That was all lies. She knew perfectly well why they could not have children: she had been sterilised. He looked at the next paragraph.

This procedure may cause depression at any age, but in your case, having it six weeks before your wedding—

Luke's mouth fell open. Elspeth's deception had begun shortly before they got married. Their marriage had been a lie. He had wanted children—yet children were the very thing she had deliberately denied him. And she had lied about it for four years.

He stepped into his study and sat at his desk, staring through the window, while evening fell over the hickory trees in the back yard. How had he let his life go so wrong? He must be a poor judge of people, he thought. He had remained close to Anthony, who had tried to kill him, yet had broken with Bern who had been a faithful friend. He had quarrelled with Billie and married Elspeth, yet Billie had dropped everything to help him, and Elspeth had deceived him.

A large moth bumped into the window, and startled Luke out of his reverie. He looked at his watch and was shocked to see that it was past seven. If he hoped to unravel the mystery of his life, he needed to start with the mysterious file. It was not here, so it had to be at Redstone Arsenal. Time was pressing. The launch of the rocket was scheduled for ten thirty. He had only three hours to find out whether there was a plot to sabotage it.

7.30PM: THERE WERE NO LIGHTS on in Luke's house when Billie drove by. It had taken her hours to get back to Huntsville and find the house. She had no idea whether either of her warning messages had reached Luke. She was furious with herself for being so incompetent.

She turned the next corner and pulled up. She breathed deeply and made herself think calmly. She had to find out what was in the house. But what if Anthony were there? On the passenger seat beside her was an attaché case. She opened it up and took out her Colt. Then she turned the car around and returned to Luke's house.

She parked outside, grabbed her gun and leaped out. She jumped the low wall and ran across the lawn to the side of the house.

She heard no sound from within. She ran round to the back and looked in at a window. The room seemed empty. She reversed her grip on the gun and smashed the glass. She reached through the broken pane, undid the latch and opened the window.

She climbed in and moved through the house in the gloom, dreading at every step that she would see Luke on the floor. All the rooms were empty. Had Luke changed his mind and decided not to come here? Or had the body been spirited away? Had Anthony somehow failed to kill him? Or had one of her warnings got through?

One person who might have some answers was Marigold.

She found a payphone and called information. She asked for a number for Marigold Clark. After a moment the voice on the line gave her a Huntsville number.

A man answered. 'She's at choir practice at the Calvary Gospel Church on Mill Street.'

Billie went out to her car. She found Mill Street on the Hertz map and drove there. The church was a fine brick building in a poor neighbourhood. There were only about thirty men and women in the choir, but they sounded like a hundred. They clapped and swayed as they sang, and a large woman with her back to Billie conducted vigorously.

They finished on a high chord, and the conductor looked around and saw her. 'Take a short break,' she said to the choir.

'I'm sorry to interrupt,' Billie said. 'Are you Marigold Clark?'

'Yes,' the woman said warily. 'But I don't know you.'

'We spoke on the phone earlier, I'm Billie Josephson.'

'Oh, hi, Dr Josephson.'

Billie said, 'Have you heard from Luke?'

'Not since this morning. I expected him to show up at the base, but he didn't. Do you think he's all right?'

'I don't know. I went to his house, but there was no one there. I'm afraid he might have been killed.'

Marigold shook her head in bewilderment. 'I've worked for the army twenty years and I never heard of anything like this.'

'He's in great danger.' Billie looked Marigold in the eye. 'Do you believe me?'

Marigold hesitated for a long moment. 'Yes, I do,' she said at last.

'Then you have to help me,' Billie told her.

9.30PM: ANTHONY WAS at Redstone Arsenal, sitting in his army Ford, watching the door of the Computation Laboratory. Luke was in the lab, searching for his file folder. Anthony knew he would not find it there, because he had already searched there.

Time was on Anthony's side. Every minute that passed made Luke less dangerous. The rocket would be launched in one hour. Could Luke ruin everything in an hour?

The door to the lab opened. Luke emerged and approached the black Chrysler parked at the kerb. He got in and drove off. Anthony switched on his headlights, and followed.

After about a mile, Luke slowed in front of a long one-storey building and pulled into its parking lot.

LUKE HAD FELT SURE he would find the folder in the Computation Lab, where his office was, but he found nothing. There was one more possibility. Marigold had said that he also went to the Engineering Building on Monday.

Engineering had an atmosphere quite different from that of the Computation Lab. Computation was spotlessly clean for the sake of the massive computers. Engineering was scruffy by comparison, smelling of oil and rubber.

Luke hurried along a corridor. At the end he came upon a large room with half a dozen steel tables. On the far side, an open door led into a laboratory. Along the wall to his left was a row of lockers, each with a name plate. One was his. Maybe he had stashed the file here.

The cupboard was locked. He took out his key ring and found a likely key. It worked, and he opened the door. Inside was a hard hat on a high shelf. Below that, hanging from a hook, were blue overalls, and on the floor, a pair of black rubber boots.

There, beside the boots, was a buff-coloured army file folder. This had to be what he was looking for.

The folder contained a large brown envelope, already open. Inside were some papers. When he took them out, he could see immediately that they were blueprints for parts of a rocket. He moved quickly to one of the steel tables and spread the papers out under a lamp. After a few moments' rapid study, he knew without doubt that the drawings showed the Jupiter-C rocket's self-destruct mechanism.

He was horrified.

Every rocket had a self-destruct mechanism so that, if it should veer off course and threaten human life, it could be blown up in midair. The explosion was triggered by a coded radio signal. An igniter rope ran the length of the rocket's main stage. At its top end was a firing cap with two wires sticking out. If a voltage was applied across the wires, the cap would ignite the rope, which would rip open the fuel tank and destroy the rocket. The blueprints showed twin plugs, one for the transmitter on the ground and the other for the receiver in the satellite. One turned the radio signal into a complex code; the other received the signal and applied the voltage across the two wires.

A separate diagram, not a blueprint but a hastily drawn sketch, showed exactly how the plugs were wired, so that anyone having the diagram could duplicate the signal. It was brilliant, Luke realised. The saboteurs had no need of explosives or timing devices, nor did they need access to the rocket. The radio signal could be broadcast from a transmitter miles away.

Written on the envelope were the words: *Theo Packman, Vanguard Motel*. Presumably Packman was, even now, somewhere in Cocoa Beach with a radio transmitter, ready to blow up the rocket seconds after it took off. But now Luke could prevent that. It was ten fifteen. He had time to call Cape Canaveral and have the launch postponed. He snatched up the phone.

A voice said, 'Put it down, Luke.' Luke turned slowly. Anthony stood in the doorway pointing a gun at Luke.

Luke stared at the man whom he had so misjudged. 'How long have you been working for Moscow?' Luke asked him. 'Since the war?'

'Longer. Since Harvard.'

'Why?'

Anthony's lips twisted into a strange smile. 'For a better world.'

Once upon a time, Luke knew, a lot of sensible people had believed in the Soviet system, but their faith had been undermined by the realities of life under Stalin. 'You still believe that?' he said.

'Sort of. It's still the best hope, despite all that has happened.'

'But you shot at me last night. Would you kill your oldest friend for a cause you only half believe in?'

'Yes, and so would you. In the war we both put lives at risk, our own and other people's, because it was right.'

'I don't think we lied to one another, let alone shot at one another.'

'We would have, if necessary. And if I don't kill you now, you'll try to stop me escaping—won't you? Even though you know that if I'm caught I'll finish up in the electric chair.'

'I guess so . . . yes.'

'So you're willing to kill a friend, too.'

Luke was taken aback. Surely he could not be classified with Anthony? 'I might bring you to justice. That's not murder.'

'I'd be just as dead, though.'

Luke nodded slowly. 'I guess you would.'

Anthony raised the gun with a steady hand, aiming at Luke's heart. Luke dropped behind the steel table. The silenced gun coughed, and there was a metallic clang as the bullet hit the top of the table.

Luke rolled under the table and he lifted himself into a stoop, so that his back was against the underside of the table. Grabbing the two legs at one end he heaved, standing upright at the same time. The table came up off the floor and teetered forward. Luke ran blindly with it, hoping to collide with Anthony. The table crashed to the floor, but Anthony was not beneath it.

Luke tripped and fell, banging his head on a steel leg. He rolled sideways and came up into a sitting position, hurt and dazed. He looked up to see Anthony facing him, braced with his feet apart, aiming his gun two-handed. Luke was now, literally, a sitting target.

Then a voice rang out: 'Anthony! Stop!' It was Billie.

Anthony froze. Luke slowly turned his head. Billie stood by the door, holding an automatic pistol, levelled at Anthony. Behind her was a middle-aged Negro woman, looking shocked and scared.

'Drop the gun!' Billie yelled.

Slowly, Anthony lowered his arms, but he did not drop the gun.

'Drop it, or I'll shoot!'

Anthony smiled. 'No, you won't,' he said. Still pointing the gun at the floor, he began to walk backwards, making for the open door that led into the laboratory. 'You don't believe that a rocket is worth more than a human life, even if it's a traitor's life.'

'Don't test me!' Billie cried.

Anthony turned and darted through the doorway.

Luke leaped to his feet. The clock on the wall said ten twenty-nine. He had a minute left to warn Cape Canaveral. He picked up the phone. 'This is Luke,' he said. 'Give me the launch conductor. Put him on, quick!'

There was a pause. In the background, Luke could hear the count-down in the blockhouse: 'Twenty, nineteen, eighteen—'

A new voice came on the line. 'This is Willy—what the hell is it?'

'Someone has the self-destruct code. They're going to blow up the rocket. You have to abort the launch.'

The background voice said, 'Eleven, ten—'

'How do you know?' Willy asked.

'I've found diagrams of the wiring of the coded plugs, and an envelope addressed to someone called Theo Packman.'

'That's not proof. I can't cancel the launch on that.'

Luke suddenly felt fatalistic. 'I've told you what I know. The decision is yours.'

'Five, four—'

'Hell,' Willy raised his voice. 'Stop the countdown!'

Luke glanced up at the anxious faces of Billie and Marigold. 'They've aborted the launch.'

A new voice came on the line. 'Luke? This is Colonel Hide. What the hell is going on?'

'I've discovered what made me take off for Washington in such a hurry on Monday. Do you know who Theo Packman is?'

'Yeah, he's a freelance journalist on the missile beat.'

'I found an envelope addressed to him containing blueprints of the Jupiter's self-destruct system. That's why I persuaded Willy to abort the launch.'

'Thank God you did.'

'Listen, you have to find this Packman character right now. The envelope was addressed to the Vanguard Motel.'

'Got it.'

'Packman was working with someone in the CIA, a double agent called Anthony Carroll. He's the one who intercepted me in Washington before I could get to the Pentagon with the information.'

'I'll call the CIA and tell them.'

Luke hung up the phone and sat back. He had done all he could.

He looked at Billie, who said, 'What next?'

'I guess I'll go to Cape Canaveral. The launch will be rescheduled for the same time tomorrow. I'd like to be there.'

'Me, too.'

Luke smiled. 'You deserve it. You saved the rocket.' He stood up and embraced her.

'Your life, you idiot. To heck with the rocket, I saved your life.' She kissed him.

Marigold coughed. 'You've missed the last plane from Huntsville airport,' she said in a businesslike tone. 'Next one is a MATS flight that leaves at five thirty in the morning. Or there's a train. It stops in Chattanooga around one o'clock tonight. You could get there in a couple of hours by car.'

Billie said, 'I like the train idea.'

They said goodbye to Marigold, who offered to return Billie's rental to Hertz, got into Luke's Chrysler and drove away.

When they were on the highway, Billie said to Luke, 'There's a question we haven't talked about.'

'I know,' he said. 'Who sent the blueprints to Theo Packman?'

'It must be someone inside Cape Canaveral, someone on the scientific team.'

'Exactly.'

'Do you have any idea who?'

With a heart full of grief, Luke said, 'I think it's Elspeth.'

11.00PM: ELSPETH COULD NOT believe it. Just a few seconds before ignition, the launch had been postponed. The triumph of her life had been within her grasp—and had slipped through her fingers.

She was on the flat roof of an administration building, with a small crowd of secretaries and clerks, watching the floodlit launch pad through binoculars. Their fears had grown as the minutes ticked by and the rocket remained on the ground, and now a collective groan went up as technicians in overalls swarmed out of their bunkers and began to the complex procedure of standing down all systems.

Elspeth left the others without a word and walked back to Hangar R. When she reached her office, the phone was ringing. She snatched it up. 'Yes?'

'What's happening?' The voice was Anthony's.

'They've aborted the launch. I don't know why—do you?'

'Luke found the papers. He must have called.'

'Couldn't you stop him?'

'I had him in my sights—literally—but Billie walked in, armed.'

'Is Luke all right?'

'Yes, but Theo's name is on those papers. They'll be on their way to arrest him. You'll have to find him first.'

'Let me think . . . he's on the beach. I know his car, it's a Hudson Hornet.'

'Then get going!'

She slammed down the phone and rushed out of the building. She ran across the parking lot and jumped into her white Corvette.

There was no regular road to the beach. From the highway several tracks led between the dunes to the shore. She planned to take the first, then continue south on the beach. That way she could not miss Theo's car. She had to go slowly for fear of missing the turn-off in the dark. Then she saw a car emerging. It was followed by another, and another. Elspeth flashed her left-turn indicator. A constant stream of cars was coming from the beach. The spectators had figured out that the launch was cancelled and they were all going home.

A car behind her honked impatiently. She saw she was not going to be able to get to the beach this way. Could she wait on the highway in the hope of spotting his car? It was too chancy. Her best option was to go to his motel and wait there.

She sped on. She wondered if Army security was already at the Vanguard Motel. She had a chance of beating them if she hurried.

The Vanguard had a large parking lot out front. There was no sign of police or army security: she was in time. But Theo's car was not here. She parked near the motel office.

She did not have to wait long. The yellow-and-brown Hudson Hornet pulled in a couple of minutes later. Theo eased into a slot at the far end of the lot, and got out, a small man with thinning hair, dressed in chinos and a beach shirt.

Elspeth got out of her car. She opened her mouth to call to him. At that moment, two police cruisers arrived. Behind them followed two unmarked cars. They parked across the entry making it impossible for cars to leave.

Theo did not see them. He headed towards the motel office. Elspeth knew in a flash what she had to do. She took a deep breath, then started walking towards him. As he came close he recognised her and said loudly, 'What the hell happened to the launch?'

Elspeth said in a low voice, 'Give me your car keys.'

'What for?'

'Look behind you.'

He glanced over his shoulder and saw the police cars.

'Stay calm. Give me the keys.' He dropped them into her open hand. 'Keep walking,' she said. 'The trunk of my car is not locked. Get inside.' She went on past him.

Elspeth recognised Colonel Hide and another vaguely familiar face from Cape Canaveral. With them were four local cops and two tall, well-dressed men who might have been FBI agents.

She reached Theo's car and opened the trunk. Inside was the suitcase containing the radio transmitter—powerful, and heavy. She dragged it over the lip of the trunk. It hit the ground with a thud. She closed the trunk lid quickly.

She looked around. At the other end of the lot, she saw the trunk of her own car slowly closing, as if of its own volition. Theo was inside. Gritting her teeth, she grasped the handle of the suitcase and lifted. It felt like a box of lead. She walked a few yards, then dropped it. She picked it up with her other hand. She managed another ten yards before she dropped the case again.

Behind her, Colonel Hide and his men were crossing the lot towards the motel office. She prayed Hide would not look at her face. The darkness made it less likely he would recognise her.

Giving up carrying the transmitter, she began to drag it across the concrete, hoping the noise would not attract the attention of the cops.

At last she reached her car. As she opened the trunk, one of the uniformed police approached her with a cheerful smile. 'Help you with that, ma'am?' he said politely.

Theo's face stared at her from inside the trunk, white and scared.

'I got it,' she said. With both hands, she heaved up the suitcase and slid it in. There was a quiet grunt of pain from Theo as a corner dug into him. Quickly, Elspeth slammed the trunk lid. 'Thanks, anyway.'

'Checking out?' the cop said.

'Yeah.'

He bent, looked into the car, then straightened up. 'Drive safely.'

Elspeth got into her car and started the engine.

The cop went to one of the cruisers and moved it out of the way.

She drove through the gap and pulled onto the highway, then floored the gas pedal.

1.00AM: THE TRAIN PULLED out of Chattanooga. In the cramped roomette, Luke took off his jacket and hung it up, then perched on the edge of the lower bunk and unlaced his shoes. Billie sat watching him. Luke undid his tie and Billie said, 'If this is a striptease, it doesn't have much oomph.'

Luke grinned ruefully. They had been forced to share the roomette: only one was available. He was longing to take Billie in his arms, yet he hesitated.

'What?' she said. 'What are you thinking?'

'That this is too quick.'

'Seventeen years is nothing?'

'To me it's been a couple of days, that's all I can remember. And I'm still married to Elspeth.'

Billie nodded solemnly. 'But she's been lying to you for years.'

'I don't like the feeling that I'm seizing an excuse.' She said nothing in reply, so he added, 'You don't agree, do you?'

'No, I want to make love to you tonight, but I know you. You've never been one to live for the moment, even when we were kids.'

'Is that so bad?'

'No. I'm glad you're like that. It makes you rock-solid reliable. If you weren't this way, I guess I wouldn't have . . .' Her voice tailed off.

'What were you going to say?'

She looked him in the eye. 'I wouldn't have loved you this much, this long.' She was embarrassed, and covered up by saying 'Why don't you climb up on top, and give me room to take off my shoes.'

Obediently, he climbed the ladder and lay down on the top bunk.

She kicked off her shoes and stood up. She slipped off her black ski pants and stood there in her sweater and panties. Catching his eye, she grinned and said, 'It's OK, you can watch.' She reached under her sweater at the back and unfastened her brassiere. Then she drew her left arm out of her sleeve and drew her bra out of her right sleeve with a conjurer's flourish.

'Bravo,' he said.

She stood on the edge of the lower bunk and raised herself to his level, tilting her face to be kissed. He touched her lips with his own. Then she pulled away.

He lay thinking about her lying a few inches below, with her bare legs and her round breasts inside the soft angora sweater. In a few moments he was asleep.

He had an intensely erotic dream and woke up slowly, reluctant to return to the world of rockets and treachery. His shirt was open and his pants were undone. Billie lay beside him, kissing him. 'Are you awake? I don't want to waste this on a guy who's asleep.'

He ran his hand along her side. 'I'm awake,' he said thickly.

He felt as if he were still half in the dream, as the train rocked and Billie kissed him and America flew by the window mile after mile. He wound his arms around her back and held her tightly, to convince himself that she was real, not a fantasy. Just as he was thinking that he wanted this to go on for ever, his body took control, and he clung to her as waves of pleasure broke over him.

 **Part Six**

8.30am: Anthony flew to Florida in a small MATS plane that bumped and bucked with every gust of wind all the way across Alabama and Georgia. The CIA did not yet believe he was a double agent. He was accompanied by a general and two colonels who would have shot him on sight if they had known the purpose of his trip.

He landed at Patrick Air Force base, a few miles south of Cape Canaveral. In his imagination he saw a detachment of FBI agents waiting to arrest him there, but there was only Elspeth.

She looked drained. She led him outside to where her white Corvette was parked in the hot sun.

As soon as they were inside the car, he said, 'How's Theo?'

'Pretty shook, but he'll be OK.'

'Do the local police have his description?'

'Yes—Colonel Hide gave it out.'

'Where's he hiding?'

'In my motel room. He'll stay there until dark. What about you? Will the CIA give your description to the police?'

'I don't think so. The Agency likes to solve its own problems. They'll think I've gone rogue, and their only concern will be to take me out of circulation before I embarrass them. Once they start listening to Luke and realising they've been harbouring a double agent, that may make them even more eager to hush things up.'

'So the three of us are still in play. That gives us a good chance to still pull this thing off.'

In twenty-four hours, it would be all over, Anthony thought. They would have struck a historic blow for the cause to which they had devoted their lives.

Elspeth glanced across at him. 'What will you do after tonight?'

'Go to Moscow. I have everything I need—passports, cash, disguises.' Anthony was a major in the KGB. Elspeth had been an agent longer—had in fact recruited Anthony—and she was a colonel. 'They'll give me some kind of senior advisory-consultative role,' he went on. 'After all, I'll know more about the CIA than anyone else in the Soviet bloc.'

'You're not nervous?

'Sure I am. I'll be lonely at first—no friends, no family, and I don't speak Russian. But maybe I'll get married and raise a brood of little comrades.' His flip answers disguised his anxiety. 'I decided, a long time ago, to sacrifice my personal life to something more important.'

'I made the same decision, but I'd still be frightened of moving to Moscow.'

'It's not going to happen to you.'

'No. They want me to stay in place. at all costs.'

For the last four years, Russian scientists had known everything about the US space programme thanks to Elspeth. She was the reason the Soviets had beaten the Americans into space. She was easily the most important spy of the Cold War.

Her work had been done at enormous personal sacrifice, Anthony knew. She had married Luke in order to spy on the space programme but her love for him was genuine and it had broken her heart to betray him.

Among the palm trees on the roadside ahead, Anthony saw a huge model of a space rocket above a sign that read STARLITE MOTEL. Elspeth slowed the car and pulled in, parking as far as possible from the road. The rooms were in a two-storey building around a large pool where some early birds were already sunbathing. Anthony wanted to be seen by as few people as possible, so he pulled his hat low and walked quickly as they went from the car to her room.

Theo was standing at the window. Elspeth introduced the two men. Theo said to Anthony, 'How did Luke find me out—did he explain that to you?'

Anthony nodded. 'He was using the Xerox machine in Hangar R. There's a security logbook beside the machine. You have to note the date and the number of copies you made, and sign the log. Luke noticed that twelve copies had been signed for by "WvB", meaning Wernher von Braun.'

Elspeth said, 'I always used von Braun's name, because no one would question the boss.'

Anthony went on, 'But Luke knew that von Braun was in Washington that day. He went to the mail room and found the copies in an envelope addressed to you. He decided he couldn't trust anyone down here, so he flew to Washington. Fortunately, Elspeth called me and I was able to intercept Luke before he told anyone.'

Elspeth said, 'But now Luke has rediscovered what we made him forget.'

Anthony asked her, 'What do you think the army will do?'

My guess is they'll change the code.'

Anthony said, 'If they change the code we can't make the rocket self-destruct.'

'I have to find out what their plan is, and figure out a way around it.' Elspeth slung her jacket over her shoulders. 'Buy a car. Drive to the beach as soon as it's dark. Park as near as you can to the Cape Canaveral fence. I'll meet you there.' She went out.

After a moment, Theo said, 'You have to give her credit, she's got a cool nerve.'

4.00PM: THE COUNTDOWN stood at X minus 390 minutes. Elspeth moved about the base updating her timetable, alert for changes in procedure. So far she had gained no clue as to how the scientists planned to guard against sabotage—and she was starting to feel desperate.

Everyone knew Theo Packman was a spy and that Colonel Hide had raided the Vanguard Motel with four cops and two FBI men. The space community quickly linked the news with the last-second cancellation of the launch. The explanation given, that a late weather report had indicated a worsening of the jet stream, was not believed by anyone inside Cape Canaveral. As midday cooled into afternoon, Elspeth's tension mounted. If she did not learn the plan soon, it would be too late.

Luke had not showed up yet. She was longing to see him, and dreading it at the same time. Her deceit had poisoned their marriage, she knew. All the same, she yearned to see his face.

The scientists in the blockhouse were taking a break, eating sandwiches and drinking coffee. She sat next to Willy Fredrickson, her boss, who had his headphones round his neck while he ate a grilled-cheese sandwich. 'I guess you know everyone's talking about an attempt to sabotage the rocket,' she said conversationally.

Willy looked disapproving, which she took as a sign that he knew exactly what she was talking about. Before he could reply, a technician at the back of the room said, 'Willy,' and touched his own headphones.

Willy listened to his headset for a minute. 'OK,' he said into his mouthpiece. Then he looked up and said, 'Stop the countdown. There'll be a ten-minute delay.'

Elspeth lifted her pencil expectantly 'Shall I say why?'

'We have to replace a feed-through capacitor that's chattering.'

Capacitors were essential to the tracking system, and 'chattering'—small electrical discharges—could be a sign that the device was going to fail. But Elspeth was not convinced.

She scribbled a note, then got up and left. Outside the blockhouse, the afternoon shadows were lengthening. The white shaft of Jupiter-C stood like a signpost to the heavens. She walked briskly across the lawn to the launch pad and entered the steel cabin in its base that housed the offices. The gantry supervisor, Harry Lane, was speaking into a phone. When he hung up, she said, 'Ten minutes delay?'

'Could be more.'

Writing on her pad, she said, 'Reason?'

'Replacing a malfunctioning component,' he said.

Just then, a technician in oily overalls walked in. 'Here's the old one, Harry,' he said. In his dirty hand he held a plug.

Elspeth knew it was the receiver for the coded self-destruct signal.

She walked quickly out of the door before Harry could see the triumphant expression on her face. Heart thumping with excitement, she hurried back to her Jeep.

She sat in the driving seat, working it out. To prevent sabotage they were replacing the plug. The new one would be wired differently, to work on a different code. The new plugs had probably been flown here from Huntsville earlier in the day. The plugs were always made in sets of four, the duplicate pair being a spare in case of malfunction. It was the duplicate pair that Elspeth had examined, last Sunday, when she had sketched the wiring. Now she had to find the new duplicate set and do the same all over again.

She drove fast back to the hangars. She entered Hangar D and went to the telemetry room. This was where she had found the duplicate plugs the last time.

Hank Mueller was leaning on a bench, looking solemnly at a complex electrical device. When he saw her, he brightened and said, 'Eight thousand.'

Elspeth suppressed her impatience. She would have to play the numbers game with him before anything else. 'It's the sum of four consecutive cubes: eleven, twelve, thirteen, fourteen.'

'Very good.' He gave her a dime and looked expectant.

She racked her brains for a number, then said, 'The cube of sixteen thousand, eight hundred and thirty.'

'I can't work that out, I need a computer,' he said indignantly.

'You haven't heard of it? It's the sum of all the consecutive cubes from one thousand, one hundred and thirty-four to two thousand, one hundred and thirty-three,' she said.

'I didn't know that! That's the first time you've ever kept my dime.' He looked comically despondent.

She asked, 'Do you have the duplicate set of new plugs from Huntsville?'

'No,' he replied. 'They put them in a safe.'

She was relieved he didn't question her need to know. 'What safe?'

'They didn't tell me.'

'Never mind.' She went out and hurried to Hangar R. There was only one safe that she knew of—in Colonel Hide's office.

She went to her desk, took an army envelope and typed on it, 'Dr

W. Fredrickson—Eyes Only.' Then she slid two blank sheets of paper into the envelope, and sealed it.

She went to Hide's office. He was alone, sitting behind his desk. He looked up and smiled, 'Elspeth,' he said. 'What can I do for you?'

'Would you keep this in the safe for Willy?' She handed him the envelope.

'Sure,' he said. He spun around in his chair and opened a cupboard behind him. Looking over his shoulder, Elspeth saw a steel door with a dial. She moved closer. The dial was graduated from 0 to 99, but only multiples of 10 were marked with a figure, the other numbers being indicated by a notch. The first number where Hide stopped the dial was easy: 10. Then he dialled a number just below 30, either 29 or 28. Finally he moved the dial to between 10 and 15. The combination was something like 10, 29, 13. It must be his birthday, either the 28th or 29th of October, in 1911 to 1914. That gave eight possibilities.

Hide opened the door. Inside were two plugs.

Elspeth smiled as he tossed the envelope into the safe, closed the door. 'Thank you, Colonel.'

Now she had to wait for him to leave his office. She returned to her own office and her phone rang. It was Anthony. 'We're leaving here in a few minutes,' he said. 'Do you have what we need?'

'Not yet, but I will. What kind of car did you buy?'

'A light green Mercury Monterey, fifty-four model.'

'I'll recognise it.' Colonel Hide passed her door. 'I gotta go,' she said, and hung up.

She went out. Hide stood in the next doorway, talking to the girls in the typing pool. Elspeth loitered, wishing he would move on. But when he did, he returned to his office and stayed there for two hours.

Elspeth almost went crazy. She did not leave her office. Her timetable was forgotten. Willy, her boss, would be furious, but what did that matter? She looked at her wristwatch every few minutes. At eight twenty-five Hide at last walked past. She sprang up and went to her door. She saw him heading down the stairs.

Another man was walking along the corridor towards her. He said, 'Elspeth?' Her heart stopped, and she met his eye. It was Luke.

8.30PM: LUKE HAD BEEN dreading this moment.

He had dropped Billie off at the Starlite. She planned to freshen up then get a cab to the base in time to see the launch. Luke had gone straight to the blockhouse and learned that takeoff was now scheduled for 10.45pm. Willy Fredrickson had explained the precautions the team had taken to prevent the sabotage of the rocket. The new plugs were locked in a safe, Willy told him.

Luke would feel less worried when he had seen Elspeth. When he looked into her eyes and asked her to tell him the truth, he would know if his suspicions were correct.

He came up the stairs in Hangar R. As he reached the top he saw a tall redhead emerge from an office along the corridor, looking anxious. She was more beautiful than her wedding photograph.

He spoke to her, and then she noticed him. 'Luke,' She came quickly towards him. Her smile showed genuine pleasure, but he saw fear in her eyes. She threw her arms around him and kissed him.

He cut short the kiss and detached himself from her embrace. She frowned and looked hard at him, trying to read his expression. 'What is it?' she said. Then she sniffed, and sudden anger suffused her face. 'You've been with a woman.' She pushed him away. 'You screwed Billie Josephson, you bastard!'

Her betrayal was worse than his, but anything he said was going to sound like a pathetic excuse. So he said nothing.

Her mood switched again, just as quickly. 'I have to go. We'll talk later.' She looked up and down the corridor, seeming impatient.

'I don't think so,' he said. 'When I was at the house I opened a letter addressed to you.' He took it out of his jacket pocket and gave it to her. 'It's from a doctor in Atlanta.'

She pulled the letter out of the envelope and began to read it. 'Oh, my God,' she whispered.

'You had your tubes tied six weeks before our wedding,' he said.

Tears came to her eyes. 'I didn't want to do it,' she said.

He led her into her office, closing the door. She sat down at her desk, fumbling in her purse for a handkerchief. He pulled a chair over close to her.

'I almost didn't have the operation,' she said. 'It broke my heart.'

He looked carefully at her, trying to be detached. 'I guess they forced you to.' He paused. Her eyes widened. 'The KGB,' he went on, and she stared at him. 'They ordered you to marry me so that you could spy on the space programme, and they made you get sterilised so that you would not have children to divide your loyalties.' He saw a terrible grief in her eyes and knew he was right. 'Don't lie,' he said. 'I won't believe you.'

'All right,' she said.

She had admitted it. He sat back. It was all over.

'I kept changing my mind,' she said, and tears rolled down her face as she spoke. 'In the morning I'd be determined to do it. Then at lunch time I'd call you and you'd say something about a house with a big yard for children to run around in, and I'd make up my mind to defy them, but I couldn't in the end. What are you going to do, now? Call the FBI?'

'Should I?'

'If you do, I'll end up in the electric chair, like the Rosenbergs. But there's an alternative.'

'What?'

'Let me go. I'll go to Europe. From there I can get a flight to Moscow.'

'Is that what you want to do? Live out your days there?'

'Yes.' She gave a wry grin. 'I'm a KGB colonel, you know. I'd never be a colonel in the US.'

'You'd have to go now, immediately,' he said.

'OK.'

'I'll escort you to the gate, and you'll have to give me your pass so you can't get back in.' He looked at her, trying to imprint her face on his memory. 'I guess this is goodbye.'

She picked up her purse. 'Can I go to the ladies' room first?'

'Of course,' he said.

9.30PM: ELSPETH WALKED out of her office, passed the door of the ladies' room, and entered Colonel Hide's office. It was empty.

She closed the door behind her and stood leaning against it, trembling with relief. The office swam in her sight as her eyes filled with tears. The triumph of her life was within her grasp, but she had just ended her marriage to the best man she had ever known, and she was committed to leave the country of her birth and spend the rest of her days in a land she had never seen.

She closed her eyes and made herself breathe slowly. Then she turned the key in the office door, went to the cupboard behind Hide's desk and knelt in front of the safe.

Carefully, she repeated the actions Hide had performed when she watched him opening the safe. She dialled 10, 20, 14. She tried to turn the handle. It would not move. She heard footsteps outside, and a woman's voice, but the footsteps receded and the voice faded.

She knew the first number was 10. She dialled it again. The second number could have been 29 or 28. She dialled 28 this time, then 14 again. The handle still would not turn.

She had tried only two possibilities out of the eight. Next she tried 10, 29, 13, then 10, 28, 13. She was halfway through the list.

She heard a siren give a warning blast—two shorts and a long. This meant that all personnel should clear the launch-pad area. The launch was an hour away.

The combination 10, 29, 12 did not work. But 10, 28, 12 did. Jubilant, she turned the handle and pulled open the heavy door. The two plugs were still there. There was no time now to dismantle them and sketch the wiring. She would have to take them to the beach. Theo could use the actual plug in his own transmitter.

Someone tried the door and Elspeth stopped breathing.

A man's voice called, 'Bill, you in there?' It sounded like Harry Lane. The doorknob rattled. Then she heard departing footsteps. She grabbed the plugs from the safe and stuffed them into her purse. Then she closed the safe, spun the dial, and shut the cupboard.

She went to the office door, and opened it. She re-entered her office. Luke was sitting where she had left him, looking grim. 'I'm ready,' she said.

He stood up. 'After you leave here, you'll go straight to the motel,' he said. 'In the morning, you'll drive to Miami and get on a plane out of the United States.'

'Yes.'

He nodded, satisfied. Together they went down the steps and out into the warm night. Luke walked her to her car. As she opened the door, he said, 'I'll take your security pass now.'

She handed it over.

'I'll follow you to the gate in the Jeep.' She realised this was good-bye. She found herself unable to speak. She got into her car.

The lights of Luke's Jeep came on and followed her as she drove off. Passing the launch pad, she saw the gantry inching back on its tracks, leaving the huge white rocket standing alone in the flood-lights. She checked her watch. It was a minute before ten. She had forty-six minutes left.

She drove out of the base without stopping. The headlights of Luke's Jeep diminished and finally disappeared as she rounded a bend. 'Goodbye, my love,' she said aloud, and began to cry.

The lights of other cars swept by in blurred streaks. She almost overshot the beach road. When she saw it, she jammed on her brakes and slewed across the highway in the path of the oncoming traffic. A taxicab braked hard and swerved, honking, and narrowly missed the tail of her Corvette. She bumped onto the uneven sand of the beach and drove on, more slowly, to the beach.

AFTER ELSPETH LEFT, Luke stayed at the gate in his Jeep, waiting for Billie. He felt stunned. He had been married to a spy for four years. He could hardly take it in.

Billie arrived at ten fifteen in a taxicab. He signed her in, then they headed for the blockhouse. 'Elspeth has gone,' Luke said.

'I think I saw her,' Billie replied. 'Is she in a white Corvette?'

'Yes, that's her.'

'My cab nearly hit her car. I saw her face in the headlights. She was turning off the road in front of us.'

'She told me she'd go straight back to the Starlite.'

Billie shook her head. 'No, she was heading for the beach.'

'Damn,' said Luke, and he turned the Jeep around.

ELSPETH DROVE SLOWLY along the beach, staring at the groups of people who had gathered for the launch. She was looking for a Mercury Monterey. Anthony had told her it was green, but there was not enough light to see colours.

She started at the end of the beach nearest to the base, but Anthony and Theo were not there. She guessed they had chosen a more isolated spot. She checked her watch. It was ten thirty. She was almost out of time.

Elspeth drove close to a car that looked right, but it seemed to be empty. She accelerated again—then it honked. She slowed down and looked back. A man had got out and was waving at her. It was Anthony. 'Thank God,' she said. She reversed back to him and leaped out of the car. 'I've got the duplicate plugs,' she said.

Theo got out of the other car and opened its trunk. 'Give them to me,' he said. 'Quickly!'

10.45 PM: THE COUNTDOWN reaches zero.

In the blockhouse, the launch conductor says: 'Firing command!' A crewman pulls a metal ring and twists it. This is the action that fires the rocket. Prevalves open to let the fuel start flowing. The liquid oxygen vent is closed, and the halo of white smoke around the missile suddenly vanishes.

The launch conductor says, 'Fuel tanks pressurised.'
For the next eleven seconds, nothing happens.

The Jeep tore along the beach at top speed. Luke scanned the cars, ignoring the cries of protest as his tires showered people with sand. Billie was standing beside him, holding the top of the windshield.

The last connection hose drops away from the missile. A second later, the priming fuel ignites, and the first-stage engine thunders into life. A huge orange firelick bursts from the base of the rocket as thrust builds.
With painful slowness, Jupiter-C lifts off the launch pad.
In the blockhouse, someone yells, 'Go, baby!'

Billie saw a white Corvette parked next to a darker sedan. 'There,' she screamed.

'I see them,' Luke shouted back.

At the rear of the sedan, three people were clustered around the open trunk. Billie recognised Elspeth and Anthony. The other man was presumably Theo Packman. Their heads were raised and they were staring across the sand dunes towards Cape Canaveral.

Billie read the situation instantly. The transmitter was in the trunk. They were in the process of setting it to broadcast the detonation signal. She turned towards Cape Canaveral. There was nothing to see, but she heard a deep, rumbling roar like the sound of a blast furnace in a steel mill. The rocket was taking off.

'We're out of time!' she yelled.

'Hold tight!' Luke said.

She gripped the windshield as he swung the Jeep around in a wide arc.

The rocket picks up speed suddenly. At one instant it seems to be hovering hesitantly over the launch pad. At the next it moves like a bullet out of a gun, shooting into the night sky on a tail of fire.

Over the roar of the rocket, Elspeth heard the scream of a car engine. She looked up and saw a Jeep heading for them at top speed. 'Hurry,' she screamed.

Theo connected the last wire. On his transmitter were two switches, one marked ARM and the other DESTROY. Theo threw the ARM switch.

On the beach, a thousand faces tip backward, watching the rocket rise straight and true, and a huge cheer goes up.

Luke drove straight for the back of the Mercury. The Jeep had slowed as he turned, but he was still travelling at about twenty miles per hour. Billie jumped out, hit the ground running, then fell and rolled.

At the last second Elspeth threw herself out of the way. Then there was a deafening bang and the crash of breaking glass. The Mercury's rear end crumpled and its trunk lid came down with a bang. Luke was thrown forward violently. The bottom of the steering wheel caught his lower chest, and he felt the sharp pain of cracked ribs. His forehead hit the top edge of the wheel, and he sensed blood flowing down his face.

He pulled himself upright and looked at Billie. She seemed to have fared better than he. She was sitting on the ground rubbing her forearms, but she did not appear to be bleeding.

He looked across the hood of the Jeep. Theo lay on the ground, not moving. Anthony was on his hands and knees, looking shaken but unhurt. Elspeth had escaped injury and was scrambling to her feet. She dashed to the Mercury and tried to open the trunk.

Luke leaped out of the Jeep and ran at her. As the trunk lifted, he shoved her aside.

Anthony yelled, 'Hold it!' Luke looked at him. He was standing over Billie with a pistol to the back of her head.

Luke looked up. The red firetail of the missile was a bright shooting star in the night sky. As long as that was visible, Jupiter-C could still be destroyed. The first stage, which contained the explosive detonator, would burn out when the rocket was sixty miles high. It would separate and fall away, eventually to splash down in the Atlantic Ocean. Separation would take place two minutes and twenty-five seconds after ignition. Luke figured the rocket had been ignited roughly two minutes ago. There had to be about twenty-five seconds left, plenty of time to throw a switch.

Luke looked at Billie. She was on one knee, like a sprinter at the starting line, frozen in position with the long silencer of Anthony's gun pressing into her curly black hair. He asked himself if he was ready to sacrifice Billie's life for the rocket. The answer was No.

Elspeth again bent over the trunk of the car.

Then Billie threw herself backward, hitting Anthony's legs with her shoulders.

Luke lunged at Elspeth and pushed her away from the car.

The silenced gun coughed as Anthony and Billie fell in a heap.

Luke stared in dread. Had Anthony hit Billie? She rolled away from him, apparently unhurt. Then Anthony lifted the gun, aiming at Luke.

Luke looked death in the face, and a peculiar calm possessed him. He had done all he could.

There was a long moment of hesitation. Then Anthony coughed, and blood came out of his mouth. Pulling the trigger as he fell, he had shot himself, Luke realised. Now his limp hand dropped the gun and he slumped back on the sand, his eyes staring up at the sky but seeing nothing.

Elspeth sprang up and bent over the transmitter a third time.

Luke looked up. The firetail was a glow-worm in space. As he watched, it winked out.

Elspeth threw the switch, but she was too late. The first stage had separated. Luke sighed. It was all over. He had saved the rocket.

Billie put her hand on Anthony's chest, then checked his pulse. 'He's dead,' she said.

At the same moment, Luke and Billie looked at Elspeth. 'You lied again,' Luke said to her.

'We weren't wrong!' she yelled hysterically. 'We were not wrong!'

Behind her, families of spectators and tourists were beginning to pack their belongings. No one had been close enough to notice the fighting; all eyes had been turned to the sky.

Elspeth got into her car, slamming the door, and started the engine. Instead of turning towards the road, she headed for the ocean and drove straight into the water.

The Corvette stopped, waves lapping at its fenders, and Elspeth got out. In the car's headlights. Luke and Billie saw her begin to swim out to sea. Luke moved to go after her, but Billie grabbed his arm and held him back.

'She'll kill herself!' he said in agony.

'You can't catch her now,' Billie said. 'You'll kill yourself!'

Elspeth passed out of the headlights' beam, swimming strongly, and he realised he would never find her in the dark.

Billie put her arms around him. After a moment, he hugged her back. Standing on the beach, with their arms around one another, they both looked up.

The sky was full of stars.

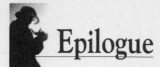

Epilogue

1968: Luke was on the NASA team that put Apollo 11 on the moon.

By then he was living in a big, comfortable old house in Houston with Billie, who was head of Cognitive Psychology at Baylor. They had three children: Catherine, Louis and Jane. (His stepson, Larry, also lived with them, but that July he was visiting his father, Bern.)

Luke happened to be off duty on the evening of 20 July. Consequently, at a few minutes before nine o'clock, Central time, he was watching TV with his family, as was half the world. He sat on the big couch with Billie beside him and Jane, the youngest, on his lap. The other kids were on the carpet with the dog, a yellow Labrador called Sidney.

When Neil Armstrong stepped on the moon, a tear rolled down Luke's cheek.

Billie took his hand and squeezed it.

Catherine, the nine-year-old, looked at him with solemn brown eyes. Then she whispered, 'Mommy, why is Daddy crying?'

'It's a long story, honey,' Billie said. 'I'll tell it to you, one day.'

Explorer 1 was expected to remain in space for two to three years. In fact it orbited the earth for twelve years. On 31 March 1970 it finally re-entered the atmosphere over the Pacific Ocean near Easter Island, and burned up at 5.47am, having circled the earth 58,376 times and travelled a total of 1.66 billion miles.

KEN FOLLETT

Ken Follett was just under thirty years old when his novel, *Eye of the Needle*, hit the best-seller lists in 1978. He has been a name to reckon with ever since, as well as being a great favourite with Condensed Books readers—this is the tenth time one of his books has appeared in the series. *Code to Zero* is Follett doing what he does best: combining heart-stopping fiction with historical fact.

The novel is set in 1958 during the early days of the space programme in the United States. The Soviet Union had already successfully launched the Sputnik satellite in 1957 and the US were attempting to regain their position in the space race with the Jupiter-C rocket. It's a historical fact that Jupiter's launch was delayed twice, and Follett has taken this information, let his imagination run riot, and plotted an exciting thriller around it. Another important element in the novel, the CIA mind-control programme, is also based on fact. Between 1953 and 1963 the US Central Intelligence Agency carried out top-secret research into mind control using drugs, electric shock treatment and sensory deprivation to artificially induce amnesia. It's a chilling but fascinating episode of the Cold War era, and one that Ken Follett has put to good use in *Code to Zero*.

One of the author's great passions in life is politics and he has long been involved with the Labour Party at both local and national level. He has been famously dubbed a 'champagne socialist'—a description he cheerfully accepts. 'I deserve both halves of that label. I've always been enthusiastic about champagne!' His wife Barbara shares his interest in politics and was elected Labour MP for Stevenage in 1997.

Follett's other passion is jazz, and he plays regularly in a blues band. Fans may be interested to know that he can be heard performing vocals and bass guitar on a CD aptly titled *Stranger than Fiction*.

Winter
Solstice

Rosamunde
Pilcher

When actress Elfrida Phipps retires to a cottage in a Hampshire village, she quickly feels at home. With her dog Horace for company and friendly neighbours Gloria and Oscar Blundell nearby, life is tranquil.

Until terrible tragedy befalls Oscar. Suddenly Elfrida is called upon to help her dear friend in his darkest hour of need.

Elfrida

Before Elfrida Phipps left London for good and moved to the country, she made a trip to Battersea Dogs Home, and returned with a canine companion. It took a good—and heart-rending—half-hour of searching, but as soon as she saw him, sitting very close to the bars of his kennel and gazing up at her with dark, melting eyes, she knew that he was the one. She did not want a large animal, nor did she relish the idea of a yapping lap dog. This one was exactly the right size. Dog size.

He had a lot of soft hair, some of which fell over his eyes, ears that could prick or droop, and a triumphant plume of a tail. His colouring was irregularly patched brown and white. When asked his ancestry, the kennel maid said she thought there was border collie there and a bit of bearded collie, as well as a few unidentified breeds. Elfrida didn't care. She liked the expression on his gentle face.

Her new companion travelled away with her, sitting in the passenger seat of her old car and gazing from the window in a satisfied fashion, as though this were the life to which he was happy to become accustomed.

It took some time to decide on a name for him, but in the end she christened him Horace.

ELFRIDA, WITH A BASKET in her hand, and Horace firmly clipped to his lead, closed the front door of her cottage, walked down the narrow path, through the gate, and set off down the the pavement towards the Post Office and General Store.

It was a dull grey afternoon in the middle of October. The last of autumn's leaves were drifting from trees, an unseasonable wind was too chill for even the most ardent of gardeners to be out and about, the street was deserted and the children not yet out of school. She walked briskly, Horace trotting reluctantly at her heels, knowing that this was his exercise for the day and he had no alternative but to make the best of it.

The village was Dibton in Hampshire, and here Elfrida had come eighteen months ago, leaving London for ever to make a new life. At first she had felt a bit solitary, but now she couldn't imagine living anywhere else. From time to time, old acquaintances from her theatre days came to stay with her, sleeping in the tiny back bedroom where she kept her sewing machine and earned a bit of pin money making elaborate cushions for an interior-decorating firm in Sloane Street.

When these friends departed, needing reassurance—'You're all right, aren't you, Elfrida? No regrets?'—she had been able to set their minds at rest: 'Of course I am. This is my geriatric bolt hole where I shall spend the twilight of my years.'

And there was now a comfortable familiarity about it all. She knew who lived in this house, that cottage. Some of the inhabitants were commuting families, the man of the house setting out early each morning to catch the fast train to London. Others had lived there all their lives in small stone houses that had belonged to their fathers and grandfathers. It was all very ordinary, and so undemanding. Just, in fact, what Elfrida needed.

She passed the newly furbished pub, the Dibton Coach-house, then the church, with its yew trees and lich gate, and a notice board fluttering with parish news. The street curved, and at the end of it, by the dull bungalow that was the new vicarage, she saw the village shop with newspaper placards propped against the wall. There were bars over the shop window to stop vandals breaking the glass and stealing the tins of biscuits and arrangements of baked beans that were Mrs Jennings's idea of tasteful decoration. Elfrida tied Horace's lead to one of the bars. He hated being left on the pavement, but Mrs Jennings didn't like dogs in her establishment.

Inside, the shop was bright, low-ceilinged and very warm. Refrigerators hummed and there was strip lighting and an up-to-date arrangement of display shelving that had been installed some months ago—a huge improvement, Mrs Jennings insisted, more like a mini-market. Because of all the barriers, it was difficult to know, at first glance, who was in the shop and who wasn't, and it was not until Elfrida rounded a corner that she saw the familiar back view, standing by the till and paying his dues.

Oscar Blundell. Elfrida was past the age when her heart leaped for joy, but she was always pleased to see Oscar. He had been almost the first person she met when she came to live in Dibton. She had gone to church one Sunday morning, and after the service the vicar had stopped her outside the door, his hair on end in the fresh spring breeze, and his white cassock blowing like clean washing on a line. He had spoken welcoming words, and then was diverted. 'And here's our organist. Oscar Blundell. Not our regular, but a splendid spare wheel in times of trouble.'

Elfrida had turned, and saw the man emerging from the church. She saw the gentle, amused face, the hooded eyes, the hair thickly white. He was as tall as Elfrida, which was unusual. She towered over most men, being five foot eleven and thin as a lathe, but Oscar she met eye to eye, and she liked what she saw there. He wore a tweed suit and a pleasing tie, and when they shook hands his grip had a good feel to it.

She said, 'How clever. To play the organ. Is it your hobby?'

And he replied, 'No, my job. My life.' And then smiled, which took all pomposity from his words. 'My profession,' he amended.

A day or two later, and Elfrida received a telephone call.

'Hello, Gloria Blundell here. You met my husband after church. The organist. Come and have dinner on Thursday. The Grange. Turreted redbrick at the end of the village.'

'How very kind. I'd love to.'

'Splendid. See you Thursday, then. About seven thirty.'

'Thank you so much.' But the receiver at the other end of the line had already been replaced. Mrs Blundell, it seemed, was not a lady with time to waste.

The Grange was the largest house in Dibton, approached through hugely pretentious gates and up a drive. Somehow none of this fitted Oscar Blundell, but it would be interesting to meet his wife and see his background. You never really got to know people properly until you had seen them in the ambiance of their own home.

On Thursday morning she had her hair washed, and the colour given its monthly tweak. The shade was officially called strawberry blonde but sometimes it came out more orange than strawberry. This was one of those times, but Elfrida had more important things to worry about. Clothes were a bit of a problem. In the end she put on a flowered skirt, which reached her ankles, and a long cardigan-type garment in lime-green knit. The effect of hair, flowers and cardigan was fairly dazzling, but looking bizarre was one of Elfrida's best ways of boosting her confidence.

For once, she was dead on time. She found a bell and pressed it, hearing it ring in the depths of the house. She waited, gazing about her at well-tended lawns. Footsteps. The door opened. A local lady in a flowered apron, clearly not the mistress of the house. 'Good evening. Mrs Phipps, is it? Come along in. Mrs Blundell won't be a moment, just went upstairs to fix her hair.'

'Am I the first?'

'Yes, but others'll be here soon. The drawing room—'

But they were interrupted. 'You're Elfrida Phipps . . . I'm sorry I wasn't here to greet you.' Looking up, Elfrida saw her hostess descending the wide staircase. She was a large lady, tall and well built, dressed in black silk trousers and a loose, embroidered Chinese jacket. She carried a tumbler of what looked like whisky and soda. 'I got delayed,' she went on. 'And then there was a telephone call. Hello.' She held out her hand. 'Gloria Blundell. Good of you to come.'

'Good of you to invite me.'

'Come along in by the fire. Thank you, Mrs Muswell.'

Elfrida followed her into a large room, panelled in the style of the thirties, furnished with hugely padded and patterned sofas and chairs. A log fire burned in a vast redbrick fireplace, the curtains were plum velvet braided in gold, and the floor was covered with richly coloured Persian rugs.

'Have you lived here long?' Elfrida asked.

'Five years. The place was left to me by an old bachelor uncle. Always adored it, used to come here as a child.' She dumped her glass on a handy table and went to hurl another enormous log onto the fire. 'I can't tell you the state it was in.'

'Where did you live before?'

'Oh, London. I had a house in Elm Park Gardens.' She picked up her glass and had a restoring swallow, then set it down again. 'My dressing drink. I have to have a little boost before parties. What would you like? Sherry? Gin and tonic? Yes, it was a good place to be and marvellously spacious. Oscar's church, St Biddulph's, where he was organist, was only ten minutes away. I suppose we'd have stayed there for ever, but my old bachelor uncle was gathered, as they say, and the Grange came to me. And we have this child, Francesca. She's eleven now. I've always thought it's better to bring a child up in the country. I don't know what Oscar's doing. He's meant to pour drinks. Sorry, did you say sherry or gin and tonic?'

Elfrida said gin and tonic, and watched as Gloria Blundell went to pour her one at a table at the end of the room. She also generously replenished her own glass with Scotch.

'There. Now, sit down, tell me about your little cottage.'

'Well . . . it's little.'

Gloria laughed. 'Poulton's Row, isn't it? They were built as railway cottages. Are you frightfully cramped?'

'Not really. I haven't got much furniture, and Horace and I don't take up much room. Horace is my dog.'

'And what made you come to Dibton?'

'I saw the cottage advertised in the *Sunday Times*. It looked rather dear. And not too expensive.'

'I shall have to come and see it. And what do you do?'

'Sorry?'

'Garden? Play golf? Good works?'

Elfrida hedged slightly. She knew a forceful woman when she met one. 'I'm trying to get the garden straight, but it's mostly shifting rubbish so far.'

'Do you ride?'

'I've never ridden a horse in my life.'

'I used to ride when my sons were boys, but that's long ago. Francesca's got a pony, but she's not all that keen.'

'You have sons as well?'

'Oh, yes. Grown up now and both married. Oscar's my second husband, you see. Of course, we had known Oscar for years at St Biddulph's. He played divinely at my husband's funeral. When we married, everybody was astonished. "That old bachelor," they said. "Do you have any idea what you're taking on?"'

It was all marvellously intriguing. 'Has Oscar always been a musician?' Elfrida asked.

'Always. He was educated at Westminster Abbey Choir School, and then went on to teach music at Glastonbury College. When he retired he moved to London, got the post at Saint Biddulph's. I think he'd have continued there until they carried him out feet first, but then my uncle died and fate decreed otherwise.'

Elfrida felt a little sorry for Oscar. 'Did he mind saying goodbye to London?'

'It was a bit like pulling an old tree up by the roots. For Francesca's sake, he put a brave face on it. And here he has his music room where he does a little private coaching. Music is his life. He loves it when there's an emergency and he can play for morning service in Dibton church. And, of course, he's always sneaking over to have a little quiet practice on his own.'

Behind Gloria, the door from the hall opened. She turned in her chair and peered over her shoulder. 'Oh, there you are, old boy. We were just talking about you.'

THE OTHER GUESTS arrived, filling the house with the sound of their voices, and the dinner party was under way. It was a formal evening, lavish and traditional, with excellent food and a great deal of splendid wine. They ate smoked salmon and a beautifully presented crown of lamb, and there were three puddings with bowls of thick cream, and then a creamy, blue-veined Stilton was served and the port was handed round. Soon, Mrs Muswell was putting her head round the door to say that coffee was ready in the drawing room.

Gloria led the way across the hall. She and her guests gathered around the fire, but Elfrida, lifting her cup of coffee from the tray, saw through the uncurtained window a sky of deep sapphire blue. There was a window seat and she went to sit on it, cradling the cup and saucer in her hands.

Presently she was joined by Oscar. 'Are you all right?' he asked.

'Of course. Such a lovely evening. And your daffodils will very soon be out.'

'Would you like to take a little stroll? It's still not quite dark.'

She glanced at the others, settled in the deep chairs and in full flood of conversation.

'Yes, I would like that, but wouldn't it be rude?'

'Not at all.' He took her cup from her hand and carried it back to the tray. He set it down. 'Elfrida and I are going to have a stroll around the garden.'

'At this hour?' Gloria was astounded. 'Make sure the poor girl's got a coat—it's chilly and damp.'

In the hall, Oscar lifted from a chair a thick leather coat lined in sheepskin. 'It's Gloria's—you can borrow it,' and he draped it gently over Elfrida's shoulders. Then he opened the front door and they stepped outside into the chill and purity of the spring evening.

They walked. At the far end of the lawn was a brick wall fronted by borders and broken by an archway with an imposing wrought-iron gate. Oscar opened this and they were in a spacious walled garden, neatly divided into geometrical shapes by box hedges. One quarter was a rose garden and clearly, when summer came, there would be something of a display.

'Is this all your work?' Elfrida asked.

'No. I plan, but I employ a labourer.'

Side by side, they strolled down the gravelled pathway. He said, 'I hope you didn't feel too distanced at dinner. I'm afraid we're something of a parochial lot.'

'Not at all. I enjoyed every moment. I like to listen.'

'Country life. It teems with intrigue.'

'Do you miss London?'

'From time to time, enormously. Concerts and the opera. My church, St Biddulph's.'

'Are you a religious person?' Elfrida asked impulsively, then wished she hadn't. Too personal a question.

But he remained unfazed. 'I don't know. But I have spent the whole of my life steeped in sacred music, and I would find it uncomfortable to live in a world where I had no one to thank.'

'For blessings, you mean?'

'Just so.'

'I understand, but even so I'm not a bit religious. I only went to church that Sunday because I was feeling a bit isolated and needed the company of other people. I didn't expect the lovely music.'

'The organ is a new one, paid for by countless bring-and-buy sales.'

They trod in silence for a moment. Then Elfrida said, 'Do you count that as a blessing? The new organ, I mean.'

He laughed. 'Yes, of course I do.'

'What else?'

He did not immediately reply. She thought of his wife, his lavish house, his music room, his friends. It would be interesting to know how Oscar had come to marry Gloria. Had he, after years of bachelordom, meagre salaries and dusty academic rooms, seen, looming in the future, the emptiness of an elderly bachelor's old age, and taken the easy way out? The wealthy, forceful widow, the capable hostess, competent mother. Or perhaps it was Gloria who had done the stalking and she who had made the decision. Perhaps they had simply fallen madly in love. Whatever. It seemed to work.

Finally, Oscar broke the silence that lay between them. 'I married late in life and for some reason it never occurred to me that I should have a child of my own. When Francesca was born, I was amazed, not simply that she was *there*, a tiny human being, but so beautiful. And familiar. As though I had known her always. A miracle. Now she is eleven and I am still astounded by my good fortune.'

'I would like to meet her.'

'You shall. I think you'll be charmed by her. When Gloria inherited this house, I kicked against leaving London. But for Francesca I went with the tide and complied. Here she has space and freedom. Trees, the smell of grass. Room to grow. You, I believe, also fled London?'

'Yes. I'd lived there all my life. From the moment I left home. I was at RADA. I was on the stage, you see. Much to my parents' disapproval. But I didn't mind about disapproval. I never have, really.'

'An actress. I should have known.'

'And a singer too. And a dancer. Revues and big American musicals. I was the one at the back of the chorus line because I was so dreadfully tall. And then years of fortnightly Rep, and bit parts on television. Nothing very illustrious.'

'Do you still work?'

'Heavens, no, I gave it up years ago. I married an actor, which was the most dreadful mistake for every sort of reason. And then he went off to America and was never seen again, so I kept myself by doing any sort of job that came my way, and then I got married again. But that wasn't much use either.'

'Was number-two husband an actor as well?' His voice was amused, which was exactly the way Elfrida wanted it to be. She seldom talked about her husbands, and the only way to make disasters bearable was to laugh about them.

'Oh, no, he was in business. Terribly expensive vinyl flooring. He had that disagreeable Victorian conviction that if a man feeds and houses his wife and doles out some sort of a housekeeping allowance, then he has kept his share of the marital bargain.'

'Well,' said Oscar, 'and why not? An old-established tradition, going back centuries. Only then it was called slavery.'

'How nice that you understand. Turning sixty was one of the best days of my life, because I got my pension book, and knew that I could walk down to the nearest post office and be given money, cash in hand, for doing nothing. I'd never in my life been given something for nothing. It was like a whole new world.'

'Did you have children?'

'No. Never children.'

'You still haven't explained why you moved to this particular village.'

Elfrida looked back towards the house and saw the glow of the drawing-room windows. 'I haven't told anybody, but there was this man. So special, so loving, funny, and perfect. Another actor, but successful and famous this time and I won't say his name. We lived together for three years in his house in Barnes, and then he got Parkinson's disease and it took him two years to die. It was his house. I had to leave. I saw an advertisement for the cottage in Poulton's Row and the next week I bought it. I have very little money, but it wasn't too expensive. I brought my dear dog Horace with me for company; I have my pension and a little job making cushions for a rather snob interior designer in London. I always liked to sew, and it's good to work with lovely, expensive materials. I don't know why I'm telling you all this. It's not very interesting.'

'I find it fascinating.'

'I don't see why you should. But you're very kind.' It was getting too dark now to see into his face or read the expression in his eyes. 'I think perhaps it's time we went back to the others.'

'Of course.'

'I love your garden. Thank you. Some time I must see it in the daylight.'

That was Thursday. The following Sunday morning, the rain was drumming against the windows of Elfrida's cottage, darkening the tiny rooms. She had made a cup of tea and was intending to spend the morning reading and finishing the crossword, but just after eleven she was interrupted by the ringing of the front-door bell and Horace let out a couple of barks.

Elfrida made her way to the front door and there she found a girl in jeans and a dripping anorak. Her auburn hair was braided into plaits, and her face was rosy from the chill, damp outdoors.

'Mrs Phipps?'

There were bands on her teeth, a mouthful of ironmongery.

'Yes.'

'I'm Francesca Blundell. My mother said it's such an awful day, would you like to come for lunch? We've got an enormous piece of beef and there's heaps—'

'I think you'd better come in before you drown.'

'Oh, thank you.' Francesca stepped indoors.

Elfrida closed the door behind her. 'This is Horace, my dog.'

'He's sweet. Do you mind if I take off my anorak?'

'No, I think it would be a very good idea.'

Francesca unzipped it and draped it over the newel post at the bottom of the banister. She looked about her. 'I always thought these were the dearest little houses but I've never been inside one of them. When Mummy said you were living here I couldn't wait to come and look. That's why I biked over. Do you mind?

'Not a bit. It's all rather cluttered, I'm afraid.'

'I think it's perfect.'

It wasn't, of course. It was cramped and filled with the few personal bits and pieces Elfrida had brought from London: the sagging sofa, the little armchair, the battered desk and too many books.

'Where does that door go?' Francesca asked.

'Into the kitchen. I'll show you.'

She opened the wooden door with the latch and pushed it ajar. Her kitchen was no larger than a ship's galley. A small Rayburn simmered away, a wooden dresser was piled with china and a wooden table and two chairs filled the rest of the space.

'I love it.' Francesca looked about her with a housewifely eye. 'But you haven't got a dishwasher. I think Mummy would die if she had to wash dishes.'

'It's not very arduous when you live on your own.'

'I love all your china. Blue and white. My favourite. What's upstairs?'

'A tiny bathroom, a bedroom for me and a workroom where I do my sewing. If I have a guest, they sleep there.'

'I think it's exactly right. For one person and a dog. Like a dolls' house. I'd better go now. Thank you for letting me see your house.'

'A pleasure. Thank you for bringing that kind invitation.'

'You will come, won't you?'

'Of course.'

'Mummy said a quarter to one.'

A moment later she was off on her bike with a wave of her hand, pedalling furiously through the puddles.

OSCAR, GLORIA AND FRANCESCA were Elfrida's first friends. Through them, she met others like the Foubisters, who were old-established and held the annual summer church fête in the park of their rambling Georgian house, and Commander Burton-Jones

(Retired), principal chorister in the church choir. Others came into her life one by one: Mr Hodgkins, who did the rounds once a week with his butcher's van and was a reliable source of gossip; Albert Meddows, who answered her advertisement for garden help and tackled the sad disarray of the paving in her back garden; the vicar and his wife.

They were all amiable enough and welcoming, but Elfrida found none of them as interesting or as stimulating as the Blundells. She spent Christmas with them, and New Year's Eve, and when she threw her first little party for her new friends it was Oscar who volunteered to be her barman.

However, there had to be limits if she was not to be utterly absorbed by, and beholden to, the Blundells. She knew that it would be only too easy to be swept along (and possibly drowned) in the churning wake of Gloria's social energy. So, from time to time, Elfrida stepped back, kept to herself. Every now and then, she escaped the confines of Dibton, packing Horace into her old Ford Fiesta and driving across country to some other county, where she could climb a sheep-grazed hill and relish her precious solitude.

On such occasions, with perceptions sharpened by a sense of perspective, she realised she liked Oscar immensely, perhaps too much. She was well past the age of romantic love, but from their first meeting outside Dibton church she had been instantly taken with him, and had come to enjoy his company more and more.

Elfrida also realised that Francesca, at eleven years old, was the kind of daughter she would have liked to call her own: independent, open and totally straightforward, yet possessed of a sense of the ridiculous that could reduce Elfrida to helpless laughter, and an imagination that was fed by voracious reading of books. During the school holidays Francesca frequently turned up at Poulton's Row, to play with Horace, or ask endless questions about Elfrida's theatrical past, which she clearly found fascinating.

Her relationship with her father was unusually close. He was old enough to be her grandfather, but their delight in each other's company went far beyond that of the average parent and child.

As for Gloria, she was a man's woman, and so closer to her grown-up and married sons than to her lately conceived daughter. Elfrida had met these sons, Giles and Crawford Bellamy, and their pretty, well-dressed wives, when they turned up at the Grange for a weekend, and she got the impression that neither of them approved of her. Their mother doted on them, and it was clear that in her eyes neither son could do wrong. But Francesca, Elfrida decided, was not that important to her, not as absorbing or fulfilling as her own hectic lifestyle, her parties, her friends, her position as social mentor.

Only once had Elfrida fallen from grace. It was during a convivial evening at the Foubisters' home, a dinner party of great formality and style, with candles lit and silver gleaming and an aged butler waiting at table. After dinner, Oscar had moved to the grand piano to play and had suggested that Elfrida should sing.

She had been embarrassed. She had not sung for years, she protested. But old Sir Edwin Foubister added his persuasion.

At that moment, Elfrida caught sight of Gloria's face, set in an expression of disapproval and dismay. And she knew that Gloria did not want her to stand up with Oscar and entertain the little group. She did not like others to steal attention away from herself.

However, emboldened by delicious wine and a tiny flame of self-assertion, Elfrida decided she would not allow herself to be bullied. So she smiled towards Gloria's threatening frowns, and then turned her head and let the smile rest upon her host. She said, 'If you want, I should like to, very much.'

'Splendid.' Like a child, Sir Edwin clapped his hands.

And Elfrida crossed the floor to where Oscar waited for her.

'What will you sing?'

She told him. An old Rodgers and Hart number.

A chord or two for introduction. It had been a long time. She straightened her shoulders, filled her lungs . . .

> 'I took one look at you,
> That's all I had to do.
> And then my heart stood still.'

All at once she was consumed by reasonless happiness, and felt young again, standing by Oscar and, with him, filling the room with the music of their youth.

While everybody marvelled and congratulated Elfrida on her performance, Gloria drank her brandy and scarcely spoke. When it was time to leave, Sir Edwin accompanied them out to where Gloria's powerful car was parked. Elfrida got into the back, but it was Oscar who slipped behind the driving wheel, and Gloria was forced to take the passenger seat of her own vehicle.

'How did you enjoy your evening?' Oscar asked his wife.

Gloria replied shortly, 'I have a headache,' and fell silent.

Elfrida saw the sad truth. Gloria, hard-headed and with a stomach like a tin bucket, drank too much. She was never incapable, never hung over. But she drank too much. And Oscar knew it.

OSCAR. AND NOW, here he was, in Mrs Jennings's shop on a grey October afternoon, picking up his newspapers. He wore corduroys, a thick, tweedy-looking sweater and sturdy boots.

Mrs Jennings looked up. 'Afternoon, Mrs Phipps.'

With his hand full of change, Oscar turned and saw her. 'Elfrida. Good afternoon. How are you?'

'Oh, surviving. A bit fed up with this weather.'

Elfrida unloaded her basket so that Mrs Jennings could run the prices of its contents through the till. As she loaded her bag, Oscar said, 'I'll give you a ride home, if you like.'

'I've got Horace with me . . .'

'He's welcome to join us. Thank you, Mrs Jennings. Goodbye.'

'Cheerio, Mr Blundell. Regards to the wife.'

Outside, Elfrida untied Horace's lead and he wagged his tail as the three of them made their way to Oscar's car. Elfrida got into the passenger seat and Horace sat on the floor between her feet. As Oscar switched on the ignition, she said, 'I never expect to meet anyone in the shop in the afternoons. Mornings are the social time. That's when you get all the chat.'

'I know. But Gloria's in London and I forgot about the papers.'

He nosed out into the main street, where the pavements were busy with a procession of tired, grubby schoolchildren making their way home.

'When did Gloria go to London?'

'Yesterday. For some meeting or other. Save the Children, I believe. I've got to meet her off the six-thirty train.'

'Would you like to come back and have a cup of tea with me? Or would you prefer to return to your gardening?'

'How do you know I've been gardening?'

'Woman's intuition. Mud on your boots.'

He laughed. 'Perfectly correct, Mr Holmes. But I wouldn't say no to a cup of tea. Gardener's perks.'

He drew up at her gate, and they decanted themselves. Horace, freed of his lead, bounded up the path, and Elfrida followed him, lugging her shopping bag. She opened the door.

'Don't you ever lock it?' Oscar asked, behind her.

'Not for a village shopping spree. Anyway, there's little to steal. Come along in, shut the door behind you.' She went through to the kitchen, filled the kettle and set it on the stove.

Oscar looked about him. 'You know, you have made this little place very charming.'

'It's a muddle. Not enough space. Possessions are a quandary, aren't they? They become part of you, and I'm not very good at throwing things away. And there are one or two little bits and pieces I've been carrying about with me for years, dating back to the giddy days when I was on the stage. A silk shawl, the odd knick-knack.'

'I particularly like your little Staffordshire dogs.'

'They were always part of my luggage.'

'And the little travelling clock.'

'That travelled, too.'

'It appears well worn.'

'"Battered" would be nearer the truth. I've had it for years; it was left to me by an elderly godfather. I . . . I have one thing I think might be very valuable, and it's that little picture.'

It hung to one side of the fireplace, and Oscar found his spectacles and put them on to inspect it.

'Where did you get this?'

'A present from an actor. He'd picked it up in a junk shop and I don't think paid all that much for it, but he was excited because he was sure that it was a David Wilkie.'

'Sir David Wilkie?' Oscar frowned. 'A valuable possession.' He returned his gaze to the painting, which was only about eleven inches by eight, and depicted an elderly couple in eighteenth-century dress sitting at a table on which lay a huge leather Bible. The background was sombre, the man's clothes dark. But the woman wore a canary-yellow shawl and a red dress, and her white bonnet was frilled and ribboned.

'Is it insured?'

'It *is* my insurance. Against a rainy day. When I find myself on the streets with only a couple of plastic bags and Horace at the end of a piece of string, then, and only then, will I think about selling it.'

'A hedge against disaster.' Oscar smiled and took off his spectacles. 'Whatever. It is the manner in which you have put your possessions together that makes such a pleasing whole. I'm sure you own nothing that you do not think to be beautiful or know to be useful.'

'William Morris.'

'Yes. Perhaps the measure of good taste.'

'Oscar, you say the nicest things.'

At this moment, Elfrida's kettle let out a startling toot, which meant that it was boiling. Oscar watched while she made the tea in a round brown teapot and set it upon the wooden table.

They sat facing each other across the table and Elfrida busied herself cutting some gingerbread. She said, 'Oscar, I am going away.'

'For ever?' he asked, fearfully.

'Of course not for ever.'

His relief was very evident. 'Thank God for that. What a fright you gave me.'

'I'd never leave Dibton *for ever*. But it's time for a holiday. Autumn always depresses me. A sort of limbo between summer and Christmas. And I'm going to have another birthday soon. Sixty-two. Even more depressing. So, time for a change.'

'Perfectly sensible. It will do you good. Where will you go?'

'To the very end of Cornwall.'

'Cornwall? Why Cornwall?'

'Because a cousin of mine, Jeffrey Sutton, lives there. He's exactly two years younger than me. We've always been friends.'

Oscar shook his head in some bewilderment. 'I never knew that you had a cousin. Or any sort of relation.'

'I am a bit denuded of family. But Jeffrey's a special person and we've always kept in touch.'

'Has he a wife?'

'Actually, he's had two. The first was a pain in the neck. She's called Dodie. I suppose he was charmed by her pretty looks and sweet air of helplessness, only to to discover, poor man, that he had tied himself to a woman of such self-absorption it beggared belief. She was, as well, idle and undomestic, and most of Jeffrey's hard-earned salary went on paying the wages of cooks, cleaners and au pairs. He remained constant and enduring, but when his two daughters were grown, he walked out. When the very acrimonious divorce was over, he married Serena, a girl he'd known for years, and almost at once started another little family. A boy and a girl. They live on a shoestring in Cornwall, keeping hens and doing bed and breakfast for summer visitors.'

'What about his daughters? What happened to them?'

'I've rather lost touch. The eldest, Nicola, married some man and had a child. She was always dissatisfied, perpetually complaining about the unfairness of life. I think she was jealous of Carrie.'

'Carrie being her sister.'

'Precisely so. And a darling. Jeffrey's nice personality all over again. About ten years ago, when I had to have an operation, she came to take care of me. She stayed for six weeks. Took it all in her stride and we got on like a house on fire.' Elfrida frowned. 'She must be about thirty now.'

'Did she marry?'

'I don't think so. Last time I heard, she was working in Austria as a ski rep. She always loved skiing.' She poured his tea and gave him a slice of the crumbling gingerbread. 'So you see I do have a family, if not a particularly close one.' She smiled. 'How about you? Do you have any dotty relations you can boast about?'

'Well, I had a Scottish grandmother. How's that for starters?'

'Hoots toots.'

'She had a great big house in Sutherland called Corrydale. Enormously comfortable. Huge meals, and gumboots and fishing rods lying around the place. Smells of flowers and beeswax polish and grouse cooking. I used to spend summer holidays with her. She was totally unpretentious and enormously talented.'

'In what way?'

'I suppose a talent for living. And music. She was an accomplished pianist. I think I inherited my small talent from her. She set me on the road to my chosen career. There was always music at Corrydale.'

'What else did you do?'

'Fish for trout. Play golf. If it was warm enough, I might bicycle to the beach and fling myself into the North Sea. At Corrydale it didn't matter what you did. It was all very relaxed. Good fun. Then my grandmother died and I never went back. My uncle Hector McLellan inherited and went to live there.'

'Didn't he invite you for summer holidays?'

'I was sixteen. Into music. Taking exams. Other interests. A different life.'

'Does he still live there?'

'No, he's in London now. He's very old.'

'And Corrydale?'

'He made it over to his son, Hughie. My cousin. A feckless fellow whose one idea was to live a grand life and do things in tremendous style. Hughie decided that life north of the border was not for him, so he sold up and scarpered off to Barbados. As far as I know, he's still there, leading the life of Reilly. We used to put up with each other, but we were never friends.'

'So everything's sold up, and you'll never return?'

'Actually, I could go back. When my grandmother died, she left Hughie and me a house in the middle of the little town. It used to be estate offices, but then it was converted to a dwelling house. It's been let for years to some old couple.'

'How exciting. I wish I had a house in Scotland.'

'Half a house. I suppose one day Hughie will either offer to buy me out or suggest that I buy him out. But it's not something I worry about. Now, when are you off to Cornwall?'

'Next Wednesday.'

'For how long?'

'A month.'

'We shall miss you,' said Oscar, and she felt warmed.

JEFFREY'S HOUSE was called Emblo Cottage. It stood with its granite face to the north wind and the Atlantic and its windows were few and deep-set, with windowsills wide enough for potted geraniums and scraps of driftwood. On the south side there was a sheltered lawn where wisteria climbed the wall and a camellia bush still flowered.

Jeffrey, who had been waiting outside the house when she arrived, leaped out from the side of the road and waved her to a halt. If he hadn't been so immediately recognisable, she might have been frightened out of her wits, but there was no mistaking that tall, lanky figure, still lithe and active despite his advancing years. Now he opened the door of the Fiesta. 'You made it! What sort of journey did you have?' he asked.

'All right. I was a bit nervous. It's years since I've done such a long drive; unknown motorways and thundering lorries I find a little unnerving. This car isn't exactly a Ferrari.'

'Good enough.'

Elfrida climbed out of the car and let Horace free, while Jeffrey opened the boot of her car and heaved out a battered suitcase. Doors were slammed and he led the way up a slate path and round the corner of the house. The wind from the sea pounced upon them and yellow squares of light, from windows and a half-glassed door, lay upon the cobbles. Jeffrey set down Elfrida's suitcase and opened the door and she went through and into the kitchen. The children,

Ben and Amy, looked up from the table and Serena turned from the stove and came, aproned and open-armed, to greet them.

'Jeffrey, you found her! What a perfect bit of timing! Did you have a frightful drive, Elfrida? Would you like a cup of tea? Or would you like to unpack and have a bath? There's plenty of hot water.'

'Bless you. Then that's what I'll do.'

'Come on,' Jeffrey said, and led the way up the creaking wooden stairs. He showed her round, said, 'See you in about an hour,' and left her, closing the door behind him.

Elfrida unpacked and set her few belongings about the simple room. Then she undressed, wrapped herself in her old dressing gown and went next door to the little bathroom, where she soaked in a scalding bath. When she got out she felt active and cheerful and ready for the evening ahead. She dressed and went downstairs to join Jeffrey and Serena by the blazing log fire in the sitting room.

In later months, when she came to look back at those weeks spent at Emblo Cottage, the thing Elfrida most clearly remembered was the wind. It blew perpetually, at times pounding in from the sea at gale-force strength, rattling doors and window panes.

October moved towards November and the nights drew closer every evening. The daily routine of the little household took Elfrida over and she slowed herself to its pace. There was always washing to be pegged out, potatoes to be dug, hens to be fed and eggs washed. Some evenings she took over the kitchen and cooked supper for Ben and Amy, so that Jeffrey and Serena were able to grab a chance of dinner out by themselves. And she taught the children to play rummy or mesmerised them with stories about her theatre days.

WHEN THE DAY came for her to return to Dibton, Elfrida could scarcely believe that she had been in Cornwall for a month, so swiftly had the weeks sped by. But it was time to pick up the thread of life again. To return to her own little nest.

Dibton church clock stood at half past two as she drove into the village. She parked outside Mrs Jennings's and went into the shop. She picked up a basket and moved up the aisles, taking what she needed from the shelves. Finally, she presented herself at the counter. Mrs Jennings looked up.

'Mrs Phipps. Well, what a surprise. Have a good holiday, did you?'

'Wonderful. Just back. Haven't even been home yet.' She put the wire basket on the counter and looked up. Mrs Jennings was staring at her, biting her lip and looking much troubled. 'Is anything wrong, Mrs Jennings?'

'You haven't heard?'

Suddenly Elfrida's mouth was dry. 'No.'

'Mrs Blundell. She's dead. A car smash at Pudstone roundabout. She was bringing the little girl home from a firework party. November the 4th, it was. A great articulated lorry. She couldn't have seen it . . . It was a dreadful night. Pouring with rain.'

Stunned, Elfrida said, 'And Francesca?'

'She died too. Only good thing was the police said it was instant.' Mrs Jennings's voice shook a little. 'You've gone white as a sheet, Mrs Phipps. Would you like a cup of tea?'

'No, I'm all right.' Which she was, because she was numb, shocked beyond horror. She said, 'Was there a funeral?'

'A couple of days ago. Here in the village. Huge turnout.'

So she had missed a chance to mourn and comfort. She said, 'And Oscar? Mr Blundell?'

'Hardly seen him. At the funeral, of course, but not since then.'

Elfrida thought of Francesca, laughing and teasing her father, playing duets with him on the piano, curled up in his big armchair.

She said, 'Is he at the Grange?'

'Far as I know. The vicar went to call, but he didn't even want to see the vicar. Mrs Muswell goes up there each day, but she says he just stays in his music room. She leaves a tray for his supper on the kitchen table, but she says most times he doesn't touch it.'

'Do you think he would see me?'

'I wouldn't know, Mrs Phipps. Except that you and them were always friends.'

'I should have been here.'

'Not your fault, Mrs Phipps. I feel I've spoilt your homecoming. I'm sorry.'

Elfrida went out of the shop, got back into her car and sat there for a moment, feeling as though her life had been snapped into two pieces. Heavy-hearted, she started up the engine, drove down the main street and passed her own house. Then she came to the great gates of the Grange, turned up the drive and saw the elaborate face of the house and a large black limousine outside the front door, a uniformed driver behind the wheel.

She parked, and went up the steps. She did not ring the bell, but opened the door and went inside. She stood for a little, listening, hoping for comforting, domestic sounds from the kitchen, or a thread of music from upstairs. Nothing. The silence was suffocating.

She crossed the hall, thick carpets blanketing her footfall, and went through to the drawing room. A man was sitting in the wing chair by the empty fireplace. Tweed trouser legs, polished brogues. Not much else was visible.

'Oscar,' she said softly. She moved forward to look down at him, and experienced the second stunning shock of that dreadful day. For here was Oscar, aged beyond belief, all at once an old man, wrinkled and hunched, a gnarled hand clenched over the ivory handle of an ebony stick. Instinctively, her hand went to her mouth.

He looked up at her, and said, 'My word,' and instantly relief flooded through her. He was not Oscar, aged beyond belief, but someone resembling Oscar, an old gentleman well into his eighties, with a strong Scottish accent.

He went on, 'I never heard you coming in. Did you ring a bell? I'm a bit deaf, but I'd have heard the bell. I'd have come to the door.'

'No,' she told him. 'I didn't ring the bell. I just walked in.'

'You'll forgive me not getting up. I'm a bit stiff and slow these days. Perhaps we should introduce ourselves. I am Hector McLellan. Oscar is my nephew.'

Hector McLellan. Who had once owned Corrydale, but now lived in London, and whose son Hughie lived in Barbados.

She said, 'Oscar told me about you.'

'And you, my dear?'

'Elfrida Phipps. I have a house in the village. I live on my own. Gloria and Oscar were endlessly kind to me. I'm sorry I was so rude when I first came in. I thought you were Oscar, and then, of course, I realised my mistake.'

'Oscar, aged by grief?'

'Yes. I suppose so. You see, I haven't seen Oscar yet. I've been in Cornwall for a month. I've only just heard about everything from Mrs Jennings in the village shop. What happened?'

The old man shrugged. 'Gloria drove her car onto the roundabout, right into the teeth of this great articulated lorry.'

'Mrs Jennings said she'd been to a party with Francesca.'

'That's so.'

Elfrida bit her lip. After a little, she said, 'Sometimes, at the end of a party, she'd have a strong drink.' And immediately wished she hadn't said such a thing.

But the old man was unfazed. 'I know, my dear. We all knew. Sometimes she overdid it a wee bit. And then to drive home . . . Oscar knows this, better than any of us. He is consumed with guilt because he didn't take Francesca to the firework party himself.' He spread his hand. 'Finished. Lives wiped out.'

'I've even missed the funeral.'

'I missed it too. I had a touch of flu, so my doctor forbade it. This is my first visit, though of course I have been in touch over the telephone. It was while I was speaking to Oscar that I became aware of his situation. As soon as I could, I made the journey down from London to talk things through. I am aged, but I am still his uncle.'

'Yes.' Elfrida frowned. 'You said "his situation". Does that have special meaning?'

'It most certainly does.'

'Am I allowed to be told?'

'No secret, my dear. Gloria has left everything, including this house, to her sons. They intend selling.'

'And where do they imagine Oscar's going to live?'

'They suggested some old folks' home. The Priory, I think it's called.'

'You mean, they're throwing him out? Into an old folks' home? *Oscar*? They must be mad.'

'No. Just avaricious and without heart. And they've got two hard wee wives as well, probably pushing from the back line.'

'Then Oscar must buy another house.'

Hector McLellan regarded Elfrida over the top of his spectacles. 'Oscar is not a man of means. A pension and a little put by. But not enough to buy a decent house.'

'Gloria's sons must know that.' Another thought occurred to her. 'And Gloria must have known too. Surely she could have left Oscar *something*. She was so generous.'

'Maybe she intended to. In all likelihood, it never occurred to her that she would die before Oscar. Perhaps she simply never got around to making a new will. We shall never know.'

'But he can't go and live in an old folks' home. I won't let it happen. He can come and live with me.' But even as she said it she knew that this was an impractical suggestion. There was scarcely space for one at Poulton's Row, let alone two.

'My notion,' said the old man. 'is that he should move away. This house, this village is too filled with memory. That's why I came down here today. I put forward my suggestion. But he seems unable to make any sort of decision. Doesn't seem to care what happens.'

'Where is he now?'

In the garden. Some problem with the greenhouse heating system. I said I would wait until he returned, then start back for London.'

'What was your suggestion?'

'That he goes back to Sutherland for a bit. Corrydale and the Estate House. Half of it belongs to him, and my Hughie, the co-owner, lives in Barbados and is likely to stay there. At the moment it's empty. An elderly couple were living there but the old man died and his wife went to stay with her daughter. I discovered this from our erstwhile factor, Major Billicliffe. He's retired now, but he still lives on the Corrydale estate. He says the place is in good condition. Furnished. No frills, but all the essentials of day-to-day living.'

Sutherland. Elfrida imagined it: peat bogs and sheep, remote as the moon. She said, 'It's a long way for Oscar to go, all on his own.'

'He's known at Corrydale and Creagan, the little town. He's family and people are kindly. He will be remembered, even though he's not been back for fifty years.'

But is he up to such an upheaval? Elfrida wondered.

They gazed sadly at each other. The silence was disturbed by the slow tread of someone crossing the gravel in front of the house and Elfrida saw Oscar pass by the long window. The front door opened and closed. They waited. Then he was there, surveying the pair of them, his thick white hair falling across his forehead. She had imagined him diminished, felled by tragedy. But heartbreak is a hidden thing and Oscar was a private man.

'Elfrida. I saw your little car.'

She went to meet him, and he took her hands in his own and leaned forward to kiss her cheek. His lips were icy against her skin. She looked into his eyes. 'Dear Oscar. I'm home again.'

'How long have you been here?'

'About fifteen minutes. I drove up from Cornwall this morning. I went into the shop, and Mrs Jennings told me. I came straight here and walked in on your uncle.'

'I see.' He let go of her hands and turned to Hector, who sat in his chair and watched their reunion. 'I am sorry I kept you waiting, Hector. But you have had Elfrida for company.'

'And very pleasant it has been, too. Now I must be on my way.'

They all moved, at the old gentleman's pace, to the hall.

'It was good of you to come, Hector, and I really appreciate it.'

'Dear boy. Give thought to my suggestion. It may seem a little drastic, but it would give you a breather. You mustn't stay here.' Then he remembered something. 'Billicliffe's got the key of your house, by the way. All you have to do is give him a ring. Now I must be off.' He turned to Elfrida. 'Goodbye, my dear. I *have* enjoyed meeting you. I hope one day we'll be able to renew our acquaintance.'

'I hope so too. We'll come with you to the car.'

Oscar put a hand beneath Hector's elbow and they walked through the front door and down the steps onto the gravel. The chauffeur got out of the car and went round to open the door of the passenger seat. Oscar embraced the old man. 'Thank you again for coming, Hector.'

The car started up. They stayed until it was out of sight, then Oscar said, 'Come indoors.'

'Are you sure you don't want me to leave as well?'

'No. I want you to stay with me.'

'Would you like me to make us a cup of tea?'

'I think that would be an excellent idea.'

Oscar led the way into the warm kitchen. Elfrida found the kettle, filled it, and put it on the Aga to boil. She turned to face Oscar. 'I wish I was articulate and brilliant at thinking of things to say. But I'm not, Oscar. I'm sorry. I just wish I'd known. I would have come back from Cornwall. I would at least have been at the funeral.'

He sat at the kitchen table, and as she spoke he buried his face in his hands. For a dreadful moment, she thought that he was weeping. But slowly he drew his hands from his face, and she saw that his eyes were filled with an anguish that was almost worse than tears.

He said, 'I would have been in touch, but I had no idea where in Cornwall you were.'

'That was because I had no idea that you might need to know.' She took a deep breath. 'Oscar, I *do* know about loss and bereavement. I know, too, that there is nothing I can do to help, to ease you.'

'You are here.'

'I can listen. If you want to talk, I can listen.'

'Not yet.'

'I know. Too early. Too soon.'

'The vicar called very soon after the accident. Very soon after I had been told that both Gloria and Francesca were dead. He tried to comfort, and mentioned God, and I found myself wondering if he had taken leave of his senses. You asked me once if I was religious, and I don't think I was able to answer your question. I only knew that my music and my choirs meant more to me than any churchly dogma. Thundering away on the organ, hearing the boys' voices soar to the rafters. That was when I truly believed, when I knew a faith that I thought nothing could rock.' He fell silent.

'And now, Oscar?'

'I cannot believe in a God who would take Francesca away from me. I sent the vicar home. He departed, I think, in some umbrage.'

'Poor man.'

'He will, no doubt, survive. The kettle's boiling.'

It was a welcome interruption. Elfrida busied herself finding mugs, spooning tea. She carried everything over to the table and sat facing Oscar, just as they had sat that day, an eternity ago, before she went to Cornwall, in her little house in Poulton's Row.

'You like builders' tea, don't you?'

'Strong and black.'

She poured her own mug and left the pot to stew. She said, 'Hector told me about your stepsons and the house. About selling the Grange, I mean.'

'They think that I should book into the Priory, a Victorian mansion converted for the benefit of desiccated gentlefolk.'

'You won't go there.'

'I admit, I would rather not.'

'What do you want to do?'

'I would like to be left alone, to lick my wounds. But I can't be left alone *here*, because Giles and Crawford want me out of the way so that they can put the house on the market.'

'Brutes.' She poured his tea, black as ink, and pushed the mug towards him. 'Hector McLellan told me his suggestion.'

'I had a suspicion that he might have.'

'Is it such a bad idea?'

'Elfrida. It's mad. Sutherland is the other end of the country. And I haven't been there for years. I would not know a single soul.'

Elfrida persisted. 'Is it very isolated? Your house, I mean.'

'No. It's in the middle of Creagan, the little town. It's just that I can't imagine what the hell I would do with myself.'

'Well, you can't stay here, Oscar. And you go into the Priory over my dead body. So you must consider any available alternative. Scotland,' she mused. 'It would at least be a fresh start.'

'I am sixty-seven and in no shape to start anything. And although I can scarcely bear to speak to anyone, I dread being alone. Empty rooms. Even before I married Gloria, there were always colleagues, choristers, a whole world of lively company. My life was full.'

'It can be again. Never the same, I know. But you have so much to give people. A generosity of spirit. We mustn't waste it.'

He frowned. 'You said "we".'

'A slip of the tongue. I meant *you.*'

Oscar reached out for the teapot and poured himself a refill.

'Suppose . . . suppose I did go to Scotland, to Sutherland. Would you come with me?'

She stared into his face, wondering if she had heard right. 'Come with you?'

'Why not? Is it such a bad idea? To go together? Somehow we'll get there. We shall collect the key from Major Billicliffe, take possession and spend the winter there.'

'Christmas?'

'No Christmas. Not this year. I probably won't be a very lively companion. But, by spring, perhaps, I shall be stronger. Time will have passed. Here, as you so clearly stated, I have no future.'

'And my house, Oscar? What should I do with it?'

'Let it. Or shut it up. It will be safe.'

He meant it. He was asking her to go away with him. He needed her. She, Elfrida. Eccentric, disorganised, not beautiful any longer, even a little raffish. And sixty-two years old.

'Oscar, I'm not sure that I'm that good a bet.'

'You underestimate yourself. Please come, Elfrida. Help me.'

All her life she had made decisions without thought for the future and had regretted none of them. All she regretted were the opportunities missed, either because they had come along at the wrong time or because she had been too timid to grasp them.

She took a deep breath. 'All right. I'll come.'

'Dear girl.'

'I'll come for *you*, Oscar, but I owe it to Gloria as well. You and Gloria and Francesca were my first friends when I came to Dibton. I feel ashamed. We've been talking, and this is the first time I've said their names to you.' A lump had swelled in her throat, and it became difficult to talk. She was crying, but the tears, strangely, were something of a relief. 'I . . . I've only been to Scotland once. To Glasgow, ages ago, with a touring company . . .' Fumbling up her sleeve for a

handkerchief, she found one and blew her nose. 'I couldn't understand a single word anyone said to me.'

'There's Glaswegian for you.'

'It wasn't funny at the time.'

'It's not funny now, but you've always made me smile.'

'Like a clown?'

'No. Not a clown. Just a dear, funny friend.'

Sam

At seven o'clock on the first dark Friday morning of December, Sam
Howard wheeled his trolley of luggage out into the arrivals hall of
Heathrow Airport. There was nobody to meet him. No wife, no
driver. No welcome. He knew that outside the heated terminal building it would be very cold, partly because they had been warned of
the temperature before the plane landed, but also because everybody
was bundled up in padded jackets, gloves, scarves and woollen hats.
It had been cold in New York, but a dry crisp cold that stimulated.

His trolley was laden with two suitcases, a huge American golf bag
and his briefcase. He manoeuvred it towards the exit doors and out
into the cold and wet. He joined the queue for taxis and had only to
wait five minutes or so.

The taxi driver was a morose man with a walrus moustache.

'Where to, guv?'

'Wandsworth, please. Fourteen Beauly Road.'

''Op in.'

Sam opened the back door of the taxi, humped his luggage
aboard, shoved the empty trolley out of the line of trouble and
climbed in. The taxi trundled forward.

The short wait had chilled him. Sam turned up the collar of his
navy-blue overcoat, leaned back and yawned. He felt tired and
unclean and was grateful that his first appointment was not until
Monday at twelve thirty, when he had to present himself for lunch
with Sir David Swinfield, chairman of Sturrock & Swinfield, and
Sam's ultimate boss. Until then, his time was his own.

The taxi drew up at a red traffic light. Suddenly the driver spoke,
flinging the question back over his shoulder.

'Golf clubs. Been on 'oliday?'

'No,' Sam told him.

'On business, then?'

'You could say. I've worked in New York for six years.'

'Not much of a mornin' for comin' 'ome.' Green light. They moved forward again.

'No,' Sam agreed. He did not add, And I'm not coming home. But right now, he did not have a home. For the first time in his life, and he was now thirty-eight, he found himself without bricks and mortar to call his own. The house in Beauly Road was a semidetached three-storey Victorian villa belonging to his old friend Neil Philip and his wife Janey. Neil had been part of Sam's life since the day they first met at boarding school, becoming a regular visitor at Sam's Yorkshire home in the holidays. Sam's mother had ended up calling him her second son. When Sam had phoned to say he was coming to London for a few days, Neil had insisted that he stay with them for as long as he liked.

Bundled gloomily in his overcoat in the back of the taxi, Sam thought of homes, remembering Yorkshire and Radley Hill, where, as an only child, he had been born and brought up. A large, comforting family home, filled with the smell of wood smoke and cakes baking. It was a place as comfortable as an old tweed jacket, which he had thought would never change, but of course it did. During his last year at Newcastle University his mother died, and after that nothing was ever quite the same again.

The family business was a small woollen mill in a small Yorkshire town. After Newcastle, Sam had intended to spread his wings, perhaps get a job abroad, but with his mother gone he hadn't the heart to abandon his father and, with a degree in engineering under his belt, he went home to Yorkshire and the mill. For a few years, father and son boxed along happily together and business boomed. But then recession hit, and the mill, which specialised in fine worsteds and lightweight tweeds, came up against sophisticated competition from Europe. At the end of the day, Sturrock & Swinfield, the huge textile conglomerate based in London, moved in and the little mill was taken over. Sam was given a job under the new umbrella, but his father, too old a dog to learn new tricks, took early retirement. Unable to fend off the stress of loneliness, boredom and enforced inactivity, he died twelve months later of a massive heart attack.

Radley Hill was left to Sam and, after some heart-searching, he put it on the market. It seemed the only sensible thing to do for he was now London-based, working for Sturrock & Swinfield. Then, out of the blue, came a summons from the Chairman. Sam was told that he was being transferred to New York. The head of the New York office, Mike Passano, had particularly asked for him. It was a promotion, responsibility, the opportunity for which he had subconsciously yearned ever since university.

He took to New York like a duck to water, relishing every aspect of the stimulating, cosmopolitan melting pot that made up the city. Home, there, was a walk-up in Greenwich Village, but after he married Deborah she persuaded him to move and they ended up in a fancy duplex on East 70th Street, where she engaged the services of an interior designer.

Homes. East 70th Street had been the last, and that, too, had gone. Along with Deborah.

She had never been a moral coward. She told him, face to face, that she was leaving. She was tired of playing second fiddle to Sturrock & Swinfield, and tired of being married to a workaholic. There was, of course, another man.

He was furious, but he was hurt, too, bewildered and abased. But in a way he understood.

He soldiered on for six weeks. At the office he found every excuse to stay at his desk long after the others had left, returning late to an empty apartment. Mike Passano said, 'Take a vacation,' but that was the last thing Sam wanted. Instead, slowly, it was borne upon him that he had had enough of New York. He wanted England. He wanted to go home. He wanted misty skies and temperate green fields and warm beer and red buses.

And then one evening, at the nadir of his despair, the telephone rang in the apartment, and it was Sir David Swinfield from London.

'Hear things aren't running too smoothly for you.'

'Bad news travels fast.'

'Do you feel like a change?'

Sam was cautious. 'What do you have in mind?'

'Sam, I want you back in the UK. I need you to be general manager of a place called McTaggart's Mill in Buckly, Sutherland. We bought them out a few months ago. They're an old-fashioned set-up, been going for at least a hundred and fifty years, making classic tweeds. But, as you know, that market has shrunk. I want you to get the mill back on its feet again. Run the place.'

It had rained most of the weekend, and so on Monday morning Sam buttoned into his overcoat and set off, armed with one of Neil's umbrellas, for St James's Street. At twenty-five past twelve he presented himself to the porter at White's and asked for Sir David Swinfield, who was expecting him.

Carrie

Carrie dreamed of Austria and Oberbeuren. In the dream, the sky was a deep blue and the snow so dazzling that every frozen flake glittered like a jewel. She was skiing on an empty piste, floating down through white fields that spread to infinity on either side. And then, far ahead, she saw another lone skier, a black silhouette, hurtling away from her, down the slope. She knew that the skier was Andreas, and she called his name. *Andreas. Stop, and let me be with you. Let us ski down together*. She topped a rise and saw that he had heard her call and was waiting, leaning on his sticks, watching for her.

He was smiling. White teeth in a deeply tanned face. She reached his side and stopped, and only then saw that it was not Andreas at all, but another man, with a wolfish grin and eyes hard as grey pebbles. And the sky was not blue any longer but storm-dark and she was afraid . . .

Her eyes flew open in the darkness. She saw a strip of uncurtained window, the street lights beyond. Not Austria, not Oberbeuren, but London, the spare bedroom of her friends, Sara and David Lumley. The dream receded. Andreas, who had never been truly hers, was gone. It was all over.

She reached for her watch on the bedside table. Six o'clock on a dark December morning. She found herself overcome with a desperate yearning for Andreas, for his smooth, muscular body close to her own. To be back in the huge carved bed beneath the sloping beams; lovers, bundled in goosedown and bliss. She closed her eyes, turned her face into the pillow and slept again.

At nine o'clock she awoke once more. By now, David and Sara would have departed for work and she would be alone in their house. Already she had been here for a week, and in that time had accomplished little: seen nobody, done nothing about finding a new job.

Carrie's only contact with her family had been to call her father in Cornwall and have a long and comforting conversation with him. 'You will get in touch with your mother, won't you?' he had said. She knew that it could be postponed no longer. Today she would telephone Dodie.

She did not look forward to seeing her mother or her sister Nicola. She knew that they would have much to tell her, none of it good news. However, the sooner it was over with, the better.

She pulled on her dressing gown and went downstairs. In the neat kitchen, she found a note, propped against the pot plant that stood in the middle of the kitchen.

Have a good day. There's bacon in the fridge and orange juice. I'll be home usual time. If you go to Safeway could you buy a veg. for supper? Cauliflower would do. And some Lapsang Souchong teabags. Love, Sara.

Carrie boiled a kettle, made coffee, put bread in the toaster. Then she reached for the telephone and punched the number.

'Hello.'

'Ma, it's Carrie.'

'*Carrie*? Are you ringing up from Austria?'

'No. London. With friends. Putney. Just across the river from you.'

'How long have you been back?'

'About a week. But there's been a lot to do, otherwise I'd have called before.'

'A *week*? Is this a holiday?' Dodie's voice was querulous, as though in some way her daughter had pulled a fast one on her.

'No. I chucked my job in. Decided I'd done it for long enough.'

'I always imagined you were there for good. We haven't seen you for years. What happened?'

'Nothing happened. Just a whim.'

'Will you get another job?'

'Have to. Look, Ma, I thought I'd come and see you. How about lunch?'

'Here, you mean?'

'I'll take you out if you'd rather.'

'No, I can manage. Soup and pâté. Would that be all right?'

'Perfect. How's Nicola?'

'Oh, my dear girl, such dramas.'

Carrie's heart sank. 'Dramas?'

'I think she's gone mad. I'll tell you all about it when you come.' A pause, and then Dodie added, 'Actually, all this might be rather fortuitous. You coming home, I mean. She'll be back for lunch, but perhaps you could get here a bit earlier and we can have a private chat about it.'

Carrie began to wish she hadn't telephoned. She said, 'And what about Lucy?'

'Lucy's here too. She's got a morning off school, something to do with a boiler being replaced. She's in her room swotting for some exam. Spends most of her time in her room so she won't disturb us.'

'I'd like to see her.'

'Oh, you will, you will. What time will you be here?'

'Eleven thirty?'

'I'll expect you.' Dodie rang off.

The chill and ambiguous welcome was exactly what Carrie had both dreaded and expected. It had always been thus. A lack of communication, an antipathy, perhaps, that Carrie had learned to accept even before she entered her teens. Being with other families, seeing how they behaved with each other, had compounded her perception and, had it not been for the presence of her father, she could well have grown up with no knowledge of loving or being loved. She had never quite worked out why Jeffrey Sutton, her father, married Dodie in the first place. Perhaps because she was pretty and flirtatious and had the ability to turn herself into exactly the sort of companion any potential husband would wish to spend his life with. But it was all a calculated act.

Nicola was their first child, and then, five years later, Carrie arrived. So different were the sisters, it seemed that each belonged solely to one of their parents. As though Dodie had produced Nicola without cooperation from Jeffrey, and Jeffrey had fathered Carrie, in some miraculous fashion, entirely by himself.

He was her father, her friend, her ally. It was Jeffrey who drove his daughters to school, while their mother lay in bed, sipped China tea and read novels. It was he who had first taken Carrie skiing at Val d'Isère when she was only ten—one of the best holidays of her life, and the start of a passion that had never left her. Nicola had turned down the invitation, partly because she was hopelessly unathletic, but also because she liked being on her own with Dodie so that the two of them could go shopping and buy new dresses for all the Christmas parties, which Nicola had no intention of missing. Clothes, boys and parties were her passionate interests and it surprised nobody when she became engaged, at twenty-one, to Miles Wesley, who held a respectable job at the London office of Hurst & Fieldmore, an old-established estate agent with branches all over the country.

CARRIE WAS THE FIRST person to whom Jeffrey confided that he was leaving Dodie. She was nineteen and at Oxford reading English and philosophy, relishing every moment of her new life. When he met her for lunch to tell her the news, he looked less stressed than she had seen him for ages.

But he was in for a traumatic experience, and Dodie's resentment and recrimination were to echo for a long time. At the end of the day, though, most people had to agree that Dodie had done very well for herself. She let Jeffrey get away with nothing and ended up with the family home. He could scarcely have done more to make amends.

Dodie put the house on the market, sold it at a socking profit and moved to an apartment in Fulham, looking south over the river to Putney. 'My little lonely nest,' she told her friends, sounding wistful and plucky, and everyone said she was marvellous. In truth she was as content as she had ever been, with her bridge and her little drinkie parties and the unfailing panacea of shopping and holidays abroad.

Then, seven years after Dodie's divorce, Nicola Wesley discovered that her husband, the mild-mannered Miles, was having it off with another woman, and grabbed the opportunity to flounce out of a marriage that had become both predictable and boring. She flounced, of course, to her mother and her mother's spacious and pretty apartment. All of which might have been quite fun and companionable, had not Nicola brought with her her nine-year-old daughter Lucy. Dodie knew that her halcyon days were over.

THE DREGS OF HER COFFEE had grown cold. Carrie got to her feet and went to take a shower and dress. Lately she had not bothered too much about how she looked, but this morning she knew that the time had come to take a bit of trouble.

So, slim camel-coloured trousers, a polo-necked cashmere sweater, polished boots, gold earrings, gold chains around her neck. She sprayed scent, checked her leather shoulder bag, took her coat from the wardrobe and went downstairs.

In the hall was a long mirror, and she paused, regarding herself. Saw a tall, slender, dark-haired girl. Or perhaps, more accurately, a woman. After all, soon she would be thirty. Her short, chestnut-brown hair shone with cleanliness, a lock like a bird's wing sweeping across her forehead. Her eyes, accentuated by eye shadow and mascara, were large and dark as coffee, her face still tanned from the slopes. She looked all right. Confident. Not a person to be pitied.

She did up the buttons of her coat, a dark grey loden piped with forest green that had been bought, a year ago, in Vienna. Andreas had helped to choose the coat, and then insisted on paying for it. 'You will wear it for ever,' he told her, 'and you will always look a million dollars.'

It had been a day of bitter cold and thin snow, and when they had bought the coat they had walked through the streets, arm in arm, to Sacher's and there lunched in some style, and . . .

Don't think about it.

She strode down Putney High Street towards the river. Once over the bridge, it was only a short way to the ornate Edwardian block where Dodie had her flat. Carrie ran up the steps, went in through the heavy main doors, got into the lift and sailed upwards. She opened the doors with a tremendous clanging sound, crossed the hall and pressed the bell.

Dodie had been waiting for her, She was there almost at once, dealing with the double lock and flinging the door open.

'Carrie!'

She looked much as she always had—small and trim with dark, neatly dressed hair flashed with a streak of white that was entirely natural. She wore a little cardigan suit, the skirt fashionably short, and court shoes decorated with square gold buckles. A still-pretty woman, with apparently everything going for her. Only her mouth gave her away, moulded by the years into an expression of constant discontent. Carrie had always been told that the eyes are the mirror of the soul, but had long ago decided that a person's mouth is the true giveaway of character.

She stepped through the door, and Dodie closed it.

'Hello, Ma. How are you?' Carrie asked, shedding her coat. 'You're looking marvellous.'

'Thank you, dear. You're looking well, too. So brown.' They kissed, formally, touching cheeks.

Dodie led the way into her sitting room. It was a pleasant room, with large windows facing south onto a balcony and, beyond it, the river. In the white marble fireplace there flickered a small mock-coal electric fire. Dodie settled herself beside this, in her own chair.

'It was good of you to come so promptly. I wanted to tell you about everything, this ridiculous drama that's suddenly blown up.'

'Nicola?' Carrie lowered herself into the chair on the other side of the white sheepskin hearth-rug. 'Where's she gone?'

'Travel agent.'

'Is she planning a trip?'

'I think she's gone mad. I said that, didn't I, over the telephone. She met this American at some party a few weeks ago, and they've been seeing each other ever since.'

Carrie thought it sounded quite hopeful, and not at all mad.

'What sort of American?' she asked cautiously.

'Oh, quite presentable. A businessman. Railways, or steel or something. He's based in Cleveland, Ohio, wherever that is. He's called Randall Fischer. He's divorced. And now he's invited Nicola to go and spend Christmas with him at his place in Florida.'

'So what is so dire about that?'

'Don't you see, Carrie? It's Lucy.'

'You mean Lucy is not included in the invitation?'

'She most certainly has been included, but she refuses to go. She says she won't know anybody and Randall doesn't really want her. He's only asked her because he feels he has to.'

Carrie was sympathetic. 'I see her point. What age is she? Fourteen. She'll feel like a fish out of water and, admit, it's a bit embarrassing watching your own mother in the throes of a love affair.'

'But what will she do?'

Now, thought Carrie, we're getting to the nub of the matter.

'For Christmas, you mean? Stay with you, I suppose. Where else would she go?'

Dodie did not reply. Instead, she got to her feet and stood at the window, gazing down at the river. Carrie waited. Then her mother turned. 'I can't deal with her on my own. I have a life to lead. I have plans made. The Freemans go every year to the Palace Hotel in Bournemouth. They've invited me to join them. And I'm not going to change my plans for a stubborn little girl.'

No, Carrie thought, I don't suppose for a moment you'd even contemplate such a thing. She said, 'What about her father? Miles. Can't she spend Christmas with him and his new wife?'

'Miles and his wife are going to St Moritz to ski for Christmas, with a grown-up party. Miles said it was out of the question.'

Carrie said, 'In that case, you seem to have come to a deadlock.'

'That's what I meant on the telephone. About your abrupt return from Austria coming at a fortuitous time.'

'You mean *me*? *I* take Lucy off your hands?'

Dodie looked up. 'Have you plans laid?'

'Ma, I'm only just back from Austria. I haven't had time to lay a plan. I'm living out of a suitcase. I'm not really in a position to have someone to stay.'

'I didn't mean that. I thought maybe . . .' She hesitated. 'Your father . . . He's Lucy's grandfather. Surely . . .'

'Look, Ma. I've spoken to Jeffrey. We talked about Christmas then, but he's got Serena's brother and his wife and baby coming to spend the holidays with them. Emblo is going to be bursting full. There's not an inch for two more people.'

Dodie let out a sigh and sat back in her chair, as though at the end of her tether. 'I really can't go on like this. No cooperation from anybody, least of all my own family.'

'But, Ma—'

She did not finish. There came the sound of a key in the lock of the front door.

'Nicola's back,' Dodie said unnecessarily.

When Nicola came into the room, Carrie got up and turned to face her sister. 'Hi.'

'*Carrie!*' Nicola's jaw dropped. 'I thought you were in Austria.'

'I was,' Carrie told her, 'but I'm back now.'

The sisters eyed each other. They had never been close, never been friends, never shared secrets. And it occurred to Carrie that Nicola, as she matured, was growing to look even more like their mother. The same height, the same neat figure, thick dark hair. The same small, mean-tempered mouth. Put side by side, and they could easily have been mistaken for a pair of cross little twins.

Whenever she thought of Nicola, Carrie always had a mental picture of her wearing some coordinated little outfit. Shoes matching a handbag, a silk scarf exactly toning her lipstick. Now, Nicola did not let her down, for there was the immaculately tailored trouser suit, beneath a car coat of *faux* leopard. Her bag was chocolate-brown suede of exactly the same shade as her high-heeled boots.

Nicola shrugged out of her jacket and gave Dodie a cold look. 'I suppose Mother's been telling you about all the drama. Getting you on her side.' Dodie and Nicola were clearly, at this moment, on the worst of terms. Carrie decided that Lucy must have been having a hellish time between the pair of them.

Dodie looked hurt. 'Nicola, that's not fair,' she protested.

'No, but I bet it's true.' Nicola settled herself with a thump in the middle of the sofa. 'Anyway, it's too late now. I've booked my flight. I'm going on the 18th of December. For two weeks.'

Carrie said, 'There seems to be a problem with Lucy.'

'She was asked to Florida, but she refuses to come with me.'

'Ma suggested that I look after her for Christmas. But I can't.'

'Why not?'

'No house. No home.'

Nicola chewed her thumbnail. 'Anyway, I'm going. I'm going to Florida with Randall, and nobody's going to stop me.'

Carrie, sympathetic in a way, but thinking of Lucy, tried reasoning. 'But, Nicola . . .'

She got no further. Nicola rounded on her. 'It's all very well for you.' Carrie wondered how many thousands of times in her life she had heard that familiar wail. 'You've never had a family, you don't know what it's like being tied, day in, day out, to a child. Term time and holidays. Keeping Lucy amused, dealing with problems at school. As far as I can see, your life has been one long holiday. Nothing but skiing and having a good time. Not a care in the world.'

Carrie, with some difficulty, kept her voice even. 'Nicola, you haven't the faintest idea what I've been doing. My job was public relations officer for a travel firm, and each morning nine people had to report in to my office. I very often worked seven days a week. So let's hear a little less about irresponsibility.'

'It's not the same.' Mulish, Nicola stuck to her grudge. 'Not the same as bringing up a child.'

Carrie gave up. 'Look, this isn't getting us anywhere.'

Nicola ignored her. 'It's up to you, Mother. You'll have to forget about Bournemouth.'

Dodie became incensed. 'I shall do no such thing.'

Suddenly Carrie knew she could listen to this pointless sniping no longer. 'Do *stop*,' she told them sharply. Rather surprisingly, they did. 'If you don't mind, I'd like to go and have a chat with Lucy, since she could hardly talk less sense than her mother and grandmother. Where's her room?'

'Next to the kitchen.' Nicola jerked her head. 'At the back.'

Carrie went from the room and closed the door behind her.

Lucy

Lucy Wesley, when she came to live with her grandmother after her parents' divorce, had been given a room that had originally been designed for a housemaid or cook. She did not really care, though, that it was cramped and sunless, looking out onto the well at the centre of the building, because it was her own. The walls were yellow, which imparted the illusion of sunlight, and the curtains yellow and white striped, and Lucy had her bed, piled with teddies, a large table with drawers for doing her homework, and lots of shelves for her huge collection of books. Her computer sat on the table, and a small television set, and when her schoolfriends came to visit they were always loud with envy and admiration, mostly because the space belonged to Lucy only, and she didn't have to share it with some tiresome younger sister.

Lucy was an extremely tidy person. On the shelves, her books stood in straight lines, her bed was smooth, her clothes folded. Once a week, Mrs Burgess, who came to clean for her grandmother, went through the room with Hoover and duster, but Lucy herself polished the mirror of her dressing table and the silver frame that held the photograph of her father.

She missed him dreadfully. Like a piece of furniture that had lost a leg, the family had collapsed with his going, fallen sideways, crooked and useless, and Lucy knew that it was unmendable and would never be the same again. From time to time she saw him, but his new wife, Marilyn, was wary of involvement and clearly had no interest in children or stepdaughters, or anything except her absorbing job.

Lucy felt she could no longer confide in her father, because of divided loyalties on both their parts. Sometimes she felt that she would burst if she didn't find someone adult to talk to.

Now, at a quarter to twelve on a Friday morning, she had finished her homework and was writing in her diary, a fat leather-bound book with its own tiny lock and key. It had smooth thick paper that was a pleasure to write on, and had been a present from Cornwall. *Happy Christmas, Lucy* was written on the flyleaf, *from Grandfather, Serena, Amy and Ben.* She had kept up the diary ever since the day she had received it. There were no dates, just lovely clean pages, which meant that you wrote the date yourself, and then the day's doings underneath. Sometimes there was little to record, but other days she used up two or three pages.

She wrote now, *Mummy went to the travel agent this morning. She and Gran are scarcely speaking to each other because of Christmas. I wish they would understand how I would hate Florida. You can't swim all day in a pool, and I don't like Randall that much.*

The diary was better than having nobody to confide in, but a person would be better. She thought about Carrie, Mummy's younger sister, and a splendid aunt. Carrie would be perfect, because she talked to you as though you were a grown-up and yet was always prepared to do exciting things. Once they had gone down the Thames together in a boat, all the way to Tower Bridge, and had lunch on board.

Every now and then during the course of the morning, Lucy had heard the telephone ring, and Gran's low voice, chatting away. About an hour ago, someone had rung the bell and come to visit. She had no idea who it could be, and did not particularly care. Later, she heard the rattle of a latchkey in the front door, and knew that her mother had come back from the travel agent.

After about five minutes, she heard somebody approaching her door. Her mother, come to impart the latest news about plans for Florida . . . Lucy felt almost sick with apprehension. But then, there was a soft knock, and she knew it wasn't Mummy, because Mummy never knocked, just barged in.

Before she could bring herself to say 'Come in', the door opened slowly, and a head came around the edge of it.

'Am I interrupting?' Not her mother. Not Gran. But . . . Carrie. Carrie? Lucy found herself dumbfounded, astonished that such a marvellous event was actually taking place. She felt the warm blush of sheer pleasure creeping into her cheeks.

Carrie said, 'Don't goggle. It's really me.'

Slowly, Lucy got to her feet. She said, 'Goodness.'

Carrie came into the room, closed the door behind her and planted a kiss on Lucy's cheek. She looked about her. 'What a pretty room. It used to be very gloomy.'

'Gran did it up for me. She let me choose the colours.'

'Perfect. All sunny.' There was a small blue armchair by the bed, and Carrie sank into this. 'Have you been working?'

'Yes. Homework.' Lucy picked up her diary, stowed it away in a drawer, and then sat down again, swivelling her typist's chair round so that she faced her aunt. 'How long are you home for?'

'Indefinitely. Chucked the ski job in. I'm both homeless and unemployed, but it doesn't matter. How's everything with you?'

Lucy shrugged. 'All right.'

'There seems to be a certain crisis. Poor child, you must be wondering what on earth is going to happen next.'

This was in character, and Lucy was grateful. Carrie had always been completely direct, coming straight to the point of any dilemma. Suddenly Lucy felt much better, even strong enough to ask, 'Mummy didn't buy *two* air tickets for Florida, did she?'

Carrie laughed. 'Don't worry, she's going on her own. So that little battle you've won. It must have been something of a fight.'

'Do you think I'm being stupid, not wanting to go with her?'

'No, I think you're absolutely right. You'd be a gooseberry. Much better for Nicola to be on her own. But it does pose problems. What do *you* want to do for Christmas? I bet nobody's even asked you that.'

'Not really.'

'I suggested you go to your father, but apparently he and his wife are off to the ski slopes. You haven't got cosy schoolfriends with cosy mothers you'd want to go and be with?'

Lucy felt a bit abashed, because she hadn't. She had schoolfriends, but nobody special, nobody with a motherly mother. 'I did think perhaps I could go to Cornwall. To Grandfather. The only thing is I've never been there.'

Carrie's dark eyes were filled with kindness. 'I think it's a wonderful idea, but not this Christmas. I spoke to Jeffrey on the telephone when I got back from Austria, and they're expecting a houseful. Their house isn't very big, anyway.'

Hope died. 'Oh, well. It doesn't matter. . . .'

'But you should certainly go one day. In the spring, perhaps. They'd love it, and you'd love all of them. So we'll have to come up with something else.'

We was significant. 'We?'

'Yes. You and me. Orphans of the storm. What shall we do for Christmas? Perhaps we should go away.'

'But where?'

There seemed to be no answer to this. They gazed at each other, and then Carrie got to her feet. She said, 'I've an idea. Have you ever heard of Elfrida Phipps?'

Lucy shook her head, wondering what was coming next.

'She's heaven. A cousin of Jeffrey's. Your gran could never stand her, because she was rather wild and an actress, and had lots of boyfriends and husbands. But I always loved her, and when I was at Oxford I started seeing her again, and we became terrific friends.'

'How old is she?'

'Oh, ancient. Over sixty. But more fun than anyone you ever knew. Once, ages ago, she was ill after an operation, and I stayed with her until she was better, and we've always kept in touch. Now she's living in a little village in Hampshire. She says the house is weeny, but Elfrida would make space for you and me. Would that be a good idea, do you think? Shall we give it a try?'

'For two weeks? Would she mind?'

'I would bet my bottom dollar that she'll jump at it. I can ring her. I've got her number.'

'Now?'

'No, not now. When I get back to Putney. We don't want the others to know our plans until they're all cut and dried.' Carrie pushed back the cuff of her sweater and looked at her watch. 'Heavens, it's nearly one o'clock. I'm starving, aren't you? Your gran said she'd give us soup and pâté, but I'm not sure if that's going to sustain me. Why don't I take all four of us out to lunch. Is there somewhere cheap and cheerful not too far away?'

'There's Rosetti's. It's a five-minute walk.'

'Italian?'

'Spaghetti and stuff.'

'My favourite food. What do you say? Shall we go and round up our mothers and tell them they're in for a treat?'

Lucy felt as though, suddenly, she had walked from a dark and cold corner into a blaze of warm sunshine. All part of having Carrie back again, a benevolent presence who was making everything all right.

BY THE TIME Carrie reached the Lumley's little terrace house later that cold December afternoon, carrying the cauliflower and the tea bags that Sara had asked her to buy, dusk was already falling. Her hands were frozen and it was quite painful to remove her glove and struggle with the latchkey.

She went into the kitchen, made a mug of tea and settled down by the telephone with her address book. She punched in Elfrida's number and waited. There was no reply. After two more tries later in the evening, Carrie began to be a little concerned. It was, after all, a long time since they had been in touch. But she knew that if anything had happened to Elfrida, her father would have let her know.

She would ring him. Jeffrey would surely know the whereabouts of his cousin. He did.

Oscar

In midwinter, it was an alien land. Monotone beneath a sky scoured white by the wind. The hills, sweeping down to the coast, were already topped by an icing of snow and the snow merged with the clouds, so that the summits of the hills were lost to view, veiled as though absorbed by the doleful heavens.

It was alien because Oscar did not remember the landscape thus. Always, as a boy, he had come in the summer to visit his grandmother at Corrydale, and in summer, so far north, the afternoons had stretched on until ten or eleven o'clock at night. At bedtime the shadows of trees fell across golden, sun-washed lawns.

He had left the house after lunch, setting out with a stout stick to help him on his way, and insulated against the cold by a fleece-lined jacket and tweed hat pulled low over his brow. His boots were sturdy, and once he had traversed the streets of the little town and climbed the hill to the gate above the golf links, he was able to step out at some speed.

Horace bounded cheerfully ahead, and they followed a footpath high above the links, winding between thickets of gorse. After a mile or so, this path led over a stile and along the track of a disused railway. The sea lay to his right, beyond the dunes, and he heard the breakers on the beach and the cry of gulls.

The old railway track petered out into a thicket of broom, and rounding this Oscar saw that they had reached the end of the links, the turn of the course, and the ninth tee.

It was then that he heard the voices. Below him, a group of four men were making their way to the tee. Oscar was instantly wary, fearing that one of them might be Major Billicliffe, and he would be spied and forced into introductions and convivial chat. His fears were, thankfully, ill-founded. Major Billicliffe was not one of the group.

Major Billicliffe was the main reason why Oscar had kept a low profile ever since he and Elfrida had arrived in Creagan. From time to time, he nipped across the road to the supermarket to stock up on beer or buy a loaf of bread, and his daily outing was a trip to the newsagent. But on these occasions he kept an eye open, just in case Billicliffe should be bearing down upon him, loud with greeting and invitations to his terrible house. This walk with Horace was Oscar's first real foray into the countryside, and he had started out because all of a sudden he was restless and needed to stretch his legs. Even the prospect of encountering Major Billicliffe did not put him off.

It was all very unfortunate. Because Billicliffe, retired factor of Corrydale, was the man who had custody of the key to the Estate House, and calling upon him, to take possession of this key, had been their first priority.

The occasion had not been propitious. At the end of the long drive from Hampshire, which had taken two days, both Oscar and Elfrida were exhausted. Crossing the border into Scotland, rain had turned to sleet, and then snow. Darkness was falling as they crossed the new bridge that spanned the firth.

Somehow they found the main gates to Corrydale, which was now a country house hotel. They went through the gates and turned left onto a rutted lane that seemed to lead nowhere, but all at once they saw a small stone house with a single curtained window, lit from within. They drew up outside and at once the quiet was ripped apart by deep-throated barking.

Then the barking stopped. The door of the cottage was opened. A lanky, gangling figure stood there, sagging at the knees to peer out beneath the low lintel. 'That you? Blundell? Been waiting . . .'

Oscar and Elfrida got out of the car. 'I'm sorry,' Oscar apologised. 'Difficult, driving in the dark. It's all unfamiliar. We've come for the key, and then—' He had been going to say, 'We'll be on our way,' but Major Billicliffe overrode him.

'Of course. Got it here. Come along in. Just going to have a snifter. You'll join me.'

'Well . . .'

'Splendid to see you. Come in out of the cold.'

He stood aside, holding the door open in a hospitable manner, and after a moment's hesitation Oscar capitulated. 'Thank you,' he said weakly, and put out a hand to steer Elfrida in front of him. 'This is my friend, Elfrida Phipps. She came to share the driving with me.'

'Splendid. Splendid. Charmed to meet you, ma'am.' Billicliffe took Elfrida's hand, and for a moment Oscar thought he might be about to press a kiss upon it, so courtly was his manner.

They followed him into a small, low-ceilinged sitting room, where a tiny fire in a tiled grate did little to warm the air. All seemed to be in a state of sad confusion: sagging leather chairs, a carpet covered in dog's hairs, ashtrays brimming with pipe ash.

At the back of the room was another door, behind which the dog had been shut away. Whines and heavy breathing emanated from it, and every now and then they heard a thump as the imprisoned brute flung its weight against the door.

Elfrida began to look nervous. 'What kind of dog is it?' she asked.

'Labrador,' Major Billicliffe told her. 'Wouldn't hurt a fly. Now, what can I get you?'

He made his way across the room to an old trolley on wheels, laden with bottles and one or two smeary glasses.

Oscar longed for a cup of tea, but knew that that would take much longer to prepare. 'A Scotch would be splendid. Very small.'

'And the lady?'

Elfrida, too, was longing for tea, but she said bravely, 'A sherry?'

Pouring drinks, Billicliffe talked. Oscar and Elfrida stood by the miserable fire and did not interrupt. ''Fraid the housekeeping's a bit hit and miss these days. Wife died, couple of years ago. Miss her like hell, but what can one do?' To look at, Major Billicliffe was something of an old wreck, knock-kneed as a horse on its way to the knacker's yard, with thin, stockinged legs that ended in a pair of enormous black unpolished brogues. His head was bald, sparsely covered with a few strands of grey hair, his eyes rheumy and his moustache tobacco-stained. It was hard to imagine him as a dapper officer in any regiment of the British Army.

'Hector rang me and said you'd be coming. Delighted. About time we had a bit of new blood about the place. Funny we've never met before, you and I, but then, it's years . . . I've been here since the sixties. Came straight out of the army and trained as a factor.' He came shambling over to deliver their drinks and returned to the trolley to deal with his own thirst, which seemed to require an enormously dark whisky in a small tumbler.

'Sit down, make yourselves comfortable.'

'We mustn't be too long.'

'Won't take you five minutes to get to Creagan.' Without much alternative, Oscar and Elfrida perched on a sofa, side by side. Major Billicliffe lowered his tremendous height into the only armchair.

'I'm retired now, of course. Good of Hector to let me buy this cottage, but it was standing empty anyway. And Hughie couldn't care less. Buggered off to Barbados and sold the place up. Hotel. You probably saw the sign. All plate glass and bathrooms. And the bar prices are daylight robbery. Never go near the place. Take my pleasures in the golf club. Do you play golf? You should join. Put your name up if you like. Short walk from the Estate House.'

Oscar nodded and feeling desperate, said, 'The key? To the Estate House. If you could let me have it, we'll get out of your way.'

'Ah, yes. Got it somewhere.' Major Billicliffe crossed the room, to an old roll-topped desk, standing open. He rootled around, feeling into pigeonholes. 'Eureka!' he exclaimed at last, and held up a large old-fashioned key tied to a crumpled label.

Oscar and Elfrida finished their drinks and rose to their feet. Oscar took the key. 'Thank you. I am sorry we disturbed you.'

'Didn't disturb me at all. Splendid to have a bit of company. Remember, I'm at the club most days. And perhaps I'll pop in at the Estate House. See how you're settling in.'

Elfrida smiled. She said, 'Of course. But don't come *quite* right away. Oscar's not been very well, and we'll need a little time.'

'Of course, of course. But we'll certainly see each other around.'

Now, in the middle of his walk, Oscar was beginning to feel a bit weary. When he spied a small wooden shelter provided for the convenience of golfers, he decided to sit for a moment to get his breath.

He thought about the men on the rolling fairway, companionably playing their game deep into the dusk of a dying afternoon, and knew an envy that was almost resentment. They were together. Friends. Talking, joking, competing. They would have a drink in the clubhouse, part, return to their families. Ordinary men.

He wondered if he would ever be ordinary again.

He had always despised self-pity, and now, sitting huddled in the shelter, he fought it like a lion, striving to be positive, to count present blessings. First was the Estate House, the fact that he owned a bit of it and that it stood empty, a timely sanctuary to which he had fled. Second was Elfrida. Her companionship had saved his reason, and in her own uncomplicated way she had got him through the blackest times, comforting by simply accepting his limitations.

When he fell silent, she left him alone. When he felt compelled to talk, Elfrida listened.

I must go on, he told himself. 'I must go on.' This time he said the words aloud, and Horace, who had been lying at his feet, sat up and looked hopeful. 'Come on, old chap. Time we headed for home.'

By the time he finally reached the clubhouse it was dark, and Oscar was very tired. He saw the blaze of lights shining out from wide windows, behind which figures could be seen, relaxed as though in a friendly pub. In the car park, on the bumper of a well-worn estate car, a man was perched, in the act of changing his studded golf shoes for a pair of brogues.

The man tied the last lace and got to his feet. By now Oscar was alongside. For an instant, he hesitated, debating as to whether to stop and exchange a friendly word. Even as he wavered, the decision was taken out of his hands.

'Hello there. Did you have a good walk?'

Oscar paused, then turned to face him. 'A bit too far, perhaps. I'm out of practice. How did you get along?'

'We gave up on the fifteenth. Chickened out. Too dark and too cold.' The man chucked his golf shoes into the car and slammed the boot. He came forward and Oscar saw a ruddy face, a head of thick greying hair, and a pair of piercingly blue eyes. 'Forgive me, but you're Oscar Blundell, aren't you?'

Oscar found himself disconcerted. He said 'Yes,' and it sounded like an admission.

'I knew you'd come back to Creagan. I've only been here for twenty years, so I never met your grandmother, Mrs McLellan. But I did have the pleasure of a good friendship with Hector. Just for a short while, before he handed Corrydale over to Hughie and went south to live. I'm Peter Kennedy, by the way.' He stuck out a hand, which Oscar took in his own gloved one. 'Welcome to Creagan.'

'Thank you.'

'You must be exhausted. That's a long hike in the teeth of the wind. I'm just going in for a cup of tea. Would you care to join me?'

Oscar was torn by conflicting emotions. It was true. He was bone weary and the thought of sitting down for a bit in the warmth with a restoring, hot cup of tea was a very tempting one. On the other hand, he was not sure if he felt brave enough to go into that brightly lit and convivial clubhouse. But there was something so warm and genuine about his new friend, so disarming and sincere, that he could not bring himself to refuse the invitation.

'Yes. I would like to join you. Thank you very much.'

They incarcerated Horace in the back of Peter Kennedy's car. He gazed at them reproachfully through the rear window.

'I won't be long,' Oscar told the dog.

In the foyer, lined with cabinets containing silver trophies and shields, portraits of former captains glowered down at them. To the right, glassed doors fed into the main room, furnished with tables and comfortable chairs, and with a small bar in the corner. As they entered, one or two people looked up, but nobody took much notice of them except an elderly waitress in a black skirt and white blouse.

Spying them, she was all smiles. 'Mr Kennedy. I didn't think we'd be seeing you this evening.'

'Hello, Jessie. Are we too late for a cup of tea?'

'Never too late.' Her eyes turned to Oscar.

'Jessie, this is Mr Blundell. He's come to stay at the Estate House.'

'Oh, my, that's who you are. I'd heard you'd moved in, but I haven't seen you around. Are you a golfer too?'

'I'm sorry, no.'

'We'll have to rectify that. Now, Mr Kennedy, where do you want to sit?'

But before there was time to tell her, an interruption occurred. From across the long room there came a shout, a deep voice ringing out like a clarion, startling everyone. '*Peter*! Come away over and have a word. I haven't seen you for a week.'

Peter Kennedy swung around, and Oscar, following his gaze, saw, in the far corner, a heavily built man sitting in a wheelchair, waving a knotted stick.

'Would you mind, Oscar, if I left you for a moment? It's old Charlie Beith, and I must go and pay my respects . . .'

'Of course.'

Jessie took charge. 'Come and sit down and get comfortable. Would you like a scone? And do you prefer Indian or China tea?'

Oscar said, 'I'm sorry, but can you tell me who Peter Kennedy is? I've only just met him, in the car park. He knew my uncle. But I don't know . . .'

'You mean you don't know what he does or who he is? He's our minister. The minister of the church.'

The minister. The vicar. Whatever. The man whose job it was to comfort. Peter Kennedy's spontaneous friendliness had seemed genuine, but this new knowledge rendered it depressingly suspect. Did he already know why Oscar had returned to Creagan? Had Hector been in touch with Peter Kennedy? Suggested, perhaps, a pastoral visit? Comforting chats, counselling, a gentle urging back to a church in which Oscar no longer believed?

Jessie said, 'Are you all right?'

He looked into her concerned and motherly face and realised that his own was suffused with heat. A heat kindled by an inner turmoil that was frighteningly akin to panic. He knew that he could not stay there, or he would suffocate.

With a huge effort, he made himself speak. 'I am sorry. I've just remembered . . .' His voice sounded unreal, like a voice from another room. 'I must get home. A telephone call.' Backing off, he apologised again. 'I'm sorry. Please explain to Mr Kennedy.'

He turned away from her, and carefully, slowly, made for the door. He crossed the foyer and stepped out into the bitter air. The cold wind was an assault, and he stopped to steady himself, to let the icy air fill his lungs. He pulled on his old tweed hat. He was all right. He was surviving. All he had to do was get himself home. To be safe. Alone with Elfrida. He went down the steps and crossed over to the car park and retrieved Horace from Peter Kennedy's car. Then he was on his way, walking at a tremendous pace. Escaping.

Elfrida

In Dibton, the Women's Institute was great on mystery tours. These usually took place on a Saturday afternoon, and entailed the ladies' being piled into a bus and whirled off to some unknown destination, quite often a stately home. Spirited away so abruptly, by circumstances outside her control, to the north of Scotland, to Creagan and the Estate House was, Elfrida decided, the mystery tour of all time. From the moment she and Oscar departed from Dibton, she had no idea of what lay in store for her, and there never came an appropriate moment to ask. So precipitant had been their departure, so swift the packing process, that nit-picking details of their destination lost all importance. They just had to get away.

Elfrida had handed the key of Poulton's Row over to her

neighbour, with as few explanations as possible. She telephoned her cousin Jeffrey in Cornwall and explained to him the circumstances of what she was about to do. He said, 'Good luck.'

Without any clear idea of what sort of clothes she would need, she packed a suitcase with an assortment of garments (warm) and shoes (stout), then an ancient, squashy, zipped bag for her most precious things, the possessions that had always travelled everywhere with her. The silk shawl, wrapped round the little painting by Sir David Wilkie; the Staffordshire dogs; her clock; her current piece of tapestry. On top went a few photographs in silver frames and half a dozen books. Oscar's luggage was a leather holdall and his fishing gear.

'Do you intend to go fishing, Oscar?'

'No idea. But I can't travel to Scotland without my rod. It would be almost sacrilegious.'

There was space for all this in the back of Oscar's Volvo, and still room for Horace, his blanket, his biscuits and his water bowl.

The encounter with Major Billicliffe had been the final hurdle. With that accomplished and the key safely in Oscar's pocket, the hard grind of the two-day journey was behind them, and the last few miles were easy, almost carefree. The dark road ran downhill towards the sea, between dense stands of conifer. Elfrida opened her window and smelt pine and a sturdy whiff of salty air. Then the trees fell away and ahead could be seen a straight and silvery line that was the sea. Far away, across the water, a lighthouse blinked, a pinprick in the darkness. Then, ahead, the glow of street lights and houses with windows lit behind drawn curtains. She saw the church looming, the lighted clock like a round lantern, high in its tower. The hands stood at seven o'clock. Now larger, handsome houses, set back behind tall stone walls. Creagan.

Another turning, another street. Oscar drew up at the pavement's edge. Then he laid his hand over hers. 'Dear girl. We're there.'

The Estate House: square and solid, set back from the road behind a wrought-iron railing and a forecourt of sea pebbles. The face of the house was a child's drawing, with a door and five windows. Above these, from the slope of the slate roof, two dormers jutted. They got out of the car, and Elfrida set Horace free. He leaped down into the road, and began to sniff for unfamiliar smells.

Oscar unlatched the gate and went up the path. Elfrida and Horace followed. With the key he opened the door. He felt for a light switch, found one and turned it on.

They entered, and Elfrida instantly felt the warmth and smelt the cleanliness of a place newly scrubbed and polished. Ahead, a staircase rose to a half-landing and an uncurtained stair window. On either side, doors stood closed, but at the end of the hall a third door was open, and Oscar went through this and turned on another light.

Elfrida closed the front door behind her. She followed Oscar into a kitchen with an old-fashioned painted dresser and a wooden table. Beneath the window was a clay sink, and at its side a capacious gas cooker, dating back, perhaps, forty years or more.

Oscar said, 'Hardly all-singing, all-dancing.' He sounded a bit apologetic.

'It's fine,' Elfrida assured him, and meant it. 'Someone has left us a letter.' It lay in the middle of the table, a sheet of lined paper, weighted down with a jam jar. Elfrida picked it up and read it aloud: *I have turned on boiler. Beds made up. Bath water hot. Coal and wood in shed. Milk in fridge (scullery). Yours, J. Snead (Mrs).*

Oscar said, 'Mrs Snead. She keeps an eye on the house and she knew when we were arriving.'

'Yes.'

'Elfrida, are you about to cry?'

'I might be.'

'Why?'

'Relief.'

THAT HAD ALL happened three weeks ago. Now, at five o'clock on a dark December afternoon, Oscar, who had set out after lunch with Horace at his heels, had still not returned.

Blotting out images of him dead of a heart attack, Elfrida made a mug of tea and took it upstairs to the sitting room. They called it the sitting room, but it was a drawing room, formal and spacious, with a huge bay window looking out over the street and the church. Hours could be wasted simply sitting on the window seat, watching the world go by: cars and delivery vans coming and going; shoppers pausing on the pavement to chat; strings of chattering children, walking to and from school.

The room was furnished, as was all the house, with the bare minimum of furniture. A thick Turkish carpet. A sofa and two chairs. A table against the wall, a glass-fronted bookcase, in which a few old books leaned against each other. No pictures, no ornaments—until Elfrida had put her modest stamp upon the place. The David Wilkie now hung opposite the fireplace above the heavy oak table that Oscar used as a desk. The Staffordshire dogs and her clock occupied the empty marble mantelpiece. Her half-done tapestry lay across the seat of a chair. Earlier on, she had lit the fire. Now, she fed it with coal and logs then went to the window, to sit and watch for Oscar. But no sooner had she settled herself than the telephone rang. She went to answer.

'Hello.'

'Elfrida. It's Carrie. Carrie Sutton.'

'*Carrie!* Where are you?'

'In London. How are you?'

'All right.'

'Jeffrey told me you were in Scotland. Gave me your number. Elfrida, I've got something to ask you. It's a favour, a huge favour. It's about Christmas.'

IT WAS, NECESSARILY, a very long telephone call. Finally they were finished. Elfrida replaced the receiver; at the same moment she heard the front door open and knew that Oscar and Horace were home. She went downstairs and found Oscar, in the hall, shedding jacket and hat, hanging them on the bentwood hat stand.

'You've been ages.'

'We went for miles. The other end of the links and back. I'd forgotten it was so far.' He put up a hand and ran it over his hair. He looked, she thought, exhausted.

'A cup of tea?'

'I think I'm ready for something stronger.'

'A Scotch. Go upstairs. There's a fire. I'll bring it to you.'

In the kitchen, she poured his drink and made herself another mug of tea because she knew that the first one would be cold by now. Upstairs she found Oscar standing with a hand on the mantelpiece, gazing down into the fire. He turned his head and smiled gratefully. 'How good you are.'

He took the drink and lowered himself into one of the armchairs, stretching his legs. Elfrida went to the window and drew the curtains. 'I didn't draw them before because I was sitting in the window, watching for you,' she said.

'I was delayed. Outside the golf club I met Peter Kennedy, the minister. We talked, then we went into the club for a cup of tea.'

Elfrida waited. Finally, 'So, Oscar?'

'It occurred to me that perhaps Hector had forewarned him about Gloria and Francesca. I had thought him simply a friendly chap. But I am afraid he was being kind. Sorry for me. I don't want to be helped. I don't want to have to speak or to listen. I want to be left alone. So I left. I came home.'

'Oh, Oscar.'

'I know. Rude and mannerless.'

'I'm sure he'll understand.'

'I hope so. I liked his face.' He took a deep breath that sounded like a terrible sigh. 'I hate myself.'

'Oh, my dear, never do that. I understand.' She drank some tea and sat, facing him, in a little wide-lapped Victorian chair. 'Perhaps this isn't an opportune moment, but I have to ask you something. I had a telephone call. Jeffrey's daughter, Carrie Sutton. She has returned from Austria. She wants to come and spend Christmas with us.'

'But we are not having Christmas.'

'I told her, a lamb chop for lunch and no tinsel. She understands. She says she's not interested in Christmas either.'

'Then let her come.'

Elfrida hesitated. 'There is a complication. Jeffrey's grandchild. Carrie's niece, Lucy. If Carrie comes, then Lucy must come too.'

There was a very long silence. Oscar's eyes turned from Elfrida's face and gazed into the fire. 'How old is the child?'

'Fourteen.'

'Why does she have to come?'

Elfrida shrugged. 'Oh, some story about her mother going to Florida to stay with a friend and the daughter doesn't want to go with her. And Dodie, the grandmother, doesn't want the grand-daughter. The sort of selfish muddle that is always happening in that particular family.' She bit her lip. 'I can ring Carrie and tell her no, that it's too soon. A little girl around the place would be more than painful for you. It might be unbearable. I understand and I shan't think any the less of you if you say no.'

He looked at her, his gentle features filled with affection. 'It can make no difference. It can change nothing. You want them here, I think. Then tell them to come.'

'You're sure?'

He nodded.

'You are a dear, kind, brave man.'

'It's what you want. That's all that matters. Please tell them they're welcome.' He drank a bit of his whisky, seemingly deep in thought. Then he said, 'Telephone Carrie now. If they take the train or come by aeroplane, we can send a taxi to meet them at Inverness. If they're driving, warn her about the snow.'

She was filled with gratitude for his generosity of spirit. To have him sitting there mulling over such mundane details made her feel a great deal better. 'I'll ring her right away.' She pulled herself to her feet. 'Thank you, Oscar.'

ON SATURDAY MORNING Elfrida was the first downstairs. She had dressed in thick corduroy trousers and two sweaters and was glad of these when she opened the back door to let Horace out. During the night there had been a deep frost, all was iced and sparkling, and her footsteps left marks on the thick, crunchy grass of the lawn. In the east, over the sea, was the pink glow of dawn. It was going to be a fine day. Finally Horace was done, and they scurried indoors to the warmth, and Elfrida shut the door. She put the kettle on, then found the frying pan and the bacon.

She was in a good mood, enjoying the smell of bacon frying, mingled with the scent of fresh toast and hot coffee. She was drinking her first cup when Oscar came downstairs to join her, and at once Elfrida noticed his appearance. Normally, he wore a thick shirt under a warm pullover. Very informal. But this morning he had put on one of his better shirts, a tie, a waistcoat, and his good tweed jacket.

She poured his coffee. 'You're looking very smart.'

He picked up his plate of bacon and eggs from the hot plate. 'Thank you. I made an effort, because I am going calling.'

Elfrida was genuinely surprised. 'Who are you going to call on?'

He sat down. 'Rose Miller. A very old friend.'

'You've never mentioned her. Should I be mad with jealousy?'

'I don't think so. She must be eighty-five if she's a day. She was my grandmother's parlour maid. She lives on the Corrydale estate. I am going to pay my respects. Do you mind?'

'Oh, dear Oscar, I'm absolutely delighted. But I don't entirely understand your change of heart.'

'It was yesterday. Meeting the minister. If Peter Kennedy knows about me, then so will many other people. By now Rose Miller is bound to have heard I've come back. And she will be intensely hurt if I don't get in touch with her. So I have decided to go.'

Suddenly, Elfrida felt more cheerful than she had for a long time.

Things, slowly, were looking up. Oscar was going calling, and next week Carrie and Lucy Wesley would be here. She decided that perhaps yesterday had been the turning point, although she had not recognised it as such.

'Maybe while you're at Corrydale, you should look in on Major Billicliffe. He's probably dreadfully lonely. You could just drop in, casually, to pass the time of day. Perhaps ask him along for a drink or something when Carrie and Lucy are here.'

Cunningly, Oscar steered the discussion off at a tangent. 'When are they coming?'

'They're flying to Inverness on Friday morning, and I've asked the taxi man to go and get them.' Elfrida sipped her coffee. 'There isn't much time, is there? I thought Lucy could sleep in the empty attic, but I'll have to find a bed and some other furniture for it. There must be a secondhand shop somewhere. I shall make enquiries.'

THE DAY TURNED OUT to be one of dazzling brightness. The sun rose in an eggshell blue sky and there was not a breath of wind. Ladies, shopping, trod cautiously down the pavements, anxious not to slip or fall. But the cold did not stop them from pausing to gossip.

The church, behind the black lacework of bare trees, glowed golden in the sunlight. Over the spire the gulls wheeled, and jackdaws settled on the weather vane at its peak.

After Oscar had departed, Elfrida finished a little cursory housework and laid the fire. She had just sat down in the bay window when the doorbell rang. Horace, as usual, filled the house with panic-stricken barking.

'Oh, Horace, be quiet!' She ran downstairs to open the heavy door, swinging it wide to reveal an unknown female figure.

Her visitor was perhaps in her late thirties, tall and slender and marvellously unconventional in appearance. She had very dark, almost raven-black hair cut in a fringe and hanging straight to her shoulders. She wore a battered Barbour over a long red woollen skirt and what looked like Doc Marten boots. A tartan muffler was wound about her neck, framing a face beautifully boned and innocent of make-up, cheeks rosy with the cold. And she carried a basket containing eggs.

She smiled. 'Hello. You're Elfrida Phipps? I hope I'm not disturbing you, but I'm Tabitha Kennedy. Peter Kennedy's wife.'

'Oh.' Elfrida made an effort not to appear too astonished. She had never seen anyone who looked less like a minister's wife. 'How nice to meet you.' She stepped back indoors, holding open the door. 'Do come in.'

Tabitha Kennedy hesitated. 'Not if you're busy. I just brought you some eggs. From my hens.'

'I'm not busy and fresh eggs are a real treat. Come on, I'll give you a cup of coffee.'

Tabitha stepped through the door, and Elfrida closed it behind her. 'I'll put the kettle on. Oscar's gone to Corrydale to call on someone called Rose Miller.'

'Goodness, there'll be a reunion. Rose always adored Oscar. Never stops talking about him.' Tabitha followed Elfrida into the kitchen and put the basket of eggs on the table. 'One of the reasons I've come, Elfrida, is to apologise.'

'Apologise? For what?'

'Peter sent me. He's afraid he was rather crass and pushy yesterday afternoon. He hopes so much that he didn't upset Oscar.'

'I think Oscar feels he's the one to apologise. It was rude just running away like that, but he panicked. He was filled with remorse. He knew he'd behaved badly.'

'Hector wrote and told us about Oscar's wife and child dying in that appalling car accident. It takes a long while to move out of something like that, and get back into life again. It can't have been easy for you.'

'As a matter of fact, it's been hellish. I think frustration is the worst, because there is not a mortal thing one can do to help. And then impatience. And then guilt for feeling impatient. More than once I've had to bite my tongue. And another thing is, I'm quite a sociable animal. I like making friends and getting to know people, but because of Oscar I've had to keep a low profile. I've probably created a very snooty impression.'

'I'm sure not.'

'Today I have a feeling that the hellish time might just about be behind us. Perhaps going to see Rose Miller is a step forward.'

'If Peter came to see Oscar, would that be a good idea? They could put things right between them.'

'I think it's a marvellous idea, but tell him to telephone first.'

'I'll do that.'

The coffee was made, the jug set on the tray. Elfrida picked it up. 'Let's go upstairs. It's more comfortable.'

She led the way and Tabitha followed.

'I'm always impressed by this beautiful staircase. It gives such a grand feel to your entrance.' Tabitha paused on the half-landing to gaze out at the frosted garden, which climbed the slope of the hill in a series of terraced lawns, with a path and small flights of steps running up its centre.

Elfrida went on upstairs and into the sitting room. Sun streamed through the open door. 'Shall we sit by the window?'

'Let's. The sun is so gorgeous.' Tabitha unwound her muffler, took off her Barbour and settled herself on the window seat.

'Have you lived here long?' Elfrida asked.

'About twenty years. Both our children were born in the Manse.'

'How old are they?'

'Rory's eighteen. Just left school. He's got a place at Durham University, but he's not taking it up till next year. Clodagh's twelve.'

Elfrida looked at Tabitha, sitting there in her black polo-necked sweater, with her young girl's hair, and was filled with curiosity. 'Do you like being a minister's wife?'

'I adore being married to Peter. And I'm not totally a minister's wife, because I teach art at the school five mornings a week.'

'Are you an artist?'

'Yes, I paint and draw, and I teach crafts as well—pottery and sewing. The senior girls stitched all the kneelers in church. And every mother in Creagan has a wobbly pot for her begonias.'

Elfrida said, 'I was an actress,' then felt a bit shy and wished she hadn't said it because it sounded as though she was capping Tabitha's talent.

But Tabitha was gratifyingly amazed. 'Were you really? Actually I'm not a bit surprised. I can see you on the stage. Were you famous?'

'No, not a bit. But I was always working, however humbly.'

'That's what matters, isn't it? Doing what you like and being paid for it. That's how I feel, too. Really good for one's self-respect. Peter understands. It's one of the reasons I like him so much. I can't wait for you to meet him. I'd ask you up to the Manse, but perhaps we'd better wait until he and Oscar have sorted themselves out. Once they've done that, I'll issue invitations.'

'I can't think of anything I'd like more.'

'What are you doing for Christmas?'

'I don't think Oscar wants to do anything. I understand, because it can be a dreadfully emotive time. But it *is* tricky because I've got a cousin coming to stay next Saturday and she's bringing her niece.'

'How old is she?'

'Carrie's thirty. But the niece is fourteen. She's called Lucy. I hope she won't be bored.'

'There's so much going on in Creagan at Christmas. She'll have a wonderful time.'

A thought struck Elfrida. 'I've got to buy furniture. The bedroom for Carrie is all right, but I thought I'd put Lucy in the attic. It's lovely and light but there's . . .' She trailed off. 'Would you come up and look at it with me? Tell me what I have to get?'

'Of course.' Tabitha had finished her coffee and now looked at her watch. 'Then I must fly. Peter's got an early meeting in Buckly this afternoon, and I must feed him before he goes.'

They climbed the stairs to the upper floor. One windowless attic contained three old trunks and a lot of cobwebs. The other, with its huge skylight and combed ceiling, was filled only with pale sunlight.

Tabitha was enchanted. 'What a wonderful room. Any young girl would love to have this. And it's got a radiator, too. Cosy as anything. You'll need a bed, of course. And perhaps a chest of drawers. Or a little dressing table. What about a television set? Teenagers go all peculiar without something to goggle at. Rory's got an old one he doesn't use any more—I'll have a word with him. And a few lamps. And a blind for the skylight. Otherwise it might be a bit spooky.'

'I thought a secondhand shop . . .'

'There's a marvellous market in Buckly. I'll take you. You can get everything—even beds—there. Some afternoon . . . Would Tuesday be all right?'

Elfrida nodded.

'What fun we'll have. I can't wait.' Tabitha looked at her watch again. 'Now I simply must fly.'

When she had left, Elfrida did a cursory inspection of the contents of the fridge to see what was needed. She was just about to go out shopping when she heard the front door open and shut and knew that Oscar had returned. She went out into the hall to meet him.

'You're back. How was Rose Miller?'

'In splendid form.' He took his hat off and hung it on the newel post. 'We had a great crack, and a glass of elderberry wine.'

She led him into the kitchen where he took off his thick jacket and pulled out a chair and sat down. Elfrida eyed him. For a man who had just returned from sipping elderberry wine with an old admirer, he looked tired and preoccupied.

'Are you all right, Oscar?'

'Yes, I'm fine. I did what you told me. I went to see Major Billicliffe.'

'Oh, good man.'

'No. Not good. I don't feel good at all.'

'Why not? What happened?'

He told her. On his way home, as he passed Billicliffe's house, he had heard the dog howling. The sound was as arresting as a cry for help, and Oscar had been instantly concerned.

Elfrida was dreading the end of the story. 'What did you do?'

'Went to ring the bell, but nothing happened except the dog stopped howling and started barking. I tried the door and it was open. So I went in and called out. But no answer. The dog had been shut in the back. I tried the other ground-floor room. The chaos there was worse than the sitting room. Drip-dry shirts hanging over the backs of chairs, papers and boxes piled on a table. I went up the staircase and opened the door at the top and peered in. And there was the old boy, in bed . . .'

'He wasn't dead?'

'For a moment, I thought he was. And then I said his name, and he stirred . . .'

'Thank heavens for that.'

He had not been dead. But he looked ghastly, and was clearly very unwell. However, realising that he had a visitor, he had tried to rally himself, pulled himself up on his pillows and put on a brave face. Yesterday, he explained, the milkman had been so concerned by his appearance that he had telephoned the Creagan GP, Dr Sinclair, who drove immediately to Corrydale, where, after a thorough examination, told Major Billicliffe that he thought it best if he went over to the hospital in Inverness, for tests.

'He goes on Monday. Dr Sinclair's booked him in.'

'And how will he get there?'

This was the problem. Oscar realised that the old man, the old soldier, was very frightened by the prospect of hospitals, tests, illness, pain, and a possible operation. So he had suggested that he, Oscar, should drive him to the hospital and see him safely installed.

Elfrida was touched. 'You are sweet. He won't be nearly so afraid if you are there . . . What about the dog?'

'I went downstairs and let her loose in the garden. She was not fierce at all, just a dear old Labrador needing a bit of attention. I took her to Rose Miller, and filled Rose in with all that had occurred.

By the time I left, she was already girding herself up to go and do a bit of tidying up and cooking for him. At eighty-five years old, there's nothing she loves so much as a challenge. She kept saying, "He's mad on the whisky, but he's a dear, good gentleman, and too proud to ask for help." She's going to arrange for her nephew, Charlie Miller, to look after the dog.'

'Oh, Oscar, what a morning you've had.'

'But I'm glad I went.' He smiled. 'How about you?'

'Tabitha Kennedy came to see me. I've so much to tell you.'

'Then tell me over lunch. Let's treat ourselves. I need cheering up. We'll go to the pub and have a sandwich and a gin and tonic, and we'll drink to . . .' He hesitated. 'Us?'

'Oh, Oscar.' Elfrida came around the table, put her arms about him, and hugged. It was definitely a good day.

Oscar

After a late breakfast on Sunday morning, Oscar, bundled up as usual against the cold, walked down the street to the newsagent's to pick up the papers. The little town was empty and quiet.

Returning, he met Elfrida and Horace setting out for a good long walk along the beach. Elfrida wore a thick woollen hat pulled down over her ears and her blanket coat trimmed with fringe. She said, 'Come with us,' but he declined because he wished to settle down with the arts section and catch up with what was happening in London.

He went indoors and up the stairs to their magnificent sitting room. Elfrida had laid the fire, so he lit it, and settled down in comfort to read.

At half past ten, the church bells disturbed him. He dropped the paper and went over to the window seat and perched there, looking down onto the street, which was slowly but steadily filling up.

The church was coming to life, and presently he heard the tones of the organ. 'Sheep May Safely Graze'. The sound was muffled by the thick stone walls, but recognisable, to Oscar's professional ear, as a good instrument, and competently played. At first, he had found having the church so close a little disconcerting—a constant reminder of all he had lost. Sitting now, watching groups of people converging, he knew that he only had to cross the road and he would be swept up into the stream, and, like a swimmer caught in a current, sucked through those imposing doors into the soaring nave.

From outside, the colours and patterns of the stained glass in the arched windows were dimmed, and he knew that to appreciate their jewel-like beauty one had to view them from inside, with the light of day streaming through, throwing lozenges of ruby, sapphire and emerald onto worn flagstones. Perhaps this was symbolic. Perhaps, isolated from the church, there were delights, pleasures, comforts that, because of his present state of mind, he denied himself.

He did not wish to dwell on this so he left the window and went back to the fire and his newspaper. But when the congregation began to sing their first hymn, he lowered the paper and listened, staring into the flames.

> 'Hark! a thrilling voice is sounding;
> "Christ is nigh," it seems to say;
> "Cast away the dreams of darkness,
> O ye children of the day."'

A good old classic Advent hymn. He remembered rehearsing the choir at the school where he had taught, imploring them to sing as though they truly believed the message of hope.

He thought, I must get in touch with Peter Kennedy.

THAT NIGHT, Oscar lay awake for a long time, thinking about Godfrey Billicliffe. At last he had learned his Christian name in the course of helping the ward sister to fill in countless forms, before leaving the sick old man to her tender mercies. The undertaking had not been as demanding as he had feared. The drive to Inverness had gone smoothly, and old Billicliffe, encouraged by caring attention, had talked nonstop. Oscar had learned much about his life.

It was when they were speeding down the motorway across the Black Isle, and Inverness was in view across the water, that Major Billicliffe said, 'Been thinking, Oscar . . . About what's going to happen . . . Turning my toes up . . .'

'You're not going to turn your toes up,' Oscar assured him.

'Never know . . . Have to be prepared for all contingencies. Learned that in the army. Prepare for the worst and hope for the best.' A long pause. 'Wondered . . . if you'd agree to be my executor. Good to know . . . Capable hands . . .'

Oscar said, as calmly as he could, 'If it would set your mind at rest, I'd be happy to be your executor. But . . .'

'Splendid. I must tell my lawyer. I'll ring up from the hospital. Nice feller. Keen fisherman. Liked the cut of his jib.'

'Has he got a name?'

Major Billicliffe gave a snort, which perhaps was meant to be laughter. "Course he's got a name. Murdo McKenzie. McKenzie and Stout. South Street. Inverness.'

Billicliffe did not speak again until they had reached the Royal Western, and then matters were taken out of Oscar's hands. The ward sister was ready and waiting with her clipboard and admission forms. All went smoothly until she came to next of kin.

'Next of kin, Major Billicliffe?'

Suddenly he looked bewildered. 'Sorry?'

'Next of kin. You know, wife, children, brothers or sisters?'

He shook his head. 'I have none. I have no one.'

'Oh, come along, there has to be someone.'

Oscar could not bear it. 'Me,' he said firmly. 'I am Major Billicliffe's next of kin. Oscar Blundell. You can write it down. The Estate House. Creagan.' He gave her the telephone number.'

Finally, all was recorded and signed. And it was time for Oscar to leave. He said goodbye.

'You'll come again?'

'Of course. Provided we don't get snowed in.'

'Thank you for bringing me. Obliged.'

'Not at all.'

And Oscar walked away. He could have done no more. Later, when there was news of the invalid, he and Elfrida would visit Godfrey. Elfrida, if anybody, would cheer him up.

A clout of wind struck the house. Oscar turned into the pillows and closed his eyes, and all at once found himself thinking about Francesca. This often happened in the dark hours of a restless night and he dreaded the inevitable aftermath, a torment of rekindled, anguished loss. He slid his hand beneath his pillow to fumble for his handkerchief, knowing that he would probably weep. But instead of weeping, he became aware of a sort of quiet, as though he were more at ease with himself than he had felt for weeks. Francesca. He saw her running across the sunlit lawns of the Grange, towards him. And the image stayed, poignant, but especially sweet.

Holding it close. He slept.

THE NEXT MORNING dawned to dismal weather. Elfrida had bought herself a notebook, and over lunch made lists for an afternoon of shopping with Tabitha Kennedy in Buckly.

'I've got to think of everything,' she told Oscar. 'There isn't time for forgetting. Carrie and Lucy will be here on Friday. Do you think Lucy will want a dressing table?'

Oscar, who was trying to do *The Times* crossword puzzle, set it aside nobly and removed his spectacles as though the better to think. With some effort he applied himself to the problem. 'I have no idea. What about a wardrobe?' was all he could come up with.

'We'd never get a wardrobe up there. Some hooks on the wall would do. And coat hangers.' She wrote in her notebook, and Oscar watched her with amusement. He had never seen Elfrida so focused.

When Tabitha arrived to collect her and they drove off in the Kennedys' well-worn estate car like a couple of young girls, he stood at the window and watched them go.

Aware of his procrastination, Oscar made another attempt to finish the crossword. Defeated, he laid the newspaper aside. There was something else to do. He went out to the telephone on the landing, looked up the number and punched the digits.

'Creagan Manse.' The warm, familiar voice. 'Peter Kennedy.'

AT HALF PAST FIVE, Oscar set off on the stepped lane that led up the hill. He remembered the Manse from sixty years ago, when he was sometimes brought for tea by his grandmother. It was a large, stone-built Victorian building set in a spacious garden. A light was burning above the front door, and he walked up the path and pressed the bell.

He heard the inner door open and then the front door was flung wide, and Peter Kennedy stood there in a polo-necked sweater and a pair of worn corduroys, looking comfortingly unchurchly. 'Oscar! Come away in.'

Oscar went into the hall. Saw the Turkish carpet, the oak hall-stand, the antique chest on which stood a neat stack of parish magazines. A pair of football boots had been dumped on the bottom stair.

'Take your coat off. We've got the place to ourselves. I've a fire on in my study. Come along in . . .'

He led the way to a front room with a huge littered desk and two ancient leather armchairs. The walls held shelves of books and after the airy emptiness of the Estate House, it felt safe and warm. There was a marvellous smell of peat smouldering in the fire basket.

'Now make yourself comfortable,' Peter continued. 'Would you like a glass of Laphraoig? I keep it for special occasions.'

Malt whisky. Laphraoig. Irresistible.

'I'd like that.'

'I thought you might, so I am prepared.' And Oscar saw on the desk—along with a word processor, a stack of books, papers in some disarray and the telephone—a small tray, neatly set with the bottle, two tumblers and a jug of water. He was touched.

'The girls aren't back from Buckly yet?'

'No.' Oscar lowered himself into one of the chairs.

Peter handed him his drink, and then settled down in the other chair, facing his visitor. He raised his glass. '*Slàinte*.'

'Good health.'

The Laphraoig was like nectar. Clean, delicious, warming.

'Buckly's rather a depressing town at the moment,' Peter said. 'Most of the people are unemployed. The woollen mill went to the wall.'

Oscar frowned. 'Not McTaggart's? What happened?'

'The old man died, the sons weren't interested. The work force got financial help and took it over themselves. They were doing all right, and then we had a spell of dreadful weather, the river burst its banks and the place was flooded. Everything lost, destroyed.'

Oscar was appalled. 'Is that the end of it, then?'

'There's some word of a takeover. One of those big textile conglomerates. Sturrock and Swinfield, from London. But so far nothing seems to have happened.'

'What a tragedy.' Oscar frowned. 'I can't think why I haven't heard of this, but just now I don't read the newspapers properly and I haven't talked to many people. That, of course, is why I'm here. To apologise to you. I should have come before.'

'Please. Don't feel badly. I realised that I had taken you unawares, and I should have waited for a more suitable occasion.'

'I don't know what came over me. It was ridiculous.'

'Please, think no more of it. No harm done. Another time, you must join me there, for tea or a drink. The best would be if you felt like joining the club. It's such a splendid course, it would be sad to live here and not experience at least one round.'

Oscar took another sip of the Laphraoig. 'Godfrey Billicliffe also invited me to join the golf club.'

'I understand that you drove him to hospital yesterday.'

'How did you know that?'

Peter Kennedy smiled. 'There are very few secrets in this small community. Dr Sinclair rang me to put me in the picture. It was very good of you.'

'Did you know he was ill?'

'No. I don't think anybody knew. Since his wife died he's gone downhill at a frightening pace, though. I have to go to Inverness on Friday for a meeting. I'll pop into the hospital and pay a visit. See how he's getting on.'

'I said I would stand as his next of kin. So I imagine that if there is any news, I shall be informed.'

'Well, keep me in touch. Now, how is your Uncle Hector?'

'Growing older. Living in London. He came down to visit me after—after the funeral, and suggested I come back here.'

'I know, Oscar. He wrote me a long letter. I wanted to come right away to talk with you. But my instinct told me that for the time being you needed to be on your own. I hope you didn't get the impression that I was either uncaring or inattentive.'

'No. I didn't think that.'

'Sometimes it's easier to talk to a stranger, a person disassociated.'

'It's difficult to know where to start. It all seems to go a long way back. I never thought I should be married. I had my work at Glastonbury, as a schoolmaster, teaching piano and training the choir. I was very happy there. And then the headmaster retired, and I decided that the time had come for a change. I had been offered the post as organist and choir master at St Biddulph's in London. The music there had always been renowned for its excellence, so I moved to London and a flat only five minutes from the church.

'I met the Bellamys soon after my arrival and they were enormously hospitable and kind to me. When George Bellamy became ill, I used to go to their house to keep him company, play backgammon with him. When he died, I arranged the music for his funeral, and afterwards Gloria, his widow, continued to invite me to various small social affairs. Sometimes we went to the cinema together, or spent a day at Kew. I thought little of it, but much enjoyed her company. And then, one day, in a quite matter-of-fact fashion, she said that she thought it would be a good idea if we married. She explained that she did not enjoy living without a man and she felt that I, in my advancing years, would be glad of a wife. It all sounds, I know, a little cold-blooded, but the truth is that I was extremely fond of her, and she, I think, of me.'

'She was a wonderful wife, brimming with physical vitality. When she told me she was pregnant, I was incredulous. I had never, in all my life, imagined that I would become a father. And when Francesca was born, I was filled with a wonder that I don't suppose I shall ever experience again. It was as though a miracle had occurred. And she never stopped being a miracle. As she grew older, and was running about, I would watch her, and still find it unbelievable that I had helped to create this beguiling, beautiful, miniature human being.

'Then Gloria was left a house in Dibton in Hampshire, and we moved from London. I missed St Biddulph's, but from time to time I played the organ for morning service in the village church.'

Oscar paused to take another sip of the Laphraoig.

Peter spoke. 'Your friend, Elfrida. Have you always known her?'

'No. We didn't meet until she came to live in our village. She was alone, and Gloria took her under her wing. She was amusing, full of life, and we all enjoyed her company. Francesca was forever cycling off to visit her little cottage. She was staying with a cousin in Cornwall at the time of the accident. She returned after the funeral with no idea of what had happened. When Hector suggested I leave Hampshire and return to Creagan, I knew I couldn't do it on my own. I dreaded being alone. So I asked Elfrida to come with me. It is a measure of her generous heart that she agreed. She is company for me, and in the blackest moments has always been able to make me smile. When I first met Elfrida, I remember she asked me if I was religious. I told her that I felt I needed some being to thank. Because I was fortunate. I was content. The marriage of convenience was working well, and because of Francesca I could have no regrets.

'Then, a split second, and Gloria and Francesca were both dead. If a God was there . . . and I have never been totally certain that he was . . . I didn't want any part of him. I should have been with them. I should have been behind the wheel of the car. If only. If only is my nightmare.'

'If only is like hindsight,' Peter said quietly. 'A useless exercise. I hope so much that no one has sought to try to comfort you by saying that God must have needed Francesca more than you. I would find it impossible to worship a God who deliberately stole my child from me. Such a God would be a moral monster.'

Oscar was astounded. 'Is that what you really believe?'

Peter nodded. 'Thirty years in the ministry has taught me that the one thing we should never say when a young person dies is "It is the will of God." We simply don't know enough to say that. I am convinced that when Francesca died in that terrible accident, God's was the first heart to break.'

'I want to move on, to go on living, to be able to accept—to be able to give again. I don't like taking all the time. I've never been that sort of person.'

'Oh, Oscar. It will be all right. For a while, what you are probably going to need most is not people who will quote the Bible to you, but close friends who will hold your hand and lend you a listening ear when you want to speak about Francesca.'

Oscar thought about Elfrida, but did not say anything.

'Life is sweet,' Peter went on. 'Beyond the pain, it continues to be sweet. The basics are still there. Beauty, friendship, reservoirs of love and understanding. Later, you are going to need others who will encourage you to make new beginnings. They will help you move on, to cherish happy memories and confront the painful ones with more than bitterness and anger.'

Oscar remembered the dark night when, for the first time, the image of Francesca had not reduced him to the painful tears of loss, but had filled his being with a peaceful comfort. Perhaps that had been the start of his recovery. Perhaps this conversation was the continuance. He did not know. He only knew that he felt better, stronger, not so useless. Perhaps, after all, he hadn't done so badly.

He said, 'Thank you.'

'Oh, my friend, I wish I could give you so much more.'

'No. Don't wish that. You have given me enough.'

Lucy

Lucy had flown only twice in her life. Both times she had found it tremendously exciting, but today she made an effort to be consciously casual about the whole business, so as to give the impression that she was a seasoned, vastly experienced traveller.

Her clothes helped. Her mother, perhaps to assuage unadmitted stirrings of guilt, had taken Lucy to Gap, and bought her daughter a number of delectable things. She was wearing the new warm jeans, lined in red brushed cotton, and a quilted scarlet jacket. Last night she had washed her hair, and this morning had brushed it back into a long ponytail. She felt sleek and neat. A credit to Carrie.

Carrie looked, as always, immensely elegant in her long boots, loden coat and black fur hat. Lucy was very aware of heads turning to watch as Carrie walked by, pushing their trolley with the luggage. The only thing was, poor Carrie had a bit of a cold. But she said she would be fine once she started breathing the clean, cold Scottish air.

In the plane, Lucy had a window seat and sat with her forehead pressed against the little window, staring down at England spread out below like a greenish-grey quilt patterned with cloud shadows.

After they'd been served food on little trays, the plane began to lose height. The terrain below them slowly took shape, and she saw snow on the tops of mountains, then the blue gleam of the sea, boats, and a bridge over a wide firth.

They landed, huge tyres thumping on tarmac.

'We're going to be met,' Carrie told Lucy, 'by a taxi from Creagan.' And once they had reclaimed their suitcases from the carousel, there, in the arrivals hall, was a solid-looking man in a padded wind-cheater, holding up a board with *Sutton* written on it.

It was a spectacular drive. The road led through farmland and over bridges, and on the high ground the tyres of the Subaru taxi scrunched over snow. It followed the shore of a long sea loch and ran through small villages of grey stone cottages.

Once in Creagan, the taxi driver drew up at the pavement's edge before the Estate House. The next moment the front door opened and down the path came Elfrida Phipps and her vociferous dog.

'Carrie! Oh, my darling girl.' She flung her arms around Carrie. 'You're here. I've been so looking forward . . . so excited!'

Standing aside, Lucy watched. Elfrida was very tall and thin and had a lot of wild hair the colour of marmalade. She wore tartan trousers, a huge, thick grey sweater and a lot of lipstick. Lucy could understand instantly why Gran didn't approve.

Carrie said, 'Elfrida, you look wonderful. Scotland clearly agrees with you.'

'Darling, it's bliss. Bitterly cold, but bliss.'

'You have to meet Lucy.'

'But of course.' She laughed. 'Isn't this ridiculous, Lucy? We're relations, and we've never set eyes on each other. But your grand-father was my favourite cousin and we used to have wonderful, wild times together.' She put her hands on Lucy's shoulders. 'Let me look at you. Yes, I thought so. Pretty as paint. This is my dog, Horace, who has been looking forward to meeting you because he hopes you'll take him on long walks on the beach. Come along, both of you. We'll go into the house and you can meet Oscar.'

They all streamed up the path into the house, followed by the taxi driver, laden with luggage. They went down a long hall and then up a wide staircase. Lucy decided she liked the feeling of the house: solid and secure, with sturdy banisters and thick carpet. The smell of polish and well-worn furniture, and the faint suggestion of something delicious cooking in the kitchen.

They had reached the first-floor landing.

Elfrida raised her voice to call, 'Oscar! Here they are!' And then, in her ordinary voice said, 'He's in the sitting room. You two go and say hello, and I'll show Alec where to put the suitcases. Carrie's in here, Alec, and Lucy's upstairs.'

Carrie took Lucy's hand in her own and they went into the sitting room where Oscar was waiting for them, standing with his back to the fireplace. He was as tall as Elfrida but not so thin as she, and he had a fine head of silvery hair, and a quiet and kindly face, not rugged, but strangely unlined.

Carrie said, 'Oscar. How do you do? I'm Carrie Sutton.'

'My dear . . .' He came forward and they shook hands. 'How good to see you. Have you had a peaceful journey?'

'Perfect,' Carrie told him. 'No problems.'

'Elfrida's been mad with excitement all morning.'

'It's so good of you to have us.' Carrie looked about her. 'And what a marvellous house you have.'

'I own only half. I am part-owner.'

'That doesn't make it any less special.' She let go of Lucy's hand, and put an arm round her shoulder. 'This is my niece, Lucy Wesley.'

Lucy swallowed her nervousness and said, 'How do you do?' She willed herself to meet his eyes. For what seemed a long time, he said nothing. She knew that he must be thinking of his own daughter, twelve years old and now dead. And then he smiled at her, and took her hand and his clasp was warm and friendly.

'So you are Lucy?'

'Yes.'

'And you are going to have to sleep in the attic.'

Carrie laughed. 'Oscar, you don't make it sound very tempting.'

'Don't worry, Lucy. Elfrida has made it entrancing for you. Now,' he let go of Lucy's hand, 'it's half past twelve. Why don't you both go and find your rooms and get settled, and then we'll have lunch? Elfrida has spent much of the morning concocting a shepherd's pie.'

Lucy's spirits rose. The worst, the initial encounter, was over. Elfrida was funny and Oscar was kind. And they were going to eat shepherd's pie for lunch.

AFTER THE DELICIOUS PIE and a pudding made of stewed apples, meringues and cream, Oscar looked at his watch. 'If Horace and I do not set out for a walk now, we won't be home before darkness falls.' He looked at Lucy. 'Would you like to come with us?'

'For a walk?'

'We could go on the beach. And then you will know the way.'

She felt very gratified to be invited. 'Yes, I'd love to.'

'Perhaps, Oscar,' said Elfrida, 'you could wheel her round the town first and show her where the shops are. It won't take five minutes.'

'Certainly, if that's what she'd like. Have you got a warm coat, Lucy?'

'I've got my new jacket.'

'And a warm hat. The sea wind can freeze your ears off.'

'Yes, I've got that too. Shall I clear the table?' Lucy asked.

Elfrida laughed. 'How well brought up you are. Of course not. Carrie and I will do that when we've finished our coffee. Off you go with Oscar before it gets too cold.'

Five minutes later they set off together, Lucy holding Horace's lead in her gloved hand. Down the street, past the gift shop, the chemist, the book shop, the butcher, the newsagent, a shop displaying knitted sweaters, the supermarket. Beneath leafless trees, Lucy paused to look through a wrought-iron gate to where a side door of the church stood open.

'Is the church open?' she asked.

'Always. Just this side door. For visitors, I suppose.'

'Can we go inside? Just for a moment. Churches are so nice when they're empty.'

He took a deep breath, and for a moment she thought he was going to refuse. But he let it out in a deep sigh. 'All right.'

They tied the end of the lead to the handle of the outer door, and left Horace there. He did not look pleased.

Inside, their footsteps rang on the flagged floor and echoed up into the roof. Sunlight poured through the stained-glass windows and the arched ceiling soared upwards, the plaster between the curved beams painted the blue of a summer sky.

Lucy wandered off to investigate and by the time she had inspected everything, from the ornate font to the hand-stitched kneelers, Oscar had tired of standing and was settled comfortably in the front pew, waiting for her.

She went to sit beside him. 'I'm sorry for being so long.'

'I am pleased that you are interested in such things.'

'Carrie told me that you were an organist. That you taught music.'

'That's true. I was choir master as well. Do you listen to music?'

Lucy shrugged. 'Only pop and such.' She thought about this. 'Except sometimes, at school, we get taken to concerts. We went to an open-air concert in Regent's Park this summer. At the end they played the 'Music for the Royal Fireworks', and there was a fireworks display at the same time. I really loved that.' She sank her chin into her jacket and gazed up at the tall stained-glass window that faced them. Mary with the baby Jesus. She said, 'I wouldn't want a birthday in the middle of winter on Christmas Day.'

'Why not?'

'Well, for one thing, you'd probably only get one present. And for another, it's usually rather dark and gloomy weather.'

'When is your birthday?'

'July. Much better. Only thing is, I'm usually at school.'

Oscar said, 'Actually, I don't think Christ was born in wintertime. I think he was probably born in the spring.'

'Really? Why do you say that?'

'Well, the shepherds were guarding their flocks, which probably meant that it was lambing time and they were watching out for wolves, in case they came and ate the young animals.'

'Then why don't we have Christmas in the spring?'

'I think the early Christians were a cunning lot. They simply adapted what was left to them by the pagan inhabitants of the countries they converted. There had always been the celebration of the winter solstice, the shortest day of the year. Those pre-Christians lit fires, caroused, burned candles, baked cakes.' Oscar smiled. 'I suppose it was to cheer themselves up.'

'So the early Christians just used the same party?'

'Something like that.'

'But added other bits as well.'

'Their belief in the Son of God.'

'I see.' It seemed a very practical arrangement. Lucy was silent for a moment. Then she said, 'Do you like Christmas?'

'Parts of it,' Oscar told her, sounding cautious.

'I don't really like it much. There's such a build-up and then it's sort of . . . disappointing.'

'Which proves that we should never expect too much.' High above them, the church clock struck half past two. 'Perhaps we have lingered long enough. Come along. We have to get as far as the beach, and before very long it will be dark.'

Carrie

Carrie and Elfrida, left alone at the kitchen table with their coffee, smiled at each other. Two women of different generations, but old friends, who had not been together, alone, for too long, and now relished their peaceful privacy.

Elfrida, Carrie thought, for all her sixty-two years, looked as vital and energetic as a young girl.

'What a perfectly sweet man,' she said now, thinking of Oscar.

'Isn't he?' Elfrida agreed with satisfaction. 'I'm so pleased they've made friends. It's brilliant having you here. Just what we need.'

'It doesn't have to be an all-singing, all-dancing Christmas. Lucy and I both have a low expectation of the Festive Season.'

'Us, too. Though, once he knew you were coming, Oscar did order a Christmas tree.'

'Lucy will love that. She can decorate it. Poor child, my mother was never much good at creating a magic atmosphere and Nicola's too idle.'

'How is your mother?'

'Just the same.' No more needed to be said.

'And your father?'

'Haven't seen him. But we spoke on the telephone.'

'I had such a wonderful month with them all in Cornwall in October. And then I got home to hear this terrible thing that had happened to Oscar. Life can change with such shocking abruptness.'

'I know.' Carrie thought about Andreas, and said again, 'I know.'

A silence fell. Carrie knew what was coming next.

'And you, Carrie?'

She finished her coffee and set down the cup. 'I'm fine.'

'I don't think you are. For one thing, you look tired. And thin. Why did you suddenly come back from Austria?'

Carrie shrugged. 'Oh, reasons. Some time, I'll tell you. I'm fighting a cold and I'm a bit tired, but I'm not ill.'

'I feel you're unhappy. I wish I could help.'

'You are helping. By having us here.'

Elfrida ran a hand through her unruly, fiery hair. 'I will say no more. Now . . .' Her manner changed, she became cheerful, in charge once more. 'What would you like to do this afternoon? How about a little rest? I'll find a hot-water bottle.'

Bed and a hot-water bottle. Carrie could not remember how long it was since some other person had cherished her. Had said, 'You look tired.' And, 'How about a little rest?' She had spent too many years being strong, looking after others and their problems. Cancelled reservations, faulty ski lifts, lost passports, lack of snow, or too much of it . . . And then returning to London to be faced with family problems. She was tired of being the sturdy pillar against which everybody leaned. Upstairs, before lunch, she had seen the enormous double bed, downy and soft, with its white cover, and had longed, right then and there, to climb beneath the blankets and sleep. She was filled with grateful love for Elfrida.

They went upstairs. 'Lucy's in the attic,' Elfrida explained. 'You've seen your room, and there are two bathrooms, and this,' she opened another door, 'is the second spare bedroom. I could have put Lucy in here, but its very small and a bit dreary. The attic seemed a much more attractive space for her, and I had fun putting it together.'

Carrie peered into the small, undistinguished room, almost totally taken up with an enormous bed. It was clearly unoccupied, and for the first time she began to feel a bit uncomfortable, not knowing, but suspecting, what was going to happen next. 'Elfrida . . .'

Elfrida opened the final door with a flourish that had a touch of defiance about it. 'And this,' she said, 'is us.'

It was a spacious room, the master bedroom of the house, with tall windows, a looming Victorian wardrobe, a pretty dressing table and a chest of drawers. And an enormously high and wide bed. Over this was spread Elfrida's scarlet silk shawl, the embroidery faded, the fringe beginning to fray, but still marvellously opulent and recognisable from the old days.

And other possessions. A man's ivory brushes on the chest of drawers, dark blue pyjamas folded on a pillow.

There fell a small silence. Then Elfrida said, 'You're not shocked?'

'Elfrida, I'm me. I'm not Dodie. You don't have to explain.' Carrie put her arms round Elfrida and hugged her. 'It's all so sweet. Needing each other and finding each other. I'm glad.'

'Oscar still has a long way to go. Some days he's been so depressed that he scarcely speaks. But I've learned to leave him alone. He has to deal with his grief in his own way.'

'It can't have been easy.'

'Oh, darling Carrie, nothing is. And now, we must waste no more time. I shall find you a hot-water bottle, and you shall go to sleep.'

Oscar

Rather to his surprise, Oscar was having a bonfire. He had decided to clear out the potting shed and burn all the rubbish—and there was a great deal of it. The thick smoke rose and billowed and made everything smell of autumn. So intent was he on this labour that he did not hear the gate behind him open and shut.

'Oscar.'

Startled, he swung round to face Peter Kennedy, who was dressed for golf in a red jacket and peaked baseball cap.

'Heavens, I never heard you.'

'I didn't mean to sneak up on you. I saw the smoke and guessed I'd find you here. I wanted to tell you that I was in Inverness yesterday, and I saw Godfrey Billicliffe at the hospital.'

'That was good of you. How is he?'

Peter shook his head. 'Not good news, I'm afraid. He has cancer . . .'

'Oh, God.'

'I think he already had his own private suspicions, fears, but never said a word to anybody.'

'I must go and see him.'

'No. He asked me to tell you no. He's doped and frail, and already has the look of a man on his way out of this world. But he asked me to send you his regards and to say how grateful he was for your kindness.'

'I didn't do anything.'

'You did. And you were there when he most needed a friend. He really is quite peaceful. Sleeps most of the time.'

'Thank you for telling me.'

'I knew that you would want to know.' Peter paused. 'There's something else. It occurred to me that you might be missing your music.' He felt in his pocket and produced a small brass key. 'The church is always open, but the organ is locked. I have discussed it with Alistair Heggie, our organist, and he is happy for you to use it any time you feel inclined.' Before Oscar could protest, Peter had pressed the key into his palm, closing his fingers about it.

Oscar said, 'Oh, no . . .'

'You don't have to. You might not even want to. But I like to think that you can, if the impulse takes you.'

'You are too kind.'

'Just put it somewhere safe.' Peter grinned. 'It's our only spare.' He made as if to go, and then turned back again. 'I very nearly forgot— Tabitha says would you all like to come up to the Manse for a drink and a mince pie on Tuesday evening at six. Everybody's welcome. Don't dress up. Our children will probably be around.'

'Tuesday.' Oscar made a mental note to tell Elfrida. 'Tuesday at six. I think we'd like that very much.'

'Splendid.' Peter went through the gate and latched it behind him. 'We'll see you then.'

'Have a good round. Thank you for coming.'

Lucy

On Monday morning, when Lucy descended from her private eyrie in the attic, she saw that Carrie's bedroom door was closed. Downstairs, she found only Oscar and Elfrida.

'Lucy, how are you this morning?' Oscar asked, pulling her close for a friendly hug.

'I'm fine, but where's Carrie?'

'Carrie's really not well.' Elfrida got up from the table to collect sausages from the hot plate. 'I don't think she's got flu, but she isn't throwing this horrible cold off. Two sausages or three?'

'Three, please, if there's enough. Is she still in bed?'

'Yes, I looked in to see her, and she said she'd coughed all night. I took her a cup of tea, but she doesn't want anything to eat. I'm going to ring Dr Sinclair and ask if he'll have a look at her.'

Lucy sat down to her sausages. 'She must be all right for Christmas. Can I go and see her?'

'I shouldn't, until we know what's wrong.'

'We'd planned a long walk on the beach this morning with Horace. Will you come instead, Oscar?' Lucy asked.

'I can't this morning. I'm going to get my hair cut and then I'm going to pick up the meat from the butcher.'

'Oh, I see.' It was hard not to sound downcast.

'You can go on your own. Take Horace. He will guard you. You can be a lone explorer.'

Lucy mulled over this new prospect of freedom and was rather taken with the idea of setting out all by herself.

So, after breakfast, with Horace on his lead, she set off across the square and then turned up the road that led to the golf club. The right-of-way led across the links, and when she reached a shallow summit she saw the whole horizon, and a great arc of sky, grey with low cloud. Small waves washed up onto the shining wet sand, and far away she could see the lighthouse.

She unclipped Horace's lead and he ran ahead of her. In the shelter of the dunes the sand was deep and soft and difficult for walking, so she went out onto the wet hard sand and, looking back, saw her own footprints, with Horace's pawprints circling them. She was alone. Not another soul. She rather liked knowing that nobody knew *exactly* where she was, and that if she met somebody they wouldn't know *who* she was. She belonged to nobody but herself.

The beach ended at an outcrop of rocks. Lucy paused to get her bearings. Hillocky dunes separated the beach from the golf links, and as she hesitated, trying to decide which way to go next, she heard the sound of a motor and saw, above the rocks, a tractor come trundling towards her over a rise. Clearly, there had to be some sort of track. She decided that she would walk home that way, and with some difficulty hauled herself up a sandy cliff. Horace bounded ahead and out of sight. Reaching the summit she saw the track.

Coming up the slope from the direction of the town, another dog walker was striding out purposefully. She was dressed in a sheepskin coat, and wore a tam-o'-shanter slanted at a jaunty angle over cropped grey hair. Her dog, running free, spied Horace and stopped dead. The two animals eyed each other for a long moment, and Lucy was petrified, because the other dog was a Rottweiler.

'Horace.' She had meant to call him but her mouth was dry and his name came out in an agonised whisper.

Horace didn't hear. He began to bark. The Rottweiler moved forward slowly, his shining body tense, muscles flexed. A snarling sound came from deep in his throat, and his dark lips rolled back from his teeth. Horace, holding his ground, gave another timid bark, and with that the Rottweiler pounced.

Lucy screamed and Horace howled for help. He was being bitten and bruised, and however he struggled he could not escape.

The dog's owner was of no use at all. She had a chain leash in her hand, but it was obvious that she was too wary to start manhandling her pet while he was in this frame of mind. Instead she produced a whistle, which she blew sharply, and proceeded to shout orders.

'Brutus! Down, boy! To heel!'

The Rottweiler took no notice.

'Get hold of him,' Lucy wailed, hysterical with horror. Horace, Elfrida's darling dog, was about to be murdered. '*Stop* him!'

She had forgotten about the approaching tractor. Now, like the cavalry in some Western, it trundled into view in the nick of time; the door was flung open, the driver jumped down and, without showing the slightest fear or hesitation, went straight into action, landing his heavy boot into the muscled backside of the Rottweiler. 'Get off, you bloody brute!' The startled Rottweiler abandoned Horace and turned to attack this new enemy, but the young man grabbed his studded collar and hauled him away from his prey.

In a thousand years, Lucy could never have imagined anyone being so level-headed, strong and brave.

'What the bloody hell do you think you're doing?' he demanded of the dog's owner, grabbing the chain leash from her hand and somehow clipping it to the collar of the snarling, struggling beast. He then dragged the animal towards her and she took the leather loop in both her hands.

'Don't you swear at me!' she said.

'Why didn't you keep the dog on its chain?'

'He was attacked.' Now the danger was over she was belligerent.

'He was no such thing. I saw it all. You should know better than to walk a savage dog on a public footpath.'

'Don't speak to me in that tone of voice.'

'I'll speak to you any way I like. I work for the golf club. If I see that dog running free again, I'll report you to the police.'

'And I shall complain of impudence!'

But at this point, Brutus took charge. He had spied two innocent golfers striding down the fairway, and with his blood up, and a desperate need to sink his teeth into some other throat, set off on the hunt. His owner, willy-nilly, went too, trailed in his wake, her short, trousered legs going like pistons.

Lucy, by now, was sitting on the grass with Horace in her arms, his head pressed against the front of her jacket. The young man came to kneel beside her. She saw that he was very young, his face windburnt, his eyes blue. He had short, yellow hair, which looked dyed, and there was a gold ring in his left ear.

He said, 'Are you all right?'

'Yes, but Horace . . .' Lucy burst into tears.

'Here.' Gently, he examined poor Horace, making comforting noises as he did so. 'I think he'll be all right. Just superficial cuts and bruises.'

'He only *barked*,' Lucy sobbed. 'He always barks. He's so stupid. I thought he was going to be dead.'

'Lucky he isn't.'

'He's not even my dog. He's Elfrida's. We just came for a walk.'

'Where from?'

'Creagan.'

'I can take you back as far as the clubhouse. Can you walk from there?'

'Yes. I think so.'

He led the way and Lucy clambered up into the tractor's cab. There was only one seat, but she perched herself on the very edge of this and Horace was placed at her feet, where he sat and leaned heavily against her knee. Then the young man jumped up beside her, slammed the door shut and put the tractor in gear.

Lucy had stopped crying. 'Thank you so much for helping.'

'You're staying at the Estate House, aren't you? With Oscar Blundell?'

'Do you know him?'

'No, but my father does. He's Peter Kennedy, the minister. I'm Rory Kennedy.'

'I'm Lucy Wesley. Do you work on the golf course?'

'Yes, for the time being. This is the start of my gap year.'

'I'm rather dreading my gap year.'

'How old are you?'

'Fourteen.'

'You've time enough to make plans. Where do you live?'

'London. I'm up here for Christmas with my aunt Carrie. I live with my mother and my grandmother. My mother is going to America for Christmas. In fact, she's flying out today.'

'What about your father?'

'They're divorced. I don't see him much.'

'That's rough.'

Lucy shrugged. 'It's all right.'

For a bit they thumped along in silence. Then he said, 'I believe you're all coming up to the Manse for a drink tomorrow evening. There's a hooley in the school hall at seven o'clock. My sister Clodagh and I are going. Do you want to come with us?'

'What's a hooley?'

'A dance.'

Lucy was at once filled with anxiety. She had been to parties, but never a dance. She said, 'I don't know.'

'Why not? It's just the schoolkids, practising reels for the Hogmanay parties. Good fun.'

'I don't know how to do reels. I don't know the steps.'

'So it's high time you learned.'

He turned his head to smile at her, and rather to her surprise she found herself saying, 'All right. Yes. Thank you. Do . . . do I have to dress up?'

'Heaven forbid. Jeans and trainers.'

All the time they had been talking it had been growing dark. Now large white flakes of snow began to drift from the leaden sky. Rory said, 'I wondered when that would start. You could see the snow-clouds, coming down from the north. The weather forecast this morning said we're in for some heavy falls.'

'Is it going to be a white Christmas? I've never had one.'

'Good for sledging. Hard work for the roadmen.'

They were grinding up the slope that led to the clubhouse. Rory turned the tractor into the car park, killed the engine, opened the door and climbed down. 'Will you be all right now?'

Snow settled on his hair and the shoulders of his thick donkey jacket. Lucy clambered down behind him, and he lifted Horace out and set him on his feet. Horace gave himself a shake, and even wagged his plumey tail. Lucy took the lead from her pocket and clipped it onto Horace's collar.

'That's it then.' He grinned at her. 'You get home now.'

'Thank you so much.'

She walked down the hill, turning back to wave.

It had been a momentous outing. A long walk, a dogfight, a tractor ride, a snowstorm, and an invitation to a dance. She could scarcely wait to get home and tell Oscar and Elfrida all about it.

EVER SINCE THE SNOW had started, Elfrida had been blaming herself for letting Lucy go off on her own. When she heard the front door open and Lucy's voice calling, she abandoned the potatoes she'd been peeling in the kitchen and rushed out to meet her. Lucy and Horace stood on the doormat, both encrusted in snow, and with a terrible story to tell.

It was told in the warm kitchen, while Lucy shed her coat and hat and pulled off her boots. 'This horrible dog, it was a Rottweiler, went for Horace and then there was a tractor . . . Rory Kennedy was frightfully brave . . . brought us back to the golf club in his tractor. Elfrida, I am sorry, but I couldn't stop it. And poor Horace has got bites and bruises . . . It was *so* frightening.'

She was clearly upset by the whole incident but, in an extraordinary way, excited as well, having come through the entire adventure and brought Horace home alive. Her cheeks were pink and her eyes bright. She was a sweet child, of course, but serious-minded, and docility did not suit a fourteen-year-old. This metamorphosis was hopeful, and Elfrida knew that by sending Lucy off on her own she had done exactly the right thing.

As for Horace, he sat on the floor and looked sorry for himself.

'What happened, Horace?' Elfrida asked him. 'Were you attacked by a savage hound?' She turned to Lucy. 'But, darling, your jeans are soaked. You should go and get some dry clothes on.'

'All right.' Lucy started to go, but turned back. 'Elfrida.'

'What is it?'

'Rory Kennedy's terribly nice. And he's got dyed hair.'

'Dyed hair?' Elfrida put on an expression of horror. 'What *would* your grandmother say?'

Lucy told her, in Dodie's voice. '"Dis-gusting!"' She grinned and was gone, and Elfrida heard her running up the stairs, two at a time, to her attic bedroom.

Sam

They stood at the bar of the Duke's Arms in Buckly, an austere little pub that had made no concessions to either the tourist trade or trendy decor. The walls were pitch-pine tongue-and-groove, the lighting bleak and the floor worn, dark brown linoleum.

Fergus Skinner said, 'What'll it be?'

'A half of lager, please,' Sam replied.

Fergus had brought him here, crossing the snowy road from the church hall after the meeting with the mill workers. It was, he told Sam as he ordered a large Bell's for himself, his customary haunt, a place where a man could enjoy a peaceful dram without some person engaging him in conversation.

Fergus was in his early forties but looked older, with the dark hair and pale skin of a true Highlander. His features were strong—deep-set eyes, a beak of a nose, a long lantern jaw—and his expression sombre. He had been foreman at the mill in the old days and, when the McTaggart family broke up, it was he who had rallied the work-force and organised the management buy-out. Almost unanimously, he had been voted in as manager of the new enterprise, and the demise of the business had been harder on him than anyone else.

But he remained undefeated. When Sam rang him from London, from the offices of Sturrock & Swinfield, asking him to set up some sort of a meeting with the work force, Fergus Skinner had done his stuff. Because of this, the meeting had been well attended, so much so that late-comers found standing room only.

Now the two men carried their drinks to a wobbly table by the tiny fireplace. Fergus raised his glass. 'Your good health.'

'And the future.' The lager was warm.

'The future.'

To begin with, the atmosphere at the meeting had been cautious. Sam had started by introducing himself as the new general manager of McTaggart's, who would be taking overall charge of the reconstruction of the ruined mill and the restart of the business. The response to this was silence, and he knew they probably regarded him as simply a money man sent from London. So he told them a bit about his background: a Yorkshire boy, born and bred to the woollen industry and a family mill very like McTaggart's. How his family, too, had been faced with difficulties, and been rescued by Sturrock & Swinfield, which was why he, Sam, was there.

The atmosphere relaxed a little.

Sam went through the feasibility study and the restructuring. A business built on tradition and good will but moving forwards. So, new products. New markets. New machinery.

Now hands were held up. 'Will that mean retraining?'

He told them yes.

Would there be redundancies?

He said yes, to begin with. But once the new mill was up and going, there would come expansion and new job creation.

A woman asked if there would be work for her, a hand finisher, or would it all be done with this new sophisticated machinery? Sam told her that with the luxury goods they intended manufacturing there would always be work for hand finishers.

The most vital question: how soon would they get back to work?

At the soonest, nine months. There was a great deal to be done. Blueprints of the plans were on display at the back of the hall. The outward appearance of the old mill would remain the same. Inside, it would be gutted and totally rebuilt. There would be a shop to attract tourists, and the architect had made provision for a small tea shop. Both would offer increased employment.

Finally, it all became something of a general discussion, which was exactly the way Sam wanted it to be. By the end, he felt that he had won some trust and, hopefully, cooperation.

Fergus stooped to place another lump of peat onto the dying fire, 'Where are you staying?'

'At the moment in Inverness, in a hotel.' Sam glanced up at the clock. 'I should be off. It's a long drive.'

'But you have a good car. A new Land Rover Discovery.'

'I bought it in London when I knew I would be living here.'

They went outside. It was snowing again and Fergus said, 'I think, before you set off, you should phone the AA. Get a check on conditions. The Black Isle can be a hazard on a night like this.'

'Maybe. I'll see how I go.'

'It has been a pleasure to meet you.'

'The pleasure's mine, Fergus.'

They said goodbye, shaking hands. Sam climbed up into the big car, reached into his coat pocket and brought out two keys: the key for his car and the big, old-fashioned key to Hughie McLellan's Estate House, attached to its label with a knot of string.

He had met Hughie by chance when he had been staying with Janey and Neil in London. Hughie was an old acquaintance of Janey's parents and had been invited round for dinner. When he heard Sam had nowhere to live in Scotland, he had said, 'You need a house. I have one for sale in Creagan, near Buckly. No harm in going to cast your eye over the place.'

Now, for a moment, Sam debated. It would be good to get back to base, to a bath, a drink in the bar and dinner. But on the other hand, surely, while he was so close to Creagan it would be worth taking a short detour to cast an eye over Hughie's house, decide if it would be worth returning to inspect it with an eye to buying. He started up the engine and switched on the lights. Suddenly he felt adventurous.

'Creagan, here I come.'

He crossed a long bridge over a firth, and a couple of miles after that his headlights touched the luminous sign—CREAGAN: 2 MILES. He took the turning onto the single-track road and eventually came into the town. In the light of street lamps he saw the church and the square and the old walled graveyard. He drove slowly, trying to get his bearings, wondering which was the house Hughie McLellan had described. He decided to ask directions from a couple walking towards him. He rolled down the window. 'Excuse me. I'm looking for the Estate House.'

'You're there.' The man, amused, grinned. 'You're here.' He jerked his head, indicating the house behind him.

'Oh. I see. Thank you.'

'You're welcome.' They set off on their way.

Sam sat in his car and stared. It could not possibly be Hughie's house. Hughie had said the house was empty, untenanted. This house had windows that, behind drawn curtains, were filled with light. He told himself that he should simply drive on. But he did not like mysteries, and knew that this one would niggle at him. He took the house key, climbed down from the Discovery and walked up to the front door. There was a bell, and he pressed it.

An outside light came on, and the door was opened.

He was not quite sure who or what he had expected. An elderly pinafored lady? Or a man in bedroom slippers? What he didn't expect was a tall, dark girl in jeans and a pullover. A sensationally good-looking girl, who would have turned heads on Fifth Avenue.

Carrie

That morning, the doctor had popped into the Estate House to check on Carrie.

When he had gone, Elfrida came upstairs and put her head round the door. 'What did he say?'

'I'm all right, but I have to stay here for another day. I'm sorry.'

'Don't be so silly. Do you want a hot-water bottle?'

'No. Warm as toast.'

The day progressed, and through her window Carrie had watched the weather and was glad she did not have to be out in it. From time to time she heard the wind whining round the old house. It was all rather cosy. She remembered, as a child, being ill in bed, and the awareness of others getting on with the day-to-day business of life without her having to participate. Carrie had long forgotten the luxury of self-indulgence, idleness, and total irresponsibility.

At a quarter to six Oscar, Elfrida and Lucy departed for the party at the Manse. Carrie heard the back door slam behind them and got out of bed. She ran a bath, soaked for ages, then put on jeans and a sweater, did her hair, splashed on some scent, and at once felt better. *I am recovered*, she told her reflection in the mirror.

She went to the sitting room where the fire was blazing, and settled down with Oscar's newspaper. She was in the middle of a feature article about a well-known elderly actress, when the ring of the front-door bell drilled through the house.

Damn. Perhaps it was some person whose car had broken down, who now wanted to borrow a telephone. Or children all set to sing 'Away in a Manger'. She tossed the paper aside and ran downstairs, turning on light switches as she went. She flung the big door open to the snow and the cold—and the solitary man who stood there, with the beam of the outside light streaming down upon him. He had dark hair, and wore a thick, navy-blue overcoat liberally sprinkled in snowflakes, its collar turned up round his ears.

She glanced over his shoulder and saw the large and prestigious vehicle parked in the road. 'Yes?'

'I'm sorry. Is this Hughie McLellan's Estate House?'

Carrie frowned. 'No. Oscar Blundell's Estate House.'

He hesitated. And then he held up in his gloved hand a key, with a label knotted to it with string. On the label was written *Estate House*. He said, 'Perhaps I've made a mistake.'

Carrie stepped back. There must, of course, be explanations. 'I think,' she said, 'you'd better come in.'

He went past her, into the house, and she closed the door.

He looked embarrassed. 'I hope I didn't disturb you.'

'Not at all. Hadn't you better take your coat off? We'll hang it here to dry.'

He had put the key back into his pocket and now unbuttoned his overcoat. She saw that he was conventionally, even formally, dressed, in a dark grey flannel suit and a tie. She took the heavy coat from him and hung it on an old bentwood hat stand.

'Perhaps,' he said, 'I should introduce myself. Sam Howard.'

'Carrie Sutton. Come up to the sitting room. There's a fire.'

She led the way up the stairs and into the huge sitting room. Entering, he observed, as newcomers invariably did, 'What an amazing room.'

'It's unexpected, isn't it? And lovely during the daytime, because it's always full of light. Would you like a drink or something?'

'You're kind. I'd love to, but I'm driving to Inverness.'

'*Inverness*? In this weather?'

'I'll be OK.'

Carrie doubted this, but it was no business of hers. She said, 'Why don't you sit down and tell me why you have the key to Oscar's house.'

He settled himself in Oscar's chair and at once looked quite relaxed and at home. She thought that he had an interesting face, unremarkable, not handsome, but interesting. His eyes, deeply set, were unusual. He leaned back, his long legs crossed at the ankle. 'I am sure we can clear up the confusion. Tell me, did Mr Blundell once live in Hampshire?'

'Yes, he did.'

'And does he have a cousin called Hughie McLellan?'

'I'm afraid you're asking the wrong person. I'm just a guest. And Oscar and Elfrida—she's a sort of cousin of mine and Oscar's friend—they've gone out for drinks. They won't be back till about eight o'clock.' She glanced at the little clock on the mantelpiece. 'It's nearly seven now. If you wanted to wait . . .'

'No, I can't wait. I must be on my way.'

'But I still don't know why you have a key to this house.'

'I was given it by Hughie. He wants to put the property on the market. Put it up for sale.'

Carrie stared at him. 'For sale? But it's Oscar's house.'

'I think they are joint owners.'

'Joint owners. You mean the house doesn't belong to Oscar?'

'I think half of it does.'

'But Hughie McLellan, whoever he is, has no right to put a house up for sale when he doesn't even own it all.'

'It does seem a bit suspect.'

'Why would you want to look at it? Do you want to buy it?'

He said cautiously, 'I might. I have a new job in Buckly. Getting McTaggart's, the woollen mill, back on its feet again.'

'Where's Buckly?'

'About twelve miles north. I've just come from there. Now, I think I should make tracks.'

Carrie went to the big bay window. Outside, Sam's Discovery, parked at the pavement's edge, was already blanketed in snow. She thought of the long miles to Inverness. 'I don't think you should go.'

'You don't?'

'Come and look.'

He joined her, and together they gazed out at the deteriorating conditions. Carrie felt a bit sorry for him. 'It really is bad.'

'Fergus Skinner, the manager at the mill, said I should phone the AA and get a report.'

'I'll find the number for you.' She went out onto the landing, came back with the phone book and looked up the emergency number. 'Here it is.'

He took his mobile from his pocket and dialled the number. He enquired about road conditions on the A9 to Inverness. Then he listened. 'OK. I get the picture. Thank you. Goodbye.'

They looked at each other. 'You were quite right. The road is impassable. I had no idea it would be so bad. I'd better find some guesthouse, hotel . . . I'll check in there.'

'You'll find nothing at this time of year. You'll have to stay here.'

'*Here*? But I can't just come and—'

'Of course you can. Anyway, there doesn't seem to be an alternative. There's an empty bedroom, I know.' Carrie smiled. 'What do they say? Any port in a storm.'

'But . . . Mr Blundell . . .'

'He'll be delighted to have another guest. And it's important that

218

you should tell him what's happened. He'll be most interested. And Elfrida will be over the moon. She likes nothing better than impromptu house parties. There is dinner in the oven and plenty of hot bath water. What more could any man want? A toothbrush?'

'I have one in the car. And my electric razor. But if it's all right, I should make another call.'

'Feel free.' He obviously needed to ring home, explain to his wife what had happened. 'You don't want anybody worrying.'

He used his mobile once more and was speaking to the reception-ist at some hotel in Inverness. 'Just to let you know I'm stuck in Creagan, in a snowstorm. Just keep the room. Thanks.'

'Is that all?' Carrie asked. 'No more calls?'

He slipped his mobile back into his jacket pocket. 'Nope.'

'Right. Well. In that case, why don't you have that drink?'

'That would be very kind. Scotch? On the rocks?'

'Fine. I shan't be a moment.'

She ran downstairs, and in the scullery found a tray onto which she loaded the whisky bottle, the ice bucket, two glasses and an opened bottle of wine. She carried the tray upstairs and found her visitor gazing intently at Elfrida's little picture. He had put on a pair of horn-rimmed spectacles, which made him look rather scholarly.

When Carrie appeared, he took these off. 'What a dear little painting.'

'Yes. It belongs to Elfrida. It's a David Wilkie. She says it's her insurance policy against the day when she runs out of money.'

'It's a treasure . . . Here, let me have that.' He took the tray while Carrie made space on the table, shunting aside a few papers.

She said, 'I'll let you do your own drink.'

'How about you?'

'I'm on the wine.'

She went back to her chair by the fire and watched him, liking the neat movements of his hands. Intrigued, in an objective sort of way, because his appearance at the Estate House, his reason for being there and his reason for staying on all seemed like a sort of con-trivance. Like the plot of a play, perhaps.

He handed her her glass, then sat down again. 'Good health.'

'And to you, too.'

'You're visiting?'

'I live in London. I have a young niece and I brought her with me. We're staying for Christmas.'

'Has she gone out for drinks, too?'

'Yes, and then on to some sort of reel party. Do you know this part of the world well?'

'No. I don't know it at all. I come from Yorkshire. Then I was based in London for a bit, and then New York for six years.'

'What is your job?'

'I'm basically a wool-broker. I work for Sturrock and Swinfield. They bought out my father's woollen mill and I've been with them ever since.'

'This is going to be a bit of a culture change after New York, isn't it?'

'Yes,' he agreed with her. 'A bit.'

'What did you say the mill was called?'

'McTaggart's of Buckly.'

'Is it a going concern?'

He said, 'No,' and then explained the chain of events that had brought it down. And what he was expected to take on.

'And you have to have some place to live?'

'Yes.' He smiled. 'But I can't sort that one out until I've spoken to your host. You said you live in London?'

Carrie didn't really want to talk about herself. 'I've been in Austria for three years, in Oberbeuren, working for a travel firm. But I've been offered a job in their London head office.'

'Are you going to take it?'

'Yes. Why not?'

'You'll miss Austria and the mountains.'

'Yes.' For a moment, neither of them spoke, and the silence was fraught with unsaid words. Then she said, 'Your glass is empty. Would you like another drink?'

Elfrida

At eight o'clock Oscar and Elfrida, arm in arm, made their way home with tremendous caution through thickly falling snow.

Having left their snow-encrusted boots, wet coats and sodden hats in the scullery, they went out of the kitchen and up the stairs. Opening the sitting-room door, they came upon a peaceful scene: the fire blazing, the two most comfortable chairs drawn up to its warmth, and in them, looking as though they had known each other for ever, Carrie and a complete stranger. Possibilities flashed through Elfrida's mind: an acquaintance of Carrie's come in search of her; a long-time admirer . . .

Carrie turned her head and saw them, and at once rose to her feet. 'Elfrida. We didn't hear you. Did you have a good party?'

'Yes, it was splendid. But you're not meant to be out of bed.'

'I got bored.'

By now the unknown man was also on his feet, waiting to be introduced. Elfrida's first impression of this stranger was one of businesslike formality, in his beautifully cut suit. He was tall and long-legged, with a tanned complexion that accentuated hazel eyes.

'Elfrida, this is Sam Howard. Elfrida Phipps. And Oscar Blundell.'

'How do you do?' They all shook hands.

Sam Howard said, 'I'm really sorry about this intrusion. I'm in your house, unasked—'

Carrie interrupted. 'I'll get some more glasses. What about you, Elfrida? I'm having a glass of wine.'

'I'll join you.' Elfrida suddenly felt tired. She sat on the sofa. 'I've been standing for two hours, eating mince pies and chatting.'

'How about Lucy?'

'She disappeared with the Kennedy children to some other room, and hasn't been seen since. They'd gone to the reeling by the time we left. Just the way it should be.'

'That's good. I'll get more glasses and soda for Oscar.'

She left them. Oscar sat down and they were left with the strange man. Elfrida, smiling in her friendliest fashion, said, 'Now tell us exactly who you are, and why you're here. You must be an old friend of Carrie's.'

'Actually, I'm not.'

He pulled a chair near to Elfrida and began to explain.

Oscar picked up on the name Sturrock & Swinfield at once. 'Peter Kennedy told me about McTaggart's being taken over, but I didn't realise that things were already moving. That's splendid news. Have you been in this business for long?'

'All my life, really. My father owned a small mill in Yorkshire.'

'Does this mean you're going to be living up here?'

Carrie reappeared, bearing glasses and soda. Sam sprang to his feet and went to relieve her of the tray. He poured a whisky and soda for Oscar, wine for Elfrida and topped up Carrie's glass.

'What about you?' Elfrida asked him, but he said he was all right.

He rescued his drink from a table by the fire and returned to his seat.

Carrie said, 'How far have you got?' and curled up in her chair.

Sam Howard continued his story. 'This is all rather personal and very complicated. Just before I came up here, I was staying in London with old friends—Janey and Neil Philip. One evening, an old acquaintance of Janey's parents came for dinner. He was called Hughie McLellan.'

He paused, giving time for this to sink in. Then Oscar spoke. 'My cousin Hughie? But Hughie's in Barbados.'

'He was back in London to see friends and deal with various business matters, I guess.'

'What an extraordinary coincidence.'

'We talked for a bit, and then he learned that I was coming up here, to Buckly. And he asked me where I was going to live. And I said that I'd have to find somewhere. And from his pocket he produced the key to this house. He said he owned half of it, and his cousin the other half. But that he wanted to sell.'

Oscar said, 'Why the hell didn't he get in touch with me? His father, Hector, knew where I was, that I'd come back to Creagan.'

'I don't think he'd seen his father.'

'Well, what a turn-up for the books.' Oscar took an enormous slug of whisky, shattered at the perfidy of his cousin. 'Why did he suddenly decide to sell this place? We've boxed along for so many years, sharing the trickle of rent, I never imagined he'd want to put it on the market. And certainly not without discussing it with me.'

'My guess is that he needs a bit of ready cash.'

'Not surprised. Alimony for three ex-wives must cost a bomb. You knew I shared the ownership?'

'Yes, he told me. I said nothing could possibly be arranged until you had been consulted.'

'So why are you here?'

'He said, as I was coming north, why not have a look at the house? He told me it was empty, that an old couple had been renting it, but the husband had died and the wife had gone elsewhere. I suppose he reckoned a straight sale would save agents' fees.'

'Did he mention a sum?'

'A hundred and fifty thousand.'

'Split down the middle, seventy-five thousand?'

'That's right.'

'Suppose I wanted more?'

'It's negotiable. I'm simply quoting your cousin.'

'I see.' Oscar finished his drink.

Sam said, 'I really have to apologise to you both. And I'll give you Hughie's key and we'll forget the entire business. It's just that I had to tell you the whole story so that you understand.'

Elfrida, who had managed to keep silent, now felt that the time had come to get her word in. 'You've made everything extremely clear, Mr Howard. Are you staying in Buckly?'

'No. At a hotel in Inverness. This afternoon was my first meeting with the work force. I started back to Inverness, and then had this idea that I'd make the diversion to Creagan, come and case the joint, as it were. The house was so obviously lived in that my curiosity was aroused. I was never much good at unsolved mysteries.'

'I see.' Elfrida decided it was all very exciting. She could picture it. The handsome stranger, the ring of the doorbell, and Carrie, going downstairs to open the door and let him in.

She said, 'Carrie, I hope you've asked Sam to stay for dinner.'

A conspiratorial glance passed between Carrie and Sam as though they had an amusing secret to share. What had they been up to?

'Elfrida, Sam rang the AA and the roads to Inverness are blocked with snow. So we have another guest for the night. Do you mind?'

Elfrida said, 'I can't think of anything I would like more.' And could not keep the pleasure out of her voice.

IT WAS NEARLY midnight. Elfrida lay in bed and, beside her, Oscar read his book. She thought back over the events of the evening. She, Oscar, Sam and Carrie had finally sat down to supper in the kitchen at nine o'clock. They were on to coffee when Lucy and Rory Kennedy returned from their dancing.

Lucy had been introduced to Sam and his presence explained, then Rory declined a beer and said it was time he went home. He departed by the back door and Lucy saw him off. She came back, smiling, then the smile was lost in an enormous yawn.

Carrie put out an arm to draw her close. 'You're tired. Go to bed.'

'May I have a bath first?'

'Of course. You had fun?'

Lucy kissed her. 'It was the best.'

While Oscar and Sam sat over coffee, Carrie and Elfrida went upstairs to make up the last spare bed for Sam. They found sheets and pillowcases, a bath towel and an extra blanket.

'What more,' asked Elfrida, 'could any man need?'

'He's got a toothbrush. He told me. And a razor.'

'Jim-jams?'

'He probably sleeps in the buff anyway.'

'And how do you know?'

'Instinct, Elfrida. Feminine instinct.'

Suddenly they were both laughing. Carrie said, 'You're a saint. I had to ask him to stay, but the best was knowing you wouldn't mind.'

'I've always loved a full house. This is a house for parties and people. Oscar and I have been rattling around in it for too long. Now it's full.' She said this in tones of greatest satisfaction. 'Stretched to its limits. A family house. Just the way it should be.'

A family house. Elfrida lay in bed and felt the house around her, like a shield, a refuge. She said, 'Oscar. If Hughie wants to sell his half of this house, couldn't you buy him out, and then it would all be yours? For always.'

'Seventy-five thousand . . . If I sold everything I owned, I might scrape up twenty.'

'You could get a mortgage.'

'Not for that amount. Not at my age. And I've always had a horror of mortgages. I've never had much, but I've never been in debt and I couldn't start now.'

'If I had seventy-five thousand, would that help?'

'If you had seventy-five thousand, it would belong to you. It wouldn't be for bailing me out.'

'I love this house so much. It's so strong, so unpretentious, so adaptable. Can't you feel it, like a heartbeat, keeping us all going, sheltering, taking care of us? You can't lose it, Oscar.'

'I think I am not as fanciful as you.'

She lay silent, carefully framing in her mind what she was going to say. 'Oscar. Listen to me. If I sold my little picture, my David Wilkie, how much do you think that would fetch?'

'That is your treasure, your insurance.'

'If it is worth what I think it is, then we should sell it. Why keep a little picture if you can buy security? I can't bear to think of this darling place going to other people. I want you to have it. I want you to be here.'

Oscar reached for her hand. 'You are the dearest person.'

'We'll talk about it,' she told him, 'in the morning.'

Lucy

It is half past eight in the morning, and I am writing my diary. I should have written it last night, but I was so tired.

It was fabulous. We walked up to the Kennedys' house in the thick snow. Carrie didn't come with us because of her cold. When we got there, other people were there as well. We were all introduced. Then Rory and I left the grown-ups in the sitting room and went into the kitchen. There were three other boys there, friends of Rory's from school, and his sister Clodagh, who is twelve, and very skinny with bright blue eyes and fair pigtails.

We all sat around and drank Coke, and Clodagh was very flirty. We had an enormous macaroni cheese and salads, and then a very rich chocolate cake and ice cream. When that was finished, we walked down the hill to the school gym.

There were lots and lots of children of all ages, from seven up. The headmaster is called Mr McIntosh, but they all call him Waterproof behind his back, and I bet he knows about this. He was quite young and very nice. There was an accordionist, a drummer and a fiddler. There was a terrible din and everybody was larking around and then Mr McIntosh told everybody to be quiet and they were. He said it was time to get started and we were going to do Strip the Willow because it wasn't too difficult for learners (me).

By the end we were all hot and breathless, but we did a reel called Hamilton House, then the Dashing White Sergeant. The time absolutely flew, and it was so strange because, however breathless and hot you felt, as soon as the music struck up again you simply didn't want to stay off the floor.

It all ended at about ten o'clock. Rory walked back to Oscar's house with me, and he came in. A man called Sam Howard was there, and he is going to live up here, and run some woollen mill in Buckly. Very nice-looking and just about the right age for Carrie.

Rory says he is coming today with a television set for my room. Not that I need one, because so many things are happening all the time. The best is knowing that things are going to go on happening. I've never felt like this before. Here there are unexpected treats every day.

Elfrida

As usual, Elfrida was the first downstairs. At the turn of the stairs she threw back the curtains and gazed out at the day. Actually, it was the night because it was still dark, but it had stopped snowing and by the light of the street lamp she could see the garden, all shape and form obliterated. Bushes and trees drooped beneath the weight of snow. It was very still and quiet.

She went on downstairs and into the kitchen. Horace, it seemed, was beginning to recover. He clambered out of his basket and came to greet her, tail waving. She stroked him and they held a small conversation. Then she opened the back door and he stepped out. When he came indoors again his face wore an expression of indignation. He returned to his basket and sulked.

Elfrida laid the table, fried bacon, made coffee. She was drinking her first cup when Sam Howard appeared, still in his sharply cut and formal suit because, of course, he had nothing else with him. Elfrida's first thought was for his comfort. She said, 'I shall lend you a sweater.'

'I clearly look as peculiar as I feel. Overdressed.'

'Not at all, you look very nice, but a bit like a chairman about to make a speech.'

She went upstairs, raided Oscar's chest of drawers and unearthed a blue Shetland jersey. Back in the kitchen, she found Sam in his shirtsleeves, frying his egg. She tossed him the sweater. 'Too cold for shirtsleeves.' He caught it and pulled it on.

'That's much better,' Elfrida told him. 'Now you can relax.'

He flipped the egg onto a plate and added a couple of rashers of bacon. Elfrida put bread into the toaster and then filled his coffee cup. They sat at the table together and it felt companionable.

'I feel so bad about last night,' Sam said.

'Why? It was no trouble. All we did was feed you and make up a bed.'

'I didn't actually mean that, although it was very kind of you. I meant barging in, clutching the key of your house, and saying I'd come to buy it. I lay awake last night hoping I didn't offend Oscar.'

'Oscar's not that sort of a man. For a moment he was a bit cross, but with Hughie, not you.'

'I . . . I suppose Oscar wouldn't think of buying Hughie out?'

'We talked about it last night, but you have to understand, Oscar and I haven't known each other long. At the beginning of November his wife and daughter were killed in a car crash and he had to leave Hampshire. I came with him. I'm simply a sort of spare wheel to keep the car going until he's sorted himself out. So it is difficult for me even to make suggestions.'

'But wouldn't it be sensible for him to buy Hughie out?'

'Yes. Sensible, but not financially possible.'

Sam's presence was so strong and sympathetic that Elfrida went on confiding in him. 'Last night he told me that even if he sold everything he owned he couldn't raise more than twenty thousand. I said, "Oscar, I have my little picture."'

'You are talking about your David Wilkie?'

'Exactly. It was given to me years ago. I've never had it valued, because I've never insured it.'

'Would you sell it?'

'For Oscar, I would do anything. It's given me pleasure for many years, but, surely, to be able to own such a lovely house as this is of more importance.'

'I agree,' said Sam. 'You've no idea how much it's worth?'

'Not really. And this is scarcely the time and the place to start getting it appraised. I wouldn't know where to start.'

Sam was silent for a bit. And then said, 'Janey Philip—who I was staying with in London when I met Hughie—she used to work for Boothby's, the fine art dealers. I could ring her. I'm sure she'd have some bright suggestions.'

'It's a bit close to Christmas to start trying to sell pictures.'

'We don't have to do it right away.'

'And the snow precludes everything. Are you still snowed in with us, Sam? I hope so. But you obviously want to get home.'

'At this moment I haven't got one. Except an apartment in New York, but my wife and I separated.'

'Oh, Sam, I'm sorry. So what will you do for Christmas?'

'I'll stay in Inverness, and then get back to Buckly and start getting the show on the road. I'm giving celebrations a miss this year.'

'You must spend Christmas with us.'

'Elfrida—'

'No, I mean it. I couldn't bear you to be sitting in a hotel lounge wearing a paper hat and being all alone. Oscar and I didn't mean to have Christmas either. We thought we'd go pagan and celebrate the winter solstice with a lamb chop. But then Carrie and Lucy asked themselves and Oscar ordered a Christmas tree and bought some decorations. And I'm just beginning to think about food. I'm useless at this sort of thing. But we could gather a bit of holly, go and shoot a turkey, or whatever one does. And anyway, it's the people who count, isn't it? The friends you spend Christmas with? Don't go. It would be such fun for all of us to be together.'

He said, 'You're the most hospitable, generous person I think I've ever met. But I tell you what I'll do. I'll ring the AA and see what's happening on the roads. If they're clear, then I'll go back to Inverness. I really have a hell of a lot of work to do. If they're still impassable, then I'll accept, with much gratitude, your invitation.'

'Oh, good. I'll pray for blizzards. Do my snow dance.'

'What will Oscar say?'

'He'll say "Splendid", and go and read his newspaper.'

CARRIE WAS THE NEXT to appear. 'Where is everyone? I thought I heard voices.'

'You did. It was Sam. But he's gone to his room to telephone.'

'There's still the most dreadful lot of snow.' Carrie sat down and saw Elfrida had started a shopping list. 'What's this?'

'I was trying to start on Christmas. I *must* pull myself together. I've been procrastinating and now we've only got four days.'

'Why don't you let me take over? I'm a professional organiser. Where can I go and do a mammoth shop?'

'There's a PriceRite supermarket at Kingsferry—if the road's been cleared. When Sam's spoken to the AA, we'll know.'

'Is Sam going back to Inverness?'

'Depends. If he's marooned, then I've asked him to stay. Over the festive season.'

Carrie's face showed no expression. She simply said, 'In that case we'll be five in the house . . .' She drew the list towards her and picked up the pencil. 'Now. Are we going to have a Christmas dinner?'

'Oh yes. Much more festive than lunch. But we'll never get a turkey into that little oven.'

'Then we'll have chickens. Two chickens.'

She wrote furiously. Chickens. Brussels sprouts. Potatoes. Frozen peas. Carrots. Masses of fruit. Butter. French bread. Cranberry sauce. Cinnamon sticks . . . 'And the wine?' she asked.

'Oscar will want to deal with the wine.'

'Smoked salmon, nuts, Christmas cake . . .'

'I'll make the cake. And for Boxing Day a big pot of soup.'

For once, Elfrida felt competent and efficient. Soup was her speciality, chicken stock and any handy vegetable. 'And perhaps buy crisps and dips in case we decide to have a party.'

'A party? Who would we ask?'

'Well . . . the Kennedy family. And the doctor and his wife. And the nice bookshop man and his wife. They were at the Manse yesterday and he and Oscar got on like a house on fire. . . .'

Oscar, on cue, came through the door. 'With whom did I get on like a house on fire?'

'The bookshop man. Oscar, we are going to have a little party. So we shall ask them.'

'When shall we have a little party?'

This had not been decided. Then Carrie said, 'Saturday. Saturday night is party night. The day before Christmas Eve.'

Oscar said, 'I shall have to buy some drink.'

'If the bridge is open, Carrie's going to PriceRite in Kingsferry to do all the shopping. Perhaps you could go with her.'

'Yes, perhaps I could.'

Then Lucy appeared and Elfrida, feeling happier now that plans had been made, left Carrie to feed herself and Oscar. She went into the sitting room, where the detritus of the previous evening stood about, tidied up a bit and was brushing the hearth when, from behind her, she heard Sam speak. 'I'm afraid you've got me for Christmas.'

She turned, then stood up. 'Wonderful.' She made no attempt to keep the satisfaction out of her voice.

'The roads are passable until the Cromarty Bridge, but Inverness is totally snowed up. No traffic in or out.'

'Carrie and Oscar are planning a huge shopping expedition to PriceRite. That's across our bridge. Do you think they'll make it?'

'They'll make it that far, no problem.'

'Have you telephoned your hotel?'

'Yes, and my chairman, David Swinfield. And I've spoken to Janey. There's a Boothby's representative for this part of the world, Sir James Erskine-Earle. He lives at Kingsferry House.'

'Heavens.' Elfrida was much impressed. 'How grand.'

'An appraisal doesn't mean you have to sell. And, whatever, you really should insure it. Shall I give him a ring?'

'Yes. Do that. See what he says.'

He returned to his room where he'd left his mobile and Elfrida stayed where she was, gazing across the room to where her little treasure hung. The old couple sitting at the table with their family Bible, he so sombrely attired, she proud in her red dress and yellow shawl, their faces wise and kind, their stillness emanating dignity. They had seen her through a number of desolate days. She was very fond of them.

But they were not as important as Oscar.

Five minutes later, Sam was back, looking pleased with himself. 'All fixed. He is coming over to Creagan this afternoon for some committee or other. He's going to drop in about four o'clock and cast his eye over your painting. He sounded rather interested.'

Elfrida felt nervous. 'It's rather exciting. Shall I tell Oscar?'

'I would. You don't want to start feeling underhand.'

'No. You're quite right. Thank you, Sam, for your trouble.'

'The least I can do. Now, you said Carrie and Oscar were going over to Kingsferry to shop. Instead, why don't I take her, and then I can help carting everything home?'

Elfrida thought this a marvellous idea, and for more reasons than one. 'How kind you are. Oscar loathes shopping.'

'I have ulterior motives.' Better and better. 'I must buy clothes. I can't go on going round looking like a tailor's dummy.'

Elfrida said brightly, 'Of course,' but felt slightly let down because she had hoped his ulterior motive was getting Carrie to himself.

'And I should like to buy some wine for Oscar . . . perhaps we should have a word.'

'That's a good idea. Oscar has strong opinions about wine.'

Outside, in the brightening morning, the seagulls clamoured. Watching them, Elfrida said to Sam, 'In one way, I should like you to have this house. It has such dignity and solidity, just right for the important head of a company.' She looked at him standing there in Oscar's blue sweater, and it felt as though he had been with them all for ages. 'It is very satisfactory having young people around us again. Oscar and I have both been dreading Christmas—under the circumstances I felt it could be nothing but a sad and bitter time. But now, with you and Lucy and Carrie with us, it *can't* be. There's nothing we can do to stop it happening, so we might as well make it fun. Perhaps it will be like one of those parties one longs not to have to go to that turns out to be one of the most memorable and the best. Do you know what I mean?'

Sam said he knew exactly what she meant.

Lucy

Sam and Carrie departed in Sam's Discovery for Kingsferry and PriceRite, armed with a list that went on for ever. Elfrida had taken Horace for a walk. Oscar was reading by the fire in the sitting room, much relieved he didn't have to go shopping.

So Lucy made her own plans. This morning she would buy Christmas presents. Having her holiday money made things much easier, because she wouldn't have to penny-pinch.

Elfrida, Oscar, Carrie. Now she added Sam. And Rory. And perhaps Clodagh, too; otherwise it might look a bit odd.

She put on her jacket and boots and went downstairs. Christmas, all at once, was becoming real. She went down the long hall, then paused. On an impulse, she opened the door of the disused dining room. It was gloomy and in need of a good dust and polish, but in her imagination she saw it lit by firelight and candles, the table groaning with delicious foods, goblets of wine, and crackers.

An idea took shape, but there wasn't time, right now, to think it through, so she let herself out into the snow and started off down the pavement to do the rounds of the modest shops.

In the jersey shop she unearthed a very long red cashmere scarf, which she knew would look perfect wound round Carrie's elegant neck. In the bookshop she bought wrapping paper, cards and a book for Oscar filled with colour photographs of old Scottish country houses, castles and gardens. For Sam, she got an ordnance survey map of Creagan and the surrounding district, which included Buckly.

The chemist was next. For Clodagh, little hair ornaments that she could clip to the end of her pigtails. For Rory, a big bottle of Badedas. Her father had always used it in his bath. Struck by a brilliant idea, she went into the flower shop. There she ordered, for delivery on Saturday, six Stargazer lilies. They would open slowly, spreading out into pale pink petals, filling the whole house with their heady fragrance.

She set off for home intending, once back, to wrap all her presents. However, as she pushed the front door open, she heard voices from the kitchen. Investigating, she found Elfrida stirring a pot on the cooker, and Rory Kennedy. On the kitchen table stood a television set.

Rory said, 'Hi.' He was wearing a grey fleecy jacket and rubber boots, and looked very masculine,

'Hello. I . . . I thought you'd be working.'

'Not much to do on the golf course in weather like this. So I borrowed Dad's car and brought the set down for you.'

Lucy looked at it. 'It doesn't look old.'

'It's not. It's just that I got myself a bigger one.'

Elfrida said, 'Lucy, you'd better show Rory where it's to go.'

'It's four flights of stairs,' Lucy warned him.

He grinned. 'I think I could just about manage.'

She led the way. At the top she went into her room and Rory followed her and put the television set on the table. He looked appreciatively about him. 'Hey, this is a cool room. And lots of space.'

They found a suitable power socket and Rory plugged in the set and switched it on. He fiddled with the indoor aerial until the picture became quite clear. He switched it off then looked about him. 'At home, in London, do you have a room like this?'

'No. It's not nearly so big. But it's pretty.'

'What's it like, living in a city?'

'It's all right.'

'Must be great, all those museums and concerts and plays. I've only been once, when my dad had to attend some conference.'

'It's different if you live there all the time.'

'Suppose so.' After a bit he asked, 'Are you homesick? Well, you know . . . missing your mother? Your things? Clodagh's hopeless. She won't even go away for a night. Bawls like a baby.'

'No,' Lucy heard her own voice, all at once surprisingly sharp and strong. 'No, I'm *not* homesick. I'm not even thinking about going back to London. I'm simply putting it out of my mind.'

'But . . .'

'You don't understand. My parents divorced and now we live in a flat, me and my mother and my grandmother. It's near the river and it's got a balcony and a nice view, but there's nowhere to *be*. It's not like here. It's not like this house, like your house, full of people and friends your own age coming and going. It's my grandmother's flat, and she doesn't want my friends around the place. She gets headaches, she says.' She stopped, giving Rory an opportunity to comment on this flood of confidence, but he said nothing. Lucy went on. 'It's so different here. You can do anything, you can go to the beach, or exploring, or out at night and nobody stops you. Here, they all treat me as though I were a person, not a child. I'm fourteen now, and sometimes I feel I've done nothing except go to school.'

Rory said, 'How about your father?'

'Mummy doesn't like me seeing him, and anyway he's got a new wife and she doesn't want me around much either. I've got a grandfather called Jeffrey Sutton. He's Carrie's father. But he lives in Cornwall with a second wife. She young and they have two children.'

'Can't you go and stay there?'

'Yes, I could, but Gran's bitter about him, and unforgiving, and his name is scarcely ever mentioned. One day, I'll really be brave and say I want to go and stay.'

'You don't have to wait. You have to do it now.'

'I think,' said Lucy sadly, 'I haven't the nerve.'

Rory said nothing to this and it occurred to Lucy that he was very good at listening, and was clearly sympathetic. She found herself filled with grateful affection.

'I'm sorry. I didn't mean to say all this.' She met his eyes and smiled.

He said, 'Do you want to come sledging this afternoon? We'll go to the golf course—there are some really good slopes.' He glanced at his watch. 'It's nearly twelve. How about you come back home with me and we get my ma to give us some food, and then get hold of the others?'

'But won't your mother—'

'*No*, she won't mind. There'll be enough food. There always is.' He hauled Lucy to her feet. 'Stop being so worried,' he told her. 'Stop putting difficulties in your own way.'

'Is that what I'm doing?'

'Not any more.'

Elfrida

The Kingsferry shopping expedition had been highly successful. Not only had Sam and Carrie brought back with them cardboard boxes stuffed with food, but Sam had kitted himself out with some country clothes including Timberland boots and a Barbour jacket.

After lunch, he and Oscar set off to walk to the golf club, where Sam had made an appointment to talk about becoming a member.

Elfrida, watching them stride side by side down the snowy pavement, thought it was good for Oscar to have a bit of masculine company.

She and Carrie were left to prepare for the arrival, at four o'clock, of Sir James Erskine-Earle.

'Shall I make some scones?' Carrie asked.

Elfrida was impressed. 'Can you?'

'Of course.'

On the table in the bay window of the sitting room, Elfrida laid plates, knives, cups and saucers, the butter dish and the jam jar.

A short while later, Oscar and Sam returned from the golf club in good heart. They had been introduced to the captain, admired portraits and trophies, and then walked home.

When he came, on the dot of four o'clock, Sir James Erskine-Earle was something of a surprise. The front-door bell shrilled and Elfrida ran down to let him in. She was a little taken aback to be faced by a man so young. His mousy hair was cut like a schoolboy's.

'Mrs Phipps?'

'Yes. Sir James. Please come in.' She led him upstairs, 'It is so good of you to come at such short notice.'

'Not at all.' He had a charming voice and an ingenuous smile. 'I always enjoy such occasions when I am asked to cast my eye over something special.'

She led him into the sitting room and introduced him to the others. 'Oscar Blundell. And Carrie, my niece. And Sam Howard, who is coming to run the old woollen mill in Buckly.'

'We spoke on the phone, I think. How splendid to meet you.' He moved over to the window and looked across to where Christmas lights shone like jewels against the old stone face of the church. 'What an outlook.' He turned back to face them all. 'But I mustn't waste your time. Where is this picture you want me to see?'

'It's . . .' Elfrida cleared her throat. 'It's here.'

'May I take it down?'

'But of course.'

He gently lifted it off the wall. 'What a lovely thing. Sir David Wilkie. A portrait of his parents. Painted about 1835.'

'I didn't know it was his parents.'

A silence fell as they waited for his verdict. Sir James Erskine-Earle took his time. He put on a pair of rimless spectacles, turned the painting over and closely inspected the back. Finally, he laid it carefully down. 'How did you come by it, Mrs Phipps?'

'It was a present. A long time ago. From a friend.'

'And do you know where he bought it?'

'I think in a junk shop in Chichester.'

'Yes.' He nodded. 'That figures.'

'I've . . . I've always believed—been led to believe—that it's an original. But I've never had it appraised or insured.'

He looked at her, took his spectacles off and said, 'I am really sorry. It's a most charming and beautifully executed work, but it's not the original. It's a copy.'

Nobody could think of anything to say.

Eventually, Oscar found his voice. 'How can you know?'

'The original passed through Boothby's about a year ago. It was larger than your little painting, Mrs Phipps, which leads me to believe that this copy was never intended as a forgery, but more as a work of respect and admiration. A student, perhaps, wishing to emulate the master's style.'

Elfrida made herself ask the dreaded question. 'What is it worth, Sir James?'

'Please. Jamie.'

'Well—Jamie—what do you think it's worth?'

'A thousand? Maybe more, maybe less, depending on the market.'

Elfrida's insurance against an impoverished and lonely future. Worth only a thousand. In a funny way, for herself, she didn't particularly mind. There was no point in selling it and so she could go on enjoying it for the rest of her life. But all her plans for buying Hughie out, and ensuring Oscar's security, were reduced to dust. For a dreadful moment she thought she might burst into tears. In despair she turned to Carrie.

'I think,' said Carrie, 'that I shall go downstairs and boil a kettle, and we'll all have a restoring cup of tea.'

And then Sam spoke, for the first time since he had been introduced to Jamie Erskine-Earle. 'I'll come with you, lend you a hand.'

Jamie Erskine-Earle said, again, 'I am so sorry.' Carefully, he rehung the picture. 'At least . . . it will continue to give you joy.'

Elfrida went to the fire and, in need of something to do that might assuage her disappointment, took a log from the basket and hurled it onto the flames. She stood, watching it catch and flare up.

And then, behind her, Jamie spoke again. 'I'm sorry, but who is the owner of that interesting little clock?'

Elfrida turned to frown at him in puzzlement. 'The clock?'

Oscar told him, 'It's Elfrida's.'

'It caught my eye. So unusual . . . May I look?'

Elfrida nodded. Jamie Erskine-Earle put his spectacles on again, took the little clock down from the mantelpiece and examined it. 'A travelling chronometer. Marvellous. How did you come by this?'

'It was left to me by an elderly godfather, a seafaring man. You can see, one dial is for hours, one for minutes and one for seconds. I have to wind it every day. I suppose I could get it fitted with a battery—'

'Heaven forbid! It's far too rare.'

'Rare? Surely it's just an old-fashioned clock?'

'Practical. But handsome, too.'

She looked at it in his hands and all at once the clock took on a new lustre. Outside, the leather was worn, but inside it was still rich and dark and the lid, which folded across like the cover of a book, was lined with coral velvet. The key, the hinges, the tiny locks were brass.

She said, 'I don't even know how old it is. Perhaps you can tell me.'

'Alas, I am not a clock expert. But,' he added, 'I have a colleague who is. If you will let me . . . I can show it to him. I think it is special.'

'It wouldn't be worth seventy-five thousand pounds, would it?' she asked bluntly, expecting derisive laughter.

'I really don't know. Mrs Phipps, would you . . . would you let me take it away with me? I shall, of course, give you a receipt for it, and will keep it under lock and key.'

'Of course.'

'If I could have a box . . . or something to wrap it in.'

Oscar unearthed a sheet of bubble wrap that he had salvaged from a parcel of new books. 'Will this do?'

'Perfect.'

Jamie Erskine-Earle sat at Oscar's desk and wrote out his receipt.

Sam

Sam opened his eyes to darkness and bitter cold. It was the cold that had woken him, and he realised that his eiderdown had slipped off the bed. He heaved himself over, reached down for it and dragged it back into place. He looked at his watch. Half past seven in the morning.

His room, by now familiar, lay about him, the corners deep in shadow. He lay there wondering why the house rendered him such satisfaction. It had felt, from that very first embarrassing evening, a bit like coming home. A little like being on board a ship, isolated from the rest of the world but intensely involved with the other passengers. It was as though the house was content to have the spacious rooms filled once more—fires lit, voices calling, footsteps on the stairs.

A good house, and Sam wanted it. That was the problem. Its location was perfect. And it would be a house with a future. His future. He would never have to leave. He would soon be forty and he didn't want to go on moving, buying and selling, starting anew. He wanted to stay here.

But half of it belonged to Oscar Blundell. He liked Oscar enormously and this made nothing easier. And yet he couldn't get rid of the feeling that this solid Victorian town house was where he was destined to spend the rest of his days.

Losing Deborah, returning to London and his new job, the last thing on his mind had been the possibility of another woman coming into his life. But Carrie had been waiting for him, the last link in an extraordinary chain of coincidences. It was Carrie who had opened the door of the Estate House to him. Carrie, with her smooth cap of chestnut hair, her dark, expressive eyes, her slenderness, her long neck. Her voice deep-toned, with an underlying suggestion of laughter. She was totally without artifice. If she had nothing to say, she said nothing. If she spoke or aired an opinion, it was deliberate, considered, intelligent. Her relationship with Elfrida and Lucy was deeply affectionate and caring.

Sam found it impossible to guess what Carrie thought of him. She was totally at ease, in charge of the situation, but at the same time reserved to the point of withdrawal. When they had driven to Kingsferry to do the huge supermarket shop, he had thought that he could break through this barrier, but every time the conversation veered round to Carrie and her private life she had turned the conversation in a different direction. He found himself wondering if she had once been married, but knew that he could never pluck up the nerve to ask. Some time, somewhere along the line, something had gone wrong. And Carrie was not about to confide in Sam.

The less she gave away, the more he longed to know. He wondered if this obsession was the beginning of falling in love with her. Otherwise, why should it matter so much? And what was the point of falling in love with a woman deeply committed to her career and her ill-assorted family, who would never jettison the lot and come to live in the north of Scotland with Sam Howard. Quite apart from the fact that he was still married to Deborah.

The sun drained darkness from the sky. The new day had begun, and Sam was ravenously hungry.

From the kitchen flooded mouth-watering smells of bacon and coffee. He made his way down there and found only Carrie, reading *The Times*. She looked up, and said, 'Good morning.'

This morning she wore a red cashmere sweater and the bright colour rendered her vital, radiant and more attractive than ever. In his present mood of well-being he felt an urge to sweep her up into his arms and embrace her.

She laid the newspaper down and got to her feet. A plate sat on the warmer, covered by another plate. She set it down on the table before him and removed the top plate. He saw bacon, eggs, a sausage and a fried tomato.

He looked at the feast in amazement. 'Who cooked this?'

'I did. I reckoned you'd be hungry.'

He felt touched. 'You are sweet.' He sat and buttered a slice of toast. 'Where is everybody?'

'Around and about. We have to fetch the Christmas tree this morning. Oscar wondered if you would do that in your car—easier to load trees in.'

'We? Are you coming with me? Where . . . ?'

'The Corrydale estate. Oscar's drawn a map. I shall have to come, to be your navigator. Besides, I want to see Corrydale. Oscar says the grounds and the garden used to be amazing, but of course it's different now because it's a hotel. It's closed, so we could have a nose around.'

Sam could think of no better way of spending this fine morning than driving Carrie to Corrydale, collecting the Christmas tree and having a nose around the place. But he only said, 'Right,' and started to eat, because he didn't want Carrie to sense his pleasure and start backing off.

OSCAR'S LITTLE MAP proved to be a meticulous plan of all that lay within the Corrydale boundary wall. A small maze of roads, woodland and a long shoreline. Each estate worker's house had been drawn and named: Billicliffe's house; Rose Miller's house; the gamekeeper's house; Home Farm; the gardener's house. A little way off, along a winding driveway, and standing all on its own, he had drawn Corrydale House. The map reminded Sam of the endpapers of a Winnie-the Pooh book.

The boundary wall appeared on the left-hand side of the road, then the notice: CORRYDALE COUNTRY HOUSE HOTEL.

Sam turned in through the gates, and the formal drive led downhill between an avenue of huge oak trees. They moved on, slowly, past Major Billicliffe's stone house, Rose Miller's snug cottage, a field of sheep, the gamekeeper's cottage, and finally reached the gardener's house. Sam drew up and they climbed out of the car. As they did so, a young man appeared. He wore a deerstalker.

'Charlie Miller?'

'Yes, that's me. You'll be Sam Howard.'

Leaning against an aged Ferguson tractor was a cut tree.

'Oscar phoned. He said six foot would be tall enough, so I picked this one out. It's a good shape and no broken branches.'

'Looks fine to me.'

'Two pounds a foot. Twelve pounds. And a stand. Two fifty. That's fourteen fifty you owe me.' He was obviously not a man to beat about the bush. Sam dug out his wallet.

Carrie now spoke. 'Charlie, we've never been to Corrydale before, and we wanted to look around, see the house. But if it's private, or we're not allowed. . . .'

'Go anywhere you please. The hotel is closed anyway. While you're walking I'll net the tree and load it.'

'Thank you.'

'No trouble. Have a good walk, now.'

THEY SET OFF, footsteps scrunching on frozen ruts, the air sweet as chilled wine, the thin sunshine warming their backs and causing flurries of melted snow to drift down from the trees.

Carrie said, 'There must once have been a lot of money. This is a huge establishment. Yet Oscar doesn't seem to have anything.'

'No. I don't think he does have much.'

'What's happened to it all? Why didn't Oscar inherit? He would have made a lovely laird.'

'Hughie was the son of the eldest son. Primogeniture.'

'Oscar deserves better. He and Elfrida. They deserve some place to live together that they can call their own. I would like to be rich so that I could take care of them both.'

For a bit they fell silent, trudging through the snow. To their left, snowfields swept down to the water of the loch, and on their right a small wood of ancient beeches revealed dells and paths between the massive tree trunks.

Carrie said abruptly, 'I would like to see your mill.'

Sam had never imagined her being interested. '*Would* you?'

'You told me it was a beautiful building. Shall we go one day?'

'If you want.'

'I like seeing buildings and houses stripped down. Empty places, bare walls. I like imagining how they were, what they could become. You must feel excited about it all, getting it going again.'

'Yes. It's a daunting prospect. But difficulties can be stimulating. And in Buckly, I have a good man, Fergus Skinner, on my side.'

'It's still a long stride from working in New York.'

'Yes, but, you see, I was born and bred into the woollen trade and I secretly believe that there is nothing so good-looking, so comfortable and so exactly right as a well-tailored tweed jacket. It'll stand up to anything the elements choose to hurl at it and, of an evening, be perfectly acceptable at a dinner table. I love the smell and the feel of tweed. I love the sound of well-tuned cog-wheels, the clack of looms, the monstrous pistons of the carding machines. And I like the people who work them. So, I am in my own world.'

'I think you're fortunate. Coming to live up here, in this enormous, clean, unsullied place.'

Ahead they could see the wall of the formal garden. The path led to a wrought-iron gate flanked by gate posts bearing stone armorial lions and entwined by thorny roses. They paused, gazing through the lattice of intricate curlicues, at the lawns beyond, climbing in stepped terraces towards Corrydale House. It was a Victorian mansion, gabled and turreted, built of red stone, some of which was smothered in Virginia creeper.

'Nice,' said Carrie, after a bit. 'Oscar must have had good times.'

'Would you like to live here?'

'Do you mean in this house? In this place?'

'No. I just mean here. In Creagan. In Sutherland.'

'I have a job. In London. I have to earn my living.'

'Supposing you didn't? Would you be content? Could you bury yourself in such an environment?'

'I don't know. To leave London, I'd need to be free. No commitments. No responsibilities.'

'Aren't you free?'

'There's Lucy.'

'Lucy?'

'Yes, Lucy.' She unlatched the gate and opened it. Beyond was a wide path leading across the garden towards a stand of beech trees. In the middle of the path, in line with the flights of steps that climbed the terraces to the house, stood a sundial and wooden seat.

'Lucy is the main reason for taking this London job. Somebody has to winkle her out of that dull, enclosed, totally female life she's forced to lead.'

Sam considered this. He said, tentatively, 'She seems to me to be quite well-adjusted. Happy, even.'

'That's because she *is* happy. Here. With Elfrida and Oscar and people coming and going. And, of course, Rory Kennedy. Going back to London is going to be a real let-down.'

Sam found himself resenting this maiden-aunt attitude. Carrie was too young, too beautiful, to start structuring her life simply for the sake of one niece. 'So, what will you do with Lucy?'

'Oh, I don't know. Just be around, on the end of the telephone. *There*. Perhaps at Easter I'll take her away again. To Cornwall to stay with her grandfather. Or maybe we could go skiing.'

'Will you go back to Oberbeuren?'

'No.' She had said the word almost before he had finished asking the question. 'Not Oberbeuren. Somewhere else.'

'You could go to the States. Colorado or Vermont. Sounds a long way to travel, but it would certainly be cheaper.'

Carrie strolled beside him. 'Have you skied in Vermont?'

'Yes. A number of times. We used to drive up for weekends.'

'We,' Carrie repeated. 'You and your wife, you mean?'

So this was it. The nub around which they had both been circling, the moment of truth. He said, 'Yes, with my wife, Deborah. We're separated now.'

'Elfrida told me. Did you have children?'

'No. She didn't want babies. Not so soon. Some day, perhaps, she promised me. Anyway, last summer, she met this guy. I never guessed. I never knew until she told me she was leaving. I was devastated.'

'Are you still in love with her?'

'Oh, Carrie . . .'

'If you've been married to a person, they're part of you. You can never be free. You belong to them.'

She spoke with such bitterness that Sam all at once knew that he only had to push a bit further and the closed door which had stood between them would finally open. He turned to her. 'Carrie . . .'

But she strode on, and he had to catch her up and take her by the arm and jerk her round to face him. He saw that her dark eyes were shining with tears. 'Carrie. Tell me.'

'Why?' She was angry, blinking the tears away. 'It's not worth talking about. And you wouldn't understand.'

'I could try. And I think I would understand. I've been through bad times myself. Trying to come to terms with a total rejection.'

'I wasn't rejected,' Carrie shouted at him, and all at once she was in floods of tears. Furious with herself, she pushed at him, trying to escape from his grip, but he held her shoulders and would not let go. 'I wasn't rejected. I was loved. We were in love, and all we wanted was to be together. But the odds were too great. Too many demands, responsibilities, traditions. His job, his family, his wife, his children. I didn't stand a chance. And finally, when Andreas walked away from me, I went to bits. So now you know, Sam. And perhaps you can accept the fact that I'm really not very interested in married men.'

He opened his mouth to protest, but at that moment, with a wrench of her body, she slid out of his hold and set off at a run, stumbling in the snow. He went after her, and caught her once more. 'Carrie . . .' and this time she did not fight him. He took her into his arms and she leaned against him, her shoulders heaving, weeping into the front of his Barbour.

Holding her, having her in his arms, was something he had been wanting to do all day. She felt slender, weightless, and he told himself that he could feel the beating of her heart through all their layers of winter clothing. The fur of her hat tickled his cheek and her skin smelt sweet and cool.

'Oh, Carrie.' It was shameful to feel so elated when she suffered from such desolation and wretchedness. Trying to comfort her, he said, 'It will be all right.'

'It *won't* be all right.'

So cold, so adamant was her voice, that he realised it was hopeless to continue mouthing platitudes. Standing there, with his arms about her, Sam found himself confused and disorientated. Carrie was beautiful, intelligent and desirable, but also complicated. To truly understand her was going to take patience and a lot of time.

He accepted this. He said again, 'It will be all right.'

'You don't know.'

He had the good sense not to argue. After a bit, her furious weeping calmed down. She made motions as though to pull herself together. Gently, Sam put her away from him, and watched as she wiped at tear-stained cheeks with her padded glove.

He said, 'I'm sorry.'

'What for?'

'Because this wasn't what I had planned. I didn't mean to upset you so. This was simply an outing, to pick up a Christmas tree and go for a walk. No ulterior motives. It just went wrong.'

'Not your fault. Let's forget it. Pretend it never happened. Walk on, the way we'd planned.'

'We did talk. To talk is always good. I thought we never would.'

'Is talking so good? I'm not so sure.'

'Clears the air. Makes things easier to understand.'

'I don't know that I want to be understood. Just left alone. Perhaps right now I'm better off not belonging to any person.'

Sam thought, Don't be too sure about that, but did not say it aloud.

Lucy

This morning Carrie and Sam went and got the Christmas tree, and I spring-cleaned the dining room and found four silver candlesticks, tarnished but very handsome after I cleaned them. Then I went out and bought some candles, tall and cream, a bit like church candles.

I didn't want anybody to know about it, so that it would be a surprise, but just before lunch Carrie and Sam got back with the Christmas tree, and there was a great discussion as to where we should put it. So then I had to admit about the dining room, and they all trooped downstairs, to inspect what I had been doing, and it was lovely because everybody was thrilled, and it all smelt polishy, and Elfrida said she had no idea the dining room could ever look so festive. And, of course, that was exactly the right place for the tree. So Sam brought it in.

In the afternoon, we tied the decorations on the tree, and Sam fixed the lights and the star on the top branch. And Elfrida produced a whole roll of tartan ribbon so we made lovely bows and put them all over the tree, and with the tinsel and the lights turned on, it is the prettiest I think I've ever seen.

Tomorrow we have to get started on the party. I shall wear my new black miniskirt and my black tights and my new white sweater.

Oscar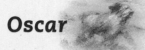

'Oscar. I am about to leave you on your own.'

Oscar, settled by the fire, looked up from the newspaper. 'For ever?'

'No. For about half an hour. I'm going up to the Manse to borrow some extra glasses for our party.'

Elfrida had not been gone for ten minutes when the telephone rang. Heaving himself out of his chair, Oscar went to answer.

'Estate House.'

'I wonder, is Mr Blundell there?' A female voice, very Scottish.

'Speaking.'

'Oh, Mr Blundell, this is Sister Thomson from the Royal Western in Inverness. I'm afraid it's sad news. Major Billicliffe died early this morning. I have your name as his next of kin.'

Old Billicliffe. Dead. Oscar found himself struggling to think of something to say. All he could come up with was, 'I see.'

'It was all very peaceful. He had a quiet end.'

'Thank you very much for letting me know.'

'There are personal possessions you'll want to collect. And any other arrangements . . .' Sister tactfully did not finish her sentence. But Oscar knew exactly what she was driving at.

He said, 'Of course. Thank you. I'll be in touch.'

All at once he needed to sit down. Billicliffe was dead, and he was not only his next of kin, but his executor. He pondered for a bit as to what he should do next. The lawyer. Oscar had made a note of the lawyer's name. He found his diary in the sitting room. He turned the pages. Murdo McKenzie. It occurred to him that only Billicliffe would have a lawyer with such an outlandish name. Murdo McKenzie, McKenzie & Stout, South Street, Inverness. He looked up the firm in the telephone book, then punched in the number.

There will have to be a funeral, he thought. A church. People will have to be told. I must tell Peter Kennedy. And an announcement in the newspaper. Just a few lines.

'McKenzie and Stout.'

'Oh, good morning. Could I speak to Mr Murdo McKenzie?'

'Who shall I say is calling?'

'Oscar Blundell. From Creagan.'

'Hold on a moment, please.'

Murdo McKenzie came on the line almost at once. 'Mr Blundell. Good morning. What can I do for you?'

'Good morning. I'm sorry to bother you, but I've just heard that Major Billicliffe died this morning.'

'Oh, that's sad news. I am sorry.'

'Major Billicliffe asked me to be his executor.'

'He told me you had agreed to take the duty on.'

'I suppose there will have to be a funeral, but where, when and how? He has friends in Creagan who will certainly want to be there, but as far as I know the roads are still impassable and there's no hope of anybody getting to Inverness.. An undertaker will have to be approached, of course, and the bank notified, and the registrar—'

Murdo McKenzie smoothly intervened. 'Mr Blundell, why don't you leave all this to me? Major Billicliffe wished to be cremated, so that precludes many headaches. There's an excellent undertaker in Inverness I know well. I can make the necessary arrangements.'

'That's enormously kind of you. And all the other details, probate and the bank and such. Freezing his account . . .'

'We'll deal with those details.'

'And his personal possessions.' Oscar thought of Billicliffe's battered leather suitcase. He felt a ridiculous lump grow in his throat. 'They will have to be collected from the hospital.'

'I'll telephone and have a word with the ward sister.'

'I really can't thank you enough. You've taken a great weight off my shoulders.'

'I know that Major Billicliffe did not want you to be inconvenienced. If any problems should arise, I'll give you a ring.'

'It is more than good of you. Now, I'll waste no more of—'

'Mr Blundell! Don't ring off. I shall be writing to you, but as we're talking now, perhaps I should put you in the picture.'

Oscar frowned. 'Sorry, I don't understand.'

'Once he was settled in hospital, Major Billicliffe wanted to see me. I called in early last Monday morning. He was very frail, but perfectly lucid. He wished to make a new will. You are his sole beneficiary, Mr Blundell. He wants you to have his house at Corrydale and his dog. He had, as well, a few savings, which, once all bills have been settled, should come to about two thousand five hundred pounds.'

Oscar could not think of a thing to say.

'Major Billicliffe was anxious that you should know how much he appreciated your kindness to him.'

Oscar said, 'I wasn't kind.' But the lawyer ignored this.

'I don't know if you know the house?'

'I knew it in the old days, when it was the forester's cottage.'

'I did the conveyancing when Major Billicliffe bought it from the estate. It is quite a modest establishment, but I would say it has distinct possibilities. I'll put it all in a letter to you, and then you can decide what you do next.'

'Thank you so very much.'

'A pleasure, Mr Blundell. Goodbye. Have a good Christmas.'

Slowly Oscar replaced the receiver. He thought for a long time about the little house on the Corrydale estate. Years ago, when the head forester and his wife had lived there, it had been a hive of activity, with four children underfoot, three dogs, and strings of washing flapping on the line. There was always a welcome for a small boy and a plate of hot drop scones dripping in butter.

Now, it belonged to him.

The front door opened. 'Oscar!' Elfrida, returned. 'Can you come and help me?' He went out to greet her. 'I've got two huge boxes in the back of the car—'

'We'll bring them in later. I have something to tell you.'

Her eyes went wide. 'Oscar, you're looking quite flushed and excited. What *has* been going on?'

They went through to the kitchen and sat at the table. 'If I tell you, quite slowly, because it's rather complicated, will you listen and not ask questions until I've got to the end?'

'I'll try.'

'Right. The first thing is that Major Billicliffe died this morning. I had a phone call from the hospital.'

Elfrida put her hand over her mouth. 'Oh, Oscar.'

'I know. We never got to see him but he was surrounded by kindly nurses and people all the time. Not nearly so alone as he's been since his wife died.'

'I suppose so.' Elfrida sighed.

He told her about telephoning the lawyer, Murdo McKenzie, and having all responsibility removed from his shoulders.

'But that's not the end. Billicliffe wrote a new will. He has left me his house, his dog and two thousand five hundred pounds.'

'His house? He's left you his house? How terribly touching. Did he really have no other family?'

'Nobody.'

'Poor, lonely man. Oh, Oscar, and we were so horrid about him.'

'Don't remind me.'

'What will you do with the house?'

'I don't know. I haven't had time to think. Sell it, I suppose.'

'What's it like?'

'You know. You saw it. A tip.'

'No, I mean, how many rooms?'

'I suppose, in estate agent jargon, you'd say two up, two down, kitchen and bathroom probably added on after the war.'

Elfrida was silent for a moment, and then, astonishingly, she said, 'Why don't you go and live there?'

Oscar stared at her in disbelief. 'Live there? All on my own?'

'No, stupid, I'll come with you.'

'But you thought the house was horrible.'

'There's no such thing as a place that cannot be improved, enlarged, redecorated.'

'But I have a house. I have this house.'

'Only half. You could sell your half and then you'd have seventy-five thousand pounds and you could spend that on Major Billicliffe's house and live happily ever after.'

'You mean, sell up here?'

'Oh, Oscar, don't sound so horrified. It's really quite a good idea. Sam Howard wants it, and Hughie McLellan is obviously agog to get rid of his half. I know you love it here, and I do too, but when Sam and Carrie and Lucy have gone, we're going to be rattling around like a pair of peas in a drum. I think of *here* as a family house. It should have young people, and children . . .'

'Sam hasn't got any children.'

'No, but he's bound to get married again . . .' Elfrida did not finish her sentence. In the silence which followed, with some reluctance she looked Oscar in the eye.

'Not Carrie. You mustn't matchmake.'

'It's impossible not to. They're so perfect together.'

'They're not perfect at all. He never stops being amiable and Carrie is remote and prickly as a gorse bush. All that's happened is that they have been flung together by circumstances.'

'Maybe so.' Elfrida sighed. 'But even discounting Carrie, this is exactly the right establishment for a man like Sam Howard, for the manager of the resuscitated woollen mill, an important member of the community. And Sam really wants this house. I think he feels *right* here, he feels at home.'

'Elfrida, I am not a man of means. If I did sell the Estate House, that money would have to be squirrelled away for old age. I couldn't be mad enough to sink that money into Major Billicliffe's cottage and leave myself with nothing put by.'

'We don't know how much we'd have to spend . . . Supposing I sell my house in Hampshire, and we use *that* money for—'

'No. It's about all you own, and you must not sell it. Rent it out if you can, but you must never sell.'

'Oh, well.' She became resigned and Oscar felt a brute. 'It was a good idea while it lasted, but I suppose you're right.' Then she perked up again. 'Whatever, we must inspect it from attic to cellar. What shall we do with the dog?'

'Perhaps I can bribe Charlie Miller to keep the dog.'

On the landing above, the telephone began to ring. Elfrida pulled herself to her feet and ran upstairs.

OSCAR SAT ON, waiting patiently for her return, mulling over her wild ideas, and wishing he could go along with them. They would certainly go and look at Billicliffe's house. But still, it would be a poky, dark place in which to live after the spacious grandeur of the Estate House. He would miss, unbearably, the airy, sunny rooms, the sense of space. It would be painful to sell up, even to a friend like Sam.

When Elfrida came downstairs, he had never seen her eyes so bright, never seen her look so young.

'Oscar.' She put her arms around him and pressed her cheek against his own. 'Something simply, utterly wonderful has happened.' She took his hand and sat, once more, facing him across the kitchen table.

'That was Jamie Erskine-Earle. About my little clock. You know he said he was going to show it to a colleague at Boothby's? Well, the colleague is in London, and in this weather there was no way Jamie could get it south. But he sent him a fax, a detailed description and some photographs, and the colleague telephoned back this morning.

He said the clock was a very rare timepiece. French, made by one J. F. Houriet, about 1830. Its official description is a silver chronometer tourbillion. Just imagine, Oscar, all these years I've owned a tourbillion, and never had the faintest suspicion. So I asked what it was worth, and he said at auction . . . possibly . . . Guess, Oscar!'

'Impossible. Put me out of my misery. Tell me.'

'Seventy to eighty thousand pounds!' Elfrida shouted gleefully.

'I have misheard you. It can't be true.'

'You haven't misheard me and it is true. Don't you see? With that money we can really transform Billicliffe Villa into the most desirable of residences. Build a conservatory—'

'Elfrida, that money, if you sell the clock, belongs to you.'

'Oscar, it belongs to *us*. And we'll end our days in a charming little cottage. We shall have Rose Miller for a neighbour, and a four-star country-house hotel in the garden. Who could ask for more? It's so exciting. Isn't it tremendously, wonderfully exciting?'

'But, dear girl, we must be practical. We must be sensible.'

'I hate being sensible. I want to go out and dance in the street. Shout our good news from the rooftops.'

Oscar considered this, as though it were a perfectly viable suggestion. And then he said, 'Not until I've had a chance to get Sam on his own, and explain the situation. He must know we are thinking about selling up here. I am certain that he will want first refusal.'

'Yes. You're right. When will you tell him?'

'I shall take him down to the pub this evening.'

'What if Billicliffe's house proves to be a total disaster?'

'Then we shall have to think again.'

'I can't wait to go and look at it. You and I. But we can't go tomorrow because of getting ready for the party.'

'Sunday?'

'Christmas Eve! As good a day as any.'

'All right. We'll go on Sunday morning. Perhaps we should ask Sam to drive us. We'll all go. Carrie and Lucy as well. I'm sure Sam will be wonderfully practical. He'll talk about things like soffits and rap walls, and be knowledgeable about rising damp. I've had another brilliant idea. If we went to Corrydale in the morning, we could take a winter picnic. Oscar, have we got a key for Major Billicliffe's house?'

'Rose Miller will have a key, or know some person who has. I have to ring her anyway, to let her know that the old boy has died. And I must call Peter Kennedy.'

Carrie

They drove to Buckly to view the woollen mill that was to be Sam Howard's future. McTaggart's of Buckly.

It stood on the outskirts of the small town, set back from the main road behind a stone wall and an imposing wrought-iron gateway.

The gate stood open and the snow beyond was unmarked by footprints or tyre tracks. They were, it was clear, the first and only visitors of the day. The main building was impressive and good-looking, built of local stone and pleasingly symmetrical. A central pediment was topped by a clock tower. Beneath this was an important double door, over which arched an elegant glass fanlight.

Sam drew up in front of the big door, and they stepped down into the snow. After a bit he asked, 'What do you think?'

'It's very handsome.'

'I told you. No question of bulldozing the lot and starting anew.'

Carrie said, 'It all looks in such good order. Hard to believe it suffered a fatal flood.'

'Well, brace yourself. You're in for a shock.'

He fitted a key into the brass lock, turned it, and pushed the door open. Carrie went past him and into a square, high-ceilinged reception hallway. And devastation.

The high-tide mark of the flood water reached to nearly five feet and the floor was much damaged: old planks rotted and broken, gaping holes revealing the dark cavities of deep foundations.

A door at the back of the hallway led into a big, stone-floored space, glass-roofed for light. It was empty, echoing and piercingly cold.

'This was a weaving shed. They salvaged what they could—the spinning frames—but financially the worst disaster was the ruin of all the finished goods, orders worth thousands, packed and ready for delivery. It was that loss, really, that finally finished off McTaggart's.'

'What happened the next day? The work force?'

'All laid off. No alternative. But as soon as the waters subsided, about a hundred men turned up to save what they could. Some of the older, less sophisticated machinery did survive. The engineers stripped down the carding machine and cleaned it off before the rust set in.'

Carrie, fascinated and attentive, was nevertheless starting to feel tremendously cold. She shivered. Sam saw this and was remorseful.

'Carrie, I'm sorry. Do you want to go?'

'No. I want you to show it *all* to me, and tell me what you're going to do. It's mind-boggling. Like being given charge of a totally impossible task. And being the guy in charge.'

'Yes, but with the resources of a huge conglomerate behind me. That makes a hell of a difference.'

'Even so. They chose *you* to take on the job. I wonder why?'

Sam grinned, and all at once looked not simply boyish but bursting with eager confidence. He knew what he was talking about. He was on his home ground. 'I suppose because, basically, I'm a Yorkshire boy. And where there's muck, there's brass. Now, come, before you freeze, and I'll show you the rest.'

By THE TIME the tour was finished, and they stepped once more into the outdoors, Carrie was chilled to the bone.

Sam looked at his watch. 'It's half past eleven. Would you like a heartening drink? A Whisky Mac?'

'Coffee would do the trick.'

So they drove into Buckly and Sam drew up outside a gloomy-looking establishment called the Duke's Arms.

Inside, a coal fire glowed and flickered in the old-fashioned hearth and over the mantelpiece hung an enormous fish in a glass case. There seemed to be only two other customers, both of them silent, male, and very old.

'Come on,' Sam said. 'Sit here, close to the fire.' He pulled a chair away from a table. 'Would you try a Whisky Mac? It's the most warming drink in the world.'

It sounded more tempting than coffee. 'All right.'

Sam went over to the bar, and he and the barman fell into conversation, their voices low.

Carrie watched them as she pulled off her gloves and fur hat and laid them on the chair beside her. She thought that this morning she had seen, for the first time, the other side of Sam. Back in his own world, he was no longer the amiable house guest of the last few days, but a man in charge, a man to be reckoned with.

He returned to her, bearing their drinks. 'Sorry. Conversation.'

'What were you talking about?'

'Football. Fishing. The weather. There's a thaw on the way. And the road to Inverness is open again.'

'Does that mean you're going to disappear instantly?'

'No.' He shook his head. 'I've been asked for Christmas, so I'm staying. Anyway, I've nowhere else to go. But on Boxing Day, I must come down to earth with a bang, pack my bags and leave. I have to be in London next week. David Swinfield's set up a meeting.'

'Lucy and I go on the third. We're on the morning flight.' She bit her lip, thinking about this. 'I'm not looking forward to it. I think Lucy is going to be desolate, going back to that dull flat and a mother who won't be particularly delighted to see her.'

'I shall buy her a splendid Christmas present.'

Carrie was amused. 'Have you still not done your shopping?'

'I shall go to Kingsferry tomorrow morning and get the lot.'

He fell silent. The quiet lay between them, and felt comfortable

'I sympathise with Lucy,' he said. 'I decided the other morning that life at the Estate House is a bit like being on a cruise, marvellously removed from all the stresses and strains of everyday life. I could happily jog along, in low gear, for weeks. Achieving nothing.'

Carrie reached for her glass, took a mouthful of her fiery, reviving drink. 'I suppose it's all been a bit of a waste of time for you.'

He frowned. 'A waste of time? Never a waste of time.'

Carrie looked into Sam's face. *Never a waste of time* . . . And an extraordinary thing happened, because all at once it was as though she had never truly seen him before, and now all she knew for certain was that her recognition of him was too late, because he would go away and it would be all over, and she would probably never see him again.

Suddenly she felt dangerously emotional and quite unsure of herself. Yesterday, at Corrydale, after her outburst of words and her angry weeping, Sam had taken her in his arms and held her until the tears ceased. And she had felt no warmth for him, no physical reaction to his closeness. Only a grudging gratitude for his comfort, and shame for herself for behaving like a fool.

But now . . . the beginning of recovery, perhaps. The melting of the coldness that had been her only armour. To love. To be loved again . . .

'Carrie. Can we talk?'

'What about?'

'You and me. Us.' Carrie said nothing, so he went on, 'It seems to me that we've met each other at a bad time. Neither of us is free. You've taken on the moral responsibility for Lucy and I'm still married to Deborah. Perhaps we both need a bit of space to get our houses in order.'

He watched for her reaction, and his expression was both anxious and serious. Carrie's response was clearly of great importance to him.

'What are you telling me, Sam?'

'Just that perhaps we should give ourselves a bit of time. You have to get on top of your new job in London. I shall get in touch with Deborah's lawyer. I don't know how long it will take . . . I have to sort out the past before I can embark on a new future. Then I'll be living and working here in Buckly. You'll be in London. We'll be hundreds of miles apart. But I shall be flying up and down to London like a yo-yo for meetings and such. I thought perhaps . . . we could see each other again. Go to a concert; out to dinner. Start over. Afresh. As though none of this time had ever happened.'

Start over. Afresh. The two of them. Carrie said, '*I* wouldn't want this time not to have happened.'

'I'm glad. It's been extraordinary hasn't it? Magic. Like days stolen from another life, another world. When it is over, how shall I find you in London?'

'The travel company I work for is in the phone book. I'll give you details and you can always get me there.'

'No promises. No commitments.'

'No promises.'

'So we leave it like that?'

'We leave it like that.'

Sam said, 'Good.' And, as though he were sealing their agreement, he covered her hand with his own. The two old men, heads sunk into the collars of their overcoats, sat on, ancient and silent as a pair of hibernating tortoises, unaware that, as they whiled away the last of the morning, the whole world had changed.

Elfrida's Party

By half past five that evening, the Estate House stood ready for Elfrida's party. The front door wore a wreath of holly, and guests, once through the door, would see the dining-room Christmas tree revealed in all its glory, lit up and standing knee-deep in packages. At the far end of the hall the staircase rose, entangled with holly and ivy and sparkling with white fairy lights.

Above, the landing had been turned into a bar, where the big table from the sitting-room bay window was spread with a white cloth. On it bottles and rows of polished glasses were neatly set out.

From behind closed doors came sounds of running taps, the buzz of electric razors and the steamy fragrance of bath oil.

Oscar was the first to emerge. He closed the bedroom door behind him and stood alone, for a moment, to savour the Christmas transformation of his house, prepared and ready for an influx of guests. He saw the green and gold of champagne bottles jammed into a bucket of ice, the crisp white linen tablecloth. The stairwell entwined with dark ropes of greenery, red-berried holly and starry lights. So much, he thought wryly, for the bleak winter solstice, which was all he had promised Elfrida. And he decided that the Estate House, normally so minimal and austere, but now dressed and adorned to the nines, was a bit like a strait-laced, elderly but much-loved aunt, who had put on her best finery and precious jewels for some special occasion, and ended up looking not bad at all.

Oscar, too, had made an effort, and wore a favourite old smoking jacket and his best silk shirt. Elfrida, whom he had left at her mirror, had insisted he wore his gold-embroidered black velvet slippers.

As he had bathed and dressed, Oscar had not allowed himself to think back to his last Christmas at the Grange. But now, in a moment of solitude, he did. He thought of Francesca, running down the great staircase wearing a black velvet dress, and with her hair flying loose. She had always seemed to be running, as though time were so precious that there was not a moment of it to be wasted.

Only a short while ago this memory would have shattered him with grief. But now Oscar simply felt grateful, because Francesca would always be part of his life, part of his being. And because, after all that had happened, he had somehow survived. And, more, found himself surrounded and sustained by friends.

The sitting room looked warm and welcoming. Every lamp had been turned on and Elfrida had filled jugs with holly and white chrysanthemums, but the best was the huge vase of Stargazer lilies that little Lucy had given Elfrida for Christmas. Elfrida had nearly burst into tears, so touched and delighted had she been.

ELFRIDA, with the final eyelash tweaked into place, gazed at her reflection in the long mirror of the wardrobe. She had put on black silk trousers and a filmy little black blouse, over which she wore a loose green silk coat. Dangling earrings and long strings of beads were the same jade green as the coat, her eyelids were blue, her mouth scarlet, and her hair a blaze of flame.

She went to join the others. They all looked wonderfully sophisticated and glamorous. Lucy had somehow put her hair up, and with her long black legs and her elegant neck, looked about seventeen. As for Carrie, she was ravishingly beautiful with a glow to her skin and a shine in her dark eyes that Elfrida had not seen for years. She had put on a sleeveless black dress, simple as a T-shirt, but with a skirt that flowed softly from her slender hips to her ankles.

Seeing her, Elfrida could not imagine how any man could stop himself falling in love with her. Elfrida wanted above all else for Carrie to be happy again, but Oscar was right. This was too early for matchmaking. One just had to be content that Sam and Carrie seemed, at last, to have made friends.

They were all talking, but Oscar, standing by the fireplace, saw Elfrida as she came through the door. Their eyes met, and for an instant it was as though it were just the two of them, alone in the brilliantly lit room. He came across to take her hand.

'You look *quite* wonderful,' he told her.

'*I* thought I looked a bit like a battered old actress. Which of course I am. But a happy one.' She kissed his cheek cautiously, so as not to leave a smudge of lipstick. 'And you, Oscar?' They understood each other very well. 'All right?'

He nodded.

Downstairs, the doorbell rang.

Elfrida's party, at last, was on its way.

A QUARTER PAST EIGHT and it was all over. Only the Kennedys lingered, and that was because they had been late arriving, coming to the Estate House from a party at the old people's home.

Now a certain languor prevailed. Sam had built up the fire, and all had collapsed into chairs. Rory and Lucy were down in the kitchen doing the last of the clearing up.

Elfrida sank gratefully into cushions and said, 'I can't believe it's gone so quickly.'

'That's the sign of a good party,' said Peter. He looked at his watch. 'Tabitha, my love, we should be on our way.'

'Oh, don't go,' Elfrida begged, 'unless you have to. This is the best bit of a party. Talking it all over with the last of the friends. Stay, and we'll have kitchen supper. We've got some soup, and there's more smoked salmon and a delicious Stilton.'

'Are you sure?' Tabitha was clearly tempted.

'Of course you must stay.'

Carrie took over. 'In that case, *I* shall be in charge.' She got up from the sofa. 'I'll go and see what's happening in the kitchen and find something for us all to eat. No, Sam. You stay and chat.'

As Carrie went out of the room, the telephone began to ring. She picked up the receiver. 'Hello.'

'Who's that?' The female voice was clear as a bell, but there was a tiny hiccup of hesitation on the line.

'It's Carrie.'

'Carrie. It's Nicola. From Florida.'

'For heaven's sake. How are you?'

'I'm great. Fine. What are you doing?'

'Just had a party. We're all sitting around recovering.'

'Is Lucy there?'

'Yes. She's been having the time of her life. She's in the kitchen helping with the clearing up. I'll go and find her.'

Carrie laid the receiver on the table and went downstairs, where she found Rory leaning against the sink and Lucy sitting on the kitchen table, their work accomplished.

'Lucy, your mother's on the telephone,' Carrie said.

Lucy's head jerked round. 'Mummy?'

'Yes. From Florida. Go quickly, because it costs a bomb.'

Lucy looked at Rory, slipped down from the table and went out of the kitchen and up the stairs.

Carrie said, 'Elfrida's asked you and your parents for supper.'

Rory asked, 'Do you want me to help?'

'I think you've already done your share.'

'I don't mind. What would you like done?'

'Well, if you really mean it, could you get the smoked salmon from the fridge in the scullery? I think it's all sliced. You could maybe put it on a plate, and then we'll have to butter some bread.'

In the scullery Carrie found an enormous pot filled with Elfrida's latest brew of soup. She lit the gas ring on the cooker and put the pot on top of it to heat through slowly.

Behind her, Rory said, 'Lucy talked to me.'

Carrie turned. 'Sorry?'

'Lucy. She talked to me about London and everything. About not really wanting to go back. Couldn't she go to a boarding school?'

'Perhaps she should, Rory. But, you see, I am simply a maiden aunt. I don't dare make too many controversial suggestions in case I'm cast out into the wilderness as well.' She thought about this. 'And her school is good. She has a splendid headmistress. Now, where's the smoked salmon?'

Rory went to the scullery to get it. Carrie meanwhile took a loaf of brown bread from the bread crock, then returned to the cooker to give the soup a stir. When Rory returned, she found a large oval dish and he began to separate the slices of salmon and lay them out in overlapping layers. Carrie took a couple of lemons from the fruit bowl and cut them into wedges.

Rory worked on, intent and businesslike, and Carrie watched him, saw his unlikely bright yellow hair, the ring in his ear, the blunt features, youthful but strong, well on his way to manhood. He had rolled up the sleeves of his dark blue cotton shirt and his forearms were tanned, his hands strong and capable. She could perfectly understand why Lucy liked him so much.

She said, 'You've been kind to her, Rory. A lot of guys your age simply wouldn't have bothered.'

'I felt sorry for her.' He shrugged. Then he stood back to survey the plate of salmon. 'There. Is that going to be enough?'

'Have to be. We're keeping the other lot for Christmas Day. Now, perhaps I'd better go and see how Lucy's getting on. You come too.'

'No. I'll stay here, be the chef. I quite like cooking. You go back to the others. I'll butter the bread. And there are still some pizzas left over. I'll put them in the oven.'

Carrie left Rory to it and went upstairs. The landing stood empty. The receiver back in the cradle. No sign of Lucy. She hesitated for a moment, experiencing a pang of disquiet. And then, just as before, the telephone rang.

Carrie picked up the receiver. 'Hello?'

'Is that the Estate House? I want Carrie.'

Carrie's heart sank. 'Yes,' she said, 'I'm here. Hello, Ma.'

'It's you. Oh, thank heavens. Has Nicola been on to you?'

'Yes. She rang from Florida. But she wanted to talk to Lucy.'

'Did she tell you?'

'Tell me what?'

'Oh, my dear, she's married Randall Fischer. This morning. They had some sort of whirlwind ceremony.'

'She rang you before she rang Lucy?'

'Yes. She wanted to make arrangements. For Lucy. When she gets back from Scotland and that sort of thing. . . .'

Oh, God, thought Carrie. Here we go again.

'She's talking about a honeymoon, not flying back to London until the end of the month. And she expects me to be in London so that I can get Lucy back to school. But I've planned to stay here in Bournemouth until the end of January, and I cannot see why I should change all my arrangements.'

'Is she going to spend the rest of her life in America?'

'I suppose so. If you marry an American, I suppose that's what you have to do.'

'What about Lucy?'

'Lucy will just have to do what she's told. The immediate problem is who is going to look after her until her mother gets home?'

Carrie did not answer this question. She simply stood there, aware of a great wave of fury directed at her mother and her sister. She knew that if she made any remark it would be wrong, precipitating a slanging match that would solve nothing.

'Carrie?'

'Ma, I think it would be better if I rang you back.'

'Have you spoken to Lucy?'

'No. Not yet. This is the first I've heard of the happy news.'

'You've got my number here in Bournemouth?'

'Yes. I'll call you. Tomorrow, maybe.'

'Don't leave it too long. I'm worried sick. Oh, and darling, you will have a lovely Christmas, won't you?'

'Lovely,' Carrie told her.

She put the receiver down and stood for a moment, giving herself time to cool down, gather her wits and face facts. Nicola was now Mrs Randall Fischer, and there was so much emotional debris littered around, waiting to be picked up, that Carrie felt she scarcely knew where to start.

Lucy. Lucy was the first. She had been given the joyous news over the telephone by her mother, put down the receiver and disappeared.

Carrie took a deep breath and climbed the stairs to Lucy's attic. The bedroom door was firmly closed. She knocked. No reply. Gently she opened the door. All was darkness. She reached for the light and switched it on. 'Lucy?'

A hump under the blue and white duvet did not move or answer.

'Lucy.' Carrie crossed over to the bed and sat on the edge of it.

'Go away. I don't want to talk.'

'Darling, I know. Gran rang from Bournemouth. She told me.'

'I don't care if she told you. It doesn't make any difference. Everything's spoilt now. Everything. It always is. They always do.'

'Oh, Lucy . . .' Carrie laid her hand on the duvet, but Lucy jerked her shoulder and spurned the tentative touch.

'I wish you'd go away and leave me alone.' Her voice was filled with tears. She was angry and resentful, and Carrie understood, but still felt loath to leave her.

'To be truthful, I think your mother shouldn't have sprung this on you over the telephone, expecting you to be delighted. But I suppose we have to try to see her point of view . . .'

All at once, Lucy flung the duvet aside and turned her face to Carrie's. It was swollen and stained with weeping and Carrie realised, with despair, that the anger was directed not simply against her mother but at Carrie too, because they were all adult and there was not a single adult who could be trusted.

'Of *course* you take her side,' Lucy shouted at Carrie. 'She's your sister. Well, I hate her. I hate her because of all this, and because I've never mattered. I matter even less now. And I won't go and live in America. And I hate Randall Fischer and I don't want to talk about it and I just want to be left alone! So *go away*!'

And she flung herself away from Carrie, pulled the duvet over her head and buried her face in an already sodden pillow.

Feebly, Carrie tried again. 'The Kennedys are staying for supper.'

'I don't care if they are. I want you to *go away*!'

Carrie, knowing that it was hopeless to persist, got to her feet, went out of the room and closed the door once more.

She felt completely shattered, and without any idea of what to do next. She stood at the top of the stairs, hearing the voices of the others in the sitting room.

What she wanted, above all, was for it to be yesterday, for none of this to have happened. To be with Sam Howard in the Duke's Arms, with the hot fire and the warming drink, and no one to think about but herself.

She straightened her shoulders, walked downstairs and opened the sitting-room door. They were all talking peacefully among themselves, but when Carrie came in, heads turned.

'Here I am. Sorry to keep you all waiting.'

Elfrida said, 'Darling, what's been going on? So many telephone calls. Nothing wrong, I hope?'

'I don't know where to start.' Sam got up and came over to her side. 'Would you like a drink?'

She shook her head. He reached for a chair and drew it forward, next to Elfrida, and Carrie sat down and felt Elfrida take her hand.

'Darling Carrie, tell us.'

So she did, and they all listened attentively. She concluded, 'So the crisis is immediate and also long-term. Immediate, because there is nobody in London to take care of Lucy and get her to school. Except, of course, dogsbody me. But the long-term problem is Lucy's future. She doesn't particularly like Randall and, to be truthful, I don't think she's all that fond of her mother.'

'She doesn't *have* to go and live in America,' Elfrida ventured hopefully. 'How about her going to her school as a boarder?'

'It's a day school, Elfrida. And there are still holidays.'

'Your mother?'

'Ma would never cope on her own. Wouldn't even try.'

'Perhaps Lucy's father . . .'

'No way. Number-two wife would never consider it.'

'This is all ridiculous.' A new voice broke into the argument, taking everyone by surprise. Rory Kennedy had got to his feet, his blue eyes blazing with indignation. Nobody interrupted him.

'It's ridiculous. You're all taking in circles, taking it for granted that Lucy will go back to London, just as though nothing had happened. But she can't go. She's miserable there, she told me so, and what's happened just now only makes everything more impossible for her. She has no proper home and she's never felt loved. What has made her really happy has been staying here with Elfrida and Oscar. In Creagan. She told me she'd never been so happy as she is here. So don't send her back. Keep her here. She can stay with Elfrida and Oscar, and Mum and Dad will be around, and Clodagh, and she's made friends with our friends, and she can go to day school in Creagan. I think if you let her go back to London, without any sort of plan for the future, it would be criminal. Unhappy teenagers do terrible, stupid things. Lucy belongs to you all far more than she belongs with her mother. So this is where she should be.'

He stopped, red-cheeked from the passion of his feeling. For a moment an astounded silence filled the room. Rory, perhaps feeling that he had gone too far, looked a bit sheepish and apologised.

'Sorry,' he said. 'I didn't mean to speak out of turn.'

Silence again. Then Peter Kennedy got to his feet to stand beside his son. 'You didn't speak out of turn,' he told him, laying a hand on the boy's shoulder. 'I think you're right. Well said, Rory.'

LUCY LAY AND STARED at the sloping ceiling of her bedroom, exhausted by weeping and beginning to feel remorseful about the way she had behaved towards Carrie. Listening to her mother burbling on, lyrical with excitement and as insensitive to others' feelings as she had always been, had all at once become too much, and Lucy, unable to listen to one more word, had put the phone down.

A tap on the door. It opened. 'Lucy?'

It was Oscar. He came to sit on the edge of her bed. His weight was strangely comforting, pulling the duvet tight around her body.

'How are you feeling?'

She said, 'Awful.'

'Carrie came down and told us what happened.'

'I was horrible to her. I shouted at her and told her to go away. I feel dreadful about her.'

'When we're really upset we always take it out on the people who are closest and whom we love the most.'

'Do we?'

'Always.'

'I can't imagine you ever shouting at anybody.'

He smiled, his rare, warm smile that always seemed to change his whole demeanour. 'You'd be surprised.' He reached into the breast pocket of his velvet jacket and produced a linen handkerchief. She took it gratefully and blew her nose.

'I don't know what will happen. That's the worst. I don't know what I'm going to do.'

'I don't think you have to do anything. I think others have to do it for you.'

'Who?'

'Now, just listen. Downstairs we've all been having a little chat, and we've come up with an idea. Supposing, after the New Year, you don't go back to London with Carrie? You stay here with Elfrida. And *I* shall go back to London with Carrie, and go to see your grandmother in Bournemouth.'

Lucy was alarmed. 'What are you going to say to her?'

'I am going to suggest that, until your mother's new life is sorted out somewhat, you should remain in Creagan with Elfrida and myself. Just for the time being.'

'But what about school? I have to go back to school.'

'Yes, of course you do, but how about taking a term off from your school in London and going to school in Creagan instead?'

'You mean . . .' Lucy felt she had to get the facts right because what Oscar was telling her sounded almost too good to be true. 'You mean I wouldn't go back to London after the New Year? Just stay on with you and Elfrida?'

'If you want to. The decision must be yours.'

She was silent for a moment, mulling this over. 'Gran doesn't approve of Elfrida,' she told Oscar bluntly.

Oscar laughed. 'So I believe. But she will, I am sure, approve of me. I shall present myself as a schoolmaster and a church organist, with an impeccable background and an unsullied reputation. Will she be able to resist that?'

Lucy said, with a touch of humour, 'Not if it means getting rid of me.'

'And your mother?'

'She won't care either. She never did care, much. She'll care even less now that she's got Randall.'

'Carrie's going to telephone them both tomorrow. She can outline our plans. Stay on, with Elfrida and me, in Creagan. Go to the local school. Get your GCSEs. After that you should spread your wings a bit. Maybe a co-educational boarding school where you could take your A levels.'

'That's what Rory said, when we talked about things. A co-educational boarding school.'

'He's a wise lad. He is your champion. It was he who stirred us all to action.'

'But, Oscar . . . Would you *want* me living with you for two years?'

'More than anything. We love you. Perhaps I am being selfish, but I don't want to let you go. I need a young person about the place. I've got used to the sound of your voice, and footsteps on the stairs.'

Lucy said, 'When I first came here, when Carrie and I flew up from London, I was terribly nervous because she had told me about your daughter . . . I was afraid that I would remind you of her and make you dreadfully sad again.'

'You do remind me of her, but it didn't make me sad.'

'What did she look like?'

'Like you, I suppose. Long fair hair and freckles on her nose. She was two years younger than you. Always on the go. Never still except when she and I settled down in my armchair to read to each other.'

'My dad and I used to do that. We read *The Borrowers*. What was Francesca good at? The piano?'

'Not very.'

'Was she good at lessons?'

'Not very.'

'What was she good at?'

'Living.'

Their eyes met, and they gazed at each other, both silenced by the enormity of what Oscar had just said. The word hung between them like a lie. To her horror Lucy saw Oscar's eyes fill with tears, his mouth tremble. Then, in an abrupt movement, he covered his eyes with his hand.

She had never before seen a grown man weep. She stared at him, wondering what she could do to comfort. After a bit, to her huge relief, he took his hand from his face, then made an effort to smile at her, reassuring. He said, 'Sorry.'

'It doesn't matter, Oscar. I don't mind. I understand.'

'Yes, I think you do. Death is part of living. I have to remember that, but from time to time the truth eludes me.'

'Living is important, isn't it? And remembering?'

'More important than anything else. That first day, the day you arrived, you and I sat in the church and talked about Christmas and the winter solstice. It was then that I remembered Francesca, for the first time, without total desolation. I remembered having exactly the same conversation with her a year or so ago. Trying to explain about the Christmas star and the scientist's theory of time. And she listened, but was not convinced. She didn't want to be convinced. She liked the story just as it was. Because the snow and the carols and the presents were all part of a time when the whole world soared to the stars.'

Lucy said, 'That's how this Christmas is going to be.'

'Stay with us.'

'I do love you, Oscar.'

'There's a lot of love around. Don't ever forget that.'

'I won't.'

'Do you want to come downstairs now, and have some supper?'

'I have to comb my hair and wash my face.'

He went to the door. 'Don't be too long.'

Christmas
Eve

In this fickle northern climate, one woke each morning without any idea of what the elements were about to reveal, but Christmas Eve dawned astonishingly pure and gentle, like a day stolen from spring. The thaw had melted the snow away from streets and fields, and only the hills still wore their white mantles, summits glittering in the light of the low sun, streaming down from a cloudless sky. A sun that, because there was no breath of wind, even managed to engender a faint warmth. Birds sang from leafless trees, and in the Estate House garden a few early snowdrops pierced the rough, untended grass beneath a lilac bush.

Because of the fine day, and the fact that the roads were clear, Elfrida and Oscar had come to Corrydale on their own in Oscar's car. The others were driving over later, because Carrie reckoned she had to wait until noon before getting on the telephone to her sister in Florida. She had already spoken to Dodie, who was clearly much relieved to shed responsibility for Lucy.

Now they were standing in the open gateway of Oscar's new property. They walked up the driveway and Oscar put the key in the lock. The door swung inwards, and Elfrida followed him, fingers crossed, into the little sitting room.

It felt very cold and a bit dank, but not nearly as bad as Elfrida had remembered and feared. The window at the back of the room let in a flood of sunshine, and Betty Cowper, the tractorman's wife, and Rose, between them, had scoured, cleaned and polished. In the fireplace were laid paper and sticks, all ready for kindling.

Oscar said, 'First things first,' and knelt to set a match to the paper. At the back of the room stood a door. Elfrida went to open this, and found herself in a mean, chilly little kitchen. It had a clay sink, a tiny refrigerator, a gas cooker, and a small table spread with an oilcloth. A half-glassed door led out onto a bit of paving.

She went back to Oscar, who was piling coal onto flames, and said, 'How did the major keep himself warm?'

'We'll find out. Come. Let us go and explore.'

They went into Major Billicliffe's dining room, then up very steep and narrow stairs to the upper floor. They inspected the two

264

bedrooms. In Major Billicliffe's bedroom, the bed was covered with a fresh cotton counterpane, and rag rugs had been laundered.

The second bedroom was smaller, and the bathroom spartan and not conducive to long soaks. The bath, which stood on feet, was stained and rusted, the basin cracked and the linoleum beginning to turn up at the corners. But the good thing about the bathroom, like the kitchen, was a view of the sloping fields, dazzling blue water, and the distant hills. And, Elfrida thought, the house did have a good feel to it. It had been neglected, but was not without hope. It simply needed, like any human being, a bit of laughter and some tender loving care, and it would leap into life again.

From behind her, Oscar spoke. 'I am going to go out of doors.'

She crossed the narrow passage into the smaller bedroom for a quick reassessment: this would have to be for Lucy. She tried to decide if there would be space to put a desk for homework. There would, if they replaced the double bed with a single divan.

She heard the sound of Sam's Discovery approaching down the drive and drawing to a stop. The back door opened and Lucy tumbled out. 'Elfrida!'

She sounded joyous. Elfrida, feeling ridiculously hopeful and happy, ran down the narrow stairway to fling open the front door and hold wide her arms.

Lucy bolted into them. 'Oh, Elfrida. It's all right. Carrie got hold of Mummy and she was frightfully surprised and had to have it all explained twice before she understood. And Carrie was marvellously persuasive. Mummy's going to ring Miss Maxwell Brown and ask her to keep my place at school open for me next summer just in case I want to go back. Elfrida, isn't this the sweetest house? Is this the sitting room? And look, you've already lit a fire! Where's Oscar?'

'Out in the garden.'

With no hanging about, Lucy went galloping down the garden and calling Oscar's name. Then Carrie appeared, with a huge basket slung over her arm. She was joined by Rory and Sam hefting a heavy grocery box close to his chest.

'Is this all picnic?' Elfrida asked in some amazement.

'A feast,' Sam replied.

THE CHRISTMAS EVE PICNIC at Corrydale started with a glass of wine by the fireside, then slowly progressed out of doors because the day was so beautiful that it seemed sacrilegious to be inside. Rory and Lucy were first out, and the others joined them one by one to perch on kitchen chairs or sofa cushions, or the rug from Sam's car.

Carrie and Sam had done a splendid job. They had brought hot soup laced with sherry, fresh rolls filled with thick slices of ham and English mustard; a bacon quiche, chicken drumsticks, tomato salad, crisp green apples and chunks of Cheddar cheese.

Elfrida, sitting on a cushion with her back against the wall, turned her face up to the sun and closed her eyes. 'That was the best picnic ever. Thank you, Carrie.'

Rory and Lucy had disappeared indoors to inspect the little house. Now, they appeared again.

'It's so nice, Oscar,' Lucy told him. 'Now we thought we'd take Horace for a walk, down to the water and the beach.'

Oscar tipped back the last of his coffee. 'I shall come with you. After that feast, I need exercise. Who's coming with us?'

'I shall,' said Carrie.

'I shan't,' said Elfrida firmly.

'I shall stay with Elfrida,' said Sam. 'I would like to do a building inspection.'

SHOWING SAM HOWARD round Major Billicliffe's house was quite different from looking at it with Oscar. Sam tapped walls, turned taps, inspected window frames and power points.

Finally he sat down with Elfrida on the sofa. 'Now,' said Sam, 'do you intend living in the place just as it is, or do you want to change a few things?'

'It depends,' said Elfrida, 'on how much it would cost.'

'Supposing . . .' He began to draw a plan on a scratch pad. 'Supposing, to begin with, you demolished the existing kitchen and bathroom. My suggestion would be that you make the dining room into a kitchen, and maybe build a small dining area out to the south. Glass-walled to the south and west—you'd get all the view and every ray of sun. And there's a chimney in the kitchen so you could install an Aga or a Rayburn for continual, steady heat.'

'Bathroom?'

'A new one.' He sketched it. 'Over the dining room.'

Elfrida gazed at his sketches. 'Would it . . . would it cost more than eighty thousand pounds?'

He laughed, his face creasing up with amusement. 'No, Elfrida. I don't think it would cost as much as that. You're not, after all, rebuilding. And the roof seems to be sound.' He looked at her. 'Have you *got* eighty thousand?'

'No. But I hope to have. Jamie Erskine-Earle is going to sell my little clock for me. We never told you, but apparently it is very rare.'

'In that case you have no problems. Go for it, Elfrida.'

'How long will it take?'

'I suppose six months. I don't know.'

'We'll have to stay in the Estate House until the work's done.'

'Of course.'

'But you, Sam? You want the Estate House.'

'I can wait. I'm not about to throw you out onto the streets.'

A brilliant idea occurred to Elfrida. 'You can live with us. At the Estate House. You and Lucy and Oscar and me.'

Again, Sam laughed. 'Oscar may not like the idea.'

'Oh, Oscar will love to have you. And so shall I. It will be a new job for me. Letting out lodgings. Oh, please say yes. I feel as though you were always meant to come and live there.'

'In that case, I accept,' said Sam, 'subject to Oscar's approval.'

THE SUN WAS BEGINNING to dip down out of the sky by the time the walkers returned. 'How was it?' Elfrida asked.

'Perfect,' Carrie told her. 'All the birds! Ducks and cormorants and gulls . . . How did you and Sam get on?'

'Sam is brilliant. He's practically drawn the plans. You must come and look, Oscar.'

It was half an hour before Rory and Lucy finally joined them, by which time Oscar had seen and listened to all Sam's ideas, been persuaded, and given his consent. Carrie approved as well. 'You know, Sam, you *are* very clever.'

Now, the light was fading, and it was time to go back to Creagan. 'Are we going to the midnight service, Elfrida?' Carrie asked.

'I think so. Oscar doesn't want to come, but I'll go.'

'Me, too. And Lucy and Sam are coming, as well.'

Having packed up the remains of the picnic, the first party took their leave in Sam's car. Elfrida, Oscar and Horace went out of doors to see the others off, then walked back inside.

Elfrida said, 'I don't want to leave. I don't want today to end.'

'Then we'll stay for a little.'

He sank tiredly onto the sofa. He had walked further than he'd intended. Elfrida put the last bit of wood on the fire and sat beside him.

She said, 'We will live here, won't we, Oscar?'

'If you want.'

'I want. But do you want?'

'Yes. I admit I had reservations, but now that I have seen it again, and Sam has come up with all these ideas and possibilities, I think it is exactly what we should do.'

'It's exciting. A new start.'

The shadows lengthened. Beyond the window the bare trees faded into darkness. Elfrida sighed. 'We should go.'

'Wait. I want to talk.'

It sounded so serious that Elfrida got up from her chair and went to sit beside him on the sofa. He put out his hand and laid it upon her own.

'I'm listening,' she told him.

'This is a new step we're going to take. Together. A real commitment. Don't you think perhaps the time has come for us to be man and wife? It's a formality, I know, because we could scarcely be more married than we already are. But it would put a seal on our union . . . an affirmation of our trust in the future.'

Elfrida's eyes were filling with tears. 'Oh, Oscar . . .' She drew her hand away and began to search for her handkerchief. 'You don't need to do this. I will stay with you happily for the rest of my life, but I don't want you to feel you have to marry me.'

'I don't feel that. I love and I honour you just the way things are, and all things being equal, I should happily settle for carrying on just the way things are. But we have Lucy to consider now.'

'What difference does she make to how we live our lives?'

'Oh, my dearest Elfrida, just think. So far the people of Creagan have accepted us with great kindness, even forbearance. No questions. Not a single soul has cast a stone, not even a tiny pebble. But for Lucy it is different. She is going to the local school. Children are not always very kind. Rumours can be started and, even in this day and age, parents can be mean-spirited. I wouldn't want any of that sort of thing to rub off on Lucy.'

'So for her sake, we should be married?'

'Put baldly, yes.'

'But Gloria . . .'

'Gloria, of all women, would understand.'

'You're sure?'

'Yes, I'm sure. Because one thing is truly certain, and that is that you have helped me to start again, and it is you who have made a dark and painful time not only bearable and possible but even joyful as well. I told you a long time ago that you could always make me laugh. And you have made me love you. Now, I cannot imagine an existence without you. Please marry me. If I wasn't feeling so bloody stiff, I'd get down on one knee.'

'I'd hate you to do that.' Elfrida, having at last found her handkerchief, blew her nose. 'But I'd like to marry you very, very much. Thank you for asking me.'

'So. Shall we break the news or keep it to ourselves?'

'Let's keep it to ourselves. Secretly relish. Just for the time being.'

'You're right. There's so much going on. Let's get Christmas behind us, and then I shall take you to Kingsferry and buy you a diamond ring.'

'I have to be truthful. I'm not all that keen on diamonds.'

'What would you like me to buy you?'

'Aquamarine?'

Oscar laughed, and kissed her, and they might have sat on, in the gloaming, for the rest of the evening, but the last of the logs had burned and the house had grown cold. It was time to leave.

Oscar locked his front door and took Elfrida's arm and, with Horace at their heels, they walked, in the deep blue evening light, down the pebbled path.

Lucy

It's nearly eight o'clock in the evening and so much has happened. The worst was Mummy ringing in the middle of Elfrida's party to say that she has married Randall Fischer. All I could think about was having to go and live in America, or else have to live with Gran in London on my own. I had horrible hysterics and was beastly to Carrie, but that's all over now. It's all sorted out, and I'm going to stay here, in Creagan, with Elfrida and Oscar, anyway, for the time being, and go to day school in Creagan.

Carrie rang Gran and told her about her plans, and she went along with them. Later on she rang Mummy in Florida, and persuaded her, too. And then I had a chat with Mummy, and

*managed not to sound too delighted, in case she took offence
and changed her mind.*

*Then Rory appeared, and we got a picnic together, and Sam
drove us over to Corrydale. Oscar's little house is sweet, tucked
away on the estate with great big trees, and a long view of the
water and over hills. Sam thought up lots of clever ideas for alter-
ations and when it is finished it will look really nice.*

*We all came back with Sam, left Rory at the Manse and then
came home. Carrie made supper and while she did this I finished
laying the table for Christmas dinner tomorrow, and put on the
candles and the crackers and dishes of chocolate. There's a bowl
of holly in the middle and it looks really festive. When we've lit
the fire the room will look exactly right, like a Christmas card.*

*It's lovely here. And Sam is going to be our lodger until every-
thing is sorted out. I can't believe that I could be so miserable and
despairing one day, and so utterly happy the next.*

IT WAS TEN PAST ELEVEN, and Elfrida was endeavouring to fan out
her enormous hand of cards for the last game of canasta when the
telephone rang.

Oscar said, 'That damned telephone. Who's ringing us at this hour?'

He laid down his cards and went out of the room and Elfrida
heard him say, 'Estate House.'

And then silence, as the caller spoke, and then a murmured reply.
The next moment, he was back.

Elfrida was curious. 'Who was it?'

'Nothing much. A mistake.'

They played on and ran out of cards. Then Sam pulled the score
pad towards him and totted up all the figures and announced that he
and Elfrida were the overall winners.

With that, Oscar got to his feet and said, I'm going to take Horace
for a walk.'

Elfrida stared at him in some astonishment. He often took Horace
out in the garden last thing at night but never for a walk.

'A walk? Where will you go?'

'I don't know. I just feel in the need of some fresh air. I may not be
back by the time you set off for church, but leave the door open and
I'll still be up when you all return. Have a good time.' He left.

Elfrida's expression was puzzled. '*Funny.* You'd have thought he'd
had enough exercise today to last him for a week.' She went round

the room puffing up cushions. 'We shouldn't be too long making our way to church, I think. There's bound to be a huge congregation, and we want to be able to get a seat.'

They all went away to get coats and a few minutes later, Lucy ran downstairs from her attic to find Sam and Elfrida waiting on the landing. 'All ready, Elfrida, but Carrie's still in her room.'

'Well, you and I will go, Lucy, and bag a pew for the four of us . . . Sam, will you wait for Carrie, and come over with her?'

'Of course.'

Sam heard them slam the front door. He stood on the landing and waited for Carrie. He felt no impatience. He had waited, during his life, for countless women to appear. So now, in the house which would, one day, belong to him, he waited for Carrie.

'Oh, Sam. Have the others gone?'

She came out of her room wearing her loden coat, a silk scarf, all pinks and blues, softly wound around her slender throat. He had never seen her more beautiful.

He said, 'Yes,' and put his hands on her shoulders, and drew her close and kissed her. Something he had been longing to do ever since that first night when she had opened the door to him and found him standing on the doorstep in the falling snow. When at last they drew apart, he saw that she was smiling.

He said, 'Happy Christmas.'

'Happy Christmas, Sam. Time to go.'

ELFRIDA AND LUCY crossed the street. The square, lamplit, was already busy with people converging on the church.

'Elfrida!'

They stopped and saw Tabitha, Rory and Clodagh behind them.

'Hello! I thought we were early, but it seems we're not. I've never seen so many people.'

'I know. It's fun, isn't it?' Tabitha wore a tartan coat and red muffler. 'People come from miles away . . . The only thing is, we've had a bit of a setback. Alistair Heggie, the organist, has got flu, so we won't have any proper music. We're going to use taped music.'

'Oh, that is disappointing . . .'

'It can't be helped. Come on. With a bit of luck we'll get a pew to ourselves.'

They went up the path which led to the wide flight of stone steps and the double doors of the church. Tonight these had been flung open. Light from inside streamed onto the cobbles and Elfrida could hear the taped music from within the church. A choir singing: '*God rest you merry, gentlemen, let nothing you dismay . . .*'

It sounded a bit mechanical and tinny, thought Elfrida.

'*Remember Christ our—*'

Silence. Either the tape recorder had broken down or someone had inadvertently switched off the electricity.

And then it started. A great surge of sound from the organ. Huge chords and waves of music filled the church, overflowed out through the open doors, resounded up and out into the night.

Elfrida stopped dead. She looked at Tabitha, whose eyes were wide and innocent. For a long moment, neither of them spoke. Then Elfrida said, 'Did Peter ring Oscar? About a quarter past eleven?'

Tabitha shrugged. 'No idea. Come on, kids, see if we can find somewhere to sit.' She ran up the steps with her two children and Lucy at her heels.

After a moment, Elfrida followed. The church was already nearly filled, the congregation shuffling into their places. The music thundered all about her, filling the huge void of the soaring arched ceiling, echoing down the long nave. She began to move down the centre aisle. Walking into the music was like stepping into a pounding sea of sound.

A hand touched her arm. She stopped.

'Elfrida. Here.' It was Lucy. 'We're keeping seats for you and Sam and Carrie.'

She took no notice. Did not move.

The Christmas tree, lavishly decorated and twinkling with lights, stood in the middle of the transept, between the pulpit and the lectern. Beyond this, against the north wall of the church, the organ pipes soared. The organist's seat was enclosed by an oaken stall, so that he was not visible to the seated assembly. But Elfrida was standing. And she was tall. An overhead spotlight shone down upon him, and she could clearly see his head and his profile and the thick white hair, rendered unruly by the unselfconscious exuberance of his own performance.

Beethoven. 'Ode to Joy'.

And Oscar Blundell, playing his heart out. Reconciled. Returned. Back where he belonged.

ROSAMUNDE PILCHER

Charming, elegant, down-to-earth, the septuagenarian Rosamunde Pilcher might have stepped straight from the pages of one of her own novels. Like Elfrida in *Winter Solstice*, it is easy to imagine that she is immensely practical and would not be thrown by the arrival of a houseful of unexpected guests for Christmas. In fact, she *prefers* to be spontaneous when it comes to entertaining.

'We always made a big thing of Christmas for the children when they were young, but I never really enjoyed it,' she confesses. 'It's difficult because expectations are so high. In *Winter Solstice* none of the characters plans to have a proper Christmas, so everything's done just a couple of days before, the way it always was before everything got so commercial.'

Rosamunde Pilcher was born and raised near St Ives in Cornwall. Growing up in a house filled with books she read voraciously, and at fourteen decided she wanted to be a writer. An aunt gave her a subscription to *Woman's Home Journal* and she devoured its short stories, teaching herself the techniques of fiction writing. She was just eighteen and serving in the WRNS when her first story sold for eighteen guineas.

At twenty-two she married a Scot, Graham Pilcher, and moved with him to Dundee where, while bringing up four children, she kept up a steady output of stories for the publishers Mills & Boon and women's magazines. Then her American editor suggested that she might try a longer book—something autobiographical, and *The Shell Seekers* was the result. At sixty, Rosamunde Pilcher found herself catapulted to fame.

This year she will be spending Christmas in Cornwall with her son and his family, among the idyllic landscapes of her childhood.

On a satellite link between Mount Everest and her home, Josie Turner hears news from her husband Sebastian as he makes a bold attempt on the summit.

'If the weather holds and all goes to plan, I'll be on top at about midnight your time,' he confidently predicts.

But the weather doesn't hold—and nothing goes to plan . . .

Hal scooped a final shovel of snow from the makeshift grave and clambered out to address the group. He stood, panting a little, a thin vapour of steam rising from his cheeks, feeling at home here in the wild mountain country, the jagged peaks of the Alaskan Chugach range jutting skywards around him.

'This morning,' he told them with a smile, 'I'm going to bury one of you alive.' He walked down the line, making eye contact with the five shivering clients. 'Now, who wants to volunteer?'

There were no takers. Hal looked at Rachel. 'Want to get those shots?'

Rachel clutched at the Nikon strung round her neck, unable to keep the alarm from her face. 'Maybe I'll do them another time.'

'This is the last course of the winter. If you don't do it now . . .'

Rachel looked down into the icy grave and suppressed a shudder. 'I'm not so sure it'll produce a worthwhile picture . . .'

'That's not what you told me before. All those faces of the rescuers as they dig you out? The point of view of an avalanche victim? Sounds like a pretty unique shot to me.'

She looked at him pleadingly. 'The camera might get snow in it.'

'Rachel? If you want that photograph, get in the hole.'

'Oh God . . .' Rachel stepped down into the snow hole and lay flat on her back, her hands cupped over the camera to protect it.

'Move your head and shoulders into that cavity in the side wall,' Hal told her. 'There's enough oxygen to keep you going for a while.'

Rachel wriggled herself into the scooped-out hollow.

'OK.' Hal clipped a transmitter onto her ski suit. 'Your beacon's in place. Hopefully we'll find you before the battery runs out.'

'Ha ha. Will you just bury me and be done with it?' Rachel turned her face to look at Hal, smiling as she saw his reassuring wink.

'It'll be OK. Just breathe slow and relax,' he whispered. A shovelful of snow landed with a thump on her shin.

As the clients took up their shovels and joined in, snow began to rain down on her. The weight was extraordinary, the snow pushing down on her body with a terrifying pressure. Then there was just the muffled thud as the shovels pounded away above her.

Then silence. Rachel tried not to panic.

Hal led the group across the snowfield. 'Let's assume that this area has just been the scene of a big slide and that one of your party is under that snow somewhere. You have no idea where she is.'

He began to zigzag, then turned them in a series of circles until they were disorientated. 'Now find her as fast as you can.'

The clients looked out across the snowfield. The snow was falling fast—fast enough to cover the tracks they had just made. They realised they no longer had a fix on where Rachel was buried.

Remembering their training, they organised themselves into a search line, and beginning a methodical sweep of the target area, their avalanche transceivers set.

Three feet under the snow, Rachel forced her mind to think of other things . . . of the surprise news she had for Hal, which, somehow, she had failed to find a moment to tell him. She wanted the timing to be right. Tonight she would cook for him back at the cabin, buy some wine . . .

Rachel could feel the cold beginning to seep into her bones. What if they couldn't find her? If the transmitter failed? A brief surge of claustrophobia embraced her. The snow was too hard; there was no way she could dig her way out. 'Trust,' she whispered to herself. 'Hal knows what he's doing.'

Suddenly she became aware of a distant noise, a shout, barely audible. Then the sound of digging, directly above her, as the rescuers worked their way carefully down to her.

Rachel waited until the top part of her body was free and then raised the camera to her eye. She fired off the motor drive—seventeen shots in rapid succession as the rescuers reached down towards her. Finally she allowed them to pull her free.

'You see?' Hal said, kissing her chilled lips. 'We had you out of there in less than fifteen minutes.'

'I just hope the shots are worth it.'

Hal called a coffee break, bringing out his flask and filling plastic mugs for Rachel and the clients. 'Get some warm fluid inside you. Then we're going to that steeper slope over there to learn a little about avalanche prediction.'

'You're not going to get us all avalanched now, are you?' A client forced a laugh as she sipped her coffee.

Hal held out his bare hand, watching intently as the huge crystals fell to rest on his palm. 'Not if I know my snow,' he told her.

'He does,' Rachel told them reassuringly. 'Know his snow, I mean.'

JOSIE WAS OUT on the London streets at 4.00am, her body warming to the rhythm as she jogged north through Kensington and up into Hyde Park. She always ran before dawn when she was working on the show. Normally she struggled to drag herself out of bed, but today had been different.

It's not easy to sleep when you know the person you love is climbing into the death zone on the highest mountain in the world. Josie had been restless all night.

The circuit took forty minutes if she was feeling lazy . . . thirty-five minutes if she wanted to break a sweat. Today was a thirty-five-minute day: Josie was in a hurry to get back for Sebastian's satellite call at five. She felt her muscles tighten as she pushed the pace. When she got back to the leafy Kensington Square that was home, she let herself in the back door, away from the prying lenses of the newsmen who waited at the front. She took a shower, dressed quickly and went to the kitchen to fix coffee. While she waited she stood in front of the freezer and looked at the photograph of Everest that Sebastian had pinned there the day before he left for Nepal.

Josie kissed her finger and imprinted it on the picture where she knew Sebastian was. 'Just come home,' she whispered. 'I don't care about anything else.'

A glance out of the window told her that the photographers were still waiting. Sebastian had been right when he'd predicted his Everest expedition would create a lot of media interest.

The telephone rang. The faraway echo on the line told her it was the satellite connection—Everest calling.

'Josie, this is Base Camp. I have Sebastian on the walkie-talkie from the South Col. I'm going to link him up, OK? Just hold the line.'

Josie waited while the connection was made.

'Hey, Josie. Can you hear me OK?'

'Loud and clear, Bas. How beautiful to hear your voice. Where are you and how's the expedition going?'

'We reached the South Col a couple of hours ago and I tell you I've never been so tired. And I've been feeling as sick as a dog for the last few days. But we're still going strong.'

'Are you sleeping?'

A sound like a snort came down the line. 'I don't remember the last time I slept for more than two hours at a stretch. But you get beyond tiredness. Like you get beyond the pain. It's awesome, Josie, the whole thing. I wouldn't be anywhere else. I'm living the biggest dream of my life here. I can see getting on for a hundred of the world's most beautiful mountains right from where I'm sitting and somehow that makes it all worth while.'

'What about the weather?'

'It's perfect. We have a blue sky with virtually no wind.'

'So are you definitely on for the summit?'

'You bet. If the weather holds and all goes to plan, I'll be on top at about midnight your time.'

'You scare me, Bas. The whole thing scares me.'

'Come on. I'm in good hands here. We have a mountain of oxygen cylinders, loads of strong Sherpas and it's roped all the way. How's the publicity going?'

'Great. We have big picture spreads lined up with the dailies, just as soon as you can wire back some shots. I'm not going to sleep a wink until I know you're back in Base Camp.'

'I have to go. There's a queue of climbers waiting to use this sat-phone.'

'Yeah. Me too. Darling, listen, you take so much care, OK? Just come back in one piece. For me.'

'I love you.'

'Love you too.' Josie blew him a kiss down the telephone and replaced the handset.

She quickly packed her small leather case. The intercom buzzer rang, the chauffeur calling to drive Josie to the studio. It was 5.15am.

She walked out into the pre-dawn chill where the photographers were waiting on the pavement. 'Good morning, gentlemen.'

'Any news from Everest?'

'There is. It looks like Sebastian is definitely going for the summit.'
'How's he feeling?'
'He's feeling confident and calm. Ready for the challenge, I'd say.'
'Are you nervous for him, Josie?'
Josie laughed as she climbed into the limousine, relaxing back into the leather-clad rear seat. 'Sorry. I have nothing more to say. You'll have to wait for this evening and we'll see how he gets on.'

HAL RUBBED HIS HANDS to get the circulation going in his frozen fingertips. 'Right. What we're going to do next is create our own personal avalanche zone, like a miniature test bed to check how stable the pack is.

He gave each of the clients an aluminium shovel and showed them how to cut a vertical profile into the snow. They dug for fifteen minutes, creating a sheer wall cut into the mountainside.

'OK. What you have now is a cross-section through the season's snowfall. He selected one of the female clients. 'Wendy. Take this plastic ruler and start to probe it into the snow. Start at the top and move down. Call out when you feel something change.'

The woman did as Hal said.

'What you're doing is checking out how stable the snow pack is.'

Wendy paused. 'It's harder here,' she said, 'more like ice.'

'Good. As snow falls, it creates layers, some hard, some soft, some granular. A deep overnight frost after a fresh fall would create a hard, polished layer like the one you just found. That layer remains in the snow pack for the entire winter, offering little adhesion for the weight collecting on it. Keep going lower.'

Wendy continued probing with the ruler. 'Now it's gone all soft.'

Hal bent down and showed the group what she had found. 'You see this? Now this is potentially deadly. Just nine inches from the ground there's a thin layer of sugar snow—big, round crystals, loosely packed. This stuff is inherently unstable. And right beneath it is a layer of wind-polished slab as slippery as glass. That means that the whole winter's snowfall is sitting on the crystalline equivalent of ball bearings.'

He climbed higher up the slope. 'This is the acid test which proves the true stability of the pack.' He jumped as high as he could in the air to let his full weight slam down onto the slope.

Nothing happened. The slope held. 'Goddamn.' Hal slid down on his backside, a disturbed look on his face. 'Now that is weird. My guess would have been that weak layer would have given way. This has been one of the strangest avalanche winters I've known.'

He checked the thermometer tied to his backpack. 'The only explanation,' he told the group, 'is that it's still four degrees below freezing. The pack is frozen solid.'

'What if the temperature rises?' one of the clients asked.

'Well, avalanche prediction isn't the exact science we'd like it to be. But if the temperature rise was fast enough, the fragile layer of sugar snow could let the whole winter's pack go all at once. We could be looking at a climax avalanche scenario.'

'What the hell is that?' Rachel felt her stomach lurch as she saw the serious expression on Hal's face.

'A climax avalanche is when every slope that *can* possibly avalanche *does*—virtually simultaneously. It can strip an entire mountain range of its mantle of snow in less than ten minutes. It probably won't happen. Last time it did was in 1873.'

Hal checked his watch. He would have to be in his office by midday to give his avalanche report to the local radio station. 'OK, guys. That concludes the morning session. See you next week.'

As the clients moved away, Hal bent to examine the weak layer once more, sticking his finger into the crystals.

'What do you think?' Rachel asked.

'I really don't know . . . But I don't like it at all. I'm going to call an amber alert just in case.'

Hal and Rachel skied the mile or so to the road where the Toyota was parked and began the journey to the cabin—the wood-built home Hal had constructed five years before.

It sat on the edge of one of the prettiest valleys in the Chugach with a picture window looking out across the range. On a clear day you could see sixty miles from the living room, but today the visibility was no further than you could toss a snowball. When they arrived, the shingle roof of the cabin was buried beneath the heaviest fall of the winter.

Rachel made for her darkroom to process her film.

Hal went straight to his office, put on headphones and switched on the direct feed to Anchorage radio. He waited for the familiar voice of Angie, the studio producer, to cut in.

'You with us, Hal?'

'I'm here, Angie. How you doing?'

'Busy show. You're on in twenty seconds.'

Hal watched the seconds tick past on his wall clock. Then he had the presenter, Ben Owen, direct on the line. 'We go now for our regular avalanche update with Hal Maher at Alaskan Avalanche Control. Good morning, Hal.'

'Hi, Ben. But I wouldn't call this good. We've had more than six feet of snow in under seventy-two hours and it's sitting on top of some pretty dubious foundations. As if that weren't enough, there's a high-pressure front coming in right behind. If it hits us with some warmer weather then we'll be looking at some monster slides. I'm issuing an amber avalanche warning for the entire state.'

'We going to see your famous climax avalanche, Hal? The big one?'

Hal forced a laugh. 'I hope not. That's a once-a-century scenario. Last time it happened more than two hundred people were killed in Alaska in one day alone.'

'Scary stuff. There you have it: amber avalanche alert for the entire state. You have been warned. Thanks, Hal. We'll check in with you same time tomorrow.'

'GOOD MORNING!' The receptionist greeted Josie with a smile.

'Hiya.' Josie never lost the thrill of being a part of the *Daybreak TV* studio. It was, after all, only by chance that she was here at all. Every time she walked in she flashed back to her first visit five years ago.

She had been twenty-two, a cub reporter looking for a scoop and with the mighty Sebastian Turner in her sights. Sebastian was hot news. Josie was no one. She had to bluff her way past the security guards to get to the receptionist. 'I'm here to see Sebastian Turner.'

'Do you have an appointment?'

'I don't, but I'm sure he'd want to see me. I want to do a profile on him.'

'Are you the same one who called six times last week?'

Josie gave a hopeful smile. 'Yes, that's me.'

'I'm afraid Mr Turner is extremely busy at the moment.'

Suddenly a figure in motorbike leathers was standing next to her. Josie found herself looking into a dark pair of eyes set beneath a tousled head of sun-bleached hair.

'Is this the reporter you told me about?' Sebastian asked the receptionist in his American accent. 'The one who's a pain in the neck?'

Josie flushed bright red. 'I know I've made myself a bit of a pest. But I really want this interview.'

Sebastian looked more closely at the girl before him. She was blonde, fit-looking. Her eyes were lapis blue. He held her gaze, noticing the way her mouth creased attractively into a smile at the edges, locks of hair curling around her ears in untamed wisps. 'What magazine do you work for?'

'*New Icons.*'

'Never heard of it. What's the circulation?'

'About four thousand a month.'

Sebastian frowned. 'You're prepared to doorstep me on spec . . . for a magazine that barely anyone reads?'

Josie nodded.

'You're the features writer, right?'

'Yeah.' Josie fixed him with her most winning smile. 'Well, I am at the moment. In fact, the magazine is about to go bust.'

Sebastian laughed and looked at his watch. 'Fifteen minutes. But I won't answer questions about my private life.'

Josie held eye contact, trying to keep the tremble out of her voice. 'Fifteen minutes and I can ask any question I like.'

The words hung in the air for a moment before Sebastian laughed. 'Holy shit. You're something else, aren't you? What's your name?'

'Josie Cameron.' Josie held out her hand.

Sebastian shook it, laughing as he led her into his office.

'So,' he said, 'what's your angle?'

'I'm doing a series of articles called "Homemade Heroes". Profiles of people who make it big against the odds. You know, find out who's really behind the public image you try to promote . . .'

'Whoa! Wait just a minute. I don't *try* to promote a public image. My face just has a habit of ending up in the newspapers.'

Josie opened her case and brought out a file of press cuttings. 'How about all this? Sebastian Turner arriving at a premiere with actress Miranda DeLane . . . posing naked on a motorbike for a women's magazine. . . standing on the summit of the Eiger. All that doesn't happen by accident, now does it?'

Sebastian gave her a disarming smile. 'So what's your point? I'm not the only person with a public profile who runs a business.'

'My point is there are about six different personalities jostling for prominence in these pages—playboy, mountain climber, television executive, businessman . . . So which is the true you?'

'You don't mince words.'

'Well, you did say I only had fifteen minutes.'

Sebastian relaxed into his chair. 'OK. All defences down. You can have me in my entirety, probe beneath my skin, penetrate my soul . . .'

'Let's start from the beginning. When did you come to the UK?'

'Eight years ago. I came to do some climbing with my friend Mike. He's my business partner now. We were broke, looking for a way to make some money, and we had the idea of starting up a magazine. It was obvious, really. There we were in the midst of a community of people who were obsessed about climbing, hang-gliding and extreme sports but there was no magazine covering all that. So I persuaded Mike to borrow a camera—then we just went out and did profiles on kids doing stuff. Mike did the photos, I did the words.'

'How did you fund it?'

'We did the whole thing on zero budget, borrowed the word processors, got the paper on credit, promised the printer the world. We sold three thousand of the first copy, then ten thousand of the second, then a distributor picked it up and we were flying. Then we got into fashion titles, then into photography and travel. We now have a turnover in excess of one hundred million dollars a year.'

Josie scribbled notes. 'And the television franchise?'

'We were looking for ways to diversify, and television seemed like the most exciting way to go ahead. So we applied for the franchise. And here we are, three months into *Daybreak* and going strong.'

An assistant called through the door: 'We're waiting for you, Bas.'

'One more question.'

'OK, OK.' Josie was flustered as she tried to think. 'Oh, I have it. If you had to choose one key moment in your life—something that changed everything—what would that be?'

Sebastian thought carefully. 'I would say that came when I opened a climbing magazine one day and saw a picture of Everest, and decided to climb it.'

'Climb Everest? Just like that?'

'Climb it . . . and fly a paraglider from the summit. A Japanese guy did it a few years back but no American has ever done it.'

Josie looked at him, not sure if he was joking or not. 'Seriously?'

'Sure. Why not? It's a life mission. Everyone needs one.'

'What do you think that decision says about you?'

He turned to her, his face set, no trace of humour now in his eyes. 'I dare to live the dream. I believe that no target is out of reach if you want it enough.' Sebastian looked at her. 'How about you, Josie? You dare to live the dream, too?'

For a moment their eyes locked and Josie knew that beneath his penetrating gaze she could not lie. 'I'd like to think I could. But there's no Everest in my life, if that's what you mean.'

'So tell me about yourself.'

'I thought you had a meeting to get to?'

Sebastian picked up his telephone, punched three numbers and spoke into it. 'Start without me. I'll be through in a while.' He leaned back in his chair. 'I spilled my beans, now you can spill yours.'

HAL AND RACHEL had also met by chance, two years earlier, when Rachel had been sent on a six-month photographic assignment to Alaska. Hal's name kept cropping up. 'You have to meet this guy,' she was told. 'He's like Mr Adventure around here. He teaches people to fly paragliders, he climbs big time, he skis—oh, and he runs the Alaskan Avalanche Control unit.'

It was the avalanche work that interested her the most. She'd left a message on his answering machine: 'Hi, Hal. I'm a photographer doing a picture book about Alaska and I've heard about your avalanche control work. So, if it might be possible to spend a day with you to get some shots, please get back to me . . .'

Hal agreed to meet Rachel at a steakhouse in downtown Anchorage. 'How will I recognise you?' he'd asked her.

'I'll be stinking of walrus fat.'

'I'm sorry?'

'I'm flying up to Barrow tomorrow to shoot a traditional Inuit walrus hunt.'

'Some people get all the luck.'

Rachel had arrived late, offering a flurry of apologies, with a battle-scarred Nikon round her neck. She was dark, and prettier and younger than Hal had imagined from her voice. 'Just got back from the north,' she told him. 'Five-hour flight. My ass is going to be shaped like an airline seat by the end of this shoot.'

'Economy or business?'

She laughed and offered Hal her hand.

To her surprise, he raised it to his nose to inhale her scent. 'You were wrong about the walrus grease. Unless they've started marinating them in Chanel.'

'You're an endangered species—an Alaskan with a sense of humour. If you must know, I managed to get a shower.'

'How was the hunt?'

'Incredible. I've done some work in war zones and it felt kind of the same. The matter-of-fact business of dealing out death. It's frightening how normal it becomes.'

'I'd like to see some of your work.'

'Be my guest.' Rachel pulled a small portfolio from her bag.

They ordered the food and Rachel watched Hal as he flicked through the black and white prints. He was not what she'd expected, a mountain man with a beard and a thousand-mile stare. Instead, he was clean-shaven with a strong, intelligent face and a head of wavy brown hair. Cute, Rachel realised, seriously cute.

He turned his blue eyes back to her. 'These are excellent. I can see why they gave you this assignment.'

It took Hal approximately three ounces of a ten-ounce steak to fall in love with Rachel. What really captivated him were her eyes. They were deepest brown, with tiny slivers of honeycomb-coloured pigment set in the irises. They had a sparkling intensity, a teasing quality that was utterly disarming.

'So. Are you happy for me to join you for a day?' she asked him.

A week. A month. A lifetime. Why set a limit? Hal wanted to ask. 'What did you have in mind?'

'Something visual. Something dynamic.'

'Well, we do some helicopter stuff. That might be suitable. We go out to known avalanche slopes and detonate explosives. It makes them shed their load before it gets big enough to be destructive.'

Rachel had joined Hal on his next assignment. And the one after that, too. Hal loved having her around, so much so that the days started to feel empty when she went off on another shoot.

Winter ran into spring, the thaw marking the end of the avalanche period.

'So what do you do now?' Rachel asked him.

'In the summers? Different things. I get jobs as a mountain guide. Sometimes I run paragliding classes,' Hal told her. 'But this year's looking quiet.'

'How about you invite me on another shoot for my book? I'd like a shot of a bear. A bear in the wild, with her cubs.'

Hal considered his hands, suddenly shy. 'Well, I could take you out to a few places if you'd like. I reckon I know where to find them.'

Rachel smiled. 'I'd really like that.'

As soon as the river ice was broken up enough to allow a kayak to pass, Hal took Rachel for a trip down the Evans River. It was a day of crystal clarity, the sunlight punching through the water so powerfully that Rachel could see the rocky river bottom. For lunch, they built a fire on the river bank, pan-frying the arctic grayling that Hal pulled out of the water by the dozen.

They sat side by side in the early sunshine, savouring the silence of the wilderness.

'I could really get into this place,' Rachel said quietly.

'You are really into it.'

'But it'll be over soon.'

'It will? I thought you had plenty more to do on the book.'

'I do. I haven't started writing the text yet. But that's going to have to happen back home in Seattle. I don't have the money to stay much longer. I'll have to go back to the agency work, freelancing.' She flicked a tiny stone onto the glassy surface of the river, watching as the concentric ripples quickly pulsed and died. 'Still think we'll get that bear?' she asked him with a smile.

'Not here. This wood smoke will make them wary.'

After lunch they floated with the current. They saw a mink, moving with liquid grace along a lichen-encrusted branch overhanging the river and heard the telltale alarm slap of a beaver as it dived. Finally, while they drifted noiselessly, a black bear with two cubs came down to the river edge to drink and bathe. Rachel and Hal watched from close by until the animals shook themselves dry and melted back into the dark shadows of the forest.

Rachel turned to Hal, wide-eyed with wonder. 'That was . . .' she struggled for the words '. . . a very Alaskan moment.'

'Happens all the time,' he said, but she could see from the flushed excitement on his face that he too had been thrilled. 'Did you get it?'

'Get it? Those were the best pictures I've taken since I got here.'

'Well, I'm glad.'

Rachel looked at him intently. For a second, Hal thought she was going to lean forward and kiss him. 'I love it here,' she said finally, 'and I don't want this to end.'

'SO LET'S START at the beginning,' Sebastian had said to Josie in that first meeting at the *Daybreak* studio. 'Where did you grow up?'

Josie inhaled deeply to calm her nerves. Hesitantly, she began. 'Well . . . I lived in Durham. My father was the university rowing coach.'

'Your mother?'

'She left my father early on . . . She's been living in Buenos Aires for the last twelve years. I don't see her much.'

'And the big life-changing moment?'

There was an awkward silence. Josie looked at him appraisingly. What was it about Sebastian that made her instinctively trust him? She took a deep breath. 'When I was eighteen my father committed suicide. That pretty well changed everything for me.'

Sebastian let out a low whistle, his face creased with concern. 'That *is* heavy. Did you expect he might do that?'

'No. It was a total shock. I knew he'd been depressed when my mother left him but not that he was suicidal.'

'How close were you to him?'

'I worshipped him. After my mother left we were a team.'

'It must have turned your life upside-down.'

'Well, it did that all right. Everything was so clear up to that point. I had a college place to do sports psychology but I didn't last a year. It all seemed so pointless. So I went travelling round the world. Then found myself back in England wondering what to do.'

'How did you get the *New Icons* break?'

Josie's eyes lit up. 'Now that *was* a great moment. I saw this ad in a local newspaper and went along. I discovered I love interviewing people and writing about them.'

'But you say the magazine is on the way out?'

'It's probably going to fold. It's a shame . . .' Josie paused, aware that she had opened up far more than she had intended.

Sebastian appeared to be thinking for a while. Finally he asked her, 'You ever thought of working in television?'

Josie felt a knot of excitement form in her throat. 'In my dreams.'

'We've been looking for a researcher on the show-biz desk. You'd have to come up with ideas for guests, persuade them to come on the show and discuss what they want to talk about.'

'I don't know what to say.'

'Say yes or no.'

Josie flushed bright red. 'Well, yes.'

And that was the beginning.

AFTER THE TRIP down the Evans River Hal had invited Rachel back to his cabin for the first time. She had explored the house at Hal's side, pausing in front of the many expedition photographs hanging on the walls, enchanted by the stunning view from the living-room window and the worn tribal rugs from Afghanistan and Iran laid here and there on the wooden floor.

'This is my office.' Hal showed her into the smallest and untidiest of the rooms. The walls were lined with books devoted to avalanche science and the desk was home to a powerful computer and a radio transmitter.

'Do you ever write about the stuff you do?' she asked him.

'Not yet, but I have thought about that. There's a gap in the market for a popular book on avalanche avoidance and rescue.'

'Hey! I could do the photography. That would be a great way to stick around in Alaska and . . .' Rachel bit her lip.

'Well, yeah.' Hal grinned. 'That would be neat.'

'You'd have to let me come on the real rescues. And I'd want to get some awesome avalanche shots.'

'We'll see.'

'What are these?' Rachel picked up a handful of pebbles, which were sitting in a small dish near the computer.

'Just a memento. Souvenir of a climb.'

'Oh, yeah. I heard that you're a climber. So where are these from?'

'Everest.'

'You've been to *Everest*?'

'Sure. That used to be the main part of my business, but I don't guide any more. I . . . well, let's just say I retired.'

Hal turned to head for the kitchen but Rachel blocked him, determined not to let the subject go. 'So how high did you get?'

'Twenty-nine thousand and twenty-eight feet.'

'Wow. And how high is the mountain?'

'Twenty-nine thousand and twenty-eight feet.'

'*No way!* You've stood on the summit of Everest? But that's . . . stupendous. How many times were you there?'

'Six expeditions. Four times to the summit.'

'How many people did you get to the top?'

'Thirty-five.'

'That's incredible. It sounds like a real success.'

'It was. Then I lost one of my clients.'

Rachel could not keep the shock from her face. 'One of your clients died?'

'Yes,' he answered finally.

Hal unpinned a photograph from the pinboard and handed it to her. It showed a lone climber, standing in front of his tent. 'His name was Alex. He was a nice guy. His death was the worst incident of my guiding career. I still blame myself even now. I couldn't face going back. There are too many ghosts on that mountain for me.'

She held his gaze. 'Will you tell me about it one day?'

'Definitely.'

Hal summoned his courage to ask her a question he'd been thinking about all day. 'How long will it take you to write your book?'

'Well. I have to deliver by Christmas. That gives me six months.'

'Stay here if you like. I have to go to South America with a trekking group for a month this summer so you'll have plenty of peace and quiet. After that . . . well, we can see what happens.'

Rachel was delighted. 'Are you serious?'

'Yes.'

She reached up her hand to caress his cheek. 'I wanted to kiss you when we were down by the river,' she told him, 'but I didn't have the nerve.'

Hal gathered her in his arms. 'Got the nerve now?'

'Sure. Suddenly I feel very brave.'

Josie's rise through the ranks of *Daybreak* was meteoric—researcher to producer to presenter in three years flat. Her relationship with Sebastian had the same heady momentum, from long, lingering nights in Soho wine bars to marriage on a Bahamian beach less than a year after they'd first met.

Josie had a photograph from that happiest of days, pinned to the side of her dressing-room mirror. Nearby was a gold trophy: '*TV Times* Television Presenter of the Year'. Josie touched it for luck before each show—twice this morning for extra luck for Sebastian.

Josie went down to the studio, savouring the familiar electric charge of adrenaline as she walked beneath the rack of lights, the glare dazzling her for a moment until her eyes adjusted. 'When you lose that buzz,' Sebastian had told her right at the start of her career, 'that's when you have to stop.'

Through the studio monitors came the familiar opening title music. As the final chords died, the red light flickered into life on top of camera one. Josie stared straight into the lens and gave her best early-morning smile as she launched into her welcoming piece.

As a presenter, she was witty, with a cheeky line in backchat that could turn even the most staid interview into something fun. Today, she wrapped up the show with a beaming smile as three hours of live television came to a successful close.

As she left the set a production assistant called out: 'Mike wants to see you in his office.'

Josie's heart sank. A session with Mike was enough to blow out the high of the show. It was never about the good news.

She entered the deep-pile opulence of his office, which was already filled with cigar smoke. Mike was always immaculately groomed, with a year-round tan that could only come from a sunbed. His eyes, hawkish, appraising, set behind elegant gold-wire spectacles, were focused on a copy of *Broadcast* magazine. His jacket was off, revealing a pair of tartan braces which, along with the Disney cartoon character tie, said, 'I'm fun.'

Actually Mike wasn't fun, as Josie well knew. In fact, the faster the business had grown, the less fun he'd become. Mike was responsible for finding the advertisers who were the lifeblood of the show. Which meant his eyes were forever glued to the ratings sheets.

'Check this out.' He tossed the copy of *Broadcast* onto the desk. 'We slipped two percentage points against the BBC last week. Peaked at three point two million on that Tuesday when we did the live link-up with Sebastian. Slumped on Thursday with the fashion special. Generally not good enough, Josie. You're letting it slide.'

'Thanks, Mike. You really know how to lift a girl.'

'Come on. We all know what you can do when you really turn it on. You light up the screen. What's up?'

'Well, it doesn't help to have Sebastian out on Everest.'

'Don't worry about him. He's having the time of his life. And the ratings shoot up every time we do a progress report. We're all set for the party tonight. I've invited all our principal advertisers, plus some movers and shakers from the ITC. It'll be massive and the press will go crazy when he reaches the top . . .'

'Fantastic. He'll be really pleased.'

'Be here by nine thirty,' Mike said. 'And, Josie, be a darling and put on a short skirt, won't you? Doesn't do any harm to remind our male viewers what a great pair of legs you've got.'

She turned and fired a mock salute. 'Yes, sir.' He didn't hear her murmur 'asshole' beneath her breath as she walked away.

EVEREST. Josie had decided early on that it was pointless to fight Sebastian's fixation with the mountain—she could see that it was something akin to a love affair. Sebastian thought of the mountain as he pumped iron in the gym each morning. He thought of it as he spent his weekends walking for miles with a heavy pack on his back. He devoured the literature of past expeditions.

'Have you ever thought you might be obsessed?' Josie had asked.

He had considered the question quite seriously. 'Not obsessed. I'd say more . . . committed.'

Sebastian did research to find his guide, getting recommendations from summiteers. Two names kept coming up: Rick Fielding of Himalayan Objectives and Hal Maher of Mountain High. And the two were close friends, apparently.

Sebastian was keen to get Maher involved, mainly because he was a qualified paraglider pilot. But Maher turned Sebastian down flat, telling him he no longer guided Everest. Fielding, on the other hand, was super-keen, knowing that the high-profile client would be good for business. A wild-looking man, with a mane of shoulder-length golden hair and restless blue eyes, he had flown to London and briefed Sebastian about what he would need to do.

'How serious are you about the paraflight from the summit?' Fielding asked Sebastian.

'Totally serious. I need to create the maximum possible publicity and the flight element will guarantee that.'

'One thing worries me. How the hell do you get enough speed to take off when you're that high?' Rick wanted to know. 'Because you won't have the breath to run at twenty-nine thousand feet.'

Sebastian put a VHS cassette in a video player. 'Take a look at this. This is the documentary film of the Japanese guy who did it.'

Fielding watched as the Japanese climber laid the paraglider flat on the ice. He checked the lines, then strapped himself into the harness and shuffled forward on his backside until he was balanced right on the edge of the steeply sloping drop before him.

'Is he going to do what I think he's going to do?'

'Watch.'

The Japanese man lifted his legs and let himself go, accelerating fast on his back for ten, twenty, fifty yards. The paraglider canopy was dragging behind him, inflating as air filled it. Just before the final ten-thousand-foot drop, the crescent of nylon plumped up and began to rise. Within seconds the Japanese pilot was flying stable and true, out across the Western Cwm, heading for his landing site far below.

'That's the technique I want to use,' Sebastian informed Fielding. 'I've been practising it in the Alps and it's not as lethal as it looks. Just get up enough speed and that chute will open. It has to.'

'Rather you than me.'

Fielding pulled together a detailed training plan. Sebastian paid $40,000 to join up for preliminary climbs to Argentina, Alaska, Nepal—short, three-week expeditions that were gruelling and tough. With other Everest hopefuls, he learned how to control breathing at 25,000 feet; how to cope with temperatures down to forty degrees below freezing; how to pitch a dome tent in a force-ten gale.

Finally, the last training expedition over, Sebastian was ready. He wrote a cheque for $50,000 and mailed it to Himalayan Objectives in Vancouver. 'That's it,' he said to Josie with an excited smile. 'In four months' time I'll be standing on the top of the world.'

Josie smiled back but couldn't help noticing a tiny pool of cold fear somewhere deep inside her.

'I love you,' he told her, as they parted company at Gatwick, 'and I'm coming back in one piece.'

NOW, ON THE FIFTH FLOOR of the *Daybreak* studios, more than 100 guests gathered for the party to celebrate Sebastian reaching the summit of Everest.

At ten, Mike ushered Josie up onto the podium. 'Ladies and gentlemen, welcome to the *Daybreak* studios for what should prove to be a momentous night. As you all know, Sebastian is now well into his final summit attempt and we hope to be getting confirmation that he has reached the top of Everest in a very short while. When he gets there, assuming he does get there, we'll be establishing radio contact so we can speak to him direct.'

One of the journalists raised his hand. 'Josie. How do you feel about Sebastian joining the expedition?'

'I feel excited for him. The mountain has been a part of him since he was a child and now he's finally got the opportunity to go there. It's a dream come true.'

'The statistics show that, for every six people who summit, one dies.'

'Sebastian won't fail,' Josie told him straight. 'No matter how tough it gets out there, he won't back down. I don't think he's ever walked away from a challenge in his life. It'll be really hard but that's what he thrives on. He'll be having the best day of his life.'

EIGHT THOUSAND miles away, on the highest flanks of the summit ridge, Sebastian crouched over his ice axe and vomited. He fought for breath, drawing the oxygen into his lungs in great convulsive gasps, his head pounding with an altitude headache.

In front of him and behind him, strung out along the rope, the rest of the team members were locked in nightmares of their own. Hazily, he could see a figure looming in front of him. It was Rick, leader of the team.

'Dig deep, Bas.' Rick's words were muffled through his oxygen mask. 'It's in there. You just have to find it.'

Sebastian nodded, feeling a resurgence of strength.

'Let's go,' Rick said. He looked ahead for a target Sebastian could aim for, and spotted a discarded black cylinder about thirty yards up the ridge. 'The oxygen cylinder. OK? Then rest.'

The guide turned and began to climb, kicking the front points of his spikes into the ice as the ridge steepened into a series of steps. Sebastian kicked in behind him.

Kick in. Breathe. Lungs aching as the freezing-cold oxygen flowed into them from its icy cylinder. Kick in. Breathe and breathe. The nagging pull of cramp tightened the muscles in his thighs. Kick in. A stumble as hollow ice fractured beneath the spikes of his crampons, leaving him for a split second with no firm foothold. He felt the rope go taut as Rick held the fall.

Breathe. Breathe. Breathe. Sebastian found a firmer placement and kicked in once more, levering himself up on his ice axe as he found his balance. He expected the guide to start moving straight away but something had caught Rick's attention.

Something had changed. A gust of wind had embraced them. Up until then the night had been perfectly still. But now ice crystals were beginning to circulate along the skyline. The plume—the streamer of vaporised ice that was so characteristic of Everest's highest ridge—was beginning, barely detectably, to move.

FOUR HOURS after Hal had issued the avalanche warning on the radio, he went outside for another look at conditions. The snowfall had gradually eased off and he could see that the sky was clearing—precisely what he had feared: a sure sign that the warm front was moving in fast. He checked the thermometer by the back door.

'It's getting warmer,' he called to Rachel. 'It's one degree below freezing. I'm going to dig a test pit.'

He fetched a shovel from the store and headed for the slope behind the cabin.

When it was finished, Hal took out his plastic snow probe. There was only one layer of snow he was interested in this time: the volatile layer of sugar snow right at the bottom of the pack. It had changed dramatically with the temperature rise. Hal scooped out some granules and was astonished by its texture. It didn't feel like snow at all, more like a teaspoon of caviar—greasy, almost oily. He checked the thermometer once more, the mercury showing just a fraction below freezing. It was rising fast.

In a flash, he knew, with horrifying certainty, exactly how this snow pack was going to behave. For a moment he was awe-stricken, paralysed by the implications.

He hurried back to the kitchen door and called in to Rachel, 'Hey, come out the back. I want you to see something.'

Mystified, she came to the door.

Hal picked up a pickaxe handle from the woodpile and crossed to an old oil drum that lay nearby. He rolled the drum out to the bottom of the avalanche test area. 'I'm going to try something I've never tried before. Are you ready?'

He paused, with the pickaxe handle raised in the air.

'I think you've finally cracked,' she said.

Hal beat a single blow into the side of the drum, producing a sharp booming resonance that cut through the still winter air. Almost simultaneously, in a single fluid movement, the entire test bed avalanched into a pile at the base of the slope.

'My God,' Rachel said, joining Hal by the debris. 'It seemed almost . . . animal, the way it shot forward. What does it mean?'

Hal turned, his face drained of colour. 'It means that every single avalanche slope in Alaska is primed right now and ready to go just like this one.'

As THE CLOCK hit 11.00pm in the *Daybreak* studios, Mike was beginning to get restless and so were the waiting newsmen. It was getting late and most of them had already put in a long day's work. There was a limit to how long they could be expected to wait. 'Where's the call?' he asked Josie impatiently.

'I don't know, Mike. I have as much idea as you do.'

'I think we should try to contact Base Camp direct, at least get an update.' They retreated to Mike's office.

3

At the top end of the Khumbu Glacier, the portable satellite unit rang in the mess tent. A Sherpa called across the glacier: 'Telephone, Mr Tony.'

Within seconds Tony Keller, Rick Fielding's Base Camp manager, was out of his tent. As he crossed the moraine to the mess tent he happened to glance down the glacier to the south. He stopped dead, perplexed by what he saw.

Normally the view was one of the most spectacular in the world, jagged ice peaks, stretching away as far as the eye could see. Now there was only a fast-moving cloud, pulsing up the glacier. It was a cloud unlike any Tony had ever seen, supernaturally dark, almost maroon. 'Hey, Gyaltsen! Come out here and have a look at this.'

The laid-back sirdar ambled unhurriedly from the Sherpa tent.

'You ever seen anything like that before?'

The Sherpa's normal inscrutable expression changed to one of surprise as he saw the cloud racing in. 'No, never seen. Not like that. I think we have to close the tents,' he said.

The two men began to run back towards the mess tent. As they reached the entrance the first hammer blow of the storm hit the camp.

Inside the tent Tony paused for a moment, unsure what would happen as the screaming intensity of the wind ripped into the canvas. Less than a second later he found out, as the front panel caved in towards him, sending the table flying. Tony watched in disbelief as the heavy white canvas bulged, then split with a rending crack as a seam gave way. The stinging whirlwind of driven ice particles filled the interior within seconds.

'Hold it down!' he shouted.

Running from their tents, the Base Camp team joined in as he threw himself at the front end of the tent, snatching at the wildly flapping wall of canvas. A side wall began to flare out, the skirt starting to lift free of its heavy rock anchors as the wind took control. Two of the Sherpa support team began to load it with more rocks.

The metal side poles began to bend as the full weight of the wind bore down on the open structure. The interior was being stripped out before their eyes as maps, files and plastic cups were spun into the air and transported away.

'The satphone!'

Tony found the satellite communications set behind the over-turned table, already covered in snow. The ringing had stopped. Cradling it in his arms, he exited the tent just as one of the corner legs collapsed. The tent billowed and twisted, the frame groaning as the metal poles snapped out of their securing points. The 100-pound structure cartwheeled into the whiteout and was gone.

SEVEN THOUSAND FEET above Base Camp, Sebastian tried to will himself into finding the strength to continue the ascent. Looking ahead he could see a line of climbers waiting at the foot of the Hillary Step—the thirty-foot-high ice cliff that posed the last serious technical obstacle before the summit. There were five teams making their ascent that day. There was going to be a long wait here, he realised. A wait he could ill afford, as his body was cold to the core, far colder than he had ever been in his entire life.

Rick was just above him and, to take his mind off the nagging frost pain in his fingers and toes, Sebastian fixed his concentration on Rick's mask. The guide's goggles were mirror-coated and Sebastian could see an image of himself in the lens, distorted as if by a funfair mirror. Fascinated, he leaned closer, studying the rows of great white teeth rising up behind him as if the mountain was about to be engulfed. Between the sharp fangs he could see a boiling mass of black and violet. Was that shadow? He couldn't tell.

A trail of icy vapour passed overhead at that moment, blanking out the sun. Rick tensed, stiffening as he focused on something. A high-pitched roar was approaching, a sound like the rip of a jet fighter passing low overhead.

'Oh my God.' The guide's words were barely audible.

Sebastian felt the hair on his head stiffen; an electric charge seemed to be running through him. 'What's happening?'

Rick held up his hand. 'Get down,' he muttered.

Sebastian shifted his body, planted a crampon into the ice and turned round. There was not a single mountain to be seen. Instead, the entire sky was filled with a racing mass of black cloud, rising up from an unseen world below. Sebastian watched in mute fascination as the ridge was engulfed at phenomenal speed. He barely had time to crouch for cover as the maelstrom hit the ridge.

BACK AT HIS DESK, Hal called up Anchorage FM. Once he explained the situation, he was patched, live, into the studio, the presenter cutting the music abruptly.

'I got a newsflash here. Seems we've got an urgent message from Hal Maher at the Alaskan Avalanche Control unit. Hal?'

'I have some important news for anyone planning to travel in the next twenty-four hours and for anyone who lives or works in a designated avalanche risk area. The heavy snowfalls have combined with a rise in temperature so that we now have a critical situation. This is now a state of red alert. I'd like you to broadcast that in your hourly news reports from now on.'

'What does this mean in practical terms, Hal?'

'Unless your journey is absolutely essential, do not travel until the alert has been lifted. If you live or work in a high-risk area, evacuate as quickly and as calmly as you can. If you are in doubt as to what to do then call your local police department.'

'Are we going to see some big slides in the next couple of days?'

Hal paused. 'I believe we are entering a period of intense avalanche activity. Perhaps the most intense for many decades.'

'Thanks, Hal. We'll spread the news.'

Hal didn't hear the final words as he was already accessing his computer to update the website. He typed in the carefully worded report and activated the code that would automatically send it, in the form of a fax, to more than 450 connections throughout Alaska. Within minutes, as the modem hummed into action, the warning notice was printing out in mountain rescue centres and in every police station in Alaska.

'What can I do?' Rachel was at the door.

'You can help me with the AMRs.' Hall pulled a file down.

'At Most Risk' was the file containing details on the hundreds of properties that Hal had identified as sitting in the path of prime avalanche routes. There were twenty-seven that Hal regarded as potential deathtraps. 'Take half these numbers and call the owners,' he told Rachel. 'Tell them to get the hell out.'

'OK.' Rachel went to use the living-room telephone.

Hal began working through his own quota of telephone numbers. It wasn't an easy task to tell home-owners to evacuate but Hal had built such a strong rapport with them that they knew he would only ask *in extremis*. He reached the last name on the list: Stan Carroway.

Hal had lost count of the number of times he had tried to

persuade that stubborn old bastard about the risk of avalanches. But would he listen? Carroway and his wife Louisa spent every winter in their remote cabin in Cooper Valley. They were happy there, Louisa painting delicate watercolours of the winter landscapes, Stan curing the fish he caught during the summer months. 'This is what keeps us alive, son,' Carroway told Hal the first time they met. 'You won't get us out of this cabin come hell or high water.' Still, they came to have a grudging respect for Hal and he developed a fondness for the cranky old couple.

Now, he dialled them. 'Stan? It's Hal Maher.'

'Thought you might be calling. No sooner do we get a few flakes of snow up here than you start squeaking.'

'This is prime avalanche weather, Stan. I know I sound just like a scratched record to you two but I want you to get out of there.'

'No chance in hell. We're staying put.'

'You can see how much snow you have on that hillside just outside your back door?'

'It's heavy all right, but I don't see no harm in that. We're—'

With the softest of clicks the line went dead.

'Stan . . .?' Hal felt a cold spasm turn his guts. 'Stan? Answer me!'

'What's wrong?' Rachel came into the office.

'I was talking to the Carroways and the phone went dead.'

He dialled the operator and gave the number. 'Can you tell me what's wrong with this line?'

The operator came back to him after thirty seconds: 'It's cut off. They've probably got a post down in Cooper Valley.'

'Thank you.'

'You think they've already been hit?' Rachel asked.

'I don't know. But if they're still alive I want them out of there.'

'Why don't you call up the helicopter?'

'It's too risky. The rotor noise alone could be enough to set off that slope. I'm going over to get them.' Hal picked up his car keys.

'Let me come with you.'

'No chance. I don't want you to risk getting injured.'

Rachel stood in the doorway, blocking him. 'I need the photographs for our book, Hal. I need an evacuation. You promised me when we started the project together. No restrictions, remember?'

Hal could see from her face that she was not going to back down. He sighed. 'I'll put in a quick call to Robbie McGowan at the State Troopers office to tell him where we're going.'

At 11.30 JOSIE DIALLED the Inmarsat number again. This time it did not ring. Instead she heard a continuous tone.

'That's odd. It sounds like the machine has been switched off.'

Mike looked through the glass door at the party where the champagne was beginning to take effect and the noise level and the sound of laughter were rising. 'Bloody satellites,' he said. 'We have to give them some news soon or they'll start to leave.'

'Don't panic. We'll get through.'

The telephone rang. Josie leapt across the room to get it. 'Yes?'

'Josie. This is the switchboard. I have a gentleman from CNN on the line. He says it's absolutely urgent that he speaks to you.'

'Very well. Put him through.'

The caller was connected. 'Josie Turner? My name is Ron Purdey, I work for CNN's London bureau. I just got an email from one of my stringers in Kathmandu that could be interesting to you.'

'What email?'

Purdey took a deep breath. 'Apparently, the mother of all storms is raging on Everest as we speak. Virtually all the lines into Base Camp are down. My stringer got one of the last calls out of a Malaysian team but since then, nada.'

'Is there any news of Sebastian and the rest of his team?'

'According to my stringer, he's missing. And so are about thirty other climbers. I'm sorry to bring you this news.'

'Jesus. Have they reached the summit?'

'According to our guy no one reached the summit. The weather turned before they got there. We'll be running a report at midnight on this. Can I get a quote from you?'

'I haven't got time for that now.' Josie put down the telephone and turned to Mike. 'It seems a storm has hit the mountain. I don't think Sebastian's going to reach the summit now. Not today at least.'

Mike pursed his lips. 'That's all we need. We're going to look bloody stupid now, aren't we?'

'I'm sorry?' Josie's voice was cold and emotionless. 'You're worried about looking foolish in front of your guests? Hasn't it occurred to you to wonder about Sebastian? About the fact that he's probably going through hell on that mountain?'

'You didn't say he was in trouble. You just said there's a storm. They'll just retreat to a lower camp and hang out for a bit before they try it again.'

Mike strode from the office into the conference area. 'Thank you for your patience, ladies and gentlemen. Some minutes ago we got a message from Everest to inform us that weather conditions have deteriorated rapidly and it seems that Sebastian's summit attempt is postponed for the moment.'

There was a collective groan from the audience.

'Since we have no more news at present, we have to call this press conference to a halt.'

A dozen hands were raised as a babble of conversation erupted. 'Can we have a word from Josie?' someone called.

Mike glanced to where Josie stood. She shook her head firmly from side to side. 'Josie will be leaving right away. But we'll all be here tomorrow to resume the conference, hopefully with good news from Everest. Thank you.'

THE LIGHT WAS FADING fast as Hal and Rachel entered the narrow confines of Cooper Valley. The valley sides were steep and forbidding, with exposed black rock jutting out through the trees.

As they powered along in second gear along the snow-covered road Hal switched on the headlights, the brilliant yellow beams illuminating a haze of tiny crystals falling from the pine trees on the lower slopes.

'It's snowing again,' Rachel said.

'That's not snow. It's tiny droplets of water. The temperature's still rising.'

They passed through the narrowest part of the valley, a section so choked with massive glacial boulders that a tunnel had been dug through them. It was only fifteen yards long, but Hal knew it had taken Carroway three years to excavate it. The sides of the Toyota scraped along the rock walls as they drove through.

Boulders and slippery rocks snatched at the Toyota's wheels, rocking it violently. With its engine groaning under the strain, the vehicle made it up onto the plateau at the end of the valley. Hal brought the car to a halt.

The Carroways' wooden cabin was clearly visible, dwarfed by the immensity of the valley walls above it.

JOSIE CHECKED her answering machine—one message, sent ten minutes earlier: 'Josie, this is Deborah Fielding at Himalayan Objectives. Can you call me in Vancouver?'

If anyone would have news it would be Rick's wife, running the

Himalayan Objectives office. Josie punched in the numbers. 'Deborah. This is Josie.'

'Oh, thank goodness you called. You've heard about the storm? I'm just calling all the clients' families. As soon as we get any news we'll be straight in touch.'

'Why can't we get them on the satphone?'

'I don't know. I've never known that happen before.'

Josie felt a sudden surge of anger. 'How could Rick let them get caught in this way, Deborah? Haven't they got weather information? It sounds crazy to go for the summit on a day like that.'

Deborah sighed. 'Josie, I don't know what went wrong. But I do know how you feel. My husband is up there, too.'

'Sorry. You're right. I just . . . I just can't stand not knowing.'

Deborah was soothing. 'Don't worry. If I know Rick, he'll have the whole team snugged up at Camp Four. In a few hours' time we'll get a call to say they're fine. I'll get Base Camp to call you direct.'

Josie put down the telephone and ran to the sitting room, where the resonant tones of Victor Melzac, CNN newscaster, boomed out of the television. 'News just in from Mount Everest indicates that up to forty climbers are missing in what has been described as the storm of the century. Among them is media mogul Sebastian Turner. Let's go to our Kathmandu correspondent, Pia Rothwell, for the latest.'

An image of the stringer came up on screen next to Melzac. 'Pia, what can you tell us about the storm?'

'Well, it seems weather reports had not predicted the storm, so the expeditions had little warning that it was on the way. The Malaysian expedition base camp told me they have recorded wind speeds of up to one hundred and forty miles an hour and temperatures as low as seventy degrees below freezing, and that's thousands of feet beneath the high camps where many of the climbers are.'

'Are the climbers still stuck out on the peak?'

'There's no way of telling that as of now, Victor, but initial indications are that a significant number of climbers have not made it back to the top camp after their abortive summit attempt.'

'Pia, thank you for that. We'll be talking to you later as this story develops. In the meantime we have Ed Haston on the line.'

A still picture of the bearded climber came up on screen. 'Ed, you were one of the early pioneers on Everest. What is your expert assessment of their situation?'

'Their oxygen bottles will be running out and they'll almost certainly be without life-sustaining fluids or high-energy foods. Not many people have survived a night at those sort of altitudes and they'll be desperate for shelter.'

'How about a rescue team coming up from Camp Four?'

'No one will be moving up from Camp Four in those conditions.'

'Are you saying that a rescue is impossible?'

'Nigh on impossible. Once you're in the death zone, by which I mean above twenty-five thousand feet, you are truly beyond reach.'

'A final word. How do you rate their chances?'

'It depends on the storm. If it blows out, then they've got a fighting chance of survival. But if it doesn't then I'm afraid that many people are going to die on Everest tonight.'

As HAL AND RACHEL reached the cabin, Stan Carroway emerged. 'What the hell are you two doing up here? You didn't need to drive all this way to give me the same old lecture.'

'I did. Your telephone's out of action.'

Stan beckoned them into the living room, where the wood-burning stove had pumped the temperature up to something just a shade below the average sauna. Louisa emerged from the bedroom.

'We're coming with you,' she said. 'We've already got the bag packed.' She gestured to a suitcase standing by the door.

Hal paused, surprised. 'I'm sorry?'

'I heard something about an hour ago that fair made the hairs on my neck stand up,' Stan said. 'I tell you, Hal, the quicker we get out of here, the happier I'm going to be. I would have driven us out myself but I couldn't be sure we'd make it down the track. I figured you'd be along soon enough.'

'What did you hear?' Hal asked, the hairs on his own neck rising.

'After you rang I went out to check the wood store and I was just standing there when there was this terrifying noise from the mountain. A "whoomph", a thunderous great boom, and it was all around the valley. And I saw the whole goddamn snow pack move in a single mass. It dropped about a yard, then it stuck.'

Hal felt his stomach turn. 'It's worse than I thought. Get your boots on now. We haven't got a moment to lose.'

The sky was darkening rapidly as night fell and a crescent moon rose over the ridge. They walked towards the Toyota without a word. Rachel went ahead, turning occasionally to fire off a photograph.

When they reached the Toyota, Hal opened the tailgate to let Stan place his bag inside while Rachel helped Louisa into the back.

Hal took his place in the driving seat, slipped the clutch and put the Toyota in gear. 'Let's go, Stan.'

The old man paused, standing at the back of the vehicle, looking back at the cabin.

'I'll get him in,' Rachel said. She walked round to Stan and placed a hand on his shoulder to usher him gently into the car. Then she placed her hand on the tailgate and slammed it down hard.

And that was all it took. The wave of sound created by the slamming door sprung the mountain into life with all the explosive force of a finger triggering a gun. An answering retort came back, a detonation that rent the air like the crack of some celestial whip—nature's ultimate fury unleashed. The crack became a rumble. Hal squinted out into the half-light. Terror gripped him as ink-black fracture lines ripped across the valley walls.

'Avalanche!' he yelled in the split second after the slope began to move. He turned to Rachel, shouting, 'Get into the car!'

Rachel was transfixed, scarcely able to comprehend the magnitude of what she was witnessing, as millions of tons of snow began to race down towards the valley floor. She raised her camera and started to shoot.

'Rachel! Forget about the shots!' Hal shouted.

As he spoke the avalanche swept down towards the cabin like a hawk tumbling out of the sky onto its prey, and obliterated it into matchwood. Then it was hunting across the plateau towards them.

Next thing Rachel knew, Hal was bundling her into the front seat of the Toyota. He slammed the vehicle into gear and the 4x4 leapt forward and began to forge across the plateau. In his rearview mirror Hal could see the avalanche gaining on them, the roar intensifying with every second as the pressure wave powered after them.

Suddenly Rachel screamed, 'Hal look to the side!'

He spun his head to glance through the side window for a split second. Coming towards them, illuminated by the blue-grey cast of the moon, was a second avalanche.

A beat later Hal made eye contact with Rachel. Her face was white, the proximity of death in her eyes. Over her shoulder, Hal saw the third avalanche tumbling across the plateau.

He realised in that heart-stopping second what had happened: all three sides of the bowl had been released at the same time—the entire amphitheatre had ripped out in one avalanche.

SEBASTIAN LAY on Everest's summit ridge, locked in a state somewhere between confusion and terror, with Rick huddled next to him. They were buried in fast-drifting snow, out of oxygen, out of fluid. Of the other climbers there was no sign.

The storm had grown in ferocity as the hours had passed, the wind rising to a hurricane force blast of 150 miles an hour.

Sebastian tried to focus, a niggling pulse of life force telling him that if he let his mind drift away he would be finished. He was hovering on the borderline of acute mountain sickness—the altitude-related condition that begins with disorientation and ends inevitably in death, if the victim does not descend. His feet and hands had lost all sensation some time before and now, dimly, he was aware that the cold was eating into his core.

In the early stages, Rick had yelled words of encouragement. Now Rick wasn't yelling anything at all. He couldn't; earlier, he had taken off his oxygen mask to give Sebastian his last air and in the course of inhaling a deep breath had frost-burned the tissue in his lungs. He was having severe trouble breathing as he hauled Sebastian to his feet and dragged him blindly in a direction chosen at random.

Neither of them could see further than a few feet ahead; there was too much wind-whipped ice in the air for that. As he stumbled after Rick, Sebastian could physically feel his tendons cracking where the frozen flesh in his legs was tearing itself apart. He closed his eyes as the wind picked up in a new assault.

Rick shook him. 'Don't sleep,' he tried to shout. 'Sebastian, don't sleep . . .'

But Sebastian merely buried his head in the crook of his arm, trying to find refuge from the ferocity of the storm. He slumped onto the ice and sensed Rick lying down beside him, shivering violently—a phase Sebastian had experienced himself as he passed through the early stages of hypothermia.

Slowly an image seeped into his mind, a picture as cruel as it was beautiful. It was Josie. Suddenly he was overwhelmed with an unbearable sense of loss.

ONE GLANCE in the rear mirror told Hal everything he needed to know. His entire rear vision was filled with a cloud of pulverised snow as the avalanche snatched at their back bumper and the steering wheel fought against his grip. Suddenly the rush of noise increased massively and in that instant he saw that the avalanche that had come from the left-hand wall of the bowl was going to collide with the one behind them.

The crescendo reached its peak as Hal gave up his battle for the steering wheel. All hell broke loose as the shock wave of the two avalanches colliding caused the rear windows to implode one by one.

Hal threw himself across the cab, using his body to protect Rachel as best he could, as the entire vehicle slewed sideways. Then the Toyota was airborne, tossed into a 360-degree roll, which crushed the roof down in a scream of rending metal. Next thing he knew, Hal felt the car dumped back upright, then sent spinning into a glissading skid that ripped them backwards at awesome speed. A bone-jarring impact shook them, as the vehicle was pounded into something hard, then slipped sideways down an incline and ground to a halt.

Hal shook himself free of the snow covering him and raised his head. He could sense from a movement beneath him that Rachel was still alive. The Carroways were both crying in the back, Louisa screaming in short bursts as Stan tried to help her upright in her seat. Both were bleeding profusely.

Hal tried to orientate himself. Some 100 yards away, a white mushroom cloud was now racing *away* towards the other side of the valley. The side avalanche had not only demolished the one coming directly down the valley, it had swallowed it whole, changed its direction and the combined force of the two was now running into a head-on collision with the slower-moving third arm.

It happened a second later: a cataclysmic clashing of forces. Sixty million tons of ice travelling at 140 miles an hour smacked straight into 40 million tons of ice travelling at 90 miles an hour and caused a climax avalanche.

On both sides of the valley, avalanches were beginning to shoot down towards them, the sides peeling away neatly in a funnelling effect, which formed a perfect trap. Bruised and dazed, Hal watched with a mixture of wonder and terror as the world came in towards him. Far off, in unseen valleys, he could hear a distant rumble as slope after slope was fired into action.

Hal realised he had just two options: sit there and wait to be destroyed . . . or drive. He pulled himself upright in the driver's seat, and turned the key.

The Toyota lurched forward with a screeching protest of twisted metal. Hal ignored it, gunning into high revs and steering directly down towards the forest at the base of the valley. Just a short distance inside it was the rock tunnel and Hal fixed every part of his being on one single intention—to get the Toyota into that tunnel before the next wave of avalanches hit them.

Both headlights were shattered. He had to punch the remains of the windscreen out to give himself any vision. The slope was peppered with embedded boulders and hollows, the Toyota careening from one impact to another.

Then he was in the forest, weaving round the larger trees, smashing down the smaller. The tunnel was just ahead. He pushed harder on the accelerator. Suddenly the Toyota was sliding out of control, a mass of snow catching the rear and spinning the vehicle backwards towards the tunnel mouth.

In his last moment of consciousness Hal realised that they had been spun around to face the avalanche. Out of the oblivion the splintered end of a seventy-year-old pine flew vertically towards the Toyota, its trunk at least a yard wide. As it punched through the front of the vehicle, Hal felt the first particles of powder snow enter his lungs in one suffocating breath, then all was black.

Josie retreated to the living-room sofa, wrapped herself in a blanket and switched on the television to see if there was any more news. There was, but not from Everest. CNN had switched its focus to another breaking story, this time in Alaska. Pictures showed terrible devastation: houses, cars and railway tracks shattered and twisted.

Josie turned up the sound. '. . . Early reports indicate that more than forty people have been killed this evening in the worst series of avalanches to hit Alaska since records began.'

A shaken-looking police officer flashed up on the screen. 'We're only beginning to gauge the true scale of this disaster. Seems like just about every valley in the south of the state has avalanched all at once. We believe that there may be a hundred or more people still missing.' The picture cut to a photograph. 'Among the missing is Alaskan avalanche expert Hal Maher. Police fear he may have been caught himself as he tried to warn others of the impending disaster.'

THE IMPACT HAD smashed several teeth. Hal spat out the pieces of broken enamel, coughed up the powder snow and pushed his right arm into ice around him to create an air pocket.

All was silent. He tried to move his head, only to find that it was pinned tightly in position. Blood was dribbling into his eyes, a steady, thick fluid tracing a warm path from his mouth. That was when Hal figured he was upside-down, which would explain why his temples were tight with the rhythmic pulse of his heartbeat.

The final moments came back to Hal in a series of vivid images: the speed at which the avalanche had swept the Toyota backwards towards the tunnel, the tree coming out of the wall of white, the impact of his face against something metal as he was dragged, spinning uncontrollably, out of the vehicle. Then the blackout.

Experimenting, he moved his left leg above him, finding to his astonishment that it was free. So was the right. Hal paused to summon his strength, then jammed his left leg into solid terrain and tensed the knee to push. The movement twisted his torso round at the waist, forcing his head and shoulders free from the snow in which they had been buried. He lay on his side, shocked and bruised, panting with the exertion.

Rachel. The Carroways. The thought of them brought Hal to his feet. The moon had risen higher in the night sky and, as his eyes adjusted, he was able to make some sense of his location. He was standing a few yards from the tunnel entrance, which was now partly clogged with snow and the debris of broken trees. Around him, not a single tree had been left standing.

Inside the tunnel he could see the glow of a red light—one of the taillights of the Toyota. Hal screwed up his eyes, struggling to pick out detail in the dim light. Now he could see it, the wreckage of the vehicle was partly crushed beneath the weight of the huge tree that had hit them in the final seconds.

He started to fight his way through the splintered trees, clambering over and under the confusion of broken branches. He reached the vehicle, his heart sinking as he saw that it was upside-down, half buried in snow. He tapped the wing section, praying for a response.

A muffled cry came back. It was Stan Carroway's voice.

'I'm getting you out, Stan.' Hal began to dig as fast as he could, knowing that if Stan was alive there was still hope for Rachel and Louisa. The smell of petrol was strong—the fuel tank must have been ruptured as the vehicle rolled. He concentrated on scraping away the compacted snow until he got to the window frame and could reach into the back seat.

A bony hand grabbed him with a feeble grip as he heard Stan's voice, weak and shaking with shock: 'Louisa's still alive . . . I can hear her breathing next to me. For Chrissakes get us out of here.'

'You're going to be all right, Stan,' Hal told him. 'I'm digging you out as fast as I can.' Then he eased his hand in towards the front, reaching up into the constricted footwell of the passenger side where snow had failed to penetrate. An air pocket.

At first he felt nothing. He moved his body headfirst down into the cavity to get better access to the space. Then he felt a tiny movement—and a groan of pain. Rachel was also alive.

Hal pulled back and began to dig once more, slicing into the frozen pack with a piece of torn metal until he had exposed one entire side of the Toyota. It took him an hour to achieve this and a further hour to extract Stan and Louisa.

Stan was in deep shock, Louisa alive but unconscious. Hal found the bag they had brought with them and spread clothes on the snow before laying Stan and Louisa them side by side. Stan pulled Louisa into his arms to warm her as best he could.

Then Hal returned to Rachel. It was a delicate job to manoeuvre her out of the constricted space, but finally she was free. She was deeply concussed, and Hal could see immediately that one of her legs was broken. He placed her gently next to the Carroways. She would live. They would all live if he could get them to hospital.

Suddenly Hal heard a noise, the muffled clatter of rotorwash as a helicopter flew overhead sweeping up and down the valley. A rescue team was out looking for them. Hal remembered his last-minute call to Robbie McGowan at the State Trooper's office—he'd told Robbie where he was going. But how could they possibly be seen in the dark?

Strapped in the back of the Toyota was a gallon can of spare fuel. Hal retrieved it quickly then shook Stan Carroway by the shoulder. 'Stan! You have a lighter?'

Stan looked at him in confusion and did not respond as Hal began to search his pockets. He found a brass Zippo in the old man's back pocket and made his way as fast as he could to the tunnel entrance. The helicopter rotor was already getting fainter as the aircraft searched further down the valley.

A safe distance from the tunnel Hal began to shake out the petrol. He took some paces back, ignited a flame on the Zippo and tossed the lighter onto the fuel, stepping back as it combusted with a roar. Soon, the flames were rising into the night sky.

Hal sat on a tree trunk, praying the helicopter would make one more pass. Slowly the sound of the rotorwash increased once more as the machine made its way back up the valley. Abruptly, it changed tack, heading directly for the fire. Hal stood, feeling dizzy and weak, waving his arms as the searchlight of the rescue helicopter picked him out. Then it was hovering directly over him, the propwash creating a mini whirlwind of leaves and broken fragments of bark.

Hal saw a figure being lowered on a winch cable. He wanted to shout a greeting, but the world was spinning too much. By the time the paramedic reached him, he had collapsed in a faint.

DESPITE HAVING had no sleep, Josie decided she would go ahead and present the show. If nothing else, it would give her a chance to escape the pressure of this endless wait.

As she went down to answer the chauffeur's call, the telephone rang once more. It was Everest Base Camp again. 'Sebastian and the others are still not back at camp,' Tony told her, his voice flat and emotionless. 'Another team have reported seeing bodies huddled together near the South Summit.'

'Oh, Christ. Can't you get them on a radio?'

'We did get a snatch of radio from Rick about four hours ago. We think he's still alive—possibly with Sebastian.'

'What did he say?'

Tony sounded strangled by his own grief. 'He was distressed. He didn't make sense. He said he was in trouble and wanted oxygen before he could move. He told us he can't feel his feet.'

'Can anyone get to them?'

'I think not. There's no chance in hell of anyone making it up there in these conditions even if they were willing to try. We're preparing for the worst, Josie, I can't pretend otherwise.'

Josie wanted to lash out, to swear at the only voice she had to rage at. But she knew it would not help.

'Thank you for telling me.' She put down the phone.

AT ANCHORAGE General Hospital, Hal, revived by the paramedics during the flight, watched as Stan and Louisa were examined and pronounced to be in no serious danger. Rachel was worse. A surgeon took one look at her injuries and had her spirited away to an operating theatre. Hal sat outside the operating room, stubbornly refusing to get his own injuries treated.

It was an hour before the surgeon emerged. 'Your partner has suffered multiple trauma. We pulled a six-inch piece of metal out of her thigh and she has numerous fractures to the legs and ribs. There are superficial injuries to the head but so far as we can ascertain there will be no lasting effects. I believe she will make a complete recovery . . . in time. I'm afraid for the baby there's no hope.'

Hal looked at him in confusion. 'The baby?'

'Your partner was pregnant, Mr Maher, but I fear that her abdominal injuries are such . . .' He gave a small shrug, the gesture of a professional man used to the imparting of bad news. 'Now may I suggest that you get your own injuries seen to?' He took Hal by the elbow and led him through to the casualty ward.

THE MAKE-UP GIRL toned out the bags beneath Josie's eyes, just in time for her to take her place on the sofa. As the red cue light came on, Josie forced her face into a smile. 'Good morning and welcome to *Daybreak* . . .' Her voice suddenly faltered as she saw herself reflected in the lens of the camera. For a brief instant she thought she could see the figure of Sebastian by her side.

And that was when she knew. He wasn't coming back. Sebastian was dying, probably dead. Everest had killed him.

The tears began: agonised, rending sobs that came from a deeper place than she knew she had inside her.

The camera lingered on her face for a while before the gallery realised Josie was not going to recover. They faded to black as she ran from the studio.

Twenty-four hours after the avalanche, Hal discharged himself from hospital. He was as stiff as hell, beaten and bruised from being ripped out of the Toyota, with one fractured rib, two broken fingers and a mouthful of sawn-off teeth.

At his cabin he went straight to the computer. There were more than ninety email messages. Hal knew that every one of those callers would be seeking his help or advice.

The telephone rang. 'Hello?' he said.

'Thank God I got you, Hal. This is Deborah. I've been trying to get you all through the day. I heard that you'd been caught in one of the avalanches. I didn't know if you were dead or alive.'

Deborah. Rick Fielding's wife. Hal was relieved it was a friend on the line. 'I'm sorry. I've been at the hospital and only just got back.'

'Is Rachel all right?'

Hal decided he could not hide anything from her. 'She was pregnant, Deborah. But not any more.'

'Oh God, Hal. I am so sorry. What's her condition?'

'She'll be in traction for quite some time. Her left leg is well smashed up but it seems they saved it. She's heavily sedated.'

'Have you seen a paper or the news today, Hal?'

'I've deliberately avoided them . . . so many people have died.'

'I know you've just been through hell, but I have more bad news for you and I want you to hear it from me.' There was a sob from the other end of the line.

Hal realised for the first time that she was calling not merely to commiserate. He sat down heavily on his chair. 'It's Rick, isn't it? You heard something from the expedition?'

'The climb was a total wipe-out, Hal. Six died in a storm. Rick was one of them. I know this is . . .'

'Rick *died*? I can't believe it.'

'You're not the only one, Hal. I can't believe it, but he's not coming back and neither are five of his clients.' Deborah's voice broke.

'How did it happen?'

'Don't ask me. I've spent the last twenty-four hours on the telephone trying to find out. Most of the time the satphone's been down in the storm.'

There was a long pause, finally broken by Hal. 'How are the children taking it?'

'Totally distraught and in shock, like me. Rick was invincible, Hal, we all knew that. How could that happen to him?'

'I can only think he must have been trying to save some clients. It must have been one hell of a storm.'

'Why, Hal? Why?'

Hal knew there was little more he could say. 'Anything I can do, just tell me, OK? Anything, you hear?'

'Thank you. I have to go, Hal. I need to make some more calls. But listen, whatever happens, you must come down to Vancouver for the memorial service for Rick . . . for the whole team, everyone who died. Rick always told me that that's what I should do if the worst ever happened. Will you come?'

'I'll be there.'

THREE DAYS after Sebastian's death Josie finally summoned the courage to return to work. A question of pride, she told herself. She knew it was what Sebastian would have wanted.

At the studio, a volley of flashes blinded her as photographers jostled with security guards to try to get prime position. Josie kept her head down and ran for the entrance.

Mike was there, along with the show's senior producers. 'My deepest sympathies, Josie,' he said, 'and from everyone here at *Daybreak*.'

'Well, what can I say? Sebastian lived on the edge . . . we all knew that. And sometimes people who live on the edge pay the price.' Josie bustled away, moving quickly towards her dressing room. She found a black outfit on the rail—Jacqui, the wardrobe assistant, had been sharp enough to think that one through.

The technicians were gentle with her when she walked through to the studio, the soundman miking her up while at the same time telling her, 'It takes a lot of courage to do what you're doing here today. Not many people could sit in front of that camera after what you've been through.'

His words boosted her confidence.

As Josie took her place on the sofa, she breathed in deeply in a final bid to calm her nerves.

The red light flicked on and with it Josie's face came to life as it had done hundreds of times before. 'It's six o'clock on the 28th of April and a warm welcome to the *Daybreak* breakfast show.'

And so the first days passed, filled with flowers, telephone calls and grief. Each morning Josie held it together through the programme and then collapsed as soon as she reached the sanctuary of her home.

The press was insatiable and the sensational story of Sebastian's death ran on and on. The quality broadsheets went for in-depth analysis of the disaster—bringing in 'experts' and reconstructing the final hours of the climbers. Josie saw Rick's wife Deborah quoted frequently, defending his record and rebutting the critics who were already accusing the dead leader of negligence.

Every day Josie added an extra loop to her habitual run. It was the only therapy she could think of. Before long, she was out there running for two or three hours a day.

RACHEL WAS ASLEEP, the lighting in the room subdued. Her left leg was heavily plastered, hauled up in a complicated traction device.

Hal pulled up a chair and sat looking at her, seeing that despite her black eye and swollen lips she was still as beautiful as ever. He ran his hand over her forehead.

Her breathing altered, becoming shallower as she came out of sleep. 'Hey, Hal,' she whispered.

'Are you OK?' he asked her gently. 'You want some painkillers?'

'No. I'm stacked up with pills. I can't feel a thing.'

'Listen. They told me about the baby. You don't have to worry about telling me about that, OK?'

Rachel closed her eyes. 'I don't know why I hadn't told you . . . I was meaning to . . . that night . . .'

Hal brushed away the tear that welled from the corner of her eye.

'I never even asked you,' she continued. 'Do you like the idea?'

'I love the idea,' he told her, 'and when we get you out of here we can start again.'

'It was the camera, Hal. It was the camera that killed our baby. They told me the injury was caused by a blunt object being punched into my stomach when the vehicle was crushed. The camera . . . I had it in my lap. Oh, Hal, I'm so sorry . . .' She reached out to hold his hand as she began to sob. 'And the worst thing is the avalanche was my fault. I slammed down the door.'

'Anything could have set it off, Rachel. I told you . . .'

'But it was me. I was so stupid I didn't think . . .' She looked at him for a long while. 'Hal. How many people died?'

'They're still counting. It's going to be more than forty. But those lives are on my conscience, not yours.' Hal stood, pacing the room, agitated now. 'If only I'd been faster off the mark. I should have called the red alert twenty-four hours earlier.'

'No one in the world could have known for sure, Hal. It was a freak event, like you said yourself.'

'Maybe.' Hal returned to the seat and laid his head close to Rachel's. Finally he broke the silence: 'There's one more thing you have to know. On the same day as the avalanche there was a storm on Everest. Rick Fielding was killed.'

Rachel was stunned. 'My God, I never would have imagined that could happen to Rick . . . Deborah must be destroyed.'

'Pretty much. We'll go down to Vancouver when you're healed and spend some time with her. She may need help.'

SEBASTIAN'S MEMORIAL SERVICE was held three weeks after the storm. 'Sebastian wouldn't have wanted this to be miserable,' Josie had told the organisers. 'Let's try not to make it too morbid.' But the weather was conspiring against her; it rained solidly all day, drenching the congregation as they hurried through the London streets to the church.

The interior was dark and sinister and she found the hymns deeply depressing. She was relieved when they were able to spill out into the street and breathe fresh air.

A reception was held afterwards at the *Daybreak* studios. Josie drank a glass of wine fast, trying to numb the feeling that she had let Sebastian down with this lacklustre day. 'I've never seen such a totally despondent crowd of people,' she told Mike.

'They're all scared,' he said. 'No one knows what the future is going to be like now Sebastian's not around. Just about everyone in this room depends on *Daybreak* for their jobs and I suppose they're terrified that there are going to be some big changes.'

Josie wasn't slow to pick up on his words. 'Are there?'

'Between me and you, yes, there might have to be. *Daybreak* isn't yet as profitable as we'd projected.'

'So what are we looking at. Cuts?'

'Well, we'll see. Sebastian was very much the public face of the company. His profile made things like raising money relatively easy. Without him, we're going to have to fight twice as hard. The advertising revenue is critical.'

Josie left the reception early, driving herself away from the studios. At Hyde Park Corner she should have branched off towards Kensington. But a sign for the M1 caught her eye. On an impulse she followed it. There was nothing for her at home. The memorial service had left her feeling empty and it wasn't hard to figure out why. There had been no body. Sebastian's grave was on some unknown, godforsaken part of Everest. What did the shrinks call it? Closure. Definite lack of closure around here, she realised.

A hundred miles clocked past. Two hundred. She left the rain clouds behind, hitting blue skies in the midafternoon. Then Josie was in the hills of Northumberland, the familiar territory of her childhood. Sebastian had been here with her, in the early days of their relationship. Josie turned off the motorway and headed for the wild coastline that had excited him so much. 'Great flying conditions,' he had told her. 'Onshore breeze and rising hills.' Rounding a corner, she saw the headland where he had taught her to fly.

Josie drove up the track, parked, and lay on the grass, surprised at the warmth of the early summer sunshine. Her mind drifted back.

It had been a glorious summer day, just the two of them together, Sebastian's dual paraglider in the back of the car. Josie had helped him to unravel what seemed to be a cat's cradle of strings, and within a few minutes they had the bright-yellow and red canopy stretched out on the grass.

Sebastian helped her into the harness and then buckled himself in. As soon as he judged the wind right, he pulled on the guide lines. The canopy unruffled and filled with wind, and a few moments later was flying, suspended above their heads like a kite.

'Now!'

They took a series of stumbling steps forward. Then they were airborne, swooping out across the sea.

'Wow! This is incredible!' Josie screamed in delight.

They were flying parallel to the coast, with the mountains to the left and the shore directly below. Josie could see the white surf beating against the beach and feel Sebastian next to her.

'I love you,' he told her.

It was the first time he'd said those words. As they began to soar upwards on a thermal, Josie had never been happier.

ON THE JOURNEY south, Josie's mobile telephone rang—Deborah, calling from Vancouver. Damn, Josie cursed herself. She had forgotten about the memorial service for the expedition. She had promised her a decision a week ago. 'I don't want to pressure you,' Deborah said, 'but I need to know for numbers. Can you make it or not?'

Josie hadn't planned to go to the ceremony. But after the sheer depression of Sebastian's memorial, the more she considered it, the more she realised that the journey might help. There would be other families of those who had died. Perhaps with them she would find more solace than she had done so far and maybe even the answers to some questions.

'I'll be there,' Josie told her.

FIVE WEEKS after the avalanche, Rachel was finally ready to go home. Her left leg was still pinned but she was mobile enough to get around in a wheelchair. Hal picked her up from the hospital.

They drove out of town, Hal noticing every detail of the newly arrived summer: the rivers flowing strong with meltwater, the shoots of cotton moss standing tall next to the road. At Eagle Junction he stopped at the post office to pick up the mail.

The postmaster was new and looked at Hal curiously when he gave his name. 'You're the avalanche man, aren't you?'

'Some people call me that.'

'Your postbox is pretty much bursting at the seams.'

The man fetched the mail. Hal knew that most of the letters would be from insurance companies—all wanting his expert testimony on avalanche claims following the disaster.

Hal climbed into the new Toyota. 'You know what he called me?' he asked Rachel. '"The avalanche man". That's what I'll always be around here. Isn't that frightening?'

'Just drive, Hal. Let's get home.'

They finished the journey in silence, Hal pondering over the postmaster's words—Rachel trying not to show the pain she felt every time they hit the smallest bump in the road.

'Looks like you haven't had much time for housekeeping,' Rachel told him, seeing the state of the cabin.

In the frenzy of the clear-up operation Hal had not had time to devote to the property and he was ashamed, as he saw its tatty state, that he hadn't thought to do something about it before Rachel's return.

He lit the wood stove to take the chill off the air as Rachel wheeled herself from room to room. Everything was as she remembered it: the tiny handful of stones from Everest on the desk; the bottle of wine on the shelf—the wine they had been going to drink that evening, she realised, on the day of the avalanche.

What had been stolen from them that day? Rachel wondered, as she wheeled herself into the bedroom. Bones would mend in time but what unseen damage was still to be discovered? They had a lot to adjust to, she knew, and an unborn child to mourn.

Hospital had not seemed the right place to talk. Hal had visited as often as he could, but their conversation had been stilted. They talked about Rachel's progress as her legs healed, the work Hal was doing with his team and the long sessions at the dentist's which had restored his teeth so that he could smile without making people scream.

Rachel had longed to get home, to be in Hal's arms, to talk freely and openly about the deeper wounds they had both suffered. But that night their conversation was anything but easy. Hal was distracted and monosyllabic, Rachel overtired and on the verge of tears. They ate together but neither could enjoy the meal.

'I'm going down to Vancouver next week,' Hal told her, 'for Rick Fielding's memorial service. Will you be OK?'

'I'll be fine. It'll give me a chance to get the cabin straight.'

Finally Hal helped her into bed and they fell into an awkward silence. They had not shared such close contact for a very long time but there was no spark of physical desire between them.

'You wondering what I'm wondering?' Rachel asked him. 'Like, who's feeling worse?'

'Yes. I hope you have the strength to begin talking about all this, because I'm not sure I do.'

'We don't need to rush in. Best to spend some time getting used to being around each other again.'

Neither had the emotional energy to say anything more that night.

'Sleep,' Hal told Rachel, 'that's what you need.'

But Rachel could not sleep. Every time she closed her eyes she saw the avalanche tearing down the valley towards her. She listened to Hal's fitful breathing, and wondered if things were ever going to be the same.

POLICE CHIEF Robbie McGowan looked at the envelope that Hal had placed on his desk. 'Is this what I think it is?'

'I want out, Robbie. I'm quitting the avalanche work.'

'You sure this isn't a knee-jerk reaction?' the police chief asked him. 'I know how tough the last month has been for you.'

'I can understand why you might figure that,' Hal answered, 'but something happened the other day to make me question what the hell I was doing. Some guy at Eagle Junction called me "the avalanche man". There's hardly a family in the state won't know someone who died in that slide. And when they see me coming I'll be the public face of that catastrophe, the guy who was right in the middle of it all.'

'They know you did your best. You got all the AMRs out safely.'

'The AMRs, yes. But plenty more died . . . It was my job to get the prediction right. But I didn't predict that the slide would be so huge. How do you think that has made me feel when I've been pulling the bodies of children out of shattered buildings these last weeks?'

'You want me to arrange for you to see a counsellor?'

'That's kind of you, Robbie, but I don't think it's the answer. I just can't face another winter of avalanche work.'

There was a long pause before McGowan rose and offered Hal his hand. 'I respect your decision, Hal, but I want you to know that there's a job for you here. Any time you want it.'

HAL MADE IT to the memorial service in Vancouver with an hour to spare, the flight down from Anchorage having been delayed. Deborah met him at the airport, looking more drawn and exhausted than Hal had ever seen her before. 'Hal, I'm so glad you could get here.' She held him in a tight embrace.

Deborah drove Hal back to the home she had renovated with Rick over the years. It was on the coast about ten miles from the city—a converted yacht club, situated on a quiet wooded bay.

Seeing Rick's old boat moored out front fired happy memories for Hal. He and Rachel had spent long days sailing in it with Rick and Deborah—days that passed in a haze of red wine and laughter.

'Where are the kids?' Hal noticed the house was quiet.

'At my mother's. I didn't want to force them to come today.'

'Rachel sends you all her love,' Hal told Deborah, 'and said she's sorry she can't be with you today.'

'How is she?'

'Oh . . . healing, I guess. Slowly.'

While Deborah went to change for the service, Hal took a look around the Himalayan Objectives office. It was neat, the files packed away tidily, a tall pile of brochures waiting to be mailed out in the corner. Hal could not imagine that the company would survive now Rick was dead.

Hal and Deborah drove to the church, where they met the other mourners—more than a hundred. Most were close family, but some were climbing friends of Rick's, people Hal had known for years.

The service began at three in the afternoon. Hal took the pulpit after the first few hymns. He paused and looked around the church. 'Rick Fielding was one of the finest high-altitude climbers in the world. I know that for sure because on more occasions that I can remember he proved himself to be stronger, braver and more committed than anyone around him. He was generous to a fault, to the point where he was prepared to risk his life for others. There are many climbers alive today who would otherwise be dead if it had not been for Rick's assistance.

'Rick loved Everest. He truly believed that every step he ever made on that mountain was a privilege to be earned. He was gentle with Everest. Perhaps his only mistake was to assume that Everest would always be gentle with him. Rick, you will always be in our hearts and our memories of you will be ones we will treasure for all time.'

Hal left the pulpit, taking his seat next to Deborah who, finally, had dissolved in tears.

'That was so beautiful,' she whispered to him. 'Thank you, Hal.'

After the service was concluded, Deborah invited the guests back to the house for food and drinks. Finding himself claustrophobic in the crowd, Hal went down to the jetty to breathe a little sea air. There he found one of the mourners, looking out across the calm water. 'Mind if I join you?' he asked her.

'No, go ahead.' Josie turned to scrutinise him, sure she had seen him somewhere before. 'I was really moved by your speech,' she told him. 'Almost made me want to forgive the mountain.'

'You lost someone in the storm?'

'My husband Sebastian. We had a memorial service for him in London. But this has a much better feel to it. I'm glad I came.'

They sat in silence for a long while.

'I admire Deborah,' Josie continued. 'This has to be the most diffi-cult day of her life. Everyone here has lost someone they loved. She must know that deep down we can't help blaming Rick.'

'She knows that. But she's got the courage to face it.'

'I keep getting this terrible urge to point the finger at someone—at something. To begin with, I was angry with Sebastian. Then I was mad at Rick. Then I got furious with the mountain. I fantasised about destroying it, smashing every last stone with a sledgehammer.' She sighed deeply. 'And I blame myself. I encouraged him to go.' She thought for a while. 'You know Everest, right?'

'I know a bit about it. I've been to the summit.'

'Can the bodies ever be recovered? I'd do anything to get Sebastian back.'

'That's a difficult thing. I'd say not. I've never heard of anyone being retrieved from high on Everest.'

'It's hard for me to understand that.'

'It's hard for anyone who hasn't been there to understand that.'

At that moment Deborah came down from the house.

'How's it going in there?' Hal asked her.

'Oh, warming up. People are starting to talk, starting to drink a little. That's how Rick would have wanted it.'

'Have I missed the food?'

'Not yet you haven't. Speaking of which, Hal, you look like you haven't eaten for a month. You'd better do it now or it'll be gone.'

'I'll do that.'

Hal left the two women and returned to the reception.

Josie watched Hal as he walked back to the house. 'I'm sure I've seen him somewhere recently,' she told Deborah.

'Hal? Well, his face was all over the television when the big avalanche hit Alaska.'

Suddenly Josie remembered the shot of Hal, bloodied and bruised. 'I do remember seeing him. That was the same day as the storm.'

'His girlfriend, Rachel, was injured in the avalanche. She lost the baby she was carrying.'

'Oh my God. And here I am talking about nothing but Sebastian. He didn't even mention his girlfriend.'

'That would be about right. I remember an expedition when three of his best friends had been killed. All he said was "I'll speak about it when I'm over it." But he never did.'

'I feel the opposite. All I want to do right now is talk about Sebastian, how he died, how it happened . . . Hal told me that the bodies will never be recovered.'

'I know. It's brutal isn't it?'

'It makes it harder to grieve, when you can't even picture where your loved one died.'

'I know. At least I've been there. I went to Base Camp one year with Rick. It really helped to understand what it was that meant so much to him. Now it helps even more. I'm thinking about trying to organise a memorial of some type at Base Camp. A cairn, with a plaque . . . At least it would be something.'

'I hadn't thought of that. It's a really good idea,' said Josie.

'I'll contact you with the details when I know.'

'Thank you. I'd appreciate that.'

THE GUESTS LEFT before midnight, Josie returning to her hotel by taxi. Hal was the only one of Rick's friends Deborah invited to stay. As they sat in front of the fire, drinking the last of the wine. Deborah asked, 'You think Rick would have been happy with today?'

'I reckon he'd have been delighted. You did it just right,' Hal said.

'There's something I wanted to ask you. Another favour, in fact.'

'Go ahead,' Hal replied.

'If I organise a memorial plaque, will you take it up to Base Camp for me?'

Hal hesitated for a few moments as he thought it through. 'Of course. I'd like to do that for Rick.'

'Thanks. I know you said you'd never go back but it's only to Base Camp. I could get someone else to do it but it wouldn't be the same.'

'Don't worry about it. If the same thing had happened to me I'd sure as hell expect Rick to drag his ass up there on my behalf.'

Deborah smiled. 'How long would you need to sort it out?'

'We'd have to wait a couple of months for the rains to finish. I'd have to be sure Rachel was going to be OK.'

'She can come and stay here, if she likes. I'd love to have her here.'

'That would work out well.'

They sat in silence for a long time, staring into the dying embers of the fire. Finally Deborah stirred. 'It's been a long day. I prepared the spare room for you.'

'Thanks.'

In his room, Hal opened the window. Outside he could hear the sound of the sea breaking gently on the pebble beach.

Base camp. Everest again. History repeating . . . Hal fell into an uneasy sleep.

JOSIE'S DECISION to ask Deborah if she could join the trek to Base Camp took the entire summer to make. It had begun with the barest seed, sown in Vancouver, but for weeks she ignored it.

She ignored it as her performance on *Daybreak* gradually lost its edge. She ignored it as her relationship with the show's producers deteriorated to the point where they barely spoke.

Mike was not slow to bring up the subject. 'You look terrible, Josie, and your appreciation index is way down. I know you're having a hard time after Sebastian's death but, hell, you have to get back on form or I'm telling you we're heading for a problem.'

Josie sat there despondently. One of Mike's lectures was the last thing she needed before she broke the news.

'After Sebastian died there was a huge amount of sympathy for you, Josie,' he continued. 'Your appreciation figures even went *up* for a couple of weeks. At that stage I thought we'd all pull through it.

But now I'm not so optimistic. And because our audience figures are dropping the advertisers are getting jumpy.'

'I know, Mike. But morale in the whole building has been steadily going downhill. It's not all down to me.'

'But you're the figurehead. You have to make it look like a party.'

Josie plucked up her courage. She knew Mike would not react well to the news she had to give him. 'I'm thinking about taking a break.'

Mike gave her an exasperated look. 'Running away won't help.'

'I think it might. Particularly the journey I have in mind.'

Mike's curiosity was piqued. 'What journey?'

'To Everest Base Camp, to put up a memorial to the climbers.'

'What! You don't know the first thing about mountains.'

'Apparently any reasonably fit person can get to Base Camp.'

'So how long will this take you away for?'

Josie looked sheepish. 'I think it's about a month.'

'A month! Jesus. The viewers will have forgotten who you are by the time you get back.' Mike lit a cigar. 'So what is this really about?'

'A chance to get my head together, perhaps.'

'Hell of a long way to go. Can't you do it at a health farm?'

'It's deeper than that. I think it will help. I'm having the most dreadful nightmares about Sebastian lying there all abandoned and frozen. I want to get close enough at least to say goodbye.'

'I don't know, Josie. I think you should think about this. It's against *Daybreak*'s interest. Unless . . .' Mike suddenly brightened. 'Maybe we can work this to our advantage.'

'How?'

'Send a cameraman out with you to wire back video. Run it as a series of daily updates on the show! "Josie goes to lay memorial at Everest Base Camp." Brilliant. Shots of you in front of the mountain. I can just see it.'

Josie blanched. 'Well, I was thinking of it more as a private thing.'

'It would just be one guy. He wouldn't get in the way. I think the viewers will be very touched. It's perfect . . . you get your journey and *Daybreak* gets a publicity-generating special series.'

Josie thought for a few moments. 'I suppose you're right. It does make a kind of sense.'

'You do understand I'm not talking about a travelogue? The viewer is going to want innermost thoughts as well.'

'That's what frightens me, having three million people watching my every step on what is supposed to be a personal trip.'

'You can handle it,' he insisted. 'Whatever happens I want the ratings up . . . and this could be a good way of doing it.'

'I'll sleep on it and let you know tomorrow.'

Later that day Josie called Deborah in Vancouver. They had talked frequently since the memorial service and Deborah had already agreed in principle that Josie could accompany Hal on the journey to Base Camp. Now, Josie confirmed that she would do it.

Putting down the telephone, there was a pulse inside her that she hadn't felt since Sebastian's death . . . a bright core of something so close to optimism it almost felt like a betrayal.

Kathmandu was a shock, louder, more polluted and yet in some ways more charming than any other city Josie had ever been to. She flew with Hal and cameraman Jeremy, arriving in the first week of September and checking into Hal's old haunt, the Yak and Yeti, where, despite his long years of absence, many of the staff still remembered his name. 'Welcome back to Kathmandu, Mr Hal,' the manager greeted him. 'You have been gone for too long.' Garlands of sweet-smelling flowers were placed round their necks and they were offered a rough china bowl of raki to drink.

'I feel like I've stepped into another world,' Josie whispered to Hal as they waited for the receptionist to give them their room keys.

'You have,' he said. 'The most special country on earth.'

Josie wandered the streets in a daze, which was part disorientation and part intoxication with the exotic city laid out before her. Hal was busy chasing up old contacts so she was left with Jeremy. He didn't waste any time in starting the first of his video sequences: Josie on a bicycle rickshaw; Josie outside a temple; Josie bargaining for trinkets.

'This is going to be *some* assignment,' Jeremy told her, dripping enthusiasm. 'That's it. Just lean back against that temple wall and look wistful.'

Josie was a nervous flyer. She had to resist the temptation to hold on to Hal's hand, two days later, when the tiny Twin Otter unevenly lifted off the runway at Kathmandu airport. She steeled herself to look down from the tiny aircraft window. Thousands of feet below them terraced fields were etched into the mountainsides, green with the shoots of a late Himalayan harvest. The rounded foothills soon gave way to rugged valley sides. Deep in shadow-filled canyons Josie could see silver threads of light, rivers dancing their way to the plains of India.

'Take a look ahead,' Hal said.

Josie peered over the pilot's shoulder through the front window. The plane was now heading straight towards the dreaming snow-capped peaks of the Himalayas.

IN THE HOUR before sunset, Hal took Josie on a walk around Lukla. The Sherpa village was shrouded in a haze of wood smoke, the air filled with the laughter of children kicking a ball around. Josie found herself enchanted by the beauty of the Tibetan faces that surrounded her, the jet-black, elegantly plaited hair of the women, the ready laughter that filtered from doorways and windows.

They climbed up a small trail leading away from the village as the chill of evening set in. There was just enough light left for Josie to see a low wooden building surrounded by a stone wall. A woman and several children came out to greet them. Hal spoke to her in her own tongue. They were escorted into the house.

It took Josie's eyes a while to adjust to the low level of light—the only illumination came from the flames of the hearth. They sat cross-legged round the fire as the woman chatted amiably to Hal. They drank tea and ate a simple meal of rice and lentils.

Suddenly the door burst open and a figure appeared, panting for breath. It was a Sherpa boy—strikingly handsome, perhaps eighteen years old. On seeing Hal his face lit up. 'I heard you were here!'

Hal stood, with a smile, to embrace him. 'Nima! Great to see you. Did you run down the valley?'

'As soon as I heard you landed.'

'Josie, this is Nima, the oldest son of the family.' Josie could not miss the glimmer of pride in Hal's voice.

'Pleased to meet you, Josie.'

'He just ran about six miles in the last couple of hours,' Hal explained, 'but that's not unusual for Nima. He's as strong as a lion.'

Nima's mother handed him a bowl of tsampa—the glutinous barley paste that is one of the staple foods of the Sherpa people. 'So where you go?' Nima asked through a mouthful.

'Base Camp. Slow trip. No hurry.'

Nima nodded. 'I come with you.'

Hal laughed. 'Wait a minute! What about school?'

'Not first time I leave school to go to Base Camp,' Nima said.

'Nima's following in his father's footsteps,' Hal explained to Josie. 'His dad was Ang Phurba, one of the all-time greats. Pretty well the strongest Sherpa I ever knew. He was killed in the Everest icefall on my second Everest expedition and I've kept in touch with the family ever since.'

'This good man.' Nima laughed, punching Hal playfully on the shoulder. 'Hal look after us. He like a father to me.'

'And if I was your father I'd be insisting you got back to school.'

'No. I come to Base Camp. Have to train. Last year I go to Everest with Italian team—twice above twenty-six thousand feet, big loads, no problem for me. Only weather stopped me from going to top.'

'You want to go to the summit?' Josie asked him.

Nima looked at her as if she were mad. 'Of course. My father reach summit three times. I will go there for him very soon.'

'When you've finished your education,' Hal protested.

'Everest twenty-nine thousand and twenty-eight feet high. What else I need to know?' Nima gave him a cheeky smile.

Later Josie learned that Hal had supported Nima's family financially since the death of Ang Phurba, paying for Nima's education.

'If you think you can square it with the teachers, you can come with us,' Hal told him.

'Very good. And next time you go on the mountain you make me sirdar, yes?'

'I'm not going back on the mountain.' Hal's voice was firm.

'You not resist.' Nima spoke earnestly. 'One day you will go back.'

THEY TREKKED for eight days through the Khumbu to Namche Bazaar, then struck out on the narrower and steeper trails beyond. The physical process was harder than Josie had anticipated; her body struggled to adjust to the rigours of hard walking for eight to ten hours every day. The altitude was another shock. Even at 10,000 feet she found herself breathless when she moved too fast.

'Slow down,' Hal advised her. 'Imagine you're moving in a type of slow motion. That way your muscles will be able to cope.'

Gradually, once her body had begun to acclimatise and she had mastered the art of packing endless amounts of fluid into herself to prevent dehydration, Josie settled happily into the rhythm of the trek. She began to notice the landscape, to appreciate the green intensity of rhododendron forests, to drink in the majesty of Ama Dablam, the icy sentinel towering over the approach to Everest.

Cameraman Jeremy was her constant companion, snapping her at every opportunity and consoling her by having an even tougher time on the trek than she was. He was kept busy filming scenes in the villages and recording Josie's diary pieces along the way. Each night he set up the satellite transmitter and beamed five minutes of material back to the *Daybreak* studio.

Hal kept himself to himself, choosing to trek alone and spending his evenings with Nima and the rest of the Sherpas, rather than with Josie and the photographer. On the trail he was just as elusive, either leaving long before Josie and Jeremy, and setting such a pace that they could not possibly catch up, or lagging far behind.

ON THE TENTH DAY of the trek they rested at the village of Pheriche, an untidy collection of stone-built houses on a high plateau just a few days from Base Camp. It was a chance for the small team to recuperate and to garner their strength before the final three-day stint.

'We'll leave at six tomorrow morning,' Hal informed them.

Josie was in a good mood as she left Pheriche, and by late morning, with Jeremy lagging far behind, found herself following Hal up the trail, which was so rocky that she needed to concentrate hard to avoid twisting an ankle. The sky was clear and blue, and the warmth of the autumn day was such that she was trekking in a T-shirt and shorts.

After a while, the path eased off into a grassy valley with stone-walled fields in which yaks and the occasional horse could be seen. Hal selected a comfortable-looking spot and they stopped to rest. They sat without speaking for a while, the only sound the clanging of the yak bells as an expedition passed by on the trail.

'So,' Josie asked him, 'how do you feel I'm doing? Think I'll make it to Base Camp?'

'You're looking a lot stronger than you were,' Hal admitted, offering her a swig of his water bottle.

'I'm feeling better, too,' she said. 'The altitude really knocked me for six but I feel like I'm adjusting.'

'I'm a bit worried about Jeremy,' Hal said. 'He's not coping so well.'

'I noticed that. But he's still adamant he's going to get there.'

'I'll keep a careful eye on him,' Hal promised.

THAT NIGHT Jeremy coughed violently and vomited several times.

When Hal had a good look at him the next morning he decided to send him back. 'Your lips are starting to look blue,' he told him, 'and that's the first sign of acute mountain sickness. Your blood is not carrying enough oxygen to keep your organs going.'

Hal appointed one of the Sherpas to accompany Jeremy back down to Namche Bazaar.

'But what about the filming at Base Camp?' Josie asked.

Hal thought it over, then said, 'I'll do it.'

'You mean that?' Josie gave him a hug. 'Thanks, Hal.'

Hal, Josie, Nima and two other Sherpas trekked up through Gorak Shep—the final human habitation on the route—and for a long and, for Josie, memorably painful day, made their way alongside the decaying ice spires of the Khumbu Glacier, arriving at Base Camp just after 4.00pm on a cold and bleak afternoon.

'Oh. Is that it?' Josie stood, panting and light-headed, as they saw a sprawl of colourful domes, vivid against the dirt-grey of the ancient ice. 'But we can't see the mountain!'

Hal laughed. 'Everyone expects Base Camp to be at the foot of some great pyramid. In fact, the route goes up there to the right, through the icefall.'

'So am I going to get to see the mountain?'

'Don't worry. We're going up to Kala Pattar, the classic viewpoint where all the photographs are taken from. That's where we're going to put the memorial plaque.'

'Oh.'

While Nima set about building their small camp, Hal took some video footage and stills of Josie with the icefall behind her, then, with night falling, they retreated to the mess tent.

'So,' she asked Hal, 'when was the last time you were here?' She saw Hal and Nima exchange a glance.

'Six years ago,' Hal told her. 'That was when I decided I wouldn't be coming back.'

Josie looked at him searchingly. 'Will you tell me about it?'

Hal thought for a while, then began . . .

ALEX CHESMAN HAD been a star client—Hal liked him greatly, right from the first phone call.

'Let me get this straight,' Alex had said, his crisp East Coast accent loaded with the pleasure of an impending joke. 'I pay you thirty-seven thousand dollars so I can spend three months puking my guts up on the highest mountain in the world? I get cerebral oedema, my lungs fill up with fluid, my fingers and toes shrivel up and then drop off? Or have I missed something?'

Hal smiled. 'You might get a summit photograph thrown in.'

Alex was what he called a 'corporate mountaineer'—one of the growing band of high earners who had an Everest-sized disposable income to help them take their pick of the world's summits.

'I see this as part of my personal development,' he told Hal, 'and it's kind of a unique item to put on a CV!'

But Alex was slow to acclimatise—so much so that it was only in the very last days of the expedition that he was ready for a summit bid. Hal's other clients, and the exhausted Sherpas, were already back down at Base Camp by the time he and Alex left Camp Four. On that day they were the only people on the mountain.

Not long after sunrise they came to a rising bluff of blue ice—a wind-polished wall steeper than anything they had tackled so far. Hal called to Alex. 'You OK to climb this section unroped?'

Alex looked up at the dauntingly steep terrain. 'You sure you don't want to fix it?'

If Hal had been sharper, he might have spotted the tiny catch of uncertainty in Alex's habitually optimistic voice.

'We can't afford to lose the time. Just take care and you'll be fine.'

Shards of ice showered down the slope towards Hal as his client kicked into the glassy surface of the blue ice with his sharp crampons.

Alex was no more than thirty feet above Hal's position when he tripped and fell, but it happened so fast that Hal was caught completely off his guard. Alex shot down the slope past Hal with a scream of abject fear.

'Use your axe,' Hal shouted.

But the axe had already been ripped from Alex's hand. Now he was tumbling in a series of cartwheels towards the crevasses at the foot of the slope. Hal had the sickening certainty that his client would not survive. He could barely bring himself to watch as the tiny figure was flung in the air. Then Alex plunged out of sight into the cobalt-blue interior of the first crevasse.

Silence. Hal was shaking, looking down in shock. It took him more than an hour to climb down into the crevasse. Alex was lying on a bank of powder snow not far below the lip of the crevasse. He was still alive, but only just.

His physical condition was as bad as Hal had feared—a compound fracture of his left thigh, massive contusions and internal bleeding. Hal knew that to move Alex could cause more damage, but leaving him where he was would mean certain death. Hal called Base Camp on the walkie-talkie. Three Sherpas immediately offered to come and assist and, although Hal knew it would take them two days to get back up, he asked them to try in case, by some miracle, Alex lasted that long.

For the next five hours Hal manhandled Alex's dead weight across and down the west face—a feat of enormous physical strength fired by desperation.

Finally on reaching their tent, he tended to Alex's injuries as best he could, injecting him with morphine against the pain. 'Sleep, Alex. Help is on the way.' Hal gripped Alex's hand as the injured man passed once more into oblivion.

Hal had little hope that Alex would survive. By midday on the following day the food supplies were finished and Alex's pulse was becoming weaker, his breathing shallower as he passed into a coma. Hal radioed the Sherpas and told them to turn back.

By three that afternoon Hal was aware of the pressing need to make a decision. If he stayed another night at that altitude he would be risking his own life. He was already extremely debilitated and he was a long way from the safety of the lower camps.

Alex was already effectively dead, Hal told himself. There was no way he would ever regain consciousness. He probably wouldn't last for more than another hour. But what if Alex *did* regain an awareness of where he was, even for a fleeting moment?

Hal prepared his rucksack for the descent.

To find that Hal had abandoned him?

Hal put on his boots.

To find he was dying alone?

Hal forced himself through the entrance of the tent and set off for the route that would take him down. He didn't look back.

And there the story of Alex might have ended—if it hadn't been for the two climbers who loomed out of the cloud as Hal descended. They were from a Catalan expedition—Hal recognised Miguel Font, the expedition leader.

'Where is the other?' Font pointed up into the cloud. They had heard at one of the camps that two of Hal's team were overdue.

'He's not coming back.' Hal could think of nothing else to say.

'You want us to help you? You need something?'

'No. I'm OK.'

The Catalan shrugged. 'So, we go now.'

Hal continued his descent and didn't give the two Spaniards another thought, although he would have done had he known the identity of the second man.

Font's fellow climber was Xavier Pujol, a photojournalist for the Spanish newspaper *El Periódico*, there to cover the Catalan expedition. When, out of curiosity, he unzipped the front of Hal's tent and found Alex was still—just—alive, he was not slow to spot the opportunity. Pujol shot photographs of Alex's dying face and wired back his pictures and story by satellite transmission.

The following day *El Periódico* ran it front page under the banner headline, LEFT TO DIE. The piece was a scathing indictment of the guide who abandoned his client to a lonely death: 'Hal Maher lost no time in accepting Alex Chesman's dollars,' Pujol wrote, 'and lost no time in turning his back on his wounded teammate when he needed him most.' A London-based syndication agency picked up the feature. Within twenty-four hours the story of Alex Chesman was distributed around the world.

There was no defence, of course. To stress how close he himself had been to that critical point at which the effects of altitude become irreversible was something only those who had been there would truly understand. A few big guns of climbing wrote spirited defences of Hal. But from the layman's point of view it seemed that Hal Maher had a case to answer.

Hal had returned to Anchorage, closed the office for a couple of months and embarked on a series of long solo treks through his beloved Chugach Mountains. At the end of the lonely summer he decided he would close down the company and concentrate on avalanche work.

HAL DRAINED his hot drink and looked at Josie. 'And that was the story of my last Everest expedition,' he told her. 'And the reason I decided not to go for the summit again.'

'I'm so sorry,' she said. 'Watching him die before your eyes like that . . . I really can't imagine what it must have felt like.'

'About as bad as it gets.'

An uneasy silence fell over the mess tent, which not even the cheerful Nima could dispel.

NEXT MORNING, after forcing down some muesli and hot chocolate, Josie followed Hal across the glacier and onto the ash cone that would take them to the summit of Kala Pattar—the outcrop of rock that would, she hoped, give her the longed-for sighting of Everest itself.

The effects of altitude were more noticeable with every passing hour. Josie's chest tightened as her breathing rate increased to cope with the thin air. She climbed, her eyes fixed on the shallow impressions Hal's boots left in the trail, trying not to raise her hopes too high. Hal had already warned her the mountain could be covered in cloud.

Hal suddenly stopped and waved Josie through with a theatrical bow. 'Welcome to Kala Pattar and your first view of Everest.'

And there it was. The mountain that until now had existed for her only in photographs was sitting right there, terrifying, impossibly huge. *This* was what she had come for. They sat side by side in silence, watching the perfect triangle of rock and ice that soared effortlessly above the jagged ridges of its neighbours.

'Have you really stood on that summit?' Josie was the first to break the silence.

'Yes. And it's the most beautiful place in the world.'

'Is that why you climbed it so many times?'

Hal placed his lightweight rucksack behind him and rested back on it with his hands behind his head. 'I guess so.'

Josie arranged her own pack and leaned back next to him. The mountain made her feel intimidated and small. 'How can anyone seriously contemplate climbing that,' she said, transfixed by the mass of ice and rock.

'Too many people do,' Hal said.

A cold realisation hit her. 'I'm looking at where Sebastian is. I'm looking at his grave. He's up there somewhere.'

Hal said nothing.

Josie concentrated on Everest, registering every feature—the gullies, the couloirs, the hanging glaciers of ice poised to avalanche—as if by knowing them she could find an answer to the question that had haunted her since the journey had begun. What was the hold this mountain had had on Sebastian?

Time passed. A hint of cloud began to play around the face, thickening rapidly even as they watched.

'We should put the plaque in place,' Hal reminded her. In his backpack he had the brass plate that Deborah had designed. It was fourteen inches by twelve, etched with a motif of the mountain and the names of the members of Rick's expedition, along with the date on which they had all died.

Josie held it in her hands, looking at it for the first time. 'It's nice. Deborah did a good job.'

Nima had been up a couple of hours before them to deposit a small one-kilo pack of cement. Now Hal scooped a hollow out of the ground and poured the powder in before adding a cupful of water from his bottle and mixing it with a small trowel.

They decided to fix the plaque to a rock face nearby, on a small ledge cut into solid rock and facing the mountain. Hal smoothed the cement and pushed the plaque into position. It was a neat job. Then he took out the video camera and filmed Josie looking at the plaque.

'So, that's it?' she asked.

'Yep. That's it. Now we go home.'

The mountain was now behind a mass of cloud, depriving Josie of the one last look she craved. She said a prayer for Sebastian and followed Hal down the slope to the trail that would take them back towards the lush valleys and Kathmandu.

THAT NIGHT, when Josie closed her eyes to try to sleep, all she could see was that great pyramid of rock and ice as it was revealed from behind the clouds. What had she understood from that fleeting glimpse of Everest she wondered. Why had that awesome vision imprinted itself so indelibly in her mind? What had it done to her?

It would be many months before she understood.

Hal watched the Rockies rise out of the dawn, the familiar ridges of the continental divide reduced to a mere wrinkle on the surface of the earth. He massaged his neck with the fingers of both hands, stiff from the sixteen hours of air travel, and breathed a sigh of relief when the captain announced twenty minutes to landing and began the descent into Vancouver airport.

In the Vancouver airport terminal, Rachel and Deborah were waiting for him, Rachel walking with a stick.

Hal kissed them both.

'You lost some weight,' Rachel said.

'And you learned to walk.' Hal was pleased. Rachel's leg had healed well. There was a distinct limp but that was nothing considering the damage the leg had sustained. 'You'll be dancing by Christmas,' he told her.

They drove back to Deborah's place and sat round the kitchen table to catch up with news.

'So did you get the memorial put up?' Deborah asked.

'Everything went fine,' Hal answered. 'I shot a couple of stills of the plaque for you. I'll get them processed in the next few days.'

'Oh, thank you, Hal. You don't know what a relief it is that you managed to get that done . . .'

'How was Josie?' Rachel enquired. 'Was she a pain in the neck?'

'She was OK. I think the journey helped her quite a bit.'

'Did she have trouble with the altitude?' Deborah asked.

'Her cameraman did—I had to turn him back before Base Camp, but Josie made it up to Kala Pattar like it was a Sunday-afternoon stroll.'

'And the filming?'

'Oh, we got the occasional bit of feedback from London. It seems that millions of viewers were following the updates. How about here?'

Rachel gestured to a stack of correspondence sitting on the kitchen table. 'Guess what they are?'

'Letters of condolence?' Hal suggested.

Deborah laughed bitterly. 'Not quite. These are requests for Himalayan Objectives brochures. Everyone wants to climb Everest. We've never had as much interest in that mountain. It's almost as if the disaster has made people more keen to go there.'

'Have you decided to hold on to the company?'

'I don't know what else I *can* do. We have a loyal clientele and I could find leaders to take on McKinley, Aconcagua and so on. At least I'd make a living that way.' Deborah stood. 'Anyway, enough of my problems. You two probably want to spend a bit of time together. I'll take the kids into town.'

When they were alone, Rachel cupped Hal's face in her hands, kissing him tenderly. 'I'm so glad to get you back. I missed you.'

'I missed you too.'

'You didn't fall madly in love with Josie? She's quite beautiful from what I've heard.'

Hal laughed. 'I don't go for blondes, remember?'

They kissed again.

'So how has Deborah really been?' Hal asked.

Rachel sighed. 'Courageous, but I think she's closer to cracking up than she lets on.' She took Hal's hand in hers. 'Hal, do you mind if we spend some more time here? From what I've seen, Deborah desperately needs more help over the next few months. There's the kids, the business, the house.'

'That's fine by me,' Hal agreed.

Rachel looked at him intently. 'What are you going to do next, Hal? Did you come up with any great ideas on the trek?'

'Not exactly.' He laughed. 'All I know right now is that we should spend a big chunk of time together.'

'You really mean that? While you were away I had this strange idea that you'd want to end our relationship when you got back.'

Hal looked shocked. 'Why?'

'I don't know . . . I guess I just can't quite see where we're heading at the moment and that makes me nervous.'

Hal reached out to hold her. 'I know what you're saying. We still haven't straightened things out after the avalanche. But don't worry, it's just a question of time.'

JOSIE GOT BACK to find that plenty had changed at *Daybreak*. The first clue was the black cab that arrived to take her to the studio—limousines were out, in Mike's new regime.

'We were losing a quarter of a million a month,' Mike told her by way of explanation. 'So certain things have had to go.'

Josie could scarcely hide her dismay. 'I really couldn't give a damn about the limousine but have you cut any of the staff?'

'Oh, a couple of lighting technicians, a few sound people, a handful of researchers. The producers have been very good about it.'

'Why did you wait until I was away to do all these things? Because you knew I'd object?' Josie could not disguise her anger.

'Not at all. That was just an accident of timing.'

Josie picked up her running order for the day and could see at a glance that the show would be bland. She went through to make-up.

'Morning, ladies!' Tarik, the producer of the day, put his head round the door, his smile vanishing as he saw Josie's expression.

'That's a B-grade running order and you know it.' Josie tossed the script onto the make-up desk. 'I can't work miracles out there. You have to give me the quality guests. No one is going to watch this.'

'There's nothing I can do about that now,' he countered. 'Mike booked most of those guests.'

'And what is "Junior Commando"?' Josie pointed to the script and a ten-minute item scheduled in the second half of the show.

'A cartoon series.'

Tarik retreated before she could respond.

Josie blinked as she entered the set. The lighting was too harsh and would have her squinting into the camera. Everyone seemed stressed.

'One minute.'

Josie let her mind wander back to Nepal. She imagined herself in one of the rhododendron forests, trekking up a cool mountain trail, with the glistening peaks of the Himalayas ahead. The trek to Base Camp had been a great healer, she now realised. Getting back to this was the last thing she needed.

She snapped out of the daydream just as the transmission began.

'Good morning and welcome to *Daybreak* . . .' She smiled as she read the autocue.

Her gut instinct had been right, the show *was* tedious, so much so that in the middle of an interview with a politician Josie lost the thread of the conversation. As he droned on, she found herself daydreaming once again about Everest—and about returning there.

'Are you listening to me?' he asked. 'I have the impression you haven't heard a word I've said.'

Josie went white, stammering as she tried to recover the situation.

And that was the new *Daybreak* for Josie as the weeks went by: a constant fight to keep her mind from wandering, falling staff morale and an ever-increasing diet of cartoons introduced by Mike to disguise the lack of quality guests.

No wonder Mike was looking increasingly sour. 'We slipped eight places on the top one hundred last week,' he told her one morning.

'We need better guests,' Josie retorted.

'Or perhaps it's the viewers responding to your evident lack of interest. One way or another we need to solve this problem . . .'

THEY SETTLED EASILY into the pattern of life at Deborah's, Hal running the Himalayan Objectives office, Rachel helping Deborah with the children and the house. During the days they were happy, relishing the busy routine, but when they were alone the fragile world of their own relationship was difficult to escape. Each night they would lie in each other's arms, wanting to erase the black void that had existed between them since the avalanche, wanting the passion back. But it was elusive. They had not made love since the accident. The loss of the baby—and the blame they shared for it—weighed more heavily on them both than they could express.

One morning Rachel was up at dawn, early enough to catch the sunrise. There was a thin layer of sea fog sitting in a perfect blanket over the water and, in the places it had drifted over the islands, it had left cedars standing as if on cloud. She had a camera with her, but she realised that a photograph would be as nothing compared with the grandeur of what she was witnessing. She lowered the camera and drank in the scene.

A moment later Hal was beside her.

'Isn't that the most beautiful thing you've ever seen?'

Hal wrapped her close in his arms. 'Perfect.'

She turned to look him in the eyes. 'Hal, do you think we can sort things out between us?'

'Maybe.' Hal gave her an awkward smile. 'I think there's two ways we can be. One is to be in a sort of suspended animation, like now, going neither forward nor back.'

'I don't want that way.'

'Nor do I,' Hal said. 'The other way is to go on the offensive—realise we do still love each other and try to start again.'

Rachel watched the sea fog shift as a breeze wafted through it. For the first time in a long time, she felt a flash of happiness inside her. 'You mean it? You really want to start again . . . a clean slate.'

'Yes. Yes, I do.'

Rachel threw her arms round Hal's neck. 'Will you take me back to bed?' she whispered.

EARLY IN THE NEW YEAR a letter arrived for Deborah at Himalayan Objectives. 'Come up to the office,' she invited Rachel and Hal. They followed her upstairs.

'Take a look at this.' She handed Hal an official-looking document with the address of a legal firm in New York on the letterhead.

'What is it?'

'Himalayan Objectives is being sued by the families of the victims over the Everest disaster. They believe they can prove negligence.'

'What's their case, exactly?' Rachel asked.

'That Rick had a professional duty of care. That he should have known not to keep the team going forward when the storm was coming. There's even a suggestion in there that he cut and ran when the storm hit, that he died alone . . . trying to save his own skin.'

Hal was outraged. 'Rick would never do that. He would have fought until the bitter end.'

'That's something I may have to prove.'

'How?'

'I'm not sure. Get some hard data on which members ended up in which spots on the mountain. No one has really looked. I'll do any-thing to prove that Rick was a fine and honourable man, a total pro-fessional. That's ultimately what I care about, not the money.'

'You don't deserve this,' Hal said. 'I'll give you any help I can.'

Deborah turned, looking at him intensely. 'If I asked you to go to Everest and map out where the bodies were, would you do it?'

Hal let out a long sigh. 'I did say never again . . .'

'I know that, Hal, and the last thing I would ever want to do is pressurise you into it. I just don't see how we can make a defence until we map out the sequence of events as far as we can and prove that Rick died protecting those people.'

'How are you going to fund it?'

Deborah sighed. 'I'm not sure. We could get a bunch of clients together but then you'd have your work cut out looking after them.'

'How about Josie Turner?'

'What?'

'Get this,' Hal said. 'A while back she approached me about the idea of a private expedition. Just the two of us. She's talking about the possibility of visiting the site where Sebastian died. It's only an idea but—'

'That's virtually the summit. She'd need to be in pretty good shape to get that high. You think she's got what it takes?'

'I think she has. She was surprisingly strong.'

'It'll give you a chance to get up and find Rick's body.'

'Yes. And the good part is that she said she inherited money when Sebastian died and would cover the cost herself.'

'You think she's serious?'

'I'd say she's deadly serious.'

'There's something else I'd want you to do,' Deborah said. 'I'd like to get Rick's ring back. It would mean so much to me. If we do go ahead . . . What do you think?'

Hal hesitated and looked at Rachel questioningly. 'I think Rachel and I need to have a long hard talk about this.'

Rachel shook her head. 'No, we don't.' She put her arm round Deborah. 'You could lose everything if these people win their case against you. We can't let that happen.' She looked at Hal. 'Do you want to do it?'

'For the chance to get something right? Maybe. Can you bear it?'

'It's not a question of bearing it, it's a question of what's right. How long would the expedition be?'

'Three months.'

'You can continue to stay here if you want,' Deborah told Rachel. She stepped towards the door. 'I should leave you two to talk about it. I'll go and put some coffee on.'

Rachel took Hal's hands in hers. 'Hal. You have to do it. Without us, she hasn't got a hope.'

'I know, but Everest . . . ?'

'Think about it. You make a big success of this and we can go back up to Alaska and make a completely fresh start. Everest is something you know intimately, you told me before that you feel alive there—renewed.'

Hal looked at her, thinking. 'I'll do it. For Deborah and for Rick.'

Rachel kissed him softly on the lips. 'And for me. Please.'

JOSIE WALKED into Mike's office, feigning a confidence she definitely didn't feel. Hal's telephone call had been a bolt from the blue—she'd almost given up hope that he would agree to take her to the mountain. But would Mike give her the three months she would need?

She sat opposite him at the desk and watched him working at his computer for a while until it was clear that he wasn't going to be the one to speak first. 'Mike, you remember the trek to Base Camp? How I had it in mind that it would help me put Sebastian behind me?'

Mike glanced up and gave her a blank look. 'And?'

'It didn't. If anything, it left me feeling more restless than before.'

Mike put on his bored voice. 'I can't sanction you going on another holiday, Josie. If you've got itchy feet, why don't you wait until the summer holidays like everyone else . . . ?'

Josie let him finish. Then she went on: 'I'm thinking about climbing the mountain. For real this time.'

He looked at her in shock as the words sank in. 'You can't be talking about *Everest*, for God's sake?'

'What other mountain is there?'

Mike burst into laughter. 'Don't be absurd, Josie.'

'This isn't a joke, Mike. I'm completely serious about it.'

'You're prepared to risk your life . . . ?'

'I feel I might as well not *have* a life unless I do it.'

Mike looked at her intently. 'When would it happen?'

'In the spring. I've asked Hal Maher if he'll take me up. It takes three months.'

Mike scribbled some notes on a pad. 'The ITC meet to decide on our franchise renewal in July. If we play our cards right, we can get three months of sky-high ratings out of this before they meet. The timing is spot on.'

Josie got a familiar sinking feeling. 'You want me to cover the expedition for the show?'

'Of course.' Mike gave her a quizzical look. 'Why on earth would we agree for you to do it if it wasn't for the ratings? You did it for the journey to put up the memorial. What's the big deal?'

'That was a lot less serious. I'm not totally sure I can handle this climb and report on it at the same time.'

'So where does that leave us? A show without its star presenter for three months? At a time when the BBC is catching up on us?'

'I know the show's in trouble. But I don't want to promise you a series of reports that I can't deliver.'

'You're a pro, Josie, that's your job. Besides . . . how often do you think I can put a stand-in presenter in your seat before I feel I have to offer them something more permanent?'

'Is that a threat?'

'Just trying to make you see sense.'

'This expedition is different, Mike. It's my dream to go there, not *Daybreak*'s. Maybe I want something for *me*.'

Mike pursed his lips and Josie knew she had made him angry. 'Look at it another way. Sebastian made you what you are, Josie. You owe everything to him. You think he would have wanted you to stand by and watch his business slip away before your eyes?' Mike's eyes were cold as stone. 'This new project can give *Daybreak* a real shot in the arm. But only if you play the game. Now, yes or no?'

Josie bit her lip. 'What choice do you give me?' she said quietly.

'That's my girl!'

Mike picked up the telephone and barked an instruction to his secretary. 'Get the press in for four o'clock. Tell them we've got a surprise announcement.' He was smiling as he put down the receiver.

BACK HOME, JOSIE found the adrenaline pumping strong. She put on her running gear and hit the streets, aiming for a four-hour session. She would have to squeeze every last ounce of fitness training out of the next three months if her body was to stand a chance of the summit.

As for her mind . . . Josie had no real idea how to prepare herself for the enormous strains the expedition would bring. Even as she ran, she was already wondering if Everest was going to be the biggest mistake of her life.

In late March, three days before they left for Nepal, Hal flew into London with Todd, the high-altitude camera operator he had chosen to shoot the *Daybreak* reports. Todd, a native of Denver, had trained as a professional cameraman and now specialised in wilderness documentaries. An experienced expeditioner and climber, he would also act as logistics and communications manager while Josie and Hal were climbing together. He was blue-eyed, bearded, with the physique of a rugby player and a handshake that left Josie's eyes watering.

'We're not talking about a Jeremy clone here,' Hal told her with a smile. 'Todd's an old friend. He has filmed on K2 and plenty of mean mountains.'

Todd was taken into the *Daybreak* studio for a briefing from Mike while Josie and Hal went shopping for last-minute pieces of personal equipment she would need.

The following day an on-air party was thrown in the studio to mark Josie's departure. Hal was invited in to talk about some of the highlights the viewers could expect over the coming three months and the party went surprisingly well.

Josie said emotional goodbyes to the staff and walked out of the studios knowing she would not be back for three months. It was a great feeling. The atmosphere at *Daybreak* had deteriorated yet further in the weeks of waiting and she was desperate to get out.

On the Royal Air Nepal flight she ordered three glasses of champagne and proposed a toast: 'To the expedition.'

'I'll drink to that!' said Todd.

Hal smiled and chinked her glass.

When they landed in Nepal, Nima was waiting for them. Having finished his schooling, he'd trekked down from the mountains to join the expedition and to help Hal with the provisioning in Kathmandu. He was delighted see Josie again, clasping her in a tight bear hug. 'Now I go to summit! I'm very happy.'

Josie laughed. 'Well, if you're happy, I'm happy too.'

'I take good care of you. With me and Hal you are very safe, very good. All come back alive. All reach summit. Keep fingers and toes.'

Nima introduced Josie to the six other Sherpas who would be accompanying them, and to Tashi, the expedition cook. They were all seasoned Everest hands; some—like the veteran high-altitude porter Lhakpa—had summited numerous times.

Nima, smiling fit to bust, shuttled backwards and forwards between the market and the hotel with sacks. He was astoundingly strong, never once complaining. Every day, the mountain of supplies grew: tons of food, 150 oxygen bottles, twenty-eight equipment barrels stuffed with ropes, tents and climbing hardware. Hal was quartermaster, accountant and quality-control supervisor rolled into one, waiting to log in and count every item.

At last he pronounced they were ready to roll. The boxes, barrels and containers were loaded up into two green trucks and driven to the airport, where a helicopter was waiting to take them to Lukla.

THE TREK TO BASE CAMP was very different from the time before. It was not yet spring, the land bearing the remnants of deep drifts, the high peaks around them still wearing their winter plumage of ice. The last journey had been seven months before, in the lush warmth of the Himalayan autumn, with green terraced fields of barley and millet surrounding each village. Now the crops were gone.

In the lodge at Lukla there was no sugar, flour or tea—all had run out long ago and the owner was grateful to Hal for a few of the expedition's supplies as payment for accommodation.

Hal was busy recruiting, haggling with porters and yak drivers for the long haul up to Base Camp. Josie chose this for her first video report for *Daybreak*, knowing the viewers would enjoy the spectacle as he was surrounded by the crowds of Sherpas, each claiming he could earn more working for other expeditions. She was pleased to find that Todd was competent and relaxed behind the camera and the rushes were successfully beamed out that night.

Eventually Hal ticked the last of the items off his list and saw them loaded onto the backs of the yaks. When they set out they had no fewer than thirty-eight beasts of burden and twenty-nine porters carrying loads.

'It's always a relief to finally hit the trail,' Hal told Josie as they walked side by side out of Lukla.

The trails were quiet compared with the autumn, when the tracks had been alive with merchants, porters and trekkers. Now, the only people using them up into the deeper part of the Khumbu were those who had Everest in their sights.

Past Namche Bazaar the cold set in with a vengeance. Big sections of each day were spent trekking through falling snow, often accompanied by a wind that cut to the bone. By the time they got to Base Camp Josie's everyday wear consisted of three sets of silk long johns and thermal gear, jogging trousers and top, fleece layer above that, an all-in-one Gore-Tex and down wind suit and sometimes more. On her head she wore a silk balaclava and a wool cap, on her hands three layers of gloves, on her feet four layers of socks. Nevertheless, she felt her teeth chatter when she stood still for too long. 'Base Camp is cold in early April, make no mistake,' she said to camera on one of her daily reports.

After a few days she began to feel her body slowly adjusting to the altitude, her appetite returning. 'That's good,' Hal said approvingly every time he saw her eating. 'Feed yourself up. The higher we go, the sicker you're going to be. The more calories you can get inside you down here the better.'

When it came to fluids Josie also took Hal's advice, drinking copious amounts of liquid a day to combat the dehydrating effects of the dry air. Hot chocolate was her favourite, as the cook Tashi soon discovered. 'Hot chocolate! Hot chocolate for Josie!' he would sing from the mess tent, luring her in to drink and chat.

'Get to know your gear, Josie,' Hal warned her, and she did. There were the crampons—the savage metal spikes strapped to her plastic boots—the harness, and the ice axe wrapped round her wrist with a small sling. Everything had to be fastened, clipped and doubled back with frozen fingers. Nothing could be lost or dropped. Hal drummed into her the perils of mislaying even the smallest piece of kit.

He took her out to learn some of the basic mountain craft she would need. He taught her how to arrest herself with the ice axe by rolling so that her body weight forced the sharp end into the surface.

He showed her how to walk properly with the crampon spikes.

'At least twenty per cent of people who fail on Everest do so because they have a problem with equipment,' he lectured. 'Always treat every last thing as if your very life depends on it.'

Josie's mind buzzed as she sat in the Base Camp tent for hour after hour, going through each piece of gear again and again. 'Got to get this right,' she told herself. 'No mistakes at all.'

JOSIE TUGGED the sleeping-bag tightly around her as she heard footsteps approaching across the glacier. It was the twenty-fifth day of the expedition and the climbing was about to begin in earnest.

Nima spoke softly from the entrance as he unzipped her tent: 'Josie. It's four o'clock. Here's your tea.'

Ripping herself out of the snug warmth of her sleeping-bag into the freezing pre-dawn required a colossal act of will-power. This was the day Josie had dreaded: the first trip up through the Khumbu icefall to Camp One. She ate a fast breakfast of Granola in the mess tent and then joined Hal, Todd and Nima as they prepared their equipment for the climb.

'How are you feeling?' Hal asked her.

'Dead scared.'

'I understand. I still get freaked by the icefall myself.'

'Icefall very bad place,' Nima added. 'My father killed there.'

Josie felt the knot in her stomach take another twist. What the hell was she doing here? she asked herself as they walked away from the tents. A novice climber, she was about to enter one of the most dangerous mountain environments on earth.

The night was clear and the stars created enough light to see the silver silhouettes of the mountains. The silence was broken by the creaking and groaning of the flowing ice of the glacier. At random intervals a report like cannon fire signalled that a new fissure had opened up, putting Josie's already stretched nerves more on edge. Hal set a slow but steady pace. Josie followed, with Nima and Todd behind her.

They reached the first of the fixed ropes and Josie learned to clip herself onto the line with her carabiner.

By dawn they were deep in the icefall, amidst a shifting maze of crevasses and séracs, and massive blocks of teetering ice leaning at impossible angles prior to collapse.

Todd brought out the camera and filmed Josie as she moved as fast as she could beneath a gravity-defying tooth-shaped mass of ice the size of a large house. Her heart pounded with the knowledge that it could fall at any time.

A tortuous trail of fixed ropes had been laid through the maze. Where crossing large crevasses was unavoidable, aluminium ladders were in place. Josie crossed them with her eyes trained resolutely on the far side, trying not to think of the chasm beneath her.

They were two-thirds of the way through the icefall when an ear-splitting 'whoomph' rent the air, as a thousand-ton chunk of glacier split free and fell.

Josie saw Hal's head whip round as he tried to compute whether the debris was going to sweep down on them.

Terror ran through Josie. She heard a roar like water rushing from a burst dam, then the air became still as the avalanche died somewhere down the glacier.

Silence. They stood side by side, Josie trembling as the adrenaline subsided.

At last Hal spoke. 'We were lucky there.' He led on, giving Josie no choice but to follow.

Five hours later they made it to the top of the icefall, where the Sherpas had prepared four tents on the Western Cwm.

They sat side by side, sipping hot tea, looking up at the Lhotse Face—the next big obstacle, revealed in all its fearsome glory.

'When I see how much climbing we still have to do, it seems like mission impossible,' Josie said.

'You'll be fine,' Hal told her. 'That was an impressive day's climbing for a novice. I think you're going to go high.'

'You really think so?'

'Yeah. If you can handle four more trips through the icefall.'

Josie sat there, sinking quickly into a depression at this prospect. Then she thought about Sebastian, how it would feel to be with him again, and knew that she would find the strength.

THEY RETURNED the next day to Base Camp, where Josie lay on her back in the tent for twenty-four hours to recover.

'Feel like you've run a marathon, eh?' Hal asked her. 'That's what oxygen deficiency does to your body. If we did that same trip at sea level you'd probably have recovered in half the time.'

Josie thanked God she'd taken her fitness campaign seriously.

Five days later it was back up through the icefall to Camp One again: one night there and then the nine-hour climb to Camp Two; one night there, then back down to Base Camp and so on . . . a programme that would give their bodies maximum chance to adjust to the altitude. Each excursion demanded a longer recovery period, pushed muscles and tendons harder than the one before. Each time Josie had to dig deeper to find reserves of strength.

At last they pushed up the steep flanks of the Lhotse Face towards Camp Three. They were higher than 25,000 feet, and still not using supplemental oxygen.

Josie was so drained by the ascent that she collapsed straight into the tent without a word. Todd tried to do some filming, but he, too, was gasping for breath and badly dehydrated. Hal brewed them both tea and forced them to eat some food.

That night was unpleasant. The tent was pitched on an incline, with Hal and Todd jostling for space beside her. When Josie did fall asleep she soon lurched out of it with a horrible gasp—gulping down lungfuls of air to fight the sense of suffocation.

'That's a syndrome known as Cheyne-Stokes,' Hal told her. 'It's when your brain has a sudden panic attack because there's so little oxygen. It wakes you up to make sure you're breathing.'

'Can't we use some of the bottled oxygen?' she begged.

'Not yet. We haven't got the gas to spare this low down.'

This low down. Josie pondered those ominous words. Later, she vomited every last morsel of food from her stomach, only just making it to the tent door in time. 'Hal, I'm sick,' she told him, feeling weaker than she could ever remember.

'That's normal,' he answered. 'Don't worry about it.'

She lay without sleeping, wondering, dreading, what it would be like when they got really high. Camp Three was the turning point, the end of the acclimatisation programme.

'Next time we come up, it'll be for real,' Hal promised them as they began the return descent through the Western Cwm.

Two days later they were back in Base Camp, resting and letting their bodies recover.

'There could be a bit of hanging around now,' Hal warned. 'There are a lot of teams trying for the summit right now and we don't want to get caught in the rush hour up there.'

The days stretched into a week. Josie found the waiting difficult. Team after team went for their summit attempt and still Hal held back. 'Are you sure we're doing the right thing?' she demanded.

'Josie, I know how you feel,' he assured her. 'But believe me, we'll be better off without them. They'll get stuck one behind the other on the summit ridge, and we'll have a clean run at it, no delays.'

'OK. You're the boss.' Josie threw him a mock salute.

Hanging around at Base Camp, she began to get cravings—for oranges, bananas, fresh croissants, steak. Instead there was just end-less beans, rice and pasta. The weight was falling off Josie. 'You're missing a trick, Hal,' she teased him. 'The real money isn't in climb-ing . . . it's in the Everest weight-loss programme.'

'That's normal for someone your size,' Hal told her. 'Your body is burning up its own fat.'

She began craving butter, fats. Tashi tried her on the local tea, which was prepared with rancid yak butter, and despite its foul taste Josie found her body accepting it for the fats it gave her. From then on, it was yak butter tea rather than hot chocolate for her.

Hal spent hours sitting outside the tent watching the mountain through his binoculars. One day he sauntered casually into the mess tent. 'We go tomorrow,' he said. 'That OK with you?'

'Well . . . yes.' Josie felt a spasm of terror run through her.

Hal handed her the binoculars and took her to the tent door. 'See that crocodile of climbers retreating through the icefall?' he asked. 'That means it's time to go for it. A nice empty mountain waiting there just for us.'

A FROSTED MIST of ice coated the polarised glass of Josie's mask, causing her to squint as she tried to focus through the distorting rime.

'Look at that.' Hal was holding his pocket altimeter in front of her face. 'We just reached 26,000 feet.'

Josie did not have the breath to reply at that moment, or the strength to feel the excitement she knew she should feel. Hal had told her how few people reached this high. Altitude, and the eight hours of climbing since dawn, had dulled her awareness of every-thing other than the depth of her own pain.

'Can you see the tents?' Hal's voice was hoarse and frayed.

Josie looked up and saw a cluster of red domes far across the flat expense of the South Col. Camp Four. Beyond was the brutal, intim-idating mass of Everest's final pyramid.

Josie fixed her eyes on the red domes of the camp. 'They're miles away.' Her voice was flat, emotionless.

'One hour, maybe less.'

He was lying, she knew. One of Hal's hours was invariably two.
'Let me rest.'

'Not now. Rest at the camp.'

Hal shifted his position so he faced her, his vivid blue eyes locked
onto hers. 'You still got the chant going?'

Josie nodded. She felt an encouraging pat on her back, then came
the tightening tug of the short rope on her waist harness as Hal
moved up.

The mantra was so much a part of her now that she no longer
knew whether the whispered words were real, or merely a series of
brain impulses.

'Every yard up . . .' One step. No more than one plastic boot's
length. 'Is a yard . . .' Another. The muscle tissue of her calves and
thighs protesting. 'Less to go.' Another. Dig the metal crampon
spikes hard into the ice. 'Every yard up . . .'

The slope they were climbing was at the top end of the Geneva
Spur, the bulging ridge of snow that forms a natural ramp between the
Lhotse Face and the South Col of Everest. The angle was not steep
but, at 26,000 feet, their progress was little more than crawling pace.

By 3.00pm the cloud had cleared and they were cresting the rise
onto the flatter terrain of the col. Josie followed Hal as he picked his
way across the gently undulating plateau. Even though she was no
longer ascending, she still found herself struggling to put one foot in
front of the other. The camp stayed obstinately in the distance until
she feared she would never reach it.

Suddenly there was a cry from ahead. A figure in a yellow jacket
was approaching from the camp, his face obscured by an oxygen
mask. It was only when he stood just inches in front of her that Josie
recognised the laughing eyes. 'Nima?'

'Yes, ma'am. Welcome to South Col.'

Hal slapped him on the back. 'How you guys doing up here?'

'Lhakpa tired, maybe sick, but me and Todd OK. You want tea?'

'Definitely.'

Nima took the small rucksack from his back and brought out a
flask. He poured the sweet brown liquid into the plastic top and Josie
sipped it slowly.

Twenty minutes later they reached Camp Four, where Todd and
Lhakpa—the team's second climbing Sherpa—were waiting. Todd
was filming as they arrived. 'Hey, Josie. How are you feeling?'

Josie wanted to be bright, to say something meaningful for the camera but all she could manage was: 'I'm a bit sick.' She sat down heavily on the ice, fought the wave of nausea for a few seconds, then succumbed, vomiting up the tea in a violent spasm.

Todd laughed. 'I don't think that shot's going to make it to prime-time TV.'

'We'd better get her on the gas.' Hal took a full bottle of oxygen from the small pile next to the tent, screwed the thread of an aluminium regulator valve into the bottle and connected the rubber hosing leading to the face mask. 'Welcome to wonderland.'

Josie held the mask against her face and took a tentative breath. Then another with more confidence. 'That's incredible.' She could scarcely believe the chemical changes as the oxygen took effect. Within a minute she could feel the pounding sensation in the back of her head subsiding. After three minutes the nausea was also easing off. 'I feel warm, Hal. I can feel my toes!'

Hal assembled his own oxygen equipment. For some time they sat saying nothing, letting their bodies recover.

Todd brought out more tea. 'Lhakpa's having a pretty hard time. He can't hold down any food or drink.'

'Lhakpa too old,' Nima said quietly. 'He no good for big mountains any more. Should buy shop in Kathmandu and rest.'

'Let me see him.' Hal crawled into the tent and found Lhakpa lying in his sleeping-bag. 'Hey, Lhakpa. What's the problem?'

'No eat. No drink. Only sick. Headache. Everything ache.'

'Do you think you can climb tonight?'

'Maybe. Not sure.'

'All right. You try and sleep.'

Hal consulted with Todd. 'You think he's up for tomorrow?'

'I'm not sure. Let's see how he feels at midnight.'

'OK. How's the weather looking?'

'Pretty good. Some slightly odd patterns lurking around in the north but I don't think they'll affect us.'

Hal crossed to Josie. 'It looks like the weather window we need is with us. You still want to go through with it?'

Josie gave a small nod.

'Because if there are any doubts inside you then maybe just to be here is enough.'

'No. I'm sure about it. I can handle it. I feel Sebastian is waiting for me up there. I want to finish what we've started.'

'OK. We leave at midnight.'

THE ROAR OF THE GAS stove dragged Josie out of her half-sleep just before midnight. Hal was sitting up in his sleeping-bag, tending to the stove, which was in the front alcove of the tent. Josie watched him as, illuminated by the soft blue light of the gas, he broke fist-sized chunks of ice off a larger block to add to the meltwater.

Summit day. The very words created a cold pit of terror deep inside her. She suddenly remembered something Sebastian had said before leaving for Nepal: 'It only takes one tiny mistake up there. And that's it.' One tiny mistake: one dead body. What gave her the insane idea that she would be one of the lucky ones?

She buried herself in her sleeping-bag, trying to ignore her fear, but before long Hal was offering her a warm drink and making her eat two foil sachets of high-energy food. He supervised her as she dressed, making sure every layer of clothing was right.

It was 1.15am by the time they had wriggled into their huge down suits, zipped a wind layer over the top and exited the tent. Hal checked that Josie's oxygen cylinder was correctly positioned in her rucksack and fastened her harness for her.

Todd came out of the adjoining tent where the two Sherpas were preparing themselves.

'How's Lhakpa doing?' Hal asked him.

'He's grumbling a bit, but it seems he's going to try.'

'How much oxygen are they carrying?'

'Sufficient to leave two bottles at the South Summit.'

'Good enough.'

Nima and Lhakpa joined them. 'This the most exciting day of my life!' Nima told Josie, 'Maybe go to summit with you.'

'Oh, I hope so, Nima, I really do,' Josie said.

Hal ran a final check on his equipment.

'Got the dexamethasone?' Todd asked.

Hal patted his pocket, feeling the outline of the syringe case.

'What's that?' Josie asked.

'A steroid for treating acute mountain sickness. Just a contingency.' Hal checked to see if the two Sherpas were ready. 'Shall we?'

Josie nodded and gave Todd a hug. 'You sure you don't want to come with us?'

'Someone's got to man the radios. Besides, I quite like the thought of climbing back in my sleeping-bag.'

Hal gave Todd a thumbs-up sign, then turned his back on the camp to begin the trek across the col, their route lit by head torches.

The four of them moved unroped on the flat plateau, picking their way with care across frozen fields of ice and rock.

Ahead of them were a mammoth sixteen to eighteen hours of unrelenting physical activity. They would barely have time to rest, save the short stops to cram calories and fluid into themselves. Josie had read somewhere that summit day put the human body through the equivalent of five marathons. She prayed that she would not fail.

By 2.30AM they were leaving the flat terrain of the col. Hal cut across the snow ramp at an angle until his head torch picked out the first of the fixed ropes. Nima was right with them but Lhakpa was already lagging behind.

They waited fifteen minutes for Lhakpa to catch up, Nima getting increasingly impatient. 'Why he so slow?' he said.

'I want you to stay with him,' Hal instructed Nima. 'I'm worried he might not make it if he's on his own.'

After allowing Lhakpa time to get his breath, they began the climb. They clipped their jumar clamps onto the fixed ropes—the sliding device would lock into position in the event of a fall.

Josie was deeply shocked by how little oxygen she seemed to be getting. 'Hal. I think there's a problem with my oxygen.'

Hal stopped and shone his head torch onto the oxygen line. 'Everything's OK with the equipment. It's the way you're breathing. It's a common mistake to pant too fast. Then you're just recycling exhaust gases and not getting any new oxygen. You have to breathe as slow and deep as you can.'

Josie tried to calm herself down. She took a long slow breath, inhaling as deeply as she could. Then another. 'OK. I see what you mean. That feels better already.' Reassured, she stepped up behind Hal once more. Gradually they pulled away from the two Sherpas, Nima staying alongside Lhakpa at the back.

At 4.00am Hal called a rest, pouring Josie a cup of hot chocolate and insisting that she eat a high-energy bar. 'Look. There're the Sherpas' head torches.' He pointed down at Nima and Lhakpa. 'I don't like the speed Lhakpa's moving at. And hey. Look behind them. There's another light down there, just coming off the flat ground.'

'Oh, yes. That's weird. I wonder who it can be?'

Hal thought. 'Maybe it's Todd. Perhaps the Sherpas left something behind.' He retrieved the walkie-talkie from his jacket pocket. 'Hal to Camp Four. Come in, Todd.'

Todd came on the line. 'Go ahead, Hal.'

'That's not you coming up behind the Sherpas, is it?'

'You got to be joking, mate. I'm snug in my sleeping-bag.'

'You bastard. So who is it?'

'I think it's a Russian climber called Andrei Vasylenko. He's a bit of a lone wolf, apparently, who bought into one of the other team's permits but they don't want him to climb with them because he's got a chequered history. He's been rescued off more mountains than I've had hot meals. He was moving bloody fast when he left.'

'He'd have to. He left very late. Over.'

Eventually the two Sherpas arrived, Lhakpa breathing hard and looking increasingly ill.

'I'm sorry, Hal,' Nima said. 'Nothing I can do to make him faster. I try everything, persuade him, but he no go fast. He too old.'

'Not too old!' Lhakpa pulled his oxygen mask to one side and spat into the snow. 'Too sick today.'

'I think he not get higher than South Summit,' Nima said sadly. 'We drop oxygen bottles there for you, then I take Lhakpa back.'

'Oh, but, Nima, that means you won't get to the summit today.' Josie was distraught, knowing how upset he would be.

'Plenty other time for summit,' he said, 'but I don't leave sick friend alone on mountain.'

Hal nodded. 'Thank you, Nima. Your chance will come soon.'

'When the gods wish. Now you go, we rest.'

Hal kicked his front crampon points into the ice and continued up into the night. 'He's like his father, generous to a fault. The finest people on earth, the Sherpas, and Nima's one of the best.'

JUST AFTER 10.00AM Josie and Hal completed the long climb through the ice gullies and emerged onto the sharply defined terrain of the ridge. One hour earlier they had switched to their second oxygen bottles.

'I've got to sit down, Hal. Let me rest.'

'I can't let you do that. Last time you sat down we were stopped for fifteen minutes. We're getting slow.'

Josie knew he was right. The consistent pace of the first five or six hours had slowed to a crawl, punctuated by frequent stops as she sought to control her breathing. She slumped over her ice axe, trying to restore some strength to her legs by resting them for a few moments.

'Let's go. The South Summit is just past this section of ridge.'

Josie willed herself to carry on, fired by the thought that Sebastian was not far away. Sebastian. She had become so wrapped up in the process of the climb that she had almost forgotten him. Focus, she told herself. Remember what this is all about. But that was hard.

When they finally reached the flat terrain of the South Summit she stood, blinking and confused, staring around her as if she expected Sebastian to be there, a ghost of ice.

But there was no sign of any bodies.

They both rested for a while before Hal said, 'I'll take a look around.' He moved off, his crampons cutting crisply into the ice.

Alone, the sheer exposure of the place suddenly struck Josie. She was lying on a patch of snow just a few hundred yards from the summit of Everest. Looking up, she could see the notorious summit ridge with its steep sections. The summit pole itself was out of her eyeline.

Hal returned. 'I found Sebastian and Rick,' he said. 'They're together just the other side of that snowbank.' He pulled Josie to her feet and led her away towards the ridge. At its far end two bodies were lying half buried by snow.

'I'll leave you alone for a while,' Hal said, retreating.

Sebastian was curled in a foetal position, his face half nestled into the faded nylon of his wind suit. Josie pulled the fabric back from his face so she could see him more clearly.

She had thought about this moment so many times that there was no sense of horror, no feeling of revulsion at the partly mummified corpse of the man she loved. The features were still recognisably Sebastian despite the tightening of the skin against the skull. The eyes were frozen shut and what remained of his hair had been bleached pure white by the intensity of high-altitude radiation.

Josie took off her outer gloves and stroked his face, whispering, 'I can't tell you how much I miss you. It's been so difficult to get over all this when I didn't know where you were . . . didn't know anything about the place that killed you. But now I do and I think I understand what made you come here.'

For a while Josie stayed very still. 'Do you remember the poem you sent me once?

'They who are near me do not know that you are nearer to me than they are.
They who speak to me do not know that my heart is full with your unspoken words . . .'

Josie paused as the emotion of the moment overcame her. 'That's how I'll always feel. That my heart will always be full of unspoken words for you.' After some minutes she stood, her legs shaking.

Hal came over to join her. 'You OK?'

'Yes, I'll be fine.'

Hal kneeled by Rick's body and searched the pockets until he found the guide's camera. 'There might be some useful shots on this. Then he searched until he found the hand bearing the ring Deborah had asked him to retrieve. He slipped it off easily and put it carefully in his pocket. Then he turned his attention to Sebastian.

'Look at this.' Hal pulled open the rucksack to reveal the top of an empty oxygen bottle, Rick's name written on it in black marker. 'Rick gave Sebastian his last oxygen bottle.'

'But where are the other clients?'

'I don't know. They could have stumbled off the ridge in the white-out. You see how steep it is here.'

Hal reached further into the rucksack. 'There's something else in here. It feels like Gore-Tex or Dacron.' He pulled out a corner of brightly coloured fabric. 'Oh, maybe it's the paraglider.'

'You're right. I forgot he was planning to fly that.'

Hal stood to take out his camera. 'Do you mind if I take a photograph of the bodies? That bottle is exactly the type of thing that might help Deborah when she gets to court.'

'Of course.'

Hal took a few pictures.

Josie brushed a flurry of snow from Sebastian's face. 'You'll always be in my heart, Sebastian.' She stood. 'I'm ready,' she told Hal.

He looked up the ridge, considering for a while. Eventually he asked: 'How about the summit? Sure you're up for it?'

Josie did not hesitate. 'Yes.'

The summit. The words set her heart racing. If she had to crawl there on her hands and knees, Josie wanted it now more than ever. She let her head drop, watching Hal's crampons as he began to move relentlessly up the slope. Josie braced herself for the pain.

IT SEEMED only moments passed before Josie fell to both knees to rest. A wave of nausea threatened her, the taste of bile filling her mouth. She breathed in her oxygen, relishing the purity of the taste as it cleaned away the acid rancour of the bile. Then she looked ahead, her heart sinking. The ground here was steep with big exposed drops on each side. Fixed ropes snaked along its length.

Hal pulled out an energy bar and passed Josie half. 'Take it. Come on. You have to force this stuff down, right? You're going to need this energy later on.'

Josie eased the oxygen mask just far enough away from her face to slip the frozen tablet of food into her mouth. She let the warmth of her mouth thaw it out before chewing and swallowing.

'Let's go.'

Josie hauled herself up on the rope and shakily continued, forcing herself to concentrate on the thin red filament of nylon, trying not to let her eyes be pulled to the sides.

Step and breathe. Breathe. Breathe. Step and breathe.

Hal stopped. They were standing at the foot of the steepest section yet. Hazily, Josie realised this would be the Hillary Step, thirty feet of demanding climbing, protected by a fixed rope. He checked that her jumar clamp was in place and began to ascend.

Josie waited for his call, then forced her body upwards, swinging her ice axe into the face and levering herself onto it with shaking arms. Panting uncontrollably she pushed her crampon spikes into the crumbling snow and stretched her leg up onto a protruding rock. Her whole body was shaking with the strain as she pushed up.

Another blow of the ice axe, two more moves and she made it, collapsing onto the flatter ground at the top.

The walkie-talkie suddenly crackled to life in Hal's pocket.

'Todd here. How you going up there, Hal?'

'Slow but good. Just made it up the Hillary Step.'

'You know what the time is, don't you? It's almost one o'clock.'

'It is? Shit, I lost track of that one.'

'One o'clock is turnaround time. What are you going to do?'

Hal looked up along the ridge. The summit pole was still not visible. 'Let me talk to Josie.'

'What's he talking about?' Distracted by pain, Josie had not concentrated fully on the conversation.

'We've got a problem, Josie. We hit the turnaround. You remember I told you if we hadn't topped out by one we were out of here? I don't want to risk bringing you down in a night descent.'

Josie stared at him dumbly as she tried to register the implications of his words. A sense of disbelief engulfed her. 'You're not serious. Tell me you're not serious about that.'

Hal said nothing.

Inside Josie the disbelief escalated rapidly into anger. 'No! You can't do that to me. Not now. Look how high we are.'

'It's brutal, I know, but you are moving too slowly.'

'I'll get faster. I can do it. I promise you I can make it. There's nothing to stop us. How far are we from the summit, anyway?'

'If you pick up the pace we can make it in thirty minutes. If.'

'Please, Hal. Please.'

Hal clicked on the walkie-talkie. 'Hal to Todd. We're going up.'

'That's pretty bold, mate.'

'I know that. What's the status of the Sherpas?'

'I can see them through the binoculars. They made it to the South Summit. Oh, and Andrei is still behind you. He's getting late too.'

'Well, that's not our problem. We'll call from the summit.'

'Good luck. Over and out.'

Josie reached out and touched Hal's arm. 'Thank you.'

'Thank me when we're back down in Camp Four.'

'ALL YOUR POINTS IN! Keep moving.'

Dimly, Josie could sense that the angle of the ice now sloped awkwardly away from the face. The rope pull intensified. She placed her feet carefully sideways, bending her knees in a crabbing motion to plant home every one of the ten crampon spikes.

Kick in. Breathe. Kick in. She could feel her kidneys throbbing inside her. Breathe.

She plunged in her ice axe and fell to one knee, her head resting on her gloved hands as she struggled to draw in life-giving air. She felt Hal's arms under her shoulders and found herself on her feet. They stood there for some minutes until her dizziness subsided. Then Hal half pulled and half pushed her along the now-flatter terrain of the ridge. Then he paused. 'Look up ahead.'

Josie squinted through the frozen lenses of her goggles and saw the flags of the summit pole for the first time, sitting above a final rise in the ridge. A rushing wave of adrenaline engulfed her.

Hal took hold of her harness and they began again.

'Every yard up . . .' Move. Breathe. 'Is a yard less to go.' Rest.

She could hear Hal, strangely distant above the rising bluster of the wind: 'OK, Josie. OK! Look how close. One more time.'

Josie squinted up the ridge. He was right. The summit pole, with its fluttering garland of prayer flags, was now just a few yards further up. Adrenaline coursed once more through her body.

She looked steadily in front of her, lifting her head as high as she could and straightening her back. As she took the first step, Hal fell in behind her. Breathe. Another step, swing the feet out in an arc to avoid snagging the other boot. Breathe. Breathe.

'Don't . . .' Josie punched through the pain barrier with an explosive grunt. Breathe. Breathe. Breathe. Breathe. '. . . Stop.'

Two more steps. The ridge was levelling off now and Josie was laughing silently to herself.

She took one more step, placed her hand on the summit pole and used it to pull herself up. Hal moved steadily up beside her.

'Everest is yours, Josie!'

They stood side by side, recovering. The view was the most perfect in the world. Josie was speechless with awe as she looked to the south. The ridges of the mountains around her appeared to be sharpened steel razor edges ripping the sky. To the north clouds filled the sky. Nothing could dull the intense joy of the moment.

'For you, Sebastian,' she whispered, 'with my love.'

'I'm going to bump up your oxygen level for a short time.' Hal opened her rucksack. 'For the interview.' He clicked the regulator round from its flow rate of two litres a minute to four.

Josie felt the extra gas suffusing warmth into her body, bringing a wave of euphoria with it. She sucked it down deep, relishing its richness, then pulled Hal gently towards her. They embraced clumsily, oxygen masks clashing. 'We made it, Hal. We really made it.'

He looked out to the north. 'We've got work to do. Then we move fast. I'm not so happy about the look of those clouds.'

Hal sat facing Josie on the other side of the pole, pulled the walkie-talkie out of his rucksack and clicked onto TRANSMIT. 'Hal to Camp Four. Todd, do you read me? Over.'

'Loud and clear, baby. This is Todd. You'd better have good news.'

'We're on the summit.'

A cheer erupted from the handset. 'That is the best news ever, Hal! Josie OK?'

'Pretty good.'

'OK. Listen. Just a minute ago I had Rachel call up. I think she's still on the satellite line. I'll patch her through.'

'Hal?' Rachel's voice sounded hesitant and nervous.

'On the top of the world.'

'Hey, fantastic! Oh, I'm so pleased for you, Hal, and for Josie too . . . Oh, and did you find Rick?'

'Rick's and Sebastian's bodies were together . . . it seems that Rick gave Sebastian his last oxygen bottle. We got Rick's camera. We haven't found any of the others.'

'All right. I'll tell Deborah. We'd better get off the line now.'

'Hey. One last thing. Will you marry me?'

'What? Hal, you're outrageous. You ask me that from the summit of Everest? How wonderful. The answer is yes.'

Hal laughed. 'I love you.'

'Me too.'

'Over and out.'

Josie patted Hal on the back. 'Congratulations,' she said. 'I never knew you were such a romantic.'

The walkie-talkie crackled again, this time with Todd's voice. 'I'm going to patch up the satellite link to *Daybreak* right now . . .'

'CAN SOMEONE get these lights turned down? It's like a sauna in here.' Mike padded a handkerchief against his brow.

The *Daybreak* studio was way too hot and the only person in the room who didn't seem to be feeling the heat was the stand-in presenter, Tim, who was sitting on the sofa looking as cool as a cucumber.

'We've got the call!' The words from the director fed into Tim's earpiece. 'Connecting you in five seconds.' Tim turned to the camera. 'We've just had the news that Josie Turner and Hal Maher are standing on the top of Everest right now! Thanks to the wonders of modern technology we should be able to speak to them direct. Do you hear me, Josie?'

'Tim?' Josie's voice came across the studio speakers loud and clear.

'Josie. You're a hero! Everyone here at *Daybreak* sends you heartiest congratulations. What's it like up there? What can you see?'

'Right now I'm looking out across the greatest peaks of the Himalayas and I'm the happiest woman in the world. I want to thank everyone at *Daybreak* for their support. I could never have reached the summit without you.'

'How was the final section?'

'More exhausting than I can tell you. And terrifying . . .' There was a loud crackle of interference on the connection.

'Sorry, Josie, we didn't quite catch that. Can you repeat, please?' This time there was no answering voice.

'Hello? Josie? Do you hear me . . .?'

HAL CALLED CAMP FOUR. 'What's happening, Todd?'

'Satellite link went down.'

'Goddamn.'

'Soon as we have it, I'll be back on.'

Hal shifted impatiently. 'Let's do the filming.'

He brought out the lightweight digital video camera and took several careful steps back down the slope to frame up some shots.

'Hey. I nearly forgot the flag.' Josie rummaged through the internal pockets of her down suit, retrieving a crumpled square of cloth. She unfurled it, turning it so the words '*Daybreak* Everest Expedition' faced the camera.

Hal shouted up, 'Can you take the oxygen mask off so I can see your face?'

'Oh God. OK.'

Josie unclipped her mask and tried to turn her convulsive gasping into a smile. She held up the *Daybreak* flag in a triumphant sweep of her arms. 'Made it!' she shouted. 'Feeling on top of the world!'

'OK. That'll do it.'

Josie replaced the mask, experiencing a surge of relief as the flow of oxygen resumed.

'Camp Four to summit. Do you read? Camp Four to summit.'

Hal grabbed the handset. 'This is Hal.'

'Todd here. We still can't get a response on the satellite link.'

'This is a major pain in the ass, Todd. Tell them if they can't make the connection in the next five minutes we're starting down. Out.'

'No!' Josie snatched the radio from him. 'Todd! You have to get that link. We can hang on if that's what it takes.'

'Roger that. Wait my call. Out.'

Hal looked out into the void for a few moments. 'I say when we leave, Josie. That's my decision, not yours.'

'The summit broadcast is part of the package. I owe it to *Daybreak*.'

'And I have to get you off this mountain alive.'

A sudden rush of wind whistled across the summit, causing them both to hunch down for protection. The prayer flags flew momentarily into life, then died again as calm returned.

Hal stood and moved away. Josie could hear the faint click and motorwind of his stills camera as he photographed the scene behind her.

Trying to extinguish the tight knot of anger inside her, she stared out to the north where, she now realised, Everest's plume was starting to run. For minutes she sat motionless, mesmerised by the ebb and flow of the curling mist as it stretched away to infinity.

She closed her eyes as a flash of pain seared the back of her retinas. She clutched wildly at her forehead, fearing for a terrifying second that the goggles were gone. Her frozen fingers snatched clumsily against the plastic frame, trying to drag the tinted glass down. The elastic was snagged onto some part of the oxygen headband.

Josie pulled the goggles from her head to reposition them. She held them in front of her to brush away the ice with her glove. One fumbling moment, one split second as her deadened hands moved a nerve pulse slower than the signals from her brain.

The goggles fell, skittering down the steep ice before dropping over the edge of the ridge out of sight. Josie felt panic well up within her as she imagined them tumbling, impacting hard against ice and rock. She placed both hands round the summit pole and gripped with all her strength.

She heard the crisp ice steps as Hal worked his way back up to her. Please God he didn't see, Josie prayed.

'Can you still feel your feet?' he asked.

'Yes,' Josie lied.

'How about your hands?'

'Bit cold. But I'm keeping the circulation going.'

'Another two minutes and I'm taking you down.'

'Really. I'm fine.'

'You're fine because I pumped up your regulator to four litres. When we leave here I'll have to knock you back to two. Then you're going to feel it.'

Needlepoints of pain danced across nerve endings in the back of Josie's eyes. She screwed then shut, until the sensation passed.

The walkie-talkie suddenly clicked on.

'Here we go.' Hal said.

Tim's voice came on the line, startlingly clear: 'This is *Daybreak* expedition control in London. Do you hear us, over?'

'This is Hal Maher on the summit of Everest reading you loud and clear.'

'Yes!' The sound of cheers rang from the walkie-talkie. 'Josie, how are you feeling? Does Everest live up to your expectation?'

Josie laughed. 'You might say that. Climbing this mountain has been the most incredible challenge of my life. I had no idea it would be so tough. But standing here now, it all seems worth while.'

'As I understand it, you visited the resting place of your late husband today. If you can bear to talk about such a deeply personal moment, can you describe how you felt?'

Josie paused, searching for the words. 'I know a lot of people have accused me of being ghoulish for wanting to visit Sebastian's body. All I can say is that those moments with him today were the happiest I have had since he died.'

'Amen to that, Josie. I think we all understand how you feel. Hal, how long will it take you to get down now?'

'Hard to say but we should be moving right away.'

'We'll leave you to it. Godspeed from *Daybreak* and over and out.'

THE WIND WAS RISING. And as it did so, the cold was cutting deeper.

Then the pain hit. Josie screamed as the burning stab rippled across the back of her retinas. She could not see.

The weather was deteriorating fast and they had descended just thirty yards down the ridge. Josie felt so tired she could barely move. Now she had to sit.

'Hal! My eyes!'

Hal crouched over her on the windward side so she could hear his shout. 'Where are your goggles?'

'I don't know. They're gone.'

'You lost your goggles? I told you *never* to take your goggles off! Now you're becoming snowblind.'

'Give me yours,' she begged him. 'Let me borrow them.'

'The damage is already done,' he told her. 'If I give you mine we both get snowblind and then we really have got a problem.'

A blast of wind hit her. Only the steady grip of Hal's hand on her harness prevented her from being blown backwards off the ridge.

'Move!' Hal said. 'This weather is coming in fast.'

Josie pulled her legs up beneath her, willing the frozen muscles to move. The pain in her eyes subsided to a dull ache.

She felt Hal lift her bodily to her feet. Leaning into him for protection, she took one faltering step. Then another. Hal shuffled forward into the whiteout, dragging her, bent double, at his side with her head buried deep in the down hood of her wind suit.

She sensed the uncertainty in Hal's step as they hit a steeper incline. Then he stopped. She risked a look out from inside the hood and by chance caught a moment when the blizzard faltered, revealing a drop in front of them.

The sickening realisation churned in her guts. Breathe. Breathe. Breathe. 'Hal! We're on the edge.'

'I know that.' Hal let her rest as he stared intently into the blank whiteness, searching for the smallest visual clue to orientate him.

Just a few yards away, a climber emerged from the blizzard and headed slowly towards them.

'There's someone climbing up,' Hal told Josie.

The climber was less than an arm's length away before he showed any sign of recognising their presence. Then he stopped.

'Andrei?' Hal said.

The climber leaned forward. 'How far to the summit?'

'You'll get blown off the ridge! Go back down.'

'No!' Vasylenko pulled a yellow plastic camera from his pocket and waved it, ranting, 'I need a photo. On the summit. Come back up with me.'

'No way. Do you think I'm crazy? We're going down.'

Andrei grabbed Hal by the shoulders. 'I have to have the photograph. They won't believe me.'

Hal yelled, 'Andrei. Listen. If you keep going up into these conditions you are going to die. Get off the mountain while you still can.'

'The summit is here. You think I can turn round now?'

Hal manoeuvred Josie around Vasylenko and took her several steps down the ridge. When they looked back, Andrei was little more than a grey shadow moving through the driving snow.

Josie sucked as hard as she could on the mask. There seemed to be so little air. A ring of stars danced around her head as she fell on the ice. She tried to move but her legs would not obey the command. Hal hoisted her upright. She stood unsupported for a few seconds, then lunged forward again onto her knees.

Hal bent down next to her. 'I can't carry you, Josie. You have to get off this mountain on your own two feet. Now get up and walk.'

Josie shook her head slowly from side to side.

Hal looked at her in confusion for some moments, then reached for her oxygen line. He saw immediately that the red ball inside the valve indicator was lying idle. 'Shit! You're out of oxygen. I never put you back down to two litres when we left the summit. How could I have been so damned stupid?' He began to unclip Josie's oxygen mask. Then, removing his own mask, he placed it against Josie's mouth. 'Hold it to your face.'

Josie did as he instructed, feeling the miraculous gas permeating every cell in her body with new life.

Hal brought out the walkie-talkie. 'This is Hal to Todd at Camp Four. Do you read?'

A barely audible voice replied. 'Hal. This is Todd.' Hal paused to draw breath, beginning to feel dizzy as the loss of his oxygen supply took effect. When he spoke, his words were slurred. 'We're about halfway along the ridge. We're on the last quarter-bottle of gas. Listen, I need to know exactly where those two cylinders are at the South Summit. Talk to Nima and find out where he left them. I may have to dig them out. I'll call you when we get down there.'

'Roger that.'

Hal helped Josie to her feet. The oxygen had restored some strength to her legs. 'We're going to share this, OK?'

Josie nodded but he could see the fear in her eyes. He gently pulled the oxygen mask from her and placed it over his own face for a minute or so. Then he returned it and indicated they should move. Josie felt him lead her onwards into the wind, the two of them bent double against what was rapidly becoming a full-out storm.

THE LIGHT WAS FADING and Hal was struggling to make out anything through the darkened glass of his goggles. 'Keep moving, Josie.'

Crying out in a sudden howl of pain, Josie began to scrape at her eyes with the frozen fabric of her outer gloves.

Hal had to take his hands away from the rope to force her to stop. He put his arms round her, holding her tightly against him. She pushed her head into the protection of his shoulder, her body stiffening as each wave of agony hit.

Lifting the goggles from his eyes, Hal scanned the section of ridge beneath them. All he could see was the fixed rope descending into a shifting world of blacks and greys. 'Josie. Time to go.'

Josie looked up at him, the whites of her eyes shockingly red from retinal haemorrhage. 'Rest?'

'No.' Hal moved a few steep steps down the ridge. He hit her hard on the back of the leg with his ice axe. 'Move this leg. Now!'

Josie moved the frozen limb forward a few inches. Hal grabbed the front of her waist harness and pulled her down towards him. Then, moving to her side, he forced her as fast as he dared down the steep section of ridge, using the fixed rope for support.

Out of the gloom, the level terrain of a snow platform appeared, marking the dip between the sharp section of ridge and the rise of the South Summit. Hal could see the huddled shapes of Sebastian and Rick nearby. He unclipped Josie from the rope and she collapsed onto her side. She curled up instinctively into a ball, to retain as much body heat as she could.

Hal crouched down close to her to shout into the walkie-talkie: 'Hal to Todd.'

'Go ahead, Hal. Where are you?'

'Near the South Summit. Todd, how do I find the gas? We have less than three yards vis up here.'

'On the west side. About five yards down.'

Hal turned off the unit. 'Stay here. I'll be back as fast as I can.'

Standing too fast, Hal had to pause as stars flickered across his vision. Then he stepped over Josie onto the slope beyond. The bottles were higher than his current position and the thought of coercing his deeply fatigued body to ascend once more sent a wave of despair through him. He tried desperately to remember the topography of the summit. Then he took the first step back up the slope, his body aching, protesting as it had never done before.

JOSIE LET HER mind drift—away from the excruciating pain of her eyes; away from the biting cold that was seeking to destroy her. Time and place had ceased to have any meaning. She had given up trying to imagine how many minutes, hours or days Hal had been away, given up trying to remember where she was—or why. The shivering had stopped. That has to be a good sign, she decided.

Through the distortion of ice that had grown around her eyes, she could see a dark shape lying on the terrace. It was just visible through the driving snow. *Sebastian.*

Was that really Sebastian or was she imagining it? She rolled onto her front and began to crawl towards the body.

He was so cold. Why was Sebastian so cold? Josie placed her cheek against his. She would warm him with her body, she decided, as she entwined herself as closely as she could.

She dreamed their embrace into a sleeping-bag, into a cocoon of warmth so intense it was almost too much; she dreamed of Sebastian laughing, kissing her tenderly.

Then she felt the wind rushing around her face, the patter of the snow granules against her skin. She tried to open her eyes but could see nothing. She could sense that she was alone with Sebastian. Utterly alone, only the roar of the storm for company.

She curled herself back into the foetal position by his side, content. She took one of his hands in hers, curling the warmth of her living flesh around fingers that were frozen as hard as iron.

I love you.

What did the shrinks call it? Josie had a moment of lucidity before slipping away once more. Closure. That was the word.

HAL PLACED his hands against his temples, trying to squeeze away the pulse of the altitude headache. The climb had driven new blood into the frozen cells of his hands and feet, stirring them painfully back to life. He had to keep the fingers working.

As he fought to remember what Todd said about the position of the bottles, he began to traverse, striding ten steps one way then dropping down one pace and returning for the same distance in the other direction. Knowing the oxygen cylinders would be at least partially buried, he dragged his feet, hoping to knock against metal. Then his crampon spikes struck an unseen obstacle. His hopes rising, Hal scraped away the snow and shone the torch onto the exposed metal cylinder. It was olive green and obviously old—one of the thousands of discarded empty bottles littering the peak.

He resumed the search. Ten minutes passed, fifteen. He could feel his entire body running down into a sluggish form of slow motion. Increasingly frustrated, he began to probe in the snow with his ice axe as he moved. 'Help me find them!' he screamed.

Soon he was on the verge of blacking out. It was now nineteen hours since they had set out from Camp Four and his body was desperately short of oxygen. Instinct told him he was out of time. He couldn't risk leaving Josie any longer. He set off down the slope.

Fifteen minutes later he stepped onto the snow platform, his head torch illuminating the still figure of Josie where she lay immobile in Sebastian's arms, the bright colours of her outer clothing barely visible beneath the crystallised shroud of ice that now covered her.

'Oh God. Josie!' She did not respond.

'Wake up!' Hal pulled the stiffened fabric of the wind suit back, shining the torch directly onto her.

Josie's eyes were two inflamed slits, the skin around them grotesquely puffed. The pupils barely dilated as the light hit them.

'Who is it?' Her voice was a rasping croak. 'I've been having such beautiful dreams.'

For the first time in hours the wind dropped for a few moments. Hal could speak without having to raise his voice. 'We're going to get you back safely, Josie.'

'Why? What's the problem?'

Hal hauled her a few yards away from Sebastian.

She turned towards him in confusion. 'Where's Sebastian? What have you done with him?' The wind began its furious assault once more as Josie started to scream: 'I'm blind! I want the pain to go away! Sebastian!'

Hal hustled her to her feet. 'Don't lose it now, Josie.'

She stumbled one awkward step forward, reaching the slope where the fixed ropes began. Then she lost the support of her legs, crashing down on her backside and forcing Hal to step back to keep his balance. They were still on the platform, but only just.

She lay prone, making no attempt to protect her face from the wind. Hal yelled at her, hitting his hands repeatedly against her cheeks to get her attention. Desperation and anger gave him the strength to raise his voice so he was sure she could hear. 'Listen. If you stay here you are going to die. Do you hear me, Josie? Get up and move!'

Josie's face remained impassive, as serenely indifferent as a death mask. Hal had seen it before, the terrifying finality with which the human body could switch off at altitude.

He had gone beyond the point where will-power alone could keep him standing. He lowered himself and rested with his back to Josie, his eyes close, burying his head between his knees.

'THIS IS CAMP FOUR to Hal. Is that you?' The hiss of transmission noise came back. 'Hal Maher. Do you read?'

Hal's voice came through: 'That you, Todd?'

'Yes.' A wave of jubilation ran through the tent. It had been more than four hours since the last transmission from the summit team. 'Where are you, Hal?'

There was a long pause before Hal responded. 'At the South Summit. I couldn't find the gas.'

'Shit! You're still at the *South Summit* now?' Todd could not keep the crack of emotion from his voice. 'How is Josie?'

There was no reply. The seconds ticked by. 'Do you read me, Hal?'

'Josie's right here.'

'Is she conscious?'

'She's sleeping.'

'That's not good, Hal. Can you wake her up and get her moving?'

There was no reply. Then Todd remembered the syringe of dexamethasone. The benefits were temporary, but it might get Josie on her feet. 'Hal. Can you give her the dexamethasone shot?'

Hal's breathing came through for several seconds, laboured and fast, before he replied: 'There's no point while it's dark and we can't move. I'll save it for daylight when we can see where the hell we're going. We'll make it through the night and come down at first light.'

'You've got no shelter up there. You'll be dead by morning, Hal. You know you can't do that.'

'Can you send anyone up with some more bottles?'

'With the conditions the way they are? If Nima and Lhakpa go out into this whiteout they'd never find the other side of the col. If the Sherpas leave at dawn they won't be at the South Summit until one, two o'clock in the afternoon—they're both exhausted, Hal.'

Hal made no reply.

Todd looked at Nima and Lhakpa. 'God help me,' he whispered, 'for what I'm about to do.' He clicked on TRANSMIT. 'Hal. If Josie's unconscious then perhaps she can't be saved. No one's going to blame you if you have to leave her. You did everything you could.'

'No way, Todd. I can't leave her, you know that. I've got a stove with me and some food. I'm going to dig out a bivouac.'

'You stubborn idiot. Don't waste your strength. If you've got anything left inside, use it to move down.'

'I'm turning the walkie-talkie off, to save battery power.'

'No you're not. Don't you do that. Listen to me, Hal.'

A faint click came through the speaker. The line was dead.

Todd turned to Nima.

The Sherpa held his head in his hands.

There were tears in his eyes. 'I go to find Hal,' he said, anger sweeping across his face. He made to leave the tent.

'Are you crazy? If you go out into that we'll never see you again. Be sensible, wait for light, then go with Lhakpa.'

Nima slumped back, knowing in his heart that Todd was right.

'Then I pray to the gods.' He began to mutter beneath his breath.

Seconds later the satellite phone began to ring. Todd braced himself and picked up the receiver.

'Todd? Do you hear me? This is Rachel in Vancouver.'

Oh God, Todd thought, this is going to be bad. 'Yes, I read you.'

'Can I speak to Hal? Or is he sleeping?'

'Rachel. Hal and Josie are not back in the camp yet.'

Rachel stuttered, 'Not back? Then . . . where are they?'

'Rachel, we have whiteout conditions here. Just after they left the summit a storm blew in. They can't see to find the route right now. But I'm sure they'll make their way down as soon as it clears up . . .'

'Like Sebastian and Rick,' Rachel said. 'It's all going to happen over again, isn't it?'

A new voice suddenly broke in: 'Todd?' It was Deborah. 'What the hell's happening?'

'They're benighted on the summit ridge.'

'In what conditions?'

'It's not the worst I've seen on Everest, but it's bad. Hal was talking about digging a bivouac.'

'Oh my God. Can you patch us through to Hal?'

'I don't want to do that. His batteries are getting low.'

'OK. I understand. All right.' Deborah was going to be the strong one, Todd recognised from the way she sounded.

'We'll call you when we have more news.'

HAL PUSHED the sharpened tip of the ice axe into the steeply angled ice wall. It was iron hard, too dense to be easily cut away. He swore, taking two more steps onto the incline and shining the head torch onto another section. He tried it with the axe. The same story. He began to doubt that he would find a suitable place to dig. He had been testing the face for almost half an hour.

He pushed the tip in again. This time the ice felt different, softer. He raised the axe to strike a blow. The broad edge bit deeply into the face, producing a quantity of loose crystals. Three feet to the right the conditions were the same. Encouraged, he began to scrape away at the compacted snow. After ten or fifteen minutes he had made a hollow about ten inches deep.

'Too slow.' He picked up the ice axe and began again, increasing the frequency of the blows. Breathe. Breathe. Breathe.

Unexpectedly, the ice axe plunged in with no resistance. Confused,

Hal shone the head torch into the scraped-out area. He could scarcely believe what it revealed. A hole had opened into the face. There was a hollow area behind. He pushed in the axe and began to pull at the edges. After three or four minutes he had excavated it wide enough to push his head inside.

It was the best sight of his life. A coffin-shaped space about three feet high which, with some work, would allow two people to lie side by side. Hal realised he had been cutting into the entrance hole of an old bivouac site. He was stunned by his good fortune. Now he had a fighting chance of getting Josie through the night.

He opened up the entrance with his hands, scooping out the loosely packed snow so that he could push his upper body into the cavity. He began to clear out the drifted snow from the far end of the shelter.

When he was satisfied he had created enough space, Hal wriggled out of the bivouac and crossed the slope back to the platform where Josie lay. 'Josie. I found a shelter. Do you hear me?'

She made no movement.

Hal bent down and placed his hands under her arms. Shuffling awkwardly backwards, he dragged Josie against the full force of the wind for several steps. Breathe. Power backwards a few more inches. Rest. And so on. And on. Hal had no idea how long it took him to haul Josie across the ten yards but it felt like hours. By the time he got her to the bivouac his world was spinning. He drew a few enormous breaths and with a last supreme effort hauled her up so that the top part of her body was leaning into the bivouac entrance.

He released the straps of her rucksack. 'Now, Josie, push yourself up into the shelter.'

'Hal? I don't understand.'

'Just lift your leg up and move inside the hole.'

He pushed her from behind as Josie lifted her knee stiffly onto the lip of the entrance. She slid into the snow hole headfirst and lay full length on her side. Hal pushed her pack in and followed it with his own. Then he climbed in beside her.

Hal took Josie's rucksack and jammed it across the entrance. The worst of the punishing wind was excluded.

He collapsed onto his back, a wave of relief overwhelming him as he lay by Josie's side, close to tears. 'I'm going to make you warm now, Josie. Going to get you through the night.'

'Are we in the camp?'

'Yeah. We're in a camp. A five-star camp.'

10

Hal pulled off his gloves and scrutinised his fingers. They were frozen but had sustained no more than frostnip. He undid the front of his wind suit and unzipped the down suit beneath it. He placed his hands into the warmth of his armpits. The relief that he had not so far suffered frostbite went some way to compensating for the pain as his fingers thawed out.

Leaving Josie to sleep, he opened his rucksack and brought out the basic emergency kit he carried with him: a superlight Gore-Tex survival bag, a foam sleeping mat, a burner unit for cooking with, a full canister of butane gas, a small aluminium pot and two red survival packs, each containing 1,500 calories of mixed high-energy rations.

He began the awkward task of placing the survival bag along the length of the shelter floor. He had to roll Josie against the ice wall to push the fabric beneath her. Then he did the same with the foam mat.

Next, fluids. Hal knew he had to get at least a litre into each of them. He picked up the burner unit and screwed it into the gas container. Snapping an ice screw off his belt, Hal used it to scrape shavings of ice off the wall of the shelter into the aluminium pan. When it was half full he placed the lid on top and put the pot on the cooker in a niche that had been carved out of the ice wall. Hal found his lighter in an inside pocket and held it against the burner unit. Deprived of oxygen, the gas was reluctant to fire even when he did manage to make a spark. The shelter filled with the stench of uncombusted butane as he repeated the process over and over. Finally, he got the burner to catch.

Hal watched the ring of blue flame roar into life, then—despite himself—fell asleep, waking with a start ten minutes later.

The last of the ice was just melting in the pan. He poured a little of the warm liquid into a plastic mug and ripped open one of the emergency sachets of chocolate powder. He tipped it into the mug, stirring it into a paste with his knife, then added the rest of the fluid. His body craved the sugar and the warmth it would bring. But Josie had to come first. 'Josie.'

She stirred next to him.

'You have to drink.'

He raised her head and tried to hold the mug to her lips. Josie turned her head away.

'It's hot chocolate. I want you to drink it now.'

Josie parted her lips, swallowing the fluid in small gulps.

When the mug was empty, Hal packed the pan with more snow and put it on the burner to begin the process once more.

Getting calories into Josie was his next priority. Sugar would provide the fastest hit. He fed a 200-gram bar of mint cake to her in small pieces before eating his own. Within minutes, Hal could feel the sugar being absorbed into his bloodstream. Later he would boil up the foil sachets containing ready-cooked food.

Next he pulled off the four gloves on Josie's right hand, struggling with the last silk layer, which was frozen stiffly in place. Josie was passive, still only half aware of what he was doing.

He let out a low whistle as her fingers were revealed. Only her little finger and thumb were untouched. The other three fingers were grossly distorted with fluid-filled blisters that indicated first-degree frostbite. At the edges Hal could see the telltale encroachment of black tissue—gangrene would set in if he didn't act fast. Josie's left hand was even worse: all four fingers were blistered. He lay next to her and placed her hands under his armpits, shivering as the frozen tissue drew heat away from his skin.

Josie began to murmur, calling his name several times. Hal knew that the pain of thawing out her hands was pulling her out of whatever dream state she was in.

Ten minutes later, Josie was conscious enough to talk. 'What's happening? My hands are burning.' Instinctively she tried to pull them away.

Hal locked them in position. 'Stick with it. Just a little longer.'

Josie pushed her face into Hal's shoulder and bit into the fabric of his suit as the warm blood seeped back agonisingly slowly into the tissue of her hands, capillary by capillary, cell by frozen cell.

As soon as Josie could move her fingers Hal let her withdraw her hands to continue the warming process herself.

Now the second pan of water was ready. He prepared the chocolate, this time adding a sachet of muesli to the liquid. He allowed himself half the warm mixture. The rest he spooned into Josie's mouth.

'Josie? We're going to have to do the same thing with your feet.'

She said nothing.

Hal was deeply fearful of what state her feet would be in. He knew that finding the bivouac had dramatically increased their odds of survival. But if she couldn't walk, Josie was as good as dead.

He unlaced the double-ring fastener on the crampons, praying under his breath . . .

JOSIE PROPPED HERSELF on her elbow to drink as Hal offered the mug once more. Her fingers felt alien, bloated and distorted. She drank the liquid quickly and felt Hal take back the mug.

'I'm going to heat up the meals,' he told her.

Josie nodded. Speaking was a big effort for her.

Her feet were still aching from the brutal process of defrosting, but Hal had told her she would be able to walk in the morning. Her eyes had stabilised, the searing attacks having been replaced by a dull pulse of pain. There was a gritty texture to the tissue, as if someone had thrown a teaspoon of sand into each eyeball.

Josie shivered. The snow shelter was just warm enough to keep her body core at a level to sustain life but she was definitely not warm.

'You're going to come through this, Josie, OK?' Hal told her.

She held out her hand and felt him take it in his. He raised it upwards and she could feel the warmth of his breath on her fingers.

He let her rest. He had forced as much food and liquid as he could into her body and the sleep would help restore her strength for the descent. If she had any strength left to give.

He checked his watch. It was 3.30am. He found the walkie-talkie and switched it on. 'Come in, Todd.'

'What's happening, Hal?'

'I found a bivouac site near the South Summit. We're going to leave here at first light. Get the Sherpas to come up and meet us as high as they can with some oxygen and fluids. Do you copy?'

'I read that. Are you sure Josie'll be strong enough to get down?'

'I'm loading her up with calories, so she has to be in with a fighting chance. I'll give her the dexamethasone shot just before we leave.'

'Hey, Hal. I'm so sorry for what I said earlier. Maybe it was too soon to tell you to bail out. But if it gets to the stage where Josie can't move . . .' Todd struggled to find the words.

'I know what you're saying. I'm signing off now.'

Hal sat for a few minutes trying to work out what had changed. Then he realised—the rumble of the wind had eased away. The storm had blown itself out.

NIMA TIGHTENED the shoulder straps on his rucksack and stared up into the night sky as he waited for Lhakpa. Todd was standing beside him outside the tent, shifting from one foot to the other as he attempted to keep warm. 'What's the time?' Nima asked him.

Todd checked his watch. 'Four thirty.'

'Storm finished,' Nima said. 'But now plenty soft snow. Not good for fast climb. You have walkie-talkie for me?'

'I don't. This is the last one with any power left.'

Nima pulled back the flaps of the tent to see if Lhakpa was ready. He spoke in his own language: 'Get moving. The day is nearly here.'

'I'm moving as fast as I can,' Lhakpa snapped.

Nima tried to quell his anger. He knew that Lhakpa had suffered badly over the last two days. Nevertheless, his recalcitrance was beginning to wear Nima down. 'Let me help with those,' he offered, crouching to assist Lhakpa with his boots.

Finally Lhakpa was ready. He emerged from the tent. 'How high we go?' he asked Todd aggressively.

'I don't know. If Hal manages to get Josie moving then they'll come down towards you. If he doesn't, you have to get to the South Summit. Their lives are depending on you.'

'Why you no go?' Lhakpa stabbed Todd in the chest with his hand.

'My job is here,' Todd said. 'If I leave there's no one to run the communications. Then no one knows who is dead or alive.'

'Are we on or not?' Todd turned to Nima, unsure whether Lhakpa was even now about to pull out.

'We go.' Nima pushed Lhakpa gently away from the tent.

Uttering a silent prayer to the gods, Nima led the way.

'JOSIE. IT'S LIGHT. Time to move.'

Josie's mind ripped her back to the last place in the world she wanted to be. Her eyes had improved a little; now she could see dim images of her surroundings, the light filtering from the entrance of the snow shelter, Hal crouched over her.

'We're going down,' he said, then kicked out the top layer of snow from the hole, pulled Josie's pack inside and poked his head out. 'Want to know what I'm looking at?'

'OK.' Josie forced herself up into a sitting position.

'A clear day. Not much blue sky but clear enough to navigate our way down the ropes. We'll meet the Sherpas in a couple of hours.'

'I still can't see much.'

'That won't stop us. I'll get you clipped onto the ropes and guide you down every step of the way.' Hal took out the syringe. 'Now don't move while I give you the dexamethasone.'

He injected it right through Josie's many layers of clothing, directly into her thigh. The effects were fast and dramatic.

'God, I can feel that working,' she told Hal. She felt a tingling sensation as the steroid ran through her, energising every exhausted tissue in her body.

'It doesn't last long,' Hal warned her. 'So we have to move fast.'

'My fingers feel like they're going to burst.'

'Let me see them.'

Josie let Hal pull off her gloves. The blisters had increased in size, the skin at the edges blacker than before. Hal knew that giving her that news would not be good for her morale.

'They've stabilised. They should work out fine.'

'I'm going to lose them, aren't I?'

'Not if you're prepared to fight. I want you to be positive about what we're about to do, OK? Compared with how it could be we're in very good shape. We've had a full night of shelter, fluid and food.'

Hal checked his watch. It was 6.17am. He packed his rucksack and turned to the tricky task of getting Josie dressed. Her feet had swollen in the night so he had to use force to get her plastic outer boots fully on. The laces had frozen together in a ball. Hal picked at the iron-hard strands with the numb ends of his fingers. It took a good five minutes blowing on them to defreeze his fingers enough to tackle his own boots. Finally he snapped on the crampons.

'OK. I'm going to exit first. You crawl out after me.'

Hal turned his head to the entrance. And froze.

A face was staring into the shelter.

'Oh my God.' Hal recoiled, breathing heavily from the shock.

'What is it?' Josie was confused by Hal's sudden cry.

'It's OK. Just stay calm. I'll sort this out.'

The face staring at Hal was ravaged by frostbite. The eyes were nothing more than slits in the midst of huge swellings, the whites bloodshot and the pupils dull. The nose and cheeks were blistered jet black—the frostbitten skin the colour of charcoal. The lips were blue, indicating severe hypoxia, and the beard beneath them was stained red from the blood that seeped from the mouth.

With some effort the climber parted his lips, ice cracking around them as he did so. 'Help me.'

Then Hal realised. 'Andrei? Is that you?'

The climber made no response, merely swayed from side to side.

Josie was disturbed by the long silence. 'Are the Sherpas here?'

'It's not the Sherpas. It's Andrei. He's been out all night in the storm. He's in a hell of a state.'

'Are we going to move?'

Hal made a fast decision. 'Andrei. We're going down to Camp Four. I'm going to help you as far as I can. I'll be looking after Josie on the fixed ropes but if you can descend with us I'll make sure you stick on the right route. Do you understand?'

'No!' Andrei began to scramble into the shelter.

Hal placed his hands on Vasylenko's shoulders, blocking him. 'Andrei, you don't have time to come in here.'

'Don't tell me this.' Andrei began to push hard against Hal's arms, forcing his head and shoulders into the shelter and pinning him against the back wall. Hal pushed back as strongly as he could but the Russian was too strong. He began to beat his hands wildly at Hal. 'Let me! Let me!'

Using his knees to lever himself against the entrance wall, Andrei forced the rest of his body into the space, half smothering Josie.

'I can't breathe, Hal.' Josie was struggling to free herself from the weight that constricted her.

Hal pushed Andrei to the side so that the Russian was lying along-side Josie. Hal was now jammed right by the entrance.

'Are we going now?' Josie's voice was thin and filled with fear.

Andrei reacted violently as he heard her words. 'No leave! Help me!'

'Hal. Let's go now.' Josie's voice held a new urgency. 'The shot's not going to last for ever. I feel strong enough to get out.'

Hal felt nausea welling up in his throat. The brief struggle with the other man had left him dizzy and exhausted.

'Let me think,' he said.

'About what?'

Hal exploded in a burst of anger. 'Give me a chance, Josie! I have to think my way through it, all right?'

'No, it's not all right.' Josie shuffled her way forward in an attempt to reach the entrance. 'We're leaving. I am *not* going to die here.'

'And Andrei?'

Josie swung her boots awkwardly over the Russian but could not get past him in the confined space of the bivouac. 'Hey! Wake up. Out of my way. Move!' She beat at his legs in frustration. Andrei remained motionless. Josie pushed angrily at Vasylenko's legs once more, then slumped back, gasping for breath. 'We were *ready*, for God's sake,' she told Hal. 'Why the hell did you let him in?'

'I couldn't stop him.'

'And now? What do you suggest? We stay and freeze to death?'

Hal thought for some time. 'Option one. The two of us leave now.' Hal gestured at Andrei. 'And if we do that. He dies. Option two. We do everything we can to keep him alive. The Sherpas arrive with fresh oxygen in about four hours and we all go down. Nobody dies.'

'He's nothing to do with the equation. He got himself into this shit. He's not our responsibility.'

'And what if it were Sebastian?'

A hiss of breath was exhaled icily into the air. 'How can you possibly say that now?'

'Because it's the only way I can think of to make you see. Someone is out there, waiting on the end of a telephone line to hear if this man is dead or alive, just as you did.'

Even now, Josie could feel the effects of the steroid wearing off. She watched Hal as he turned his gaze back to the entrance. 'So?' she asked him, deflated.

Hal remained silent, staring out of the snow-hole entrance. 'I can't leave him,' he said finally. 'I'm going to radio Todd and tell him there's a change of plan.'

Josie had no energy left to fight. With infinite weariness she wriggled backwards into her horizontal position against the wall.

'I will never forgive you if you let me die.'

Hal patted Josie's leg. 'Priority number one,' he murmured, fighting a wall of fatigue. 'Everyone goes home.'

He tried to fix his mind on the task—use the walkie-talkie. He tried to raise his hand but it felt as heavy as lead. Then an overwhelming desire to sleep overcame him. 'Everyone goes home . . .' He muttered the words before passing into a state somewhere between deep sleep and unconsciousness.

NIMA CURSED LHAKPA as he watched him fighting to make progress up the fixed rope towards him. It was already mid-morning. Since leaving the camp the pattern had been the same: Nima painfully breaking the trail through soft snow, and then having to wait interminably while Lhakpa made heavy weather of following.

Nima turned to look above him. He had expected to see the two climbers coming down towards them by now. He wondered for a moment if they had somehow missed Josie and Hal in the dark. But looking down at the col he could see no sign of movement.

Some minutes later, coughing and retching dramatically, Lhakpa finally reached the small snow platform Nima had chosen to stop on.

'Where are they? We should have met them.'

'I don't know. Maybe the woman can't move.'

Nima pulled the Thermos flask from the side pocket of his rucksack and poured a small measure of the sweet tea into the lid.

Lhakpa took it with shaking fingers. 'I won't go on,' he said. 'I'll leave my oxygen here. This is the limit.' He turned his head, ashamed to meet Nima's eye.

Nima glared at him angrily. For a moment he felt like shaking him, so intense was his fury. But then he crouched down, brushing the snow away from his friend's cheek. 'I understand,' he told him. 'Don't be ashamed. You got the oxygen as high as you could.'

Now Lhakpa turned to face him, grateful for the sympathy. 'I would climb if I could, Nima. But I am no longer young like you.'

Nima pulled off Lhakpa's rucksack and took out the two full oxygen bottles. 'So go,' he told him. 'I will continue.'

'HAL. COME IN. Hal. Come in. This is Todd.'

Hal came slowly out of sleep. He somehow got his thumb against the TRANSMIT button. 'Hi,' he croaked.

'Hal, I couldn't hear your voice, but we heard a click. I think what's happened is your walkie-talkie battery is too weak to transmit. If you can hear me click once.'

Hal clicked the TRANSMIT button again.

'That's great. Can you confirm that you have left the bivouac?'

Hal made no response.

'I don't hear a click,' Todd said. 'Does that mean you are still in the bivouac?'

Click.

'Shit. Is Josie still alive?'

Hal tried to lift his head to check her but was saved the effort when she suddenly coughed.

Click.

'Thank God. Listen, Hal, Lhakpa has turned back but Nima is on his way up. Is Josie going to be able to walk?'

Click.

'That's good. Now when Nima gets close, Hal, I'm going to ask you to get out of the shelter onto the South Summit so that he can locate you. Do you think you can do that?'

Click.

'Over for now.'

The line died. Hal lay for a long time looking at the walkie-talkie. He knew he was losing it. And he knew also that he should do something about it. But what *could* he do?

Then Hal saw Andrei's rucksack. With a sudden shock he realised he had not checked it.

The rucksack was heavier than he had expected. Taking off the glove on his left hand, he used what sense of touch remained in his fingers to undo the plastic clips on the restraining straps.

Inside was an orange oxygen cylinder.

He looked at it in confusion. Josie's name was written in black marker on the side. He checked the gauge. It was full.

Hal pulled out his regulator from the pile of gear next to him and, painfully slowly, managed to screw it onto the cylinder. Holding the mask against his face, he breathed deeper than he had ever done before. The oxygen re-energised him almost immediately.

He kicked the Russian's body. 'You thief, Andrei! If you weren't half dead already I'd kill you.'

Then he shook Josie's shoulder to rouse her. 'Josie. Wake up. Wake up and have some air.'

Hal let Josie breathe for ten minutes, then switched the mask to Andrei. Ten minutes later it was his own turn once more. He checked his watch. Eleven o'clock. The oxygen would keep them alive for a few more hours but not much longer. Where the hell were the Sherpas?

NIMA FOUND himself wading in softer snow, heavy powder that had collected in the lee of the slope. Each step broke through the thin crust of ice on top, plunging him in up to his waist. He tired rapidly; lifting each leg—and its heavy boot—required more strength than his exhausted thigh muscles could supply.

He could feel his will-power draining as he thought of Lhakpa reaching the camp. He flexed his back to ease some of the nagging pain of the rucksack, then looked up the slope. It looked hours more work. He was on the edge of giving up. But he didn't. With an enormous effort he pulled himself upright.

One painful step after another, he began to climb.

THE OXYGEN was long gone. Hal watched the faltering rays of light through the entrance hole. Night was just a few hours away. And then?

He could not project his mind forward to think of the following dawn if they had to stay in the shelter. They were already in the most fragile margin between life and death.

The walkie-talkie buzzed into life, the signal incredibly faint as the batteries gave their last pulse of power. 'Hal? This is Todd. If you can hear me, click the button.'

Click.

'OK. We can see Nima through the binoculars and he's just a few minutes from your position. Be ready for him.'

Click.

Todd was in tears. 'We're praying for you both. Over for now.'

Feeling dazed and weak, Hal tried to move his legs. The creeping effects of frostbite had—he was now sure—begun to strike his feet. He sat back, feeling nauseous. What next? He decided to try to get the Russian out.

'What are you doing?' Josie half raised her head in confusion as Hal began to shift.

'Nima is almost here. I'm getting Andrei out first.'

Vasylenko flinched as he recognised his name.

'Andrei, we're going to go down. Oxygen is on the way.'

The Russian moaned loudly, sucking on his frostbitten fingers and rocking back and forth in his agony.

Suddenly there was a noise from the slope outside. It was faint, but Hal thought it was a shout.

'Nima!' The first attempt was little more than a whisper. 'Nima! In here!' Hal's voice found some residual power.

'Hal?'

Suddenly, Nima's face appeared at the entrance, his eyes clouding with confusion for a second as he saw the three figures, then filling instantly with relief when he spotted Hal. 'I not too late?'

Hal held Nima's outstretched hand in his own. 'You made it . . . you made it . . .'

'Who's this?' the Sherpa asked, gesturing to Andrei.

'He came in for shelter. We have to get him down too.'

'Josie,' Nima called. 'I have tea. I have oxygen. We go down.'

Josie roused herself so she could see him. 'Nima? is that really you? You came for us?'

'Don't talk. No time. Nearly dark. I get this one out, OK?' Nima began to enlarge the entrance hole rapidly with his ice axe, then reached in to grab the Russian's shoulders. With difficulty, he manoeuvred Andrei so that one big pull would slide the semiconscious climber out of the entrance.

He took Vasylenko's waist harness in his hands. Then with all his strength he hauled him out of the bivouac.

'What happens?' Andrei cried out, staring around in shock.

'Be still,' Nima told him. He unclipped a titanium ice screw from his harness, screwed it into the slope and fastened a short sling onto Andrei's harness to secure him. He turned back to the shelter, where Hal was struggling to straighten his legs. 'Let me help you,' he said.

As slowly and awkwardly as an insect emerging from its cocoon, Hal let Nima drag his protesting body out until he was sitting on the snow platform next to Andrei. Hal sat massaging life back into his cramped limbs, then he rose. Nima embraced him tightly and for a long moment they stood holding each other. 'Thank you, Nima. Thank you from the bottom of my heart.'

'No problem.' Nima smiled at him. 'You my father.'

With just thirty minutes of daylight remaining, Hal and Nima were putting the final touches to the equipment. Nima had done the lion's share of the work, fixing the oxygen masks to the new cylinders and installing them in the individual rucksacks. Hal had forced Josie to drink a full cup of heavily sweetened tea and she now lay resting. She was looking more alert as each minute passed.

Hal was also benefiting from the hot tea and oxygen, but Andrei had rejected it. 'No give me!' he yelled at Nima. 'I no need.'

'Take it,' Nima told him calmly, 'or you not get down.'

Andrei thrust his grotesquely swollen fingers in Nima's face. 'You see?' he screamed. 'Don't care,' he told them. 'Don't care anything now.' Then he went back to sobbing in his native tongue.

'He crazy,' Nima said.

'I know, but we take him,' Hal replied. 'I take Andrei, you take Josie.'

Nima glared at the Russian. 'OK,' he agreed reluctantly.

They helped Josie to stand. She gasped with pain as blood began to circulate in her feet.

Andrei did not resist as Hal took a short length of rope and attached it with a carabiner to his harness.

Nima did the same with Josie. 'You can walk?' he asked her.

'I don't know.' Josie began to shuffle forward, gaining confidence as she felt her body starting to work.

Between the bivouac and the top of the fixed ropes was a narrow ledge some thirty yards long. It was the logical way to traverse the steep ground back to the South Summit. They set out along it.

Suddenly, Andrei stopped dead. 'Summit!' He gestured to the rising ground ahead.

'That's not the summit, Andrei. We're going down.'

The Russian pulled hard on the rope as he tried to climb directly up the slope, jerking Hal at the waist.

'No!' Hal reached towards him to restrain him.

Andrei took two clumsy steps up the incline.

Hal grabbed his shoulder to block him.

'I go summit . . . I go summit. For photo! For photo!' Andrei began to nod rapidly. 'Yes, that good idea now.'

'Not a good idea.' Hal tried to twist Andrei back. Andrei began to scream, turning and kicking Hal with his spikes.

'Nima! Help me!' Hal cried.

Before the Sherpa could come to Hal's aid, Andrei leapt up on the steeper ground once more, his steel crampon spikes scraping against the ice as he scrabbled for a purchase on the iron-hard slope. He was pushing strenuously against Hal now. One foot slipped but he threw his weight forward to compensate, stumbling back for a yard or so and clasping Hal's leg with both hands.

For a heart-stopping moment Hal's leg held Andrei's entire weight as the Russian scraped the sides of his spikes against the ice.

But Andrei twisted his body away, snatching at Hal's waist harness. They fell, locked together, down the ice run.

HAL FELT HIMSELF fly through the air, and strike the ice a shattering blow with his right side. Then they were glissading down the face, their bodies turning and spinning. Outcrops of rock flashed past. Hal hit one, the stone slicing through his clothing and ripping into his leg. He felt the bone break, then he braced himself for the sickening plunge into the depths.

It didn't happen.

Instead, he felt himself lurch to a stop, his pelvis twisting abruptly as the waist harness bit hard into his midriff. In the violence of the impact every scrap of breath was forced from his lungs. Winded, he gulped for air as he tried to comprehend what had happened.

He looked down to find that the Russian, still attached to him, was hanging beneath him, dangling over the ten-thousand-foot drop on the short length of rope tying them together. His weight was straining Hal's spine to the point where it felt like it was about to break.

Hal forced his frostbitten fingers to snap open the carabiner holding them together. With a last guttural gasp of terror Andrei vanished into the tumbling black void of the southwest face.

Hal lost consciousness as he watched Andrei fall.

NIMA AND JOSIE stood motionless as Hal and Andrei slid away from them. The two men were out of sight in seconds. There was no scream of terror, no impact of flesh on rock, nothing.

After a while, Nima leaned forward as far as he dared to try to see down the fall line. From his vantage point he could see nothing that would stop the two men from pitching into the abyss.

He unclipped his oxygen mask so he could call: 'Hal!' His cry echoed around the vast amphitheatre of the Western Cwm. 'Hal!'

They waited, praying silently for a response.

When none came they were not surprised; the two men had fallen to their deaths, of that they were certain.

Nima was the first to speak. 'Camp Four,' he said, gesturing to the narrow trail to safety. 'Walk, please.'

Josie stepped forward towards the fixed ropes, replaying the horror in her mind: the sound of the sharpened spikes scrabbling against the ice, Andrei screaming for the summit. Hal was gone in that violent moment of insanity. There was no sense of sorrow, just the brutal knowledge that the mountain had taken him as it had taken so many others.

THE PAIN of his broken thigh brought Hal back to consciousness just as the sun was setting. He turned, looking frantically up the slope. 'Nima!' But there was no movement above, just the jutting, angular presence of whatever had caught his fall. A tree? A branch? Then he focused his eyes and realised.

His harness had snagged on the frozen torso of a climber half buried in the snow, one arm sticking out at a crazy angle, the face twisted into a mummified contortion of horror, the skin black from relentless solar radiation.

Hal reached up and grasped the dead man's hand. He thrust the ice axe in next to him and hauled himself up against the corpse. Trying not to faint from the pain in his leg, he levered himself higher and twisted the harness free.

He waited while his breathing recovered a little. Then he swung the ice axe into the ice again, kicked in his left crampon as hard as he could and inched his way upwards, the broken leg trailing behind. He used an ice screw as a makeshift second axe, digging it into the face with his left arm. He knew that if he made the slightest error he would die there and then. His good leg shook uncontrollably every time he pressed his weight onto it, the muscles close to their limits. He was beyond exhaustion but he kept the ice axe swinging, one blow after the other, gaining a few inches of precious ground.

He paused for a considerable time, resting on an easier gradient, blacking out once more for he knew not how long.

By the time he reawakened, a sliver of moon was moving across the night sky. When clouds weren't obscuring it, he could just make out the dark shadow of the bivouac entrance against the snow. He began to traverse, heading for the mouth-like shape, oblivious to everything but the all-consuming desire for shelter.

Hal dragged his shattered leg up the final steep mound and collapsed into the flat sanctuary. Nima had left very little. Half a foam mat, two empty oxygen cylinders and the dead walkie-talkie. Hal laid his head on the foam mat. Then he took the walkie-talkie and after a painful battle with his swollen fingers, retrieved the battery. He unzipped his wind suit with difficulty, placed the battery against his chest and zipped it up again.

Would a few hours of warmth regenerate the battery to make just one call? And would anyone be listening?

He slipped rapidly into unconsciousness.

JOSIE WOKE IN A COCOON of green light filtering through the side wall of the tent, a sleeping-bag of snug down wrapped in a tight embrace around her.

Half-constructed images flickered in her mind: torchlights bobbing across the col; the texture of fabric as she was helped into a tent; the white bandages being wound around her fingers; the hypodermic syringe as it entered her arm. Morphine. That was why she could feel no pain in her hands or feet. A moment later Nima's head came through the tent flaps. He unzipped her sleeping-bag and propped her upright, unclipping her oxygen mask before helping her to drink some tea. Her lips were so swollen with blisters she could barely sip the fluid. 'Nima. Thank you,' she whispered.

Nima left as Todd came in. He looked as if he hadn't slept for a week. 'Josie, are you strong enough to talk?'

Josie nodded. 'Go ahead,' she croaked.

'I got what I could from Nima but he's too upset to say much.' Todd looked at her hard. 'I have to ask you. Is there any way Hal could have survived that fall? Could he still be up there, injured, in a crevasse, for example? I have to make decisions here. I have responsibilities to the Sherpas, to myself and not least to get you to medical care. But once we pull out of this camp that is it for Hal.' Todd looked away, tears springing to his eyes. 'Could he still be alive?'

'I don't think so,' she whispered.

'OK, I'm going to tell Rachel. We've released the news that you've been brought down to Camp Four. All we've said so far is that Hal is still missing. She may want to speak to you.'

Josie did not reply, but allowed herself to be pulled to her feet and half carried to the communications tent.

Todd put on the loudspeaker option so Josie could hear. 'Rachel?'

Rachel sounded strained but composed. 'Go ahead, Todd.'

'I have to tell you that Hal is dead. He was killed in an accident on the South Summit yesterday evening.'

All the confidence drained from Rachel, her voice catching as she spoke. 'Hal wouldn't fall. He knew the mountain too well.'

'He was trying to help another climber. There was someone else up there. He sheltered with Josie and Hal in the bivouac.'

'And that climber fell with Hal?'

'Correct.'

'Can I speak to Josie?'

Todd held the handset to Josie's face. 'Rachel, this is Josie. I . . .' She trailed off, knowing that any words were pathetically inadequate.

'Don't worry, I don't want the words, I want the facts. Did you see Hal's body?'

'Well, no . . . you see he fell far away down the slope.'

'So he *could* still be alive? No one saw his body, right?'

'We called him. There was no reply.'

'Have you tried the walkie-talkie again?'

Todd took the handset. 'The walkie-talkie's dead. It has been for more than twelve hours.'

'Is there anyone who can go up one more time?'

'No way. We've pushed it to the limit, Rachel. No one has the strength now. We've got to get Josie down.'

'So even if Hal is alive you're abandoning him?'

'That's not fair. We're ninety-nine point nine per cent certain that Hal died in that fall.'

'And that point one of a per cent?' Suddenly, Rachel was crying. 'Oh shit. It's just if there's a chance . . . If you were going to try one more walkie-talkie contact when would it be?'

Todd checked his watch. 'On the hour. In thirty-five minutes, but there's no—'

'Let me try it. Patch me through so I can try one last time.'

'It'll delay our departure. Let me talk to Josie.' He turned to her. 'It's your call. An extra thirty minutes might mean another toe or finger lost by the time we get you out of here. That's the bottom line.'

'Let her do it,' she told him.

HAL WAS SO COLD when he came round that he could not tell where his flesh ended and the ice began. He registered daylight, blinking as his eyes pulled the world into a blurred sense of shape. He took his hands out from inside his down suit. Frostbite had eaten another few millimetres into the flesh, but after a little clenching he found he could still move them.

He checked his watch. It was five minutes to ten.

The battery. He had to get it into the walkie-talkie or he would miss the 10.00am call. He retrieved it, slotted it into place and watched the seconds ticking past on his watch.

Hal turned the ON switch. The unit beeped faintly. He placed it against his ear, waiting for a voice to come out of the ether. He did not waste power trying to transmit.

He waited. Ten o'clock came and went. Thirty seconds, forty.

Then: 'This is Rachel calling Hal Maher. Rachel calling Hal Maher. Can you hear me, Hal?'

Heart racing, Hal clicked on the TRANSMIT button, hearing the static fade as the battery dribbled out its last milliamps of power.

'I'm not sure if that was a response or not—it was a click but it was so faint.' Rachel's tone had changed; Hal could hear her trying to maintain her composure. 'Hal. Maybe your battery is dying. If you can hear me, click now.'

Hal clicked so hard he burst the frostbite blister on his thumb.

The volume fell away until it was barely audible, but he could still hear the desperation in Rachel's next words.

'Hal, I believe you might be alive. Fight for me . . . don't give up . . .'

With a small pop of interference the walkie-talkie died. Hal stared blankly at the lifeline. He had failed. The signal had not been strong enough for Rachel to be sure she had heard it.

He looked out of the bivouac, experiencing for the first time the fear that he was going to die in this place. Across the slope he saw Sebastian's body. To die here like that?

WHILE THE TWO Sherpas began to dismantle the tents, Josie scanned the slopes, hoping against hope that something would move.

'It was nothing.' Todd touched her gently on the shoulder.

Josie turned angrily to confront him. 'It was a click. Rachel heard it. We all did. He's alive.'

'I don't think it was Hal. It was just a random bit of static.'

'He's up there, waiting to be rescued. We have to do something.'

'Like I just explained to Rachel'—Todd tried to keep the impatience from his voice—'no one here is in a position to go up again.'

'Rachel's right. You're abandoning him.'

Todd snapped: 'Josie. We're all dying here, OK? We're out of food and cooking gas. We have no more oxygen. Hal's dead, Josie. You have to come to terms with that and think of yourself now. You need hospital treatment. Fast. I've ordered up a helicopter. It's going to pick you up at Camp One and take you straight to Kathmandu.'

Josie felt a wave of intense fatigue. 'I'm sorry. I'm too tired to think. I just couldn't face Rachel unless we had done everything.'

Todd prepared a syringe of dexamethasone.

'I know how she feels, you see,' Josie murmured as the needle went into her thigh.

BETWEEN THEM, Todd, Nima and Lhakpa half carried, half manhandled Josie along the thousand yards of fixed ropes leading down the Lhotse Face. It was a retreat of fifteen hours, an exercise of brute strength as the three men took turns to take her weight.

Josie's awareness diminished as the afternoon became a bitterly frigid night. Sliding for the most part on her back, her spine and coccyx became bruised, even through the padding of her down suit.

At some point she was aware of arriving at a tent, of hot tasteless fluid being poured down her throat, of a choking mouthful of cloying chocolate. New voices joined them, other Sherpas from the team who had come up to Camp Three to assist with the evacuation.

Then they were out into the night, mobile again, Josie lowered yard by yard down the face.

With daylight came the bergschrund, the crevasse that marked the end of the Lhotse Face and the beginning of the glacier. Josie descended the short ladder herself, with Todd guiding her frozen feet onto the rings. Then they were on easier ground, with six hours of hard walking between them and Camp Two.

Nima and three other Sherpas took it in turns to carry Josie on their backs. She rode in darkness, a scarf tied round her face to protect her eyes. The miles were measured in a succession of boneshaking passages, the Sherpas gradually tiring beneath her until they could manage less than five minutes in each session.

They finally reached Camp One at the top of the icefall.

Josie lay, unflinching, as a doctor from one of the other teams unravelled the bandages on her fingers. She tried not to notice his sharp intake of breath as the damage was revealed. 'Nothing we can do here,' he told Todd.

There were urgent conversations into a radio. Todd's voice raised in an intense tirade with someone in Kathmandu. 'We pay cash,' he kept repeating. 'We pay dollars to pilot. Dollars.'

Then, unbelievably, the muffled clatter of a helicopter coming up the valley, the distinctive rotor chop echoing around the cwm.

Numerous hands began to carry her across the ice towards the waiting aircraft.

'Stop!' Josie forced the shout. The downwash of the helicopter rotors was creating a small blizzard of noise.

'What's up?' Todd stooped to hear her better.

'Let me see the mountain.'

'The helicopter can't wait at this altitude.'

'I want to say goodbye.'

Todd instructed the Sherpas to help Josie to stand.

The mountain was clear of cloud, bathed in the bronze light of late afternoon. Josie let her eyes follow the familiar fluted lines up that serpentine, glittering ridge to the summit.

Hal was there somewhere, she knew. She didn't feel separate from him; she had travelled too close to the edge of her own destruction for that. Instead, she felt absolutely in tune with where he was, so much so that there was no need to say a goodbye out loud.

Fighting against the light, Josie shifted her eyeline down to where a haze of heat shimmer was hanging lazily above the glacier. It was pulsating, distorting the air into impossible pools of water, a mirage.

Then she saw it.

A shape was rising from the mirage. Josie blinked. For a second she thought she must have been mistaken. Then it moved again. An arm raised, almost hidden among a confusion of moraine and boulders, bearing an ice axe. 'Todd. There's someone out there.'

'Don't be ridiculous.' He scanned the glacier but could see nothing.

Josie saw the arm again. 'There is! There's someone there.' Insanely, she set off across the glacier, her frozen feet tripping her into a fall. Todd and the Sherpas picked her up.

'Josie. Stop it. You're going to damage yourself more.'

'It's Hal!' Josie pointed.

Then one of the Sherpas gave a cry and began hurrying away.

Now Todd could see it. 'My God. There *is* someone there.'

Josie watched as Todd picked his way through the maze of crevasses and threaded round the boulders in pursuit of the faster Sherpas. She saw them stop, huddle close round something. Then they were coming back, bearing a figure swaddled in a bright fabric, which was hung between them like a hammock. The procession came to a stop. Josie locked onto Nima's face, noticing that it was shining with shock and amazement.

'Hal alive! Hal alive!' he cried.

They placed the bundle on the ice. Inside was Hal, wrapped in what she took initially to be the fabric of a tent. His eyes, clouded with pain, shone with recognition when he saw her.

'How could I ever doubt?' she told him. She rested her face against his, her bandaged hands clutching him clumsily in an embrace as she held herself tight to him.

'I wouldn't want you to be the only one to walk away from this,' he whispered.

He was crying, pulling Josie closer again. 'Call Rachel,' he managed to croak. 'Tell her I'm alive.'

'Give him fluid,' Todd instructed.

Josie stood back as Nima took an insulated bottle of meltwater and pressed it to Hal's lips. He gagged as he forced it down.

'But how . . . ?' Josie looked up at Todd in confusion.

'It's a paraglider,' Todd said, 'but God knows where it came from.'

Then Josie understood. 'It's Sebastian's. It was in his rucksack.'

Todd stared at Hal in amazement. 'He flew down. With Sebastian's paraglider?'

A Sherpa ran across from the helicopter, shouting as he came: 'Pilot say two minutes. No more.'

Todd was galvanised into activity, organising the Sherpas to cut Hal from the harness he was tangled in and pick him up once more. It was clear from the way his legs lolled strangely to one side that both were broken.

Todd and Nima lifted Josie and bundled her into the rear of the cockpit, lying her on the aluminium floor. Hal was heaved in beside her. Nima held his hand until the final moment, then turned away with tears in his eyes.

Todd waved everyone clear. The rotors changed pitch, the brittle roar of the jet engine becoming a scream as the Alouette rose into the air. Then it was gone, heading down the Khumbu Glacier.

Josie drew Hal closer to her. Wordlessly, they watched as the grey ice gave way to green fields, the terraces caught in relief by the last dying rays of the sun.

Then Hal was pointing.

Through the window Josie could see what he was gesturing towards. It was Everest, visible for a fleeting moment amid darkening clouds. She watched the clouds race across the mountain's face until it was gone.

MATT DICKINSON

Few people could claim to have climbed Everest by mistake, but that's what happened to film-maker Matt Dickinson. He was on Everest to make a documentary about sixty-year-old actor Brian Blessed's third summit attempt. Blessed had made it to just under 25,000 feet, but could go no further.

Dickinson decided to switch the focus of the film to expedition member Alan Hinkes, who was also making a third attempt on the summit and who would have filmed Blessed's final assault. 'That left me to carry the camera,' Dickinson explains. 'I was inexperienced and out of my depth as a mountaineer, but I made it! It was a mistake that turned into the greatest adventure of my life. I've been climbing since I was sixteen, but until I went to the summit of Everest I'd never been above twenty thousand feet.'

His ascent of the technically difficult north face of the mountain took place during the spring of 1996, a season notorious for the ferocious storms that killed twelve climbers. The author recounted his experiences in his best-selling book *The Death Zone*, before using them as the background for *High Risk*, his first novel.

Matt Dickinson has made more than forty mountaineering and adventure documentaries for various television companies, including the BBC, and has won many prestigious awards. Recent projects have taken him on a sea voyage to Antarctica, a white-water rafting trip on the Brahmaputra River in India, and on an expedition on foot across the Namib Desert. Home is in St Albans, where he lives with his wife and their three children. They take his hair-raising adventures in their stride. 'When I came through the door after Everest the children were playing Nintendo. I'd been away for three months, I'd cheated death, had frostbite and lost eleven kilos. They just looked up and said, "Hi dad," and went back to their game.'

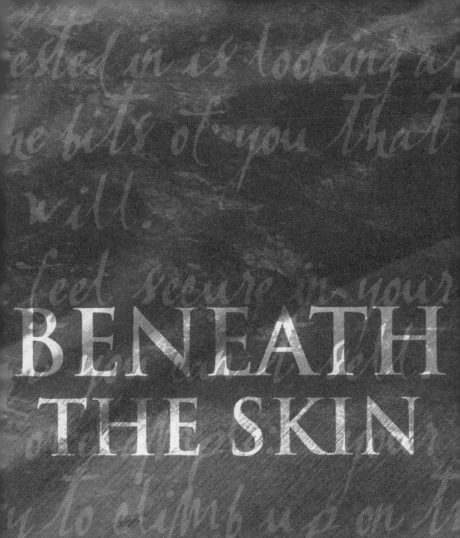

BENEATH THE SKIN

Nicci French

In the scorching heat of a London summer, a killer watches the city's women. He notices every detail — the clothes they wear, where they live, the way they move, even the blemishes they try to hide. Then he chooses a victim, his perfect woman.

*I*n. the summer, their bodies catch heat. Heat seeps in through the pores on their bare flesh; I imagine it rippling round inside them, stirring them up. They take off their clothes, all the thick, closed layers that they wear in winter, and let the sun touch them: on the arms, on the back of the neck. It pours down between their breasts, and they tip back their heads to catch it on their faces. Heat throbs on the pavements where they walk, light skirts fluttering to the rhythm of their stride. Women. In the summer, I watch them, I smell them, and I remember them. I see them when they think they are invisible.

The heat can make women disgusting. Some of them get all dried up, like insects in the desert. Dry lines on their faces, stitching their upper lips, crisscrossing under their eyes. Other women get rank, rotten; when they come near, I can smell them: under the deodorant and soap and the perfume they've dabbed on their wrists and behind their ears, I can smell the odour of ripeness and decay.

But some of them open like flowers in the sunlight; clean and fresh and smooth-skinned; hair like silk, pulled back, or falling round their faces. I sit on a bench in the park and look at them as they walk past, singly or in groups, pressing their hot feet into the bleached grass.

I see them when they think they're alone.

Getting in a car, the dress hitched up, a flash of underwear. Dimpled thighs. The love bite under the carefully arranged scarf. Pregnant, and I can see the tummy button through the thin material of the dress. The *first sign of varicose veins on the white leg, like a purple worm under the skin.*

Sometimes I stand among them in the underground; the press of hot flesh in the stale air. Sometimes I sit beside them, my thigh just touching theirs. Sometimes I open a door for them, watching the way they walk, turn their heads or push their hair behind their ears. The way they smile and look away. Sometimes they do not look away. Sometimes they do not look away.

Part One: Zoë

One

I wouldn't have become famous if it hadn't been for the watermelon. And I wouldn't have been in possession of the watermelon if it hadn't been for the heat. So I'd better start with the heat.

It was hot. But that may give you the wrong impression. It may make you think of the Mediterranean and deserted beaches. Nothing like that. The heat was like a fat, smelly, mangy, dying dog that had settled down on London at the beginning of June and hadn't moved for three horrible weeks. Holloway Road now felt like a giant exhaust pipe, the car fumes held down at street level by a weight of even more harmful pollutants somewhere above. It had felt good at first to put on a summer dress and feel it light against my skin. But my dresses were grimy and stained by the end of each day and I had to wash my hair every morning.

Normally the choice of books that I read to my class is dictated by the government, but this morning I'd rebelled and read them a Brer Rabbit story I'd found in a box of battered childhood books when I'd cleared out my dad's flat. I kept all the books because I thought one day I might have children myself, and then I could read them the stories that Mum had read to me before she died. Whenever I read aloud to kids, there's a bit of me that feels that I'm reading to the child I once was.

I wish I could say that the class was enthralled by this classic piece of storytelling. But what mainly emerged as I asked them about the story afterwards was that nobody knew what a watermelon was. I drew one on the blackboard for them in red and green chalk. A watermelon is so like a cartoon anyway that even I can draw them. A complete blank.

So I said that if they were good—and for the last hour of the afternoon they were alarmingly well behaved—I'd bring in a watermelon for them the next day. On the way home I got off the bus a stop later than usual, after it had turned up Seven Sisters Road. I walked back down the road past the greengrocers and stalls. It was just after five o'clock, so the traffic was already starting to grind to a halt. The fumes were hot against my face, but I was feeling almost cheerful. I was fighting my way through crowds of people as usual, but many of them were in good spirits and wearing bright colours. My urban claustrophobia meter was down from its usual eleven to a more manageable six or seven.

I bought a watermelon the size of a basketball and the weight of a bowling ball. It needed four carrier bags one inside the other and there was virtually no practical way of carrying it. Very gingerly I swung the bag over my shoulder, almost spinning myself into the traffic as I did so, and carried the melon like a man with a sack of coal on his back. It was about 300 yards to the flat. I'd probably make it.

As I crossed Seven Sisters Road and turned into Holloway Road, people stared at me. Goodness knows what they thought I was up to, a skimpily dressed young blonde hunched over and carrying what must have looked like her own weight in iron ore in a shopping bag. Then it happened. A bus was coming towards me on the inside lane of the road. It had almost reached me when a person jumped off the platform at the back, almost losing his balance.

Then I saw there were two of them, apparently joined together by straps. The one behind was a woman, older than him. But not really old. She really did lose her footing, horribly, when she hit the ground, and rolled over. I saw her feet crazily high in the air and she crashed against a bin. I saw her head hit the pavement; I heard it. The man wrenched himself free. He was holding a bag. Her bag. He held it in two hands, chest high. Somebody shouted. He ran away at full speed. He had a strange, tight smile on his face and his eyes were glassy. He was running straight for me, so I had to step out of the way. But I didn't just step out of the way. I let the watermelon slip off my shoulder, leaned back and swung it. Its circular progress was suddenly halted as it hit the man full in the stomach, with the most amazing thud. There was a whoosh of ejecting air and he went down as if there were no body inside his clothes and they were attempting to fold themselves up on the pavement.

He clawed at the pavement a bit, but he wasn't able to get up, and then we were all surrounded by a crowd and I couldn't see him any longer. The woman was slumped and twisted on the pavement, her face down. There was quite a lot of blood on the stone. Suddenly I thought of her having breakfast this morning and going to work, then heading home thinking of what she was going to do this evening, and this suddenly happening and her life being changed. People were standing around her looking uncomfortable. We all wanted somebody official—in a uniform—to step forward and take charge. But there was nobody.

'Is there a doctor?' an old woman next to me said.

Oh no. I'd done a two-day first-aid course in the second term of my teacher-training. I stepped forward and knelt down next to the woman's body. I knew about administering medicines to toddlers but I couldn't think of anything relevant here except one of the key maxims: when in doubt, do nothing.

'Has anybody called an ambulance?' I said.

'I done it on my mobile,' a voice said.

A groan came from somewhere inside the woman. A good sign, probably. Very loud and close by I heard a siren. I looked up. I was pushed aside by a man in uniform. Fine by me.

My melon. I didn't have my melon. I wandered off in search of it. The man was sitting up now, with two police officers, a man and a woman, looking down at him. I saw my blue plastic bag and picked it up.

'She did it,' a voice said. 'She stopped him.'

'That right?' said the WPC, looking a bit suspicious.

'Yeah,' I said warily. 'But I'd better be getting on.'

The male police officer stepped forward. 'We'll need some details, my darling.'

'What do you want to know?'

He took out a notebook. 'We'll start with your name and address.'

That was another funny thing. I turned out to be more shocked than I realised because I just couldn't think of my address, even though I own the place and I've been living there for eighteen months. I had to get my diary out of my pocket and read the address out to them. They must have thought I was mad.

Two

I had reached E in the register, E for Damian Everatt, a skinny boy with an anxious gappy mouth and scabby knees, when Pauline Douglas pushed her head round the already open classroom door. 'Can I have a quick word, Zoë?'

I stood up, smoothing my dress anxiously, and joined her. There was a welcome through breeze in the corridor, though I noticed that a bead of sweat was trickling down Pauline's carefully powdered face and her normally crisp greying hair was damp at her temples.

'I've had a call from a journalist on the *Gazette*. They want to talk to you about your heroics with the melon.'

'What? Oh, that. It's—'

'They want to send a photographer, too. Quiet!' This last to the circle of children fidgeting on the floor behind us.

'I'm sorry they bothered you. Just tell them to go away.'

'Not at all,' Pauline said firmly. 'I've arranged for them to come round at ten forty-five, during break-time. It might be good publicity.' She looked over my shoulder. 'Is that it?'

I looked round at the huge striped fruit, innocent on the shelf behind us.

'That's the one.'

'You must be stronger than you look. All right, I'll see you later.'

I sat down again, picked up the register. 'Where were we? Yes. Kadijah.'

'Yes, miss.'

THE JOURNALIST WAS middle-aged, and short and fat, with hairs growing out of his nostrils and sprouting up behind his shirt collar. Never quite got the name, which was embarrassing as he was so aware of mine. Bob something, I think. All the time he was asking me questions, the photographer who accompanied him wandered round the classroom, staring at me from different angles through the camera lens. They made me uncomfortable.

'What thoughts went through your head before you decided to hit him?'

'I just did it. Without thinking.'

Bob was scribbling away in a tatty notebook and his plump fist kept slipping down the pen. I had a feeling that I should be making cleverer, more amusing comments about what had happened.

'Where do you come from? Haratounian's a strange name for a blonde girl like you.'

'A village near Sheffield.'

'So you're new to London.' He didn't wait for me to reply. 'And you teach nursery children, do you?'

'Reception, it's called.'

'How old are you?'

'Twenty-three.'

'Mmm.' He looked at me musingly, like someone assessing an unpromising item of stock at an agricultural auction. 'How much do you weigh?'

'What? About seven and a half stone, I think.'

'Seven stone,' he said, chuckling. 'Fantastic. And he was a big chap, wasn't he?' He sucked his pen. 'How does it feel to be a heroine?'

Up to then it had been amusing in a way, but now I felt a little irritated. 'It just happened,' I said. 'I don't want to set myself up as anything. Do you know if the woman who was mugged is OK?'

'Fine. Just a couple of cracked ribs.'

'I think we'll take her with the melon.' It was the photographer. He pulled the fruit off the shelf and staggered across with it.

'Blimey,' he said, lowering it onto my lap. 'No wonder you took him out. Now, look at me, chin up a bit. Give us a smile, darling. You won, didn't you? Lovely.'

Next he wanted the melon and me with the children. He suggested cutting it up, so I did. Thirty-two wedges: one for me, one for each child. They stood around me in the sweltering concrete playground, holding their melon and smiling for the camera.

The local paper came out on Friday and the photograph was on the front page. 'Miss Heroine and the Melon'. Not very snappy. Daryl had a finger up his nose and Rose's skirt was tucked into her knickers, but otherwise it was all right.

Pauline seemed pleased. She pinned the piece on the notice board in the foyer, then told me that a national paper had rung, interested in following up the story. She had provisionally set up an interview and another photo opportunity for the lunch-break. If that was all right with me, of course. She had asked the school secretary to buy another melon.

I COULD HARDLY recognise the woman on an inside page of the *Daily Mail* next day, weighed down by a vast watermelon, topped by a large headline. She didn't look like me and she certainly didn't sound like me. Wasn't there enough real news in the world?

'Crap,' said Fred, when I said as much to him later that day, eating soggy chips doused in vinegar after seeing a film. 'Don't do yourself down. You had a split second to decide and you did the right thing.' He cupped my chin in his slim, callused hand and kissed me. 'Let's go back to your place, shall we? It's still early.'

'I've got a stack of marking and forms about a yard high.'

'Just for a bit.'

He chucked the last of the chips in an overflowing bin and wrapped his long arm round my shoulder. Through all the exhaust fumes, he smelt of mown grass. His forearms, where he had rolled up his sleeves, were tanned. His pale hair flopped down over his eyes. He was cool in the industrial warmth of the evening. I couldn't resist.

FRED WAS my new boyfriend. We were past the difficult, embarrassing first bit where you're like a comedian going out before a difficult audience and desperately needing laughter and applause. But we hadn't remotely got to the stage where you walk around the flat and don't notice that the other person hasn't got anything on.

He had been working most of the year as a gardener and it had given him a wiry strength. You could see the muscles ripple under his skin. He was tanned on his forearms and neck and face, but his chest and stomach were pale, milky.

When we got into my flat—and it always seemed to be *my* flat—there was still an urgency about getting at each other.

We lit cigarettes afterwards, lying in my little bedroom and listening to music and car horns in the street below. Fred turned on the bedside lamp and all the dreary, dingy nastiness of the flat was illuminated. How could I ever have bought it? How would I ever manage to sell it? Even if I made it look nicer—got rid of the flimsy orange curtains the last owner had left behind, put mirrors and prints on the walls, no amount of clever interior design could disguise how cramped and dark it was. In a spasm of grief and loneliness and the need for a place I could call home, I'd used up all the money my father had left me when he died. It had never felt like home, though, and now, when property prices were soaring, I was stuck with it.

'Beer in the fridge?' Fred asked hopefully.

'No.'

He was pulling on trousers in a businesslike way that I recognised. He was about to give me a peck on the cheek and leave. Purpose of visit over.

'Tomorrow,' he said. 'With the guys.'

'But of course.'

I sat up in bed and contemplated the marking I had to do.

'Sleep well. Here, there's some post you've not opened.'

The first was a bill, which I put on the pile on the table with the other bills. The other was a letter written in large, looping script:

Dear Ms Haratounian,

From your name I gather you are not English, though you look it from the photographs I have seen. I am not a racist, of course, and I count among my friends many people like yourself, but . . .

I put the letter on the table and rubbed my temples. A mad person. All I needed.

Three

I was woken by the doorbell, just after seven. I couldn't think of anyone who could possibly be calling at this time. I wasn't wearing anything so I pulled on a bright yellow plastic mac before going downstairs to see who it was.

I opened the door just a fraction. It was the postman and he was wearing rather fetching blue serge shorts and a crisp, light blue short-sleeved shirt.

'Flat C?' he asked.

'Yes.'

'There's mail for you,' he said. 'It wouldn't go through the box.'

And there was. Lots and lots of different envelopes arranged in piles held together with elastic. Was this a joke? It took some complicated manoeuvring to take these bundles with one arm while holding my mac closed with the other.

'Happy birthday, is it?' he said, with a wink.

'No,' I said, and pushed the door shut with a naked foot.

I took them upstairs and spilled them onto the table in the main room. I picked a dainty lilac envelope to open but I already knew what they were. One of the things about having an Armenian great-great-grandfather is that you're very easy to look up in the phone book. Why couldn't he have changed his name like other immigrants? I read the letter.

Dear Zoë Haratounian,

I read of your heroic exploit in this morning's newspaper. First may I congratulate you on your courage in tackling that person. If I may trespass a little longer on your patience . . .

I looked ahead, then over the next five pages. Janet Eagleton (Mrs) had written on both sides of the paper in green ink. I'd save that one for later. I opened an envelope that looked more normal.

Dear Zoë,

Congratulations. You did brilliantly, and if more people behaved the way you did, London would be a better place to live. I also thought you looked lovely in the photograph in the paper and that's really why I'm writing. My name is James Gunter and I've always had trouble meeting the right girl . . .

I folded the letter and placed it on top of Mrs Eagleton's. Another letter was more like a package. I opened it. There was a bundle of paper half folded, half rolled up. I saw diagrams, arrows, subjects arranged in columns. But on the first page it began as a letter addressed to me.

Dear Ms Haratounian,

(That's an interesting name. Might you be a Zoroastrian? You can let me know at my box number (below). I will return to this subject (Zoroaster) below.)

You have defences against forces of darkness. But as you know there are other forces that are not so easily resisted. Do you know what a kunderbuffer is?

I put the letter on top of James Gunter's. I went into the bathroom and washed my hands. That wasn't enough. I needed a shower. The shower in my flat involved squatting in the bath and fiddling with decaying valves and twisting the cable. Still, I lay back for several minutes with a flannel over my face showering it. It was like lying under a warm wet blanket.

I got out and got dressed in my work clothes, made a mug of coffee and lit a cigarette. I felt a bit better. What would have made me feel *really* better was if the pile of letters had gone, but it was still stolidly present on the table. All those people knew where I lived.

At that moment the phone rang, which made me jump.

It wasn't a fan. It was Guy, the estate agent who was allegedly trying to sell my flat.

'I've got a couple of people who want to look around the property.'

'Fine,' I said. 'You've got the key. What about that couple who saw it on Monday? What did they think?'

'They weren't sure about the location,' Guy said breezily. 'A bit on the small side as well. Not keen, basically.'

'The people today shouldn't come too late. I'm having some friends round for a drink.'

'Birthday, is it?'

I took a deep breath. 'I'm having an anniversary party because it's six months since this flat went on the market.'

'It's not, is it?'

He took some convincing. After the call I looked around the room rather desperately. Strangers were going to be coming in and looking at it. I made my bed, straightened the rug by the door, found a cardboard box and tipped all the letters into it.

I was late at the school. Sweatily late. Again. And the day was only starting to get hot.

'I WANT TO KNOW about this new man. Is he coming tonight?'

Louise was standing at the window with a bottle of beer.

She had come early to help me get things ready and to have a proper talk.

'They're all coming.'

'What do you mean *all*? Have you got more than one?'

I giggled. 'No. He goes round with this gang of boys. I think they've all known each other since primary school or something ridiculous. They're like those six-packs of beer. You know, not to be sold separately.'

Louise frowned.

'This isn't some sort of strange five-in-a-bed sex thing, is it? If so, I want to hear about it in detail.'

'No, they leave us alone some of the time.'

'How did you meet?'

I lit a cigarette. 'A few weeks ago I went to a party at a gallery over in Shoreditch. The person I knew turned out not to be present, but there was a group of good-looking young men round a pinball machine. One of them—not Fred, as it happens—looked round and asked me if I wanted to play. So I did. We had a great time and the next evening I met them again in town.'

Louise looked thoughtful. 'So you faced the difficult choice of which one of them actually to go out with on a one-to-one basis?'

'It wasn't like that,' I said. 'The day after *that*, Fred rang me at home and asked me out. I asked him if he had the permission of his gang and he was a bit sheepish about that.' I leaned out of the window. 'And here they are now.'

Louise peered out. 'They look like nice boys,' she said primly.

'That's Fred in the middle carrying the large bag, the one with brown hair, almost blond.'

'So you grabbed the nicest-looking one.'

'The one in the very long coat, that's Duncan.'

'How can he wear it in this heat?'

'Apparently it makes him look like a gunman in some spaghetti western. He never takes it off. The other two are brothers. The Burnside brothers. The one in the glasses and the cap is Graham. The one with the long hair is Morris. Hi!' This last was yelled down at them.

They looked up, startled.

'Here, catch.'

I dropped my bunch of keys and, with what I have to say was remarkable style, Graham took off his cap and caught the keys in it. The boys disappeared from view as they let themselves in.

'Quick,' said Louise. 'We've got thirty seconds. Which one of them should I marry? Who's got the best prospects?'

I thought for two seconds. 'Graham's working as a photographer's assistant. Duncan and Morris work together, stuff to do with computers. Duncan's the life and soul of any party; Morris is rather shy when you actually get him on his own.'

'They're the ones who're brothers, right?'

'No, that's Morris and Graham. Duncan has red hair. He looks completely different.'

And then they were in the room, filling it. Fred came over and gave me a lingering kiss, which I couldn't help thinking was a public demonstration to everyone in the room. Was he showing affection or marking territory? Then he produced a brightly coloured drape. 'I thought this would be helpful. It's to hang over the damp patch,' he said.

'Thanks, Fred.' I looked at it dubiously. It was a bit bright and the colours clashed. 'But I think that surveyors are allowed to move bits of cloth out of the way to see what's behind them.'

'Let's get you to the surveyor stage first. Hang it up, then.'

'Oh. OK.'

'Zoë says you're geniuses with computers,' Louise was saying to Duncan and Morris.

Morris blushed slightly, which was sweet.

'That's just because we showed her how to use her own computer,' Duncan said, pulling the ring top off a can of beer. 'Admittedly it was an impressive achievement. It was like teaching a squirrel how to find nuts.'

'But squirrels are brilliant at finding nuts,' Morris objected. 'You should have said it was like teaching a squirrel to juggle.'

Duncan looked puzzled. 'But you can't teach squirrels how to juggle.'

I topped up Louise's drink. 'They can go on like this for hours,' I said. 'It's a bonding thing.'

I went off to get some crisps from the kitchen and Louise came with me. We could see the boys in the room.

'He's lovely-looking,' she said, nodding at Fred. 'Is it serious?'

I took a sip from her glass. 'I'll have to get back to you about that,' I said.

A few other people arrived. There was John, a nice teacher from our school, who had asked me out just a few days too late, and a couple of women I had met through Louise. After a few drinks I was feeling benevolent. A year ago I was lonely and lost and hadn't met a single one of this new circle of people and now they were all coming to my so-called home on a Friday evening. Suddenly my thoughts were interrupted by the ring of the doorbell.

I opened the door to find a man dressed in a brown corduroy suit with rubber boots.

'I've come to see the flat,' he said. 'Is that all right?'

'Yes, yes,' I said eagerly. 'Come on up.'

As I led him up the stairs, the talking of the guests became audible.

'You seem to be having a party,' he said.

'Yes,' I lied. 'It's my birthday.'

Four

The letters gradually fizzled out. The first flood turned into a trickle, then stopped altogether. For a little bit it had seemed funny. One time I took a bunch of them with me when I was meeting Fred and the guys. We sat at a table outside a bar in Soho, drank very cold beer and passed them between us, occasionally reading aloud choice phrases. Then while Morris and Duncan were conducting one of their impenetrable conversations, which involved them challenging each other to name the Seven Dwarfs or the Magnificent Seven or the Seven Deadly Sins, I talked about it with Graham and Fred.

'It's the thought of these people all over Britain writing eight-page letters to someone they don't know. Haven't they got better things to do with their lives?'

'No, they haven't,' said Fred. He put his hand on my knee. 'You're a male fantasy. You and your melon. We all want someone like that to walk up and down our bodies wearing high heels.'

'Stop it,' I said. 'It's not funny.'

'Now you know what it's like to be a celebrity,' said Graham. 'Enjoy it while you can.'

'Oh, for God's sake, is nobody going to give me any sympathy? Morris, what have you got to say on my behalf?'

There was a sudden silence. Morris blinked in the face of our attention and ran his fingers through his long, thick hair. 'Who can name ten films with letters in them?' he said.

'Morris!' I said furiously.

'*Letter from an Unknown Woman*,' said Graham.

'*The Letter*,' said Fred.

The serious conversation was over.

After that I stopped reading them. I chucked them in the box with the rest. They weren't even funny any more. A few were sad, a few obscene. Most were simply tedious or deranged.

Madness came through the door in the shape of prospective buyers of the flat as well. There was one man, of about fifty, who insisted on kneeling on the floor and knocking against the skirting boards, like a doctor checking a patient for a chest infection. I stood ineffectually beside him, wincing at the music pounding into the flat from the pub next door. One young woman, probably about my age, with dozens of silver studs in a bumpy ridge around the rim of her ears, brought her three huge, smelly dogs into the flat while she looked round. The thought of what it would be like after a week with them in residence made my stomach heave.

Most of the visitors stayed only a few minutes, just long enough not to seem rude, before beating a retreat.

Perhaps on superficial, casual acquaintance Guy was more like a normal member of the human race. Anyway, due to his failure to sell my flat, we were becoming long-term associates. I would have assumed my flat would come to symbolise failure and that he might have avoided it, but he kept accompanying viewers, even in the evening or at weekends. He was always smartly dressed in a variety of suits and colourful ties, some of which had cartoon characters on them. However hot the weather became he didn't sweat. Or, rather, he sweated discreetly. There would be just one single drop running down the side of his face.

So maybe it should have been less of a surprise when, after a thin, anxious-looking woman had scuttled out, he looked me deep in the eyes and said, 'We must get together for a drink one evening, Zoë.'

I should have come up with some monumentally savage put-down to reflect my hatred of him and his infuriating euphemisms, but instead I blurted out, 'I think we should lower the price.'

The man who had come to look around on the evening of my not-moving party returned with a tape measure, a notepad and a camera. It was early evening and Fred was away on some regional TV assignment transforming a large, overgrown garden in the Yorkshire Dales. He'd rung me from a pub, his voice thickened by alcohol and lust, and told me things he would do to me when he returned. Not what I needed to hear: I was struggling with the literacy-hour report on the computer. I was trying to produce a pie chart. It had seemed so easy when Morris had done it. 'A type 19 error has occurred' kept flashing on my screen. So I smoked and cursed while the man who might or might not buy my flat poked around. When he went into the bedroom and I heard the sound of drawers beings opened, I followed him.

'What are you doing?'

'Checking things out,' he replied, quite unconcerned, gazing into my jumble of knickers and bras and laddered tights.

I slammed the drawer shut, returned to the computer and typed: 'A Whole School Curriculum Plan ensures that all pupils reinforce ...'

Oh God. This wasn't what I became a teacher for. Soon I'd be writing words like 'satisfactory attainment levels' and 'inputting'.

Crossly I picked up the homework—if that's not too grand a word for it—that I had set the class and brought home that evening. I had asked them all to draw a picture representing one of their favourite stories. I went through them, wrote encouraging remarks on them, then put them all in a folder under the table.

'I'm going now.'

The man stood in the doorway, camera round his neck, gazing at me.

'Oh, right.' Not a word about coming back. Bastard.

I left a few minutes after him, to go to see a film with Louise. It was lovely sitting in the dark eating popcorn and giggling. It was so safe.

I came back quite late, pushed open the door and there was a letter on my doormat. Neat italic writing, black ink. It didn't look like it was from another nutter. I opened it standing in the doorway.

Dear Zoë,

When does someone like you, young and pretty and healthy, become frightened of dying? I wonder. You smoke (there's a nicotine stain on your finger by the way). You eat bad food. You stay up late. Probably you think that you will live for ever, that you will be young for a long while yet.

Zoë, with your white teeth and your one small dimple when you smile, you will not be young for much longer. You have been warned.

Are you scared, Zoë? I am watching you. I am not going to go away.

I stood on the pavement while people flowed past me, and stared at the letter. I lifted up my left hand and there was a yellow stain on the middle finger. I crumpled the letter into a tight ball and threw it into a bin with all the other rubbish.

Today, she is wearing a pale blue dress with straps. It comes down to her knees, and there is chalk dust near the hem that she has not noticed yet. She has shaved under her arms; her legs look smooth, soft. There is a pale nail varnish on her toes, but it is beginning to chip on her left big toe. Her sandals are flat, navy blue, old, scuffed. She is tanned; the hairs on her arms are golden. Sometimes I can glimpse her milky underarms; the whiter skin behind her knees; if she stoops down I can see that the honey colour on her shoulders and throat fades between the beginnings of her breasts.

When she laughs, she makes a pealing sound, like a doorbell. If I told her that I loved her, she would laugh at me like that. That is what women do. They turn what is serious and big into a small thing, a joke. Love is not a joke. It is a matter of life and death. One day, soon, she will understand that.

She talks very quickly, in a light, husky voice. She has grey eyes. She is not frightened yet.

The big joke when people discover I'm a teacher is how they envy me the short hours and the long holidays. Fair enough, of course, since this was one of the less worthy motives that brought me into this job. But I also liked children, their transparency, their eagerness and sense of possibility. And I liked the idea of standing around a sand-pit all day or helping mix paints.

Instead I found myself in a job that was more like being an accountant in the middle of a zoo. And the hours were longer than an accountant's. The official school inspection was coming at us like a train. After the kids had been collected and taken back to their housing estates and tower blocks, we had meetings, form-filling, planning. We stayed on until seven, eight, nine o'clock, and Pauline would have been better off installing a camp bed and a Primus stove in her office, since she never seemed to leave.

I got away earlier that evening because I had an appointment to meet a man at the flat. Naturally the bus didn't arrive for ages, so when I ran panting along the pavement only five minutes late, he was standing there in the doorway. Bad start. I had already given him too much time to look at the area. He was in his late twenties, wearing a suit that was a slightly odd shape, so it was probably very expensive. His hair was cut very short, and he looked cool in the blistering heat.

'I'm really sorry,' I panted. 'Bus.'

'That's all right,' he said. 'I'm Nick Shale. You're Miss Haratounian.' We shook hands. He smiled.

'What's so funny?'

'I pictured you as a grim old landlady,' he said.

'Oh,' I said, trying to smile politely.

I opened the street door. There were the usual pizza and taxicab leaflets on the doormat, and one hand-delivered letter. I recognised the writing immediately. It was the creep who had sent me the letter before, when was it? Five days ago. I looked at it for a moment then at Nick, who had a puzzled expression.

'What did you say?' I said.

'Your bag,' he said. 'Can I take it for you?'

I handed it to him without speaking.

I had my guided tour of the flat down to a skilful three minutes, brilliantly taking in all the points of interest while deftly avoiding areas that were not necessarily to the advantage of the property. Occasionally Nick asked questions I had now become used to.

'Why are you moving?'

Did he think he could trap an old hand like me so easily? 'I want to be closer to my work,' I said, falsely.

He looked out of the window. 'Is the traffic a problem?'

'I've never thought about it.' That was laying it on a bit thick. At least he didn't laugh. 'It's handy for the shops.'

He put his hands in his pockets and stood in the middle of my living room, as if he were rehearsing being the owner. He looked like the squire of a very small estate indeed.

'I'm trying to place you,' he said. 'With your name you should be Armenian. But you don't sound Armenian. Not that I know what Armenians sound like. Maybe they all sound like you.'

I felt oddly sensitive when people looking around the flat turned personal, as if we were going to be good friends, but I couldn't help smiling. 'I grew up in a village near Sheffield.'

There was a pause for mutual thought.

'I'd like to think about this,' Nick said, with an earnest expression. 'Would it be all right if I came back and had another look?'

I was dubious about whether it was the flat he was interested in, but even a crumb of enthusiasm was something. 'Fine.'

'Your number,' he said. 'Can you give it to me or do I need to go through the estate agent?'

I told him and he typed it into what looked like a chunky pocket calculator.

'Good to meet you, erm ...?'

'Zoë.'
'Zoë.'

I heard him trip down the stairs two at a time and I was left alone with my letter. I pretended to myself to be casual about it for a bit. I made myself a coffee and lit a cigarette. Then I opened it and spread it out on the table before me:

Dear Zoë,
I may be wrong but I think you aren't as scared as I mean you to be. As you know, I'm looking at you. Maybe I'm looking at you as you read this.

It was stupid but I glanced up and around, as if I might catch someone next to me.

As I said before, what I'm really interested in is looking at you from the inside, the bits of you that you'll never see but I will.
Maybe it's that you feel secure in your horrible little flat that you can't sell. You're not secure. For example: your back window. It's easy to climb up on the shed in the yard behind and then through it. You should put a proper lock on it. The one you've got at the moment is too easy. That's why I left it open. Go and look.
PS You look happy when you're asleep. Being dead is only like being asleep for ever.

I put the paper back on the table. I walked across the room and out onto the landing. Sure enough, the window that looked down on the garden I wasn't allowed to go into was raised a couple of feet. I shivered though it was a clammy, hot evening. I went back into the living room and sat by the phone. I wanted to be sick. But was it an emergency? Was it anything?

I compromised. I looked up the nearest police station in the phone book and called it. I had a slightly complicated conversation with a woman at the desk, who seemed to be looking for excuses to put the phone down. I said there had been a break-in and she asked what had been stolen and what damage had been done. I said no damage and I wasn't sure what had been stolen.

'Is this a police matter?' the voice said wearily.

'I've been threatened,' I said. 'Threatened with violence.'

The discussion went on for quite a few minutes more, and after a conversation with a third party, inadequately masked by a hand over the receiver, she said that somebody would call round 'in due course', whatever that meant. I went from window to window then, locking them, fastening bolts.

It was over an hour later that the doorbell rang. I walked down to the street door, pulled back the stiff sprung opening of the letterbox and looked out. I saw dark blue cloth. Two police officers. I opened the door. Their car was parked behind them.

'Do you want to come in?'

They didn't reply but stepped forward, removing their caps as they entered. I led them up the stairs. Pointed to the letter on the table. One of the officers leaned over, reading it. It took him quite a time.

'You've had another letter from this person?' he asked finally.

'Yes, I got one a few days ago. On Wednesday, I think.'

'Where is it?'

I'd been waiting for this. 'I threw it away,' I said, a bit guiltily. 'I'm sorry, I know it was a stupid thing to do. I just got upset by it.'

But the officer didn't get cross. He didn't seem worried at all.

'Did you check the window?'

'Yes. It was open.'

'Can you show us?'

I led them out of the room. They followed in rather a heavy way, as if they were being asked to do too much for something so trivial.

'The pub garden's down there,' the other officer murmured, peering through the window. 'He could've seen the window from it.'

They turned and walked back to the living room.

'Can you think of anybody who might have sent this? Old boyfriend, someone at work, that sort of thing?'

I took a deep breath and told them about the melon and the mail it had provoked. They both laughed.

'That was you?' said the first officer, rather cheerily. 'Nice one. We've got your picture up in the station. Quite a heroine you are to us.' He chuckled. 'That's it, then.'

'What?'

'You get your face in the paper, this sort of thing happens.'

'But he's broken in, he's threatened me. Hasn't he committed a crime?'

'Are there any signs of forced entry?'

'Not that I could see.'

He looked across at his companion and gave a little nod towards the door, which clearly meant, Let's get out of here as soon as we can shut this little woman up.

'If anything serious happens'—he put a gentle but unpleasant stress on the word 'serious'—'give us a ring.'

And they went. I looked out of the window as their car pulled out into the hubbub of the hot city.

There was loud music and laughter outside in Holloway Road, as if there were a slightly sinister late-night street party going on. A car horn blared. The hot night air held the smells of frying onions, garlic, exhaust fumes, cinnamon and the unexpected drift of roses. It was the middle of the night but there were no stars, no moon, only the streetlamps, which cast a dirty orange glow round the room. And noise. People. Cars. I felt for a moment that I'd like to be out in the middle of a forest or on the open sea.

I looked at Fred and he looked back, smiling, sure of himself. Even after an evening of dancing and then sex, he smelt clean, yeasty. Lemon soap and earth, grass and beer. I pulled the damp sheet off us and he stretched out his slim, smooth, rather soft body on the narrow bed and put his arms under his head and grinned at me.

'That was nice,' I whispered.

'Thanks,' he said.

'You're not meant to say that,' I said. 'You're meant to say something like, yes, it was nice.'

He shook his head. 'Have you ever had sex as good as that?'

I couldn't help giggling. 'Are you serious? You want me to say, "Oh, Fred, I never realised it could be like this."'

'Shut up.'

I looked at him. He wasn't smiling. He looked humiliated and angry. I'd hurt his feelings. Men.

I sat up, legs crossed, shook two cigarettes out of the packet lying on the floor, lit them both and handed one to him.

All evening I'd been trying not to think about the weird letters, about people I'd never met having fantasies about me. Maybe there was someone standing outside the flat at this moment, looking up at my open window, waiting for Fred to go.

I dropped my cigarette into the glass by the bed and heard it sizzle. 'Those last letters . . .'

'Ignore them,' Fred said briskly. He closed his eyes.

'But they scared me. They were . . . oh, I don't know, purposeful.' There was a silence. 'Would you stay the night, Fred? I mean the whole night. If you'd like to, that is.'

It was as if I'd told him there was a bomb under the pillow. His eyes snapped open and he sat up. 'Sorry,' he said. 'I've got to be at some old lady's house near Wimbledon first thing tomorrow.' He stepped into his boxer shorts, his cotton trousers. What a speedy dresser he was. Shirt on, buttons done up, patting his pockets to make sure his change was in there. Jacket from the back of the chair.

'Your watch,' I said drily.

'Thanks. Look at the time. I'll ring tomorrow. Don't worry about things.' He ran his hands over my face, kissed my neck. 'Beautiful woman. Good night.'

'Bye.'

AFTER HE'D LEFT I got up and closed the living-room window, in spite of the heat. The room felt more claustrophobic than ever. I checked the landing window, which I'd already checked several times that evening, got my watch from the bathroom: one forty-five. If only it were morning already. I was tired, but not sleepy, and time creeps when you're scared. My sweat prickled on my skin, suddenly chilly, and I picked up the sheet from the floor and wrapped myself in it. Then I lay down in bed and tried not to think. But I couldn't help it. I turned over the two last letters in my mind. The first, of course, I'd thrown away. But I remembered most of it. The second I had put on my desk.

Despite myself, I got it out and read it again, lying in bed. I knew this man had looked at me; I mean, really looked at me. He'd seen things that even I hadn't bothered to notice about myself, like the stained finger. He was learning me, the way we never even learn lovers. He'd been in here, I knew he had, whatever the police said, and looked at my things, touched them.

I closed my eyes and put one arm over them so I was in complete darkness. London crouched outside my window, full of eyes. My mind wouldn't stop, I couldn't make it slow down. I went over and over the letter in my mind.

As I said before. That was the funny thing. What was it? He would like to see inside me. As he had said before. But he hadn't said it before, had he? What could that mean?

A thought stirred, something I wished I could ignore. I sat up, dry-mouthed, swung my legs out of bed and went into the living room where I dragged the cardboard box out from under the sofa. There were dozens of letters in there, some not even opened. I just needed to glance at each one to make sure it wasn't from him . . .

And there it was. Suddenly I could hear my heart beating hard, too fast. My throat felt too narrow to breathe. The handwriting, black italic. I picked up the envelope and tore it open. The letter was short but to the point.

> *Dear Zoë,*
> *I want to see inside you, and then I want to kill you. There is nothing you can do to stop me.*
> *Not yet, though. I will write to you again.*

I stared at the words until they blurred. My breath was coming in little ragged gasps. I jumped to my feet and bumped the sofa over the floor, until it was rammed against the front door. I picked up the phone and dialled Fred's number with shaky, inept fingers. It rang and rang.

'Yes.' His voice was thick with sleep.

'Fred, Fred, it's Zoë. I got another letter.'

'Zoë, it's three thirty.'

'He says he's going to kill me. Can you come round? I'm scared. I don't know who else to ask.'

'Zoë, listen.' I could hear him strike a match. 'It's all right.' His voice was gentle but insistent, as if he were talking to a small child who was worried about the dark. 'You're quite safe.' There was a pause. 'Look, if you're really scared, call the police.'

'Please, Fred. Please.'

'I was asleep, Zoë.' His voice was cold now. 'I suggest you try to sleep yourself.'

I gave up then. 'All right.'

'I'll call you.'

I called the police. I got a man I'd never talked to before who took down all my details with painstaking slowness. In the end he told me to come into the police station in the morning. I suppose I was reassured by the tone of dullness and routine in his voice. Things like this happened all the time.

At some point, I fell asleep. When I woke it was nearly seven o'clock. I looked out of the window. It had rained heavily in the night and the downfall had cleaned the road; the leaves on the few plane trees looked less bleached and shrivelled, and the sky was actually blue. I'd forgotten about blue.

Seven

I got to see more important policemen this time, so that was something. Detective Sergeant Aldham was smartly dressed in a blue suit and sober tie. He was large, heavyset, his brown hair cut short and precise.

He led me to his desk and sat me down by the side of it, which made me feel like an awkward pupil going to see her teacher after school. Or before school, in this case. I had had to phone Pauline to say I'd be in late and she wasn't pleased about it.

Aldham read the two letters very slowly with a frown of concentration. I spent five minutes fidgeting and staring around the open-plan office at people arriving, talking on the phone. He looked up. 'So what do you think?'

'What do *I* think? Well, but I—that's your job, isn't it?'

'I don't know. What did the other letter say?'

'It was horrible so I threw it away. It had some weird stuff about what I ate. And there was something about being afraid of dying. It sounded as if it were someone who had been spying on me.'

'Or somebody who knows you? It might be a joke. Don't you think you might have some friend who's doing this for a laugh?'

I hardly knew what to say. 'Someone's threatening to kill me. I don't see any joke.'

Aldham shifted in his chair. 'People have a funny sense of humour,' he said. 'Hang on a moment. Let me have a word with someone.'

He took a folder out of his desk, inserted the two letters, and walked heavily across the room and out of my sight.

When Aldham finally returned, he was with a smaller, slighter man, greying, who looked as if he were a bit further up the food chain. He introduced himself as Detective Inspector Carthy.

'I've looked at your letters, Miss . . . er . . .' He mumbled an attempt at my name. 'These are certainly nasty pieces of work.' He looked around and pulled over a chair from an unoccupied desk. 'The question is, what's actually going on here?'

'What's going on is that somebody is threatening me and this person hasn't just written letters. He's been in my flat.'

'He *may* have been.' Carthy gave a long-suffering sigh. 'Do many people visit your flat?'

'Well, I've got friends. A bunch of them came round for a drink last week. I've got a new boyfriend. He's been round quite a few times.' Carthy wrote something on a large pad of paper that was balanced on his knee. 'Oh, and the flat's been on the market for six months.'

Carthy raised an eyebrow. 'How many people have been to see the flat?' he said.

'A lot. Over the six months there must have been sixty, seventy.'

'Have any of them seemed strange in some way?'

I couldn't help laughing grimly. 'About three-quarters of them. I mean, they're complete strangers rummaging through my cupboards. That's what it's like trying to sell your home.'

Carthy didn't smile back. 'There are various motives for harassment of this kind. The most common is of a private nature.' He was sounding embarrassed. 'Do you mind if I ask you some personal questions?'

'Not if they're relevant.'

'You said you have a new boyfriend. Does that mean that a previous relationship ended?'

'I wasn't in a relationship.'

'But have you had a recent personal, that is, er, sexual, liaison?'

'Well, fairly recent.' I was blushing hopelessly. 'I've seen a few people at different times.'

'A few?' He and Aldham exchanged a significant look.

'Look, that sounds wrong.' I was flustered. I knew what they were both thinking, and what made it so ludicrous is that, compared to almost anyone I know, I'm a nun: an awkward, embarrassed, inarticulate nun, too. 'I've gone out with, seen, whatever you call it, two men in the last year or so.' They both went on looking at me as if they were not at all convinced by this low number. 'The last of them was months ago.'

'Did it end badly?'

I thought of sitting opposite Stuart in a café near Camden Lock and gave a sad laugh. 'It just fizzled out, really. Anyway, the last I heard he was hitchhiking across Australia. You can cross him off the list of suspects.'

Carthy gave a loud click of his ballpoint pen and stood up. 'DS Aldham will help you fill out a case form and take a brief statement. If anything else happens give Aldham a ring and we'll take it from there. Take sensible precautions in your private life for a while.'

'I told you, I've got a boyfriend.'

He nodded curtly and turned away, muttering something I couldn't hear under his breath.

WHEN I WALKED OUT of the police station into the glare of the sunlight my eyes throbbed painfully. My skin felt dusty, gritty, under my cotton dress. My shoulders were full of vicious little knots, bubbles of stress. For a moment, I thought of going back to the flat and having a bath, pulling myself together, before going to school.

Instead I slunk guiltily into a greasy-spoon café, ordered two cups of black coffee and a poached egg on toast. I ate slowly, watching people pass outside the smeary window. A Rasta in a yellow cap. A man carrying a baby in a sling; I could just see its tufty head. A woman screaming at the red-faced child at her side. An Indian woman draped in a scarlet sari, picking her way in delicate sandals through dog shit and litter.

He could be looking at me at this moment. What had I done, that this should happen to me?

Before catching my bus up Kingsland Road, I passed a phone box and had the stupidest impulse to phone my mother. My mother who hadn't been alive for twelve years. I just wanted her to tell me everything was going to be OK.

Pauline was politely chilly with me when I arrived at school. She told me a man named Fred had called. She didn't seem happy to be collecting messages for an absent member of staff.

The primary assistant who was sitting in for me had the children in plastic pinafores, mixing paints with thick brushes, so I told them they all had to draw a portrait of themselves, before parents' evening. Eric, who never smiles, gave himself a red mouth that stretched from ear to ear. Stacey spilt water all over Tara's efforts and Tara hit her in the neck. Damian started crying, tears dripping onto the paper.

In the break, I phoned Fred. He wanted me to come and watch

him play five-a-side football that evening. They played every Wednesday, he said. A regular lads' feature. He was cheerful and laid-back, as if nothing had happened last night. He told me he was dead-heading roses in suburbia but kept thinking about my body.

Pauline reminded me I had to have my literacy-hour material ready by the end of the week and did I think that was possible. 'Oh, yes,' I replied, unconvincingly, head throbbing. I usually buy a roll at the sandwich bar on the way to school, but today I'd forgotten, so while the other teachers ate healthy sandwiches and fruit for lunch, I had boiled potatoes and baked beans from the obese dinner lady, followed by steamed pudding and custard. Comfort food: it made me feel better.

IT'S AMAZING HOW MUCH noise ten men can make. I was amazed not to see blood gushing, bodies on stretchers, fisticuffs. But at the end of the hour they were all sweaty, smelly, fine, clapping each other round the shoulders. I felt a bit stupid, standing on the sidelines and watching them like part of a fan club. I guess I was meant to have cheered Fred on as he rushed past me in a hot blur, eyes glazed, yelling something, but I couldn't quite bring myself to do it.

Afterwards, he came over and draped an arm round my shoulder and gave me a kiss. 'Mmmm. You're all cool and lovely.'

After work, I'd been to Louise's flat to have a bath and she'd lent me a pair of grey cotton trousers and a sleeveless knitted top to put on. I hadn't wanted to go back to my place.

'Coming for a drink?'

'Sure.' The last thing my body needed was a drink but I wanted company. Just the thought of it getting dark again, and me in my flat, on my own, made me breathless.

'I'll see you after the shower.'

ONE DRINK TURNED into several, in a dark pub whose landlord obviously knew all the team well.

'And she's been getting all these mad letters,' continued Fred, as if it were all a big joke. His hand moved round to my side, feeling its way down my ribs. I shifted nervously. I didn't want to talk about it. 'Including ones that threaten to kill her. Haven't you, Zoë? What did the police say?'

'Not much,' I said. I made an attempt at lightness: 'Don't worry, Fred. I'm sure you'll be suspect number one.'

'It can't be me,' he said cheerfully.

'Why not?'

'Well . . . er.'

'You've never seen me asleep,' I said, and immediately wished I hadn't, but Fred just looked puzzled. It was a relief when Morris started telling me how they used to come here on quiz night.

'Are you together with any of . . .' I said in a subdued voice, giving a discreet nod in the direction of the various young women around the table.

Morris looked evasive. 'Well, Laura and me are, in a way . . .' He leaned over very close to me and whispered into my ear. 'It's over. It's just that she doesn't know it yet.'

I looked across at Laura, a large woman with brown hair pulled back in a bun, as she sat there, unaware of the sentence hanging over her head. 'Why?' I said.

He just shrugged and I couldn't bear to talk about it any more.

'How's work going?' I said, for want of anything better.

Morris lit a cigarette before answering. 'We're all waiting,' he said.

'What do you mean?'

'Graham is a photographer's assistant who wants to be a real live photographer. Duncan and me go around showing stupid secretaries how to do things with their software that they should have read in the manual. We're waiting for one or two of our ideas to, well, come to fruition.'

'And Fred?'

Morris looked reflective. 'Fred is digging and sawing while trying to decide who he is.'

We sat there for a long time and drank too much, especially the boys. Later Morris moved across to be close to Laura, at her request, which sounded more like a command, and Duncan sat next to me. He talked about his work with Morris, how they taught idiots with too much money how to operate their own computers. Then he told me about Fred, how long they'd known each other, their long friendship. 'There's just one thing I can't forgive Fred for,' he said.

'What's that?'

'You,' he said. 'It wasn't a fair fight. We think you're the best.'

'We?'

'The guys.' He gestured around the table. 'Fred always chucks his women in the end,' he said. 'Can I have you afterwards?'

'What?' I said.

'No, I want her,' Graham said from the other side of the table.

'What about me?' said Morris.

'I was first,' said Duncan.

Maybe at some other time I might have laughed and made a flirtatious attempt to play along, but this wasn't one of those times. All of a sudden I felt nauseous. The thick, noisy atmosphere of the pub was curdling around me.

'Time to go,' I said.

Fred gave me a lift back to my flat in his van.

I told him how the police had asked about my personal life. 'They made me think it was my fault,' I said. 'They asked about my sex life.'

'A long story?' There was a gleam in his eye.

'Don't be stupid.'

'So they think it's one of your ex-lovers?'

'Maybe.'

'Did any of them seem like nutcases?'

'No.' I hesitated. 'Except, when you start thinking like that, of course, everyone seems odd, a bit sinister. Nobody's just normal, are they?'

'Not even me?'

'You?' I looked across at him as he drove, thin hands on the steering wheel. 'Not even you.'

He seemed pleased. I saw him smile.

I'd learned my lesson from last night. I didn't ask him in. I waved him off, in a reasonably convincing charade of cheerfulness, but instead of going into the flat I dithered on the street for a few minutes, then told myself not to be so stupid. I walked to the front door, opened it. There were no hand-delivered letters.

Eight

'I really think he's interested, this man who's coming back to see the flat. God knows why, but I think he might like it. If only he did. I hate it here, you know, Louise. I dread coming back at night. If I could only get out of here, maybe all the letters would stop.'

Louise looked round the room. 'What time is he coming?'

'About nine. Strange time to be viewing flats, don't you think?'

Louise rolled up her sleeves, looking, rather alarmingly, as if she were going to scrub the floor. 'That gives us nearly two hours. Where shall we start?'

I love Louise. She's down-to-earth and generous; even when she's acting outrageous and reckless, I know she's got her feet on the ground. She eats too many cakes and goes on mad, hopeless, completely unnecessary diets. She wears skirts that make Pauline raise her beautifully shaped eyebrows, high platform shoes and a stud in her navel. She is small, stubborn, sure of herself. Nothing seems to get her down. She's like a pit pony.

When I arrived at Laurier School, Louise took me under her wing, for all she had been there only a year herself. She gave me teaching tips, warned me which parents were troublesome, shared her sandwiches with me at lunch when I forgot to bring any. And she was my one point of stability in the whole fluid mess that was London. Now she was putting my life in order.

In the living room, twelve foot by ten, she emptied ashtrays, pushed the table under the window so that the peeling wallpaper was partly obscured, vacuumed the carpet, while I stacked bits of paper and mail into piles, threw away junk.

'Are those the letters?' asked Louise, pointing at the cardboard box.

'Yep.'

'Creepy. Why don't you throw them away? Treat it all like the trash it is.'

So she held open the neck of a bin bag and I shoved all the lavender envelopes, green-ink letters, instruction manuals on self-defence and sad biographies into it. My spirits rose.

Louise went down Holloway Road to buy some flowers while I cleaned the bath. She returned with yellow roses for the living room, a pot plant with fleshy green leaves for the kitchen.

'Can I use this jug for a vase?' she said. 'There, doesn't that look better?'

It did. It felt better, too, now that Louise was with me. Just an ordinary poxy room backing onto a pub, not a coffin, after all.

'I've been really thrown by all this,' I said.

Louise filled the kettle. 'Where does this plug in? There's no spare socket.' She pulled the other plug out of the socket with a flourish. 'You can always come and stay at my place, if it would help. I haven't got a spare bed but I've a spare bit of floor. Come this weekend, if you want.'

'That's nice of you.'

The bedroom looked more or less OK. Wandering around, Louise paused and looked at objects on top of my chest of drawers.

'What on earth is this strange collection?' she asked.

'Things people sent me.'

'Bloody hell,' she said, picking them up and examining them.

There was a whistle, which one letter-writer had said I should wear round my neck at all times as an alarm. A comb, a pair of tiny pink silk knickers. A round smooth stone that looked like a bird's egg, a small brown teddy bear.

'This is pretty.' She was looking at a dainty silver locket on a thin chain.

'If you open it up, there's a piece of hair inside as well.'

'Who sent it?'

'Dunno. It arrived wrapped in a newspaper article about have-a-go heroes. It's beautiful, isn't it?'

'And these are exciting.' She was looking at a pack of porno-graphic playing cards. 'Men,' she said.

I shivered in the heat.

NICK SHALE ARRIVED just after nine, by which time I had had a bath and changed into jeans and a yellow cotton shirt. I wanted to look neat and clean, to go with my flat. I piled my hair on top of my head and dabbed perfume behind my ears.

He was wearing running shorts and when he took his canvas backpack off, I saw there was a dark V of sweat down the back of his singlet.

He wandered from room to room, staring up at ceilings as if he could see interesting patterns on their surfaces. In the bedroom, he opened the fitted wardrobe and gazed for a moment into my laundry basket, a funny little smile on his face. Then he straightened up and looked at me. 'I could do with a glass of wine.'

'I don't have any.'

'Then it's lucky I brought my own.'

He stooped down and opened the backpack, bringing out a slim green bottle. I touched it: it was still cold, dribbles of moisture run-ning down its neck.

'Do you have a corkscrew?'

I wasn't feeling especially pleased about this—I didn't think prospective flat-buyers were meant to give presents to the owner—

but I gave him one. He turned his back to me to open it. I handed him a glass and a tumbler and he poured the wine.

He told me he lived in Norfolk but needed to buy a flat in London because he stayed two or three nights during the week.

'So my flat could become a *pied-à-terre*. What an honour.'

'Cheers.'

'I've got to go out now,' I said, lying, of course.

'It's a bit late, isn't it?' he said, draining his glass.

I didn't reply. I didn't see why I needed an excuse for a man I didn't know. 'You should take your bottle,' I said.

'No, you keep it,' he said, turning to leave.

'What about the flat?'

'I like it,' he said. 'I'll be in touch.'

I heard the door close downstairs. I liked him well enough. I wondered what his handwriting looked like.

THE NEXT DAY I felt like a robot in class. The robot got on with a lesson on letter formation while somewhere inside I was going over things in my mind. I needed to get rid of the flat. I'd been too young when I'd bought it. The money I'd been left by Dad when he died had felt like Monopoly money. He had said to me to buy somewhere to live; it was almost like a deathbed command. He was a man who thought that if you owned property, then you were safe. So I did as he had told me. Very quickly. And since I'd moved to London from a quiet village, my only impulse had been to buy something that was in the real city, where there were shops, markets, people, noise. I'd certainly found that.

'Zoë?'

I was woken up out of what felt to me like sleep, and I was almost surprised to look at my hand and see a piece of chalk. I looked round. It was Christine, one of our special-needs teachers.

'Pauline asked to see you,' she said. 'I'll take over here.'

'Why?'

'There's a mother with her. I think she's very upset.'

'Oh.'

I felt a dull ache in my stomach, that sense of an imminent blow. I looked at the class. What could it be? I made a quick count. Thirty-one. They were all here. Nobody was foaming at the mouth. I felt better. How bad could it be?

As I walked the short distance to Pauline's office, I thought how, if

I hated my flat, at least I loved the school. Even when the children were running around screaming it felt like a refuge.

Pauline was standing by the half-open door with a woman I recognised. Elinor's mother. I nodded a greeting at her but she didn't catch my eye. I tried to picture Elinor this morning. Had she been upset? I didn't think so. Nothing unusual occurred to me.

'Shut the door behind you,' Pauline said, leading me in. The mother stayed outside. She waved me to a chair in front of her desk. 'That was Gillian Tite, mother of Elinor.'

'Yes, I know.'

I noticed that Pauline was white-faced, trembling. She was either deeply upset or so angry that she could barely control herself.

'Did you give the class homework last week?'

'Yes. It was just for fun. I asked them to draw a picture of one of their favourite stories in their art book.'

'What did you do with the homework?'

'I collected the books up on Wednesday. I looked through them immediately.' I remembered doing it—sitting there while that peculiar man who came to view the flat went through my knicker drawer. That was the day I'd found the letter on the doormat. 'I wrote nice comments on them and gave them back the next morning.'

'Elinor's mother came in to see me in tears,' said Pauline. 'This is Elinor's drawing. Take a look.'

She pushed a familiar large-format exercise book across her desk. It was open and I recognised my writing at the bottom of the page. 'Sleeping Beauty'. The drawing wasn't like a toddler's drawing. There were traces of Elinor's pencillings here and there but they had been embellished, drawn over and filled out. The figure of the girl was lying in a carefully rendered room. More than that, I could see what Pauline couldn't. It was my room. My bedroom.

On the bed, Sleeping Beauty wasn't asleep and she wasn't Sleeping Beauty. She was me. The bed looked more like a mortuary slab. I mean that there were huge incisions in the body, with bits of internal organ, guts, trailing out. Parts of the body were so mutilated as not to be recognisable. Suddenly, I started to be sick, bitter bile came up in my mouth, but I managed to hold it down, swallow it. I pushed the book back to Pauline.

She looked at me earnestly. 'Just tell me, did you do this?'

My eyes were burning. I had to stop myself crying. I had to be strong, not collapse. 'Call the police,' I said.

PAULINE WAS DUBIOUS and reluctant at first but I insisted. I wasn't going to leave her office without something being done.

'It's happened before,' I said to her in explanation. 'In a way.'

I was put through to Aldham and I said he had to come over now, here, to the school, right away. Aldham was reluctant but I said if he didn't come then I would make an official complaint, so he agreed. I gave him the address of the school and quickly put the phone down.

There was quite a long silence. Pauline stared at me as if I were an unpredictable wild animal that needed careful handling. Finally she gave a shrug. 'I'll talk to Mrs Tite outside,' she said quietly.

'Yeah,' I said, hardly taking in what she was saying.

Pauline stopped at the door. 'Are you saying that someone else did that? That picture?'

I lit a cigarette. 'Yeah,' I said. 'Something horrible's going on. Horrible. I've got to get it sorted out.'

Pauline started to say something then stopped and left me alone in her office. It must have been half an hour later that I heard voices outside and Aldham came in, escorted by Pauline.

'Look,' I said, pointing at the art book, which was still open where I had left it. 'That's me. That's an exact copy of my bedroom. You can't see that from the pub.'

He looked stunned. 'Where was this done?'

'How do I know?' It took an effort to slow myself down, to make myself concentrate. 'It was just in a pile of school books. I took them home last Wednesday and brought them back the next day.'

'Were they ever out of your sight?'

'Of course they were. What do you think? I didn't sit and guard them all night. Sorry. Sorry, sorry, sorry. Let me think. Yes, I went out to see a film with a friend. I must have been out for two, nearly three hours, I guess. It was the day I found the letter on my doormat.'

Aldham wrinkled his nose and nodded. He looked baffled and anxious. 'And it wasn't discovered until today?'

Pauline stepped forward. 'The mother only looked this morning,' she said.

'Have any other books been tampered with?' Aldham asked.

'I don't know,' I said. 'I don't think so. I—'

'We'll check the other art books,' Pauline said.

I could feel my heart beating fast. My pulse seemed to be everywhere, in my face and arms and legs.

Aldham took a mobile phone from his pocket and retreated into a corner. I heard him ask for DI Carthy then begin a murmured conversation. I heard fragments. 'Shall we talk to Detective Inspector Stadler? And Grace Schilling? Can you give her a bell? And send an officer along with the file. Send Lynne, she's good at this kind of thing. We'll meet her there. Right, see you later.'

Aldham put the phone away and turned to Pauline. 'Is it all right if Miss Haratounian comes with us for a while?'

'Of course,' Pauline said. She looked at me with a new concern. 'Is everything all right?'

'It'll be fine,' Aldham said. 'We just need to go through some routine procedures.' He took a handkerchief from his pocket and used it to pick up Elinor's art book. 'All right?' he said.

IT WAS QUITE a long drive across London. After almost an hour we drove along a residential street and arrived at what looked like a school but had a sign outside identifying it as the Welbeck Clinic.

'We're seeing a woman who knows about psycho stuff like this,' explained Aldham.

A female officer was sitting in reception reading a file. When she saw us she snapped it shut, came forward and handed it to Aldham.

'You stay here,' he said to me. 'WPC Burnett will stay with you.'

'Lynne,' she said to me, with a reassuring smile. She had a purple birthmark on one cheek and big eyes. On another day, I would have liked the look of her.

I started to light a cigarette, but this was really *verboten* so Lynne and I stood out on the steps and she had one of my cigarettes as well. I think she did it to keep me company. And she didn't speak, which was a relief. It was ten minutes before Aldham emerged with a tall woman, not much older than me, in a long grey coat. She had blonde hair tied up casually on her head and was carrying a leather briefcase and khaki canvas shoulder bag.

'Miss Haratounian, this is Dr Schilling,' Aldham said.

We shook hands. She looked at me with narrowed eyes as if I were an unusual specimen that had been brought in for examination.

'I'm really sorry,' she said. 'I'm already late for a meeting, but I wanted a quick word.'

I suddenly felt crushed. I'd been driven across London to talk to a woman as she accelerated past me on the steps of a clinic.

'So what do you think?'

'I think this should be taken seriously.' She gave Aldham a sharp look. 'I want us to have a proper meeting on Monday morning at nine o'clock to consider this in detail. I've got to go now but . . . That drawing, that really is your bedroom?'

'I've already said that.'

'You've got a boyfriend, right?' she asked.

'Yes, Fred.'

She looked at Aldham. 'Talk to him.'

'If you're thinking it might be Fred,' I said, 'you can stop right now. Apart from the fact that it can't be him, because, oh, well, just because, you know.' She nodded, kind but quite unconvinced. 'Well, he was away the night it must have happened. He was in the Dales, digging a garden with several other people. I think you'll find he's even caught on camera by Yorkshire TV to prove it.'

'Talk to him anyway,' she said to Aldham. Then to me, 'I'll see you on Monday, Zoë. I don't want to panic you, but I think it would be a good idea if you didn't spend the night alone at your flat for a while. Doug?' That must be Aldham. 'Look at her locks, all right? Bye, see you Monday.'

Aldham and I walked back to his car.

'That was . . . er, quick,' I said.

'Don't worry about her,' said Aldham. 'She's ten per cent bullshit, ninety per cent covering her arse.'

'You don't want to talk to Fred, do you?'

'We've got to start somewhere. Where are we now?'

'Hampstead.'

'I think he's working fairly nearby. He said north London. I could ring him on his mobile.'

'Please,' said Aldham, offering me his phone.

I found the number in my diary and started to dial.

I saw Fred before he saw me. He was at the far end of an amazingly grand garden, moving sideways along a border with a Strimmer that was suspended from his shoulders by straps. He had an eye visor and ear protectors, so that the only way I could make myself known to him was to tap him on the shoulder. He started slightly, even though I had rung ahead to warn him I was coming, switched off the machine and pulled off the visor and ear protectors.

'Hello,' he said, making the greeting a question. He wasn't pleased.

'Hello,' I said, kissing him, touching his cheek. 'Sorry. They said they wanted to talk to you.'

'Now?' he said warily. 'We're in the middle of a job.'

'That's nothing to do with me,' I said. 'I just wanted to say to you face to face that I was sorry you're being dragged in.'

He seemed suddenly unyielding. 'What's all the fuss about?'

I gave him a potted version of what had happened at school but he didn't seem to be taking it in. He was like one of those awful people at parties who glance over your shoulder at a better-looking girl over by the drinks. In this case Fred kept looking at Aldham who was hovering at the other end of the garden by the door into the house.

'And she said I should stay away from my flat for the next few days.'

There was a pause and I looked at Fred. I waited for him to say that of course I could stay with him until all of this had been sorted out. I waited for him to put his arms round me and tell me everything was going to be all right and he was here for me. His face was like a mask.

Then his eyes dropped to my breasts. I felt myself beginning to flush with humiliation and the first stirrings of a hot anger.

'I . . . All right. I'll talk to them for a minute. Nothing to say, though.'

'Another thing,' I said, without even knowing I was going to, 'I think we should stop seeing each other.'

That stopped his wandering, mildly lecherous eyes; his vague and disconnected air. He stared at me. I could see a vein throbbing in his temple, the muscles of his jaw clenching. He looked me up and down, as if I were on display in a shop window, then he allowed a little sneer to twitch at his mouth. 'And why would that be, Zoë?' he said at last, his voice icy.

'I'm scared,' I replied. 'And I need help, and I'm not going to get if from you, am I?'

'You bitch,' he said. 'You stuck-up bitch.'

I turned and walked away. I just wanted to get away from there, to be somewhere safe.

Her hair is hanging loose on her shoulders. It needs washing. The parting is dark, a bit greasy. She has aged in the past week. Her skin is looking slightly unhealthy, pale and a bit grubby. She smokes all the time, lighting one cigarette from another.

The feeling inside me is growing. I will know when she is ready. There is nothing more certain. Certainty fills me up, it makes me strong and purposeful. She gets weaker and smaller. I look at her and I think to myself, I did this.

Nine

I banged at the door. Why didn't she come? Oh, please, come quickly now. I couldn't breathe. I took some shallow gasps, felt an unbearable pressure growing in my chest. There was a tight band of pain round my head and I couldn't stand up any longer. Everything was going blurred and grey-black. I sank to my knees at the door.

'Zoë? Zoë! For Chrissakes, Zoë, what's happened?' Louise was on her knees beside me, wrapped in a towel and with wet hair. She had her arm around my shoulder and the towel was slipping away but she didn't mind, darling Louise.

She took me in her arms and rocked me. Nobody had done that to me since Mum had died. Oh, how I'd missed that; how I'd missed having a mother. She was telling me that everything was going to be all right. Gradually I started to be able to breathe once more. I felt warm tears slide under my closed lids, onto my hot cheeks.

Louise lifted me to my feet, holding her towel round her with one hand. She led me up the stairs into her flat and sat me on the sofa and sat beside me.

'It was a panic attack,' she said. 'That's all, Zoë.'

I STAYED WITH LOUISE at her flat in Dalston. There was nowhere else for me to go, and while she was around I felt less scared. Nothing would happen to me while Louise was with me.

First I had a bath, much better than the bathroom in my flat. I lay in the hot water and drank tea.

Later Louise phoned out for a pizza to be delivered. I borrowed her dressing gown, and we sat on the sofa and ate dripping slices of pizza and drank cheap red wine and watched *Groundhog Day* on video. We'd both seen it before, of course, but it seemed a safe choice.

A couple of times her phone rang, and she answered it and spoke in a low voice, hand over the receiver, glancing at me occasionally.

Once, it was for me: Detective Sergeant Aldham. For a stupid moment, I thought perhaps he was going to say that they had caught him. Desperate hope. He was just checking up on me. He reiterated that I shouldn't go back to the flat unaccompanied, that I shouldn't be on my own with any man I didn't know well. 'Be alert, Miss Haratounian,' he said, and the fact that he'd managed to get my name right scared me almost as much as his earnest, respectful tone. I'd wanted them to take me seriously. Now they were serious.

Louise insisted on giving me her bed, while she rolled herself up in a sheet on the sofa. I thought I wouldn't be able to sleep, and I lay for a while with thoughts whirring in my head like bats that had lost their radar. But I must have gone to sleep quite soon, and the next thing I remember is the smell of burnt toast, and daylight flooding in through the striped blue curtains. Then Louise poked her head round the bedroom door. 'Tea or coffee?'

'Coffee, please.'

After I'd eaten, I phoned Guy to find out if anything was happening with the flat. He sounded self-conscious and warily solicitous, not a bit like his usual chirpily ingratiating self.

'I hear you've been having a bad time,' he said.

Of course, the police would have interviewed him by now.

'Not brilliant. Any news on the sale?'

'Mr Shale wants to see the flat again. I think we've got him sniffing our hook. It's just a matter of landing him.'

'What are you talking about?' I asked wearily.

'I think he's ready to make an offer,' Guy said. 'The point is, he wonders if today, midday, would be at all convenient.'

So we arranged to meet at the estate agent's office at midday, Guy and me and Nick Shale. Safety in numbers.

We walked up the road to my flat, and Guy opened the door with his set of keys and went in first. Nick stood back to let me enter. There was a funny smell. Nick wrinkled his nose and looked at me questioningly.

'I must have left something out,' I said. 'I haven't been here for a bit.'

It was coming from the kitchen. I pushed open the door. The smell was stronger in here. I opened the fridge. The light didn't come on.

The milk was sour but there wasn't much else the matter. But I knew where the bad bit would be. I opened the small freezer on top of the fridge. All I could do was groan. A tub of coffee ice cream lying on its side had spewed its contents out over an opened packet of prawns. The smell and sight of day-old prawns and melted ice cream in my hot kitchen almost made me gag.

'Oh God,' I said.

'Zoë.' Guy put his hand lightly on my shoulder and I jumped back from him.

'Wait,' I said. 'I've got to call the police.'

'What?' he asked, his expression puzzled, almost embarrassed.

I turned on him. 'Just shut up. Don't come near me, keep off.'

He put up his hands in surrender. 'All right, all right.'

He glanced across at Nick with the apprehensive expression of a man watching a sale ooze away between the floorboards. It didn't matter. All I cared about now was staying alive. I knew the number by heart. I dialled and asked for Carthy and he was there in less than ten minutes, with Aldham and another man carrying a large leather bag who started pulling on thin gloves as soon as he got through the door. They stared at the mess, muttered to each other. Carthy was asking me questions, but I couldn't seem to understand them.

Aldham spoke very calmly and quietly. 'Zoë, there was no note, was there?'

'I don't know. I didn't see one but I didn't look.'

'We've looked. We haven't found one. The fridge had been unplugged and the kettle had been plugged into the socket instead.'

'Why would he do that?'

'I think it was a mistake. It's easy to do.'

'But I wouldn't . . .' And then I stopped myself and remembered Louise making me tea, pulling out the plug so that she could plug in the kettle. Oh, shit. I felt my face going red.

There was a silence. Aldham looked at the carpet, Carthy looked at me. I stared back. 'You told me to be alert,' I said. 'It's easy for you. I keep thinking I'm going to die.'

'I know,' said Aldham. He put his hand tentatively on my shoulder. 'I wonder whether we're alarming you too much. I'm sorry.'

I shook myself free. 'You . . . you . . .'

But I couldn't think of anything rude enough. I turned and ran out, conscious as I did so that I was leaving them all in my flat.

LOUISE WAS WAITING for me when I got back. As I was telling her what had happened, I realised I was assuming she would continue to let me stay with her. But she made it easy for me. 'Stay as long as you like.'

'I'm taking the sofa, though.'

'Whatever.'

I was feeling better. The gripping fear of yesterday was loosening.

I need never sleep in my flat again, need never set eyes on Guy again or show strange men round the rooms. I need never see Fred again either, or his laddish friends. I felt as if I'd shed a dirty, suffocating skin. I'd stay with Louise; we'd eat supper in front of the TV in the evening, paint each other's toenails. On Monday, I'd see Dr Schilling. She'd know what to do. She was an expert.

Louise insisted that she had no plans for the weekend, and although I suspected that she had actually cancelled everything for me, I was too relieved to make any but the feeblest protest. We bought French baguettes filled with cheese and tomato and walked to the nearby park, where we sat on the dry, baked-yellow grass.

Louise lay back, arms pillowing her head. I sat beside her, smoking cigarette after cigarette, and watched the people, waited to glimpse a face that was looking at me as if they knew me.

'You know what?' I said.

'What?' she said dreamily.

'I've been passive,' I said. 'I've wanted other people to sort this out for me. I couldn't be bothered.'

'Don't be silly, Zoë.'

'It's true. I've got to look at myself and think why somebody would pick on me. Who would do it.'

'Tomorrow,' said Louise. 'Look at yourself tomorrow. Today just look after yourself.'

I let the sun soak into my skin, under my grubby clothes. I was more tired than I'd ever been, with gritty, aching eyes and heavy limbs. I wanted to have deep baths, sleep for hours, eat healthy food, raw carrots, green apples, drink orange juice and herbal tea. The hot, sweaty, frantic life I had led in London filled me with vague, pervasive horror. Maybe, I thought, I'd even give up cigarettes. Not yet.

WE PASSED a cheery shop selling things for children—bright cotton dungarees and stripy tops—and Louise dragged me in. 'You're a child's size,' she said, looking at me. 'You've lost too much weight; we've got to fatten you up again. But in the meantime, let's buy you a couple of things.' So, while the salesgirl looked on rather disapprovingly, I selected a few objects off the rack, and took them into the changing room. I put on a lovely white T-shirt, decorated with tiny stitched flowers.

'Let's have a look,' shouted Louise. 'Come on, you can't go shopping with a friend if you don't make it into a fashion show.'

I pulled the curtains open, giggling, doing a turn for her. 'What do you think?'

'It looks lovely on you.' She put a hand on my shoulder. 'Like a flower, sweetheart.'

Later, Louise and I went in her rattling car to the supermarket to stock up. 'I'll make us a meal tonight,' I said boldly. I felt as if I were playing at domesticity. It had certainly been weeks, probably months, since I had actually cooked anything, with a recipe and real ingredients that you have to put together. I put fresh pasta into our trolley, large garlic bulbs and Italian plum tomatoes; lettuce hearts, cucumber, mangoes and strawberries. A tub of cream. A bottle of Chianti. I bought an economy pack of knickers, some deodorant, a flannel, a toothbrush and toothpaste. I hadn't cleaned my teeth since yesterday morning. I'd have to collect stuff from the flat.

'Tomorrow,' said Louise decisively. 'Leave it for now.'

I picked up some cellophane-wrapped roses from the check-out area, which I added to our trolley. 'I don't know how to thank you, Louise.'

'Then don't.'

A FRIEND OF LOUISE'S, called Cathy, came round for supper. Louise lit candles and melted them onto old saucers. I sat at the kitchen table, light-headed. There was a hollow feeling in my stomach, but I couldn't eat very much. I couldn't speak very much either. It was enough to sit there, listening to them; words buzzing lightly over the surface of my mind. I went to bed before Cathy left, lying curled up on the sofa in the tiny sitting room, wearing Louise's skimpy night-dress. I could hear them in the kitchen, the comforting hum of conversation, and I drifted off to sleep feeling safe.

THE NEXT MORNING, after breakfast, we went to my flat to collect a few clothes. Louise couldn't find anywhere to park near the flat, so she stopped on a double yellow line a few yards down from the front door and I said I'd run up.

'I won't be more than a couple of minutes,' I said.

'Sure you don't want me to come with you?'

I shook my head and smiled. 'I'm just going to say goodbye.'

There was an air of general squalor and neglect about the place, though I'd only been gone one day, as if the flat knew that nobody cared about it. I went into my bedroom and gathered two pairs of trousers, four T-shirts, several knickers, bras and pairs of socks.

Some trainers. That would do for now. I shoved them all in a large holdall. Then I went into the bathroom, took off the dirty clothes I was wearing and threw them into a corner.

I heard a click, like a cupboard door closing. It's nothing, I said to myself. Imagination plays nasty tricks. Back in the bedroom I found some clean underwear. I pulled my knickers on, and took my new T-shirt—the one Louise said made me look like a flower—out of the bag I had brought with me and pulled it over my head.

Without any warning at all, I felt a grasp around my neck and a weight on my back, someone on me. I lost my balance and fell with my face pushed hard into the carpet. I was stunned, in pain. I felt the hand holding my mouth, a warm hand smelling of soap, apple soap from my bathroom. An arm wrapped round my rib cage, just under my breasts.

'Bitch, you bitch.'

The grip on my neck slackened, I tried to move and to scream, but then it was on my throat. There was nothing I could do. I thought about Louise sitting in the car outside, waiting for me, though she seemed a long, long way off. How stupid, to die like this, before I'd even begun.

I felt my head bounce on floorboards, my feet slide across the wood. I couldn't speak, no words left to be said now, no time to say them any more, but somewhere deep inside a voice was saying: No, please, no. Please.

Part Two: Jennifer

One

Everything seemed to be happening, but then our house at breakfast-time always seems to be rather like one of those medieval castles with donkeys and pigs and all the serfs coming in for shelter at the first sniff of trouble. In the weeks since our move it had become even more chaotic, if that's possible, and now the medieval castle had a building site slap bang in the middle of it.

Clive had left the house at six, which is even earlier than usual, because at the moment he's working on some sort of horrific takeover bid. Just before eight Lena drags the two older boys into the Espace for the school run. Lena's our nanny stroke au-pair thing, lovely-looking girl, Swedish, infuriatingly blonde and slim and young, though she has this thing through her nose that makes me wince every time I see it. Goodness knows what it must feel like when she blows her nose.

Then people started arriving. Mary, of course, our priceless cleaner who came with us to Primrose Hill. She's a treasure, except that I have to spend so much time telling her what to do and then checking she's done it that I've said to Clive I might as well do the cleaning myself. And then all the people who were meant to be improving the house but instead have been reducing it to a slum full of brick dust.

I was satisfied, though, despite everything. This was what I had always wanted, what Clive had always promised me. A project. The house was down to bare boards and walls, and now I was going to turn it into a home we could be proud of.

I'd spent four months with Jeremy, our clever architect, head down over plans. It was just a matter of being simple. Rip out everything. Then put kitchen and dining room in the basement, living rooms on the ground floor, Clive's study on the first floor at the back, then bedrooms on top.

This morning Jeremy popped in at around half past eight to go over a problem with an arch or beam or something, closely followed by Francis, who we'd brought with us to do—by which I mean completely redo—what passed for the garden. Tea and coffee all round, of course. Somewhere in the middle of all this I pop Christopher—who's four—along to his playschool thing.

Finally a sit-down, another coffee and the quickest of glances at the paper and the mail before getting down to work—i.e. walking around stopping people knocking through the wrong wall and doing some liaising. Then the mail. In general 90 per cent of the mail is for Clive. The remaining 10 per cent is divided between children, pets and me. Not that we've got any pets just at present. I'd been thinking of getting a dog now that we're two minutes from Primrose Hill. Haven't mentioned it to Clive yet, though.

I made a pile of anything with Clive's name on it or variations thereof. All bills ditto. That left two letters to Josh and Harry from Lascelles School about sports day. And then, after all that, there was one letter addressed to me. The name and address were neatly hand-written. And I couldn't recognise the handwriting. It wasn't Mummy's or a friend's or relative's. This was interesting. I opened the envelope, smoothed out the folded slip of paper on the table:

Dear Jenny,

I hope you don't mind if I call you Jenny. But you see I think you're very beautiful. You smell very nice, Jenny, and you have beautiful skin. And I'm going to kill you.

It seemed like the silliest thing. I tried to think if someone was playing a practical joke. Some of Clive's friends have the most awful sense of humour. Anyway, Jeremy came down and we started talking about some of the problems with the kitchen. Then I remembered the letter and I showed it to him.

He didn't laugh. He didn't find it funny at all. 'You'd better call the police,' he said.

'Oh, don't be so silly,' I said. 'It's probably just someone playing a joke. I'll make a fool of myself.'

'Doesn't matter. You must call the police.'

'Jeremy . . .'

He was an absolute pig about it. He dialled the number for the local police station himself then handed me the phone as if I were a toddler talking to her granny.

The phone rang and rang. 'Probably nobody's home . . . Oh, hello? Look, this is going to sound really stupid, but I've just been sent this letter.'

I SPOKE FOR A FEW minutes to a girl who sounded bored and she said she'd arrange for somebody to call round but there might be a bit of a delay. I said it didn't matter to me and went back to Jeremy, who was helping himself to more coffee.

We were right in the middle of discussing his latest bit of clever-ness with a tricky pillar that we had to work round when there was a ring at the door. I left it to Lena since the only people coming into the house were carrying pots of paint or strange copper pipes.

I heard her yelling for me at the top of the stairs. Being shouted at in my own house is an experience I rank alongside chewing tinfoil. I walked up to the ground floor. Lena was standing at the open front door with two policemen in uniform.

'Mrs Hintlesham?'

'Yes, yes, it's very nice of you to come round. I can't think that it's necessary, but come in. Since you're here.'

They both wiped their feet with immense care on the mat before following me down the stairs to the rudiments of our kitchen.

'This will only take a minute,' I said. I pointed out the letter where it still lay on the table. 'You'll see it's just something stupid.'

The two of them looked down at the note while I got back to work with Jeremy. After a few minutes I saw one of the officers step outside the French windows into the garden, talking into his radio. The other was looking around at the room.

'New kitchen?' he said.

'Yes,' I said, and pointedly turned back to Jeremy. I wasn't in the mood for a conversation about interior decoration with a junior police officer. The first one stepped back inside. 'Are you finished, then?' I asked.

'No, Mrs Hintlesham. Someone else is going to come over to have a look at your note.'

'Really!' I said, in a reproving tone. 'Isn't this just a waste of everybody's time?'

They answered only with shrugs.

'We'll be in the car outside until the detective sergeant arrives.'

'Oh, all right.'

They shambled out. I went up with Jeremy, which was just as well because a tin of National Trust paint had arrived in entirely the wrong shade. While I was on the phone trying to sort it out with a gormless female at the other end, I heard the doorbell ring, and I was still talking when a man in a grey suit was shown into the room. It's embarrassing to get cross with somebody you've never met while someone else you've never met stands right next to you, so I brought the call to a close. He introduced himself as Detective Sergeant Aldham and I took him down to the basement.

He looked at the note and I heard him swear under his breath. He looked up. 'Have you got the envelope?'

'What? Er, no. Well, I think I chucked it in the bin, there.'

I couldn't believe it but he started rummaging in the bin like some down-and-out. He lifted out a scrunched-up envelope, which looked a bit damp and brown from the coffee grounds, and held it very delicately, by a corner, and put it on the side near the letter.

'Excuse me a moment,' he said, and took out a mobile phone.

I retreated across the room and put the kettle on. I heard fragments of his conversation: 'Yes, definitely' and 'I haven't talked to her yet'. Apparently from then on it was bad news for Sergeant Aldham, because his side of the conversation turned into squeaked questions. 'What?' 'Are you sure?' At last he gave a resigned sigh and replaced the phone in his pocket. 'Two other detectives are on their way,' he said, in a sullen tone. 'They would like to interview you, if that's possible.'

Things were a bit sticky after that. Aldham hung around looking embarrassed. I tried to get on with things but his doleful face put me off. It was quite a relief when the doorbell rang. This time the doorstep was positively crowded. At the front were two slightly more up-market-looking detectives. With them were a couple more uniformed officers and two more people, one a woman, were coming up the steps behind them.

The older man was balding with grey hair cut very short.

'Mrs Hintlesham?' he said, with a reassuring smile. 'I'm Detective Chief Inspector Links. Stuart Links.' We shook hands. 'And this is Detective Inspector Stadler.'

Stadler didn't look like a policeman at all. He looked more like a politician, or one of Clive's colleagues. He had a smartly cut dark suit, a discreet tie. He was rather striking-looking, in a way.

'This is Dr Marsh,' Links continued. 'He's from our forensic department. And he's brought his assistant, Gill Carlson. You're probably wondering why there are so many of us.'

'Well—'

'A letter of the sort that you have received is a kind of threat. We need to ensure your safety.'

Links had been looking me in the eyes. But with that he slowly shifted his gaze towards Aldham. 'We'll take over from here.'

Aldham mumbled goodbye to me, eased his way past us and was gone.

Links looked around. 'You've recently moved in?'

'In May.'

'We'll try not to cause too much disturbance, Mrs Hintlesham. I'd like to see the letter and then I'd like to ask you one or two questions.'

'Downstairs,' I said faintly.

And so, a few minutes later, I found myself sitting at my table with two detectives in the middle of a half-completed kitchen. The letter was read and then lifted with tweezers into a transparent folder, as was the sodden envelope. The scientists left, clutching the items.

'Look,' I said, 'can I just say that I don't think there's anything remotely I can tell you? It's a horrible silly letter and that's all there is to it. I don't know anything about it.'

'You've recently moved into this house,' said Links. 'Did you live in this area before?'

'No. We lived south of the river, in Battersea.'

'One of the things we try to do is to establish connections with other threats that may have been made. Do you have children?'

'Yes. Three boys.'

'Do you know Laurier Primary School in Hackney, or maybe you've met one of the teachers? A woman called Zoë Haratounian, for example.'

'No. What can the school have to do with this letter?'

'There were . . . er, incidents associated with the school, letters like the one you received. But can we continue with our questions? Has this letter come out of the blue? You don't connect it with anything else, no matter how remotely?'

'No.'

'I would like to assess how many people have access to this house. I see that you're having work done.'

'That's right. It's like Waterloo Station here.'

He smiled. 'Did you use Clarke's estate agents?'

I shrugged. 'I must be on the books of almost every estate agent in London.'

They looked at each other.

'I'll check it out,' Stadler said.

One of the uniformed officers came down the stairs with a tall woman. Tall, with long blonde hair, some of it pinned up on top of her head. She was carrying a case and had a raincoat over one arm. Both detectives looked round and nodded at her.

'This is Dr Grace Schilling,' said Links. 'She specialises in the psychology of, well, of people who do things like this. I'd be very grateful if you'd talk to her.'

I looked at Dr Schilling. She was looking at me with narrowed eyes. I felt like something stuck to a card with a pin.

'Mrs Hintlesham,' she said, 'can we go somewhere quiet?'

'I'm not sure there *is* anywhere quiet,' I said, with a forced smile.

'SORRY ABOUT THE MESS.' We tiptoed across the room between packing cases towards a sofa. 'This is going to be a drawing room in about twenty years.'

She sat down in an uncomfortable old basket-weave chair and took a notepad and a pencil out of her bag.

'Thank you for giving me your time, Mrs Hintlesham.'

I was feeling agitated. I wasn't quite sure what was going on, why she seemed so serious.

'I don't want to give you a psychology lecture. I just want to do anything I can to help you.' She paused, as if she were trying to make up her mind. 'Look, as you know there are men who just attack women at random. This letter you received is obviously something different. He's seen you. Been close to you. He says that you smell nice. That you have beautiful skin.'

She leaned closer. 'You do have beautiful skin,' she said, as if it were an interesting scientific observation.

'Well, I try hard enough with it. I have this special cream.'

'Are you often aware of people finding you attractive?'

'What a question. I can't think how this is going to help you. Let's see. Some of Clive's friends are awful flirts. I suppose there are men who look at me, you know, the way men do.'

Grace Schilling just gazed at me with that calm expression on her face. 'Do you work, Jenny?'

'Not in the way you mean,' I said, almost belligerently. 'I have children, and this house. I haven't worked since I got pregnant with Josh, fifteen years ago. Clive and I always agreed that I would give up. I used to model hands.'

She looked baffled. 'Hands?'

'You know, in posters for nail varnish and things like that, consisting of nothing but a giant hand. In the early and mid-eighties lots of those hands were mine.'

Dr Schilling smiled for the first time. 'Maybe you could describe your life to me.'

'Oh dear, you mean a day in the life?'

'I want to get an idea of the things that are important to you.'

'This is ridiculous. You can't catch somebody by finding out what I think about my life.' She waited but this time I beat her at her own game. I just stared back.

'Do you spend a lot of time with your sons?'

'I'm their mother, aren't I? Though sometimes I feel more like their unpaid chauffeur.'

'And your husband?'

'Clive is madly busy. I hardly see him at the moment.'

'You've been married how long? Fifteen years?'

'Yes. Sixteen this autumn.' God, was it that long?

'And would you describe it as a happy marriage, close?'

'I wouldn't describe it to you at all.'

'Jenny. There is a man out there who says he wants to kill you. However ridiculous this sounds, we have to take it seriously.'

I shrugged. 'It's a marriage,' I said. 'We have our ups and downs, like everybody.'

'Have you told your husband about the letter?'

'I left a message at work; he'll phone later.'

She looked at me as if she could see through me. 'Jenny,' she said finally, 'I know that one of the things that you feel, or will feel, is violated. And what's worse is that some of our efforts to help you may feel like a violation as well. But there are things I need to know.' She leaned forward. 'Has your husband been faithful, Jenny?'

'*What?*' I glared at her and felt my face going red. My head was starting to hurt. 'I think you should ask him,' I said, coolly.

She made a mark on her notepad. 'What about you?'

'Me?' I snorted. 'Don't be stupid. When on earth would I find time for an affair, even if I wanted one, unless it was with the gardener or the odd-job man or the tennis coach?'

'Do you find these questions intrusive?'

'Of course I do. I know it's an unfashionable view, but I like to keep private things private.'

She stood up at last, but she wasn't ready to leave quite yet. 'Jenny,' she said. I was irritated by the way she kept using my first name. 'If anything comes to mind that seems significant in any way, let the police know or let me know. Don't be embarrassed to tell us, will you?'

She seemed almost to be pleading with me.

'All right,' I said. 'I'll put on my thinking cap.'

'Do that.' She turned to go. 'And, Jenny?'

'Yes.'

She hesitated, then thought better of it. 'Nothing. Take care.'

LATER, THEY ALL WENT—except that Stadler man. He told me they would be opening my mail in the morning, just to be on the safe side.

'And,' he added, as if it were an afterthought, 'we're leaving a couple of police officers outside the house, and during the day there will be a woman officer here most of the time.'

'This is getting beyond a joke,' I said.

'Just a precaution,' he said soothingly. 'She's here now. Hang on a minute.' He strode to the door and shouted, 'Lynne! Lynne, can you come in here for a minute? Mrs Hintlesham, this is WPC Burnett. Lynne, Mrs Hintlesham.'

The woman was almost as small as me, but much younger, with light brown hair, pale lashes and a birthmark on her left cheek. She smiled at me. 'I'll try to keep out of your way,' she said.

'Do,' I snapped. I pointedly turned my back on her and Stadler until they had both left the room and I was blessedly alone again.

Lena brought Christo and Josh back. Harry was being dropped off by another mum after football practice. I told Josh, in vague and reassuring terms, about a stupid note and there being policemen outside. But he just shrugged before loping off to his bedroom with two peanut-butter sandwiches and a tankard of milk. He's grown up all of a sudden. His voice has broken, he's got little pimples on his forehead, soft hair on his upper lip. And he's so tall.

Christo is too young to understand, of course; I just gave his squashy little body a hug. He's my baby.

Clive rang to say he wouldn't be home until late, so after Harry got back, and after I had put Christo to bed with a story, I had supper with Josh and Harry. Lasagne that I'd taken out of the freezer earlier, with peas, and for pudding ice cream with chocolate sauce. I didn't eat very much. It was too hot.

The boys drifted off into their own rooms again, so I poured myself a glass of white wine and sat downstairs with the TV on.

Eventually, I heard the key turn in the door. Clive kissed my cheek. He looked grey with tiredness. 'God, what a day.'

I looked at him: expensive charcoal-grey suit, purple and grey tie, slight paunch beneath his well-ironed white shirt, little threads of silver in his dark hair. He took off his jacket and lowered himself into the sofa, sighing. I went to the kitchen and came back with two glasses of white wine, very cold from the fridge.

'I've had an extraordinary day,' I began.

'Oh, yes? Tell me.'

I think I told it badly. I couldn't convey how strange it felt, how seriously the police had taken it. When I finished he took a sip of wine. 'Well, it's nice that someone appreciates your skin, Jens.' Then: 'I'm sure it's just some crank. I don't want crowds of policemen running all over the house.'

'No. Mad, isn't it?'

two

I never go downstairs before I put my make-up on, not even at the weekend. As soon as I hear Clive leave in the morning, I get out of bed and have a shower. I sit at my dressing table, which Clive says looks like something in a starlet's trailer, and examine myself. There are lines I didn't have last year, horrible little ones above my upper lip. My skin no longer has the bloom of youth, whatever that stupid man wrote in his letter. When Clive first met me, he told me I had skin like a peach. But that was a long time ago. He doesn't say things like that any longer.

I make sure there are no stray hairs between my eyebrows, then I start with foundation, followed by a tiny smudge of beige eye shadow, mascara, maybe lip gloss. Then I feel better. I like the face that looks back at me, ready to face the world.

Breakfast was awful as usual. In the middle of the chaos there was a knock on the door. WPC Lynne Burnett. 'Call me Lynne,' she said. Everybody says that. Everybody wants to be your friend. I wish they'd just get on with their job. She told me that her first task was to look at my mail when it arrived.

'Will you be tasting my food as well?' I asked sarcastically.

She blushed so her birthmark became livid.

The phone rang and it was Clive, who was already at work, to say that Sebastian and his wife were coming to dinner on Saturday.

'But we haven't got a dining table,' I protested.

'Jens, the documentation we're preparing for next month's merger is over two thousand pages long. If I can coordinate that, I think you can organise a dinner party for a client.'

'Of course, I'll do it, I was just saying …' But Clive had rung off.

I put the phone down and looked round. Lynne was still there, of course.

'I'm going out to talk to my gardener,' I said frostily. 'I suppose you'd like to come and meet him.'

'Yes,' she said.

With his long plaited hair down his back, Francis may look like he should be in a caravan heading for Stonehenge, but in fact he's an absolute genius.

I introduced him to Lynne, who blushed. But then she seems to blush all the time.

'Lynne is here because someone's written me a mad letter,' I said. Francis looked puzzled, as well he might. 'And Francis is here full time for the next month at least,' I said.

'Are you doing this on your own?'

Francis smiled.

'Of course not,' I said. 'There's a whole subculture of gardeners drifting around London who come and work for Francis when he needs them.'

Lynne actually got out her notebook and wrote down the names of all the casual workers he used.

ALL IN ALL, it was a relief to leave the house. Or that's what I thought, until Lynne told me that she would be coming with me.

I was about to get cross when the doorbell rang. It was Stadler, so I protested to him instead. He just gave his official smile.

'It's for your own safety, Mrs Hintlesham. I'm just here to touch base and make a couple of routine checks. We want to compile a register of people you have dealings with. So, over the next day or so, I'd like you to sit down with Lynne and go through your address book, diary, that sort of thing. Is that all right?'

'Is this really necessary?'

'The more effective we are now, the quicker we can wind this up.'

FIRST STOP WAS at the reclamation centre for brass hooks. At least Lynne didn't come into the shop.

In Hampstead, she stood just outside the shops staring neutrally into windows full of women's clothes. God knows what the shop assistants made of her. I pretended to ignore her.

I had arranged to meet Laura for lunch, so I drove down the hill, Lynne's car in my rearview mirror. Laura was already waiting. It should have been fun but it wasn't. Lynne sat in the car outside eating a sandwich. I could see her as I fiddled with my rocket and roasted red pepper salad. She was reading a paperback. I couldn't quite concentrate on anything Laura was saying to me. I cut the lunch short, saying that I had to dash.

Next stop, Tony in Primrose Hill. Normally I love having my hair done, but today I felt hot, cross, out of sorts. My clothes stuck to me and I didn't like the way I looked after the cut. In the traffic on the way home a kind of road rage engulfed me, so that I revved impatiently at traffic lights. Lynne kept patiently behind me. I stuck out my tongue in the mirror, knowing she couldn't see it.

For the rest of the day she followed me like a faithful dog—the kind you want to kick. She followed me when I took Chris to play with a chum of his down the road. Then I had to collect the boys because it was Lena's night off. Wednesdays are always a nightmare. Josh was at the school after-hours computer club, which is always held in a Portakabin that stinks of boys' sweaty feet.

When I got there, Josh was sitting slumped in a chair and the rather sweet young man who came in to teach them every week was crouched down beside him, talking to him intently. I remembered that when I'd first met him a few weeks earlier, he told me that everybody in the club called him Hacker—Hack for short.

All the boys were still in their uniforms but Hack was wearing ancient torn jeans and a T-shirt with lots of Japanese writing on it. He was pretty young himself, with long, curly dark hair. He could have been one of the sixth-formers. As I drew nearer they both looked up and I saw that Josh had been crying. His eyes were red-rimmed. This startled me. I couldn't remember when I last saw Josh cry. It made him look much younger and more vulnerable.

'Josh! Are you all right? What's wrong?'

'Nothing.' The tone was cross rather than miserable.

'It's no big deal, Mrs Hintlesham,' Hack said.

'Jenny,' I corrected him, as I do every week. 'Call me Jenny.'

'Sorry. Jenny.'

'He seemed upset.'

Hack looked unconcerned. 'It's probably school, summer, all that stuff. Plus he just got whipped onscreen.'

'Maybe his blood sugar's low.'

'Yeah, that's right. Give him some sugar. Jenny.'

I looked at Hack. I couldn't tell if he was laughing at me.

HARRY WAS ROUND the other side of the school, in the large and draughty hall that doubled as the theatre once a year for the school play. When Josh and I went in, he was standing by the side of the stage with a yellow dress over his trousers and a feather boa round his neck. His face was scarlet. The sight of him seemed to cheer Josh up considerably. Up on the stage were a motley crew of boys, a couple of whom were also wearing frocks.

'Harry,' called a man with a small moustache and hair cut brutally short. 'Your lovely lady mother has arrived. Good evening, Mrs Hintlesham. You light up our dingy hall.'

'Jenny. Good evening.'

'Try to get your son to learn his lines, will you?'

'I'll try.'

She's dead. Of course. As I wanted. But I feel cheated of her. Forget it. Another one. Another she.

She wears too much make-up. It is like a mask, smoothed over her face. Everything about her face is glossy and cared-for—shining lips, dark lashes, creamy skin, neat and glossy hair. She is an image presented to the world. But she can't hide from me. I have watched her. I see beyond her smile that is not a real smile, and her laugh that, if you listen very carefully, is forced and brittle. She does not realise she is not happy. Only I realise. Only I can see inside her and release her.

Fate smiles on me. I see that now. At first I did not understand that I had become invisible. Nobody can see me. I can go on and on.

IT'S VERY LATE, almost midnight, but it's still indecently hot. The house is quiet. Clive still isn't back. Lena's out doing God knows what until God knows when. The boys are asleep. I've started to pack for Josh and Harry, who are catching the plane tomorrow. It's going to be quiet in the house over the next few weeks.

A second note has arrived. Just after lunch today, Lena found an envelope addressed to me lying on the doormat. I opened it straight away.

Dear Jenny,

You're a beautiful woman. You bite your top lip sometimes when you're thinking. You look at yourself and I look at you. But one day I'll look at you when you're dead.

It gave me the creeps a bit, naturally, but mainly I was furious. I'd had two days of Lynne hovering about being nice enough, but always hovering, always being just a bit irritating, a bit too determined not to be offended when I snapped at her. And then the police car parked outside. People always watching me, keeping an eye on my day. And this was all the good it had done. So when I had read the letter I went in search of her. She was on the phone. I stood in front of her waiting until she got embarrassed and hung up.

'I've got something you might be interested in,' I said, handing her the letter.

That lit a rocket under her. It was barely ten minutes before Stadler was sitting in my kitchen, staring at me across the table.

'On the mat, you said?' he asked, in a mumble.

'That's where Lena found it,' I said tartly. 'Clearly he's making private arrangements for his mail. To be honest, it makes me wonder what the point is of all this disruption if he can still walk up to the house and deliver a letter.'

'It's disappointing,' he said, pushing his hands through his hair. Handsome—and he knows it, my grandmother used to say of men like that. 'Did you see anybody approaching the house?'

'People have been approaching the house all day, tramping in and out. Forgive me for being stupid, but just spell out for me what you're actually *doing* about all of this?' I said.

He put his hand on mine and I let it lie there, hot and heavy. 'Mrs Hintlesham, Jenny, we're doing everything we can. We're doing forensic tests on all the letters, we're going through all your friends, acquaintances, contacts, to try to establish any connections between you and the, er, the other people who have been targeted by the writer of these letters. Until he is caught, we are making quite sure you are safe and protected.'

I took my hand away. 'Is there really any point in carrying on with all this fuss?'

Stadler looked at me with his dark eyes, almost too dark. 'This is serious,' he said. 'You've read the letters. This man has threatened to kill you. I think we need to make this environment more secure. All the work being done here must stop. Just for the time being.'

'Are you crazy?' I was aghast. 'These builders have a six-month waiting list. Jeremy's off to Germany next week. This isn't something I can just shut down and start up again when you feel like it.'

'I'm sorry, Jenny, but it's essential,' he said. 'I'm sorry we haven't caught this lunatic. But it's difficult. Normally there's a procedure, knocking on doors, looking for witnesses. But when a madman picks on somebody at random, there's no normal procedure. You just have to hope you get a break.'

I almost laughed but stayed coldly silent. This ridiculous man wanted me to say, 'There there,' because it was so hard to be a policeman.

'The alternative,' he continued, 'would be for you to move away from this house to somewhere more protected.'

The second prospect was even worse so I agreed, in a sort of cold fury. I asked when he wanted the builders to leave and he said straight away, while he was in the house. So I briskly ejected everybody. Then there was an awful hour of phone calls and half explanations to baffled people, attempts to make vague commitments for the future.

Three

I'm good at packing. I always pack for Clive when he has to go away for a few days. Men are hopeless at folding their shirts properly. Anyway, now I was packing for the boys, who were off into the wilds of Vermont for their summer camp. Three weeks of abseiling and windsurfing and sitting round campfires and, in Josh's case, probably eyeing up nubile young girls in skimpy shorts. I said as much to him as I was carefully laying his things into his case.

He looked glum. 'You just want us out of the house,' he muttered.

Everything he says now is in a mutter that I can't quite catch. It makes me feel as if I'm going deaf.

'Oh, Josh, you know you loved it last year. Don't say you're going to miss me,' I said teasingly.

He gazed at me. He's got huge dark brown eyes, and he can use them to look pathetically reproachful, like some donkey. I noticed how pale he was looking. 'You could do with some fresh air. As could this room. Don't you ever open your windows?'

He didn't answer, just stared moodily out at the street below.

I clapped my hands to wake him up. 'Your father is taking you to the airport in about an hour. Why don't you go and see Christo before you leave? He's going to miss you.'

Josh sat down at his computer. 'In a minute. I want to look at this new game. It's only just come.'

I started to leave the room then stopped. 'Josh? Will you miss me?'

Silence. 'Oh, for God's sake, Josh.' I was shouting now.

He turned sulkily. 'What?'

'Oh, nothing.'

I left him locked in a form of unarmed combat in which every blow sounded like a falling tree.

I HUGGED HARRY, though he seems to think that eleven is far too old to be hugged, and I kissed Josh's cheek. 'Have a wonderful time.'

'Mum . . .'

'Darlings, you've got to go, your father's in the car. Bye, darlings. Bye.' I waved to them until they were out of sight.

'Come on, Chris, it's just you and me for the next three weeks.'

'And Lena.'

'Well, yes, of course, Lena too. In fact, Lena's going to take you to the zoo soon. Mummy's got a busy day.'

A BUSY DAY cooking for this wretched dinner party that Clive had foisted on me. I couldn't remember the last time I had been alone in the house. It was oddly quiet, echoey. No banging of hammers, whistling of workmen as they slapped paint onto plaster. No ringing of the doorbell as gravel, or wallpaper lining, or electric cables were delivered. Well, almost alone. Lynne was always around somewhere.

At least I had loads of time. Lena wouldn't be back till teatime and Clive was going straight from the airport to a golf course. Because of the heat I had decided to go for a real summer meal. The canapés with wild mushrooms I'd have to do at the last minute but the main course—red mullet in a tomato and saffron sauce, to be served chilled—I could do now.

For pudding I was doing a huge apricot tart. It always looks spectacular, and apricots are gorgeous at this time of year. The wine and the champagne were already in the fridge. The butter was cut into little knobs. The brown rolls I was going to pick up this afternoon.

We were going to have to eat in the kitchen, but I pulled out the Chinese screen so the room was divided in half, and covered the table with a white tablecloth. With our silver cutlery and a mass of orange and yellow roses in a glass vase, it was a brilliant improvisation.

I had invited Emma and Jonathan Barton along as well. We've known them for ever. God knows what this Sebastian and his wife would be like. I had a picture of a fat City type, and a hard-bitten, bottle-blonde, power-dressing wife.

At six o'clock I had a long bath and washed my hair. Downstairs, I heard the door open and Lena come in with Chris. I put on a dressing gown and sat in front of my mirror. Lots of make-up this evening. Blusher. Dark grey eyeliner, plum-coloured lipstick. My favourite perfume behind my ears and on my wrists. It gives me courage.

I put on a long black dress with spaghetti straps, and high-heeled shoes. My diamond choker, my diamond earrings. I examined myself in the long mirror, turned slowly round so I could see myself from every angle. Nobody would think I was nearly forty. It takes a lot of effort to stay young.

I heard Clive come in. I had to go and say good night to Chris, make sure he was settled before everyone arrived. He was sunburnt and fretful. I left him listening to a Roald Dahl tape and prayed he wouldn't make a fuss during the meal. Clive was in the shower.

Downstairs I put a voluminous apron over my glad rags, and shredded lettuce into the salad bowl.

'Hello,' Clive said. He looked bronzed and gleaming in his suit; there was a sheen of success about him.

'You look smart. But I haven't seen that tie before,' I said. I wanted him to tell me how chic I looked tonight.

He fingered its knot. 'No, it's new.'

The doorbell rang.

NEITHER SEBASTIAN nor his wife Gloria were the least bit as I had expected. Sebastian was tall, with a startlingly bald head. He would have been rather distinguished-looking in a sinister, Hollywood way if he hadn't been so obviously on edge. There was a faint air of contempt in Clive's manner towards him, a touch of the bully. With a sudden flash of intuition, I realised that Clive was going to shaft Sebastian in his wretched takeover bid. Gloria was a City head-hunter, in her late twenties, and her blonde, almost silver hair hadn't come from a bottle after all. She had pale blue eyes, slim brown arms, neat ankles, and wore a perfectly simple white linen shift and very little make-up. She made me feel overdressed.

She knew how pretty she was, too. She kept lowering her lashes and giving secretive smiles.

'Nice tie,' she said to Clive, giving him that smile. It made me want to spill wine on her dress.

They had obviously met before—well, I suppose they would have done, given their jobs. She and Sebastian and Clive and Jonathan stood in a group and talked about the Footsie and the futures market, while Emma and I stood by like gooseberries.

'I always think the Footsie index is such a comical name,' I said loudly, determined not to be ignored.

Gloria turned politely towards me. 'Do you work in the City too?' she asked, although I knew she knew I didn't.

'Me, goodness, no.' I laughed loudly and took a gulp of champagne. 'I can't even add up my bridge hand. No, Clive and I decided that when we had children I would stop working outside the home. Do you have children?'

'No. What did you do before?'

'I was a model.'

'A hand model,' said Emma. My friend, Emma.

Jonathan poured more champagne in our glasses. Gloria was saying something softly to Clive, who was smiling down at her.

'WHAT A MANIPULATIVE GIRL,' I said to Clive, afterwards, when I was wiping off my make-up and he was cleaning his teeth.

He rinsed his mouth carefully. He looked at me, with my one eye on and one eye off. 'You're drunk,' he said.

I had a sudden, utterly disconcerting fantasy of slapping him, plunging my nail scissors into his stomach. 'Nonsense.' I laughed. 'I'm just tipsy, darling. I think it all went quite well, don't you?'

Four

My big vice is catalogues, mail order. That's mad in a way because it's not me at all. If there's one thing I believe in it's that the objects in your home have to be exactly right, and you need to touch things before you buy them, get a feeling of how they would look.

So I shouldn't bother with catalogues. The towels that look fluffy in the picture may feel synthetic when they arrive and be just different enough in shade to clash with the wooden frame of the mirror. But I can't resist flicking through catalogues and there'll always be something that catches my eye: trainers or a baseball jacket for the boys, or a clever pencil holder or a wastepaper basket that might look good up in the den. As often as not they'll end up stuffed in the loft, but sometimes they'll turn up trumps. In any case, it's such fun when they arrive. It's like an extra birthday. Better in some ways. If I was being sarcastic, I might say that while boys—and certain men who shall remain nameless—might forget a birthday, at least Next don't forget to deliver the lampshade you ordered, even if you don't care for it quite as much as you expected to.

All of which is a prelude to what happened on the Monday when I came downstairs in the middle of the morning and saw the normal dross on the mat. And among it was an envelope that said 'Special Offer Victorian Interiors'. So I opened it.

I bet you don't know how you open a letter. You do it every day but you don't think about it. I know because I've been forced to dwell on it. You pick up the letter, turn the front of it, the address side, away from you and prise one corner of the stuck-down flap away and tear it slightly. Then you insert your index finger and push it along the fold, tearing it all the way along. That's what I did, and the curious thing was that I didn't feel any pain. I opened the envelope and saw a dull glitter of metal and that the envelope seemed to be wet in places, wet and spotted with red.

It was only then that I felt not pain exactly but a dull ache in my right hand. I looked down and there seemed to be blood everywhere. I looked stupidly into the envelope and saw the flat pieces of dull metal stapled in a line along a piece of card. Razor blades.

I lifted up my hand and inspected it. There was a deep, livid cut in the index finger, pulsing, oozing out blood. That was when it began to hurt and I felt dizzy and cold and hot all at once. My legs gave way and I slipped down and half lay there. I don't how long I was like that. Just a few minutes, probably, before Lena came down and ran to get help, and Lynne appeared with her mouth in the shape of a perfect O.

She is wearing cream slacks and a maroon shirt. Her hand is bandaged, and she holds it in her healthy hand, carefully, as if it were a wounded bird. She looks older already. I am putting on the years.

No earrings today. No perfume. Reddish lipstick that makes her face look pallid. She puts her hand against her heart. She wants to feel her life beating against her palm. She was so carefully held together and now she is coming apart. Fear turns people inside out.

Sometimes I want to laugh. It has turned out so well. This is what I have been waiting for.

'DOES IT HURT?' Detective Chief Inspector Links leaned towards me. Too close. But at the same time he seemed far away.

'They gave me pills.'

'Good. We need to ask you some questions.'

'I've had enough of your questions. It seems simple enough to me.

There's a man out there who keeps coming to the house. So can't you just arrest him while he's posting envelopes through the door?'

Links took a deep breath. 'It's not that easy. If someone really sets his mind on doing something, then—'

'Then what?'

'We want to go through some names.'

'Go on, then.'

Lynne passed a file to Links, who opened it. There was a list of names, mostly with photographs attached. It seemed almost funny to be looking at this list of drab people I'd never met.

'Who are they? Criminals?'

Links looked uncomfortable. 'I can't tell you everything,' he said, 'for legal reasons. But what I can say is that we're trying to establish any connections there may be between you and, er . . .' He seemed to be searching for the right word. 'Areas where similar problems have been reported. I mean, this estate agent, Guy Brand, to take just one example. I'm not suggesting anything, but an estate agent has access to many properties. And you have recently moved house.'

I looked. 'He might be familiar. But, then, estate agents have a sort of look in common, don't they?'

'So you might have met him?'

'I don't know about *that*,' I said. 'I just mean that if you proved that I *had* met him, then I wouldn't think it was impossible.'

Links didn't look very satisfied with that answer. 'I can leave these pictures with you, if you like.'

'Why would he do this?' I asked. 'Go to all this trouble for something so nasty?'

For the first time Links looked distressed and unable to conceal it. 'I don't know.'

'Well, I hardly need reminding of that, do I?' I responded tartly.

At that very moment there were about eight policemen crawling round the house like ants. There was practically nowhere I could go to be on my own. I raised my voice. 'What I want to know is what your lot are doing while I'm racking my brains to help you?'

'I can assure you that we are all working hard too,' he replied. Actually, he did look a bit weary, when I came to think about it.

I went into the bathroom, locked the door, and splashed cold water on my face with one hand. I was looking a bit ragged, what with one thing and another. I had to admit that this was getting me down. I wished Clive would ring back so I could speak to someone who wasn't a policeman. I had already told him about my hand and he had been very shocked but he hadn't come rushing back, as I had hoped, bearing flowers.

Then Detective Inspector Stadler wanted to talk to me about the details of my daily life. We had to retreat into the sitting room because Mary wanted to wash the kitchen floor.

On this hot day he had taken off his jacket and his shirtsleeves were rolled up to just below the elbows. When he asked me questions, he always looked me directly in the eyes, which gave me the feeling he was trying to catch me out.

'This person,' he said, 'obviously knows that you used to be a hand model.'

'Maybe.'

He picked up two books, and I saw that they were my diary and address book. We started with my diary. He leafed through each page and fired questions at me about names, places, appointments.

That was my hairdresser, I said, and that was a check-up with the dentist for Harry. That was lunch with Laura, Laura Offen. I spelled out names, described shops, explained arrangements with handymen and French tutors and tennis coaches. We went further and further back, through events I had forgotten. He kept asking where was Clive when this happened, when that happened.

Finally Stadler closed my diary and picked up my address book. We went through every blessed name. As if that wasn't enough, he produced Clive's accounts for the house. I tried to tell him that I didn't deal with any of that, it was all down to Clive. But he didn't seem to hear. I couldn't make head nor tail of the numbers. I certainly couldn't remember the quarry tiles being that expensive. Dreadful how it all adds up.

When we'd finished, he looked at me, and I thought, This man knows more about me than anyone in the world except Clive.

'Is this all relevant?' I asked.

'That's the problem, Mrs Hintlesham. We don't know. For the moment we just need information. Lots of it.'

I rang Clive again. His secretary said he'd popped out. Sorry, she said, though she didn't sound sorry at all.

DR SCHILLING WAS DIFFERENT. She looked at my hand, unrolling the bandage and holding my fingers in her slim cool ones. She said she was very sorry, as if she were personally apologising for it. To my horror, I suddenly wanted to cry, but I certainly wasn't going to do that in front of her.

'I want to ask you some questions, Jenny.'

'What about?'

'Can we talk about you and Clive? Do you mind that he's away so much?'

'No.'

She waited, but I didn't say anything else.

'Do you think that he's faithful to you?'

I gave a sigh. 'Since Detective Stadler now knows when my next period is due, I suppose I may as well tell you about my sex life as well. If you really want to know, just after Harry was born he had a—a thing.'

'How long for?'

'I'm not exactly sure. A year, maybe. Eighteen months.'

'So it wasn't just a thing, was it? It was rather more serious than that.'

'He was never going to leave me. She was just extra. Men are such clichés, aren't they? I was tired, I had put on some weight.' I touched the skin beneath my eyes. 'I was getting older.'

'Jenny,' she said gently, 'you were only, let's see, in your late twenties when Harry was born.'

'Whatever.'

'All right. Have there been others?'

I shrugged. 'Perhaps. I don't really want to know, thank you very much. If he has some stupid fling, I'd prefer he kept it to himself.' The unbidden image of Clive looking down at Gloria entered my mind. I pushed it away.

'Do you and your husband have a satisfactory sex life?'

I shook my head at her. 'Sorry,' I said. 'I can't.'

'All right.' Once again, she was unexpectedly gentle. 'Do you think that your husband loves you?'

'That's a big word.' I took a breath. 'No.'

'Likes you?'

I stood up. 'I've had enough,' I said. 'You're going to walk away from this conversation and write it up in concise notes, but I'm going to live with it, and I don't want to. Clive isn't sending me razor blades, is he, so why do you want to know all this? Now, I'm rather busy, so if you'll excuse me . . .'

Dr Schilling left and I stood alone in the drawing room. I felt as if I had been turned upside-down and emptied all over the floor.

Five

I could hear the wind rippling in the trees outside. I wanted to open the windows, let the night breeze blow through all the rooms, but I couldn't. I mustn't. Everything had to be closed and locked. I had to be secure. The air inside was stale, secondhand. Heavy, hot, dead air.

I was sweating. I turned my pillow over to find a cooler patch. What time was it? I sat up in bed and squinted across at the luminous numbers on the alarm clock. Half past two and Clive still hadn't come home. Lena was out till tomorrow morning, staying with her boyfriend, so it was just me in the house, me and Chris and, outside, a police car. My finger throbbed, my throat hurt, my eyes stung. It was quite impossible to sleep.

I padded across to Chris's room. He was sleeping with one foot tucked under the other knee and with his arms thrown up like a ballet dancer. The duvet was in a heap on the floor beside him. Maybe, I thought, I should take him to Mummy and Daddy's house down in Hassocks. Maybe I should go there myself, get away from all this ghastliness. I could just leave, get in the car and drive away. Why not?

I walked to the top of the stairs and looked down. The light was on in the hall, but all the rooms were dark. I gulped. Suddenly it was hard to breathe. Stupid. This was stupid, stupid, stupid. I was safe, absolutely safe. There were two men outside, all the doors and windows were locked, double-locked.

I went into the room that would one day be a spare bedroom, and turned on the light. Half a wall was papered, the rest just lined. The rolls of wallpaper were stacked in the corner, waiting beside the stepladder and the trestle table. The bed was in pieces on the floor. There was a hot bubble of rage in my chest; if I opened my mouth it would come out as a scream. I pressed my lips together. I had to put my life in order. Nobody else was going to do it for me, that was clear. I would just have to rely on me.

I picked up the box of wallpaper paste and read the instructions. It all seemed simple enough. I would start with this room and then I'd move through my life, putting it all back together again, just like it was before.

CLIVE ARRIVED HOME about half an hour later. I heard the key in the door and heard him take off his shoes and pad into the kitchen, where he turned on the tap. I didn't stop what I was doing. I didn't have time. I was going to finish this before morning.

'Jenny,' he called, when he went into our bedroom. 'Where are you?'

I didn't reply. I slapped the paste onto the wallpaper. The bandage on my hand was soaked and my finger throbbed harder than ever.

'What on earth do you think you're doing?' He stood in the doorway in his white shirt and red boxer shorts and the socks that bloody Father Christmas had given him last year. 'Jens, it's the middle of the night.'

'So? What does it matter if it's the middle of the night? If nobody else is going to do it, I'm going to do it myself. And you can be pretty sure that nobody else is going to do it. Had a good day, did you? Good day at the office till three in the morning, darling?'

'Jens, stop this now. It's all crooked anyway. And you've got glue in your hair. Come off that ladder now.'

'The master's voice,' I hissed.

'Jenny, I'm going to phone Dr Thomas.'

I looked down at him. 'Everyone uses that tone of voice with me, as if there were something the matter with me. There's nothing the matter with me. They just need to catch this person and we'll be back to normal. And you'—I flourished my gluey brush at him so a drop fell on his frowning, upturned face—'you're my husband, in case you had forgotten, darling. For better or for worse, and this is for worse.'

'Come to bed.'

'I'm not in the least bit tired, thank you.' And indeed I wasn't. I was fizzing with energy and rage. 'But if you want to do anything to help, you can phone Dr Schilling and tell her it is at the very best dull, thank you very much. She'll understand what I mean. You look pathetic in your socks,' I added spitefully.

'All right. Have it your own way.' His tone was a mixture of indifference and contempt. 'I'm going to bed now. You do what you want. That strip is on back to front, by the way.'

AT SIX, CLIVE left for work. He called goodbye as he left, but I didn't bother to reply. Chris got himself up and I shouted at him to get his own breakfast.

A new pretend best friend, a small woman who introduced herself as WPC Page, marched round the house, checking all the windows. She came into the spare room and said good morning in a careful voice, as if pretending that it was quite normal to find me decorating in my nightclothes. I ignored her.

When I had finished the walls, I had a bath. I applied new varnish to my nails and put on more make-up than usual, but I couldn't keep my hand steady. The lipstick kept going outside my lips, which gave me the look of a drunken old woman. I got it right eventually. It was me again in the mirror. Jennifer Hintlesham: immaculate.

I TOLD LENA to take Chris to the London Aquarium and then buy him lunch. Chris wanted to stay with me but I blew him a kiss and told him not to be silly, he would have a lovely day. I gave Mary a week's wages and told her she shouldn't bother to return.

I made a list. Two lists. The first was of things to do in the house and didn't take me long. The second was for Links and Stadler and was more complicated.

Dr Schilling and Stadler arrived together, looking grave and mysterious. I asked them both to come into the kitchen.

'It's all right,' I said to them. 'Don't look so anxious. I've decided to tell you everything. I tried ringing the Haratounian woman.'

Dr Schilling looked at Stadler, stared at him as if she were ordering him to tell me something. Stadler frowned back.

'And I've made a list of men who I think act oddly towards me.' I waved it at them. 'It's rather long, I must say. But I've put asterisks by the side of the oddest ones, to help you.'

Stadler took the list out of my hand.

'Can I have a cigarette?' I asked him. 'I know you smoke.'

He took a packet out of his pocket, took out two cigarettes, lit both, then handed me one. It felt oddly intimate.

'Clive's friends are odd,' I said. 'They look respectable, but I bet they all have affairs, or want to have them. Men are like animals. They have to be put into cages in order to keep them from running all over the place. Women are the zoo-keepers. We try and tame them. When I see the fathers at Harry's school, or when I've gone into Josh's computer club. There are some pretty odd fish there. And . . .' There was something else I was going to say.

Dr Schilling laid a hand on my shoulder. 'Jenny, come with me and I'm going to make you some breakfast,' she said.

'Whatever. I don't care. God, this kitchen's in a mess, isn't it? Everything is in such a mess. Everything. How on earth am I going to do it all, with nobody to help?'

Things got a bit misty after that. I said I wanted to go out shopping and I think I even started looking for my coat. But I couldn't find it and people all around me kept telling me not to. Their voices seemed to be coming at me from all directions. Then they stopped but I felt them gripping my arm. I was in my bedroom and Dr Schilling was saying something I couldn't understand. I felt a pain in my arm and then everything faded into darkness and silence, as if I were at the bottom of a deep dark pit. When I woke up, a policewoman was sitting by the bed. I wanted to go back to sleep, just to be unconscious, but I couldn't make it happen.

After a time Dr Schilling and Stadler came into the room.

Dr Schilling came forward clutching one of my French earthenware mugs. 'I brought you some coffee,' she said. 'Black. The way you like it.'

She pulled up a chair and Stadler stepped forward to the end of the bed.

I sat up to take the warm mug in the hollow of my hands. The bandage made it a little awkward but protected me against the heat.

'It feels like visiting time in hospital,' I said, with more than a trace of sarcasm. Neither of them spoke. They just kept looking at me with ghastly expressions of sensitivity and sympathy. If there's one thing I cannot stand it is being pitied.

'Where's Clive?'

'He saw you during the night. It's Wednesday. He had to go to work but I'll ring him in a minute and tell him how you are.'

'You must be pretty sick of me,' I said to Dr Schilling.

'That's funny,' she said, 'because I've just been thinking you must be pretty sick of me. We've been talking about you.'

'I bet you have,' I said.

'Not in a bad way. One of the things we've been talking about . . .' She glanced across at Stadler as she said this, but he didn't seem to be paying any attention. 'I feel, we feel, that we may not have been open enough with you and I want to do something to correct that, Jenny.' She paused. 'Firstly I want to apologise if you feel that I've been intrusive. You have become an object of somebody's obsessive attention. One of the ways of catching the person is to find out what it is that has attracted the attention and that can sometimes mean that I become pretty intrusive myself.'

I gave her a sort of sarcastic frown, if such a thing is possible.

'I suppose you've discovered that I'm completely batty,' I said.

Dr Schilling didn't smile. 'You mean yesterday?' she said. 'You're under a great deal of pressure. I want you to know that we appreciate that.'

I held up my bandaged hand and looked at it. 'I don't want you to be sympathetic with me,' I said with some bitterness. 'I want you to make all this go away.'

'I know,' she said. 'Detective Inspector Stadler is going to talk to you about that.'

She moved her chair to the side and Stadler shuffled forward. He had the expression of a kindly local constable giving little tots some road-safety advice. 'You're wondering why we can't just catch this man and I know what you mean. I'm not going to give you the standard lecture but the fact is that most crimes are bloody easy to solve, because most people don't put much effort into them. But the sort of person who does this is different. He's not a genius but this is his hobby and he puts a lot of effort into it.'

'He's come to the house. Under your noses.'

'That's crucial,' Dr Schilling interrupted. 'He could just attack women if he wanted. But for him the point is to demonstrate his power and control, so the main thing is to be aware of your surroundings, of anything new or out of place. He wants to show he can get things to you.'

I gave a snort. 'It's not so much a matter of new things arriving,' I said. 'It's more the old things disappearing.'

Stadler looked up sharply. 'What do you mean?'

'Nothing that will be of any help to you. Have you never moved house? It took two pantechnicons to shift us and I'm convinced that there is a small van somewhere going round the M25 with all the objects that didn't make it. Shoes, bits of food mixers, my favourite blouse, you name it.'

'This was all during the move?' asked Stadler.

'Of course,' I said. 'This man couldn't have stolen all of that unless he'd pulled up with a van. Even you would have noticed that.'

'Still . . .' said Stadler, looking lost in thought. He leaned over to Dr Schilling and whispered to her. Then he looked up. 'Jenny, could you do us a favour?'

IT LOOKED LIKE a car-boot sale organised by a blind madman. After phoning ahead, the two of them had taken me to a special room at the police station where, Stadler had told me, there would be objects on display. In the car, Dr Schilling put her hand on mine in a gesture that gave me the creeps and said that I should just look at the objects and say whatever came into my mind. The only thing that came into my mind was what a wretched lot of hocus-pocus it all sounded.

The stuff itself almost made me laugh. A comb, some rather tacky pink knickers, a teddy, a stone, a whistle, some definitely pornographic playing cards.

'Honestly,' I said. 'I can't see what you expect ...'

And at that very moment I felt as if I had been punched in the stomach and given an electric shock all at the same time. There it was. The funny little locket that Clive had bought for me. I remembered Brighton on our first anniversary. We had walked in all those little dinky shopping streets just away from the front and spotted it in a jeweller's. Clive had walked in and bought it just like that. That night in the hotel he took all my clothes off but left the locket on. It's mad, the things that stick in your mind. I almost had to stop myself crying. I picked it up, felt the familiar weight in my palm.

'Nice, isn't it?' said Stadler.

'It's mine,' I said.

'What?' he said, almost in a gasp.

'Clive gave it to me,' I said, as if in a dream. 'It was lost. There's a fiddly clip at the back that opens it up. There's a lock of my hair inside. Look, there.'

He stared. 'Yes,' he said.

He and Dr Schilling were looking at each other, open-mouthed.

Then Stadler ran out of the room.

I DIDN'T UNDERSTAND at all. Not anything. I looked over at Dr Schilling, as if she could tell me what was going on, but she just gave her meaningless, reassuring smile, the one that gave me the shivers.

'I want to go home,' I said, not really meaning it, but needing to say something to break the silence in the drab little room.

'Soon,' said Dr Schilling.

'Is anybody going to tell me how my locket got here?'

'I'm sure they'll—'

But then she was interrupted by Stadler coming back into the room with Links. They both looked intensely agitated as they sat down opposite me. Links picked up the locket by its chain.

'When did you lose this, Mrs Hintleshaw?'

'It's hard to say. I remember wearing it to a concert. That was on the 9th of June, the day before my mother's birthday. A couple of weeks later I wanted to wear it to Clive's works bash, at the end of June, but I couldn't find it.'

Stadler looked down at a notebook in his lap and nodded as if he were satisfied.

There was a hush in the room, then I raised my voice: 'Won't someone please tell me what is going on? Have you caught him? Is that it?'

'Mrs Hintlesham,' said Links, 'can we just establish—'

'Not now,' said Dr Schilling suddenly. She stood up. 'I'm taking Jenny home. She's been under great strain. Later.'

She put a hand under my elbow and I stood up.

Everybody was behaving oddly. Nobody told me anything, of course, but Dr Schilling came back with me, and Links and Stadler pitched up soon afterwards. They were all muttering things and looking at me, then looking away when I caught their eye.

'Do you think you could phone your husband, Mrs Hintlesham?' asked Stadler. 'We need to clarify a couple of points.'

'We've got a drinks party this evening. An important one.'

'The quicker we can talk to him, the quicker he'll be free.'

I picked up the phone. 'He's going to be irritated,' I said.

He was very irritated.

A BIT LATER the phone rang. It was Josh and Harry, calling from America, although they sounded as if they were just round the corner and at any moment would come charging into the house. Harry told me he had learned how to sailboard. Josh asked me how things were at home. 'Are the police still there?'

'I think they're making progress.'

'Do we have to stay out here another two weeks?'

'Don't be silly, darling, you're having a lovely time. Oh, and remember to tell Harry that there are spare batteries for his Walkman in your backpack.'

'Yeah.'

I put the phone down, feeling the conversation hadn't been a success. Christo trailed past, dragging a blanket after him. I felt a sharp pang of guilt when I saw his blotchy, sullen face.

'Hello, Christo,' I said to him. 'Can Mummy have a hug?'

He turned to me. 'I'm not Christo,' he said. 'I'm Alexander. And you're not my mummy.' Lena called to him and he raised his yellow head. 'Coming, Mummy,' he shouted, darting a glance of triumph at me as he went.

DR SCHILLING ORDERED me to eat the omelette she made. I ate it in a few forkfuls, hardly chewing it. I hadn't realised how famished I was.

Then there was a key in the lock, a door slamming loudly, heavy footsteps in the hall. 'Jenny. Jens, where are you?'

Grace Schilling stood up at the same time as me. Stadler and Links were there before us. We all converged by the staircase.

'What's going on?' Clive scowled.

'We'd like you to come with us,' said Links.

Clive stared. 'What do you mean?' he said.

'We want to take a statement. It would be better.'

Clive looked at his watch. 'For God's sake,' he said. 'This had better be important.' He turned to me before leaving. 'Phone Jan and tell her something, anything that doesn't make us both look stupid. Go to Becky's party and make sure you're jolly, as if everything is perfectly normal, do you hear?' I put a hand on his arm but he shook it off violently. 'I'm sick of this,' he said.

I LOOKED AROUND the room at all the women in their black dresses and all the men in their dark suits. I knew most of them by sight, at least, but I couldn't think of a single thing to say. I felt quite empty.

Clive didn't arrive and I felt more and more out of place standing there fiddling with the glass in my hand, so it was a relief rather than a hideous embarrassment when Becky Richards told me there was a policeman at the door for me.

Stadler was there with a uniformed officer I hadn't seen before.

'Sorry to bother you,' he said. 'I was sent to tell you that your husband won't be along. Mr Hintlesham's still being interviewed.'

'Oh,' I said. We stood there on Becky's doorstep looking at each other. 'I don't really want to go back to the party.'

'We can run you home, if you like,' Stadler said.

Back at the house, he walked up the steps with me. As I turned the key in the lock it felt, for an absurd moment, as if the two of us were coming back from an evening out together.

'Will Clive be back this evening?' I said firmly, as if to show myself how stupid that was.

'I'm not sure,' Stadler said. 'We need him to corroborate some details of the investigation. Oh, and there's one other thing. We would like to conduct a more detailed search of your house tomorrow.'

'Where do you want to search?'

'Your husband's study.'

CLIVE'S STUDY. It had been the first room we had made habitable in the new house, which was a bit rich because nobody inhabited it except Clive. It was his private lair. It wasn't exactly kept locked and bolted, but the boys weren't allowed to enter and there was a feeling of something forbidden when—after getting undressed and putting on my nightie and dressing gown—I went in.

My husband's study. What was there here that could possibly be of any interest? I wasn't going to search through his things, of course. The idea of doing that seemed terribly disloyal. I just wanted to have a look. It might be important if I had to speak on his behalf. That's what I told myself.

The study contained two filing cabinets, one tall and brown, the other short, stubby, grey metal. I opened them both and flicked through the folders and papers but they were incredibly boring. Mortgage documents, endless receipts and bills and guarantees. There was nothing that could possibly be of any interest to the police.

I sat in his desk chair and pulled out the desk drawers on either side. Chequebooks, new and empty. A whole lot of bumf from Matheson Jeffries, where Clive works. All blessedly tedious.

The bottom right-hand drawer contained some large bulky brown envelopes. I examined the top one. It was full of handwritten letters. The same handwriting. I looked at the end of one of them, a long letter on three sheets of paper. Signed Gloria. I knew I mustn't read them and what I really ought to do was replace them and go to bed and put all this out of my mind. At the same time it occurred to me that in the morning the police might be reading these letters for reasons of their own. Shouldn't I have some idea of what they contained?

I compromised by skimming the letters but words seemed to jump up off the page at me: darling . . . I miss you desperately . . . thoughts of last night . . . counting the hours. Funnily enough my initial feeling was not anger against Clive or even against Gloria. At first I just felt contemptuous at the triteness of her letters. Then I thought of her at dinner when I had last seen her, leaning over to whisper something to him, and my cheeks burned. I shouldn't have read them; it would do nothing but harm, more pain, more humiliation.

Just one more paragraph. The last one of that most recent letter. I needed to know where I stood.

And now I must close, my darling. I'm writing this at work and it's time to go home. I can't bear not seeing you but in September we'll have Geneva. Geneva. A business trip. He hadn't mentioned that yet.

It seems awful to admit, but sometimes I hate her too, nearly as much as you. I laid the letter down and swallowed hard, but the lump in my throat wouldn't go away. So he hated me. I looked down at the letter again. *But we mustn't. We'll work things out and be together somehow. We will find a way. All my loveliest love, Gloria.*

I carefully put the letters back in the envelope. I looked at the other stuffed envelopes in the drawer and lifted the top one. Underneath it was a photograph. It was a woman but it wasn't Gloria. She looked different from any woman I knew. Fun. Small and slim and very young. Dark blonde hair, short skirt, strange blouse. All quite casual-looking. I thought for a mad moment that she looked nice, that she could have been my friend, and then I felt angry and sick and I couldn't bear any more. I put the photograph back under the second bundle and closed the drawer. I left the room, remembering to switch off the light.

I was in the dark. My life was the dark place. I had thought there was someone out there who wanted to harm me, and that had seemed terrifying enough, but now I realised nowhere was safe. Not with the person I had been married to for fifteen years, not in my own house, my own bed. Nowhere.

Josh and Harry were in America, in some tent up a mountain, far from home. Christo was pretending I wasn't his mother at all. And Clive hated me: that's what he had said to Gloria.

Maybe my husband wanted me dead.

That was ridiculous. Mad, a mad thing to think. Except, why were the police holding him for so long?

At dawn, after a night of jumbled dreams, I went into Christo's room and sat beside him while he slept. Today, I thought, I would arrange to send him with Lena to my parents. I should have done it before. This was no place for a child to be.

THE POLICE ARRIVED early, three of them who moved into Clive's study like a task force. I pretended they weren't there.

I made Christo and Lena a cooked breakfast, though Christo said it was all yuck and couldn't he have his chocolate flakes instead?

He didn't ask where his father was, because Clive was usually gone before he woke up anyway. Back after he had gone to sleep.

The kitchen was a mess. The whole house was a mess. I'd clean it tomorrow. Not today.

'Are you all right, Mrs Hintlesham?' Lena asked me.

'Fine.' I put my fingers against my face; my skin felt thin and old. 'I slept badly . . .' I trailed off.

'I want to watch the cartoons.'

'Not now, Christo.'

I turned to Lena. 'Today is a bit complicated,' I said vaguely. 'Maybe you and Christo could go to the park, take a picnic, go to the bouncy castle.'

'I don't wanner picnic.'

'Please, Christo.'

'Come on, Chrissy, let's choose your clothes.' Lena stood up. No wonder Christo loved her. She never got cross.

I put my head in my hands. Dust and dirt everywhere. No one to help me. Clive in the police station, answering questions. Do you hate your wife, Mr Hintlesham? How much do you hate her? Enough to send her razor blades?

THE POLICE LEFT, carrying boxes. All except Stadler, crumpled and sweaty, with stubble on his face, looking as if he hadn't gone to bed.

'Can I just ask a question, Jenny?' He always called me Jenny now, as if we were friends, lovers. We walked downstairs to the kitchen.

'It's just a detail,' he said. 'Can you remember where you were on Sunday, July the 18th?'

I made a feeble attempt to recall and gave up. 'You've got my diary, haven't you?'

'Yes. All you wrote on that day was "Collect fish".'

'Oh, yes. I remember. I was at home. Cooking, preparing things.'

'With your husband.'

'No,' I said.

Stadler gave a visible start, then a smile of suppressed triumph. 'Do you know where he was?'

'He had to go out, he told me. Urgent business.'

I remembered the day clearly. It had been Lena's day off. Harry and Josh had lounged around and squabbled, before going out with separate friends; Christo had watched telly most of the day, and gone to bed early, worn out by heat and bad temper, and I had sat in the kitchen with the ruined day behind me and my beautiful meal spread out on the table, and he hadn't come back.

'Can you be precise about times?'

'He left too early to be able to go to the supermarket. He came back at about midnight.'

Stadler startled me by taking my hand and holding it. 'Jenny,' he said softly, his voice like a caress, 'I can tell you that all of this will soon be over, if that is of any comfort to you.'

I felt myself going red. 'Oh,' was all I could manage in response, like some village idiot.

'I'll be back soon,' he said.

I didn't want him to go, but I couldn't say that, of course. I pulled my hand away. 'Good,' I said.

I WANDERED FROM ROOM to room. Why had I ever liked this house? It was ugly, cold-hearted, unsatisfactory. I would move from here, start again. Maybe we could move to the country, to a small cottage with roses round the door. We could have a tree the boys could climb.

I wished Josh would call me, I wanted to tell him that he didn't need to stay there if he hated it so very much.

The doorbell rang.

I WAS UNABLE to speak. I just shook my head as if I could clear the confusion away.

Links leaned closer as if I were shortsighted and deaf as well as mad. 'Your husband, Clive Hintlesham,' he said, as if it had to be spelled out, detail by detail. 'An hour ago. We charged him with the murder of Zoë Haratounian on the morning of the 18th of July , 1999.

'I don't understand,' I cried. 'Who is this woman, anyway? What's she got to do with Clive? With me and the letters?'

Links looked uneasy. 'I can't tell you in detail,' he said, 'but it seems that your husband was having an affair with her. We believe he gave her your locket. Her photograph was among his possessions.'

I remembered the photograph I had seen last night: an eager, laughing face. I gulped, and a wave of nausea swept over me. 'That doesn't mean he would kill her.'

'Miss Haratounian also received letters like yours. Written by the same person. We believe that your husband threatened her, then killed her.'

I gazed at him. A jigsaw was beginning to click together, but the picture that emerged made no sense. 'Are you saying that Clive was the person writing those letters to me?'

Links was silent for some time, visibly trying to make up his mind. 'This is very painful,' he said. 'I wish you could be spared it. But it is possible that he wanted to rid himself of this woman. Then, having done that, he must have realised that nobody knew he had met her. For that reason, if you were . . . well, targeted by the person who did that murder, he wouldn't be a suspect.'

'Has he admitted it?'

'He still denies even knowing Miss Haratounian,' Links said drily.

'I want to see him.'

'YOU DON'T BELIEVE this, Jenny? You can't possibly believe this ludicrous charge?' In his voice I heard a mixture of anger and fear. His face was red and unwashed, his clothes were stained.

I gazed at him. 'Why shouldn't I believe it?'

'Jens, it's me, Clive, your husband. I know things have been shaky recently, but it's me.'

'Shaky,' I repeated. 'Shaky.'

'We've been married fifteen years, Jens. You know me. Tell them it's ridiculous. I was with you that day. You know I was, Jens.'

'Tell me about Gloria,' I said. 'Is it true?'

He flushed and tried to speak, then stopped.

'I don't think there's anything more to talk about. Goodbye.'

'You'll see,' he shouted. 'You'll see and then you'll be sorry. You are making the biggest mistake of your whole stupid little life.' His fists came down on the table between us and the moon-faced policeman at the door stood up. 'I will make you suffer for it, see if I don't.'

Seven

A day of frenetic activity stopped me from dwelling on things too much and the next morning as I sat at the kitchen table with Lynne, I felt almost calm. There was a feeling of winding down and farewells.

'So you've been busy?' Lynne asked. 'When do you leave?'

'I'm flying to Boston this evening.'

'Do the boys know yet?'

I very nearly laughed at this. 'The idea of informing Josh over the phone that his father . . . No, I'm sure that Dr Schilling would recommend doing it face to face.'

'It's probably better.'

'I spent most of the afternoon on the phone to my architect and Francis, my brilliant gardener. They're going to come and patch things up, slap some white paint on the walls, put some shrubs in the garden. Then I'm putting the house on the market.'

Lynne's eyes widened in surprise. 'Are you sure?' she said.

'I can hardly bear the sight of it. I've been unhappy here. I suppose it's not the house's fault, but still . . .'

'Have you talked to Dr Schilling?'

'Why should I talk to her?' I said, a bit belligerently. I stopped myself. 'I'm sorry.'

'That's all right.'

'In fact, all in all, this probably hasn't been the most enjoyable job you've ever had to do. Trying to look after a bad-tempered, miserable woman.'

Lynne looked serious. 'You shouldn't say that. It was awful. We all felt terrible for you. We still do.'

'I just keep remembering details of our marriage and wondering how it could have happened. What had I done to him? What had that poor girl, Zoë, done except climb into bed with him?'

Lynne gave a shrug. 'The last murder I dealt with, a fourteen-year-old boy killed his granny because she wouldn't lend him the money to buy a lottery ticket. It's like one of my sergeants used to say, you don't need qualifications to be a murderer.'

'So he *could* have done it. Do you think he'll be found guilty?'

Lynne paused before speaking. 'The Crown Prosecution Service say that we've got to be confident of a seventy-five per cent chance of conviction before we charge anybody. As far as I know, there was no hesitation about charging your husband. We've got the clear connection with the dead girl, Zoë, and his attempts to lie about it. There's the lack of an alibi. His threats against you, his affair and motivation. He won't get off,' she said firmly.

We drank our coffee.

'Have you packed?' she asked.

'I'm only taking a small bag.'

She looked at her watch. 'I think I'd better go,' she said.

'I'll feel strange being unsupervised,' I said.

'You won't be entirely unsupervised. We'll keep an eye.'

I pulled a slightly sarcastic face. 'Does that mean you're not entirely sure about Clive?'

'Just to see you're all right.'

And she was gone.

I DIDN'T HAVE LUNCH. No time. Packing was a little more complicated than I had suggested to Lynne and the phone kept ringing as well. I had rather a long conversation with Clive's lawyer. Several people rang for Josh: his violin teacher, that fellow Hack from the computer club, who said Josh had asked him to drop a game round, and a couple of my friends, or Clive's friends, who had clearly heard that something funny was going on. In each case I put them off with a series of excuses that didn't quite amount to barefaced lies.

The state I was in I thought I'd better leave in hugely good time for the plane, so I ordered a cab and ran around the house in a frenzy of closing windows and half closing curtains. One thing more. Long transatlantic flight. Soft shoes. I had a pair of nice blue canvas slip-ons. Where were they? Bedroom cupboard. At the top. I ran upstairs. In the bedroom—*our* bedroom I would once have said—I looked around. I could see nothing I'd forgotten.

There was a knock at the door. I don't mean the front door. A rap at the bedroom door.

'Mrs Hintlesham?'

'What?' I said, startled.

A face peered round the door. I was completely baffled for a moment. You know, when you see a face out of its normal setting. A good-looking young man in jeans and a T-shirt and a black work jacket. Long dark hair.

'Hack. What are you . . .?'

'That's not my real name. That just impresses the boys. I'm Morris,' he said. 'Morris Burnside.'

'Well, Morris Burnside, I'm in a bit of a rush. I'm off to the airport.'

'The game,' he said, brandishing a gaudy package. 'I rang, remember? Sorry, the door was open and I wandered in.'

'Oh. Well, you're lucky you caught me. The cab will be here any moment.'

He was panting, as if he'd been running. 'Yes, I'm really glad because . . . It's not just the game. I saw the evening paper. There's something in it about your husband being charged. You see, I've been thinking about it and Mr Hintlesham couldn't have done it.'

'That's very nice of you, er, Morris, but . . .'

'No, it's not just that. When they find your body they'll know he can't have done it.'

'What?' I asked dully, and felt a wave of alarm.

He was close to me and there was a very sudden movement, something flashing over my head and drawn tight around my neck. He was now right against me, his breath hot on my face, looking down on me.

'You can't speak,' he said to me, almost in a whisper. His face was so close to mine he could have kissed me. 'You can hardly breathe. One pull on this and you'll be dead.'

That was the last thing I was ever going to see, his face, and I wanted to ask why and I couldn't.

He tightened the cord again and held it in place with one hand. He reached to one side and the other hand reappeared. I saw a blade.

'I love you, Jenny,' he said.

All I wanted was blackness, to sink into numbness. But I didn't. I couldn't.

Part Three: Nadia

One

I was in a hurry. Well, I wasn't in a hurry at all. But I thought if I created an impression of hurry, I might trick myself into getting something done, get back in control of my life.

I found an old cotton skirt under my bed and pulled that on, with a black T-shirt over the top so that the chocolate stain was hidden. I glanced at myself in the mirror. My hair looked like a cartoon of a swarm of bees and I still had a smear of face-paint on my cheek.

Coffee. That would be a start. I found a cup and rinsed it out in the bathroom, where I also filled the kettle. The sink in the kitchen was unreachable: a tower of encrusted dishes and pans. When I'd completed my tax return, I'd wash them.

I took my cup of coffee over to my desk, along with half a bar of chocolate. I might as well get this over with. The final demand from the Inland Revenue lay on top of the computer keyboard. It had been sent several weeks ago, but I'd put it in the drawer with all my other unopened letters. Max used to say that I should go to see a therapist, just about my inability to open my mail. Sometimes I let it go for weeks. I don't know why. And it's not as if it is all stuff I don't want, like bills and library fines. I also leave unopened letters from friends, invitations to jobs interviews that I could certainly do with at the moment. Later, I tell myself. I'll do it later.

This was the moment where later had arrived. I sat down, turned on the computer and watched the screen glow green. I clicked the mouse on 'Accounts' then on 'Expenses'. I worked for an hour. I rummaged around my desk. I opened envelopes. I unscrewed old receipts and invoices. My life was taking shape. I decided to print copies to be on the safe side. A small window appeared: Unknown error, type 19. What did that mean? I clicked again, but the cursor didn't move. Everything was frozen. Now what was I supposed to do? My life, my new, ordered life, was there somewhere behind the screen, and I couldn't get at it.

I didn't have a manual. The computer had been bequeathed to me by a friend of Max's. Then I remembered the card that had been slid under my windscreen wiper last week. 'Help with your computer.' At the time I had laughed and tossed it aside. But where had I tossed it? I tipped out the contents of my shoulder bag: lots of spare change, a scrumpled ball of tissues, a couple of marbles, one earring, several rubber bands and a juggling ball. No card.

Had I stuffed it in my pocket? What had I been wearing that day? I started rifling through the clothes that were lying about my bedroom and bathroom, waiting for washday. I discovered it inside a suede boot under an armchair. It must have landed there like a fallen leaf when I'd tossed it aside. I straightened it out and looked at it: 'Computer trouble? Big or small, call me and I'll sort you.' In smaller type was the phone number, which I immediately dialled.

'Hello. Are you the computer thing?'

'Yeah.'

'Thank the Lord. My computer is paralysed. Everything's there. My whole life.'

'Where do you live?'

'Camden. Quite near the tube station.'

'How about this evening?'

'How about now? Please. Trust me. I wouldn't ask unless it wasn't a major emergency.'

He laughed. It was a nice laugh, boyish. Reassuring. Like a doctor. 'I'll see what I can do. Are you in during the day?'

'Always. That would be great.' I quickly gave him my address and phone number before he could make an excuse. Then I added, 'By the way, my flat's a complete tip.' I looked around. 'I mean, really a tip. And my name's Nadia, Nadia Blake.'

'See you later.'

Less than half an hour later, he knocked on the door. It was almost insanely convenient. He was just a bit younger than me, tall, casually dressed in sneakers, grey trousers and a T-shirt. He had pale skin, long dark hair that reached his shoulders. All-right looking, and not actually like computer nerds are supposed to be.

'Hello,' he said, holding out his hand. 'I'm Morris Burnside. The repairman.'

'Fantastic,' I said. 'I'm Nadia.' I showed him inside.

'Where's the patient?'

'Through here.' The offending machine was in my bedroom. You actually have to sit on the bed to operate it. 'Do you want some tea?'

'Coffee. Milk, no sugar.'

But I hung around, waiting for his response to my problem. In a perverse way, I wanted it to be something serious, something that would provide a challenge for Morris the Nerd and make his journey worth while. It wasn't to be.

He sat on the bed and looked at the screen. With his left hand he held down several of the larger keys on the left of the keyboard, then with his right hand he pressed the return key. The screen went black then the computer relaunched itself.

'Is that it?' I asked.

He stood up. 'If it happens again, press these three keys together and the return. If that doesn't work, pull the plug out.'

'I'm so sorry,' I said breathlessly. 'I'm just hopeless with this stuff, I feel very bad about it. One day I'll learn. I'll go on a course.'

'Don't bother,' he said. 'Women aren't meant to know how to operate computers. That's what men were invented for.'

I was in a bit of a rush but I didn't feel I could just push him out of the door. 'I'll get you the coffee,' I said.

'Can I use your bathroom?'

'Yes, it's through there. Can I apologise in advance for it?'

'How MUCH DO I owe you?' I said.

'Don't worry,' Morris said. 'I wouldn't take money for what I did.'

'How are you going to make a living if you go around doing things for nothing? You must have a call-out fee.'

'No, no, I do lots of computer stuff, software stuff, whatever. This is just a hobby.' There was a pause. 'What do *you* do?'

I always had a sinking feeling when I had to launch into this particular explanation. 'It's not exactly a job, but just at the moment I'm working as a sort of entertainer. Me and my partner, Zach—I mean, my *business* partner—we go to children's parties and do a few tricks, tie some balloons into shapes, do a puppet show.'

'That's amazing,' said Morris.

'It's not exactly rocket science, but it's more or less a living. Hence the need for keeping accounts *et cetera*. And I really am sorry, Morris. I don't expect you to be amused by my impersonation of a helpless female.'

'Couldn't your boyfriend fix it for you?'

'What makes you think I've got a boyfriend?' I said.

Morris went red. 'I didn't mean anything by it,' he said. 'I just saw the shaving foam in the bathroom.'

'Oh, *that*. Max—this person I've been involved with—left some stuff behind when he scarpered a couple of weeks ago.'

'I'm sorry.'

I didn't want to get into all *that*. 'So my computer is fully functional,' I said brightly, finishing my mug of coffee.

'I don't know how you can use it.' Morris looked at it with narrowed eyes. 'You need a bigger memory. Faster hamsters.'

'I beg your pardon? Faster *hamsters*? What are they?'

He grinned. 'Sorry. An expression. All I mean is that for a grand you could have a machine that was a thousand times more powerful. You could be on-line. And there's a spreadsheet that could handle all your accounts. I could set it up for you, if you like.'

I started to feel a little dizzy. 'That's fantastically nice of you, Morris, but I think you may have got me mixed up with a woman who can cope with the world. I don't want a computer that can do more. I've got six months' ironing to do.'

Morris looked disappointed. He put his coffee mug down.

'If you change your mind,' he said, 'you've got my card. And maybe we could meet for a drink some time.'

There was a ring on the front doorbell. Zach. Thank God.

'That's my partner,' I said. 'I'm afraid we're going to rush out. And . . .' I gave a sensitive pause. 'I'm feeling a bit wobbly at the moment. I'm not quite ready. I'm sorry.'

'Of course,' Morris said. 'I completely understand.'

That was nice of him. He followed me to the door. I introduced Morris to Zach as they passed in the doorway.

'This is a man,' I said, 'who fixes computers for nothing.'

'Really?' said Zach, looking interested. 'I'm totally baffled by mine. Any chance of taking a look?'

'Sorry,' said Morris. 'It was a once-only offer. Never to be repeated.'

'That's what I always seem to find,' said Zach bleakly.

Morris nodded at me pleasantly and was gone.

I have found her. My perfect third. She is small, like the others, but strong, full of energy. She glows with it. Skin like honey, glossy chestnut hair, but all in a tangle, green-brown eyes, copper-coloured freckles scattered over her nose and cheeks. Autumn colours for the end of the summer. She smiles easily, tips her head back a bit when she laughs, gestures when she speaks. I knew as soon as I saw her that she was right for me. My challenge. My sweetheart. Nadia.

'We ought to have another trick or something.' Zach frowned at me over his frothy pink milkshake. 'Something new, anyway.'

'Why?'

'If we get invited back to a house.'

I have two magic tricks (three, if you count the wand that collapses into segments when I depress a little lever at the base, amazing to anyone under the age of four). The first one involves putting a white silk scarf into an empty bag and then, hey presto, when I pull it out it's turned a tie-dyed pink and purple. In the second, I make balls disappear and reappear. The point is to make the audience look in the wrong direction. Then if they gasp, resist the temptation to repeat the trick. And don't tell anybody—even curious parents— how it's done.

I can juggle too. Only with three balls. Nothing hard. But I don't just use multicoloured beanbags. I can juggle with bananas and shoes and mugs and teddy bears and umbrellas. Kids love it when I break eggs juggling. I'm the clown, noisy and bright and chaotic and falling over my own feet. Zach's the glum, serious sidekick.

We'd just been to the party of a five-year-old called Tamsin—a roomful of tyrannical little girls in dresses that looked like meringues—and I wanted to go home, have a nap.

'Insects,' Zach said suddenly. 'I heard of a guy who takes bugs and reptiles to children's parties and the children just touch them. That's all there is to it.'

'I'm not keeping insects and reptiles in my flat.'

He slurped his milkshake and looked wistful.

'Don't you hate "Happy Birthday"?' he said.

'Hate it.'

We grinned at each other and I stood up to go. 'Do you want to share a cab?'

'No, it's OK.'

We kissed each other and wandered off in our separate directions.

GOING BACK to the flat has been strange for the past few weeks, since Max left. I had only just got used to him being there: the loo seat up instead of down, orange juice and bacon in the fridge, another body in the bed, at night telling me I was beautiful, and in the morning telling me to get up because I was late again. I found that I missed sharing my life. I needed to learn to live alone once more, to appreciate again the delights of selfishness: I could eat chocolate in bed, see *The Sound of Music* on video, Blu-Tack notes to the wall and be in a bad mood without worrying about it. I could meet someone new and begin the whole dizzying, delicious, dismaying round again.

All around me, friends were settling down. They were in jobs with pensions and prospects. Lots were married, several had babies. Maybe that was why Max and I had separated. It had become obvious that we weren't going to open a joint bank account and have children with his hair and my eyes.

I was beginning to make convoluted scary calculations about how much of my life I had already lived, and how much time I had left. I am twenty-eight. I don't smoke, or hardly ever, and I eat lots of fruit and vegetables. I reckon I've got at least fifty years to go. That's enough time to learn how to develop my own films, go white-water rafting and meet the man—or men—of my dreams.

Max would probably be at the party I was going to tonight. I promised myself, as I made my way home, that I was going to make myself look lovely. I would wear my red dress, laugh and flirt and dance and he'd see what he had walked out on.

IN THE END, Max wasn't there, and after a bit I stopped looking round for him every time someone new walked through the door. I met a man called Robert, a lawyer with thick eyebrows, and I danced rather wildly with my old mate Gordon, who had introduced me to Max all those months ago. I talked for a bit with Lucy, whose thirtieth birthday party this was. And at half past eleven I left and went out for a meal at a Chinese restaurant with my old friends Cathy and Mel and got mildly drunk, but in the nicest way possible.

It was past one when I came back to the flat. Camden Town comes alive after midnight. The pavements were crawling with strange people.

I stumbled in through the front door and turned on the hall light. There was a letter on the doormat. I picked it up and looked at the handwriting. I didn't recognise it. Neat black italics: Ms Nadia Blake. I slid my finger under the gummed flap and slid out the letter.

Three

'Did he ransack the flat as well?' Links gestured at the mess, the cushions on the floor, the papers piled up on the carpet.

'No,' I said. 'I've been a bit busy, I'm going to deal with it.'

The detective looked nonplussed for a moment. 'Er, Miss er . . .'

'Blake.'

'Yes, Miss Blake, do you mind if I smoke?'

'Go ahead.'

Detective Chief Inspector Links didn't look a well man. Watching him light his cigarette was an exercise in suspense, his fingers shook so much. When he spoke it was in quite a low voice, so I had to lean forward to catch what he was saying. 'It's a matter of . . .' He paused. He kept losing the thread of what he was saying. 'Of establishing who has access.'

'Yes,' I said wearily. 'You already said that. It seems like a lot of trouble to go to over one sick letter. It'll be a big job. I have people to stay quite often. My boyfriend was here a lot. There are people in and out all the time.'

Links looked round at his colleague. The other policeman, Detective Inspector Stadler, looked a better insurance risk than Links. A bit wasted, maybe, in an oddly attractive way. He had straight hair combed back over his head, prominent cheekbones and dark eyes, which he kept focused on me every second as if I were very, very interesting but in a slightly odd way. He spoke for the first time: 'Have you any idea who the note may have come from? Have you had anything similar? Any threatening calls? Strange encounters with people?'

'Oh, endless strange encounters,' I said. Links perked up and looked very slightly less like one of the undead. 'Me and my partner, we entertain at children's parties. The people you meet, honestly, you wouldn't believe it. I can tell you that being hit on by the father of the five-year-old you've just done a show for, while the mother is in the kitchen lighting the candles on the cake—well, it lowers your view of human nature.'

'Miss, erm.' Links looked down at his notebook. He seemed to be having trouble reading his notes. 'Erm, Blake. We have, erm, reason to believe that there may have been, er, other women also targeted by this person.' He kept darting glances towards Stadler, as if in search of moral support. 'So one aim of our inquiries will be to establish possible connections between them.'

'Who are they?'

Links coughed. Stadler made no attempt to fill in for him. He just sat and stared at me.

'Are you worried I might try to get in touch with them?'

Links took out his handkerchief and blew his nose. Stadler seemed to be finding something of great interest in a notebook.

'We'll keep you as in touch with our progress as we can,' Links said. 'We have a psychologist, a Dr Grace Schilling, who is an expert on, er . . . She should be here'—he looked at this watch—'any minute.'

There was silence.

'Look,' I said, 'I'm not stupid. I had a break-in a year ago, but it took the police about a day to get here and they did sod all about it. Now I get a single nasty letter and it's a major operation. What's going on?'

Stadler snapped his notebook shut and put it in his pocket. 'We take threats of this kind, against women, very seriously.'

'Oh, well,' I said. 'That's good, I suppose.'

DR SCHILLING WAS the kind of woman I rather envied. She looked intelligent and dressed pretty elegantly as well. She certainly wasn't the sort of person you'd catch standing on her head in front of a group of screaming tots. The only thing that irritated me was that she had this air of serious, almost sad, concern when she addressed me, as if she were presenting a religious TV programme.

'I understand you've been in a relationship that ended,' she said.

'I can tell you that that letter wasn't written by Max. He would have trouble composing a letter to the milkman. Anyway, he was the one who walked out.'

'All the same, that might mean you were in a vulnerable state.'

'Well, a pissed-off state, maybe.'

'How tall are you, Nadia?'

'Don't rub it in. I try not to think about it. Just a little over five foot. An emotionally vulnerable dwarf. Is that the point you're trying to make? *You* should be all right, then.'

She didn't even smile.

'Should I be worried?' I asked.

Now there was a very long pause. When Dr Schilling spoke, it was with great precision. 'I don't think it would be … well, productive to get alarmed. But you should act as if the threat means what it says just to be on the safe side. That isn't much comfort, is it?'

'It's not much comfort to *me*,' I said.

'No,' said Dr Schilling, almost inaudibly, as if she were talking to somebody else, somebody I couldn't see.

THEY STAYED AND STAYED. After a couple of hours Links received a message and shambled away but Stadler and Dr Schilling remained. While she talked to me, Stadler went out and came back with sandwiches, cartons of drink.

'There's tuna and cucumber, salmon and cucumber, chicken salad, ham and mustard,' he announced.

I took the ham, Dr Schilling took the tuna, which made me think the tuna must be vastly healthier and that there was something slightly squalid and frivolous about my choice.

'Are you some kind of medical policewoman?' I asked.

Her mouth was full, so she could only shake her head while laboriously attempting to swallow her sandwich. I felt a moment of triumph. I'd caught her looking undignified.

'No, no,' she said. 'I do consulting work for them.'

'What's your real job?' I asked.

'I work at the Welbeck Clinic.'

'Grace is being too modest,' Stadler said. 'She is eminent in her field. You're lucky to have her on your side.'

'What I really meant,' I said, 'is that you, Dr Schilling . . .'

'Please, Nadia, call me Grace,' she murmured.

'All right, Grace. I know that doctors are incredibly busy people, which I've discovered every time I've wanted to see one. I was just wondering why a grand psychiatrist like you is sitting here in a crappy flat in Camden Town. It seems strange to me.'

'It's not strange,' Stadler said, wiping his mouth. 'We want to give you protection and Dr Schilling is an authority on harassment of this kind. Her objective is to help us to find the person who has sent you this threat. To do that she needs to look at you and your life, to get a sense of what has attracted this madman.'

'I think you're being daft,' I said. 'This is a guy who gets off on sending rude letters to women. What's the big deal?'

'You're not right,' Grace said. 'A man who sends a letter like that has—well, he may have . . . crossed a boundary. He must be considered dangerous.'

I looked at her, puzzled. 'Do you think I'm not frightened enough?'

'I may advise you what you should do,' she said. 'I don't think I should tell you what to feel. I'll make us some tea.'

Subject closed. Stadler gave a cough.

'You don't look like a policeman,' I said.

He gave a slight start. Then he smiled. 'What's a policeman meant to look like?'

He was a difficult man to embarrass. I had never met anyone who looked me in the eyes the way he did, almost as if he were trying to look inside me.

'I don't know,' I said. 'You just don't have a police look about you. You look, er . . .' And I ground to a halt because what I was feeling my way towards saying was that he was too good-looking to be a policeman, which was both a deeply foolish comment and miles away from being remotely appropriate to the situation, and in any case Grace had just come in with tea.

'Normal,' I said, belatedly ending the sentence.

'That all?' he said. 'I thought you might say something nicer than that.'

'Am I interrupting something?' Grace asked, with a touch of irony.

We sat there all afternoon and I dug out the scraps of paper I call a diary, and I went through my address book and I held forth about my life. Every so often one of them would ask a question. It started to rain for the first time for days and days and all of a sudden I no longer felt like a rare specimen being examined through a microscope, but instead like someone spending time with two rather strange new friends. Sitting on the floor with rain running down the windows, it just felt reassuring as much as anything.

'Can you really juggle?' Stadler asked at one point.

'Can I juggle?' I said pugnaciously. 'You watch this.' I looked around the room. There was some fruit in the bowl.

I grabbed two wrinkled apples and a tangerine, started juggling with them, then, rather carefully walked up and down the room. I stumbled on a cushion and they fell to the floor.

'That gives you a general idea,' I said.

'Can you do more than that?' he asked.

I made a scoffing sound. 'Juggling with four balls is very boring,' I said. 'You just hold two in each hand and throw them up and down with no interchanges.'

'What about five?'

I made my scoffing sound again. 'Five is for mad people. To juggle five balls you need to sit in a room alone for three months and do nothing else. I'm saving up five balls for when I get stranded on a desert island. They're only toddlers and in any case it's only a phase I'm going through while I work out what I'm going to do with the rest of my life.'

'That's no excuse,' said Stadler. 'We want to see five balls, don't we?'

'Minimum,' said Grace.

'Shut up,' I said. 'Or I'll show you my magic tricks.'

I CAN'T EXPLAIN what happened next. Or, at least, I can't explain it so it makes proper sense.

Grace Schilling left. Then Stadler told me that they had arranged for a policewoman, WPC Lynne Burnett, to keep an eye on me.

'What about you?' I said. 'Will you be around?'

He looked at me for just a couple of seconds too long so that I almost started thinking about saying something else and then the doorbell rang. I started, blinked, smiled blearily at him.

'It'll be Lynne,' he said, and turned on his heel and opened the door. She was younger than me, although not much, and rather lovely. She had a large purple birthmark on her cheek. She didn't dress like a WPC. She was wearing jeans, a T-shirt and carrying a light blue jacket in her hand.

'I'm Nadia Blake,' I said, holding out my hand. 'Sorry about the mess, but I wasn't exactly expecting visitors.'

IT COULD HAVE been worse. After Stadler left we ate fried eggs and baked beans for supper, and Lynne told me all about her seven brothers and sisters, and her mother who was a hairdresser. Then she went and sat outside in the car. After tonight, she said, there would be other officers instead; after all, she had to sleep sometimes. I had a long bath, then I went to bed.

The next day Lynne followed me to the shops; then she sat around while I wrote letters. Early in the evening the doorbell rang and she went to answer it. It was Stadler. He was carrying a very serious briefcase and wearing a sombre suit.

'Hello there, Detective,' I said sweetly.

'I've taken over from Lynne for a spell.' His expression was impassive. No smile. 'I thought I'd ask some questions.'

He sat on the sofa, and I sat opposite him in the armchair.

'What are your questions, then, Detective?' He had lovely hands. Long, with smooth nails.

He opened his briefcase and fumbled with some papers. 'I wanted to ask you about previous boyfriends,' he said.

'You've done that already, and I don't really want to tell you any more details of my sex life.'

He gazed at me then, and I stood up and turned away from him. 'I'm going to have a glass of wine. Do you want one? And don't say, "Not while I'm on duty."'

'Maybe a very small one.'

I poured us both a glass of white wine. We walked out into what there was of the garden. My yard backs onto an industrial unit. The rain of yesterday and today had stopped and the air felt fresher than it had for weeks. The leaves of the pear tree glistened.

I took a sip of my wine. He knew a lot about me. He knew about my work, my family, my friends and my boyfriends; my exam results and my affairs. The things I wanted, like an open-top sports car and a better singing voice and more dignity, and the things I was scared of—like lifts and heights and snakes. I had talked to him and to Grace in the way that I would talk to a lover, lying in bed after sex, telling secrets and intimate nonsense. Yet I knew nothing about him, besides his name. Cameron Stadler. It made me feel giddy.

We leaned towards each other. Here I go, I thought: another big mistake about to happen.

I put my arms around his neck. He didn't look away. I couldn't tell what he was thinking; what he wanted. I kissed him full and hard on his mouth. His lips were cool; his skin was warm. He didn't push me away but he didn't kiss me back at first.

I put my hands on his back, beneath his shirt and pressed myself against him. He felt solid and huge. I picked up one of his hands, laid it against my hot cheek, then led him back through the double doors into the sitting room.

'I shouldn't do this,' he said. Then he was on top of me, on the floor, and there was a shoe under my back, a hairbrush spiking my left foot and dust everywhere, and he pulled up my skirt. Neither of us said a word.

WHEN LYNNE CAME back, Cameron was on the phone, very businesslike, and I was reading a magazine. We said goodbye to each other quite formally, but then, muttering to Lynne there was something he had forgotten to check, he followed me into my bedroom with his file under his arm, closed the door and kissed me again, and he told me he would be back as soon as he could manage it.

I spent the rest of the evening lying on my bed, tingling, pretending to read, but not turning a single page.

Four

'What's the plan?' I said to Lynne over breakfast.

I think I'm a woman of some degree of resource, but this was more than my brain could deal with. I'd had sex the day before with a man I hardly knew. Now I was having breakfast with a woman I hardly knew.

'We're taking responsibility for your protection,' she said, as if by rote.

'All the same,' I said, taking a swig of coffee, 'don't you feel this is all a ridiculous overreaction?'

'It's for your benefit,' she said.

'But I'm embarrassed,' I said. 'My life's ridiculous enough with just me here, but the thought of doing everything I do with a policewoman staring at me doesn't seem cheering.'

'We'll talk about that,' Lynne said with an earnest expression, but we were interrupted by the doorbell. It was Cameron Stadler. He looked over my shoulder and nodded towards Lynne.

'Good morning, Miss Blake.'

'Oh, please call me Nadia,' I said. 'We're very informal here.'

'Nadia,' he said, in a sort of feeble mumble, 'I've stopped in to relieve Lynne for a couple of hours. I don't know if you've got any arrangements.'

'Yes,' I said. 'At half past four me and Zach have to be at a children's party in Muswell Hill. And there are two more at the weekend.'

'That's no problem,' said Cameron. 'Lynne can accompany you.'

'It might be a bit obtrusive,' I said.

'I'll sit outside,' Lynne said. 'I can give you a lift.'

'Better and better.'

Lynne turned to Cameron. 'Nadia is concerned about our plans.'

'Basically, I don't know what they are,' I said.

'I'll discuss it with her,' said Cameron dismissively, 'and I'll see you back here about one?'

She nodded. 'Fine. See you later, Nadia.'

'See you, Lynne.'

She was out of the door. I turned to Cameron. 'About yesterday . . .'

And he was on me, holding me as if I were unbearably precious, his hands touching my face, stroking my hair. I pushed him away slightly and looked him in the eyes. 'I . . .' I stammered. 'I'm not—'

He kissed me again. 'Do you want me to stop?' he asked.

'I don't know. No.'

He took my hand and led me into my bedroom. It was different from the day before: more relaxed, more deliberate, slower. I sat down on the bed. He pulled the blind down.

'I can't stop thinking about you,' he said, as if it were a symptom. 'I see you when I close my eyes. What shall we do?'

'Take your clothes off,' I said.

He took off his clothes as if in a dream, tossing his trousers into a heap on a chair, looking at me all the time. I reached out my arms towards him, and then at last he was inside me.

LATER, WHEN WE LAY there entwined, he was still looking at me, stroking my hair, saying my name as if it were some magic spell.

'I feel confused,' I said.

A spell had been broken. He moved away slightly, a shadow crossed his face, he bit his lip. 'Can I be honest with you?' he said.

Suddenly I felt like shivering. 'Please,' I said.

'This job is my whole life,' he said, 'and this is not allowed.'

'I won't tell anyone,' I said. 'Is that it?'

'No,' he said bleakly. 'I'm married. I'm so sorry. I'm so, so sorry.'

And he started crying. I was lying there, with a naked detective crying in my bed. About eighteen hours of the relationship and we'd already moved from first lust to the weeping and recrimination.

'I'm not messing you around, Nadia, I promise you that. It means so much to me I don't know what to do. Are you furious with me? Tell me what you think.'

I kissed Cameron's chest. 'What do I think? I have a rule not to sleep with married men. But I think mainly this is your problem, not mine. And I think that Lynne is due back in about seven minutes.'

The speed of putting clothes on was almost amusing. It felt companionable. We kissed, smiling at each other through the kiss. Married. Why did he have to be married?

That was on the Wednesday. On Thursday he only had time to talk to me on the phone. On Friday morning a team of men moved into my flat and fitted new locks on every door and iron grids over each window. And after lunch he came, and Lynne was needed to provide a report. We had time for a bath.

'I'd like to see your show,' he said. 'I'd like to see you perform.'

'Come tomorrow,' I said. 'We're performing for a group of five-year-olds just up the road in Primrose Hill.'

'I can't,' he said, looking away.

'Oh,' I said primly, hating myself. 'Family business.'

'Are you cross?'

'Do you want me to be cross?'

He picked up my hand and held it to his cheek. 'I'm in love with you, Nadia. I've fallen in love.'

'Don't say that. It frightens me. It makes me feel too happy.'

She thinks they are invisible. I see them. Kissing. My girl and the policeman kissing. As he stands at the window to close the blinds, I see on his stupid face the besotted look of a man in love.

I love her more. Nobody can love her the way that I love her. Everyone looks in the wrong direction. They look for hate. Love, that's the key.

FIVE- AND SIX-YEAR-OLD girls are the best punters. They are sweet and admiring, and sit in decorous rows in their silky pastel dresses with their hair in plaits and their feet in patent leather shoes.

This party, in a large and handsome house in Primrose Hill, was for five-year-old boys, with a few girls drifting round the edges.

The birthday boy was called Oliver, and he was small and plump; his friends raged round him like random atoms while he ripped wrapping-paper off presents. His mother was called Mrs Wyndham, and she looked very tall and very thin and very rich and already seemed terminally irritated by the party that was just beginning.

She looked doubtfully at me and Zach. 'There are twenty-four of them,' she said. 'Rather boisterous. You know what boys are like.'

'No problem,' I said. 'If the children go into the garden for a few minutes, we can set up.'

There was a stampede through the French windows. Mrs Wyndham ran after them wailing something about her camellia.

Zach already knew about the letter, of course, and the police, and the precautions they were taking. He'd met Lynne, for she had given us a lift to Primrose Hill, and as we were slotting together the puppet theatre, he asked me if I was at all scared by the whole business.

'No.' I hesitated, as I hooked the curtains across the miniature stage. 'More excited, as a matter of fact.'

'That sounds a bit perverse.'

'The thing is, Zach, I'm having a thing with one of the policemen.'

'What?'

'I know. It's a bit weird but—'

'Nadia.' He took hold of my shoulders so I had to stop what I was doing. 'Are you insane? You can't do this. It's not on. It's like having an affair with your doctor. He's taking advantage of your vulnerability. Can't you see?'

'Shut up, Zach.'

'Nadia,' Zach said urgently. 'Oh, shit, here they come.'

The boys had returned from the garden.

AFTER THE SHOW, I got Oliver to help me do my pathetic magic trick, and the wand collapsed every time he touched it, and all the children shouted, 'Abracadabra!' as loudly as they could, and Mrs Wyndham winced in the doorway. Zach blew up long balloons and twisted them into animal shapes, then the children bolted into the kitchen for sausages on sticks and jam-filled biscuits and a birthday cake in the shape of a train. And it was over.

Parents and nannies started arriving. I dismantled the theatre and started to stack it into its box.

A pretty young woman came up to me with a cup of tea. 'Mrs Wyndham asked me to bring you this.' She had silver-blonde hair and a funny, lilting accent.

I took it gratefully. 'Are you Oliver's nanny?'

'No. I came to collect Chris. He lives just down the road.' She picked up a puppet and examined it. 'It must be hard, your job.'

'Not as hard as yours. Do you have just the one?'

'There are two older ones, Josh and Harry, but they're at school.'

I started loading up. She stayed, looking at me.

'Where do you come from?' I asked. 'Your English is fantastic.'

'Sweden. I was meant to go home but there was a bit of fuss.'

'Oh,' I said vaguely. Where was that wand? I bet Oliver had wandered off with it. 'Well, thanks, er . . .'

'Lena.'

She disappeared back into the kitchen, where the other nannies were gathered round their charges, talking about boyfriends and nightlife. Children started leaving. 'Say thank you,' I heard, and, 'Where's my party bag? Harvey's got a blue one. I want a blue one.'

I picked up all my stuff. Thank God Lynne was out there with her car. There were some advantages to being followed around by a blushing, stubborn policewoman. A small fair-haired boy bumped into me in the hall.

'Hi,' I said brightly, determined to make a quick exit.

'My mummy's dead,' he said, fixing me with his bright gaze.

'Oh, well,' I said, looking around. The mother was probably in the kitchen somewhere.

'A man killed her dead.'

'That can't be true.'

Lena returned, carrying his jacket. 'Come on, Chris, home.'

He took her hand.

'He says his mother was killed,' I said.

'Yes,' she said simply.

'What? Really? When did this happen?' I asked Lena.

'Two weeks ago,' she said. 'It's a terrible thing.'

I looked at her with fascination. I'd never been near someone who'd been close to someone who was murdered. 'What happened?'

'Nobody knows.' She shook her head from side to side so her silver hair swung. 'It happened in the home.'

I gawped at her. 'How terrible. How terrible for everyone.'

'He wrote letters,' Chris said.

'What?'

Lena nodded and sighed. 'Yes,' she said. 'It was horrible. Letters saying that she would be killed. Like love letters.'

'Like love letters,' I repeated dully.

'Yes.' She picked up the little boy and he wrapped his legs round her waist. 'Come on, Chris.'

'Wait. Wait one minute. Didn't she call the police?'

'Oh, yes. There were many police.'

'She still died?' I said, feeling icy cold.

'Yes.'

'What were the policemen called? Can you remember their names?'

'Remember? I am seeing them every day. There is Links, Stadler. And a psychologist, Dr Schilling. So. Why? What is it?'

'Oh, nothing important.' I smiled at her while my insides burned. 'I thought I might know them.'

Five

'You all right, Nadia?'

'What?' I looked round, startled, hardly knowing where I was. Lynne leaned across her car with the concerned look of a friend.

'You look pale,' she said.

'I've got a blinding headache,' I said. 'Is it all right if we don't talk for a while?'

I lay back in the seat with my eyes closed. I didn't want to look at her. I couldn't trust myself to speak. I'd been dropped into a new world, a horrible dark world, and I needed to work out where I was, but before that I would have to wait for the buzzing in my head to die down. A voice, somewhere far away, deep in my mind, was telling me over and over again that another woman had received letters like mine, that she was dead, murdered. A woman had gone through what I'd gone through, and at the end of it she'd been killed.

'We're home,' a voice said in my ear. 'Do you want some help?'

'I think I'll just go and lie down for a while. I think I may have a migraine.'

My mind was clear now. From now on I would just be pretending to be ill.

We went inside and I left her and retreated to my bedroom. I shut the door. And I checked that the window was firmly closed. I lay on the bed, and tried to go over the conversation I'd had with Lena. Maybe she was mad. But even in my feverish state I wasn't able to convince myself of that. She had named Links, Grace Schilling, Cameron. She'd lived nearby, hadn't she? That was a thought.

A free local paper is pushed through my door every Friday. I never even look at it; I put it straight on the pile under the sink. I walked out of my bedroom and told Lynne I was feeling a bit better. I'd make some tea for us both. I filled the kettle and switched it on. That would give me the couple of minutes I needed.

I started with the issue from five weeks ago. Nothing there and nothing in the following issue either. But in the next issue, published two weeks ago, there was the headline: PRIMROSE HILL MURDER. I tore the page out. The kettle had boiled. I poured it over the teabags.

'Biscuit, Lynne?'

'Not for me, thanks.'

I had another couple of minutes. I smoothed out the article on the work surface:

A mother of three was found murdered in her £800,000 Primrose Hill home last week. Police announced that Jennifer Hintlesham, 38, was found dead on August 3. Police suspect that she stumbled on an intruder in the late afternoon. 'It's a tragedy,' said Detective Chief Inspector Stuart Links as he announced the setting up of a murder inquiry this week. 'If anybody has any information I would urge them to contact us at Stretton Green Police Station.'

That was it. I read it and reread it as if I could suck out some more information through sheer desperation. No mention of any letters.

I picked up the two mugs of tea but my left hand was compulsively shaking. I had to put them down and carry one mug through to Lynne then return for my own mug. I sat down near Lynne and looked at her. Had she sat like this with Jennifer Hintlesham, drinking tea, pretending to be her friend, saying that everything would be fine, that she was safe? I took a sip of my tea. When I spoke, I tried to imitate a woman making conversation.

'It still seems strange to me,' I said. 'I get one letter and a policewoman stays with me for days and days. Do you do this every time anybody gets a threatening letter?'

Lynne looked uncomfortable. 'I'm just following routine,' she said.

'And if somebody came into the house to attack me, you'd protect me?' I said with a smile. 'That's the idea, is it?'

'Nothing like that will happen,' she said. For a moment I hated Lynne in a way I've never hated anybody in my life. Whose feelings was she trying to protect here? But the hatred subsided into nothing more than a dull ache.

I gulped down the hot tea. I needed time to go over things in my mind, so I went to lie down again. I tried to remember everything I could from the previous few days. Above all I thought of Cameron. Cameron taking off my clothes as if I were a precious, beautiful object that might break. What was it he had said? 'Can't I be honest with you?' that was it. Honest. I lay there listening to the noises of the street, of Saturday night in Camden Town, and I thought and thought. Finally I slept and had fragmented dreams.

When I woke, the phone was ringing. I crawled out of bed and answered it. It was Cameron. He was whispering. 'I'm desperate to see you. I've arranged that I can get away in the late afternoon. Can I come and see you around four?'

'Oh, yes,' I said.

I SPENT THE DAY in a sullen fog. Lynne and I went out for a couple of hours, walking around Camden Market, but that was just because it made it easier not to speak, and not to listen to any more lies.

Cameron arrived at exactly four o'clock. He was wearing jeans and a loose blue shirt. He hadn't shaved. He looked more rumpled, more handsome than ever, less buttoned up. He told Lynne he'd take over for a couple of hours, gently closed the front door behind her and turned to me.

'Oh, Nadia,' he said.

I walked towards him. I had prepared myself for this moment. He reached his arms out towards me. I clenched my fist as hard as I could. When I was a foot away I looked him in the eyes and then, with all my strength, I punched him in the face.

'What the hell?' I saw with satisfaction that blood was trickling down from his nostril.

'I know, Detective Inspector Stadler.'

'What are you going on about?'

'Did it turn you on, thinking that you were sleeping with a woman who was going to die?' I jabbed him in the chest with a forefinger. 'Jennifer Hintlesham. Does that name ring any bells for you?'

The first glimmering of comprehension crept across his features. 'Nadia,' he said. He took a step towards me and put out his hand.

'Stay where you are, you—you—What were you *thinking*? How could you do that to me? Did you think of me dead?'

I shocked myself then by bursting into tears.

'Nadia.' His voice was soft, with a hint of triumph in it. 'Darling Nadia, I'm sorry. I hated not telling you.'

I felt his hand on me and it made me jump. 'I'm not crying because of you!' I screamed, through my tears. 'I'm scared, don't you see? I'm so scared I feel like there's a great hole in my chest.'

'Nadia—'

'Shut up.' I pulled a tissue out of my pocket and blew my nose. Then I looked at my watch. 'Lynne's back soon. I need you to answer some questions. I'm going to wash my face.'

IN THE BATHROOM I washed my hands and face, and cleaned my teeth. There was a nasty taste in my mouth.

The heat had gone out of my hatred. I felt cold and calm and ghastly. Cameron seemed dulled, too. We sat across the table from each other and he looked at me with an expression that was both obsequious and resentful. He was scared of me now.

'How did you find out?' he asked.

'North London's a small place,' I said. 'Especially rich north London. I met the nanny. Lena.' He didn't reply but I saw a slight nod of recognition. 'She told me about the notes. And you. Are you sure they're from the same person?'

He didn't meet my eyes. 'Yes,' he said.

'But weren't you guarding her?'

'We had been. There were complicating factors.'

'Didn't you take it seriously?'

'We took it very seriously, after all—' He stopped abruptly.

'What? After all, what? Tell me.'

'We knew how serious the letters to Mrs Hintlesham were,' he muttered, so quietly I had to strain to hear him.

'Why?' He caught my eye and then I realised. My voice came out in a hoarse whisper. 'She wasn't the first, was she?'

Cameron shook his head.

'Who else?'

'A young woman called Zoë Haratounian.'

'When?'

'Five weeks ago.'

I sank my head into my hands.

The doorbell rang. It was Lynne, coming back on duty. She tried to ask Cameron some questions about next week's roster but he was scarcely able to speak or catch her eye—or my eye. He just stroked his cheek lightly as if he were trying to detect with his fingertips whether there was a revealing mark where I'd hit him. Then he mumbled something about having to get away.

'We'll talk tomorrow,' I said.

He gave a shrug and left, and I found myself alone with Lynne. I hadn't thought of what I would say to her after speaking to Cameron.

'Want a drink?' I asked.

I'm not the sort of person who ever needs a drink but, God, I needed a drink.

'Tea would be great.'

So I bustled off and put the kettle on. I seemed always to be making tea for her as if I were her grandmother. In the back of a cupboard I found a bottle of duty-free whisky that somebody had once bought for me. I splashed some into a tumbler and topped it up from the cold tap. We walked out into the garden.

'Cheers,' I said, clinking my whisky against her mug and taking a sip of my drink, which I could feel sizzling all the way down into my tummy. Now for it. 'I owe you an apology,' I said, just as she was lifting the mug to her lips. She looked puzzled.

'What for?'

'Yesterday I was asking you whether all this—I mean, all the protection—wasn't a bit much. But in fact I knew.'

Lynne froze in the act of lifting the mug of tea to her mouth.

I continued. 'You see, a funny thing happened. Yesterday at the children's party I got talking to the nanny of one of the children. And completely by chance I discovered something. She used to work for a woman called Jennifer Hintlesham.' I had to give Lynne credit. She gave no visible reaction at all. She wouldn't catch my eye, that was all. 'You have heard of her?' I said.

Lynne took some time to answer. She looked down at her tea. 'Yes,' she said, so quietly I could hardly catch the word. 'I'm sorry,' she continued. 'It felt bad not telling you but there were strict instructions. They thought it might be traumatic for you.'

'Did Jennifer know about the one before?'

'No.'

I felt that my mouth was flapping open. I was aghast. 'So, let me get this straight in my mind: she didn't know that the person sending her letters had already killed somebody. And she couldn't make decisions about how to protect herself.'

'It wasn't like that,' Lynne said. 'This wasn't my decision, but I know that they've been acting for the best. What they thought would be the best.'

'Your strategy for protecting Jennifer—and the first one as well, Zoë—it didn't quite work out.' I took a gulp of the whisky, which made me cough. I felt so miserable and frightened and sick. 'I'm sorry, Lynne, I'm sure that this is awful for you but it's worse for me. This is my life. I'm the one who's going to die.'

She moved closer towards me. 'You're not going to die.'

I recoiled. 'I don't understand, Lynne. You've been sitting here with me for days. You've been here in the house, drinking my tea, eating my food. You've seen me believing you, trusting you. I can't understand it. What were you thinking?'

Lynne stayed silent.

'I have this problem with everybody knowing something about me and me not knowing it. What would you feel, if it was you?' I said.

'I don't know,' she said.

'Did you look after the first one?'

'Zoë? No. I only met her once. Just before . . . well . . .'

'And Jennifer?'

'Yes. I spent time with her.'

'What were they like? Were they like me?'

Lynne drained her mug of tea. 'I'm sorry,' she said. 'I'm sorry you were kept in the dark like this. But it's completely forbidden to divulge details of that kind. I'm sorry.'

We walked inside, hardly looking at each other. She made some sandwiches and we sat watching the TV and not talking. I hardly noticed the programme.

I didn't know who to turn to. I thought about my parents, but quickly dismissed them. They were old and nervous. Who would be calm, strong, a rock? Who would save me?

Later, as I got into bed, without meaning to, I started to think about the women who had died. I knew nothing about them except their names, and that Jennifer Hintlesham had had three children. Two women. Zoë and Jenny. They must have lain awake in their beds in the dark, as I was doing now, and felt the same icy fear flowing round their bodies. And the same loneliness.

But even as I lay there, curled up in my covers with my heart thumping and my eyes stinging, I knew I was going to have to move on from this blind and helpless state of terror. I couldn't just huddle up and wait for other people to rescue me from the nightmare.

A small part deep inside me clenched itself in readiness.

I fell asleep in the early hours, and the following morning I didn't exactly feel braver or safer. But I did feel steelier. At ten o'clock I asked Lynne if she could leave the room because I had a private phone call to make, and when she had gone I phoned Cameron.

'I'm feeling desperate,' he said, as soon as he came on the line.

'Good. So am I.'

'I'm so sorry that you feel betrayed. I feel terrible.'

'That's all right,' I said. 'You can do something for me.'

'Anything.'

'I want to see the files on this case. Not just about me, about the other two women.'

'That's not possible. They're not available to the public.'

'I want you to listen to me very clearly, Cameron. In my opinion you behaved badly about the whole sex thing. I enjoyed it as well and I'm not interested in punishing you. But if you don't bring me the files I will tell Links about our relationship and I'll probably cry a bit and talk about having been in a vulnerable state. And I'll contact your wife and tell her.'

'You wouldn't. That would be—' He made a coughing sound, as if he were choking. 'You mustn't tell Sarah. She's been depressed, she couldn't deal with it.'

'Listen carefully to what I'm saying. There is a man who has killed two women and is now going to kill me. Just at this moment I don't care about your career and I don't care about your wife's feelings. I want the files here tomorrow morning and enough time to read through them. Then you can take them away again.'

'I'll do what I can.'

'Do,' I said.

When I put the phone down I expected to cry or feel ashamed but I surprised myself by catching sight of my reflection in the mirror above the fireplace. At last, a friendly face.

I CLEARED MY living-room table but there still wasn't enough space. After Cameron had got rid of Lynne, it took him three trips to bring in the files from his car. There were two bulging cases and two cardboard boxes. He unloaded the red, blue and grey files on the table-top and, when there was no more room, onto the carpet as well.

'You've got two hours,' he said. 'And if you mention to anybody that you've seen any of it at all, then that's my job done for.'

I picked up files at random. 'How are these arranged?'

'The grey files are statements,' he said. 'The blue files are our own reports and documents. The red files are forensic and crime scene. Anyway, it's all written on the outside.'

'Are there photographs?'

'In the albums on the floor by your feet.'

I felt cold suddenly. Was this a good idea? 'Go away,' I said. 'Go into the garden. I can't read with you here.'

Cameron paused. 'It doesn't make nice reading, Nadia.' Slowly and reluctantly, he left the room.

I opened the first file and there she was. A snapshot was pinned to a piece of paper. Zoë Haratounian. Born February 11, 1976. I looked closely at the picture. She must have been on holiday. She was sitting on a low wall with an intensely blue sky behind her, wearing a green vest and black shorts. She had blonde hair that came down to her shoulders. It was a happy picture.

Also in the file were some typed notes, contact numbers, addresses. This was what I'd been looking for. Boyfriend, friends, employer. I had a notebook ready for this, and jotted down names and numbers.

I closed the file and put it to one side. Now for the second. Jennifer Charlotte Hintlesham, born 1961, looked completely different from Zoë. She wasn't exactly beautiful but she was a woman who would catch your attention. She had large dark eyes and prominent cheekbones. Her dark brown hair was brushed so that it shone.

I had felt that Zoë was much younger than me; Jennifer Hintlesham seemed a generation older. It wasn't that she had an older-looking face; the only faces that look more haggard than mine, especially first thing in the morning, have been dug out of a peat bog after 2,000 years of mummification. She just seemed grown-up. I looked at the file again. Husband and three children, names and ages. I wrote down details.

Something occurred to me. I looked in the pile for a file with my name on it. There it was. I opened it and was looking at a picture of myself. Nadia Elizabeth Blake, b. 1971. I shivered. Maybe in a few weeks this file would be fatter.

I reached down for the first album of pictures, bound in gaudy red plastic. I opened it and mechanically turned the pages one after another. The scene of the murder of Zoë Haratounian. She was lying face down on a carpet. She wasn't naked or anything like that, but there was a ribbon or tie or something pulled tight around her neck and there were photographs showing it from various angles.

I put it down and picked up the second book. The crime scene at Jennifer Hintlesham's house. This looked quite different. It was a single photograph, but I saw it in fragments: staring open eyes, wire around the neck, clothes ripped, legs splayed. I threw the book down and ran to the sink. My stomach heaved, painfully emptying itself.

I washed my face in warm and cold water and then walked back to the table and closed the photograph album without looking at it.

I didn't have much time. I would have to be selective. I skimmed through witnesses' statements. They were so long, rambling and diffuse that it was almost impossible to extract any sense from them.

I paid a little more attention to the pathologist's reports on the two dead women. Zoë's was much simpler: ligature strangulation with the belt of a dressing gown. No sign of sexual assault.

The report on Jennifer's death was longer. I did nothing more than note details: ligature strangulation, a thin, deep furrow on the neck consistent with the use of wire; incised wounds and stabbed wounds.

There was a fat file dealing with the analysis of the letters. There had been attempts to associate the letters with people Zoë knew: her boyfriend, Fred; an ex-boyfriend; an estate agent; a potential buyer of her flat. However, the wounds (confirmed, a note added, by injuries inflicted on Jennifer Hintlesham) showed that the murderer was left-handed. The above suspects were all right-handed.

The hair and fibre samples found in Zoë's flat were only those of its recent inhabitants, namely her boyfriend Fred, and Zoë herself. The hair and fibre analysis of the Jennifer Hintlesham crime scene was more complicated because of the sheer number of people who had been on the premises. There was, however, no forensic link between the two scenes, apart from Jennifer's locket, found in Zoë's flat, Zoë's photograph found in Jennifer's house.

I also read through a bundle of internal memos that was marked 'Most Secret'. It was there I learned that Jennifer Hintlesham's guard had been removed because her husband, Clive, was in the process of being charged with the murder of Zoë Haratounian. What a foul-up.

I called Cameron back and he was in the room in a few seconds.

'So what did you think?'

'It was horrible,' I said. 'And I'm glad I know.'

Cameron started gathering up the files, putting them in boxes, cramming them into the briefcases.

'We're not very alike,' I said.

'What?'

'I thought we'd all be the same type. I know it's hard to tell from photos and a few particulars, but we seem completely different. Zoë was younger, sweeter than me, I bet. Also she had a real job. And, as for Jennifer, she looks like a member of the Royal Family. I don't think she'd have had much time for *me*.'

'Maybe not,' said Cameron wistfully, and at that moment I felt a stab of jealousy. He'd seen her, talked to her. He knew what her voice sounded like. He had seen her funny little gestures, the sort that would never get written down on a form.

'You're all small,' he said.

'What?'

'You're all short and light,' he said. 'And you live in north London.'

'So that's where you've got to,' I said. 'Nearly six weeks and two women dead and you know that this murderer doesn't choose six-foot body builders and he doesn't choose women who live randomly all over the world.'

He had finished packing up.

'I've got to go,' he said. 'Lynne's about to arrive.'

We were both acting a bit embarrassed with each other now. For me it was that embarrassment of being with someone who you've been naked with and now don't fancy in the very least.

'Nadia. I'm sorry about everything. It has all been so—' He stopped and rubbed his face. 'I've got something else.'

I could tell from his voice that it wasn't good news.

He reached inside his jacket and took out a sheet of paper. He unfolded it and flattened it on the table. 'We intercepted this two days ago.' It read:

Dear Nadia,

I don't know what the police are saying to you. They can't stop me. In a few days or a week or two weeks you'll be dead.

'I wanted to be honest with you,' he said.

'I'm going to die, aren't I?'

'No, no,' he said, moving towards the door. 'You'll be fine.'

Seven

'I'm going to Camden Market,' I said. 'Straight away.'

Lynne looked confused. It was Saturday and only just past nine o'clock and I guess she'd got used to my staying in my bed till late, trying to find ways of being alone. For the past few days I had been locked into my nightmare, seeing those photographs over and over in my mind. Zoë, looking as if she had simply gone to sleep; Jenny mutilated. Yet here I was, washed and dressed and friendly, and ready to go.

'It'll be crowded,' she said doubtfully.

'Just what I need. Crowds, music, cheap clothes. I want to buy lots of useless things. You don't need to come with me.'

'I'll come, of course.'

'You've got to, haven't you? Poor Lynne, trailing round after me, having to be polite all the time, having to lie. You must be wishing this was all over. One way or another. Come on. It's only five minutes' walk away.'

LYNNE WAS RIGHT. It was a hot day, and Camden Market was packed. She was wearing woollen trousers and heavy shoes. She must be sweltering, I thought, with satisfaction. I had put on a lemon-yellow strapless dress and flat sandals; I felt cool, light-footed. We pushed our way through the crowds and the heat rose from the pavements. I looked round as we walked and felt a wave of euphoria rise in me that I was among this great sea of people again.

There were stalls selling freshly squeezed juices and I got us each a tumbler of mango and orange and a pretzel. Then I bought twenty thin silver bangles for five pounds, and slipped them onto my wrist, where they clinked satisfyingly. While Lynne was examining wooden carvings, I slipped away. It was as easy as that.

I went quickly down the staircase that led to the canal and ran along the path until I got to the main road. It was still crowded and I was just another body in the crowd. I was on my own at last.

I felt free, quite different, as if I'd shaken off all the rubbish of the past weeks: the fear and the desire and the irritation. I knew where I was going. I had planned the route last night. I had to be quick, before anyone worked out where I was.

THE MAN WHO OPENED the front door was taller and younger than I had expected, and more handsome. He had pale hair flopping over his brow, pale eyes in a tanned face. He was wearing jeans and nothing else. He looked bleary.

'Yes?' His tone wasn't exactly friendly.

'Are you Fred?' I tried to smile at him.

'Yes. Do I know you?'

'My name's Nadia Blake. I'm here because I am being threatened by the same man who killed Zoë.'

I thought this would surprise him but it clearly hit him like a physical blow. He almost fell backwards. 'What?'

'Can I come in?'

He stepped back and held the door open. I was past him before he could say anything more. He followed me upstairs to a small cluttered living room.

'I'm sorry about Zoë by the way,' I said.

He was looking at me intently. 'How did you hear about me?'

'I saw you on a list of witnesses,' I said.

He ran his hand through his tousled hair and then rubbed his eyes. 'Want some coffee?'

'Thanks.'

He went into the adjoining kitchen and I stared around me. I thought there might be a photograph of Zoë, something that would remind me of her, but there was nothing. I wanted to feel close to her but she felt utterly absent.

'Here's your coffee.' Fred came back into the room.

'Thanks.'

Fred sat on a sofa that looked as if it had been retrieved from a dump and motioned me into a chair. He held his mug in both hands and stared into it. He didn't speak.

'I'm sorry about Zoë,' I said again, for want of anything better.

'Yeah,' he said. He shrugged and looked away.

'What was she like?'

'Like?' He looked up sulkily. 'She was nice, attractive, happy, you know, all that. But what do you want from me?'

'It's stupid, I know. I want to know silly things about her: her favourite colour, her clothes, her dreams, what she felt like when she got the letters, everything . . .' I ran out of breath.

He looked uncomfortable. 'I can't help you.'

'Did you love her?' I asked abruptly.

'We had good fun.'

Good fun. My heart sank. Good fun: what an epitaph.

'Don't you wonder, though, what she must have felt like? When she was being threatened, and then when she died?'

He reached across for a packet of cigarettes on a low table by the sofa. 'No,' he said, lighting one.

'I'm sorry, I must seem like a ghoul. It's just that I feel a connection to these two women.'

'What do you mean *two* women?'

'Zoë and then Jennifer Hintlesham, the second woman he killed.'

'What?' he said, leaping forward. He put the mug on the table, spilling quite a lot of the coffee. 'What the hell?'

'Sorry. You didn't know. The police have been keeping it a big secret. I only found out by mistake. This other woman got the same letters. She was killed a few weeks after Zoë.'

'But . . . but . . .' Fred seemed lost in thought. Then he looked at me with a completely new intensity. 'That second woman, she was killed by the same man?'

'That's right.'

He gave a low whistle.

The telephone rang, loud as an alarm, and we both started. Fred picked up the receiver and turned his back on me.

'Yeah. Yeah, I'm up.' A pause, then, 'Come round now and we'll collect Duncan and Graham later.'

He put the phone down and glanced over at me. 'I've got a friend coming round,' he said in dismissal. 'Good luck, Nadia. Sorry I couldn't be any help. Take care.'

As I MADE my way blindly towards the underground, I went over what Fred had said, which was not very much—nothing that made it worth escaping from police protection. Poor Zoë. A sudden shiver of fear went through me. I was on my own, nobody looking after me.

Suddenly my way was blocked. A man standing in my path looking down at me. Dark hair, pale face, teeth glinting behind his smile. Who was he? I stared at him.

'It *is* Nadia, isn't it? With the ancient computer?'

Ah, now I remembered. Relief flooded through me. I smiled. 'Yes. Sorry. Um—'

'Morris. Morris Burnside.'

'Of course. Hi.'

'How are you, Nadia? How have you been?'

'What? Oh, fine,' I replied absently. 'Look, I'm really sorry but I'm in a bit of a hurry, actually.'

'Of course, don't let me keep you. You're sure you're OK? You look a bit anxious.'

'Oh, just tired, that's all. You know. Well, bye, then.'

'Take care of yourself now. Goodbye, Nadia.'

THE HOUSE WAS beautiful, grander in real life than in the photographs, set back from the road with steps leading up to its porched front door, wisteria climbing up the tall white walls. Everything about it spoke of good taste and wealth. I looked upwards to the windows on the first floor. In one of those rooms, Jennifer had died. Then I walked briskly up to the door and banged the brass knocker.

'Yes?' A tall and elegant woman with blonde hair swept smoothly back. I had read about Clive's affair in the file and I had a pretty good idea of who she was. 'Can I help you?'

'I'd like to speak to Clive Hintlesham. My name is Nadia Blake.'

'Is it urgent?' she asked, with chilly pleasantness. 'As you can probably hear, we've got visitors.'

I could hear the rise and fall of voices coming from inside the house. The clink of glasses.

'It is urgent, actually.'

'Come in, then.'

The hall was huge and cool. I followed her through, and together we went into a large living room, with French windows giving out onto a newly dug-over garden. On the mantelpiece there was a photo in a silver oval frame of three children. No Jennifer. Was this what would happen to me, if I died? Would the waters just close over me like this?

The room had maybe ten or twelve people in it, all holding glasses and standing in clusters. Gloria went up to a solid-looking man with dark, greying hair and a jowly face. She put a hand on his shoulder and murmured something in his ear. He looked up sharply at me and walked across.

'Yes?' he said. 'Gloria said you had something to tell me.'

'My name is Nadia Blake. I'm being threatened by the same man who killed Jennifer.'

His face hardly altered. He looked around shiftily as if checking whether anybody else was paying attention.

'I'm very sorry,' he said evenly. 'But why are you here?'

'What do you mean? Your wife was murdered. Now he wants to kill me. I thought you could tell me about Jennifer.'

He took a sip of wine and led me towards the edge of the room. 'I've told the police everything that's relevant,' he said. 'I don't quite see what you're doing here. This has been a tragedy. Now I am just trying to get on with my own life as best as I can.'

'You seem to be managing pretty well,' I said, looking round the room.

His face turned purple. 'What did you say?' he said furiously. 'Please leave now, Miss Blake.'

I felt rage and mortification and I started to make a stammering attempt at self-justification. Even as I spoke, I saw a boy, a teenage boy, sitting alone on the window seat. He had about him all the awkward, spindly hopelessness of male adolescence; all the messy, terrified confusion of a son who has lost his mother. Josh, the eldest son. I stared at him and our eyes met.

'I'll go now,' I said quietly. 'I'm sorry if I disturbed you. It's just that I'm scared. I'm looking for help.'

'Sorry,' Clive Hintlesham said, with a helpless shrug.

In the hall a little boy on a trike pedalled furiously across my path and stopped. 'I know you. You're the clown,' he shouted. 'Lena, the clown's come to visit. Come and see the clown.'

'I'LL HAVE EVERYTHING,' I said firmly. 'Eggs and bacon, tomato, sausage, mushrooms. And a pot of tea. What about you?'

Lynne had gone slightly pale, maybe at the sight of what was being piled onto my plate.

'Oh,' she said. 'A piece of toast. Some tea.'

We carried our trays out of the café into the sunny garden on the edge of the park.

It was a beautiful Sunday morning. For a blessed few seconds I just pretended Lynne wasn't there. I took bites of my heart-attack breakfast and washed it down with mahogany-brown tea.

'Do you want me to move away from the table,' Lynne asked, 'when your friend arrives?'

'Don't bother,' I said. 'You know her.'

'What?' she asked, looking startled.

This was the bit I enjoyed. It must be the magician in me. 'It's Grace Schilling.' I took a triumphant bite of grilled tomato.

'But . . .' Lynne stammered.

'There she is.'

Dr Schilling had walked into the eating area. She caught sight of us and came across. She took off her sunglasses and looked at us warily.

I glanced over at the aghast Lynne. 'Could you get Dr Schilling a coffee?'

Lynne scampered off.

'Did you talk to Links?' I asked.

Dr Schilling lit a cigarette. 'I told him you had asked to see me. He was surprised.'

'I've seen the files,' I said. 'It wasn't exactly through the normal channels, so I'd rather you didn't talk about it too much.'

She was startled. Did she feel she had lost control? I hoped so.

'I want you to realise that I know about Zoë and Jennifer. I've seen the autopsy reports. I've got no illusions. All I want is for you to be frank with me. I need to ask you some questions.'

Lynne returned with the coffee. 'Do you mind if I sit here?'

'Sorry, Lynne, but I think this conversation had better be private after all,' I said.

She flushed and moved away to a neighbouring table. I turned back to Grace Schilling. 'I don't have any confidence in the ability of the police to protect me from being killed. You, they, whatever, have had two women under protection and they're both dead.'

'Nadia,' said Grace, 'I can appreciate how you feel but there were particular reasons for that. In the case of Miss Haratounian the degree of threat wasn't appreciated until it was too late. In the case of Mrs Hintlesham, there was a problem.'

'You mean the arrest of her husband?'

'Yes. Your situation is entirely different.'

I poured myself a new cup of tea. 'Grace, you may have misunderstood me. I'm not here to score points against you, but please don't insult me by saying I shouldn't be worried.'

'What do you want from me?' she asked impassively.

'There was no report from you in the files I saw. Maybe that's because it says things about me I wouldn't like. I need to know what you know.'

'I'm not sure I know anything useful.'

'Why me? I hoped the files would show something we had in common. I couldn't find anything beyond the fact that we're all little.'

'Yes,' she said. 'And you're all vulnerable. Sexual sadists prey on women. They choose those who hang back, who are unsure. Zoë Haratounian was relatively new to living in London and unsure of herself. Jenny Hintlesham was trapped in an unhappy marriage. You've just split up with a boyfriend.'

'Can you tell me anything about him?'

She paused. 'A French criminologist, Dr Locarde, once famously said, "Every criminal leaves something of himself at the scene of the crime—and always takes something of the scene away with him." Until we find out precisely what—all that I can say is that he's probably white. Probably in his twenties or early thirties. Above average height. Physically strong. But I'm sure you've worked most of that out for yourself.'

'Do I know him?'

Grace stubbed out her cigarette, started to speak, stopped and for the first time looked really unhappy. 'Nadia,' she said finally, 'I'd like to say it's not somebody you know well, because I hope that in that case the police would have established some connection with the other women. But it might be a close friend or somebody you've met once and forgotten about.'

'But why go to all this trouble?' I asked. 'Why not just attack women in dark alleys?'

'The trouble is part of the pleasure, Nadia. Think of the letters he sends: they are love letters, in a perverse way. He becomes obsessive about the women he chooses.'

'You mean he's the train spotter and I'm the train.'

'Well, sort of.'

'What do you think will happen?'

'He's escalating,' she said. 'The first murder was almost opportunistic. The second was far more violent and invasive. It's a characteristic pattern. The crimes become more violent and uncontrolled. The perpetrator gets caught.'

I suddenly felt as if a cloud had passed over the sun. It hadn't. The sky was a beautiful blue.

We both got up to leave. I looked round at Lynne, who avoided my gaze. I turned back to Grace. 'Are you pleased with the way you've conducted the inquiry?'

She picked up her sunglasses and her cigarette packet. 'I keep going over and over it, thinking what I could have done differently.' She took a business card out of her pocket and offered it to me. 'You can call me any time.'

I took it and looked at it in the pointless, polite way one does. 'I don't think you'd be there in time,' I said.

One thing was certain: I was going to fight. I didn't know if it would make the smallest bit of difference, but that wasn't the point. I wasn't going to cower in blind terror, feeling only the heart-thumping, stomach-churning, dehumanising dread I'd been feeling for the last few days. I'd talked to Grace. I didn't have much faith in Links and Cameron, and even Zach felt distant to me. So I was left with me. Just me.

The day after I met Grace Schilling I went ice-skating with a friend, and Lynne and another policewoman sat morosely on the side and watched me falling over myself in a wild flailing of arms and legs. Then, later the same day, I invited myself to Zach's and told him to get other friends around, which he obediently did. Lynne waited outside while we ate tacos and I drank too much red wine and tipped myself back into the waiting car at two in the morning. All the time, I was trying to think what to do next. I wanted to get a step ahead of this man.

The next morning I woke with a splitting headache, staggered to the kitchen, made a large pot of tea and returned to my bedroom.

The doorbell rang and I heard Lynne answer. Then there was a knock on my bedroom door.

'Yes?'

'There's someone who's come to see you.'

'Who?'

'Josh Hintlesham.' Lynne lowered her voice to a stage whisper. 'Her son.'

'Oh my God. Hang on.' I jumped off the bed. 'Tell him to come in. I'll be through in a minute.'

I rushed into the bathroom, splashed cold water over my face and scrubbed my teeth vigorously.

I went into the living room and held out my hand. 'Josh, hello.'

His hand was cold and limp in mine. He didn't meet my gaze but muttered something and stared at the floor.

'Can you wait outside, in the car, Lynne?' I said.

She left, casting an anxious gaze back over her shoulder as she closed the door behind her. Josh shifted nervously from foot to foot.

'Coffee or tea?' I asked.

'No. Thanks.' His voice was a mumble.

'Sit down.' I gestured to the sofa.

He perched uncomfortably on one end and I saw how bony his wrists were. His skin was pale but the rims of his eyes were red. He looked a mess.

'How did you find me?'

'I looked in the Yellow Pages, under "Entertainers". Christo told me you were a clown.'

'Brilliant.' I sat opposite him. 'Listen, Josh, I'm sorry about your mother. Have you got someone you can talk to about all of this? Friends or a doctor or something?'

'I'm all right,' he said.

We sat in silence.

'I dream about her,' he said suddenly. 'Every night. They're nice dreams, about Mum stroking my hair and stuff like that, though she only used to stroke Christo's hair. She said I was too old for all that now.' He flushed furiously. 'It just makes it worse.' Then he said, 'Nobody'll tell me exactly how she died.'

'Josh . . .'

'I can cope with the truth.'

I thought about the photograph of Jenny's corpse and looked at the awkward brave boy in front of me.

I took a deep breath. 'Josh, the truth is, I don't know. Your mother is dead. She's out of pain now.'

I was ashamed of myself but I didn't know how to do any better.

Josh took out a manila envelope. 'I've brought you something.'

There were dozens of photographs, most of them taken on holiday over the years. I leafed through them, horribly aware of Josh at my shoulder and of his laboured breathing. Jenny very slim and tanned in a yellow bikini on a sandy beach under a slice of blue sky. Jenny in well-pressed jeans and a green polo shirt, in the stiff circle of Clive's arm, smiling prettily for the camera. Jenny with a much younger Josh, holding a bald baby who was presumably Chris; sitting on a lawn surrounded by all three sons.

The one that touched me most was a photograph taken when she was obviously unaware of the camera and no longer wore her watchful look. Armour off, she looked like someone I could have known, after all. Something else hit me like a blade: there was something interesting about her. I could imagine her as a woman that people could be fascinated by. Oh God.

I laid them down in silence and turned to Josh. 'You poor boy,' I said, and he started crying then, but trying not to: gulping and sniffing and gagging on his grief; hiding his head in the crook of his arm. I put a hand on his shoulder and waited and eventually he sat up, fished in his pocket for a crumpled tissue, blew his nose.

'Sorry,' he said.

'Don't,' I said. 'It's good she has someone to cry for her.'

'I ought to go now,' he said, gathering up the photographs and pushing them back into the envelope.

'I'll give you my card so if you want to call me you don't have to look me up in the *Yellow Pages* again. Hang on.'

I went to my desk in the bedroom and Josh lounged in the doorway.

'You're not exactly tidy,' he remarked.

Lippy sod. 'True. I didn't know you were coming, so I didn't tidy up for you.'

He grinned in embarrassment. 'And your antique computer,' he observed.

'So I've been told.'

I rummaged in the drawers for my business cards.

He sat down and started tapping at my keyboard. 'How big is your hard disc?'

'You've lost me.'

'That's what it's all about. You just need more power. Faster hamsters.'

I found the card, picked it up and brandished it in the air. 'Here you are. Nadia Blake, children's entertainer . . .' Then I froze. 'What? What did you say?'

'Don't be angry. It's just that a computer is almost useless without proper—'

'No, what did you actually say?'

Josh paused and thought for a moment and then for the first time I saw him laugh. 'Sorry, that's just a stupid expression. Faster hamsters. It just means more power.'

'Where did you hear it?'

Josh pulled a face. 'Just a guy at our school's computer club.'

'What? A pupil?'

'No, Hack, one of the guys who helps run it. He's been really nice to me, since Mum died especially.'

I was trembling. 'Hack? What kind of name is that?'

'It's his handle. It's his *nom de guerre*.'

I tried to control myself. 'Josh,' I said, 'do you know his real name?'

He wrinkled his brow. *Please please please*.

'He's called Morris, I think. He knows about computers, but he'll just say the same thing I've said.'

MY HANDS WERE SHAKING so much I could hardly punch the numbers on the phone. I got myself put through to Links.

'Yes?' he said.

'I've just been talking to Joshua Hintlesham. He came round to see me.'

'How? How does he know who you are?'

If he had been within reach I think I would have leaned over and shaken him. 'It doesn't matter. The point is, I've found someone Jennifer Hintlesham and I both know.'

'What do you mean?'

'The other day something went wrong with my computer and I called a number on some card and this guy called Morris came round and fixed it. And the other day, when I slipped away, I bumped into him in the street. I didn't think anything of it. But I was talking to Josh and he goes to a computer club that's connected to his school. And one of the people who runs it is this guy, Morris.'

'What do you know about him?'

'He's called Morris Burnside. I think he's in his mid-twenties. I can't say much about him. He seemed nice, clever. Josh liked him a lot. He's not some weirdo. He's good-looking. He wasn't shy or strange with me or anything like that.'

'Has he tried to get in touch with you?'

I went through our meetings in my mind. 'I think he was attracted to me. He half asked me out and I put him off. I told him that I'd just split up.'

'Do you know where he lives?'

'I've got his phone number.'

I read it to him off the card, the card I'd been so pleased to find just two weeks earlier.

'Fine, leave it with us. Don't make any attempt to get in touch with him. We'll check him out.'

When I put the phone down I wanted to collapse in a heap, to be put to bed and looked after. But there was just Lynne, hovering like an annoying fly that I wanted to swat. I needed to get out of here. Quickly, I picked up the phone and dialled.

'You met him.'

Zach stopped, as if he couldn't walk and think at the same time. 'When?'

'The other day. When you came round and this man had fixed my computer. You met him when he was on the way out.'

'The one who wouldn't take any money?'

'That's right.'

'Sandy-coloured hair.'

'No. Quite long dark hair.'

'Have you seen *my* hair?' Zach stepped over and looked at his reflection in a shop window. Lynne was twenty yards behind, hands in pockets. 'It's going,' he continued. 'What I ought to do is shave it, if I had any integrity. What do you think?'

'Leave it as it is,' I said. 'I don't think a shaven skull would suit you. As I was saying, it turned out that this guy, who's called Morris, also knew the son of one of the women who was killed.'

'You mean he might have killed her?'

'Well, he's the only connection we've found.'

'But he couldn't have. I know I only met him for eight seconds but he just seemed a normal person.'

'So? I talked to the psychologist who's an expert on this. It probably would be someone who seemed normal. I'm just praying it's him. If he could just be locked away my life could start again.' I reached for Zach's hand. 'You know, I was absolutely convinced I was going to die. I've been so scared.'

Tears started running down my face. It wasn't precisely the time or the place for that with shoppers pushing their way past us on Camden High Street. Zach put his arms around me and kissed the top of my head. He could be nice sometimes.

Suddenly there was a presence at my elbow. It was Lynne.

'There's a message from DCI Links. He says he'd like to see you straight away.'

THEY WERE SO NICE to me at the police station. I was whisked straight through to an office and brought tea and two biscuits. Then Links and Cameron came into the room. They both looked serious and formal.

'I wanted to tell you straight away,' Links said, sitting behind the desk. 'We've interviewed Morris Burnside and we've now eliminated him from the inquiry.'

The room seemed to shift around me, leaving me queasy and dazed.

'What?'

'I want to assure you that this is a positive step.'

'But how could you clear him so quickly?'

He picked up a paperclip. First he unwound it so that it was straight. Then he was trying to twist it back into its old shape. I had tried that before. It never works as well again. But as an activity it at least preventing him having to look me in the face.

'I understand from Dr Schilling that you have found out that there are two murders involved in this inquiry. Document analysis has shown with complete certainty that the same person involved in the murders of Zoë Haratounian and Jennifer Hintlesham sent you the threats you received.' He untwisted the clip again. 'On the morning that Zoë Haratounian was murdered, Morris Burnside was in Birmingham at an information-technology conference that lasted all that weekend. We made a couple of calls. There are numerous witnesses who can place him there for the entire Sunday, morning till evening.'

'How did he react to being questioned?'

'He was a bit shocked, of course. But he was perfectly polite and cooperative. Nice young man.'

'Was he angry?'

'Not at all. Anyway, we didn't mention you had given us his name.'

Everything seemed to have drained out of me. I'd thought I was safe. Now I had to go back out into it again. 'I thought it was all over,' I said numbly.

'You'll be fine,' Links said, still not looking at me. 'The protection will continue.'

I got up and looked around for the door, in a daze.

Links stood up. 'Stadler will see you out,' he said.

It was a matter of half leading, half carrying me out. On the way he stopped in a quiet stretch of corridor. 'You all right?' he said. He touched my arm.

I moaned something and shook him off me. 'Don't touch me,' I said. 'Don't ever touch me again.'

FEAR KICKED IN. My insides felt molten with it. I crawled into bed and lay staring up at the ceiling, trying not to think. A few hours of hope and elation, and now I was back at the beginning. I slept and woke and slept again. It was dark and then it was dim and then at last light again. I peered at my watch. Six thirty. What was I supposed to do with myself today?

The first thing I did was to ring Zach. His voice when he answered was thick with sleep.

'Zach, it's me. Nadia. Sorry. But I had to. It wasn't him after all. It wasn't Morris. He couldn't have been the one. What am I going to do now?' I found I was crying. Tears were dribbling into my mouth, itching against my nose, tracking their way down my neck.

'Shit,' he said. I could tell he was trying to think of something to add that wouldn't sound so dismaying.

'I'm back at square one, Zach. He'll get me. I can't do this. I can't go on like this. It's no use.'

'Yes, you can, Nadia. You're brave. I have faith in you.'

He kept saying that: 'I have faith in you; you're brave.' And I kept crying and snuffling and saying, 'No, I can't.' But somehow the repetitions made me feel a bit better; my protests thinned out. I even heard myself giggle when Zach swore I'd live to be a hundred. He made me promise to make myself some breakfast. He told me he'd ring me in an hour or so, that he would come round to see me later.

I obediently toasted some rather stale bread and ate it with a large cup of black coffee. I sat in the kitchen, stared out of the window and thought. There was a stirring, tentative part of me that was starting to feel hatred towards him: a purposeful feeling. He wasn't a cloud, a shadow, something dreadful in the air I breathed. He was a man who had killed two young women and wanted to kill me. Him against me.

I started to make notes on the back of an envelope. What did I know? He had killed Zoë in mid-July, Jenny in early August. A locket of Jenny's, missing for weeks, had been discovered in Zoë's flat, a photograph of Zoë had been found among Clive's possessions, but those were the only things that had been found to connect the two women. The only link—weak and, as it turned out, meaningless—between me and Jenny was Morris. I thought of the other people who had been interviewed: Fred, of course, though never as a suspect since he had been cleared before Zoe's murder was even committed; Clive Hintlesham; the estate agent Guy; a businessman called Nick Shale; a previous boyfriend of Zoë's back from travelling around the world; Jenny's crew of architects and builders and gardeners. All the police had achieved, it seemed to me, was to eliminate the obvious suspects.

I went into my bedroom and found the scrap of paper on which I'd written the names and addresses filched from the files Cameron had shown me. I stared at them. Then, for lack of any better idea, I took a deep breath and picked up the telephone.

'Good morning, Clarke's. Can I help you?' A woman's voice, ringing with fake enthusiasm.

'I heard you're selling a flat in Holloway Road. I wondered if I could have a look at it.'

'Hold on, please,' she said, and I sat for a couple of minutes until a male voice announced its presence on the line. 'Guy here. Can I help you?'

I repeated my request.

'Great,' he said. 'How about this afternoon? I'll show you around myself.'

Lucky me. I rang another number from my scrap of paper. I don't really know why. Perhaps because of all the people in the files, she was the only one who had sounded sad.

'Hello?'

How do you begin? I decided to be direct. 'I'm Nadia Blake. You don't know me. I wanted to talk to you about Zoë.'

'Who are you? Are you a journalist?'

'No. I'm like her. I mean, I've been getting letters from the man who killed her.'

'Oh God. I'm sorry. Can I do anything?'

'I thought we might meet.'

'Yes, of course. I'm still on holiday. I'm a teacher.'

'How about at her flat, then, at two?'

'Her flat?'

'I'm being shown around. I wanted to see it.'

'Are you sure?' She sounded doubtful.

'I just wanted to find out about Zoë.'

'I'll be there. This is weird. You've no idea.'

I HAD FOUR HOURS before the appointment. A different WPC was with me today. Bernice. I told her I wanted to go and visit a flat on Holloway Road just before two, and she didn't even blink. Perhaps she didn't know Zoë's old address, or perhaps everybody was just getting bored of waiting for something to happen. Then I had a long bath, washed my hair, and put on a dress I'd hardly ever worn. It was a lovely pale turquoise, tight-fitting with short sleeves and a scoop neck. I put on a necklace, some small earrings, a pair of sandals. I looked as if I were about to go out to a summer party. If only. I put on some lipstick, to complete the picture.

At midday, Bernice came in and told me that two young men were here to see me. I peered out of the hall window and saw Josh standing fidgeting at the doorway. Beside him stood someone with dark tousled hair, holding a bunch of flowers.

When, for a couple of elated hours, I had thought Morris was the killer, the face I had remembered had been a murderer's face, cunning, his eyes dead, like a shark's eyes. Now I saw that he was boyish and handsome. He looked rather endearing as he held up his paper-wrapped bouquet.

'Come in, both of you.'

Josh muttered something and stumbled in, tripping over his undone laces. Morris held out the flowers.

'It should be me giving you flowers, to apologise for my suspicions,' I said. 'But thanks; they're lovely.' On an impulse I stretched up and kissed him on his cheek. Bernice closed the door behind us like a jailer.

'I hope you don't mind me turning up like this,' said Morris, watching me as I filled a jug with water and stuck the flowers in.

'Hack thought we should all get together,' added Josh, who looked dreadful, with a pallor that was almost green and bloodshot eyes. I steered him over to the sofa and pushed him back into its cushions. 'When did you last have something to eat?'

'I'm not hungry.'

'I'm going to make you something to eat. Pasta maybe, if I've got any. Do you want some?' I asked Morris.

'I'll help you,' he said. 'Just rest there,' he said to Josh.

Josh lolled back and closed his eyes. A pale smile spread over his face.

Morris chopped tomatoes. I found half a bag of pasta spirals. I poured them into a pan with a clatter and put the kettle on.

'Are you very scared?' he asked.

'It comes and goes,' I said. 'I'm trying to stay strong.'

'That's good,' he said, chopping away. 'Are the police helping you?'

'Sort of,' I said dismissively.

I didn't want to get into all of that. I had found a tin of pitted black olives. When the pasta was ready, I tossed a handful over it and sprinkled some olive oil over the top. It looked rather minimalist and elegant. Morris was still cutting the tomatoes, very slowly and methodically, into tiny cubes. 'How do you imagine him?' he asked.

'I don't,' I said, surprising myself by my firmness. 'I think about the women. Zoë and Jenny.'

He scraped the tomatoes into a bowl. 'If there's anything I can do,' he said, 'just ask.'

'Thanks.'

As we ate, I told Josh and Morris about my appointment to see round Zoë's flat. 'Why don't you two come with me?' I asked suddenly, half regretting the suggestion as soon as I'd made it.

Josh shook his head. 'Gloria's taking all of us to meet her mother,' he said bitterly.

'Yes,' said Morris with a smile. 'I'll come with you.'

'I'm meeting a friend of Zoë's there, as well,' I said. 'A woman called Louise.'

Morris looked a bit taken aback. 'That's funny. You're getting to know people who knew Josh's mother. And now people who knew Zoë. It seems strange.'

'Does it?' I said. 'It seems like something I have to do.'

He murmured something that sounded like vague agreement. When he had finished his pasta, he stood up and fished a slim mobile phone out of his jacket pocket. 'Checking my messages,' he said. He stood by the window and pressed buttons on the phone and listened, frowning. 'Shit,' he said. 'I've got an urgent call. I'll have to skip the flat. Sorry.'

'It doesn't matter.'

He took my hand and squeezed it. Then he left.

Josh left soon after. I kissed his cheek at the doorway and tears welled up in his eyes. Then, before he slouched off up the road, he blurted out, 'You take care of yourself.'

Nine

Guy wore a chocolate-brown suit, a Bart Simpson tie and a large smile. He had very white teeth and a tan and shook my hand firmly. As he unlocked the front door, a voice behind us said, 'Nadia?'

I turned and saw a woman about my size, about my age. She was dressed in a sleeveless yellow top and a very short red skirt. Her glossy brown hair was pulled back from her face in a ponytail; her lips were painted a red to match her skirt. She looked bright, alert, pugnacious. My spirits rose. 'Louise? I'm glad you came.'

She smiled reassuringly. Together we went into a dingy entrance hall and up the narrow stairs.

'This is the living room,' said Guy unnecessarily, as we stepped into a cramped space, which smelt musty and unlived-in. What a depressing little flat.

'Tell you what,' I said to Guy, 'would it be all right if we just looked round it without you? You can wait outside.'

'Don't you . . .?'

'No,' said Louise. Then, as he left, 'Creep. Zoë couldn't stand him.'
We smiled at each other sadly.

'I like the sound of her,' I said. 'I wish . . .' I stopped.

'She was great,' said Louise. 'I hate saying "was". There was something about her—she lost her mother when she was young, you know. And somehow she always seemed like that, like someone who didn't have a mother. It made you feel protective towards her. Maybe that's why . . .'

'What?'

'Who knows? Why does a woman get picked on?' She caught my eye.

'I've been wondering about that,' I said.

I walked round the room. Nothing had been cleared away yet, although somebody had obviously tidied up. A couple of pencils, a ruler and a rubber lay on top of a lined notebook on the small table by the window. I opened it up and there on the first page was a list of lesson ideas, neatly listed and numbered. On the wall was a framed page from a newspaper, with a picture of Zoë, surrounded by children, holding a giant watermelon.

'Her aunt owns the flat now,' said Louise, as if I had asked her some question about arrangements.

'Was she terrified?'

'Yeah. She stayed at my place. She had been completely out of it, but she seemed calmer on that last day. She thought it was going to be all right. I was outside, you know.' Louise jerked her head towards the street. 'Waiting on a double yellow line in my car. I waited and waited. Then I rang the doorbell. Finally I called the police. She just got out of my car and said she wouldn't be more than a couple of minutes . . .'

'Are you ladies all right in there?' called Guy from the stairwell.

'We won't be long,' I shouted back.

Together we went through into her bedroom. The bed was stripped and sheets and pillowcases were stacked on the chair.

'Did you know Fred?' I asked.

'Sure. Very charming, but not exactly supportive. It was a relief to her when she finally told him it was over.'

'I didn't know that.'

Briefly I closed my eyes and let myself see the photograph of her corpse, peaceful on the floor as if she had gone to sleep there. I opened my eyes and there was Louise, looking at me with concern.

'What are you doing here?' she asked. 'What's all this for?'

'I don't know,' I said. 'Maybe I'm just looking for Zoë.'

She smiled. 'Are you looking for a clue?'

'Stupid, aren't I? Is anything missing?'

Louise looked around. 'The police wanted to know that. I couldn't tell. The only thing I noticed was that there was a wall hanging Fred had given her. That was gone.'

'Yes,' I said. 'I saw that in the file on the murder scene.'

'It seems a funny thing to steal. It can't have been worth anything.'

'The police assumed that the killer used it to carry stuff away in.'

Louise looked puzzled. 'Why not just use a carrier bag from the kitchen?'

'I don't know. I don't suppose people are all that rational just after they've killed someone.'

'Anyway, mostly it looks just like I remember it. Dreary, isn't it?'

'Yes.'

'She hated it. Especially by the end. But it doesn't give you any idea of what she was like.' Louise went back into the living room and sat down on the sofa. 'On her last day, we went shopping together. Just to buy her a couple of things to wear until she collected all her stuff. She was a skinny thing, and she'd lost weight with all the fear. So we ended up going to this kids' shop down the road from my flat and she found a white T-shirt with little embroidered flowers all over it. Age ten to eleven, it said on the label; it fitted her perfectly. She tried it on in the fitting room and when she came out wearing it she looked so, so sweet, you know, with her thin arms and her bright face, giggling a bit, in this kids' T-shirt.'

Tears were trickling down Louise's face. She made no attempt to wipe them away. 'That's what she was wearing when she was killed. All dressed up in her brand-new clothes. Clean and fresh as a daisy.'

'Ladies,' called Guy again, putting his head round the door. He looked confused when he saw us hugging, tears streaming down our faces.

When we left, Louise put her hands on either side of my face and held me like that for a moment and stared at me. 'Good luck, Nadia, my new friend.'

JUST BEFORE SEVEN the following evening I was lying on the sofa in my flat watching television when the front doorbell rang. I opened the door. Josh and Morris were standing there. The damp, warm aroma of Indian food blew in.

Morris was in discussion with a policewoman. 'Yes, she does know us. And the other woman who was here already has our names and addresses.' He turned and saw me. 'We bought a takeaway and we were nearby, so we thought we'd drop in.'

'Come in.' The policewoman looked reluctant. 'It's all right. I know them.'

They came in, bringing the lovely smell with them, and dumped three carrier bags on the table.

'You're probably going out to a dinner party,' said Morris.

'As it happens, I'm not,' I confessed.

They both took off their jackets and tossed them to one side. They looked very at home as they started unloading tinfoil cartons.

'We didn't know about your tolerance,' said Morris, peeling the cardboard lids off, 'so we got everything from extremely mild to meat *phal*, which is dangerously hot, and various things in between. Beer for the grown-ups whereas Josh will have to make do with lager.'

I raised an eyebrow. 'Are you allowed to drink, Josh?'

'Of course,' he said truculently.

Oh, well. I had enough to worry about. I got out plates, glasses and knives.

'What would you have done if I hadn't been in?' I asked.

'Morris was sure you'd be in,' Josh said.

'Oh, yes?' I asked, turning to Morris with a mock-ironical expression.

He smiled. 'I wasn't making fun of you,' he said. 'I thought you might be a bit shaken up.'

'I was a bit,' I said. 'It's not been a good time.'

'I can see that,' he said. 'So eat.'

And we did and it was good. We challenged each other to take mouthfuls of the *phal* with glasses of very cold beer standing by. I think Morris cheated but Josh really did put a substantial spoonful of the fiery meat into his mouth and chewed and swallowed it. Beads of sweat started to pop out on his forehead.

'You're going to erupt,' I said. 'We'd better stand clear.'

'No, I'm fine,' Josh said, in a strangled tone, and we all laughed. It was the first time I'd ever seen him with any expression more cheerful than an awkward, self-conscious grimace and I couldn't remember when I'd last laughed helplessly.

Surprisingly quickly there was just the cooled wreckage of a meal. While I cleared the table, the boys wandered over to my notorious computer. They crouched over it and I heard occasional gasps and guffaws. I came back with another glass of beer, sipping it. I felt pleasantly dizzy. 'I know it's comical.'

'No, it's great,' Josh said, clicking away expertly with the mouse. 'You've got all these primeval versions of programs, all these one point ones and one point twos. It's like a software dinosaur park.'

'This is like an evening with two thirteen-year-olds,' I said.

'So?' said Josh.

He seemed to be loosening up. There was no longer any of that agonised, embarrassed respectfulness. They shouted for more beer and I brought them two cans, cold from the fridge.

I went and made a pot of coffee and poured myself a mug. Very black, very hot. 'There's coffee,' I shouted.

Josh was engrossed. For the moment he didn't know I existed. But Morris wandered into the kitchen and poured himself a cup.

'Nice flat,' he said. 'Very quiet.'

'Are you flat-hunting?' I asked. 'In which case you should take a look at the one I saw yesterday. Not very quiet, though.'

'How did that go?'

'I don't know,' I said. 'I'm not sure what I was doing there. It was probably stupid, but it felt important. I talked to Zoë's friend, Louise. She was nice. It brought me closer to Zoë.'

Morris took a sip of coffee. 'Can you really care about somebody you've never met?'

'Well, I feel slightly connected to Zoë and Jenny.'

'If you want to talk about it, that's all right. You can tell me what you're feeling. Anything.'

'That's nice of you but there's nothing complicated about it. I just want it to be over.'

Morris looked around. Josh was still engrossed in the game.

'What are your plans?' he said.

'I don't know. I had some stupid idea that I could try to look for clues myself but I think it was a waste of time. I had a brief look at some of the police files. They've combed through everything.'

'They let you look at their files?' said Morris sharply.

I laughed. 'Well, sort of.'

'What were they like? Were there autopsy reports?'

'Mostly bureaucratic stuff. There were some horrible pictures. What was done to Jenny. You don't want to know.'

'I can imagine,' Morris said. 'Did you learn anything?'

'Not really. I suppose I was hoping I would recognise something, some connection, that would link us: Zoë, Jenny and Nadia, the three strange stepsisters.'

'You found *me*,' he said, with a smile.

'Yes. Don't worry, Morris, I've still got my eye on you. And the estate agent, Guy, who seemed pretty weird. There must be some clue. There *must* be. I talked to this psychologist and she mentioned some principle that the criminal always takes something to the scene of the crime and always takes something away with him. It's a haunting idea, isn't it?'

Morris shrugged.

'Well,' I continued, 'it haunts *me*. I feel I've got the haystack inside my head, and I feel there are two straws in there and if I bring them together, maybe I'll save my life.'

'Of course you will,' Morris said. 'You mustn't give up hope.'

I was aware of a presence next to me. It was Josh. I poured him some coffee. He looked grown-up again, sitting on the sofa with two adults. We all sipped our coffee and caught each other's glances and smiles.

'I've been thinking about it,' Morris said, 'and there is an obvious connection between the three of you.'

'What?'

'It's a trick question, really, but who are the people you have in common?'

I looked from Morris to Josh. Suddenly Josh's face lit up in a smile. 'I know,' he said smugly. 'The police.'

'Has it been the same lot?' Morris asked.

'I think so,' I said. 'But, really . . .'

'Actually,' he said, 'there's a major flaw in my brilliant theory. The first victim. Zoë. The police would only have become aware of her after the first note.'

'Oh, yeah.'

We relapsed into silence. Suddenly I felt a small charge in the back of my head. 'That's not true,' I said. 'It was in the files. Zoë was in the papers just before it happened. She tackled a mugger in the street. She hit him with a watermelon. The police did know about her.'

'I didn't mean it completely seriously,' said Morris. 'But still . . . It might be worth thinking about whether there's been any strangeness in the way they've treated you. I suppose it's just been the normal detached sort of police style.'

I looked up slightly nervously. 'Yes,' I lied. 'Just the normal sort of style. But, I mean, it couldn't be a policeman, could it?'

'What do you think, Josh?'

Josh was shaking his head. 'No, it couldn't be. Except ... Well, you know, they actually picked up my dad because of something belonging to my mum that had been planted in the flat of the other woman, Zoë. Who else could have done that?'

There was a silence like a dark cavern.

'I've got to get my head round this,' I said.

'I'm sorry,' said Morris. 'I should have kept my mouth shut.'

'No,' I said. 'It's worth thinking about.'

Morris looked at Josh. 'We should go.'

I walked with them to the door.

'What do I do?' I said pathetically.

'You think about things,' Morris said. 'And we'll think as well. Maybe we'll come up with something.'

I closed the door and stood there thinking. My head hurt.

I am there, right at the heart of things. Invisible. I stand in front of her and she smiles at me in that way she has, that crinkles her eyes. She giggles at my jokes. She kissed me on the cheek: a soft, dry kiss, burning into my skin. There aren't many people that she trusts any more, but she trusts me. Yes, she trusts me perfectly. While I am with her I must not laugh. The laughter builds up inside me, like a bomb.

She is strong, resilient; she bends but she doesn't break. But I am stronger than she is, stronger than anyone. I am clever, cleverer than those fools who snuffle around for clues that are not there. And I am patient. I can wait for as long as it takes. I watch and I wait.

Ten

'You,' I said.

'Me,' Cameron said. 'I'm Lynne for the day. Orders.'

'Oh.' I had gone to the door wearing a skimpy robe and my hair was unbrushed, expecting Lynne or Bernice. I didn't want him seeing me like this. 'I'll get dressed,' I said.

I put on jeans and a T-shirt, good and plain. I brushed my hair back from my face and tied it up. It was a cooler day; I almost thought I could smell autumn in the air, a sense of freshness. I thought about walking through the coppice near my parents' house, boots crunching on leaves. Eating buttered toast. Little things.

Hearing Cameron in the kitchen, rattling the cups, familiar with all the appliances, I remembered what Morris had said yesterday, and I thought, Yes, it could be, it could be true. Should I be scared of Cameron?

I took a deep breath, went to join him in the kitchen.

'I've arranged to go and see my parents today. They live in Reading. I'd like you to wait outside. I haven't told them.'

'Fine.'

They were always anxious. That was why I hadn't said anything to them. Each time my mother heard my voice on the other end of the phone, she thought I was going to break some unwelcome event to her. But I was going to tell them today. I had to.

'Nadia, we need to talk . . .' He leaned towards me.

'No, we don't.' I tried to keep my voice businesslike.

I looked at him. Tall and solid, like a wall between me and the rest of the world. He had eyes that stared at me, undressed me.

'Tell me about Zoë and Jenny,' I said insistently. 'You've never told me about them. What were they like? You owe it to me.'

'I owe you nothing,' he said, but he put his hands up in a gesture of surrender, then closed his eyes for a moment. 'I never met Zoë, but Jenny was something else.' He almost grinned at the memory, then checked himself. 'Small, too. You're all small,' he added musingly. 'But strong, energetic, angry. Coiled wire, Jenny was. Clever. Impatient. Seriously insane sometimes.'

'Unhappy?'

'That as well.' He put a hand on my knee and I let it lie there, though his touch sent a wave of revulsion through me.

'We ought to go soon,' I said.

'I lie in bed at night and I see you, your face, your body. I've fallen in love with you,' he said hoarsely.

I stood up. 'Keep away.'

Before we left, I phoned Links, while Cameron was in the room with me, and told him that Detective Inspector Stadler was driving me to see my parents, and that we should be back mid- to late- afternoon. I repeated myself loudly and clearly, so he couldn't help but hear, so that Cameron couldn't help but hear either.

WE DIDN'T TALK MUCH on the way there. I gave him curt instructions, and he drove and looked across at me with his heavy gaze.

The house was a thirties' semi, much like all the others along the cul-de-sac. Cameron drew up outside. 'Hold on one minute,' he said, as I reached for the door handle. 'There's something I ought to tell you.'

'What?'

'There was another letter.'

I lay back in the car seat and closed my eyes. 'Oh God.'

'It was short. It just said, "You're being brave, but it won't do you any good." Something like that.'

'Well, I guess it doesn't really change much,' I said, with a sigh. 'We knew he was still out there, didn't we?'

'Yes, we did.'

MUM HAD MADE lamb stew, with rice and a green salad. Dad opened a bottle of red wine, although neither of them ever drinks at lunchtime. They were so pleased to see me. They fussed over me, as if I were a stranger. I felt like a stranger.

Always cautious, making their way gingerly through life. They were careful with me as well, waiting up for me every time I went out in the evenings, telling me to put on an extra layer when it was cold. It used to drive me insane, their care, the way they thought about every detail of my life. Now, the memory made me feel intensely nostalgic.

I waited until after lunch. We drank coffee in the living room, with mint chocolates, and I cleared my throat. 'I've got something to tell you,' I said.

'Yes?' Mum looked at me expectantly, apprehensively.

'I . . . there's a man who . . .' I stopped. I couldn't make the words come out of my mouth. 'Oh, it's nothing really.'

'No, go on. Tell us. We want to hear, don't we, Tony?'

'Later,' I said, standing up abruptly. 'First I want Dad to show me what's going on in the garden.'

There were tomato plants in his greenhouse, and he insisted on giving me a plastic tray of cherry tomatoes to take back with me.

I took hold of his arm. 'Dad, I know we've had our disagreements but I just wanted to say that you've been a good father.'

He made an embarrassed tutting sound in the back of his throat and patted my shoulder. 'Your mother will be wondering what's keeping us.'

I said goodbye in the hall. I pressed my cheek against Mum's and breathed in the familiar smell of vanilla, powder, soap and mothballs. Smell of my childhood.

'Goodbye,' I said, and they smiled and waved. 'Goodbye.'

For one moment, I let myself think that I would never see them again, but you can't keep on going if you let yourself be like that.

ALL THE WAY HOME, I pretended to sleep. I told Cameron that he should stay in his car after he had done his check round the flat. I wanted to be alone for a while.

I sat on the edge of my bed with my hands on my knees. I closed my eyes then opened them again.

The telephone rang, as if it were ringing inside my skull. I reached out a hand, picked it up.

'Nadia.' Morris's voice was hoarse and urgent.

'Yes?'

'It's me. Don't say anything. Listen, Nadia, I've found something out. I can't tell you over the phone. We've got to meet. Come to my flat, as soon as you can. Is anyone with you?'

I felt the fear growing in my stomach.

'No. They're outside.'

'Who is it?'

'Stadler.'

I heard the intake of Morris's breath. 'Get away from him, Nadia. I'm waiting for you.'

I put down the phone and stood up, balanced on the balls of my feet. So it was Cameron, after all. My fear ebbed away, and I was left feeling strong, springy and full of clarity. The time had come at last. I was ready and it was time to go.

As I WALKED through my front door my head felt very clear. I knew what I was going to do. Cameron was out of his car and beside me in a second, looking questioning, hopeful even.

'I'm going up the road to get some food for supper,' I said.

We walked along together. I didn't speak.

'I'm sorry,' he said finally. 'For everything.'

'What are you talking about?' I said.

He didn't reply. We walked across Camden High Street and along the pavement until we were standing outside Marks & Spencer. We mustn't have an argument, nothing to arouse his suspicions.

'I'm sorry,' I said. 'I'm not dealing with things in a rational way at the moment. It's not the time.'

'I understand,' he said.

I turned to go into the shop. 'I'll be out in a minute.'

The Camden Town Marks & Spencer has a back entrance. Up the travelator and out and within a few minutes I was on an underground train.

During the short journey, I tried to make sense of what Morris had said. If it had been a policeman, if it had been Cameron, suddenly what had seemed impossible became simple. The police had easy unquestioned access to Zoë's flat, to Jenny's house. My heart sank. To *my* flat. But why would they do that? Why would Cameron do that?

I only had to think of Cameron in my bed and I knew the answer. I had never been looked at like that before, never touched like that, as if I were an infinitely attractive and strange object. It had been wonderfully exciting at first and then repellent and now it seemed appallingly understandable. To be right next to the woman you were terrifying, to make love to her, to find out all her secrets. What a turnon. And yet, what evidence was there? Had Morris found something I could use?

Morris's flat was only a few minutes' walk from the tube station. I rang the bell. There was silence for a time. Could he have gone out? Then I heard a series of knobs being turned, levers pulled and he opened the door. He was wearing bulky trousers with large pockets all over and a short-sleeved shirt. There was something about his eyes, bright and alive, that was captivating. He had an energy about him that was like a force field.

'Nadia,' he said, with a welcoming smile. 'How did you get away?'

'I'm a magician,' I said.

'Come in,' he said. 'I haven't tidied up.'

It looked very tidy to me. We had stepped straight into a small and cosy living room with a doorway at the far end leading into a short corridor. The only thing out of place was an ironing board and iron to one side by the table.

I walked around the room. I gravitated with the instinct of a master snooper to a large cork board on the wall on which were pinned takeaway menus, business cards and, most interesting of all, little snapshots. Morris at a party, Morris on a beach. Morris and a girl.

'Is she someone you're seeing?'

'Well, we had a sort of thing.'

I smiled inwardly. She was someone he was seeing.

'Where are the rest of the pictures?' I said. 'Many drawing pins, few pictures.' I pointed. There were gaps all over the board.

'Oh,' he said. 'There were just some I got bored with.' He laughed. 'You should have been a detective.'

'Speaking of which, this had better be good, because Detective Inspector Stadler is going to be very angry. I'll probably be lucky if I get away with a charge of wasting police time.'

Morris gestured me to a chair at the table and he sat opposite me. 'I've been going over the interview I had with Stadler and the other one, and I'm convinced that there's something strange about Stadler. The way he talked about those other two women was really strange and I just felt I had to get you away from him.'

'Have you got any evidence?'

'What?'

'I thought you might have found something we could use against him.'

'I'm sorry,' he said. 'I wish I could have.'

I tried to think. Then suddenly I felt a wave of coldness pass through me. 'It doesn't work anyway,' I said dully.

Morris looked puzzled. 'What doesn't?'

'The police theory. I got so excited about Zoë and that watermelon and her connection with the police before the notes arrived. But that doesn't explain Jennifer. Why pick on her?'

'Stadler may have seen her somewhere.'

'You could say that about anybody. The police theory depended on the fact that they had dealings with all the women.'

I felt depressed and sick. 'It would have been so good,' I said flatly. 'It was such a nice theory, it's a pity to let it go.'

'Back to the haystack.' Morris was smiling at me as if that were funny. His teeth, his eyes, his whole face shone.

'You know what?' I said dreamily.

'What?'

'I used to feel strange that I'd never met Zoë and Jenny but more and more I think of us as the same person. We've gone through the same experiences. When I went to the flat with Louise—that's Zoë's friend—it was amazing. It was almost as if she had already been my best friend, as if we recognised each other. It was so funny when she talked of going shopping with Zoë on that last afternoon, it was almost as if she had been talking of a shopping expedition that *we* had made together.'

And at that moment, quite suddenly, the fog lifted and I could see. There was no doubt. I had been going over the forensic file in my mind ever since I had seen it.

'What is it?'

I started. I had almost forgotten Morris was there.

'You don't seem quite here,' he said. He gazed at me as if he were trying to see inside my mind. Did he think I was going a bit mad? Good. I leaned over the table and took his hand. It felt clammy.

'Morris,' I said, 'I'd love some tea.'

'Yes,' he said. 'Yes, of course, Nadia.' He was smiling and smiling. He couldn't stop.

He got up and walked out of the room. I looked across at the front door. There were several levers and knobs. Then it was fifty or sixty yards down the deserted road; no one about.

I stood up and walked over to the notice board. Below it was a writing desk with drawers. As quietly as I could I opened the first. Chequebooks, receipts. I opened the second. Postcards. The third. A pile of photographs. I picked up a couple. I knew roughly what I was going to see but still I gave a shiver of horror. Morris and someone and Fred. Morris and someone else—with Fred. I put one of them in the back pocket of my jeans. Maybe it would be found on my body. I closed the drawer and went and sat down at the table.

Morris came in, somehow managing to hold a teapot, two mugs, a carton of milk, and a packet of digestive biscuits. He put them on the table and sat down.

'Hang on a second,' I said, before he could pour. 'I want to show you something.' I stood up and walked round the table. 'It's a sort of magic trick.'

He smiled at me once again. Such a nice smile.

'I don't know very much about magic,' I said, 'but the first thing you learn is you never tell your audience in advance what you are going to do. If it goes wrong, then you can pretend you did it on purpose. Look.' I took the lid off the teapot then lifted the pot and very quickly threw it into his face. He howled like an animal and clutched his face. In the same movement I reached for the iron. I took it in both hands. I had one chance and I had to do real damage. I lifted the iron up and then brought it down with all my weight on his right knee. There was a cracking crumbling sound and a further scream. He crumpled and slumped off the side of his chair.

I moved back out of his reach. He was lying sprawled on the floor, twisted, whimpering. What I could see of his face was a livid blistering red.

'If you move one inch towards me,' I said, 'I'll break every bone in your body. You know I'll do it. I've seen the pictures. I've seen what you did to Jenny.'

I moved backwards, never taking my eyes off him and found the phone. Still with the iron in my hand, the flex trailing on the floorboards, I dialled.

Eleven

I put the receiver down and stood there, as far away as it was possible to get from him in that room. All he could do was drag himself, whimpering with the pain, so he was leaning against the bookshelf. He was badly burned on his face, blistered across his cheeks and forehead. Saliva was spilling out of his mouth, running down his chin. He coughed. 'I don't understand,' he said. 'I didn't do it.'

'One move, and I'll smash some other bit of you.'

He shifted slightly and cried out. 'You're mad,' he said. 'I didn't do it, I swear, Nadia. They told you. I was a hundred miles away when Zoë was killed.'

'I know you didn't kill Zoë. You were going to but you didn't. You killed Jenny.'

'You're wrong. I swear, Nadia,' he said, in little more than a whisper. He was crying now.

'Shut up. I've seen the pictures of you and Fred, the ones you took down before I arrived.'

He didn't miss a beat. 'I admit I hid the pictures. I got in a panic because it looked bad. But it doesn't mean I killed anybody.'

'The way you panicked when we were due to meet Louise at the flat?'

'No, that was a real message. Nadia, you're all confused . . .'

I don't know what I was expecting. Maybe I wanted him just to admit to what he'd done and to say something, however inadequate, that would make it comprehensible. Now I realised that he would never give up, and that I would never understand. I stared at him, and started to cry. I was about to fling the iron at him when there was a banging at the door and voices shouting my name. I ran across and opened the door. A blur of figures rushed past me. There were a couple of police officers in uniform and Cameron, sweating, his tie flapping over his shoulder. 'What the hell have you done? Did you call an ambulance?'

I shook my head. He shouted across at one of the officers who walked out.

'She attacked me,' Morris said. 'She's gone mad.'

Cameron walked up to me and put his hand on my shoulder. 'You all right?' he whispered.

I nodded.

He led me across the room to one of the chairs by the table. I sat so I didn't have to see Morris.

'So what happened?'

'Look in the drawer. Over there.'

Cameron stared at me. From his pocket he took thin plastic gloves, then he opened the drawer and looked at the photographs.

'He knew Fred,' I said.

The scene was becoming farcical. An ambulance arrived noisily. A man and a woman in green overalls rushed in and bent down over Morris. Cameron was staring stupefied at the photo.

Then Links arrived. 'What the hell . . . ?'

'She attacked Morris with an iron,' Cameron said. He handed Links one of the photographs. Links stared at it. Then he came over and sat by me. I was feeling calm now, clear-headed.

'Did Morris attack you?'

'No,' I said. 'If Morris had attacked me, I would be dead now.'

'But, Nadia,' Links said in a gentle tone, 'you do realise that Morris Burnside couldn't have killed Zoë Haratounian. He wasn't there.'

'I know. I know who killed Zoë.'

'What? Who?'

'It suddenly came to me. You all got it into your heads that the person who sent the notes must have killed her. But what if someone else killed her first? I was thinking about something that Grace Schilling told me. About how the criminal always leaves something of himself at the scene and always takes something away. I saw the forensic report of the crime scene. Do you remember the report on the T-shirt she was wearing when she was found?'

'Yes, I do, but how on earth do you—'

'Do you remember what it said?'

'It shared the background traces of the flat in common with her other clothes, the carpets, the beds. Just her and her ex-boyfriend.'

'But the shirt shouldn't have had traces of Fred. She had bought it the day before with her friend, Louise.' I twisted my head to look over at Morris. He was paying attention. 'Fred left traces of hair on Zoë's T-shirt while he was strangling her.'

I thought I caught the tiniest trace of a smile on Morris's face.

'But how could Fred have done it?' Links asked. 'Miss Haratounian wasn't even intending to return to her flat.'

'I don't think he planned it,' I said. 'That's what I've been puzzling about. I was thinking about that strange thing that was stolen, the crappy hanging from the wall that Fred gave her. I think Fred took it back. I think he came to collect his stuff. Zoë came back suddenly and he grabbed the cord from her dressing gown and strangled her. That's why the forensics were so difficult. The thing he took away was something that had belonged to him. What he brought to the scene was just more of what was already there. More Fred. And he had the perfect alibi as well. The police knew he couldn't have written the notes. Funny, isn't it, Morris? You and Fred made a great team, if you'd only known it.'

The paramedics had lifted Morris onto a stretcher.

'Are you going to look in his pockets?'

'Why?'

'I don't know. I think he was going to attack me.'

Cameron glanced at Links, who nodded. Morris's trousers had endless pockets and Cameron started rummaging in them. I saw something glisten in his hands. He was holding up a wire.

'What's this?' he said to Morris.

'I was doing some repairs,' Morris said.

'What repairs were you doing that needed piano wire tied into a running noose?'

He didn't reply.

The paramedics picked up the stretcher and carried it out. Links shouted at one of the uniformed officers. 'Two of you go with him to the hospital. Caution him on the way. Keep him fully secure, no access.'

I watched him go. He looked at me steadily until they turned the corner, with his murderer's face.

Then, 'What about me? Can I go?'

'We'll give you a lift home.'

'I think,' I said, as coolly as I could manage, 'I think I would feel safer on my own.'

'Very well,' Links said heavily.

WHAT DID I DO next? What does one do when a life has been given back? I spent the first day and night at my parents' house, helping my father paint the garden shed and lying face down on the faded chenille counterpane in my old bedroom, while my mother clattered anxiously round the kitchen, making milky cups of tea and baking ginger biscuits that I couldn't eat. Every time she saw me she would gaze at me with her red-rimmed eyes and press my shoulder. I had told them something of what had happened, but I had left out everything that mattered.

Then I went back home and I cleaned my flat. I threw open the French windows, and I turned the radio on so it was blaring cheerful, inane music through all the rooms. I went through every drawer. I filled bin bags with torn tights, old envelopes, scraps of hard soap, leaking pens. I put newspapers in a pile for recycling, bottles in a large box. I defrosted the fridge, scrubbed the kitchen floor. I cleaned the windows. I dusted.

It took two days. I didn't feel euphoric, and I hardly even felt relieved, but bit by bit I felt I was crossing back over into my life.

I screened all my calls—and there were a lot of them, because the first tremors of the story had reached the media. Reporters rang and friends suddenly wanted to get in touch, and Cameron called several times with a hissing, secret urgency. I didn't pick up the phone.

Not until early on the morning of the fourth day when the sun was streaming in through the open French windows. I was thinking about beginning on my garden next, when the phone rang and the answering machine clicked on.

'Nadia,' said a voice that made me stop in the middle of pouring boiling water over a teabag. 'Nadia, it's Grace. Grace Schilling.'

I crossed over to the telephone. 'I'm here.'

'Thanks. Listen, can we meet? There's something important I need to tell you.'

'Can't you tell me over the phone?'

'No. I need to see you. Can I come to your flat in, say, forty-five minutes?'

'Not here. On the Heath?'

'I'll come over to your side. Ten o'clock, by the pavilion.'

'Fine.'

I WAS EARLY, but she was already there. It was a warm morning, but she was huddled up in a long coat, as if it were winter. Her hair was pulled austerely back, which made her face look curiously flat, and older and more weary than I had remembered. We shook hands formally and started walking up the hill.

'What is it?' I asked.

She stopped and looked at me steadily with her grey eyes. 'I'm sorry, Nadia.'

'Is that the important thing?'

'Yes.'

'And what did you want me to say back? Do you want me to forgive you, or something?' I asked curiously. 'I mean, it's not me who's dead.'

She winced. 'I don't want that. I'm saying sorry because I'm sorry.'

'Did they send you, then? Is this a group apology?'

She smiled. 'God, no. Everybody has been forbidden to have contact with witnesses.' Another dry smile. 'Pending legal proceedings and internal inquiries.'

'Are you in trouble, then?'

'Oh, yes,' she said, in a vague tone. 'That's OK. We should be in trouble, Nadia. What we did was unprofessional. Stupid. Wrong.'

We turned off the path and walked down the hill, towards the pond. A small child stood with his mother, throwing chunks of bread at the fat, indifferent ducks.

'It wasn't really your fault,' I said cautiously. 'It wasn't your decision, was it? I mean, not telling us what was going on.'

She looked at me: she had decided to take the blame full on. 'It's strange,' she continued. 'I'm always talking about taking control of one's life, but it got out of control. One step taken—to keep the press out of Zoë's death, not to make ourselves look incompetent or worse—which led to the next step, then the next, and before they, we, knew it, we were on this road and couldn't turn back. And we ended up lying and lying and not looking after the people who looked to us.'

'All that fear,' I said.

'Yes.'

We walked on.

'Can I ask you a question, Nadia?'

'Sure.'

'It's been bugging me. How on earth did you get to see all the files?'

'Oh, that. I had sex with Cameron Stadler and then I blackmailed him.'

She looked at me as if I had just slapped her face.

'Don't ask,' I said. 'You don't want to know.'

She started laughing then, an unsteady and not entirely cheerful sound, but I joined in and soon we were holding on to each other's arms, giggling and chortling like teenagers.

We came to a fork in the path and she stopped, her expression grave. 'I go this way,' she said. 'Goodbye, then, Nadia.'

'Bye.'

She held out her hand and I shook it. Then I started walking back the way we had come.

'Nadia!'

I looked back. 'Yes?'

'You saved us,' she called. 'Us, yourself, the other women he would have come after. You saved all of us.'

'It was just luck, Grace. I was lucky.'

Twelve

It was too cold for snow. The sky was icy blue and the pavements still sparkled with the frost of the previous night. The wind was a knife. I walked quickly, head down.

'Nadia? Nadia!'

I turned and squinted. 'Josh?'

It was. He was with a group of boys and girls about his age, all of them muffled up in thick jackets and hats and jostling against each other, but he crossed the road to me. 'I'll catch up with you,' he shouted at them, waving them off. He stopped a few feet from me and we smiled at each other a bit awkwardly.

'Joshua Hintlesham, I've been thinking about you,' I said.

He looked around edgily. 'I should have got in touch,' he said. 'I felt bad. Coming round with Morris, all that.'

It seemed more than five months since he had sat on my sofa. I didn't know what to say to him, because too much lay between us: a great mountain of horror and loss and fear.

'Do you have time for coffee or something?' He took his woolly hat off as he spoke and I saw he had dyed his hair a bright orange.

'What about your friends?'

'That's all right.'

We walked together without talking until we came to a small Italian café. Inside it was dim, hot and smoky, and an espresso machine hissed and spluttered on the counter.

'I'm buying,' he said, trying to be casual, looking pleased with himself and jingling the coins in his pocket.

'OK, rich boy. I'll have a cappuccino.'

I sat at a table in the corner and looked at him while he ordered. Jenny's eldest son, leaning over the counter with his orange hair, trying to be a man, trying on his cool and his confidence in front of me.

He set my coffee down on the table. He had ordered hot chocolate for himself and he sipped it carefully, a small frothy moustache forming on his upper lip. We smiled again.

'I heard that you fixed Morris pretty good,' he said.

'It was him or me.'

'I guess I should be pleased about that,' he said. 'When I think of him hanging around with me and all the time him knowing what he'd done to Mum . . .'

'I think that was part of the point.'

'Maybe when he gets out I'll do something to him.'

'He won't get out until he's a doddery old man. Fred will be out sooner. I was talking to Links about it. The trial won't be until next year, but for something minor, like strangling your ex-girlfriend when you're humiliated and furious because she dumped you, he won't serve more than eight or ten years.'

He put his cup down on the table and ran a thumb over his top lip, rubbing away the chocolate. 'I don't know what I want to ask you really,' he said in frustration. 'I think a lot about asking you about it all, but now I don't know what I want to ask. I know what happened and everything, I know all of that, it isn't that.' He frowned and stared hopelessly at me, and he looked suddenly much younger.

'You think there's something I should be able to tell you.'

'Something like that,' he mumbled, and drew a finger through a small heap of sugar on the table. I took a breath.

'Your mother was murdered by Morris for fun. Then he picked on me and if I hadn't been lucky you could have been sitting here with the next woman he chose, or the one after that. There's no reason. It could have been anyone, only it happened to be Jenny. And I'm really sorry,' I added, after a pause.

''S all right,' he muttered, still making patterns in the sugar, not looking up.

'How's school?'

'I go to a different one now. It seemed a good idea to change.'

'Yeah.'

'It's better. I've got friends.'

'Good.'

'What about you? What are you doing now?'

'This and that.'

'You mean the same as before?'

'No, I don't,' I said vigorously. I gestured to the small holdall tucked under my chair. 'Do you know what's in that bag?'

'What?'

'Among other things, five juggling balls.'

'That's amazing,' he said, clearly impressed now.

'My master plan is to get out of this work altogether, but in the meantime I haven't exactly been standing still.'

'Show me,' he said.

'Do you really want me to?'

I looked around. The café was almost empty. I took them out of the bag, three in one hand, two in the other, and began. It went right for about one second and then they went everywhere. One hit Josh, one hit my empty coffee cup.

'That gives you the general idea,' I said, and scrambled under the table for one that had bounced into the corner.

'Is that it?' he said smiling.

'Well, if it was easy, everybody would be doing it.'

'No, it was great,' he said, laughing.

Maybe this was my gift to Josh, and my goodbye: Nadia the jester, the one who didn't die, throwing coloured balls around in a dark little café. A giggle, or maybe it was a sob, rose in my chest. I gathered the balls and put them back in the bag.

'I'd better get going,' I said.

'Me too.'

We kissed at the door of the café, one on each cheek, and then went out into the blasting cold. As we turned to walk off in our separate directions, he said, 'I still put flowers by her gravestone, you know.'

'I'm glad.'

'I don't forget.'

'Oh, Josh,' I said. 'You're allowed to forget some time. Everyone's allowed to forget.'

BUT AS I WENT DOWN to the canal path and walked along it, towards my flat, I thought, I can't forget. I won't forget them, the women who died. Zoë and Jenny.

I never met them, yet I miss them. I know their faces so well, like my own face in the mirror. They would have known me too. We might not have liked each other, but we are sisters under the skin, for their fear was my fear. I know what they felt. I felt it too.

I can't forget them. I have to carry them with me wherever I go now; through the life I have got back again, through the years they didn't have, all the love and loss and change they never knew. Every day I say to them again: goodbye.

NICCI FRENCH

Nicci French is the pseudonym of husband-and-wife writing team Nicci Gerrard and Sean French, both journalists, who first met when they were working for the *New Statesman* in 1989. Nicci was acting literary editor, newly divorced and coping with two young children; Sean was a weekly columnist. Within a year of meeting, they were married.

It is clear that their marriage is an exceptionally close one and that this makes co-writing easier. 'We plan out the story together, and the character and tone of voice of the narrator, during long walks or sitting at a table with a notebook and gin and tonic,' Nicci explains. 'But the writing is done separately. One of us will write a section, then hand it over to the other who is free to change, re-write, cut, add. It certainly requires an intimate kind of trust.'

Their first book, *The Memory Game*, published in 1997, was an instant success, and it was followed in 1998 and 1999 by *The Safe House* and *Killing Me Softly*. All the Nicci French novels explore the thin dividing line between passion and madness, safety and danger, in everyday life. 'One of our impulses in *Beneath the Skin*,' Nicci explains, 'was to scare people in the place they feel safest—their own home. We're overwhelmingly more likely to be killed by a partner, a lover, a friend, or an acquaintance, than by a psychopathic stranger.'

The couple continue their freelance writing careers and live in North London with their two children and Nicci's two from her previous marriage.

ACKNOWLEDGMENTS AND PICTURE CREDITS: *Code to Zero:* pages 6–8: Hulton Getty; The Photographers Library; photomontage by John Calvert; page 131: Barbara Follett. *Winter Solstice:* pages 132–134: Tony Roberts/Arena; page 273: Isolde Ohlbaum. *High Risk:* pages 274–276: Telegraph Colour Library/Kathy Collins; Sporting Pictures; Images Colour Library; photomontage by DW Design Partnership; the lines quoted on page 354 are from 'They Who Are Near Me' © Rabindranath Tagore; page 391: Colin Luke. *Beneath the Skin*: pages 392–394: Gettyone Stone; photomontage by Shark Attack.

DUSTJACKET CREDITS: Spine from top: Hulton Getty; The Photographers Library; photomontage by John Calvert: Tony Roberts/Arena: Telegraph Colour Library/Kathy Collins; Sporting Pictures; Images Colour Library; photomontage by DW Design Partnership: Gettyone Stone; photomontage by Shark Attack. Back cover: (Follett): Barbara Follett. (Pilcher): Isolde Ohlbaum. (Dickinson): Colin Luke.

Printed by Maury Imprimeur SA, Malesherbes, France
Bound by Reliures Brun SA, Malesherbes, France